CULPA

MORGAN D. JONES

Morgan D. Jones

CAPSTONE FICTION

WATERFORD, VIRGINIA

Culpa

Published in the U.S. by:
Capstone Publishing Group LLC
P.O. Box 8
Waterford, VA 20197

Visit Capstone Fiction at
www.capstonefiction.com

Cover design by David LaPlaca/debest design co.
Cover image © iStockphoto/Amanda Rohde

ISBN: 978-1-60290-055-4

To God,
whom I worship,
and to Jesus,
for His inspiration

Acknowledgments

To Capstone Fiction for recognizing the worth of *CULPA*, which no other publisher did, and to Ramona Tucker, for her skillful editing, exceptional insights, boundless enthusiasm, and immeasurable support.

"Unworthy!" O what sadder word
For human ears could e'er be penned?
What sharper, more two-edged sword
The consciousness of man could rend.

The race is run, our goal is past,
Have we not yet the victory seen?
What sorrow, what remorse, at last
For those who have "unworthy" been.

Unworthy of the Gift of Heaven!
'Twere sad if it had come from men.
Unworthy without excuses, even!
Saddest of all that could have been.

—from a poem by my grandfather,
George B. Jones
Oxford, 1908

ONE

"So you're determined to quit. To walk away from it. No discussion or sharing. No explanation."

Father Leonard wanted to pace, but the smallness of the room, cramped as it was with bed, desk, chair, and bureau drawers, denied him his habitual mode of thinking. He made do with rocking ludicrously from side to side as he stood in one corner, the only available space. His shadow on the wall behind him, cast by the lamp on the desk, rocked with him.

"Do sit down, Lenny," Brock said, chuckling as he busily packed a suitcase on the floor. "You look like you have to pee." Kneeling on the faded threadbare red rug that was standard furnishing throughout the dorm, the handsome twenty-year-old seminarian pressed a stack of socks into a crevice among the compacted clothes.

His mentor, still nervously swaying, ignored the offer and gravely pressed on. "No dialogue? No decent interval to let emotions subside and rational thought prevail? You remember what Alexander Pope wrote: 'What reason weaves, by passion is undone.'"

Brock arranged the clothes neatly in the suitcase, smoothing wrinkles, concentrating on his task, not ignoring but not replying either to the priest's intellectual sparring. When he had finished straightening a shirt and tamping it down, Brock ran his fingers through his thick wavy brown hair, then let his hands fall on his knees. He took a long deep, breath and exhaled it...slowly, wearily, patiently. For the first time in years he felt both physically and mentally calm and at peace with himself—indeed, relieved. The struggle was over.

"Yes," said Brock, nodding with a smile. "I do remember your favorite philosopher's dictum, but emotions play no part in my decision. I am totally rational." He spoke quietly, as if to himself, then looked up at

1

his friend of the past two years. Their eyes met. Father Leonard ceased his rocking and stood motionless, as if poised to speak but unable to. Brock's matter-of-fact resolve vied with the priest's anguish. Neither would yield. The priest turned away with a sigh, his head downcast, his tall frame sagging against the wall.

Ironically, this scene—Brock kneeling on the floor, the priest standing beside him—was a replay of their first meeting two years before. Brock had been in the seminary less than a week when Father Leonard entered the new seminarian's room looking for volunteers to decorate the chapel for a special evening mass. They had shaken hands, introduced themselves, and within minutes were embroiled in what became for them an almost daily routine—lively, friendly debate. Even then, and in their many subsequent dialogues, the lanky priest could not remain seated but would pace about the room gesturing theatrically with hands, arms, and head as the argument or his mood dictated—a vestige, Brock was fond of pointing out to him, of Leonardo's Italian lineage.

Their friendship grew as the weeks passed. Father Leonard was serving at St. Charles temporarily as a Romance language teacher until his appointment by the bishop could be arranged to the Vatican as diocesan research fellow. Although the priest was nine years older than Brock, they shared the same youthful penchant for practical jokes and merrymaking, within the limits permitted by the seminary's sober purpose and decorum.

Brock and Father Leonard also shared tender moments of compassion as when Brock's stepfather, his only family, passed away. Brock had never felt close to the man, but the loss hurt nonetheless because it brought home for the first time how really alone Brock was in the world. Although he drew closer to Father Leonard, it was less for friendship than for an erudite sounding-board to help Brock probe his true feelings about his stepfather, the priesthood, and life in general. But his instincts would not allow him to fully bare his innermost feelings to anyone, even a friend who was a priest. Or was it a priest who was a friend? Brock couldn't decide nor fathom the difference, though he was sure there was one.

Brock had never had close friends, male or female. He had never felt a need for any. For a time in high school his disdain for emotional involvements with girls troubled him deeply, raising in his adolescent mind the disconcerting notion that he was homosexual. Two discoveries laid this fear permanently to rest: first, that curvaceous female bodies aroused intense sexual desires in him and, second, that he had no particular interest in becoming involved with persons of either sex.

Having perceived no value in having friends, he never learned how to cultivate or sustain a friendship. Throughout his childhood his stepparents' behavior toward one another had taught him that personal relationships ultimately deteriorated into quarrels, recriminations, and lasting bitterness. It was therefore natural that the absence of intimate personal entanglements was among the factors that had attracted him to the priesthood as a vocation. In fact, it was to avoid close personal ties with any of his classmates that he had arranged through Father Leonard to secure one of the few single-student rooms in the dorm. It was not that he disliked being with people. On the contrary, he was quite the partygoer. He simply distrusted people. His early life had conditioned him to be skeptical of people's motives and to remain always on the defensive...guarded and watchful...wary of generosity and acts of kindness.

And that was his mental posture now as he knelt on the floor under Father Leonard's pained and disappointed gaze.

The priest had great admiration for Brock's intellectual and artistic gifts. A top-flight student who effortlessly tamed one academic subject after another, he was an accomplished artist, sculptor, and craftsman who unselfishly gave of his free time on weekends, holidays, and after class to repair and restore the finely carved woodwork and stained-glass windows in the chapel. It was Father Dunlap who had observed that Brock treated the sanctuary as if it were his home. The faculty had also recognized Brock's spiritual strength. It seemed to crown his many other talents with the mark of future stardom in the hierarchy of the Church. But now...this unexpected and unexplained turnaround. Father Leonard was crushed.

The two men—teacher and student—remained frozen like manikins in some macabre diorama. Then Brock spoke, breaking the fragile silence, his mellow voice controlled but indulgent. "This didn't happen suddenly. It's no childish spur of the moment impulse. I've been mulling over my decision for weeks, even months."

"Then why didn't you come to me?" implored his mentor. "Why didn't you air your concerns with me? The two of us have had so many talks...long talks." He looked reproachfully at the young seminarian. "How could you accept my devoted friendship, yet withhold from me your fundamental and critical reservations about the priesthood? I thought we shared a common commitment to honesty and frankness." He bowed his head again, too distraught to continue, and turned away.

Brock could see the priest's deep hurt. Their talks had indeed been many, long, and late into the night. So late on many occasions that Brock had to sneak back from the faculty apartments to his room in the dormitory because curfew had passed. Those secret forays into the night from Father Leonard's quarters became a humorous *cause celebre* between them, something they shared privately and that distinguished their relationship from those between other teachers and students. It bound them together as a secret always does to those who share it.

"I have kept silent about my reservations, Lenny, because I thought them premature and impertinent. If—"

"Impertinent?" cried Father Leonard, whirling about. "To whom? Me? Your trusted confidant with whom you spoke with such conviction and fervor about the joy of serving God's will, the challenge of seeking the perfection of your spirit, the thrill of embodying the holy power of our Lord Jesus to forgive sins and to preside over the miraculous transformation of bread and wine into His hallowed body and blood? Were those declarations mere deceptions? Abstractions?" The priest's face was livid, his chest heaving with emotion.

"No deceptions, Leonard," Brock replied calmly. "Inquiries. Questions. Probings. Seeking answers."

"How do you get answers if you don't voice the questions?" The clergyman was close to shouting. "If you had doubts...if you have them now...we should discuss them."

"I know you feel betrayed, but there's nothing more to discuss."

"Nothing to discuss?" Father Leonard slammed his fist against the wall. "Brock, we've discussed the Church, God's purpose, Christ's mission, the eternal mysteries. But there was something we didn't talk about. Abdication!"

Brock stood upright, his emotions finally aroused. At six feet two he still looked up to meet the priest's scowl. "I'm not abdicating! One only abdicates a duty or a trust. Where is it written that I'm to become a priest?

Where?"

The ferocity of Brock's outburst stunned the priest, who paused to collect himself. He saw that arguing with Brock was futile, since he clearly had made up his mind. A different tack was required. He clasped his hands in front of him prayerfully and smiled. "Your emotion belies your rationality, my dear friend. Why don't we go to my quarters, break out the sherry, and examine your feelings about this matter sensibly and calmly, like we have other important issues? You need time to sort this out. I understand you. I know how you feel deep down. You entered the seminary because you felt chosen, moved by the grace of God to pledge your life to His work, to His Church, and to His people. Your faith glowed like a hot ember. Students who come to the seminary without that luminescent, deeply rooted conviction and sense of mission stand out at once. And they don't last long, maybe a month or two; three or four at the most. You've been here two years! The reason—"

"The reason was self-deception," said Brock flatly, sitting down on the bed and turning away from the priest's pleading eyes. "I think differently now. The more questions I asked about God's purpose, the more ambiguous the answers became, which only led to more questions, more doubts. It ground my conviction to dust. There's nothing left."

"You mean your belief in God?"

"No, of course not." He turned about and faced the priest. "I still believe in God. I'm talking about my conviction to become a priest. It's gone."

"I simply can't believe that. This all comes too quickly. One doesn't change overnight. Something has happened."

"Yes. Something did. I awakened. I'm not sure exactly when, but I've opened my eyes and my mind. The light, as they say, has come on. My childish fantasies about the priesthood and Christianity and goodwill among men have evaporated like all fantasies should when we mature. I'm awake now in the real world. Not a make-believe, we-trust-in-God, He'll-make-it-all-right world. No, the *real* world!" Father Leonard stood transfixed, staring at Brock as if he were a stranger speaking a foreign tongue. "The physical, touchable, feelable, tasteable world where men rely on themselves, on their own labors, not on the generosity of others. Where men with ambition can fulfill their dreams and seek just rewards

5

for their achievements. Where men are not bound by dogmatic discipline with its strictures on intellectuality and freedom of thought. Where the Church—"

"You're ranting," interrupted Father Leonard, stepping over the suitcase and moving toward the door. He would hear no more of this reckless nonsense. He stopped at the foot of the bed, his rangy form made taller by his black cassock, towering over Brock almost menacingly. "I can't reason with you like this. Will you stay for breakfast in the morning and talk with Monsignor Garrity before you leave?"

"I'm not ranting, and I'm not staying overnight."

"Will you see Garrity?" His tone was cold and authoritative.

"To what purpose?"

"Will you see any of us?" The priest was almost pleading.

Brock tilted his head back to look into the priest's somber eyes and said softly, "No, Father."

His sudden recourse to Leonard's clerical title, which Brock had not used in addressing his friend since that first meeting two years ago, was a stinging affirmation of the gulf that now lay between them. Father Leonard was a clergyman and member of a holy order. Brock Stowolski was a layman, never-to-be-priest.

They studied each other in silence.

Strangers.

The clergyman solemnly held out his hand. "I'll miss you, my friend." Brock gripped it firmly without speaking. "And I'll pray for you," said the priest with a huskiness he tried to conceal. He turned and left, closing the door quietly behind him.

Brock lay back on the bed and closed his eyes. The stillness of the dorm was annoying, making his solitude more stark and cheerless. He had just bid farewell to the only person he had ever called "friend," yet strangely he felt no regret or remorse. In fact, he felt nothing. Neither sadness nor joy, neither fear nor exultation. He was blank. A chilly emptiness filled him. Or was it a new sensation? Not emptiness but...newness. A reaching out. A yearning. An awakening in him of a long-suppressed urge to achieve.

He had never felt this way before. All his life things had been laid out by others for him step by step like a multicourse dinner. First this, then this, then this. Now there was nothing ahead. Nothing planned. No obligations. No one else's rules to follow. He would go where his intuition led him and do what his will directed. He felt liberated, unchained. Over the past several months he had found the regimentation of seminary life ever more stifling and constricting. He needed mobility. He needed latitude. He needed freedom!

He stretched out his arms, his eyes still closed, and began to breathe deeply, as if learning how for the first time. Each breath brought a smile of exhilaration to his lips. He breathed harder and quicker, his excitement rising. Bursting, he sat up and, flinging his arms above his head in mock triumph, laughed aloud. "I'm free!" *Free*, he thought, *to be something. To do something. To do anything. Whatever I like. There's no limit to what I can accomplish. A world of opportunities lies waiting for me out there, and I'll need no one's permission. Nor*, he thought with grim resolve, *will I need prayers. Prayers are for priests and hypocrites.*

Nothing had upset him more at the seminary than the long daily meditation periods when the postulants silently prayed for God's grace, inspiration, and forgiveness. Brock despised being forced into the role of supplicant. It was demeaning and dehumanizing. *Let me stand on my own feet and face the world*, he thought. A raw defiance he had not sensed before suddenly surged within him. Prayers were for weaklings and the lazy. *God gave me the power to do things, so let me stand or fall on my own achievements. But I'll not beg. If I can't do it on my own, I'll not do it at all!*

Robustly he got to his feet, a look of cold determination on his rugged masculine features. He would follow his instincts from now on. It would be an exciting adventure, totally different from the orderly, predictable pattern his life had followed since he was old enough to appreciate what "serving others" meant. All his life—twenty years—he had foresworn his own pleasure and advancement to serve and obey the will of the Church as ordained by his stepparents. But not any longer. From now on he would chart a different course. He would serve himself.

He closed his suitcase. It, a clothes bag, a tennis racket, and a shopping bag filled with shoes were the only belongings he would take with him. Left behind in the desk drawers and on the shelves that lined one wall were the mementoes of his seminary life, including his books, among which was a light-blue Bible given him by Father Leonard the year before as a birthday present. Brock would have no need of the holy writ or of the other memorabilia. They would only remind him of the seminary, its strictures, and the life of servitude it would have demanded.

He opened the door and slung the clothes bag over his shoulder, gathered up the suitcase, shopping bag, and racket and hobbled out of the room, down the stairway, and out the rear entrance of the dormitory without a backward glance. What was there to look back at? His past? What might have been? A waste of time. He was cutting all ties with the past. His mind was solely on the future.

Shuffling along the poorly lighted sidewalk that led to the student parking lot, he stumbled on a water-main cover and dropped the tennis racket. It was nearly midnight. As he stooped to retrieve it, his left hand carrying the suitcase began to slip. When he set everything down to rest, he looked up and discovered he was in front of the chapel, his favorite spot on campus. What had Father Dunlap said? "Like your home."

Brock had never understood the attraction the ornate hundred-year-old sanctuary held for him. Perhaps it was the stained-glass windows he had painstakingly restored using age-old techniques taught him by one of the elder priests, a Frenchman who as a young man had learned the art from master glassmakers in Europe. Brock had a sudden urge to enter the chapel one last time. But why should he? The windows would be dark and lifeless, and he wanted to leave the grounds quickly. The urge passed, a sure sign to him that his connection with the Church had passed as well.

He grappled his luggage again and, after negotiating a half dozen flagstones up a steep rise and across a gravel path, reached his small dilapidated car. Throwing his bags haphazardly into the rear seat, he jumped in, started the engine, and sped off to the main entrance to the campus.

He braked at the flashing yellow light at the intersection with the north-south highway that cut through the small Maryland farming town that had changed little since the seminary's first buildings were constructed in the early 1800s. He sat at the light for several minutes, the engine idling while he pondered which direction to go. North or south? Where did his destiny lie? He was bereft of intuitive guides. A homing pigeon without a home.

Unsettled, he looked in the rearview mirror, then up and down the highway, waiting for some impulse that would lead him in one direction or the other. His indecisiveness irked him. If he were indeed free to make his own decisions and to follow his instincts, it was time to take charge. "I'll take W. C. Fields' advice," he said out loud. "Philadelphia, here I come!"

He pressed hard on the accelerator and spun the wheel to the right. The car jerked forward, swerved onto the deserted highway, and headed north, disappearing from sight and sound within a few seconds. Away from the seminary, away from the priesthood, away from Father Leonard.

He knew his abrupt departure would create a mild stir in the morning among his classmates and the faculty, but the measured routine of seminary life would quickly diffuse the impact, and after a few days their memory of him would fade and eventually dissolve.

For all, that is, except for his once friend, Father Leonard.

The tall priest knelt in a front pew of the chapel early the next morning praying for a dear friend who, for reasons not to be condemned nor easily understood, had given up what surely would have been a distinguished career in the priesthood to seek his life's fulfillment in the secular world. The priest blamed himself for not reading his friend's obvious signs of mounting disaffection and alienation—lapses of concentration in class, unresponsiveness, daydreaming, declining grades. He had dismissed them—too hastily, he now realized—as youthful moodiness that would pass in time. He had been wrong. Fatefully wrong. The aberrant behavior had in reality manifest fundamental changes in the seminarian's attitudes and beliefs. Had the priest only paid more attention, been more observant and not so blinded by his admiration of this bright, promising young man, the latter would be kneeling here now in the chapel with the other students and faculty members as they performed their morning prayers.

The priest bowed his head and, taking from his lap a light-blue Bible, pressed it reverently to his forehead.

TWO

B rock's pell-mell re-entry into the workaday world of opportunity awakened him rudely to the inadequacies of his professional qualifications for the high-salaried jobs he applied for: management consultant, office manager, sales coordinator, union organizer, management trainee in a bank. With only a high school diploma and two improvident years at a seminary, he had little to offer beyond an all-American physique, a promise of loyalty and hard work, and, of course, a handsome face and disarming smile. The rejections were both humiliating and enlightening, revealing his youthful naiveté.

Because he had inherited fifty thousand dollars and some stocks, bonds, and small holdings of real estate from his late stepfather, Brock was not destitute. But unless he found employment soon, he would begin depleting these valuable assets, which he was determined to preserve as a nest egg for future investment, when the right opportunity came along.

A week later the foreman on a construction job Brock had wangled, recognizing Brock's carpentry skills, asked him, "Want extra work?"

"Sure thing," said Brock. "I'll take all you've got."

"Company's opening a new upscale subdivision over by Mountain Valley. The model homes are five weeks behind schedule. We need someone like you to meet the opening. I'll raise your hourly a dollar if you do well. Time and a half over eight hours. Okay?"

"Show me the way."

The tasks he was told to perform on the model homes did not begin to challenge Brock's capabilities or to tap his reservoir of creativity, whose immense potential he himself was only beginning to discover. It was not until the interior decorator for the model homes offered him some extra work that he was given the opportunity to explore and test that potential.

She was pretty enough, he thought. A blond in her midthirties. At first glance the parts of her body did not fit well together. Her neck was too thick for her narrow shoulders, her bust was too large for her slim waist, which exaggerated her wide though well-rounded hips, and her shapely legs were disproportionately short for her overall height of five feet six. Altogether, however, they had an uncommon sexual appeal.

One afternoon while finishing the installation of a mantel over a second-floor fireplace, he recognized the familiar popping of her high heels on the hardwood floor of the foyer downstairs. To his surprise she called out his name. "Hey, Stowolski!"

"Up here in the master bedroom," he yelled. He hung his hammer on the leather tool belt slung around his waist and waited for her as she noisily climbed the uncarpeted stairs.

"I'm Frieda Steuben," she shouted, still out of sight. She had a surly-edged voice like a tavern waitress. "I do the interiors here. You've been doing such wonderful work that..." She reached the second floor and entered the room out of breath. "...that I thought I might interest you in some after-hours jobs for me." She came straight to him, her heavily mascaraed eyes riveted on his the whole time. He barely had a chance to take her in before she stood in front of him, so near that he looked down at her. Her blond hair was tied in its usual bun in back of her head. She wore a loose-fitting bright yellow dress with huge ruffles covering a low-cut bodice with matching yellow open-toed shoes.

Before he could speak, she said, "Whataya say? Interested?" It was more a challenge than a question.

"Hey, wait a minute!" He smiled. "Gimme five seconds to ask you some questions." Her perfume enveloped him.

"Okay," she said, returning his smile. "Ask me." She made fists of her hands and jammed them into her waist, throwing her elbows out in a defiant posture.

"Well, I'm busy as it is. You see, I take all the jobs I can get."

"I'll pay more."

"How much more?"

"Twice."

"You're awfully impetuous. How do you know I'm worth double wages?"

Her green eyes—made greener by her blond hair—widened in mock surprise. "Impetuous? What a big word. I'm impressed. Not only a skilled craftsman but an intelligent one. I've never met a carpenter who used that word. They don't even know what it means."

She stepped back to size up his height and build. He was magnificent. "Why are you worth double wages? I'll tell you. There's more to interior decorating than simply picking colors and fabrics. It takes know-how and skill to carry an idea through to the finished product." She stepped even closer to him, nearly nose to nose. "There are plenty of hacks around who can hammer and saw and drive nails." She raised her right fist and pointed it gunlike at his chest an inch away. "But only one in a hundred has the artistry needed for top-notch interior decoration. And you're that one in a hundred." She poked his chest with her finger.

"You think so, huh?"

"That's my business, isn't it?" She stepped back and looked around the room as if assaying his work.

"If you say so."

"Well?" She looked back at him. "Are you interested?"

Brock shrugged. "I guess so."

"Come to my office this evening around eight. I'll explain what the work entails." She gave him directions and left as abruptly and loudly as she had arrived, her high heels pop-popping down the stairs, then going silent as she exited the front door. Her perfume lingered enticingly in the air as Brock resumed his carpentry.

He went home eagerly after work to his small flat to shower and dress for his meeting with Ms. Steuben. He was delighted at finding some really well-paying employment. He could use the money. But a doubt was nagging him. He was unsure he would enjoy taking orders from a woman,

12

unsure if he could adjust to it. Having been surrounded by men and only men for the past two years, he had had little contact with females of any age. There had been several older women on the seminary's administrative staff, but they had kept to themselves, either by choice or by school policy. He never had been sure which. Now this high-powered blond appears. She'd probably be domineering and demanding, forcing Brock into a subservient role...a role he despised. But it wasn't only her position of authority that bothered him. There was also the suggestion from the way she had looked at his body that interiors were not the only designs she had in mind.

Two hours later, feeling ill at ease and apprehensive, he arrived at her office. It was disappointing. Considering her looks and style, he had expected a flashy suite in a fashionable building downtown. What he found was a shabby, cluttered, two-room office above a dingy drugstore so far from downtown he wondered how she had a Philadelphia address.

"Whataya think?" she asked, greeting him at the door in the same yellow dress of the afternoon. "Real classy place, isn't it?"

"Frankly, I expected something out of *House Beautiful*, but this will do."

"It'll have to. It's all I can afford." She laughed and pointed to a moth-eaten easy chair for Brock to sit in. "I'm no millionaire."

"At least not yet," he quipped.

"You wanna be a millionaire?"

"I was speaking of you," he replied, not wishing to discuss his own ambitions, which he held private. He took a seat feeling awkward. "You seem like a pretty sharp businesswoman."

"And you?" She sat down opposite him on a ragged sofa piled with fabric samples and wallpaper catalogues. She heaved them aside to make room. "You don't sound or act like a carpenter. More like a lawyer or maybe a doctor."

He chuckled. "You have a vivid imagination."

"That's why I'm an interior decorator." They both laughed. "Willie said you're from Maryland, you're single, and you dropped out of college there."

"What else did he tell you?"

"Not much, except you work hard, and you're the best carpenter he's seen in ten years. Coming from Willie that's a real compliment."

"Is that why you're offering me extra jobs? His recommendation?"

"That and your work I've seen with my own eyes. You're an exceptional craftsman, you know."

"I like my work, but I don't know how exceptional it is." He was growing impatient with these informalities. "What sort of jobs do you have for me?" He figured she was the kind of person who didn't beat around the bush. And he was right.

She immediately got down to business, explaining how she advertised, solicited contracts from builders, planned interiors, and hired subcontractors—carpenters, painters, rug and drapery installers, electricians, and lighting specialists—whose work she had to oversee continuously to ensure it was of passable quality. Brock was intrigued by the complexity of the whole operation, which he had assumed was a simple matter of picking paint, rugs, curtains, and furniture that matched in reasonably good taste. There was far more to interior design that he had imagined.

"And where do I fit in?" he asked.

"In several ways. First, I frequently come up with ideas that my subcontractors claim are impractical or undoable. Can't be done, they say. Won't work. Too complicated. Too costly. All kinds of excuses. I have trouble arguing with them because they're supposedly the experts. But I don't believe them. I think they either don't wanna bother with my ideas or they haven't the ingenuity to figure out how to implement them. Either way I lose. How can I produce unconventional interiors if I can't get people to build them? I need someone like you who can argue for me and my ideas, who can tell these idiots not only that my ideas are doable but how to do them. Whataya think?" She stopped talking and stared at him expectantly.

"You said I would fit in several ways. What are the others?"

"Well, some of my ideas I'll admit are novel and, like I said, require a bit of ingenuity to implement. That's where you come in. In those cases you'd do the work yourself."

"Anything else?"

"Ideas. Any usable ideas for interior designs. You've improvised several times with good results. The Melville Model, for example. You extended the tile of the master bath into the alcove, changing the color as you went. My design hadn't called for that, but I loved it."

"Thank you. It seemed like a good idea, and I knew I could rip it out if you disapproved. How come you never said anything to me about it?"

"I don't know. To be honest, professional jealousy, I suppose."

Her frankness impressed him. "You never need be jealous of me, Ms. Steuben. I think we can work well together. In fact, I'm looking forward to it."

"Wonderful. Please call me Frieda. I'll draw up a contract tomorrow and put it all down in cold legal language."

"Do we really need a contract? That seems awfully formal. I trust you, you know."

She frowned at him thoughtfully. "Let me give you some professional advice from someone who's learned the hard way. Put your trust in written contracts not in people. The guy who writes the contract writes the ticket. Oral contracts are only as good as the contracting parties' intentions and their memories. And memory has a funny way of fading when money is tight, which is most of the time. No, Mr. Stowolski, you'll work for me on a contract. I don't operate any other way. All right?"

"I bow to your professional wisdom and experience," he replied, trying to be cute. "And please call me Brock."

They talked awhile longer about the projects she was currently working on. Then they left her office and walked together to the adjacent parking lot. Stopping beside her car, a faded, unwashed, metallic green, ten-year-old Corvette, they shook hands.

"I think we're going to make a fine team, Brock. I'm very pleased."

"Thank you, Frieda. I hope I can help you as much as you think I can."

"Oh, you will, I promise. Would you like to drop by my apartment and toast our new collaboration with a nightcap?"

There it was again, he thought. That hint of a more intimate relationship. "Thanks but not tonight. We're pouring a foundation tomorrow at dawn's early light. We've got to be finished before the predicted rain hits, which could be by noon. Maybe another time."

"Sure thing. Anyway, I'll see you tomorrow after work. We have lots to discuss."

THREE

Brock had entered a new, enchanting, phantasmagorical world...the realm of interior design. He knew at once it was his natural habitat. It offered not only an outlet for the powerful untapped creative forces within him, but also independence...a chance to make it on his own. To succeed or fail, rise or fall, get rich or go broke, entirely on his own. A world of almost limitless horizons.

Frieda at first had served as his primary source of information. She was the teacher, he the pupil. They hit it off well from the start. Although his reservations about working for her were vindicated by her tendency to be domineering and temperamental, he found ways to placate these propensities, like saluting in exaggerated military style to make her laugh or going to the other extreme of being very serious and exacting about carrying out one of her directives. In either case his response defused her petulance and made working with her tolerable, even pleasant. It was a strain for Brock, however, to rein in his own strong need to dominate. He was willing to make the effort and suffer the punishment to his ego, because an opportunity like this might not come again. He had to make the most of it. Unless his instincts were woefully deceived, this was a sure route to fame and fortune.

Occasionally he asked her straightforward questions about how things were done, but mostly he remained in the background as an unobtrusive but avid and attentive observer. It would not do, he was certain, to be candid with her about his ambitions. Besides, he found her physically attractive, and though he suppressed the lustful feelings she spawned in him, they nevertheless were an inducement to work with her.

Where his commitment to religious life had been gradually eroded by lack of conviction, his new devotion to interior design was absolute.

He read everything he could find on the subject, about art, fabrics, and marketing, anything to do with design, devouring one or two books a night. The more he learned, the more he realized how little he understood and the more intense and dedicated he became to increasing his knowledge of the field.

He was jealous of every minute spent on a task not related to design. He slept very little, husbanding his free time for reading and other pursuits that would advance him toward his new goal. He enrolled in night courses in commercial art. He studied the psychology of color, how curtain fabrics are manufactured, why paint cracks and how to prevent it, the science of lighting. He attended occasional weekend design symposia. He visited model homes, furniture exhibits, and any display that featured some aspect of interior design. He subscribed to every design periodical he could find and read them all, filling the margins with comments and questions and producing reams of notes he jotted down as he read. He purchased and mastered a computer and all its routines and carried on lively correspondence via the Internet with authors of articles that had sparked questions in his mind. Twice he drove over three hundred miles on weekends to visit privately owned homes whose interiors had been the subject of articles and that were open to the public.

Throughout this months-long period of intense self-education he amassed a valuable and impressive library of reference books that would have been the envy of any designer, including Frieda, but he kept his holdings, like his growing knowledge, a secret from her. With his new knowledge had come a more discerning eye and discriminating taste. Frieda's interiors he had come to realize were tasteless and unimaginative. She had little real knowledge of the art of design, its history, or its trends. She simply followed her impulses, which at times paid off but more often produced match-ups of colors, fabrics, and furniture that from Brock's apprenticed viewpoint were incongruous, even loathsome.

As if to vindicate this perception her clients began directing questions to him on the job. Even though he strove to conceal his burgeoning knowledge, he betrayed it at unguarded moments when he gave offhand advice. When Frieda overheard his remarks, her face could not mask her chagrin. He had half expected her to scold him, a novice, for offering questionable suggestions, except the suggestions were more expert and articulate than she could have provided.

Then a profound thought struck him. Just as he was exploiting her knowledge, she was exploiting his talents to attract customers and expand her clientele. As he needed her, she needed him—his craftsmanship, his charm, his looks, but above all his imaginative ideas. But was it really an unfair trade? His ideas and artistry for her tutelage and the chance to learn the design business? He thought not.

Frieda, of course, was all too aware of Brock's rapid professional growth. His work was brilliant and his creative energies boundless. She sometimes was awed by his instinctive grasp of a design problem and its solution. She knew too that his competence as an interior decorator would eventually eclipse her own. She had stayed ahead of him by sheer guile, but the margin was narrowing. She knew her own limitations and her weaknesses. She was small-time; he was potentially a titan.

Yet there was a deeper animal magnetism about him that tantalized her. After her unsuccessful opening gambit that first night to personalize their relationship by sharing a drink at her apartment, she had not pursued that course, sensing that Brock preferred to keep their collaboration on a strictly professional level. She was content with that because she required his professional services. Her intimate needs were secondary, or so she hoped. Certainly she held no illusions about romance. She had never truly been in love with any man, and at her age it was a little late for adolescent games. She was fifteen years his senior.

Be that as it may, their relationship warmed. They were considerate of each other's feelings and moods, and they unconsciously spent more time together to talk business over lunch or dinner or in her office.

Six months after he began working for her their relationship reached a crossroads. They were seated in her office drinking coffee at the end of the day discussing an impatient client who, to accelerate completion of the remodeling of his restaurant, was urging Frieda to drop several features that, from Frieda's perspective, were integral to the design.

"If only you would talk with him," she implored. "I know he'd listen to you. You always sound so convincing."

Brock shook his head. "Frieda, babe, it ain't 'cuz I don't love yooz. I just don't have time. You have to realize that I'm only a part-timer with you. I have my regular job. I can't involve myself in this thing on a part-time basis. I need time to study it, gather the facts, meet with him, and follow it through to the end. That's just the way I am. You're working me to death as it is."

"I'm aware of that. And I've already commissioned five more projects for you to help with."

"That's madness!" he exclaimed, vigorously shaking his head. "When will I have the time? I'd have to work full-time for you."

"Well...?" She thought it over for a minute in silence. He had brought in so much business that she could afford to hire him full-time, and his total commitment and availability would enable her to take on even more jobs. Clients felt good around him, trusted him, and sought his advice. He was a natural drawing card worth his weight in future contracts. Moreover, with his expertise and talent she could venture into more ambitious and profitable design projects and perhaps compete with the larger firms for the real plums. Of course, she also enjoyed his company, but she told herself that was a minor consideration.

"Well," she repeated. "Maybe it's time you did."

"Did what?"

"Quit your job with Willie and worked for me full-time."

For some reason the idea had not occurred to Brock, but on weighing the pros and cons it would be a good move. "I think you're right." *Right, indeed*, he thought. *Working full-time on design—being able to concentrate my total energies and mind on this my chosen vocation— would be an exciting, momentous step that promises more money at once and, over the longer term, continued professional growth.* He slapped his hand on the corner of her desk. "I'll tell Willie first thing tomorrow." Striking an overly dignified pose, he leaned back from the desk and said in mock solemnity, "Ms. Steuben?"

"Yes?" she smiled knowingly.

"I accept your kind offer of employment. You will please direct your solicitor to draw up the appropriate contractual documents for my signature forthwith, in *saecula saeculorum, mutatis mutandis, ad valorem, ad libitum, ad infinitum,* and *ad nauseam.*"

"Oh, Brock." Laughing and forgetting her self-imposed restraints, she reached out and laid her hand on his. "I'm so pleased. And what's all that Latin talk?"

"Just stuff I picked up in school." He placed his other hand on top of hers and looked deeply into her lovely green eyes. For the first time they let down their defenses and revealed their mutual attraction. *It's strange,* he thought, *that in all these months our hands have never touched after that first handshake sealing our contract. In fact, we both have avoided saying or doing anything, especially touching each other, that could be interpreted as an invitation to something more intimate.*

Feeling nervous and embarrassed, Brock pulled his hands free and stood up. "This calls for a celebration," he said cheerily and checked his watch. "It's after seven. Let's highball it down to The Purple Tree and beat the rush. We won't need a reservation if we go now. Whataya think?"

She frowned playfully at his satirical use of her favorite phrase. "I say, great idea!"

She rose from her chair and walked around the desk, unconsciously straightening her skirt and adjusting the short matching jacket. Her primping drew Brock's attention to her clothes and to what lay beneath. He stepped backwards as much to let her pass as to avoid touching her. As she went by, he breathed in her perfume, savoring the aroma. The strict self-denying discipline that had sustained him during his years of preparation for the priesthood instantly sought to purge his mind of sensual thoughts, but to no avail. His motivation for purity had withered while his physical attraction to Frieda, fanned by her abounding femininity to which he was exposed nearly every day, had grown till it was constantly on his mind.

They left the office and drove in his car to the restaurant, an elegant establishment that specialized in French cuisine with tuxedoed waiters, candlelit tables with flowers, and live music. As the maitre d' led them to a table, they pretended not to notice the small hardwood dance floor they crossed, yet its presence evoked in both their minds the image of their dancing, their bodies touching for the first time, their lips only inches apart. As if the maitre d' wished to intensify this imagery, he put them at a table abutting the dance floor.

They ordered drinks and dinner selections with an exaggerated casualness that belied their shared excitement. As they struggled to make a pretense of conversation, they avoided eye contact, afraid their mutual physical attraction would somehow be revealed. Then the trio of musicians on the bandstand began playing a slow dance number. A young couple at the next table rose and moved leisurely to the center of the floor, where their bodies merged into one, swaying in perfect rhythm to the music. Brock and Frieda silently, intently watched the couple, picturing in their minds how it would feel to dance together.

Brock turned back to his drink and sipped it, methodically wiping the condensation off the glass with his thumb. So many feelings and thoughts rushed through his head that he was at a loss for words. He wanted to tell Frieda how attractive she looked, but he had never said that to anyone, and the words sounded silly and insincere as he spoke them in his mind. How did one begin an intimate conversation? He had no practice or experience to go on. Frustrated and angry at his ineptness, he could feel his normally granitelike self-composure turning bit by bit into quiet panic.

Frieda could stand it no longer. "I haven't danced in years, have you?" Her eyes searched his face, daring him to look at her.

"Not in years," he replied, his eyes still averted, focusing on his glass.

"Care to give it a try? I'll bet you're a good dancer."

He finally lifted his head and smiled. "Probably."

Without waiting for an invitation Frieda rose and extended her hand.

"Why not," he said, rising and taking her hand, his pulse suddenly racing.

The warmth of her fingers sent tremors through his body as they walked onto the floor. He held out his arm and she folded gracefully into it, giving the impression to anyone who might have been watching that they had done this a hundred times. Then they began to dance, slowly, a bit stiffly, leaving a respectable gap between their bodies.

Brock agilely guided her movements with only light pressure from his right hand, which held her loosely around the waist, feeling the softness of her skin through the sheer material of her blouse and jacket. Soon they overcame their awkwardness and moved as one around the floor. Cautiously Frieda drew closer to him, raising her cheek to his, as he was half a foot taller. Sliding his hand to the center of her back, he ever so gradually pulled her to him. Her physical closeness was a delicious mesmerizing sensation.

Frieda felt transported, swept away in a dream. It had been months since any man had held her, and years since anyone as muscular and handsome as Brock had been interested in her. His strength enveloped and overpowered her. She closed her eyes and pressed herself against him, nestling her head on his broad shoulder.

When the music ended, Brock clung to her a few seconds more, then reluctantly let loose. Feeling his hesitation, she took his hand and held it as they returned to their table. It was only then that they realized they hadn't spoken a word on the dance floor.

Brock, embarrassed, was first to break the spell. "I guess I have a one-track mind. I can't dance and talk at the same time."

"I never noticed," she replied truthfully, giggling.

The waiter served their dinner and recommended a wine which he produced with a flourish from a silver cooler beside the table. Brock sampled the wine and, without thinking, gave it his blessing by making a mini-sign of the cross over the bottle, a habit he had acquired at the seminary as a gag. They all laughed: the waiter to be solicitous, Frieda because she found the gesture humorous, and Brock to cover his concern, because he had never divulged to her that he had once aspired to the priesthood. He saw no reason to tell her now.

As they dined, a disquieting tension, heightened by their physical experience on the dance floor, permeated their conversation, like smoke from a smoldering fire. Neither one knew what to do or say to relieve the strain. Frieda had not felt so amorous in years.

She had been instantly attracted to Brock the first time she'd seen him in one of Willie's homes eight months ago. There was a latent animal power in Brock's well-proportioned physique and in the gliding, controlled way he moved. His dark eyes and rugged features were set off by thick dark curly hair that ran down the nape of his neck. Frieda had had many lovers, but had never fallen in love, even though many of her partners had been personable and attractive. Some of her girlfriends thought she was crazy for passing up such divine specimens. Yet the idea of marriage, most of all children, had always repelled her. She was too compulsive and transient, she knew, to be tied to one person and, worse, to bawling babies. The moment any man friend showed the slightest signs of marital interest, she became claustrophobic and broke off the relationship cold turkey. She would belong to no man and answer to

22

none. And that was perhaps Brock's most desirable trait. He was undemanding of her and nonthreatening, leading his own life without intruding on hers. He respected her independence, and she his. Certainly it was the most comfortable and benign relationship she had ever enjoyed with someone so deliciously desirable....

Something he said awoke her from her reverie. "What?" she asked.

"I said, do you want dessert?"

"Oh, no. I'm stuffed, thank you. Why don't we go? Let's split the tab."

"Not on your life! This one's on me."

"Well, aren't we the gallant tonight."

"I'm always gallant. You mean you haven't noticed?"

"I guess not. I'll be more observant in the future."

He paid for the dinner, and they left the restaurant and drove to Frieda's apartment building. Their conversation en route was spare and meaningless, nothing more than a time filler. On all previous occasions this would have been the end of their evening. He would have smiled, said something about the next day's work, then dropped her off at the lobby. She had not invited him up for a drink since their first meeting. Tonight Brock himself asked. "Is that invitation for a nightcap still open?"

"Of course." Her pulse surged with anticipation. "I thought you'd forgotten. And I have something special. A ten-year-old Portuguese brandy that will give new meaning to the word *mellow*."

They entered the lobby of her building and waited in nervous silence before the elevator. Neither could predict what would happen...or not happen...in her apartment, but they both knew their relationship had been permanently transformed on the restaurant's dance floor. Gone was any pretense that they could continue to disregard the powerful physical impulses driving their thoughts and actions. Their initial tacit agreement to avoid a romantic entanglement had been shattered beyond repair.

"This elevator has a mind of its own," said Frieda, impatient to reach her apartment and see how far Brock would go in the new direction their relationship had taken. "Shall we walk? It's only two flights."

"Why not? Lead the way."

She climbed the stairs hurriedly, not caring to hide her eagerness, while Brock followed two steps behind. As they left the stairwell and turned down the carpeted hallway, she withdrew from her handbag the apartment key and held it ready. She stopped so abruptly at her door that Brock bumped into her, knocking the key out of her hand. They both stooped to pick it up and knocked heads, then burst out laughing.

"Why don't you open it before we end up in the hospital," she entreated, taking a step back while he retrieved the key.

"My pleasure, mademoiselle," he replied with a curt bow. He opened the door, then stepped aside. "*Entrez vous s'il vous plait.*"

She entered...almost triumphantly. "Wanna use the little boys' room? It's off there to the left. I'm gonna change into my relaxing clothes."

She went into the bedroom while Brock used the half bath. He then removed his suit coat and, taking a seat on the large couch in the living room, surveyed its interior. It was too gaudy and harsh for his taste. *Vintage Frieda,* he mused. Glaring white walls, brilliant green-and-blue-flowered curtains, orange lamps, lavender furniture, white cushions, white carpeting. The contrasts were brazen and garish.

Ten minutes later Frieda emerged from the bedroom and strode to a wet bar in one corner of the living room, very much aware of the striking effect her changed appearance was having on Brock. She had doffed her business suit for a light pink negligee through which he could see the faint outlines of a lacy white bra and panties. She was barefoot and had unloosed her bun and let her blond hair fall across one shoulder. It had the effect she wanted. His eyes smoldered with desire.

She poured two brandies from her ten-year-old bottle, padded across the rug, handed Brock one of the glasses, and curled up beside him on the couch.

"Cheers, Brock," she said, raising her glass.

Dazed by the intoxicating scent of her perfume, the nearness of her body, and the pleasures it promised, he was speechless. They touched their glasses and sipped. The brown liquid glided down his throat, radiating a soothing exotic warmth that spread downward. He thought that, had he been standing, his body would have crumpled, melted by the heat of the liqueur.

Slowly, with impish burlesque, Frieda set her glass on a white Formica table behind the sofa. Turning back to Brock, she docily plucked his glass from his fingers and set it beside hers. Then she turned back once more, twisting sideways to face him and, taking his head gently between her hands, leaned forward and kissed him lingeringly on the lips.

Numbed by the brandy, by the luxurious moist suppleness of her lips, and by his internally raging desire, he kept his hands in his lap.

"Is something wrong?" she asked, unable to comprehend the signals she was reading. His skin was hot and his breathing labored, but he wasn't kissing her. His lips were rigid and lifeless.

"I..." He was unsure how to tell her. "I've never kissed a girl...a woman...before."

"You're kidding!"

"No. I'm not kidding. You're the first."

She was dumbfounded. This gorgeous Adonis was a virgin? A sexual infant? She would be his first? The idea aroused in her an intense feeling at once amorous and strangely maternal. "Then you've never made love to a woman?"

"Never."

"Never even kissed a woman before?"

"Never."

"That's incredible." This was new and unfamiliar territory for her. She wasn't sure how to proceed. She reached out and took hold of his hand as an adult comforts a child. She did not understand how anyone as handsome and sensual could be so inexperienced. "I have to ask you this, and I don't mean to insult you, but...are you...you know...gay?"

Brock grinned, understanding her perplexity, then laughed aloud. "No, I'm not gay. I've just led a very sheltered life, sort of saving myself for someone else."

"Someone else? You mean a childhood sweetheart?"

"Well, something like that."

"An arranged marriage?"

"I never thought of it in marital terms, but I suppose there is a similarity. You see..." He hesitated, fearful of her reaction should he reveal his background. "You see...since I was a teenager I've dedicated myself...to becoming a Roman Catholic priest." He held his breath, watching her face closely for a sign of rejection.

Bewildered, Frieda's mouth fell open and she slumped back on the couch, staring up at him in disappointed disbelief. "A priest?" she whispered.

"Oh, I'm not a priest," he said hastily, seeing the disappointment on her crestfallen face. "I quit the seminary."

"That's the college you were attending in Maryland?"

"Yes, but I gave it up."

"So, you're not gay," she purred excitedly "You're...you're just...inexperienced."

"Yeah." His voice was barely audible. "That's...that's it."

She sat up, got to her feet, and stood before him, her arms at her sides, her head lowered in a sultry pose. "May I teach you?" she cooed.

He looked up at her sheepishly but with a hunger she recognized and understood. "I'd like that."

FOUR

The next six months were a watershed in Brock's life, closing the final curtain on youth and ushering in unqualified maturity. He was now partaking fully of the fruits of manhood—a challenging and lucrative job, a new sports car, a rich flashy wardrobe, ample spending money, and a voluptuous lover whose omnivorous appetite was lifting Brock to heights of sensual pleasure he had never dreamed were possible. Above and beyond the tangible aspects of his new life, however, was the exhilarating sense of freedom and independence that imbued all of his actions, instilling in him an indomitable self-confidence that saw only limitless opportunities in the future.

A fundamental change, not apparent on the surface, had occurred in Brock's outlook on life. Perhaps less a change than a transition. Under Frieda's ministry he had sampled the good things in life...and was intoxicated. Addicted. He could no more stop imbibing in these new delights than he could stop breathing.

Because he had been spending most of every day and night at her place—some for business, mostly for pleasure—Brock had given up his flat and moved in with Frieda. It had made little sense to maintain two apartments. Moreover, to her surprise, he had brought with him from his other apartment ten computer-paper boxes containing his extensive library of books and magazines on design. The realization that he had been secretly expanding his knowledge of the many facets of her business intimidated her, proving Brock had ambitions far beyond working with her.

Nor did their cohabitation inhibit his freedom. He still came and went as he pleased, feeling no obligation to inform Frieda of his movements either beforehand and later. She, of course, deeply resented

27

this cavalier attitude but hid her displeasure for fear of antagonizing him. She knew Brock could find female companionship as easily as a postman finds mail. His gorgeous looks and manly proportions caught every woman's eye wherever he and Frieda went. She herself was past the point—several years past—when men turned to admire her appearance and figure. The subtleties and caring finesse of courting that she had so thoroughly enjoyed as a young woman were only memories, revived and savored now and then when she perused photo albums of her high school and college years.

Nor did she find warmth and enchantment in her relationship with Brock. She understood his fascination with his new possessions, among which he almost certainly included herself. He was like a child in a new world. Healthy, heady, and strong, he would follow his animal instincts in whichever direction brought him the most gratification. For that reason she knew there was no chance at all of building an enduring relationship with him. He would soon tire of her and move on, of that she was absolutely certain, for—more's the pity—she could sense he held no real affection for her. Although he was an ardent lover, he remained distant and apart, not understanding or seeming to care about her human needs outside of their sexual and business collaboration. It was all so cut and dried for Brock.

The irony of her situation weighed heavily upon her. For years she had eschewed any binding entanglement with a man, cherishing her independence and resentful of the subordinate role she believed men expected women to play. Yet, had she changed? Had she become threatened by the approach of middle age? Was she panicky over the idea of growing old alone? Was she simply lonely? Or was it Brock and his animal charisma?

She rolled over and laid her hand gently on the bulging biceps of his arm. He was asleep, his back to her. The pale light of dawn shown dimly through the drawn drapes. Running her fingers lightly back and forth across the smooth muscle, she studied the back of his head and its thick dark curly hair. So handsome, so virile, so innocent. Was it just the sex that bound her to him? Or was it something deeper? Could she truly be in love for the first time in her life...and with a man many years her junior? The question seemed irrelevant at the moment, however, because Frieda was beset by a much more imposing and ominous problem—the reason she had slept so fitfully the past three nights. Her period was overdue.

She had always been like clockwork where menstruation was concerned, even as a teenager. She could predict almost to the hour when it would begin and end. There had been occasional irregularities, but they were explained by illness or strenuous physical exertion. In her present situation, however, she could think of no factor that would explain her tardiness except the most unwanted one of all—pregnancy. Her stomach knotted at the thought, as it did each time she posed herself the question.

But of course! She sat up. How stupid of her! She was probably doing it to herself. At thirty-seven, changes in the body's functioning were normal and to be expected. Her period had been three days late, and her wild apprehension about it had by itself probably stopped the cycle.

She lay back again, relieved to have found an explanation that offered a way out of her dilemma. In any case she knew the issue could be resolved only by her physician. Frieda had to know, one way or the other. She would make an appointment as soon as the doctor's office opened. Closing her eyes, she snuggled next to Brock, reassuring herself that everything would be all right.

But what if she were pregnant, after all? Her eyes opened. How would he take it? Would he abandon her outright? Or might he accept responsibility and ask her to be his wife? He was after all a just man, a Christian. Given his deep religious beliefs—she supposed he had strong religious convictions from his days in the seminary although he never talked about them—he would naturally be disposed to sympathy for her. Surely he would not desert his own offspring.

But such thoughts were premature. Chances were very good that she was not pregnant, merely overly concerned and therefore tense. On this optimistic and restful note she fell soundly asleep.

Three days later she sat nervously on her couch awaiting Brock's entrance. He had phoned a half hour before to say he was leaving the office. She must tell him now. There was no point in waiting. Her physician had confirmed the worst. She was pregnant. She had rehearsed a hundred times how she would break the news to Brock and how she would respond to each of his possible reactions. Anger, depression, shock, happiness...

The door opened.

She took a deep breath and fought to appear relaxed.

"Hi, gorgeous!" Brock bawled, throwing his jacket on a table beside the door and picking up a stack of unopened mail she had left there. "We finished the Polynesian job. It came out perfect." He crossed the room and sat down heavily beside her as he ripped open an envelope. "Are you feeling better? You looked a little peaked this morning." He fell silent while he read the letter, a notice of a lecture series on interior lighting. "We missed you this afternoon at the showing," he said, tossing the letter on the rug and picking up another.

Aware all at once of her silence, he turned and studied her face. "Are you all right?"

"Yes, fine," she replied, almost whispering through a strained smile.

"You look tired. Maybe you should see your doctor." Brock started to open the letter.

"I did. And I want to talk to you about it." She stared straight ahead.

"Oh? Something wrong?" His eyes went to hers for information.

"I'm...I'm afraid...I...I'm..." The practiced words defied her. Tears welled in her eyes and rolled down her cheeks. "I'm..."

Brock knew at once. "You're pregnant," he said crisply.

"Yes." She was instantly alarmed at the sharpness of his voice.

He turned away and looked vacantly across the room, his face stony and impassive. "I thought you were on the pill," he challenged.

Frieda thought frantically of what to say next, but her mind went blank. "I am. I was."

"Then how did it happen!" he shouted, leaping to his feet and scattering the letters across the floor. He paced in front of his speechless lover like a caged animal. "How did it happen, Frieda, if you were on the pill? Huh?"

"I guess I forgot one time."

"One time! You *forgot?*" He spat the words out as if to strike her.

"I'm not perfect," she cried, burying her face in her hands. "It just happened."

"Not to me it doesn't *just happen!*" He shook his head violently. "Not to me!" he screamed. "This changes everything. Everything!" He picked up his jacket and stomped toward the door.

"It doesn't have to change things," she pleaded, struggling to remember the lines she had rehearsed. "I thought you should know that..."

But the door slammed. He was gone.

Frieda remained seated on the couch, weeping in the lonely silence.

Brock spent the next three days in a drunken stupor secluded in a downtown hotel, tormented by self-pity and embittered at this unexpected and unwanted turn of events. Such an irresponsible act tarnished his image of himself as a person of high purpose and ambition. How could he have let himself be used by that clawing, devious woman? What a fool he'd been. She had entrapped him from the start. Her plan was so obvious. Lure him to her apartment—she had invited him up the very first time they met. Seduce him. "Let me teach you," she had said. Teach, indeed. She had given him a complete post-graduate course. He took another drink of Jack Daniels. Oh, she was sly all right. "I forgot to take the pill." How many nights had she forgotten? More to the point, how many nights had she remembered? The truth was, she probably never took any pills. He had been so naive. Well, she wouldn't have him! Her little scheme would fail. No woman would ever again entrap Brock Stowolski. He'd make certain of that. He had to impose total control over his future relationships. Take charge. Anticipate. Give the orders. Yeah, that was it. Always be in charge.

Nodding in approval of his new resolve, he picked up the telephone beside the bed and dialed Frieda's apartment. His vision was blurred from his drinking, but his mind was clear, or at least he thought it was.

"Hello?" said a female voice softly.

"Frieda?"

"Brock. Are you all right?"

"Don't feed me the sensitivity act, honey. I've never felt better and I'm onto your game."

She started to protest.

"Just shut up and listen. I'm not going to marry you, but I'll stick around till you have the baby. We'll put it up for adoption. I'll make the arrangements ahead of time so the transfer can take place at the hospital. You understand?"

She was too traumatized to speak.

"Frieda, are you listening?"

"Yes...yes, I heard." Her voice was so soft he could barely hear her.

"Good. I'm driving to Baltimore in the morning to attend that Woodruff hardware exhibit. I'm gonna find my own place to live when I get back. Then I'll be by to pick up my things. Any questions?"

"No, Brock," she replied in a whisper. "I don't have any questions."

"Good. Take care of yourself...and the baby." He hung up and dialed room service. "Send me a pot of strong coffee and a half dozen donuts."

He was pleased with his decisiveness and display of authority. His life was on track again, and he was in command. As soon as Frieda had the baby, he would head west to California. According to what he had read in the design magazines, there was a flourishing market there for interior designers—just the place for him to get a new start. He was no longer a neophyte. He had mastered the business. Granted he was still a small-timer, but the only difference between Frieda's operation and the big rollers was scale, and he had ideas about how to break quickly into the top ranks.

When he entered Frieda's apartment four days later to collect his belongings, he found her seated on the living room rug studying some interior drawings. She smiled in an unexpectedly relaxed and friendly way and said, "I thought you'd be in a hurry, so I packed your things for you. They're in the kitchen."

"Thanks. I'll put 'em in my car."

After several trips outside carrying his belongings, he returned to the living room and sat down opposite her. "There are some things we need to discuss: medical bills, the adoption proceedings, and some legal details."

Without taking her eyes from the drawings before her, Frieda replied matter-of-factly, "Oh, I don't think there's any need to discuss those matters. You see, I'm not going to have a baby after all."

"What are you saying?" He was perplexed. "You weren't pregnant? Your doctor made a mistake?"

"Now don't get riled up," she said coyly, lifting her eyes to face his scowl. "I was pregnant, but I had an operation two days ago. It's all over. You don't have to agonize over it any longer."

Brock's mind reeled from the invisible blow her words had so casually delivered. "You killed it?" His voice was barely audible.

"Killed it? What are you talking about? I had an abortion."

"You killed it." His religious beliefs were stronger than he realized. Abortion was murder of the unborn. This was not a matter of debate but a plain and simple fact. He jumped to his feet now, poking his finger in her face. "You had no right! No right!"

"You said you didn't want marriage!" she snarled and stood up to meet his glare with her own. "You left. How was I to know you cared?"

"Cared!" he shouted back. "Cared? It was a human life, a human soul!" He stomped around the room, pounding his fist into his palm, needing to hit something. He grabbed a fancy glass ashtray and flung it angrily against the wall, tearing the wallpaper and smashing the ashtray to pieces on the wood floor.

"Who are you to talk?" she cried. "You act as if—"

"Shut up!" he shouted, glaring at her so menacingly that she stepped back from him and sat down on the rug. A powerful urge to beat her with his fists seized him, and he shook them at her violently, his face crimson. Suddenly he turned his rage against the coffee table, kicking it viciously. It crashed against the television console with a sound of splintering wood. While Frieda huddled against the couch, cowering in fear, Brock gradually regained control of his emotions. His arms fell limply at his sides, and he stood motionless before her, his face a mask.

The child was dead. Gone. There was nothing he could do about it. Nothing.

He looked around the room, deliberately, as if making an inventory of its contents. He was in control again. "Too gaudy a design," he said calmly. "Especially the curtains. I never liked it."

Without another word he walked to the door and left.

FIVE

The four-day drive across the Midwest to California was a catharsis for Brock's troubled spirits. As he traveled ever westward with the sun, the painful memory of his dead unborn child and Frieda's callous indifference gradually dissolved into shadowy opaque images that became lost amid the colorful scenery of the mid-American farmland.

Bit by bit the Rocky Mountains appeared, a giant formidable barrier inching up before him on the western horizon. How fragile and transient was man in comparison to these granite leviathans. How pitiful. His life span was a mere blink of an eye to these timeless giants. Oh, how Brock envied their serene fearless strength. A few men, a very few out of every million, made a lasting imprint on this planet. All the others were forgotten. Would he be forgotten? Would he pass unnoticed by history? Perhaps not. Brock had felt for many months an unshakable premonition of greatness in his future, a feeling that he would leave an indelible mark on future generations. He smiled, thinking of Father Leonard's inane proclamations about Brock's "bright future" in the Church. Poor Lenny. A victim of deplorably wishful thinking. Brock's achievements would, he was certain, be in the secular world, far from the rigid, restrictive culture of the Catholic Church.

Hours later, as he crested a rise, he came upon a small sign: Continental Divide 10 Miles. How appropriate, he thought, and prophetic. Just as this mountain range separated the country's water flow eastward and westward, so it would divide his life into two parts. All that had happened to him up to this point on the eastern side had been prologue. The rest of his life—his real life, the life that counted—lay to the west. He would live each day for itself, for its promise, and for its accomplishments, not counting the morrows or anticipating the pleasures and successes of the unknowable future. That was for dreamers. He would be too busy with the present to dream. He put out of his mind, as he always had, unpleasant thoughts and memories of the past that could distract him from achieving his immediate objective. He set his mind on that goal, as was his habit, with a cool singleness of purpose. By the time he arrived in Oakland on San Francisco Bay he had mapped out a detailed plan of action.

His first step, after finding an efficiency in a quiet suburb with easy access to the major highways, was to get employed at one of the renowned interior-design firms in the Bay Area through which he could study the California market, establish his reputation, make business connections, and determine where, after two or three years, he would open his own office. His initial interview was not an auspicious beginning.

The manager, a balding heavy-set effeminate man in his forties, was arrogant and aloof. "Where did you say you studied?" he asked, squinting derisively at Brock's resume.

"In Philadelphia."

"Yes, but at what school?"

"It wasn't a school. I was employed in a design firm."

"Which one?"

"It's run by Frieda Steuben. You may have heard of her. She's done some excellent work." So he lied a little.

"No," the manager replied, pouting and joggling his head. "Never heard of her. So what school did you attend before that?"

"Well, I was in a seminary..."

"No, dear fellow. Design school. What design school did you attend?"

"Well, none really. I..."

"That's all, thank you."

"But wouldn't you care to see my work?"

"What for? You're an untrained amateur. This is a professional business, not a training school. Get a degree, and come back and see us in five years."

"Anita Slavitch, Executive Vice President" read the gold nameplate on her desk. Middle-aged, thin, attractive, intense, and hyper. She had agreed to look at Brock's portfolio of interior designs, though her lingering gaze and handshake suggested she had something other than his professional qualifications in mind. He laid the portfolio before her and took a seat. She scanned the first drawing, sniffed, and made a sour face. She turned the page, passed her eyes quickly over the next drawing, closed the folder, and pushed it toward him.

"You didn't look at the others," he protested.

"I don't need to."

"Hey, gimme a break! I can tailor a design to any particular taste or period. I've been quite—"

"No need, Mr. Sto...whatever your name is. Let's drop last names." She smiled and winked. "I have no position for you now, Brock, but why don't we have dinner and get to know each other better. Then...who knows?"

"No thanks," he said curtly, gathering up his portfolio. "I haven't got time."

Her smile vanished. "What you haven't got, mister, are credentials, which you need to work in a top company like this one."

"Where did you study design?"

"Night school. An extension program of the University of Pennsylvania. And, of course, I've undertaken a great deal of independent study of all aspects of the business."

"Experience? Oh, yes, I see it here in your resume. Thirteen months with Frieda Interiors of Philadelphia." He consulted a thick leather-bound volume on his desk. "I don't find it in the industrial directory."

"Well, it's quite small. Kind of a one-woman show, but she does a fair amount of business in the Philly area."

"I'm sorry, but we can't use you. We're very particular about the credentials of our staff. You understand. Perhaps in a few years when you've had more experience."

"You say you called about an interview?"

"I not only called, I was given this date and this time."

"Do you remember whom you talked with?"

"Yes. You!"

"Well, Mr. Prentiss has no time to see you."

"Today or ever?"

"You needn't be belligerent, sir. Mr. Prentiss is very busy and hasn't time for interviews with..."

"With inexperienced applicants. Look, toots. I've been on this merry-go-round for six weeks. You made me an appointment, and I'm keeping it."

Brock picked up his briefcase and folder and strode defiantly across the plush white carpet to a paneled oak door which he opened as the secretary frantically buzzed the occupant. A tanned, bony, prematurely haggard man in his midforties wearing a white shirt and gray silk tie sat stooped behind an antique desk smoking a cigarette. He looked up at Brock coolly.

"Mr. Prentiss?" said Brock.

The secretary appeared in the doorway behind Brock and started to speak. Prentiss raised his hand. "Not to fret, Gloria. Thank you." She disappeared, closing the door behind her. "Yes, I am Roger Prentiss." He didn't rise or extend his hand but waited for Brock to identify himself and his purpose.

"My name is Brock Stowolski. I'm a designer. I'm here to interview for a job." He set his briefcase and folder down next to an easy chair facing the desk and offered his hand.

Prentiss rose nonchalantly and, reaching across the desk, grasped Brock's hand limply. He motioned for Brock to be seated and sat down himself. "It takes gall and toughness in this business. You seem to be well equipped in that area. What else do you have?"

Brock, elated by this indirect encouragement—the first he had received in California—began his spiel, which by now was well rehearsed and polished. He spoke earnestly of his desire to succeed in the design field and of his conviction that he had the artistic and professional talent required. Prentiss listened attentively, nodding as Brock made his points. Brock opened his folder and turned the pages slowly, one by one, as he described the purpose, concept, and merits of each design. When he was finished, his spirits soared. Obviously Prentiss had been impressed.

Prentiss ground out his second cigarette in an ashtray, stood, leisurely circled his desk, and went to the door. Brock started to rise.

"Don't get up," said Prentiss. "Enjoy yourself a moment. I have an appointment to keep." He took a suit coat from an antique coatrack beside the door. "This will be your last visit in this office, so make the most of it."

As he opened the door, Brock leaped up and threw his shoulder against it, slamming it shut. Prentiss stood expressionless, awaiting Brock's next move.

"Is that all?" growled Brock. "You just leave? The interview is over? *Fini?*"

"Hey, it was your show, kiddo. You forced your way in here, so I watched. Frankly I've seen Mexican house painters do better work in the rain." He pulled halfheartedly on the doorknob to signal his wish to leave, but Brock held his ground.

"What is it with you people out here? You're hung up on credentials and experience. That's all I've heard for six weeks. What about my work?" He pointed to his folder on the rug. "My designs are original, they're beautifully articulated, they're eye-catching, functional, and marketable. And you hand me a bunch of crap about their quality."

"Let me tell it to you straight, young man. Marketable designs are a dime a dozen. It's the other aspects of the business that are critical: image, style, reputation. They are what separate the big winners from the big losers. It's a matter of class, which is something you ain't got. You're crude, unpolished, abrasive, egotistical, and pushy. I don't like your style or your reputation. Now, if you'll excuse me." Prentiss pulled on the door, and this time Brock gave way.

"What reputation?" Brock asked, perplexed.

"You'll find the design community here is fairly close-knit," Prentiss said, brushing past Brock and continuing to talk as he walked through the outer office. "A bad reputation travels fast in close company. Why don't you try something else? You'll never make it out here as a designer." He left through the ornate glass doors at the entrance.

Brock stared after him, red-faced and tight-lipped, while the secretary, embarrassed, looked away, busily arranging papers on her desk. Brock, speaking softly to himself and staring at the closed door through which Prentiss had left, muttered, "Oh, I'll make it, Mr. Roger Prentiss. You can bet on that. And when I do, you and the rest of the design community will see who has real class."

Had Brock been able to study his own eyes at that moment he would have seen in them for the first time a glint of vengeance, that compulsion born of our innate sense of justice to punish those who wrong us. It was only a glint, but it was there nevertheless, part of his emerging personality linked inseparably with his ambition. It was one of the traits for which he would long be remembered.

The first step in Brock's master plan had unceremoniously foundered on the hidden shoals of the snobbery and arrogance of San Francisco's design community. In retrospect he should have expected it and been prepared, but this initial setback did not concern him, so strong were his renewed determination and self-confidence. The fact that he had failed to find employment with a leading firm merely meant he would have to skip that stage and move directly to the next—setting up his own office—which he undertook the very next day. It would require flair and imagination and, oh yes, gall and toughness. But as Prentiss had observed, those were qualities with which Brock was richly endowed.

When the California Federal Bank opened its doors, Brock, smartly dressed in a slick gray business suit and tie and highly polished black wingtip shoes and carrying an expensive black leather briefcase, was the first to enter. When he departed two hours later, he was the self-assured owner of a one-year one-hundred-thousand-dollar loan secured on the stocks, bonds, and real estate he had inherited from his stepfather. Prudent investors would regard Brock's action as foolhardy, considering his slim chance of success, but the thought that he might lose it all never entered his mind.

His next stop was the stylish twenty-story Calvert Plaza Building in Oakland to which he went directly from the bank.

"May I help you?" asked the young receptionist in the building manager's office, her face aglow with attraction for the gorgeous hunk before her.

Brock enjoyed her reaction but ignored it, keeping his mind centered on his task. Moments later, after polite introductions, he explained his purpose to the manager, a fidgety fat man with a pulpy bloated face perpetually adorned with beads of sweat. "I would like to rent a suite of offices above the fifteenth floor with a view of the Golden Gate Bridge."

"What sort of business is yours?"

"Interior decoration and design. My own firm."

"Very good." Design was a reputable business and would be in harmony with the other professions in the building. "How old is your company?"

"New. Brand-new. I'm starting it at this time."

"Oh, I see," said the manager with undisguised reservation. "You are not well-established then, I mean, with a strong clientele?"

"No, but I will be very soon."

"Well, Mr. Sto...skow..." He gave up and frowned. "The rent is steep, and we have strict criteria for leasing. You understand, I'm sure. We have a high standard to uphold for our tenants."

"Look, let's cut the bull." Brock pulled out his wallet and withdrew ten one-thousand-dollar bills which he fanned onto the blotter in front of the manager. "I'll pay cash in advance. Now why don't we go see what you've got?"

The manager's eyes widened as he smiled and scooped up the bills. "I think we have just what you're looking for."

Brock hired a skilled carpenter for the next four weeks and the two of them, working nearly around the clock and employing every decorating technique he had mastered in Philadelphia, completely remodeled his 18th floor suite. They knocked out walls, built new ones, installed a wet bar, kitchenette, and bathrooms, put in new lighting fixtures and electronic systems (computers, phone and Internet connections, fax machine, stereo, intercoms, lighting switches, television, and a security system), painted and papered walls, installed wall paneling, laid carpeting, hung drapes and pictures, and on the final day unpacked three heavy truckloads of new furnishings and office machinery. When they had arranged the last piece of furniture and hauled the empty shipping containers to the rear loading dock, Brock treated his helper to a steak dinner and a two-hundred-dollar bonus for his hard work and craftsmanship. Then, bidding him farewell, Brock returned to the Calvert Plaza.

Still wearing his working clothes, he signed in with the security guard at the entrance as was the practice after 8 PM. Before going up to the suite, he inspected the office directory on the wall of the lobby and found his new company's name—DESIGN METAPHORS Room 1801.

Step Two completed, he thought. *I'm on the map.*

He took the elevator to the 18th floor and, as he waited for the doors to open, pretended he was a prospective client on his first visit to the office. What would the person's reaction be to the entrance?

The doors opened. Brock looked straight ahead. Directly opposite the elevator was a full-length glass wall at the center of which were two shiny brass doors that opened into the reception room of his suite. Light blue floor-to-ceiling drapes behind the glass were pulled back by thick white braided cords like stage curtains allowing persons outside a clear view of the interior. Mounted on the exterior of the glass in giant brass letters in an arc above and on both sides of the doorway was the firm's name: D-E-S-I-G-N M-E-T-A-P-H-O-R-S. Soft overhead lighting in the hallway and brilliant interior lights from two crystal chandeliers in the reception room created a breathtaking display that would have dramatic impact on visiting clients as they stepped out of the elevator.

No class, Prentiss? We'll see who has class!

Brock unlocked one of the heavy brass doors and entered, surveying the reception room for shortcomings in its decor. Finding none, he conducted a room-by-room tour, a final inspection, beginning with the wood-paneled conference room behind the reception area, then through his L-shaped corner office affording a sparkling nighttime panorama of San Francisco Bay, through the design shop with its drawing tables, computers, and printers and finally his bedroom, kitchenette, and bath. The suite would be his office, workplace, and residence—the command center of his life for the indefinite future.

He went to the bar, made himself a Manhattan, and sat down in the studded leather recliner that doubled as a chair behind his crescent dark-green marble-topped desk in the corner flanked by floor-to-ceiling windows. Except for the dim spotlight over the bar the room was dark, illuminated only by the shimmering galaxy of lights in the city below. He sipped the drink and felt its warmth pervade his tired body. He was beginning to unwind. He had driven himself to the limit these past four weeks with no more than a few hours' sleep a night. Too many phone calls to be made, materials to be ordered, jobs to be done.

Thank God for his helper. Together they had achieved a minor miracle, transforming a sterile run-of-the-mill office space into a stunningly electrifying environment where creative ideas and revolutionary design concepts would virtually spring to life on their own. It would be a showplace for his daring flamboyant innovative style of design.

A supremely satisfying sense of accomplishment filled him. So these were the fruits of real achievement, he mused. Fulfillment, contentment, release. A time for reflection to savor the victory. It was a delicious feeling. Never had he felt so keenly purposeful and predestined to greatness. Eighteen months ago he was studying in a quiet seminary to become a priest; now he was head of a new design business sitting high above San Francisco Bay, twenty-five hundred miles away, in a spectacularly beautiful office that he had personally designed and built. If he could come so far in so short a time, what might he accomplish in the decades ahead?

As he dreamed of what the future might hold, the fatigue that he had tenaciously fought off during this grueling marathon finally demanded its due, and he sank into a deep restful sleep in his recliner.

Refreshed the next morning after a shower, shave, and a zestful breakfast that he prepared in his kitchenette, Brock poured himself a third cup of coffee and seated himself at his desk. He made a mental note to order a silver nameplate inscribed with his name for the desk to complete his mental picture of his office. He opened a small pocket calendar and checked the date. *Right on schedule,* he thought proudly. *This is Personnel Day, the day to begin recruiting a staff.*

He phoned a dozen secretarial agencies, accounting firms, and design schools, making appointments to visit only the latter. He wanted the others to come to him: the secretaries, so he could judge at first hand what their appearance and personality would add or detract from the special atmosphere he had created; the accountants, so they would experience the richness and vitality of his office suite and convey that perception back to their superiors. They would be the initial vectors in his publicity campaign. He must begin at once to publicize his firm among those elements of the business community critical to his success, for time was his principal enemy, as his expenditures to implement his plan would rather quickly consume his liquid capital.

By late afternoon he had interviewed eight eager motley secretaries and a few surly, unimpressive accountants. Although he was content to prolong the search for an accounting firm to get as much mileage from the publicity as possible, the quest for a secretary was a priority that could not wait. The applicants were all uninspiring until Mrs. Margaret Finley made her entrance. Brock knew at once that fortune had smiled on him.

She was thirty, taller than average, with a well-proportioned but not provocative figure that wore clothes well. Touches of prematurely gray hair and strong facial features gave her the look of elegance and maturity that Brock was seeking. Her whole appearance, set off by a snappy two-piece burgundy suit and delicate white silk blouse, told him she had discerning taste in clothes and makeup. All in all she would impart a regal quality to the reception room and serve as an impressive frontispiece for the firm. On the professional side she was equally well qualified. An untimely widow without children, she had eight years' experience as a secretary, prided herself on her efficiency and, more important, displayed considerable knowledge of the Bay Area business community, having assisted her late husband who was a commercial building inspector for the city of Oakland. Until his death from cancer two months earlier, she had worked only part-time, but now was seeking a full-time position.

"What do your friends call you?"

"Margaret...Margie...Marge," she replied in a resonant self-assured voice. "I answer to anything, especially if it comes wrapped in a smile."

Brock chuckled, warming to her gentle nature. "I'll remember that."

"My parents always called me Maggie." She liked this good-looking man. Honesty and integrity showed in his dark radiant eyes and bright smile.

"Well, then, Maggie, what do you think of this suite? Would you feel comfortable here?"

"Yes, indeed, Mr. Stowolski," she answered hastily, pronouncing his name comfortably. "I've never seen such a beautiful office."

He was impressed at how quickly she had mastered his name. A small thing, but another indication of her talents. "The salary I quoted you is the best I can offer now but, as the business grows, I assure you there will be steady increases, in keeping, of course, with the sustained quality of your work."

"You'll have no concerns there."

"I'm sure I won't. So when can you start?"

"Is that a formal offer, Mr. Stowolski?" Her eyebrows arched expectantly.

"Absolutely."

"Then anytime."

"Uh, would...now be too soon?" he asked hesitantly, almost pleading. "There's so much needs to be done."

She smiled broadly. "Let's get started. Oh, there is one thing."

"Yes?"

"I customarily address my bosses by their last name. It's more professional and businesslike. You know what I mean."

"Certainly."

"Well, you see, your last name is such a mouthful. Would you mind terribly if I called you Mr. B?"

44

Brock laughed. "Maggie, we're going to be a great team!"

He proceeded to describe the interior design business, which was relatively new to her. Maggie absorbed all of this readily. When he finished, he showed her through the suite, ending up in the reception room, her new domain where he demonstrated how to operate the various electronic locks, intercoms, and lighting systems that were controlled from a panel next to her desk.

"Are you computer literate?" he asked worriedly, realizing he hadn't posed that all-important question to her before he offered her the job.

"Of course. Isn't everyone? Why don't you leave me here for a bit so I can get organized, get acquainted with my computer, and set up some computer files I'll need. If you need anything, call or buzz me."

Brock smiled. He liked her take-charge attitude. "Sounds good to me."

He returned to his desk to draw up her contract. He'd been working only a few minutes when the intercom buzzer sounded. "Yes, Maggie?"

"Mr. B, could I have a word with you please?"

"Sure, come on in."

Maggie rounded the corner and sat down next to his desk, a quizzical expression on her noble face. She lowered her voice to a conspiratorial level. "There are no files in the file cabinets."

"Yes, I know."

"Then where are your business records?"

Brock smiled reassuringly. "Maggie, I told you. There are none. We're just beginning."

"You mean you have no clients, not one?" Her voice was still hushed.

"That's right," he replied, unconsciously mimicking her whisper. "Like I said, this is a brand-new company. My first job, once we get this place organized, is to find us clients, and rich ones too."

Her face was torn with concern. "But, if you have no clients, how can you afford to pay for all of this? Oh, please understand, I'm not worried about my salary. Please don't think that, but...well..." She swallowed. "We have no clients. How will you get them? We don't even have a staff. Who will do the work?"

Brock rose from his desk and went to one of the windows. "They're all down there, Maggie."

He waved his arm toward the window. "They haven't heard of us yet. They don't even know we exist. But the word will spread. It's already started. Even now those reps from the accounting firms are making inquiries about us. DESIGN METAPHORS? What's their credit rating? Are they a stock company? Who owns them? Oh, the big firms will ignore us. Fly-by-night, they'll call us. No competition. But I promise you, Maggie..."

He turned and pointed a finger at her. "Within twelve months DESIGN METAPHORS will be the most talked about firm in the California design industry with an expanding clientele that will include some of the biggest home and office builders in the state." His eyes blazed with fierce resolve. "That's a promise!"

He stepped up to her chair and laid his hand gently on her shoulder. "Don't worry, pretty lady. I'm not going to fail. And to ease your worries, I'm writing into your contract a one-year's guaranteed salary. How's that?"

She stood and exhorted, "Please, Mr. B, you needn't do that. You'll think I was pressuring you. That's not necessary at all."

"Yes, it is, Maggie. It's important to me and to the firm that you feel secure in your job. If you are, you'll perform at your peak. We're all going to have perform at our peak to make this company a success. You, me, and the other people I'm going to hire. As corny as it sounds, it will take a total team effort. So just stick with me, Maggie. We're gonna make it...and with style and class."

Prentiss's smug expression flashed across Brock's mind.

As he returned to his desk, she studied him. Could this young man really conquer such ambitious heights? Was it possible? Her unfailing intuition told her it was—that this man standing before her could one day be a legend...a giant. It was men with his vision and daring that had built this country.

So, yes, she would go along for the ride. No matter how it turned out, the trip would be exciting.

Brock sat down in his recliner and adjusted the back. "Any questions?" he said.

"Yes, Mr. B. Just one. Would you like some coffee? I've made a pot."

"Yes, ma'am! Black. No cream, no sugar."

Maggie took full control of the office's operation. Brock was elated with her efficiency and breadth of knowledge of administrative matters. She first cancelled further interviews with secretary applicants, with a wink at Brock when he looked in on her as she made the phone calls. Then she ordered office supplies, set up a comprehensive filing system for both hard documents and computer records, researched the watering and nutritional needs of the variety of decorative plants around the suite, sternly chastised an accounting firm by phone for their representative's failure to keep his appointment, and saw to scores of other small tasks to ensure that her employer could give his undivided attention to the substantive business of the firm without concern for the administrative end. That was Maggie's realm and Brock quickly learned to trust her knowledge and judgment in that area.

In the next days Brock paid his scheduled visits to the design schools, where he hoped to recruit an artist-designer at minimum wage. What he proposed to the school directors by phone was a co-op arrangement in which the student selected would work part-time and receive commensurate academic credit to be determined by the school. The participant would gain valuable experience, and Brock would have use of his or her skills at reasonable cost. All of the directors enthusiastically endorsed the program, advertised it, and arranged for Brock to interview the handful of students in each school who applied. As he anticipated, the directors were uniformly surprised at his young age but courteously concealed their reservations and proceeded with the interviews.

Several of the applicants, both men and women, exhibited impressive artistic skills, but of that group only one, a young woman Brock's age, showed that spark of unconventional creativity he was looking for. The color contrasts and textural variations in her work were vibrant and exciting and made the compositions of the others dull by comparison.

"Thank you so much," Brock said to the director as he entered her office and laid a stack of drawings on her desk. "You've been very helpful. I wish I could repay you in some way."

She rose and shook his hand graciously. "I'll be repaid if you hire one of my students. We welcome any opportunity to interact with the industry. It's good for our students and, frankly, enhances our image. So what's the verdict? Did any of our applicants make the grade?"

"They are all very talented, as you know, but there was one...a Miss Rollins."

"Yes, Noreen."

"I would like to see more of her work and interview her if I might."

"Oh, she'll be thrilled," said the director happily. "I think she's still in the building, if you'd care to wait."

"I would indeed."

She led him to a vacant office nearby, showed him a chair, and left. Minutes later Noreen Rollins burst through the doorway, out of breath, lugging a tattered canvas bag containing various page-size computer-designed prints as well as larger cardboards and canvases on which other of her artwork was mounted. Her disheveled appearance was vintage artist. She wore open-toed sandals, paint-spotted jeans, a ragged, faded gray sweatshirt, and no jewelry. Her wan narrow face, shrouded in a mop of long dark unkempt hair, had not seen makeup in weeks nor the sun in months, and there was a hint of discoloration in her lips that suggested anemia or, God forbid, something worse. Probably undernourished, thought Brock hopefully, but he wasn't her keeper and would not concern himself with her private affairs. It was only her art and design skills that mattered.

She set the bag of prints, drawings, and paintings down heavily on the floor and flopped into a chair to catch her breath. "I'm sorry," she panted. "I was in...the far wing." She brushed aside a tangle of hair from her face and fanned herself with one hand to cool off. "I brought...all my work...from the past...six months. Is there...anything particular...you want to see?"

"No," he said, getting up. "If I may, I'll just leaf through the materials."

"Oh, sure." She started to lift the bag to him, when he knelt beside her chair and propped the bag against his knee. "I'm embarrassed," she said, regaining her breathing, "that I haven't put together a respectable portfolio. I wasn't expecting anyone to look at my work. It's only..."

"Please don't worry. I fully understand. It's not a problem. The only thing that matters is your work."

Brock leafed through the prints and fingered through the boards, one by one, passing some quickly, lingering over others.

Noreen watched him apprehensively, her dark eyes admiring his looks and measuring his expression for signs of approval. His youth surprised and intrigued her. He looked to be about her own age of twenty-two. She had no idea who he was or what his company was all about. The director had said he was its founder and president. He was so young. Perhaps he was rich.

"I really like your style, Miss Rollins."

Her eyes glowed.

"I understand you are fully trained and skilled in the leading computer design software."

"Yes. We use the latest programs here at the school, and I've done freelance work for several graphics-design firms: ads, logos, desktop publishing, things like that. Copies of that work are among the prints there."

"Yes. I saw them. Nice work." He stood and took his seat again a few feet away. "In my meeting earlier today with the director I explained the nature of the position you've applied for and the salary and working hours. She said she had relayed all of that information to the applicants. Do you have any questions about it?"

"Did I understand," said Noreen, "that this job could become full-time if I do well?"

"Absolutely." He nodded encouragingly. "Mine is a new firm. It will be small for awhile, but as the business grows so will the organization. If your work is of a high standard, I would certainly invite you to convert to full-time when our workload warrants."

"I do want to finish school and get my degree."

"You'll have time for that, I assure you."

"It sounds great. When will I know if I get the job?"

"You just did."

"I did?" A broad smile instantly erased the worry that had clouded her face. She clapped her hands, unable to contain her joy. "This is great!"

"When can you start?"

"Whenever you say."

"Tomorrow. Eight o'clock sharp. We're across from the elevator on the 18th floor of the Calvert Plaza. You can't miss it."

By the time he arrived back at the Plaza it was 7:30 PM and Maggie had gone. She had left the reception room in perfect order, exactly as Brock had designed it, even his arrangement of magazines on the coffee table. Her neatness pleased him because it reflected clear orderly thinking. She was also a bug on cleanliness and had vowed that the Plaza's evening char force would keep the suite as clean as it was beautiful. "Eet weel be," she had said, affecting the heaviest French accent she could muster, "le zone sanitaire."

Brock locked the hallway door and went to his desk, where he found that Maggie in her meticulous fashion had arrayed a dozen messages for him in a perfect semicircle. A red PRIORITY label was stapled to one of the slips, so he read it first. On it in exquisite cursive she had written that she highly recommended the accounting firm of Winchel & Smathers, whose representative had visited the suite unannounced that afternoon. He had no appointment but had been in the Plaza on other business. (*How swiftly the word is spreading*, thought Brock. He had not contacted W&S.) She directed Brock to a corner of the desk where she had left a yellow folder containing background material and references she had obtained for a modest fee from a credit agency and a business research service giving the history of W&S, their customers, and their financial positions. She said that W&S was a prestigious, highly reputable firm and that having them as accountants would add a sparkle or two to DESIGN METAPHORS' image.

Brock grinned and shook his head. *Maggie*, he thought, *you're marvelous.*

He fixed himself a Manhattan and read through the other messages, all of which concerned mundane matters he would handle tomorrow, chief of which was retaining a lawyer to handle all of the company's legal affairs. His task tonight was to begin laying out DESIGN METAPHORS' first portfolio of interiors, which he would personally brief to potential

50

clients including the major building contractors in northern California.

He opened a low cabinet behind him and withdrew a bulging manila folder bound with string. It contained a collection of original design ideas he had produced over the past year while working with Frieda. Some were captured in full-blown color drawings; others were no more than rough pencil sketches, a few hastily scrawled on the back of a restaurant menu or scrap of paper. He had never shown these to Frieda, having jealously guarded them as a treasure trove for the day when he would need a reserve of fresh ideas. That day had come.

He emptied the contents onto his desk and methodically examined each sketch, sorting them in piles on the rug according to their theme and style and innovativeness. Occasionally he grabbed a pencil and added something or took a clean sheet of paper and recorded a new idea before it escaped him.

When he had reviewed the last sketch, he went to the design shop, got a tablet of oversized drawing paper, and returned to his office, one corner of which was outfitted as his personal studio with drawing table, stool, pencils, pens, paints, pastels, and all the paraphernalia he would need. He eschewed using a computer to do his design work, preferring to let his ideas flow directly and smoothly from his mind, down his arm, through his fingers, into a pencil, and onto paper. That way he could virtually "feel" his ideas being created. He switched on the two gooseneck lamps attached to the drawing table, laid the pad of paper on it, pushed the stool aside, preferring to stand as was his habit when he was creating, and began to outline the cover of the portfolio. He worked speedily and with decisiveness, putting onto the paper in a steady uninterrupted stream the sharp images that formed in his mind.

Finishing the cover, he ripped the page from the tablet, laid it on the floor beside the drawing table, then stood, hands on hips, in the center of the room surveying the assorted piles of drawings on the rug. After moments of deep concentration, a snap of his fingers signaled a decision, and he bent down, thumbed rapidly through the sketches in one stack, pulled one out, and hurried back to the drawing table. He set the sketch on an easel, adjusted the angle of the table and lamps, and feverishly attacked the tablet with his pencil, translating the concept of the rough drawing into a finished design.

51

And so he labored through the night, taking infrequent breaks to relieve himself, to refill his coffee cup, or to massage his stiff legs. His concentration and pace were so intense that he was oblivious to the passage of time and startled when Maggie's stern voice broke his train of thought.

"Mr. B!"

He spun around atop the stool on which he'd been forced to sit an hour earlier when his legs tired from standing.

Maggie was standing in the center of the room frowning. "Have you been up all night?" she exclaimed.

"All night?" Brock squinted out the window at the daylight and then at his watch.

"Shame on you!" she scolded. "You can't go without sleep. You'll get sick, and then where will we be?"

"Not to worry, Maggie," he replied, smiling to ease her obvious concern. "Besides..." He gestured to the stack of drawings he had drafted overnight. "We've got a portfolio to publish. I'll take a nap later." He rubbed his face and realized he should shower and shave. Noreen Rollins would be arriving any minute, and he wanted to look the part of a manager, not a hired hand. Although he was wearing a T-shirt, he suddenly felt naked, having removed his shirt and tie as well as his shoes and socks during the night.

"Do me a favor." He walked past Maggie toward his bedroom. "Make a new pot of coffee. I'm gonna take a shower." He stopped at the doorway and turned to remind Maggie to expect Rollins, but Maggie had disappeared into the reception room. He traced her steps and said, "A girl named Noreen Rollins is joining—"

Noreen was sitting in one of the easy chairs.

"Good morning," she said, shocked at the radical change in his appearance since the day before.

"Uh, good morning." He was taken aback. "Nice to see you. I've been..." He started to describe his work of last night but noticed her staring at his bare feet. "Uh, Maggie will show you around. I have to clean up. Then we can talk." He smiled gamely and retired to his room.

An hour later over breakfast in the kitchenette Brock, in shirt and tie, explained to Noreen her first project. "I'll rough out the ideas, putting

52

in as much detail as I can and as time permits. Your job is to finish them—colors, shadings, tone, highlights, the works either on the computer or on paper, as I direct. My genius is on the conceptual side. I'll accept changes you want to make in my designs, but check with me first. I make all final decisions. Questions?"

"No, I understand," she said demurely, captivated by his flashing dark eyes.

"How long will it take you to finish the fifteen layouts I did last night?"

"On computer or paper?"

"Paper."

"I would say a minimum of three hours per sketch, which may be optimistic. I warn you I'm a perfectionist."

"That's all right. That's why I hired you."

She paused for mental calculations. "That comes to about two and a half weeks, maybe three, if I work four hours a day."

"That's good. We'll plan on it. You get to work on the designs right away, while I line up a printer."

They got up from the table, and Brock moved to his desk, taking his coffee cup with him. He buzzed the intercom.

"Maggie, call that market research outfit for me. The ones who gave you that info on Winchel & Smathers. I wanna talk to them."

Brock continued to press himself and his embryonic staff to their limits as the various pieces of his master plan began to fall into place.

He visited model homes and condominiums and newly decorated offices and prepared lengthy critiques of their interiors. Through the market research firm he amassed statistics on the sales record of each model, the cost of the interiors, and the name of the design firm that did the work. He then correlated sales rates with interior-design costs for the models and ranked all of the firms by what he called "design effectiveness." These statistics showed convincingly that model homes and condos decorated by the three least "design effective" firms were regularly outsold by competitors. Noreen converted these statistics into multiple sets of colorful computer-generated briefing boards, each set individually tailored to one of the contractors who hired these three firms.

Finally, Noreen completed the design portfolio. A gifted artist, whose natural talent had won Brock over the moment he saw her work at the design school, she transformed his scribblings and rudimentary designs into brilliant lifelike renderings, so clear and sharp they looked like photographs.

One month after Brock had worked through the night sketching interiors for the portfolio, a courier from the printer delivered twenty copies of the finished product. Maggie summoned Noreen and together they brought the package to Brock's desk. He looked up from a legal document and said, "What's this?"

Maggie purred with excitement. "The portfolios."

Brock leaned back in his recliner. "You open it," he said cheerfully. "You're the mail handler."

Her eyes aglow, she slit open the wrapping and withdrew one copy, cradling it in both hands as if it were breakable. "Mr. B, it's magnificent!" She set it down before him with reverence.

He gazed at its black velvety leatherlike cover, admiring the gold embossed letters spelling DESIGN METAPHORS across the top and in the center the imprinted logo which Brock had designed for the firm: a luxuriantly plumed bird of paradise gliding through the arch of a rainbow above a pillowy bank of clouds. Maggie and Noreen gathered around his chair as he leafed methodically through the twelve-by-twenty-inch brochure, all of them oohing and ahing and applauding one another as each design appeared. When Brock turned over the final page he laid the portfolio on the desk, rose, and went to the bar.

"A toast is in order," he proclaimed. He opened the refrigerator and took out a small gold-capped bottle of champagne.

"Mr. B!" admonished Maggie. "You're too extravagant."

"This is an historic moment." He popped open the bottle, poured three glasses, handed one to each of the women, and raised his own. "To my enterprise...and its success." They sipped and savored the cold pungent liquid while Brock continued. "Do you remember a month ago, Maggie, on your first day when you revealed to me that we had no clients?"

"Don't remind me."

"Well, dear, this is D-Day. With these brochures in hand we are now ready to strike, not like that graceful bird of paradise on the cover but like a deadly taloned hawk, soaring high in the sky, patiently tracking our prey. Tomorrow, like the hawk, we'll fold our wings tightly and streak out of the sky, swooping down on our targets without warning."

"You make it sound so savage," observed Noreen more reproachfully that she had intended.

But Brock rose to the challenge. "I mean to succeed, Noreen. This is no social club we've joined. These guys are in business to make money, a lot of money, and there's only so much to go around. They aren't going to help a new competitor like us find clients, and they won't blithely hand over their customers to us; nor will they stand by complacently while we steal them. No way! It's a cutthroat business. In fact, if we're as successful as I intend to make us, one or two of our competitors—firms that have been in this business for many years—are going down the tubes." The name Prentiss leaped to his mind. "Not everyone has the stomach for it or the nerve. But I do!"

Noreen did not wish to place herself in an adversarial position with her employer, even though she disagreed philosophically with his perception of the business world. "I suppose you're right."

He went on. "To survive in this competitive environment—and let's face it, it's been called a jungle and it is—you've got to have that instinct, that urge, to go for the jugular. I know to you that sounds savage and uncivilized."

"Yes, it does, but I understand it," she lied.

"So do I. But don't you concern yourself about it. You just keep turning out these beautiful drawings and leave the jungle warfare to me."

"You're new in town then, aren't you?"

"Yes, I am," Brock replied.

"A new company."

"Yes, as I said, brand-new. But every great business has a beginning, as you well know."

The vice president for Production of the United Standard Construction Corporation of California, a hulking bushy-haired gorilla, pulled a soggy cigar from his mouth, as he did each time he spoke, and asked another question. The cigar's pungent smoke pervaded the room. His interrogation of Brock had been going on for ten minutes in an obvious ploy to make Brock admit to his inexperience. As the executive had certainly checked Brock's credentials and already knew the answers to the questions, Brock surmised that the point of this little quiz was—and his optimism rose at the notion—to establish for the purpose of negotiation that the fee for services to be rendered should be commensurate with DESIGN METAPHORS' fledgling status. If Brock were right, the vice president was seriously considering hiring DESIGN METAPHORS. Brock quickly weighed the possible gains and losses of taking a more aggressive stance and decided to follow his instincts—which in this instance told him to gamble.

"Where did you say you were from?" asked the executive, his jowls flapping.

"The moon," replied Brock calmly. "I'm also three hundred years old, and I can make gold out of lead!"

The vice president's mouth fell open. He grabbed his cigar before it fell out, the jostling knocking ashes down the lapel of his rumpled suit.

Brock continued before the executive could speak. "Look, Mr. Anglemeyer, I came here to show you some revolutionary interiors unlike anything you've seen before. I want you to evaluate these designs on the basis of their quality, innovation, uniqueness, and most of all—number one—whether they will increase sales and selling price of the new homes and condos you plan to build this year. I do not believe, sir, that knowing my age, my parentage, my childhood friends, my taste in women, my toothpaste, or how many hairs grow on my left big toe has any relevance to whether people who walk through a model home that I decorate will buy that home or how much they'll be willing to pay for it. Do you?"

Brock froze a smiling supremely confident look on his face and stared boldly at the vice president. The six staff members seated behind the executive watched the momentary stand-off in rapt silence, expecting

56

their boss to explode with invective against this brash but handsome young upstart. No one talked to the vice president in that tone of voice.

"You make gold out of lead, huh?" He laughed, setting off a chain reaction behind him. "Your point is well taken. Let's see your stuff."

As if he had given his presentation a dozen times, Brock launched into this his first briefing with the visual aids Noreen had prepared, setting forth statistics and supporting analysis that led logically and persuasively to the conclusion that the design firm that United Standard was using to decorate its model homes was losing the corporation money.

"A corporation of your reputation and standing deserves something better...and here it is!" With a light touch of ceremony Brock took from a large leather carrying case a polished brown leather box lined with blue velvet that he opened on the table in front of Anglemeyer. Nestled inside was a copy of the brochure. "Please, sir."

Anglemeyer, coerced by Brock's theatrics to treat the brochure as a precious object, carefully removed it. Brock held his silence while the vice president perused each page, his staff stealing interested looks over his shoulders as best they could. When he had finished he laid the brochure down in front of him and pondered its cover while chewing his cigar. "What other clients do you have?" he asked without looking up.

"We opened for business five weeks ago and as of this moment we have signed contracts with four companies." An unmitigated lie.

"Which ones?" The executive's eyes snapped up and locked on Brock's.

"That's privileged information, but I stake my professional reputation on it. If you insist on knowing, I'll get permission from the parties and forward that information to you privately."

"That won't be necessary. We're opening a subdivision in San Bruno in six months. Eighty lots and five models. Can you handle the five models?"

"Easily!" Brock had learned of the San Bruno deal from the market research firm and had included in the brochure designs that would fit with the architecture and layouts of the models.

"What's your price?"

Brock quoted him the price the market research firm had recommended. It was a bargain though still one thousand more than

United Standard had paid for its last models.

"That's more than we're paying now!"

"And see how well your models are selling. You get what you pay for. You want quality, you pay for it."

"That's proud talk from a company that hasn't decorated one model yet."

Brock squared his shoulders. "Pride, my foot! That's a promise!"

It was all too easy. Four of the fifteen companies Brock pitched offered him contracts...five including United Standard. His bold-faced lie to that cigar-chewing oaf, Anglemeyer, had been prophetic, and though the vice president hadn't asked for it, Brock, just for good measure, sent him by courier a letter labeled CONFIDENTIAL containing the identities of the other four new clients.

Easy or not, the five contracts gave DESIGN METAPHORS all the business he and Noreen could handle, in fact, more than they could handle. But he needed more. DESIGN METAPHORS was hanging by a thin financial thread. While the total dollar value of the fees from the new clients looked impressive, the bottom-line reality was that Brock would have to watch every penny just to break even, given the high unit cost of each of the models the firm would be decorating. The firm needed to expand its clientele, and quickly.

He would need more artists to help Noreen as well as a specialist in furniture, rugs, and drapes—someone who knew the product lines and where to find them and who could recommend appropriate patterns and pieces for special settings. After thoroughly reassessing his financial situation, however, he resigned himself to the fact that he could afford only one additional employee—an experienced commercial artist to lighten Noreen's workload. But that would not be enough.

"I need you full-time."

Noreen squirmed in her chair and pouted. "But that would mean I'd have to quit school. I can't do both. I haven't the time or energy."

Brock put on his most reasonable face. "*This* is a school. Where else could you get comparable experience?"

"But our deal was part-time so I could get both experience and my degree, too. I have three semesters to go."

"What do you need a degree for? To get a job with a design firm? You already have a job...and with a comer."

Noreen saw his point, but getting a degree had been her ambition for years, and she was the type who felt driven to accomplish a goal once it had been set. She was not a quitter.

Brock continued in a more persuasive tone. "When you decide to leave D-M, you'll have credentials to burn. Just look at that portfolio we put together. Your work is brilliant."

"Oh, yeah?" she smiled, seeing an opening. "Then why aren't you paying me more?"

"I am. I just doubled your salary...but only if you'll work full-time." He had done the calculations and figured he could afford it, though his budget would be extra tight.

She shook her head, confused and troubled, torn between completing her schooling and accepting Brock's offer. Her school friends would call her nuts for turning down a chance to join a budding firm that very likely would be a leader one day, and she would grow with it. Brock was right when he said a degree would be superfluous once her professional reputation was established. Yet as she pondered Brock's offer, she could not avoid confronting the one motive that held her powerless: her infatuation with Brock.

She hadn't wanted it. It had crept up on her like a worsening cold. At their first meeting at the school during her interview she saw that he was attractive, but so were many men she had dated. She was not given to rash emotional acts, especially since her first intimate encounter in high school had left her with a fear of either getting pregnant or contracting some vile disfiguring disease. Brock was the first man in years who spontaneously stirred her desire. It was disquieting...and irresistible.

She tried at first to dismiss her immediate enchantment with Brock as juvenile and, worse, unprofessional. A young dreamboat, he probably had dozens of eager girlfriends many times more attractive than she was. What could he ever see in a dull homely woman like her? She'd only make a fool of herself by nurturing wild dreams of romance. What's more,

Brock had given her no encouragement, not even the friendly sort of flirting that is customary among men and women in most jobs. It was maddening.

She dropped her eyes and fixed them on her hands in her lap where her fingers toyed nervously with an artist's pencil. "Well," she said, yielding as she knew she would to her unreasoning passion for Brock, "I suppose I could work full-time."

"Great! You'll never regret it."

Then ask me out to dinner, she thought, her inner voice pleading. *Treat me like a woman. Show me some affection.*

He smiled and started to speak, then held off, looking into her eyes. Noreen's heart leaped, yearning for his attention. *Now,* she thought. *Now. Ask me.*

"I'll have Maggie type up a new contract effective today. Is that okay?"

Noreen forced a smile. "Sure. I'll notify the school."

SIX

The rise of DESIGN METAPHORS in the northern California building industry was spectacular and bewildering, even to veteran designers who in their long careers had witnessed dozens of small firms like Brock's achieve stardom overnight through the brilliance of a single designer. Yet such brilliance was usually short-lived. All but a few of those companies quickly faded from prominence when, for one reason or another, the flame of genius that inspired them flickered and died. It was extremely difficult, as it is in all competitive fields, for any firm to sustain the high-energy creativity upon which dominance depends. Deprive a company of creative ideas and its competitive edge quickly dulls, allowing rivals to swarm in to fill the vacuum, crowding the company off center stage.

What made D-M different from most of its predecessors and gave it a unique characteristic among its contemporaries was Brock's breadth of involvement and inexhaustible energy. He not only made all of the design decisions, he personally supervised every step of their implementation by subcontractors, reserving for himself, as he had when he worked for Frieda, the most difficult carpentry and decorative work. His skillful workmanship inspired the men who labored alongside him and set a standard of excellence that soon earned D-M a reputation for esteemed quality to which other firms aspired and only a few claimed, mostly through exaggerated advertising, to have achieved. Brock's talent was innate. What his inventive mind conceived so effortlessly, both at his drawing table and out on the job, other less talented designers would struggle in vain to produce or even imitate.

Within ten months of landing those first contracts, his interior designs were the talk of the industry in the San Francisco area, and

DESIGN METAPHORS received its first award. It was on that occasion that Brock's relationship with Noreen entered a new and unexpected phase.

He had returned to the office from the annual awards luncheon of the Oakland Builders Association, plaque in hand, to celebrate. His staff, which now included two additional artists and a materials specialist, had received word of the award by phone and prepared a surprise party for him, decorating the office with silver garlands and the glass-walled entrance with a wide silver banner on which was painted CONGRATULATIONS. Noreen, who was now Senior Artist in charge of the two assistants, supervised the decorating, while Maggie ordered champagne and refreshments from a caterer. Late that afternoon when Brock stepped out of the elevator the staff, alerted by the security guard in the lobby, greeted DESIGN METAPHORS' creator and commander-in-chief with cheers, hugs, and a raucous chorus of "God Bless America."

Joining hands and singing, they formed a conga line with Brock at the head holding the plaque aloft and snaked through the suite, ending in front of his desk. They toasted Brock with champagne, and Maggie switched on the CD player, which boomed out a rock song to which Noreen and the three new staff members began dancing wildly. Maggie refilled Brock's glass while they watched the prancing figures.

"We should do this more often," shouted Maggie over the roar of the music.

"If we did," Brock yelled back, "we'd be out of business."

"Baloney! You work like a maniac. It does everyone good to relax once in awhile."

"I agree. And this is the once."

"Very funny. That award must have come as a big surprise. If we'd known, we would have gone with you to the luncheon."

"I must confess, Maggie, I was pretty sure I'd get it. The president of the association gave the secret away when he pestered me about attending. Wanted to be certain I would be there. It was a dead giveaway."

The smile on her face sagged for an instant as the import of Brock's casual admission hit her. If he'd known, why hadn't he invited the staff to accompany him? To share in the honor that everyone, including herself, had a part in winning? Yet Brock's haggard features reminded her of his preoccupation with the firm's grueling production schedule. The strain on him, she knew, was mind-boggling. She didn't know where he got the energy to put in eighteen- and twenty-hour days seven days a week. He was at his desk or drawing table when the last person left at night and when the first one, usually herself, arrived in the morning. On some mornings out of curiosity she checked his bedroom and confirmed that his bed had not been slept in. Here was a man driven by an obsession to succeed. All of his meals were catered except when he had business meetings at restaurants. Emulating his example the staff usually brought their lunches to work and ate on the job. She didn't think he ever noticed.

It was, as he had intended, a team operation. Each member, hired for their particular skills, performed a specific function upon which the others relied. Their interdependence molded them into a smoothly running, highly motivated machine with Brock at the controls. He drove it at a torrid pace that tested every member's endurance measured by Brock's own Herculean standard. He was like an athletic coach, rallying and urging his players on each morning, shouting instructions, critiquing their work, praising one and chastising another. He paid them well, but they sweat and toiled as no interior design team ever had before.

Maggie knew that the unrelenting pressure he placed on himself and his staff, most of whom, like Noreen, worked late every night including Saturdays, left no time for a social life or any kind of relaxation. As far as she knew, since she handled all of his calls as well as his mail, he had no lady friends. D-M was his whole life, his whole existence, morning, noon, and night.

Poor man, she thought. *We must forgive him this oversight.* He was too considerate and feeling a person to have deliberately excluded his loyal band of coworkers from the awards ceremony. She dismissed her initial doubts, and doing so, a genuine smile returned to her lips.

"Mr. B," she said, "you need a vacation."

"Only the idle rich can afford that," he teased as the CD player changed recordings.

Everyone but Noreen collapsed into chairs to sip their champagne. "Hey, come on, you guys!" she cried. "We're only getting started. Let's live it up!"

"You live it up?" said Maggie, holding her sides. "I'll watch. I'm too old for this stuff."

One of the new artists, a young man, kidded Brock. "Hey, boss. Show us how to do it." The others chorused their encouragement.

Noreen, her inhibitions neutralized by the champagne and excitement, threw caution aside and walked to Brock's chair where she took hold of his free hand and pulled him up. "Shall we *pas de deux?*" she asked, her eyes twinkling gaily.

Brock laughed loudly and slurped a last sip of bubbly from the glass in his other hand. Setting it down, he pulled off his suit coat, loosened his tie, and kicked off his shoes exclaiming, "You ain't seen nothin' yet!"

The staff cheered and, as the music began anew, Noreen and Brock danced, their bodies bending and turning in perfect synchrony, weaving a circular pattern on the rug.

They were a comely twosome, young and agile, he twenty-three, she twenty-two. Noreen was deliriously happy, floating on a cloud of months-long yearnings made real, wishing the music would never end. Brock held her hands lightly as they faced each other, their upper bodies rotating together in short jerking movements in sync with the to and fro pumping of their arms. She would prefer a slower tempo, something more romantic that would permit Brock to put his arm around her, but this would do for the moment. For the first time since they had met, Brock Stowolski was giving her, Noreen Rollins, his undivided attention. His eyes were on hers, her hands in his. The room and the other people in it whirled around them, a blurred backdrop that enhanced her feeling of being alone with him. Her fingers tingled at his touch, warming her whole body. For this brief interlude in his ever-busy, ever-so-private life, he belonged to her.

Or so she wanted to believe, but she could tell by the distant cast of his eyes that his enjoyment, though real, was not for her but for the occasion. His first really triumphant milestone for D-M had been achieved: formal recognition by the industry. He was supremely happy and deservedly so. Yet his victory only deepened her affection for him. He was a winner, a dynamic force whose energy pervaded the entire office and inspired everyone. For Noreen his dynamism only further inflamed her desire, which she successfully concealed. No one guessed, not even

Maggie, whose womanly intuition and finely honed motherly instincts were attuned to the smallest vibrations in the personal undercurrents among the staff. No one guessed.

Especially not Brock. He watched Noreen dance before him. She was a pretty woman, not beautiful, with interesting delicate features. He had not noticed before what a supple attractive figure was concealed beneath her normally loose baggy clothes. But today she wore a snug silk dress that pulled against her body as she twisted, revealing the smooth curves of her hips, her narrow waist, and full bosom. Lust stirred within him, but limply.

How changeable we are, he thought. Twenty-six months ago, when Frieda had introduced him to sex, he couldn't get enough. The wearying pace he had maintained for the past year had drained him of all other thoughts. A romantic relationship at this point in his life was a frivolous luxury he could ill afford. Perhaps later, when D-M's viability and success were assured, but not now. He needed and wanted no distractions. They would only consume vital physical and mental energy he needed for his business.

Moreover, the still bitter aftertaste of his affair with Frieda and its heart-rending quietus put him on guard against involving himself in another entanglement. Since he'd arrived in California he hadn't been able to shake the residual feeling of guilt about his dead child. Was he not an equal party to Frieda's pregnancy? His mind, however, would not accept culpability. He blamed Frieda for enticing him, surrendering to him at the slightest overture, and most of all for failing to take commonsense measures to prevent conception. He remained convinced that her getting pregnant had been either sheer stupidity on her part or a conscious stratagem to ensnare him in marriage. Either way he held her accountable and regarded himself as the victim. Nevertheless, the fact was he had not made love or even dated a woman since he'd stormed out of Frieda's apartment.

The music paused once again. He let loose of Noreen's hands, thanked her, and returned to his glass of champagne at the bar. She smiled gamely, hiding her disappointment, and quickly engaged Maggie in empty chitchat.

"Who's next?" Brock called out cheerily.

The other new artist, a heavy-set thirty-year-old black woman relaxing in Brock's recliner, raised her glass. "Brace yourself, Brock, Ginger Rogers I'm not, but I'm hot to trot!"

Laughter filled the room as the two other men on the staff pulled her up and out of the chair by her arms. Helping her to her feet, they ushered her around the desk to Brock, who bowed and kissed her hand laughing. "You're not Ginger and I'm not Fred." He groped for a rhyme. "But we'll dance all night and end up in bed!" The staff howled.

"What'll my husband say?" the woman cried in mock protest.

"Who cares?"

More laughter.

The revelry lasted another hour by which time the champagne, the dancing, and the general excitement had begun to take their toll. Maggie was the first to throw in the towel. "No more," she wailed, falling into a chair. "No more. I've had it. I'm half drunk, and I don't know if I have the energy to walk to my car much less drive home. What would my husband have said if he could see me now?"

"That this is a time to celebrate," replied Brock, smiling.

"The only celebration I need," Maggie said, "is a good night's sleep."

"Bed!" moaned the black woman. "Honey, that's the remedy for everything that ails me at this moment in my life. I don't want food or drink or hugs or kisses or lovemaking. Just my bed and a long night's sleep. I...am...pooped!" She twisted around on her bar stool and leaned toward Brock. "No reflection on your party, good lookin'."

"Hey, watch it!" he retorted, mimicking a concerned face. "You want everyone to know about us?"

"Oh, Lordy," she giggled, slapping her thigh. "I wish *I* knew about us." She tipped her head back and let loose a burst of laughter that rocked the room. The whole group joined in.

One of the male staff members slid off his stool and shook Brock's hand. "Congratulations, boss, on your award. If anyone ever earned it, you have. It was a great party, too...and this is a great place to work. Thanks for hiring me. Now I really gotta be going. I have a dinner date."

Brock held on to his hand for an extra second. "Those are kind words. Thank you. But this is only the first award. I'll get more." He released his grip and raised his arms to the group. "So go home, all of you.

Rest up. And as a special gift from me to you take the morning off. I'll see you all at 1:00 PM."

Amid the immediate chorus of shouted thank-yous and merry jibes at one another in their partially inebriated condition, the members of the staff gathered their take-home belongings and made their way to the elevator. Brock saw them out, waved a final good-bye, and closed and locked the outer glass door. Removing his loosened tie, he strolled through the office suite, turning off lights as he went. Passing his desk he picked up the plaque he had been awarded that day. "Well, Sir Plaque," he said, holding it up before his face, "I'm on my way. They know I'm here. And I'm gonna get me enough of you to cover the walls of this room." He reached up and removed a painting from the wall behind his desk and hung the plaque on the exposed hook. "You may feel a bit lonely up there by yourself, but be patient. In the coming months and years you'll have plenty of company."

I'm so tired, he thought, leaning a hand against the wall. *I have to learn to relax more, or I'll never live long enough to enjoy all the money I'm gonna make.*

He went to his bedroom, relieved himself in the bathroom, stripped off his clothes, and climbed into bed naked. It was barely eight. Although he had not eaten dinner, fatigue and the peace of mind that follows personal triumph lay upon him so heavily that he fell instantly asleep.

Noreen rode the elevator with the others to the underground parking lot. When the door opened they bid their farewells and fanned out to their cars. She intentionally walked slowly, waving to the others, stopping now and then to rummage through her purse as if looking for keys. In fact it was a stalling tactic to ensure that the others reached their cars before she did. By the time she got to hers she could hear engines starting and cars moving toward the exit. She unlocked her door and nonchalantly sat down behind the wheel, fingering her key a few seconds before inserting it into the ignition lock. She turned it and revved the engine, letting it idle while she kept count of the other four staff members' cars. One...then two...there went three...Maggie was the last. She seemed to be looking at Noreen, or was she having trouble getting started? Her car wasn't moving, nor could Noreen be sure that Maggie's engine was running. For a moment Noreen was in a quandary, her plan of action so quickly threatened. Then an idea came, an even better plan.

Noreen pulled out of her parking space and, stopping in front of Maggie's car, rolled down the window. "Are you all right?" she yelled.

Maggie lowered her window and poked her head out. "It's okay. I flooded the engine. Let me try again." She made a face while the starter growled. Then the engine came to life blasting a cloud of white smoke from the exhaust. Noreen waved and drove away, up the exit ramp and out onto the street.

She sped to the corner, made a right turn, then another immediate right into a fast-food restaurant's parking lot where she pulled into a space from which she could see Maggie's car leave the underground garage. Sure enough within a few seconds the car appeared, entered the street cautiously, and disappeared slowly in the opposite direction toward Maggie's home in the suburbs.

Noreen was sure Maggie had not spotted her, but she waited a few minutes just to be sure. Then she drove around the block to the other side of the Calvert Plaza building and turned into the entrance ramp that led down to the garage. This time she parked in a remote corner out of sight behind a cinder-block wall that housed a Dumpster. She climbed out, locked the door and, peering around at the few remaining cars, jogged to the elevator and pushed the button. Though she was certain none of the staff had seen her re-enter the garage, she feared that one of them would suddenly reappear. She tried to remain calm and remember that if she were discovered her explanation was she had forgotten her wallet and was returning to the office to retrieve it. Of course, hiding her car in a far corner of the garage was not easily explained but she had no other plan.

The doors opened and she jumped in, flattening herself against a wall, and smacked the 18th floor button, mentally screaming at the doors to close. They ignored her plea for several seconds, then reluctantly obeyed, sealing out the threat of her discovery. She exhaled and shut her eyes in thankful prayer. At the lobby the doors opened automatically. She greeted the guard as casually as she could. He squinted at her over half-rim glasses that were tilted down toward a paperback he was reading.

"I've got some work to do, Sam. I'll be very late."

"Okay, Ms. Collins." He wagged his head absentmindedly then returned to his book.

She was about to give him a smile, but he'd already withdrawn his interest in her. The doors closed again, and the elevator began its rapid ascent to the 18th floor. She stared ahead, her mouth dry, her heart pounding. She had purposely limited her consumption that afternoon to keep a clear head, having in the back of her mind all along this wild reckless plan. The champagne had indeed loosened her inhibitions, but they would have crumbled eventually under any circumstance, so powerful was her determination. The alcohol and the occasion had only accelerated the process. No, this time, this moment, her mind was sharp and alert, her objective immutably set. She was keenly aware of what she was about and, before the doors opened at the 18th floor, she had the key to the office door in hand.

She was startled by the gloomy darkness of the outer hallway, which was normally bathed in brilliant light from the reception room through the glass wall. The interior of the office was pitch-black. Her expectations instantly faltered. She hadn't seen his car leave, though he could have left by the front entrance and taken a cab. Probably on a date. She would wait for him. But what if he brought his date back to the office? After all, this was also his apartment.

She stood motionless in the hallway, immobilized by indecision, pondering her next move. Should she recall the elevator and leave, abandoning this craziness? No one would be the wiser. And what if she stayed and went through with it? What would she say to Brock when he found her there? Would he be angry at her intrusion?

The solution brought a sigh and a smile to her lips. Hadn't she told the guard in the lobby she had work to do? All right then, she'd work. She would go to her desk in the design shop and, when Brock discovered her there, she'd explain, plausibly enough, that she had come back to finish the artwork on the condominium project that was due in two days. How could he be suspicious about that? She had worked late many nights, too many, in fact, to count.

Despite her relief at improvising a way out of her dilemma should she need it, her hand shook as she unlocked the brass door of the reception room and entered. Excitement swelled within her, shortening her breath and defying her desire to remain casual about what should be a commonplace act of someone returning to their office after normal hours. But hers was no commonplace act, and she could not deceive herself about her real motive which now, as she closed the door quietly behind her, blocked out all other thoughts. She wiped her moist trembling hands on her skirt and switched on a table lamp beside the door. Although the light was comforting and soothed her tenseness, it accentuated the darkness of the outer rooms and refueled her apprehension. She walked stiffly across the room, dimly illuminated by the bright lights of the Bay city below. Stopping at the doorway, she flipped on the light switch inside. Soft indirect ceiling lights came on. She turned and went down the short corridor that led past the design shop on the left, the staff's bathroom straight ahead, and Brock's bedroom on the right. She was about to enter the design shop when she glanced into the darkened bedroom and spotted one of Brock's shoes on the floor near the open doorway. Assuming he must have changed clothes before going out and had dropped the shoe in his haste, she leaned in to check, never thinking he might be there.

The sheet exposed the upper half of his naked muscular body. The sight stunned her. She reared back, slamming her head on the doorjamb. A flash of yellow colors burst in her head causing her to drop her purse with a clatter. She froze, rubbing her head and listening for sounds of Brock stirring. The bed creaked. She flattened herself against the bathroom door, which gave way, sending her crashing backwards onto the bathroom's tiled floor.

The noise awakened Brock, who was a light sleeper. He rose up on one elbow and wondered at the light coming from his office. Someone had come in.

"Who's there?" he called, his mind still groggy.

"It's me," croaked a voice timidly. "Noreen."

"Noreen?" He peered, uncomprehending, at the doorway and the light. "I thought you went home."

"I did," Noreen murmured.

"You came back?"

"Yes."

Brock lay back on his pillow and rubbed his eyes, trying to clear his mind. "What time is it?"

Noreen, sitting up on the bathroom floor, looked at her watch. "Nine o'clock." She paused, expecting a reply, but none came. Only silence. He apparently was not fully awake. Her unscheduled return did not seem to have upset him as her worst fears had made her believe it would. Of course he had no idea what her real purpose was. She trembled. That purpose had not changed. He lay not ten feet away, in his bed. If only he would let her, she would feed his passion, indulge and satisfy it, and in the process fulfill her own need.

A lingering tenuous reservation challenged the wisdom of her plan. *What if he rejects you,* it said, *and throws you out? What then?* But the thought of his lips on hers, his hands caressing her...

Desire brought her to her feet. She stepped around the doorjamb and into his bedroom. "Brock?" she whispered. Her hands were shaking. "Brock?" A little louder this time.

"Yes," he mumbled.

She could see him in the light from the hallway. His bare muscled chest rose and fell evenly with his breathing. "I came back to give you a present."

His eyes crept open and focused on her figure silhouetted against the doorway. "A present," he murmured. It was a statement, not a question. If its meaning did not register at once, it sank home when she unbuttoned her dress and let it fall to the floor, making a silken pedestal around her feet....

SEVEN

Kelly and Brock took an instant liking for each other, drawn together by a natural affinity arising ironically from their sharp differences in personality, work style, professional background, ethnicity, and general outlook on life. While two other people with the same differences might have been alienated, Kelly Barnaby of the Irish and Brock Stowolski of the Polish, each discovered in the other an attitude, a mentality, a potential that he himself lacked and had unknowingly sought. Like two adjoining pieces in a jigsaw puzzle, their irregularly contoured edges fit perfectly together, the strength of one filling the weakness of the other.

It was one year after Noreen had seduced Brock and become his regular bedmate that the professional paths of the two men crossed. An electronics firm had commissioned Brock, ever ready to broaden the base of his operations and accept new challenges, to design and build a "spectacular award-winning" display for an industrial exhibition in the San Francisco Cow Palace. The D-M staff, fleshing out Brock's ideas, created an ingenious twenty-foot-high pyramidal structure topped by swirling lighted globes, the triangular sides gradually magically changing from one color to another across the spectrum of the rainbow. Because of its intricate design, Brock as usual took a personal hand in the construction. Work was proceeding on schedule till he encountered trouble with the installation of the globes. The mechanics of their movement had not been accurately detailed in the engineering drawings, and Brock was both angry and stumped.

"Whose idea were these lights?" he declared, addressing his question to no one in particular. He was alone atop a high ladder, having sent his entire crew to another job.

"I believe it was Thomas Alva Edison," replied a male voice from below.

Brock, a lighting fixture in one hand and a wrench in the other, looked down with a frown toward the voice. Prepared to fire off a caustic reply to this wisecracker, he was thwarted by the smile that greeted him on the pleasant face of a white-haired gentleman in plaid shirt and blue jeans. Kelly was a nondescript, ruddy-faced, burly man, several inches shorter than Brock. Kelly's thick wavy prematurely white hair, combed straight back since he was a child, was flecked with dabs of black, giving him, as he liked to say, "that distinctive Dalmatian look."

"Oh, yeah?" Brock said, grinning. "Well, maybe Edison would know how to make this confounded thing work."

"No doubt he would," said Kelly. "That was his strong suit, you know, inventing things."

"Are you any relation to him by chance?"

"'Fraid not by chance or by any other means," answered Kelly with a hearty laugh. "What seems to be the trouble?"

Brock was at once on guard, his competitive instincts roused. He treated all information on D-M designs as privileged and proprietary and was suspicious of any stranger's question that could elicit details about them. "Oh, nothing really. I'm sure I can handle it."

"Of course," said Kelly quickly, sensing Brock's wariness and wanting to put him at ease. "My name's Kelly Barnaby. I'm building the exhibit across the aisle there. The Paddington Corporation. I noticed you seem to be having difficulty with those lights."

"No problem; I'll work it out," replied Brock brusquely.

"Right." Unaccustomed to such a cold reception, Kelly spun around and walked away, cutting off what he was loath to call a conversation. But he stopped after a few steps. *The guy's obviously too proud to admit he's stymied,* thought Kelly. *I know how he feels.* "Hey, fella!"

Brock turned again in Kelly's direction.

"You might try a sling on the interior motor to displace the weight from the lighting frame."

"I already thought of that," Brock lied, turning his back on the stranger, who disappeared into the Paddington exhibit. That solution had never occurred to Brock, but it galled him to admit he could not solve his own problems. "Why didn't I think of that?" he muttered. "It's so stinking obvious!" He cursed his stupidity and the approaching deadline for completion of the display in three hours. Rigging a sling for the motor was the only way to make the lighting mechanism operate properly, but he couldn't do it alone. It would take an extra pair of hands, and his whole crew was at another job several hours away. Brock mulled over his options. There was really only one.

He climbed down the ladder and went across the aisle to the Paddington exhibit. The stranger—Brock had paid no attention to his name—was at the rear connecting some cables to a switchbox. Seeing Brock, Kelly smiled in a genuinely friendly way that made it easy for the visitor to reopen their abbreviated conversation.

"Hi," said Brock. "Hope I'm not intruding."

"You sure aren't. Always glad to have visitors. What can I do you out of?"

"Well, I've tried several different ways to rig a sling for that motor and nothing I've tried has worked well. What I really need are some heavy canvas straps. You wouldn't happen to have any, would you?"

Kelly saw through the cover-up but wanted to reward this fellow's humility. He seemed like an honest hardworking guy, and he sure needed help. "I've got something even better. Nylon rope. It'll do the trick beautifully. You get back up on that ladder, and I'll bring you the rope directly."

"That's very nice of you."

"Always glad to help. By the way, what's your name?"

"Brock Stowolski." He enunciated the syllables carefully.

"Stowolski. You're not a middle linebacker, are you?"

"Not a chance."

"You look like one. Incidentally, please call me Kelly. The last name's Barnaby."

"Okay, Kelly. I appreciate the help."

Brock returned to his ladder and before long heard a clattering below. It was Kelly setting up a ladder next to Brock's just as Brock had hoped he would. "Hey, you don't have to do that."

"No problem," called Kelly. "I like to see a job done well. Do it right or don't do it—that's my motto."

74

"Even for a competitor?"

"There's enough work for everyone. I'm not greedy. You sound a little paranoid." There was no reply. Kelly ascended his ladder and came up shoulder to shoulder with Brock and looked into his eyes wondering what sort of man this was. "You say your name's Brock?"

"Yeah. An old family name."

"I like it. It's distinctive. Here's your rigging." He pulled a coil of nylon rope from a canvas bag looped over his shoulder and began attaching it to the motor that powered the swirling globes. The two men labored side by side for half an hour till the sling was finally installed and the motor and globes were operating without a hitch. Brock admired the older man's self-assurance and skill. *No bull or make-do. Just quiet competence. With half a dozen crewmen like Kelly,* Brock thought, *D-M could take on almost anything.*

When they descended from their perch above the exhibits, he raised the subject of their working together. "We seem to make a good team."

"We certainly do. Even competitors can work together, eh?" Kelly winked, though Brock did not appear to get the jibe.

"Perhaps the next time I have a tough engineering project we could collaborate?"

"I would enjoy that. Tell you what. Why don't you let me buy you a beer and we'll talk about it." Kelly put his arm around Brock's shoulders, and they walked away toward the refreshment pavilion as Brock described a complicated stage set he had just agreed to build for a dinner theater.

And so their collaboration and friendship grew, evolving month by month into a close relationship nourished by almost daily phone conversations in which they shared both professional and personal problems and sought each other's advice. Other than Father Leonard, Brock had never had a friend in whom he could confide and never anyone his own age. Brock had always been a loner, eschewing friendships with peers, preferring, for reasons he never bothered to analyze, to look among his elders for fellowship, approval, and direction. Yet, when his own predilections clashed with their advice, as had been the case with Father Leonard, Brock felt no qualms about severing those relationships. They were conveniences not necessities. He never really gave serious thought to whether they had any special significance in his life aside from promoting his self-interest.

Kelly, being fourteen years his senior, fit the paternal role of friend and mentor for which Brock was unconsciously searching. But Kelly's perception of their relationship was worlds apart from Brock's. To a warm, sensitive, down-to-earth person like Kelly a friendship was a sacred lifelong bond in which mutual trust and caring were taken for granted. The root of this conviction was his firm belief in the fundamental goodness of his fellow man. What it came down to was that he simply liked people. He could always find a facet of goodness in even the most scurrilous scoundrels. It was this unassailable optimism that accounted for the enormous number of people who considered him their friend. He recognized Brock's selfish aims, but they were irrelevant to Kelly. "I don't befriend a man because he likes me," he once playfully scolded a skeptic. "I befriend him because I like *him*, and it seems I always find something to like in everyone, even you!"

After ten months Brock and Kelly had come to depend upon each other to a far greater extent than either realized. Although both ran separate independent businesses, Kelly bit by bit became involved in some way or other in over one-third of Brock's projects, D-M furnishing an overall design with Kelly serving as technical consultant or subcontractor. The collaboration became so intense that Kelly was spending more time in D-M's design shop than in his own office.

It was in that circumstance late one night that Brock and Kelly were pouring over rough sketches for a city-wide carnival float that the Oakland Bay Chamber of Commerce would commission in a bidding competition the next day. Brock assessed the chances of D-M's design winning the contract as very good. Kelly disagreed.

"It needs more glitter, more pizzazz. It isn't showy enough. It doesn't go *bam*!" It was late, and he was bushed. Too worn out to be imaginative.

"Why don't we dynamite it," said Brock with mock sarcasm.

Kelly bit his lip pensively. "Maybe."

76

"Maybe what?"

"Maybe dynamite." His expression was dead serious.

Brock studied his colleague a moment. "Kelly, I'm kidding."

"I'm not. What if the float did go *bam*? *Bam, bam, bam.* It would knock people on their heels."

"You mean firecrackers." Brock's cornucopic mind was awakening.

"Yeah, but louder. Bigger. Real bombs. Not big enough to break windows. Just make a big noise with a small percussive effect on the spectators."

"We could get a fireworks company to make them up special."

"We'd string them here on these two poles and set them off electronically."

"*Bam, bam!* Grand slam!" shouted Brock.

They stood up laughing and slapped their right palms together, congratulating themselves. "It's in the bag," declared Brock.

"Absolutely."

"We did it again. What a team!"

"Yeah," said Kelly, "and half of that team is about to keel over. It's after 2:00 AM. Do you think I could sleep on your couch tonight? I wouldn't trust myself driving home."

Brock looked at his friend searchingly. "You know something, Kelly?"

"What?"

"Did you hear what happened today?"

"Today?" He did not understand.

"Yeah. About the letter."

"What letter?"

"You haven't heard. You received a letter today addressed to DESIGN METAPHORS."

"So?"

"You're so involved in D-M contracts that some guy thought you were part of the firm."

"So what?"

"So why don't you join up?"

Kelly's tired mind could not fully grasp the message. "Join? Brock, I have my own company."

"I know. Why don't we merge them? Become partners?"

Kelly did not have to think hard to see the value of a merger. It made good business sense. They were obviously a winning team, and merging would significantly reduce overhead costs which had risen sharply for Kelly in recent months.

"I could handle the contract management side," Brock urged, "allowing you to focus on the engineering and construction end. You said yourself last week you despised having to be concerned all the time with legal technicalities and administrative crap. So leave those matters to me. They're my bread and butter."

Kelly listened thoughtfully, weighing the pros and cons. "Having two addresses is apparently confusing my clients," he muttered in feigned resignation. "I think I owe it to them to have a single address. Don't you agree?"

Brock rented a bachelor apartment in a nearby high-rise and converted his bedroom at D-M into an office for Kelly. Although it wasn't as spacious or well furnished as Brock's corner-window suite, Kelly insisted it was more than adequate, and Brock did not argue the point. Under the terms of their partnership, which Brock's lawyer drew up, Brock was the senior partner with majority control, and the name of the firm remained DESIGN METAPHORS. In effect, Kelly had simply joined D-M, bringing his firm with him.

But Kelly was unconcerned about who controlled whom because the merger was a welcome relief. Managing contracts, salaries, health insurance plans, and the multitude of other purely administrative tasks that attend any business operation had become tedious and taken the fun out of his work. By entrusting these responsibilities to Brock, Kelly was free to concentrate on that part of the business that gave him the most pleasure—working with his hands. Had not Christ been a carpenter?

The joining of the two men's talents had a catalytic effect on D-M. Business thrived, and the design shop was ever awash in new ideas and novel approaches. It was as if Brock and Kelly were poles on a giant battery, and their linking up had released a steady flow of enormous creative energy that empowered the whole staff to higher levels of creativity, commitment, and output. The firm prospered and expanded, not only in the size of its workforce, which now occupied the entire 18th floor of the Calvert Plaza, but also in the kinds of jobs it undertook. From interior design Brock and Kelly moved to exteriors, consulting with architectural firms and landscapers. They designed interiors of private airliners and luxury cabin cruisers, stained-glass windows for churches, a TV newsroom set, and high-priced remodelings of recreational vehicles. The sky was the limit. Wherever they turned, opportunities beckoned and money flowed. Within three years D-M was grossing well over five million dollars annually.

Kelly had never known such joy in his work. The variety and challenge of the projects they undertook were intoxicating. He felt young again, invigorated and excited. Brock, as he said he would, managed the fiscal and contractual side of the business, leaving Kelly more or less at liberty to follow his own instincts. Many projects held no special attraction for Kelly, so he delegated them to subordinates while keeping a distant watchful eye to ensure the end product met D-M's high standards of quality and was on schedule. Other jobs captivated his interest, and to these he devoted himself with a dedication and esprit that his wife, Helena, had not seen in him since the early years of their marriage. It both annoyed and pleased her. On the one hand, Kelly spent more hours away from home, but when they were together the exuberance he felt for his work carried over, infusing their marriage with a new vitality that found expression in ardent lovemaking and in the deeper warmth they felt in each other's company.

Brock's reaction to the phenomenal success of his enterprise, which he concluded was owed primarily to his own boldness and creativity, was in a wholly different spectrum from Kelly's. Brock was a daring high-roller who had bet everything he had on making D-M a success and had beaten what some thought were unbeatable odds. He had balls. His envious detractors in other design firms consoled themselves by calling him smug, conceited, and lucky, never realizing that men born with Brock's giant self-confidence can't relate to such pettiness anymore than a bird can relate to a fish, so different are the separate worlds in which they live. Whereas the world of his professional critics was a self-limiting environment dominated by fears of their own inadequacies and of their competitors' success, Brock's world had no self-imposed boundaries. His potential was virtually unlimited because he believed it to be. And nothing had yet persuaded him otherwise.

Brock was at this point twenty-eight years old and, while the basic elements of his adult personality had solidified, the final features were still being shaped by events in his life, most notably his success with D-M. It had a pernicious effect. The brilliance of his management had begun to infect his mind with the insidious notion of his own infallibility. Inexorably his self-confidence was turning into omnipotence, his pride into self-righteousness, his competitiveness into vengeance. So preoccupied was he with the firm's business operations that he was oblivious to the cumulative changes taking place in his personality. He ignored these changes because they were unimportant to him and incidental to his quest for fame and wealth. His goal was to be known for his accomplishments. It mattered little how people felt about him personally as long as they respected his achievements.

What he had not bargained for nor anticipated was the raw power that success brought him. Renown, not power, had been his objective, but power was what success had dealt him. Power to attract new business. Power to expand. Power to hire talented professionals away from competitors. Power to reward and to influence. And on the dark side of the ledger, power to punish, for with his self-ordained infallibility came a stiff intolerance to dissent.

At the first sign of opposition from his staff his temper would flare. The assumed opponents, fearing his power, would usually retreat, including even Noreen, whose intimate though still secret relationship with him would seem to give her some protection from his wrath. In fact it made her only more vulnerable. And woe to those who took advantage of Brock or who he believed had taken advantage. His retaliation was swift and stark, and on those rare occasions when the culprit escaped punishment, vengeance preyed on Brock's mind like a festering sore.

"I won't have it!" he shouted. He was standing behind his desk angrily waving a letter that he crumpled into a ball in his fist and threw across the room. It rolled on the rug and came to rest a few feet from the chair in which Kelly was sitting.

"Now, now, Brock," assuaged his dapple-haired partner. "No need to get all excited."

"Baloney, Kelly! You know that two-bit shyster stole that contract from us. Snatched it right out of our hands."

"Seemed like a straightforward business deal to me. You're just peeved 'cause he outsmarted us. Shucks, Brock, you've got to learn to shake off these little setbacks and take a lesson from them." Kelly was speaking in an almost fatherly way. "Nobody wins every contract. Sometimes you lose one, but it's who comes out on top in the long run that counts, and I have no doubt about D-M's long-term future. I don't think you have either."

"Maybe it doesn't matter to you, but I'll not be made a fool of."

Brock's condescending tone annoyed Kelly, who ignored the slight to avoid further aggravating Brock. "I never said it didn't matter to me. You're so riled up you're not listening. I'm as disappointed over the loss as you are, but I'd rather channel the energy of my feelings into some constructive future action than waste it fretting about spilt milk." He was walking a thin line of deeper and more prolonged adversity.

"I guess that's where we differ," said Brock frostily. "I realize I can't get that contract back, but I sure can make him think twice before he ever tries to con me again."

"And how will you do that?"

"Oh, I'll think of a way. I had a run-in with that guy before."

"You never told me."

"It didn't matter then, but it does now."

"You've known Prentiss a long time?"

"Six years. I interviewed with him for a job when I first came to California. He listened politely then told me flat-out that I'd never make it. Said I didn't have what it takes."

Kelly began to understand. Brock did not speak of the humiliation he must have suffered, but Kelly saw it in his eyes and his tightly drawn lips. The hate seeped through. Nor did Brock reveal the angry vow he had made to himself to run Prentiss out of business. But Kelly guessed it. It was obvious. Brock had nursed his resentment for six years and had viewed the recent contest for the contract as a chance to punish Prentiss. Unfortunately Prentiss had won, humiliating Brock again. This was no small setback as Kelly had first perceived. This was all-out war, and it unnerved him to wonder how far Brock might go to exact revenge.

"I see now," said Kelly, "what that contract meant to you." His voice was soft and warm, reaching out to console Brock. "I know how you must feel. I simply ask that, before you take any steps to redress the injustice you feel was done to you by this man, you consult with me. We're partners, and any action you take will reflect on the firm, on me, and on all the workforce."

"That sounds like a lecture," Brock said stiffly, resenting Kelly's patronizing attitude. Kelly was a hard worker and skilled in his craft, but Brock thought Kelly was a marshmallow when it came to tough business decisions. That's why Brock gave all the orders. While they did discuss things together and Kelly pretended the decisions were joint, everyone including Kelly knew that Brock was the commander-in-chief. Why then was Kelly now talking about their partnership as if they were equals? He needed to be reminded. "We'll discuss all of the firm's business as we have in the past, and you'll know exactly what I plan to do. You have my promise."

EIGHT

The mall teemed with Christmas shoppers. With Thanksgiving a week past, the stores were aglitter with decorations for the yuletide. The air vibrated with the din of Christmas music from the public address system, heels clattering on the polished tile floors, shoppers chattering, children running about yelling. The exhibit on which Brock was laboring was at the foot of a descending escalator crowded with stony-faced pedestrians laden with colorful shopping bags and gaily wrapped packages. The passengers, having nothing else to do while the stairs descended, watched Brock at work.

As he turned to look for a tool, he took in the escalator and the fifty or so blank faces staring at him. Then his eyes fell on a very attractive blond midway up the file. Their eyes met and for some reason she smiled. Never one to miss an opportunity to flirt with a beautiful woman, he smiled back, exuding a masculine charm that experience had taught him worked wonders on the female libido. To strengthen the effect he half bowed, waving his hand in a grand flourish to direct her attention to the display. She answered with an even broader grin, followed at once by a quizzical shake of her head to chide his impertinence. His charm was getting through. He locked his eyes on hers, willing her to approach him.

Conscious of his intent, she looked away, as it was not her habit to encourage flirtatious strangers, and being very attractive she had lots of experience. But the warmth and genuineness of his smile disarmed her. She looked back. His eyes were still on hers. She blushed and smiled again, unable to control her reaction. Suddenly the escalator step on which she was riding reached the bottom and she stumbled off, not having decided whether to speak to him or not. He made the decision for her.

"Whataya think? Do I win a ribbon?"

Her instinct to avoid conversing with a male stranger, especially one of the working class, was overruled by a stronger compulsion to learn more about this handsome man. She stopped in front of the exhibit, which featured a large glass box filled with Santa's elves. "It's lopsided, you know," she said, wrinkling her nose with feigned reproof.

"It's supposed to be," he replied, glancing quickly at her gorgeous figure clad in a loose-fitting white sweater and maroon slacks.

"Why?" she asked cockily, tilting her head to one side as if to get a more balanced view.

"Because that's how it was designed."

"Did you design it?" Brock noticed that her perfectly shaped lips spoke "you" like a kiss.

"Maybe. Maybe not. What difference does it make? The design speaks for itself."

"You sound defensive." Her pencil-thin eyebrows arched, drawing his attention to the deep blue of her eyes.

"I'm not being defensive. I'm just explaining the design."

"Then you did design it."

"I didn't say that."

"No, but it sounded like you did." She laughed at the inanity of their sparring. "This is crazy," she said, shaking her head and turning to leave.

"So what else is wrong with it?" he asked, baiting her, wanting to prolong their conversation long enough to learn her name and phone number.

She knew his game, but he had such beautiful eyes and broad shoulders. Though it was against her principles, she turned back. She would stay a moment...only for a moment...and play along. She studied the display, walking around it like a professional art appraiser. Brock affected an exaggerated look of concern, swiveling his head back and forth from the display to her face to identify the particular aspect she was eyeing and to read her reaction. She warmed to his playfulness.

"It's out of balance," she said finally. "The glass box is too small for the size of the elves, and there are too many on one side."

"Now wait a minute!" he exclaimed, fresh out of comebacks but still grinning.

"Then you are the designer after all?"

"And proud of it. So what are your credentials?"

"Citizen art critic." With a daring twinkling smile.

"Alas, I am victimized by an amateur." He pretended to be exasperated. "Insult to injury! Are you a plebeian or patrician amateur? I would think the latter." He noted the rich quality of her elegant clothing.

"Looks can be deceiving," she replied. "For example, I think you're late in finishing this. All the other decorations in the mall were up two weeks ago. Am I right?"

"Wrong! My contract says noon today. I still have fifteen minutes."

"So, it proves my point."

"It doesn't either."

"Are you going to finish on time?" She was enjoying this repartee.

"I will on one condition."

"What's that?"

"That you hold this reel of bunting for me while I tack in the final piece."

"Well..." She was stumped. Her scruples demanded she decline, but his eyes got the better of her. "I suppose I could."

"You're a jewel." He handed her the reel and climbed onto a chair to reach the spot where the bunting would be stapled. "I really do need the help. I'm behind schedule. Ran into some trouble with the lighting. I was supposed to be finished this morning."

"Then you *are* late in finishing! Will you get in trouble with your boss?"

Brock hesitated before replying. "Naw, I don't think so. He's a pretty nice guy. Anyway I'm glad I'm late."

"Why?" With her left hand she held up one end of the material for him to take hold of. He checked her finger for a ring and happily saw none.

"If I'd finished this morning I wouldn't have met you."

The endearing look he gave her sent an unexpected thrill through her, stealing her breath and thoughts. For a moment she was speechless, watching him work. Then she felt suddenly ridiculous. How could she explain her behavior? What was she doing helping a construction worker—good looking or not? This was absurd.

"You know something?" said Brock, arranging the bunting in neat folds and stapling the crease. "Here you are, helping me, and we haven't even been introduced properly. My name is Brock Stowolski. Don't ask me to spell it. I sometimes forget how myself." He laughed. "And who might you be?"

"Evasive," she replied curtly.

"I see. The citizen art critic wishes to remain anonymous."

"Why should I tell you my name? I don't know you. In fact, I don't even know why I'm standing here holding this thing. I came to do some shopping, not to help a common—" She cut herself off.

"A common laborer like me. Why, I do believe the critic is a snob. A patrician after all."

"I didn't mean it that way." She lowered her head to hide her embarrassment.

Brock looked down at her and said quietly and sincerely, "I know you didn't."

She turned her gorgeous face up toward him at the change in his voice.

"And I didn't take offense," he said brightly. "Why should I? I'm as common as they come."

"I can believe that," she declared merrily. "You also seem like a very nice person."

"Oh, it's more than appearances. Underneath all this blue-collar exterior is a really wonderful guy."

She smiled again. "You're making fun of me."

"No, I'm not. Honestly. You're easy to talk to. Did anyone ever tell you that?"

"No, but thank you anyway."

"So I'm finished." He snipped off the bunting, and the remnant fell into her slender outstretched hand. As he stepped down from the chair he was careful to avoid bodily contact. He could tell she was not the touching type. "We usually get time and a half for part-time work, but in your case I'm sure they'll make an exception. How about a cup of coffee? Free. On me."

Here it comes, she thought disappointedly. *He's making his move. They always do.* "Oh, I really shouldn't. I have many errands to run."

86

"Ten minutes. The coffee shop is right over there." He gestured toward the escalator. "Anyway, you haven't seen the display illuminated. I'll light it up, and you can give me a patrician-citizen critic's frank ten-minute appraisal. How about it? And I promise on my mother's grave I won't ask you your name."

His magic eyes entreated. She could not resist. "Ten minutes!" she said, with as much condescension as she could. "But then I really must go."

"Me too. I've got another job to finish."

He went behind the display and switched on the lights. The effect was enchanting, as the immediate applause from the passengers watching from the escalator testified. Brock reappeared wearing a tan suede jacket that accentuated his masculinity. He was outrageously strikingly handsome.

"Whataya think?" he asked.

She shook her head in admiration. "It's beautiful. Just beautiful." But she was thinking of his appearance.

"And lopsided?" he added.

She protested. "I'm paying you a compliment!"

"Well, warn me next time."

"You're terrible," she kidded. "Where's the coffee shop?"

"Straight ahead. Follow me." He pointed the way, minding not to touch her.

"Do you work alone or are you with a company?"

"I'm with an outfit called DESIGN METAPHORS."

They reached the shop. Tables and chairs were set up outside the door as in a sidewalk cafe. "Outside or inside? What's your pleasure?"

"Let's go inside," she decided. "It's so noisy in the mall."

He held the door, and they entered, finding a quiet table for two at a large curtained window with a view of the display. Brock ordered their coffee and fell silent while he admired his gorgeous catch.

She read his thoughts. "Feeling triumphant?"

"Should I? Are you that unapproachable?"

"You have a knack for turning questions against the questioner. You're very skillful at it."

"It's unintentional. If it offends you, I apologize."

"No need. I think I'm nervous. I've never done this before. I mean, meeting with a total stranger like this."

"I understand. The wonderful thing about two people, strangers, meeting like this is that they don't remain strangers." He saw one of her eyebrows raise skeptically as a warning. "No name. I won't ask your name. Don't worry."

"Is that what Design...what did you call it?"

"DESIGN METAPHORS."

"Is that what DESIGN METAPHORS does?" She nodded in the direction of the display.

"Not only that. The firm designs anything it's asked to including your kitchen sink. They do interior designs, industrial designs, landscapes."

"Have you worked for them long?"

Brock caught himself. He thought a moment, then replied. "About six years. They pay well, they're good people, and I enjoy the work. What about you?"

"Are you married?" she asked.

"Now who's turning questions around?"

She ignored his dig. "Are you?"

"Do I look married?"

"What does a married man look like?"

"You tell me."

"Don't you ever answer a straightforward question?"

He smiled warmly. "I did it again, huh?"

She essayed his trenchant face. The square jaw, full lips, and sparkling dark brown eyes that dared her to see anything but an honest forthright man who would cheat no one, least of all his wife. "Yes, you did, but, no, you don't look married."

"Why is that important to you? What difference would it make if I were married? I asked you to have a cup of coffee, not spend a weekend at Lake Tahoe." Then he understood. "Oh, I see. My being single alleviates your guilt about talking to a stranger."

"You know, you don't talk like a construction worker."

"Someone else once told me that." The ugly image of Frieda suddenly blocked his vision. He forced it away, resolved that her memory would not intrude. This beautiful woman was not Frieda. "And how are

88

construction workers supposed to talk?"

"Uneducated. And if that reveals a prejudice on my part it's one I've acquired through experience, not from rumors or bad jokes."

"Fact is," he said, "I'm not educated. Two years of college is all I could stand. But a lot of us construction types are college graduates. You've heard of Eric Hoffer, I presume?"

"He was a longshoreman, not a construction worker."

"Same difference, but we're off the subject. What about you? What do you do for a living?" Her ringless finger obviated a question about her marital status.

"I'm studying at San Francisco State College working on a Masters in English literature."

"I'm impressed."

"I bet."

"No, really I am. Who are your favorite authors?"

She paused to consider her answer, taken aback at his question and the knowledge it implied. It was a familiar topic among literature students. "Sir Walter Scott, Leon Uris, and O'Henry."

"Which of O'Henry's works do you like most?" Her look of surprise showed she was unprepared for his response. "We common laborers do read and write, you know."

Her cheeks reddened. "I'm sorry. Not many people, common or otherwise, have ever heard of O'Henry. I'm fond of all his short stories."

"So am I. Do you remember the one about the rich father who arranged for his son to be trapped in a massive traffic jam long enough to propose to his girlfriend? It's my favorite. The son doubted the power of money. The moral was that money is all-powerful and will buy anything." It was a story Brock had never forgotten.

"'Mammon and the Archer,'" she said as if answering a question.

"Is that the title? I'd forgotten."

"You've also forgotten the point of the story."

"Which was?"

"That it was the power of love, not money, that moved the son to make his proposal of marriage."

"Are you sure we're talking about the same story?"

As they jovially debated the message of O'Henry's famous work, time slipped away, lost in the intensity of their conversation. He was captivated by her beauty and intelligence. She was impressed with the breadth of his literary knowledge and the depth of his interpretations. Neither was motivated to terminate their meeting, so each time the thread of their dialogue seemed on the verge of running out, one or the other would introduce a new related theme to keep the encounter alive.

Both realized that their chance meeting had no *raison d'etre*, no prelude, and no justifiable future. It would be foolish to think otherwise. Their lives were on divergent tracks, wide apart and heading in different directions. There was no bond woven between them by some shared intimacy. They meant nothing to each other. Their paths had crossed by accident, not providence, and when their tête-à-tête ended they would part and resume their separate courses. Nevertheless...neither of them was willing to let it end.

The privacy of their discussion was interrupted by the waitress carrying a coffeepot. "Excuse me. Do either of you want a refill?"

Brock eyed his watch. "It's nearly one thirty! I have to go." He looked to the waitress. "Could I have the check please?"

"Sure." She fumbled in one of her apron pockets and laid the check before him.

He placed several dollars on top of it saying, "Keep the change." It was a sizable tip and she departed smiling. Brock stood to leave, then spied what he sensed was concern on the pretty face of his companion.

"Do you really have to leave?" she asked, almost pleading. Her voice conveyed an urgency, not quite a panic. This incredible man, whoever he was, was going to walk away, to walk out of her life. She had never met anyone like him and might never again.

"I have another job."

"But..." She groped for a reason why he should stay.

"But what? Hey, I've really enjoyed our talk. It's been fun. And thanks for helping me with the bunting. I'll remember you when I think of this project. You made it kind of special. So, Ms...Ms. Critic." He extended his hand, while beaming a baleful puppy-dog look at her that would melt precious glass.

She spurned his hand, digging instead into her Gucci leather purse for a notepad and pencil. "My name is not Ms. Critic," she snapped. "It's

Eleanor Dower." She tore off a page, hurriedly wrote her name and phone number, and handed it to Brock.

"Eleanor." He tested the word, measuring it against her countenance. "It fits. You're definitely an Eleanor."

"Is that good?"

"Very good!"

"And you said your name is Brock..."

"No one gets it the first time. You are speaking to Brock Stowolski."

"Brock Stowolski," she repeated, studying his face. "Polish?"

"From way back."

Then it popped out of her mouth before she could suppress it. "Maybe we could get together again over coffee some time to talk more about authors."

"Good idea. How about tonight?"

"Tonight?" The quickness of his acceptance awakened her. He was smiling broadly, victoriously. "You rat! You just pretended you were leaving so I'd give you my phone number."

"You didn't think I'd leave without it, did you?"

"You're wicked!" she declared, shaking her head and grinning.

"I hope not." His tone quickly softened, turning sincere. "I wouldn't have wanted your number, Eleanor, if I hadn't enjoyed talking with you. You're impressive...intelligent...genteel. I would really like to get to know you better."

Eleanor blushed despite herself. "Thank you."

"So how about it? Are you free this evening? I know a great French restaurant...now that sounds trite!"

"Not to me...but..." She hesitated, combating her ingrained inhibitions about dating strangers. "I'd love to only I have Christmas shopping to do. I won't finish before five or six, maybe later. Then I'll have to go back to campus to change clothes. I wouldn't be ready till after nine."

"Hey, you look great as you are. You don't need to change. Tell you what. Why don't you drop by the office when you've finished shopping? I'll wait for you there. Come as you are. We'll go to some place informal. And don't worry about the time. When you arrive, we'll go."

Flinging her inhibitions aside, she consented. He gave her directions and they parted, both of them happy and excited about the evening ahead.

At 6:30 PM Eleanor, laden with heavy shopping bags in each hand, emerged from the elevator to stand openmouthed before the breathtaking entrance of DESIGN METAPHORS. Her first thought was whether she should go directly in or if Brock was waiting for her at an employees' side entrance. Seeing none, she stepped forward, set down her bags, and tugged at one of the massive brass doors. It moved reluctantly. Grappling the bags, she walked into the reception room, stopping first to admire the two shimmering crystal chandeliers and then to await the attention of the smartly dressed lady seated behind an ornate mahogany desk. The woman finished penning an entry into a gold-embossed black ledger and looked up with a bright friendly smile. "Good evening. You must be Eleanor."

"Why, yes, I am."

"Brock is expecting you. Put your things by the door while I buzz him."

They buzz the hired help? thought Eleanor. *No wonder he enjoys working here.* Then all at once he was standing in the inner doorway, his beautiful, even white teeth glistening through a broad smile. His sudden appearance sent a tingling pulse of excitement through her, knotting her stomach and disrupting her breathing. He had changed from sloppy dungarees and soiled sweatshirt to sharply creased dark blue slacks and a light green terry-cloth long-sleeved shirt with a deep V-neck that revealed a curly tuft of alluring dark chest hair. The switch in clothing had transformed him from a handsome but rough-cut workman of that morning to probably the best-looking man she had ever seen. Their eyes engaged. Neither spoke, while Maggie looked wonderingly from one to the other.

"I'm glad you came," he said softly. The mellow timber of his voice filled the room as if he had shouted. "I wasn't sure you would."

"Why?" She swallowed. One word was all she could manage.

"You had reservations about talking with strangers."

92

"I thought we cleared that up."

"One never knows."

"I'm here, aren't I?"

"Yes." He hesitated. He wanted to tell her how lovely she looked. "You look lovely."

"Thank you." She felt self-conscious standing in the middle of the room like an actress who's forgotten her lines before a waiting audience.

There was absolute heart-stopping silence for three full seconds before Maggie, sensing their mutual unease, moved quickly, to everyone's relief, to break the spell. "Brock, why don't you show Eleanor around?"

"Yes," he said, almost startled. "The grand tour." He gestured broadly around the room. "Whataya think?"

"It's magnificent," extolled Eleanor. "Who designed it?"

"The owner," he replied, catching Maggie's perplexity from the corner of his eye. "Would you like to meet him?"

"Well, I suppose so." She was uncertain of the propriety, but it would do no harm.

"Good. I'll go tell him." He disappeared through the door, and a moment later Maggie's intercom buzzed.

"Go right in," she said, amused at Brock's playful subterfuge.

Eleanor complied, though the staged formality of her entrance made her uncomfortable. When she caught sight of Brock seated behind the huge moon-shaped desk in the corner of the office, she was at first disbelieving. *He's play-acting*, she thought, but the shiny silver nameplate on the corner of the desk plainly bore the name BROCK STOWOLSKI. Seeing him lounging in the recliner, she realized that he blended with the decor. He fit in because it was a part of him, an extension of himself. An incredibly beautiful man in an equally handsome office. There was no doubt in her mind. He was the owner and, as if to cancel out the last shadow of uncertainty, his mouth curled into a wide, pearly, self-satisfied grin.

"I should be angry with you," she said, "but I'm too..." She started to say, "Relieved," but that would only encourage his gloating. "I'm too impressed."

"At what? That a guy who works with his hands also has a brain? I must say, Ellie, you show all the symptoms of female intellectual chauvinism." He used a nickname for her as though their acquaintance dated back months instead of hours.

She, while warmed by his gesture of familiarity, felt defensive about his accusation. "Would it be too chauvinist of me," she said snidely, "to ask if I could sit down?"

Brock leaped to his feet. "Forgive me, Ellie. I'm a clod. A real oaf."

"Not unexpected of a common laborer," she teased.

"I deserve that, and I make no defense. Let's sit over here." He directed her to a cushioned sofa on the other side of the room facing the windows with a spacious view of the bright lights of the bay city spread below. "My deception about being a laborer wasn't premeditated. It just evolved as we conversed. It seemed like a fun thing to do. A spur-of-the-moment thing. I wasn't trying to prove anything...about you or me. I was just having a little fun."

She read the sincerity in his face and voice and turned her eyes down toward the heavy pile rug. "I suppose I am a snob."

"I can't say. I'll give you an assessment after we know each other better. Are you from the East?"

"Yes."

"I can hear it in your accent. You went to college there?"

"Yes."

"Let me guess. Vassar?"

"No."

"Smith."

Her eyes returned to his. "Yes."

"Your family is well off?"

"No. My father worked hard and sacrificed to put me through school. Both he and my mother are deceased."

"I'm sorry. Any brothers or sisters?"

"One older brother."

Brock chuckled. "You look like one of the Rockefellers. Your accent and clothes and, well, little things. They tell a lot about a person. For instance, your poise and posture, your erectness, reflect breeding and self-esteem. Your diction and vocabulary are cultivated. The way you're sitting now, back and head straight, hands folded in your lap, is the mark of class...high class."

94

"I'm a classic Smith graduate. Does that bother you?"

"Frankly, Ellie, I admire class. It's that intangible factor that separates those who care deeply about the quality and style of their lives from those who have no particular standards, who without question or thought take what life gives them each day. The man, the person, with class does not simply inhabit his environment like a wild animal in the forest. He plays it like a virtuoso, working it, practicing, studying, seeking in life not merely survival but elegance for its own sake. The greatest tribute we can pay our Creator for the wondrous gift of life is to endow it with as much beauty and grace as we can."

"That's a beautiful thought."

"I can't claim authorship. A friend of mine..." The learned, smiling face of Father Leonard appeared behind Eleanor like a wall painting. Brock had not thought of Lenny since...how long had it been? He wondered where the priest was. Still doing research in the Vatican? Probably not. His two-year appointment by the bishop had long since expired.

"A friend of yours?" asked Eleanor.

"Yes," said Brock, awakening from his mental excursion. "I'm sorry. I was thinking about someone." Should he tell her that Lenny is a priest? It might lead to the revelation that he himself once aspired to the priesthood. Ellie might not be ready to hear that yet. "A wise close friend who taught me a great many things about life and its purpose."

"You talk as if he's dead."

"No. Our paths separated years ago. We've lost touch."

"That's too bad. Who is he?"

"Well..." There was no way around it. He had to tell her. "He's a priest. Father Leonard."

"Is he in California?"

"No. He went to Italy to do some research about five years ago. I haven't heard from him since nor have I written. We've both been very busy."

"Where did you know him? Here in California?"

"No. We were in college together in Maryland."

"Which school?"

Brock had backed himself into a corner. He could lie to her, tell her he went to the University of Maryland, but lies only lead to more lies. "St. Charles College."

"But that's a Catholic seminary."

"How did you know that?"

"I'm Catholic. You were studying for the priesthood then?"

"Yes, but I dropped out after two years. I decided my talents and life's mission lay elsewhere."

"From the looks of your office I would say you made the right decision. It takes total commitment and self-sacrifice to survive as a priest. I know. My brother's a Maryknoll in New York."

"A Maryknoll? I can't believe it!"

"Well, it's true."

"Then I admire him," Brock said, nodding. "He's got more dedication than I ever had. I was a pretty godforsaken candidate for the priesthood."

"Oh—" she smiled coyly—"I don't think God would ever forsake you."

He laughed. "That's not what I meant."

"I know. But I did."

Brock and Eleanor were married six months later in a formal church wedding in Oakland attended by her brother, Kelly and Helena, members of D-M's staff, friends, and celebrities of California's design and building industries. Television stations covered the event, and photographs of the stunning couple and accounts of the ceremony appeared on the front pages of the society sections of the area's major newspapers. To observers the marriage seemed ordained in heaven and cast in Hollywood. The perfect couple. Young, beautiful, wealthy, successful, and with a bright future ahead. The ageless fairy tale come true.

For Eleanor, it was in fact a living dream with a fantasy ending. She had truly found her Prince Charming, disguised not as a warty frog in some bewitched forest but as a common laborer toiling in a crowded shopping mall. As their relationship deepened, she searched for but could not find, that frailty of character or weakness of purpose in Brock that would show him to be other than what he appeared. The further she probed, the more impressive his credentials became. He embodied all of the things a woman of Eleanor's upbringing and intelligence desired and needed: good-looking, virile, cultivated, charismatic, wealthy, and—a special requirement for her—a Catholic. Her infatuation with him mounted with numbing intensity each time another unexplored side of his character revealed itself, and a fervent love for him was born that would endure throughout her life.

Brock was equally taken with Eleanor, but her crowning attraction was her unparalleled suitability as homemaker and mother of his children. To achieve the towering goals he had set for himself, to scale those pinnacles of success that ever beckoned him in the distance, he needed respectability and social status. A prerequisite for both was a glamorous, dignified, socially skilled woman at his side, and a wholesome family at home. He could hunt the world over and never meet a woman who could match Eleanor's qualities. She was made for him.

And so he had explained to Noreen in the office the morning after Eleanor accepted his proposal of marriage. It was Sunday and he and Noreen were alone in the suite. She was working on a Monday deadline. Over the intercom Brock had summoned her to his office, and they were now seated side by side on the same couch where he had proposed to Eleanor the night before.

Noreen was sullen and pensive after he disclosed his engagement. "I'm not surprised," she said glumly. "I knew a good-looking guy like you wouldn't stay single forever. Actually, I knew you two would get married the first time I saw her in the office. She's a knockout, and she'd have to be running on a dead battery not to want you."

"Hey, I'm not that great a catch."

"Oh, yes you are," she countered, nodding emphatically. "Men like you come along once in a million years, and she knows it. But don't worry. I won't make any trouble for you. I never expected more from you than I got. That was our deal, remember?"

"We've shared a very special relationship, haven't we?" he said softly, stroking her cheek with a crooked forefinger.

She took hold of his hand and pressed it lightly to her lips. "It's been nearly six years and still no one suspects us."

"Nor should they," Brock reassured with quiet conviction. "We've never given anyone reason to."

For weeks Noreen had dreaded this moment, knowing it would come and she would be powerless to stop it. Now it was here. Their "special relationship," as Brock called it, was over. At an end was the wild lovemaking every month in his apartment that had become a routine part of her life and on which she had developed an addictive dependency. How could she live without it? She led a very solitary life, simple and uncluttered: her work at the office, oil painting in her apartment, visits alone to art galleries and exhibitions and lectures. She did not seek companionship, nor did her unkempt appearance, bland clothes, and retiring nature invite the interest of the men she met. Those few that paid her attention, whether innocently or with lustful ambitions, were discouraged upfront by her coldness. She was a single-channel person who felt confused and tense whenever life became complicated by competing demands. She was content to be Brock's once-a-month lover and nothing more. It was regular, uncomplicated, and gave her a deep sense of security primarily because it was a one-dimensional relationship—satisfying both of their needs without the emotional encumbrances and petty games of romance. They never went out together for dinner or a movie or a relaxing drive along the coast. They never exchanged gifts at Christmas or on their birthdays. They exacted no commitment from each other nor did they make any pretense that the relationship served any other purpose than pleasure. For both of them it was a perfect relationship.

Their private lives ran in separate lanes, converging only in Brock's boudoir for an hour or two every four or five weeks. She would drive herself to his apartment building around 11:00 PM and pass through the security gate into the underground garage using a magnetic card that Brock had given her to which were attached two tumbler keys: one silver and one gold. The silver key unlocked the door to the private elevator that serviced the rooftop apartments. The gold key opened the door to his penthouse. She kept the card and keys with her at all times in her purse— a ready reminder, whenever she needed it, of the pleasures that awaited her at their next assignation. As the date approached and her desire mounted, she would sometimes take the card and keys with her to bed, fingering them like worry beads till she fell asleep.

When she entered the penthouse she would go directly to his bedroom. If he was already in bed, she would undress and their lovemaking would commence at once. If he was working late or otherwise detained, she would change into a negligee that hung in the closet, lie down on top of the bedcovers, and read a book till he arrived. They would say very little to one another, as the singular purpose of their meeting did not stimulate wide-ranging conversation. And when their lustful appetites were sated, Brock would fall asleep and Noreen would leave. Sometimes she too would slumber, but she always awakened early enough to depart without being seen.

She never thought of herself as Brock's mistress because he gave her nothing tangible—neither gifts nor money—and she owed him nothing. What they received from each other in physical pleasure they gave freely with no emotional or palpable strings attached. It was this gratuitous nature of their affair that had prolonged it these years—much longer than either of them had expected. It cost them nothing; it posed no threat; it incurred no obligation. But most of all they both had grown accustomed to it; it had become a part of their regimens, an integral feature of their separate lives.

Now, as they sat shoulder to shoulder on the sofa, a disheartening feeling of unfairness settled upon Noreen. While Brock could indulge in the passionate gifts of his sensuous new wife, Noreen would have no one to fill the jagged void left by his abrupt withdrawal from her life...and from her body.

"What will I do?" she whimpered, staring out the window as if searching for an answer in the morning sky.

"Hey, I'm not the only guy who gets turned on by you."

"It would never be the same. You're different." A glistening tear welled up in the corner of her left eye, crested, and rolled down her cheek.

Brock leaned close to her face and wiped the wetness away with his thumb. "You know, you're sexy even when you cry."

Noreen gripped his shirt collar in both hands, rested her forehead limply against his chest, and wept. "I'm sorry...I thought I...I could handle this...but I can't. I can't live without our...our relationship." She tilted her head back and pleaded with reddened eyes awash in tears. "Please."

He looked impassively into her eyes.

"Please!" she implored. "Must it end?"

Brock's face was frozen in deliberation. Then he slowly shook his head. "No," he murmured.

NINE

Because Eleanor had expected to become pregnant soon, the question of her getting a job had not come up. She had received her Master's Degree and could have applied, and would have been accepted, for a number of professional positions, but there was no financial necessity for her to work. So she remained unemployed, occupying her time with tennis and golf in a women's group at Brock's swank country club, bridge-game luncheons, exercise sessions at a health spa, shopping trips, and a limited amount of housework, the lion's share being done by a cleaning woman who took daily care of the plush, six-bedroom house they had purchased on an estate abutting the country club's golf course. The one duty Eleanor reserved for herself was cooking Brock's meals, a task she performed with consummate culinary skill.

She was able to fit her schedule easily into Brock's, arranging her activities so she had time to bathe and change into appropriate evening clothes by the time he came home. Whether they were dining out or staying home, she made sure she looked radiant and appealing. She wanted to give him an extra incentive to break away from his first love, DESIGN METAPHORS. She realized from the start that she would have to compete with D-M for Brock's time and affection, but she accepted the challenge without self-delusion or reservation because she knew she had assets that the sexless D-M did not, and she made the most of them.

Both she and Brock were impatient to begin a family. It was a recurring topic of their conversation which, instead of inspiring lovemaking, impaired it by making intercourse a biophysical drill rather than a spontaneous act of love. After two years of disappointments, visits to gynecologists, encouraging lab reports attesting to their mutual fertility, and repeated "drills" to impregnate Eleanor—followed by the same negative results—their enthusiasm for lovemaking began to falter.

The exhilarating news that Eleanor was pregnant therefore caught them both by surprise. They lost no time celebrating, first with a private dinner with their two closest friends, Kelly and Helena, and then with a week-long vacation alone in Acapulco. It was a new higher plateau in their relationship, and they became inseparable. Brock phoned her several times a day from his office to inquire about her health and activities and to plan their evenings, always with the unspoken anticipation of the pleasures each night would bring.

Pregnancy, however, took its toll. As her abdomen swelled during the second trimester, she felt more and more grotesque and, while Brock made a great show of persuading her that he still found her attractive, the waning ardor of his lovemaking spoke for itself. In the final three months they ceased intercourse altogether—for the safety of the baby, Brock assured—while he found it more frequently necessary to be away on business trips. And when he returned he seemed to Eleanor distant and reserved. One evening as she heaved herself into bed, she asked him candidly if he had lost interest in her because she was pregnant. He adamantly denied it, embracing her and professing his love so earnestly that she wept out of guilt and relief.

Thereafter, until the baby was born, Brock was conspicuously solicitous, catering to her every need and whim. Whether this display was out of love or a self-imposed penance for having neglected her, Eleanor couldn't tell, nor did it matter at the time because she needed his affection to mitigate her feeling that she was repulsive. She loved him and wanted him and if penance was what it took to win his devotion, so be it.

Three years almost to the day of their marriage, Eleanor bore Brock a healthy, blue-eyed, curly-dark-haired son, whom they named Paul after the great Apostle. It was a joyous day in Brock's life, a day on which his ambitions reached new heights. Till then he had been working solely to establish himself, to make a name, and to secure his future. That all changed when Paul entered the world. From that moment on Brock boasted of the one possession every magnate, tycoon, plutocrat, and would-be Vanderbilt yearns for: a male heir.

Paul's arrival altered Brock's outlook in ways he had not foreseen. He had wanted children, a family, and a home, but he had never paused to consider what effect a child—a boy—would have on his own ambitions. DESIGN METAPHORS was no longer simply Brock's enterprise. D-M was Paul's inheritance, a corporation that Paul one day would head. Brock resolved at once to rear his son in a way that would prepare him to assume the leadership of a multifaceted business enterprise with global investments, widespread real estate holdings, and vast financial power. What had been Brock's vision of success would become Paul's future.

Brock did not share this vision with Eleanor. Her mind was on the present, not the future. She was understandably preoccupied with being a mother, a new, exciting, and demanding role for her and one she had eagerly awaited since their marriage. She fawned over the baby, cuddling it, cooing, nursing, nestling it with tender affection in her arms. It was the center of her world.

Whereas Paul was the fulfillment of Eleanor's maternal instincts, Brock did not have the capacity or interest to identify with them. He had no brothers or sisters nor any experience with children, let alone infants. He felt foolish holding the baby and soon refused to do it, pleading "professional incompetence." That's what mothers were for, he kidded, but more and more he kept at a distance from Paul, somewhat estranged, waiting for the boy to reach an age when Brock could talk with him, reason and communicate, teach, and explain to him his heritage and the great responsibility that one day would rest on his shoulders.

Brock did not totally ignore his son. He bought him toys and occasionally played children's games with him, but Brock was home very little. He kept basically the same work schedule he had maintained before the marriage: up at dawn and back home at eight, often later. Although Eleanor accepted this long workday without complaint, she harbored a growing resentment at his lukewarm interest in Paul and, for that matter, in herself. He went out of town frequently and once or twice a week, sometimes on weekends, called to say he was working late and would heat up a frozen dinner at the office and not to wait up for him. She felt increasingly abandoned and, worse, disturbed by the revelation of a callous calculating side of Brock's nature that had been concealed from her in the four years she had known him. Or was he reacting to a subtle change in her own behavior toward him, a change she was unaware of?

She turned to Helena for solace and advice. As the friendship between the two women had grown, they had come to share their innermost feelings. One afternoon in the older woman's kitchen, while Paul napped in his car crib on the floor, they drank coffee and chatted.

"I grew up with a brother and father in the house," Eleanor explained. "I thought I had a good idea of what living with a man would be like, but I was unprepared for this."

"The loneliness?" asked Helena. She admired Eleanor not only for her beauty and intelligence but for her self-revealing honesty.

"Oh, I expected to be alone. I wanted to be a homemaker. That's a solitary domestic role. Brock insisted we hire a cleaning woman, but I drew the line at hiring a nursemaid for Paul or a cook, which Brock had suggested. Those are things I reserve for myself, so I can be there when Paul needs me, be a part of his growing up. It's a full-time job. I wanted that and I accepted it, but I didn't expect to be deserted by my husband!"

Her sudden vehemence intensified Helena's curiosity. "He's not living at home?"

"Oh, he sleeps there and performs the minimal amenities of a husband and father. He kisses us when he comes home, kisses us good night, and kisses us good-bye in the morning."

"Are you...well...have you been intimate?" Helena was trying to be tactful.

"You mean sex?" replied Eleanor caustically. "Pardon my frankness, Helena, but Brock and I haven't had skin-to-skin contact in five weeks, and the last time we did it was—" she groped for dignified words that would not embarrass her friend—"it was perfunctory."

"No lingering kisses?"

Eleanor shook her head. "He hasn't been all that affectionate. Is it me or are all marriages like this?" She pushed herself back from the table, crossed her arms, and scowled. "I wonder if my parents had a relationship like ours. You can never tell, you know. On the surface everything can appear so chummy and cozy."

Helena smiled knowingly. "Eleanor, dear. When you're around people every day and see how they behave toward each other, you can tell whether they're in love. Love always shows through. You can't hide it. It comes through in little things: a look, a touch, a word."

A tear coursed down Eleanor's cheek. "His doesn't show through."

Helena pulled her chair next to Eleanor's and put an arm around her. "Now, now. Every marriage goes through stages. Brock is a very independent person. He's been single a good many years, coming and going whenever he wanted, keeping whatever hours suited his mood. It's probably not easy for him to be tied down."

Eleanor started to protest.

"Yes, dear, tied down!" declared Helena firmly as she stood up. "One woman. One house. Totally committed. Totally accountable to you. That's a major adjustment for a man with his energy, ego, and independence. I went through the same thing with Kelly."

"You did?" said Eleanor shakily, brushing aside another tear.

"I most certainly did!" She walked to a window and scanned the sky. "It was years before we really grew close to each other. A marriage is so filled with conflicts and challenges that once the frivolous courting phase passes, only patience and love will build a truly enduring relationship. Don't kid yourself. We've had our ups and downs. Remember, Eleanor, that unlike you I never had any children, and we tried for years before we finally resigned ourselves to the fact that we weren't blessed by God to have any. You think that didn't put a strain or two on our marriage?"

Eleanor got up and took Helena's hand. "I'm sorry. I'm being selfish. I have a lot to be thankful for, I suppose. Paul is such a beautiful baby, and Brock...I love him very much. I haven't considered how difficult it's been for him."

Helena patted her friend's hand. "Be patient. Give him time. I'm sure things will work out."

"Thank you, Helena. You're a good friend. I feel much better."

All morning Noreen had been on tenterhooks expecting her intercom to buzz, hoping it was Brock, hoping it was not, praying he would call, fearing he would. Tonight was their monthly assignation, their secret conclave, Noreen's physical and emotional deliverance. The last three months he had cancelled out each time, buzzing her at her desk in the design shop to express his regrets. His business schedule was so tight, he had told her that he couldn't get away. He had apologized and promised to make it up to her, but her anxiety remained.

She jumped as her intercom buzzed. *Is it Brock?* Ten earlier calls had been others in the office. *Please, God, let it be Brock, and let him say we're on.* She gingerly reached for the phone, afraid to pick it up, afraid not to.

"Hello," she murmured.

"Noreen?"

It was Brock.

"Yes," she whispered. "Are we on tonight?"

"Sorry, Noreen, but it's a negative."

"Not again!" she exclaimed, then covered the mouthpiece with her hand, fearful that one of her coworkers on the other side of the room would overhear. "It's been three, almost four months." she whispered. "I need you! I've thought of nothing else all week. You know how I am about this. Can't we arrange something?"

"If I could, Noreen, I would. You know that. I'm not stringing you along. I just can't break away from my other obligations right now. D-M is thriving, and I'm up to my neck in negotiations and promotions. You know how busy we are."

Noreen was mentally convulsed but struggled to maintain her composure. After a silence of several seconds in which she frantically searched for alternatives but could think of none, she sighed with utter resignation. "All right," she said morosely, drawing each word out. "How about next week?"

"I'll try. I really will."

"Could we make it sooner? Like Monday?"

"We'll see. I'm booked solid, but maybe I can postpone something. I'll let you know. Okay?"

She paused, not wanting to give up without securing a more definite commitment than "we'll see." Brock sounded sincere, and she so wanted to believe he was. "Okay," she said, defeated, and he hung up. She held the dead phone to her ear for several seconds before slowly replacing it in its receptacle.

Making love with Brock had become an obsession with her, overshadowing everything else in her life—her work, her art, her very future. A terrible feeling of emptiness welled up within her and grew larger, as if there were a hole there through which her happiness and well-being were gradually seeping out, leaving a void.

Throughout the rest of the day she remained distracted, going about her work by remote control, communicating with colleagues as if from a distance, not totally connected. At the close of the business day she sat motionless at her worktable while the office emptied. When the last person had left and the rooms were quiet, she turned off her work light and sat in the darkness, mourning the loneliness that had gradually settled over her.

Then, as she had the previous three nights, she went to the corner window behind Brock's desk, from where she could see his penthouse four blocks away atop a brightly lighted high-rise, the secret haven for Brock's monthly trysts with Noreen. He had held onto the apartment as a place where he and Ellie could entertain and as a guesthouse where out-of-town visitors doing business with D-M could stay in more sumptuous and private accommodations than were available at many of the most expensive hotels. Taking from her purse the silver and gold keys to his elevator and apartment, she fondled them absentmindedly while she gazed wistfully at the darkened windows of his penthouse. The two of them could have been there now...

Why did she torment herself? she wondered. Self-punishment? For what? Wanting him? She asked for very little. An hour or two. But then, of course, it was an hour that rightfully belonged to his wife. Noreen had no right to ask for it and certainly no right to receive it. It was wrong. She was in every sense a thief, stealing what was not hers legally to possess.

She turned from the window, unable to bear the pain. Her hand touched the headrest of Brock's recliner and without thinking she began to stroke it. The feel of the rich leather where his head had lain an hour before was soothing. She rested her head on it and closed her eyes. She knew her behavior at this moment was bizarre and maybe a trifle neurotic, but the sensation was no less pleasing. It was almost sedative.

Then the thought of lying in his bed in the penthouse popped into her mind. Why not? It was dark. No one would be there. The two keys she was holding would give her access. She could lie between the sheets and pretend he was making love to her.

Fifteen minutes later Noreen inserted the precious gold key into the door to Brock's penthouse and entered. Closing the door softly behind her, she stood in the darkened foyer, the keys in her hand, her heart beating as wildly as it had that first night in the office when she had stolen into Brock's bedroom to seduce him.

As she turned to get her bearings in the darkness, she stopped short at the sound of laughter. It was a woman's, high-pitched, sort of an excited giggle but louder. It came from the bedroom.

"Do it again!" urged a man's voice. "Once more!" The laugh resounded again more shrilly.

Noreen gasped. It was Brock's voice exhorting, speaking a line whose meaning she knew all too well. He and his wife were here. Noreen had unintentionally invaded their privacy. Instantly she reached for the doorknob to leave, when she heard Brock moan, "Oh, Maureen."

Noreen froze as her face turned crimson in the dark. Anger erupted uncontrollably inside her. She strode silently but purposefully across the heavily carpeted foyer to the open door of the bedroom and flicked on the overhead lights. Two bare intertwined bodies on the bed froze in the sudden glare. Two heads snapped towards her.

"Noreen!" cried Brock.

"A crowded schedule? Fully booked?" crowed Noreen, seething with outrage.

The bodies scrambled to disengage in almost comical confusion as Noreen watched with abhorrent fascination. Brock stepped off the bed stark naked, while a ravishing brunette in her early twenties whom Noreen had never seen before dove headfirst under the sheet.

"You have no right busting in here like this!" shouted Brock.

"I didn't bust in, buster! I have a key, remember?" She held up the silver and gold keys. "And I also have a story to tell your wife."

"I see," he said, standing brazenly before her with feet apart, arms crossed defiantly across his hairy muscled chest.

"It'll be quite a scandal. Should make all the papers. You'll be front-page news."

"Oh, really? Well, go right ahead, Noreen. Tell my wife. Tell everyone. But before you do, get yourself a sharp lawyer because I'll sue you for slander. I'll deny every allegation and defy you to prove even one.

You see, I'm very discreet about my liaisons. Very, very careful. I've never been seen in public with any woman but my wife. And no one has ever seen me in private."

"Till now."

"The only evidence you have is the keys." He lunged forward and snatched them from her before she could pull away. "And now I have them. So the next move is yours." His smug expression dared her to speak.

"I'm going to see Eleanor."

"Bravely stated, but why wait?" He stepped audaciously to the night table by the bed, lifted the receiver from the telephone, and dialed. "So you wanted a raise, and when I refused—your work has been slipping recently—you made up this cockamamie story."

Eleanor answered.

"Ellie? It's me. I'm at the office." He nodded. "Yeah, pretty busy. Listen, honey, do you remember Noreen Rollins?"

He listened to Eleanor's response.

"Yes, the senior artist on the staff."

Eleanor acknowledged her identity.

"Right, well, sweetheart, she's standing here and wants to tell you something." He held out the phone to Noreen. "Here, tell her yourself."

Seeing the futility of her position, Noreen spun about, angry tears flooding her eyes, and rushed out of the bedroom and across the foyer. Reaching the entrance, she grabbed the doorknob with both hands as if to rip the door off its hinges, then stopped, motionless. She breathed deeply several times, regaining her composure, and without turning around called out coldly, "You owe me one paycheck and two weeks' severance pay. Have Maggie mail them to me." She opened the door and left.

Brock had taken a huge gamble and won. Exposed in a compromising situation as never before, his quick mind had astutely come to the rescue, turning the situation against Noreen and calling her bluff. That was a close call. He'd have to be more careful in the future.

He looked down at the receiver, which was making funny noises, and lifted it to his ear. "Ellie, you still there? You won't believe this. Now I've seen everything. It's beyond belief. You'd think after all these years she would..."

Eleanor stood by the kitchen wall phone staring at the floor feeling desolate and forsaken. As soon as Brock had hung up, she had dialed his private number at the office. It rang and rang and rang; she didn't know how many times. He wasn't there!

Brock had explained the entire episode to her. How Noreen had burst into his office slightly drunk demanding a raise and a more important position in D-M. How, when he politely told her that her work did not merit a promotion, she had begun making wild threats about telling Eleanor that Noreen and he were lovers. Preposterous, he had said. He explained how bewildered and dismayed he was at Noreen's behavior. How the quality of her work had been declining the past few months. How he thought after all these years that Noreen would have had more loyalty to the firm and more respect for Eleanor than to pull something as despicable as this. How Brock no longer trusted his judgment of people. How he would stay on in the office for awhile and finish his project, and for Eleanor not to wait up for him.

Eleanor knew, of course, he was lying. The call to his office confirmed it. She had suspected for months that he was seeing another woman or women. He had such a strong sex drive that, since he was not making love to her, he must be bedding with someone else. She sensed his infidelity in the way he leered at other women and relished their approving glances. He was, as Eleanor was all too aware, extremely attractive, though the luster had worn somewhat thin for her.

She recalled vividly her body's reaction the first time he kissed her. Her legs quivered, her skin turned feverish, her eyes glazed. She came near to fainting. Oh, how she longed to feel that way again. It wasn't just his infidelity that had dimmed the glow. Nor was it simply familiarity and living together. It was more profound than that. Little by little, day by day, the outline and features of his true personality had begun to show through his entrancing looks, acquiring greater definition until one day, without her realizing it, his looks had become transparent. What she saw beneath the looks and the bluster and the deceptions was the real Brock: an ambitious, power-seeking, fundamentally selfish man who had the capacity to use and consume well-meaning people like Noreen. It was sad and a little frightening. And it made Eleanor feel lost and lonely.

Had he used Eleanor, too? She considered her situation. He had given her a gorgeous son. She enjoyed a standard of living known only to the rich, and his social status was what she had hoped to find in a husband: he was wealthy, respected, and successful. Until this evening he had never given her cause to be embarrassed in public or in private, and it appeared he had somehow succeeded in emerging unscathed from this evening's confrontation with Noreen, so Eleanor would be spared any public humiliation and their married life could go on without incident unless, of course, Eleanor chose to make an issue of it. The "it" was Noreen.

Eleanor shuffled across the kitchen to a chair, sat down heavily, and stared blankly at the floor. Had Noreen really been having an affair with Brock? Eleanor pondered the evidence. Surely Noreen, who looked every bit as feminine as Eleanor, would have felt attracted to him, and she had worked closely with Brock day after day for ten years, seven years before Eleanor married him.

And what of Brock's appraisal of Noreen? Would he have lusted after her? There was, Eleanor's instincts told her, a highly sensuous woman beneath Noreen's plain exterior. Moreover, Eleanor recalled the territorial look Noreen had fired at her when they were first introduced. Eleanor had attributed it to professional jealousy...the staff's having to share Brock with this new woman. Had there been more to Noreen's look? Was the jealousy of a different sort?

Yes, Eleanor concluded. Noreen had been Brock's lover. The question was whether the confirmation of something Eleanor should long have suspected justified ruining her marriage. All women who wed handsome men ran the risk of infidelity, but somehow she never believed it would happen to her. Odd, she thought, that she had always wondered how dishonored wives felt about their husband's adulteries and how they wrestled with the decision of dissolving their marriages. The choices were so painful. Would she be happier divorced? Would dissolution of the marriage be fair to young Paul? Could Brock still love her? Could she ever again sleep beside him in the same bed?

The more she agonized over her dilemma and its myriad shifting implications the more determined she became to stand firm. For one thing, she did not wish to give up the lifestyle she had acquired through her marriage. It was selfish, she knew, but she refused to sacrifice her pleasures because of Brock's wrongdoing. To do so would, she felt, be admitting some degree of complicity. Why should she be made to suffer for his unfaithfulness? Moreover, other marriages had survived philandering husbands, and hers would too. It wasn't as if he loved these other women. They were mere diversions, entertainments.

She believed that in his heart he truly loved her and her alone. To be sure, there had been wonderful moments of great tenderness between them when the soft loving sensitive inner core of his personality bubbled up through the cracks in his tough exterior crust, and it would again. She would work and live for those moments, and perhaps in time his affairs with other women would lose their appeal, and he would allow his love for Eleanor to blossom once more. She was sure his love for her was real. Every fiber of her womanly intuition felt it. Love was there. Granted, it was weak now and in need of nourishment and care, but it was there. And she would bide her time, years if necessary, for its fulfillment.

The front door chimes startled her. Who could it be at this hour? It was half past eleven. A neighbor in trouble? She went to a curtained window with a view of the stoop and looked out. It was Noreen!

Eleanor's instincts shouted for her to run and hide and hope the visitor would leave, but reason quickly took charge. She must face this woman, remain calm and dignified, and hear her out. There was no other choice.

Eleanor opened the door, and the two women gaped at one another with identical thoughts. They were facing each other over this threshold at this moment for one reason only: they both had lain with the same man, who happened to be Eleanor's husband. Happened to be. Her title as wife had never been an issue between them; Noreen had come to tell her why it now mattered.

Eleanor spoke first. "I know why you're here. Please come in."

Noreen entered, looking wretched. Hair matted and uncombed. Face pale and drawn. Eyes red and swollen from crying. Her mouth tense and frightened. Even her dingy white blouse and blue jeans looked downcast. "Thank you," she said meekly, her head bowed as if to hide her shame. "I've tried to think how to tell you."

"Why don't we get comfortable before we talk. It will make things easier."

"All right," said Noreen submissively.

"Let's sit in the kitchen. It will help us relax." She led Noreen down a short hallway to a small breakfast nook. "Would you like something to drink? Coffee?"

"No, thank you."

"Something stronger?"

"If you don't mind, I would really enjoy a glass of sherry. My nerves are shot."

"Have a seat." Eleanor busied herself with two glasses and a bottle. "You've had quite a night."

"You can say that again!" A strange camaraderie instantly formed between the two women without any effort on their part.

Eleanor poured. "Then you've come directly from wherever you were when he called?"

"Yes. The penthouse. He lied about being at the office." She said it matter-of-factly, not intending to hurt but to inform. But she saw the sting that registered on Eleanor's face. "I'm sorry. I didn't mean to."

"Don't worry about it, please," said Eleanor hastily, recovering her poise. "It's clear we have much to talk about. But before we do—" she raised her glass—"here's to life's trials. May we learn from them to understand and love one another."

Noreen nodded uncertainly, took a sip of sherry, and closed her eyes as if to draw energy and relief from the pungent liquor. "You're very kind to be so understanding," she said, opening her eyes.

"I don't have much choice, do I?" Her brittle tone made Noreen look up from her glass. "You've come to expose Brock as an unfaithful womanizer. I've suspected him for some time, you know, and you're here to dispel my doubts. Put the final nail in the coffin." Her tone was turning sarcastic despite her desire to avoid harsh words with her husband's lover of the past...how many years? Six, eight, maybe ten.

"I don't want to argue with you, Mrs. Stowolski. That's not why I came. I never meant you any harm. Brock and I had a relationship years before he ever met you. I wasn't taking him away from you. I wasn't trying to steal him from you." Noreen's eyes moistened and her lower lip began to quiver.

Eleanor quickly realized that her visitor was on the verge of a breakdown. "I know that," she said with feeling, trying to be solicitous. "I know that. I know it wasn't intentional. I can understand that." Eleanor was getting the peculiar notion that this woman had come to her for comfort, not revenge. "Why don't we start at the beginning, the very beginning when you first met Brock? How did it happen?"

Noreen launched into a tearful hour-long recitation of the history of her affair with Brock: the interview at the art school, the exciting formative days of D-M producing the initial portfolio, his award, the party, her seduction of him—the most daring adventure of her life—and the monthly trysts that followed, first in his office bedroom and later in the penthouse apartment after Kelly joined the firm.

"Only once in all that time did we ever come close to breaking off our...our get-togethers. It was the morning after he'd asked you to marry him. He told me our monthly lovemaking had to end, but I pleaded with him. I couldn't live without it. He looked at me a long time...thinking...not saying a word. My heart stopped beating waiting for his decision."

"What did he say?"

"He just grabbed me, and we made passionate love on the couch."

Eleanor's mouth gaped. "The couch in his office?"

"Yes, by the window."

The shocking image of Brock fornicating on the very spot where only hours earlier he had pledged his undying love to Eleanor tore away the last vestige of Brock's respectability in her mind. She stood and walked about the kitchen as anger hot as lava rose up within her. "That's where we sat the night before when he proposed."

Noreen drew in a loud breath. "I didn't know. I really didn't."

"He did! And he didn't care!" Eleanor's lips pursed tightly. "And you kept on seeing each other?"

"Well..." Noreen was stymied by the shocking dual image of Brock's proposing to Eleanor and only hours later making love to Noreen on the same couch. She had grievously hurt Eleanor and was unsure whether to flee or continue their conversation. After a moment's hesitation, she decided on the latter, which is why she had come. "We saw each other every day in the office, but the...the meetings...continued every month. Once a month."

"Are you in love with him?"

Noreen frowned deep in thought. It was the question she had consciously avoided from the day she had first met Brock at the art school. Love. What was love? Sexual attraction? Admiration? Devotion? Longing? "I can't say. I don't know how to define love. Is it wanting to be with someone? Wanting them to notice you? To be touched? To be missed? To be needed?" She was talking to herself now. "If that's what it is then, yes, I'm in love. But we never spoke of love. Never told each other. I'm sure he doesn't love me. To him it's always been sex and nothing more. He told me that in his bedroom that first night. I remember exactly what he said. I've never forgotten. 'It won't change our relationship,' he said. 'I don't want to be involved. No marriage. No babies.' That was it. We never spoke about it again. In fact, we say...we said...very little at all. We just made love, and I'd leave."

"You'd spend the whole night?"

"No, just a couple of hours. Once in awhile I'd sleep, but I'd be gone before morning."

The pain of discovering the truth wrenched Eleanor's heart. To suspect infidelity is one thing; to confirm it another. She stilled a sudden impulse to run from the house, to escape from her ache and sorrow. But to run now would be to condone his behavior, and she would not allow Brock the satisfaction of one more victory. One more cowed and exploited female. By God, she would stand tall and proud and fight for what was hers. Her marriage was hers. Her family. Her son. Her self-respect. Even Brock was hers, and she would not give them up so easily.

"So, you went to the penthouse tonight to confront him?"

"Not exactly. I went there...it sounds silly now."

"Nothing is silly, Noreen, where people's feelings are concerned."

"You're right. I went there to relive our...affection..."

"He had arranged to meet you there?"

"No. We had agreed weeks before to meet that night, but in the morning he called and canceled, for the fourth month in a row. I couldn't stand it. I needed to lie on that bed."

"And he was there?"

Noreen nodded.

"But not alone," said Eleanor.

"He was in bed with a girl. Her name is Maureen. A beautiful young woman I've never seen before. The penthouse was dark, but I heard their voices. It made me so angry. I just stormed in and turned on the lights. I think you know what happened after that."

"And you came straight here?"

"Yes. I had to tell you. He's been so unfaithful."

The stunning irony of her statement burst upon Eleanor like a divine revelation. It was so clear to Eleanor now, and so comical. She broke into a smile and giggled nervously. Noreen, the poor naive innocent, had come seeking comfort, not because Brock had been unfaithful to Eleanor but because he'd been unfaithful to Noreen. The giggle became a laugh. His infidelity to Eleanor over the years had never been an issue with Noreen until she herself became a victim. Noreen wasn't here for Eleanor's sake but for her own. It wasn't his love they shared but his infidelity!

Eleanor shook with uncontrollable laughter, while Noreen looked on, baffled at what was so amusing about this tragedy.

"Unfaithful, you said," gasped Eleanor between bursts of laughter as she wiped tears from her cheeks.

"Yes."

"Unfaithful to you."

"Yes."

"And to me!" She collapsed laughing into a chair, unable to continue. Eleanor struggled to get control of herself. "I'm sorry...I can't...help it. It's...so funny!"

Noreen shook her head solemnly. "I think you're hysterical."

"No, no," replied Eleanor, wiping away her tears with the backs of her hands. "I'm all right. Just give me a minute."

Eleanor prepared to explain but realized that Noreen would not comprehend. Her mind was too inner-focused, too internalized. She apparently was unable to bridge beyond her own private needs to the feelings and needs of others. It made Eleanor suddenly feel sorry for her. The impulse to laugh quickly died, replaced by tender commiseration. But there was little more to be said.

"This has all been rough on you, hasn't it?"

Noreen nodded. "I feel like my whole life has been upended. I'm leaving D-M, of course."

"That's the best thing. Get away from it all. Put it behind you. It'll be good for you. A new start. Where will you go?"

"Well, I've had a standing offer for a long time from one of our chief competitors. I never told anyone about it. I'm sure they'll take me if I ask them."

"That's wonderful. Which firm is it?"

"Prentiss Associates."

Brock came home after midnight and talked briefly with Eleanor about Noreen. Eleanor, already in bed and reading a novel, chatted amiably, pretending ignorance of the facts.

"I guess I'll have to let her go," Brock said sadly. "I hate to do it. She's become such a fixture on the staff."

"Yes," replied Eleanor with casual disdain. "I dare say she has."

Brock shot her a flickering glance to see if she had intended a hidden meaning. Her demeanor remained unchanged.

"The sooner you get rid of her the better for everyone," she added.

And they said no more about it.

The next morning Brock left on an unscheduled business trip to Los Angeles immediately after breakfast, giving Eleanor and Paul polite loving pecks on the cheek on his way out, playing the innocent, unaware of Noreen's visit to the house the night before. He had the air of one who was supremely self-confident and in control of his destiny. Eleanor bid him good-bye, waving pleasantly. He drove away smiling, believing he had successfully buried the incident. He had made only one phone call before breakfast. It was to Maggie in the office instructing her to send Noreen's paycheck plus two weeks' severance pay to her home address. He did not explain the circumstances, telling her only that he would explain it all when he returned.

Eleanor was glad at last to be alone with her baby so she could think. She had lain awake most of the night agonizing over her next move, debating whether to sue Brock for divorce, seek marriage counseling, confront him and hope for the best, or keep silent and pray that time really would heal all wounds. It had been impossible for her to be rational while Brock lay sleeping soundly beside her as if nothing had happened. His treachery screamed for punishment. The injury he had inflicted on her pride and on their sacred wedding vows demanded some kind of retribution. But what? How?

As soon as she cleaned up the breakfast dishes she phoned Kelly at the office and arranged to visit him later after leaving Paul with the babysitter.

"So what brings my favorite mother to this crazy denizen of design?" said Kelly an hour later, sitting down behind his desk after seating Eleanor opposite him.

"I came to talk to you about Brock's affairs."

He eased back in his chair and said happily, "Sure, what would you like to know? Net income? Net cash flow? Net losses? Market share? The books are open, especially to members of the immediate family."

"No, silly, not those affairs. I mean his sexual affairs. Paramours. You know, the roll-me-over-in-the-clover kind."

"Eleanor!" He glared at her sternly. "I'm embarrassed for you! Why are you talking to me that way?" He wasn't sure whether she was serious or just pulling his leg. In either case she was treading on very dangerous ground.

"Let's not kid each other, Kelly." She was very serious. "We're too good friends for that. I know all about Noreen and the others. Oh, I don't know their names and don't have times and places, but I do know Brock has been sleeping around for some time now. I need your advice on what I should do about it."

Kelly was flustered and speechless. He cleared his throat and began emptying his pipe noisily into a brass ashtray shaped like a spittoon.

Eleanor would not be put off. "Why don't you look me straight in the eye and tell me Brock has been having sex with a flock of different women, including Noreen, rather regularly for the past few years."

"Because it just isn't..."

"True? I know differently and so do you."

"I was going to say 'polite.'"

118

"Look at me. Look at me!" she demanded, raising her voice.

The weathered face with Dalmatian hair and kind gray eyes gave her a pained, rueful look. "Must we do this? What good can come of it?"

"The good of being honest with ourselves and each other."

"Honesty can be brutal and destructive, like telling an ugly child she's ugly."

"You're saying it would be cruel to tell Brock he's an unfaithful unloving husband?" Her bitterness soaked through each word.

"I've never seen you so...so venomous. It's out of character for you."

"Well, excuse me, Kelly!" Eleanor stood and leaned over the desk toward him. "Would you prefer sobs and tears and wailing?"

"No," he said, pouting. "That, too, would be out of character. Oh, Eleanor, do sit down. Let's not be confrontational about this."

Eleanor retook her seat.

"So," he continued, "let's be honest."

"That's why I came."

"When did you find out about Brock?"

She related her earlier suspicions, last night's episode, and Brock's implacable facade this morning.

"You're taking it well."

"As Brock has aptly demonstrated, looks can be deceiving."

"I'm sorry. I just don't know what to say."

"Say what I should do."

"About Brock?"

"About him, me, the baby, the family. I need your advice, as a friend...a dear friend. I feel like I'm teetering on a precipice." Her eyes teared.

"And you want me to pull you back to safety."

"Yes, I do."

"Well, I'll try. You see, without going into any details, I would say you have reason to be bitter."

"Not bitter, Kelly." She might weep after all. "Not bitter. Just so...so disappointed, and not only with Brock. With myself. If I were more feminine, more sexual, more—"

"Oh, stop it, Eleanor!" He got up, walked around the desk, and sat on its edge next to her chair. "It isn't you! You're all any man would ever want or need. I know. You give my heart a twinge every time I see your beautiful face and body, and I wouldn't be ashamed to tell Helena that either. She'd understand." He sighed again, as Eleanor watched his face intently. "But Brock isn't any man. He's unique. He needs more. He's driven like no one I've ever known. He has giant visions of the future and its possibilities that you and I and other less gifted people never dream of. These motives and drives not only make him excel; they create other appetites as well...the constant need to innovate, to have new experiences, and new conquests."

Kelly stiffened, as if mustering courage to give her a final unwelcome judgment. He took a deep breath, held it for a moment, then exhaled slowly. "If you want to keep him, you'll have to learn to live with his womanizing. He won't change. He can't."

Eleanor fought the anger and frustration that simmered inside her. "You mean I should sit by calmly and silently while he goes fornicating around town, around the whole state, with every young floozy he meets?"

"Please understand, Eleanor, I'm not condoning his behavior. I'm simply saying I understand it, and if you want to save your marriage and your family—which includes Brock—you'll have to try to understand it, too."

She rose and faced him. "Understand?" Defiance was taking over. "I had a hunch that's what you'd tell me!" She scowled darkly and strode to the window, turning her back on him while he eyed her anxiously, fearful she would take some rash, impulsive action and ruin the beautiful life she was living. "Why is there a double standard?" she asked. "If I were the one playing around, I'd be castigated by all sides, stripped, tarred, and feathered. Brock romps in the hay like a horny bull, and everyone looks the other way."

Kelly tried to explain. "But they...we...aren't against you, Eleanor. It's because we all love you and feel for you that we indulge Brock's weakness and keep silent. It's been painful for everyone who knows about it."

"Oh, yes, I'm sure you've all suffered. My heart goes out to you."

"That's not fair. We were thinking of you."

"Does everyone know?"

"Very few, I think. He hasn't flaunted it."

"Who else knows?" She was persistent. She needed to know which of the office staff were privy to her humiliation.

"Does it matter?"

She whirled about angrily. "You bet it matters! When I talk with people I want to know if they feel sorry for me. I don't want to be pitied, pampered, and patronized. I deal with everyone honestly, including you, and I expect to be treated honestly in return. Keeping Brock's affairs secret from me is not dealing honestly, is it?"

"Fair enough. As far as I can tell, only you, me, Helena, and I suppose the security guard at the Plaza know about Brock's indiscretions. The guard would have to be an imbecile not to guess why Noreen was spending so much time alone with Brock in the D-M suite after midnight."

"Anyone else?"

"One more. Maggie. She could read the mind of a spider. I'm sure she's been on to them, even though she's never said so, at least not to me or Helena."

"How did you learn about them?"

"I asked him and he told me."

"Just like that?"

"Yep, just like that."

"Oh, I see. Well, I'm just his lifetime partner. I guess I better join the business, then maybe he'd tell me, too."

"Eleanor, you have to understand..."

"Oh, Kelly," she said, giving him a pained look. "I do understand all too well." She cupped her hands over her face and wept.

Kelly rushed to her side and put his arms around her shoulders, pressing her to him. He silently viciously cursed Brock for hurting this wonderful woman.

"I lie awake most of every night thinking about it," she said. "Thinking about what my options are. What you've told me only reinforces my decision."

Kelly's face turned anxious. "Decision? You aren't going to do something you'll regret, I hope."

"I can't say whether I'll regret it or not. Only time will tell."

She stepped back, taking hold of his hands, and looked straight into his eyes. "I've decided to do nothing."

Kelly breathed more easily. "That's good thinking."

"We'll see. He wants his cake, too, you see. Well, I can play that game. You know what I want, Kelly?" She let go of his hands, turned, and walked to the window, her back to him. "I want more children. I want a traditional family. I want respectability and high station in society. I want a rich luxurious life, not only for me but for my children. I know that sounds wanton and selfish and un-Christian, but I'm being brutally frank. Brock can give us those things...and he will! A separation, a messy divorce...that would stain his public and commercial image. It wouldn't do for him. He needs me. I'm his symbol of respectability, his household fixture, his hostess and consort at celebrity events. I'm the mother and nursemaid to his child. That's my role in his life. I'm one of the supporting actors, one of the cast of thousands. Don't you agree?"

"I believe that sums it up pretty well," replied Kelly, nodding uneasily.

"But there's more to my decision than the good things in life. I want my husband back, because I still love him. In my heart I know that in time—it may take years—I can change him. That someday he'll give up his wanton womanizing and become once more the man I married."

"You mean you're going to remain silent about his affairs?"

She grinned confidently, wiping the tears. "What affairs?" She bent over and kissed Kelly's cheek, squeezing his arm at the same time. "Thank you, Kelly. I feel like a new person. I was so frightened last night, but now I know what I have to do." She went to the door of his office. "You and Helena are coming for dinner Saturday?"

"Yes, I believe that was the plan." He was a little breathless from Eleanor's swift about-face.

"Good. And don't be late. Brock likes everyone to be punctual." She gave him a wink and departed smiling.

TEN

The trauma of learning the truth about Brock's illicit affairs passed quickly for Eleanor without any noticeable impact on their marriage. On the surface their relationship appeared normal, giving no hint of the tawdry events that had so nearly driven them apart. Still, the wound to Eleanor's feelings toward Brock was deep and the scar raw and tender. She bore her malice and resentment silently, deceptively, without a formal declaration, punishing Brock in the tried and true tradition since biblical times of women betrayed by unfaithful husbands. She simply denied him the pleasure of her bed.

It was a cold, calculating denial, cunningly subtle, she thought, and masterfully executed. She fulfilled every one of her other marital obligations. She entertained his guests with the grace and humor befitting the respected station to which Brock had risen in Oakland and San Francisco society. She kept herself stylishly dressed and radiantly beautiful, exercising every day and being conscious of her diet to keep her figure shapely and her body healthy. Her popularity at the country club grew as she demonstrated her natural athletic skills in golf and tennis and her leadership ability in organizing tournaments, dinner dances, and charity events. The truth was she was more widely recognized and appreciated among club members than Brock, and not only among the women. The male membership cast a lingering covetous eye on her beauty whenever she appeared, despite or perhaps because of the fact she gave them no encouragement and maintained polite and open relations with the few men with whom she became more friendly. Her reputation, even among the most cynical and malicious dames of the club, was immaculate, a fact of which Brock was both proud and envious.

It was easy for her to resist romantic entanglements because, unlike a few of the club's young wives who had no domestic instincts or duties, she had no yearning for wanton romance. Somehow carrying out her responsibilities as Paul's mother compensated her fleshly needs, although she wondered for how long. For the time being she took her pleasure in denying herself to Brock. It was, she deemed, a fitting punishment, even though the opportunity to impose it was rare because he was so frequently away...allegedly on business.

On those rare evenings when Brock was home and Eleanor sensed his libido warming, she made the most of it. On one occasion she bathed, perfumed herself with an alluring fragrance, donned a provocative nightgown, and curled up on a sofa in the family room to read a novel while listening to soft orchestral music from a stereo. The sight of her from his den adjacent to the family room ignited Brock's desire, prompting him to stroll innocently into the room and sit down beside her to chat about inconsequential matters. Before long he began stroking her hair and touching her neck and shoulder as he talked. Eleanor pretended not to notice his tactile invitation, and when she reckoned his lust had been sufficiently aroused, she closed her book and briskly got up from the couch, leaving his fondling fingers dangling.

"I've got a lot of ironing to do," she said, feigning resignation, "so I'd best get to it."

Brock watched glumly as she left the room. Then, frowning, he returned sullenly to his desk in the den. Her message was clear. She was off limits and, though she had never explained why nor had he risked asking, he presumed she had gotten wind of his affairs. *So what! If she won't put out for me,* he grumbled to himself, *I'll get it elsewhere.* He picked up the phone on his desk, talked in a low voice for a moment, hung up, and walked out the front door to his car.

The sound of the front door closing struck Eleanor an invisible anguishing blow as she sorted clothes to be ironed. She stopped her work and let her proud shoulders sag and her head bow. An angry self-pitying tear fell on her cheek. She blinked hard several times to clear her eyes and steady her resolve, wondering how long she could continue this game of move and countermove. She demanded retribution from Brock, but each time he paid, a painful sadness came over her as now. *Who suffers more?* she wondered. The more she punished, the more she suffered, so strong was her love for him still. It somehow endured despite the contempt he had shown for their marital vows of fidelity. She wanted to believe he still loved her; she wanted to forgive him. Yet each time she rejected his advances she drove him farther away, out of reach of her absolution. It was a dismal repetitive cycle that promised nothing more than pain and unhappiness for them both. She closed her eyes tightly and prayed that God would grant her the wisdom to find a way out of this dark miserable morass.

Ironically Brock's crowded business schedule left him little time over the next two years for romantic adventures, most of which were sporadic and brief. In fact, he was beginning to find them tiresome and monotonously routine. His first love remained D-M, whose welfare and achievements were the driving force in his life. Operational expansion and capital growth were his constant preoccupations, and so successful were his initiatives that the firm was now engaged in a plethora of projects that took the staff all over the West Coast and occasionally Hawaii. The volume of business in southern California alone had become so burdensome that Brock decided it was time to set up a branch office in Los Angeles to handle the workload more efficiently.

"I want you to manage it," he told Kelly, as they discussed the plan.

"That's not why I joined the firm, remember? Managing all those details like insurance and contracts and payrolls is not my strength. You said so yourself."

"Then hire an assistant for those jobs while you shepherd the major projects, just as you do now. The point is, Kelly, we can't go on running all our southern projects out of this office. It's too much of a drain on our resources. We need someone in place at the center of that territory; someone who understands what D-M is all about and can uphold our high standards; someone who knows me and in whom I have confidence."

Kelly mulled the idea over. Moving to Los Angeles appealed to him. He was fond of southern California and had many friends there. But a more powerful incentive was getting away from Brock and his paranoid view of the world. The cabdriver who took a wrong turn did it to make Brock late for an appointment. A competitor who underbid Brock for a contract was bent on destroying D-M. A staff artist who misspelled a title on a graphic was intentionally sabotaging the project. Brock's entire outlook was riddled with suspicion and devoid of the compassion and kindness and trust that were the essence of Kelly's management style, indeed his lifestyle. Brock's philosophy was so alien to Kelly's that Helena at times asked her husband how he could work in that situation without compromising his ethics. His answer was always the same.

"I haven't compromised anything! I've been party to some very tough decisions, but this is a tough business. We're out to make profits at our competitors' expense. You don't do that by kissing them. The Mr. Nice Guys in this game not only don't win, they don't survive."

"You're pretty nice and you survive."

"Oh, yeah? Why do you think I threw in with Brock? He's the survivor. I'm just tagging along for the ride, and enjoying every minute."

"What will you do when the time comes to make that compromise with your beliefs?"

"I'll tell you when it happens."

If Kelly were in Los Angeles, his ignorance of Brock's sometimes shady machinations would shield him from ethical dilemmas, or so he believed. It did not occur to Kelly that for that very reason his acceptance of the Los Angeles position would be an unethical act. But he loved what he was doing too much to consider resigning over some flimsy ethical argument. He believed business was inherently unethical, from the purist's viewpoint, because one dedicates himself by whatever stratagem he can to depriving his competitors of income. It was such a vast gray area. Kelly brushed it all aside.

Two days later he accepted Brock's offer and began plans to set up a branch office of D-M in Los Angeles.

Kelly's departure from the Oakland office revealed to Brock how tired Brock was of maintaining the sham of partnership. It was no secret in the firm that Kelly was a yes-man and that Brock was in command and made all of the important decisions. For that reason it had annoyed Brock more and more that propriety and appearances compelled him to act out this transparent charade. It was not that he wanted to break up their partnership and expel Kelly from the firm. Kelly served a vital profitable role, for D-M was a better, closer, happier company all-around because of the warmth and humanity that Kelly brought to it, a warmth and humanity that Brock lacked and strangely felt no loss from the deficit. One cannot suffer a loss until one has lost something, and he had not been endowed with Kelly's sentimentality. Brock could only imagine what such a feeling might be. But he did not yearn for it. He was quite comfortable with his own self-centered mentality. It allowed him to make quick, hard, and sometimes even ruthless decisions from which others might shrink. For him such moments were to be cherished, not because of their cruel or unhappy effect but because of the power he felt in boldly, easily doing what others were incapable of.

However beneficial the family spirit that Kelly generated among the Oakland staff, it came at too steep a price for Brock. While the staff recognized that Brock was their leader, they had developed greater respect for Kelly. Or was it affection? Brock told himself it didn't matter. The effect was to undermine his authority, and that was something he couldn't tolerate.

So Kelly would go to Los Angeles. He was needed there. It was a sound business move, and Brock would be done with the competition for his staff's loyalty. No more pretending. No more staged dialogues with Kelly about decisions on which Brock had already made up his mind. No more wasting time which Brock could spend more productively on other tasks. Brock would once again be in full unfettered control. Of course, the contest of wills that the two men enacted was not all pretense. As their philosophies of life had clashed, so had their wills, and the tension that others sensed between them was more real than either had been willing to admit, as Brock discovered after Kelly left.

The physical distance between them allowed Brock the pleasure of indulging his pent-up animosity toward his partner. Little things Kelly had done had nettled Brock, like entertaining the staff with homey anecdotes about the old family tavern in Wisconsin. Brock had not been born with a natural gift for storytelling nor did he have waggish tales to share about his childhood. Although Brock had hidden his envy and resentment behind a condescending smile, those emotions had grown and hardened like tumors spreading through the fabric of his feelings toward

Kelly. Small incidents Brock had long forgotten reappeared in his mind. A harmless joke by Kelly at Brock's expense; a bit of friendly, constructive criticism of one of Brock's design ideas—but criticism nonetheless. One after another the memories returned, embittering his thoughts as sediment stirred up in a pond clouds and darkens the water. He realized how fundamentally he disliked the dapple-haired lover of mankind, how good he felt that Kelly was gone from the office, and how pleased he would be to see Kelly fail. What had Kelly really ever done for D-M that Brock would not have accomplished by himself? It had been a mistake to make him a partner. Brock should have hired him as an executive assistant, or perhaps not at all. It was a mistake he would not repeat.

Well, Kelly was on his own now, and they would see what he could do by himself. Brock savored the prospect of Kelly failing, showing up one morning unannounced at the Oakland office to sheepishly report the loss of a major client or the collapse of a venture involving a sizeable investment of company funds. It would happen, Brock knew. Oh, yes, it would happen, and he would relish the moment.

While he had expected to feel a renewed sense of freedom once Kelly had left the Oakland office, Brock was unprepared for the rejuvenation he experienced. It was a second wind—almost like starting over. That gnawing hunger to succeed that he had known when he first came to Oakland returned. Ideas for new projects blossomed in his mind, keeping him from sleeping and jolting him awake when he did. His mind ran free, roaming the creative landscape. It was like putting a new powerful battery in an old car.

His excitement about the design business, he now realized, had been eroded by D-M's success. He had worked tirelessly to build a viable company, but the rewards had come too easily. The challenge had dwindled like a dying fire that had burned brightly for a spell then quickly consumed its fuel. The embers still glowed but gave off little heat. Somehow Kelly's departure had refueled the fire. Brock had been granted a new lease on his quest for power and success, and he would make the most of it.

His renewed enthusiasm spilled over into his home life. He felt a new warmth in Eleanor's company and a new paternal kinship with Paul. The rancor he had nourished toward Eleanor faded, while their conversations,

128

strained and terse for so many months, became more open, personal, and philosophic. Without really intending to, he began playing the role of father and husband, which produced a pleasant change in Eleanor's attitude toward him. Intrigued by her response, which he saw as an opportunity to break through the wall of indifference she had built between them, he mounted a secret campaign to reclaim her affection...and, of course, her submission. But it was the challenge, not love for her, that inspired this effort, which he undertook like any other project, analyzing the situation, conceiving a sound plan of action, and then doggedly carrying it out with his customary zeal and dedication that all but ensured success.

His strategy relied on two tandem approaches: spending more time at home in family activities and making more outward displays of affection for Eleanor as well as Paul, for Brock knew she would react kindly to any attention he paid to their son. If Brock were to achieve his final goal, any changes in his treatment of Eleanor must be subtle, natural, and a consistent extension of his past behavior. What he wanted most to avoid was giving Eleanor the impression he had turned over a new leaf. That would be admitting culpability for past wrongs, and Brock was in no mood for criticism, nor did he feel any guilt about the dismal course their marriage had taken. His plan called for Eleanor to discover that she had been mistaken about him, that he was and always had been a sensitive, loving, caring husband and father who deserved her love and trust. And her intimacy! To that end he was careful not to overplay his part. She knew him well and would instantly see as counterfeit any exaggerated show of affection or concern. No sending of flowers or expensive gifts; that was not his nature. Instead, he would have to be patient with his low-key courtship, enduring the slow evolution of her reaction from skepticism to puzzlement to discovery to acceptance to final surrender. He was confident she would in the end succumb.

And he was right.

Eleanor had clung to the belief that the love upon which their marriage had been consecrated—romantic, abiding, God-given love— would survive the ravages of Brock's cruel infidelities and would awaken him eventually to the rich potential of their relationship. She therefore interpreted the initial subtle shifts in his attention to her as encouraging and long-awaited signs of his awakening, as Brock had correctly surmised she would. He had expected his plan to take months, but her yearning for a romantic renewal of their relationship made her more gullible than he had imagined. Realizing her vulnerability, Brock jettisoned his more intricate and deliberate plan altogether and simply played to her expectations, which lay hidden but discoverable in her conversation. If she mentioned at breakfast that she would be shopping downtown, he would invite her to lunch. If she read him a notice of a new restaurant opening, he took her there soon after. He listened for clues to her needs and pleasures, then satisfied them, without fanfare or reward. These acts of kindness and affection were to millions of happily married husbands commonplace expressions of love; to Brock they were simply ploys in a game-winning strategy.

These activities, however, did not include making love. That was sacrosanct territory Brock astutely avoided, knowing how Eleanor had used it as a weapon to punish him. Only when she invited him to bed— only when she took the initiative and yielded to him of her own free will—could he claim victory in his campaign. Sex would be the victor's prize and trophy—the laurel wreath. Everything else was part of the contest.

For Eleanor, the thought of making love with Brock generated wildly conflicting emotions. She sensed that the wall of hostility that stood between them was gradually wearing away, forcing them to re-examine their feelings toward each other and freeing them to reach out and to love, if they chose. It was scary for Eleanor. The wall had been a crutch on which their wounded marriage had leaned. Now, with health restored and no crutch to lean on, their marriage, which had survived on her hate, must renew itself on love. But how to begin? She longed to touch him, to feel his embrace, to kiss his lips, but the dread of his rejection immobilized her. She was afraid to test his love for fear there was none. Then where would she be? Adrift. Alone. Abandoned.

She had vindictively denied herself to him for over two years, never imagining how difficult the transition back to a normal married life would be once the conflict between them was reconciled. She had assumed there would be a reconciliation, although she hadn't given much thought to how it would come about. As Brock became more attentive and affectionate, her resistance to his masculinity grew weaker. But she dared not broach the subject with him.

So each evening as they dressed for bed she nervously preened and perfumed herself like a jittery virgin on her wedding night, wondering whether this would be the night and, if it was, how he would manage it. Would he flat-out ask her to make love? He had not done so yet, even though she nightly gave him the opportunity by dawdling at her dressing table till he got in bed. She would comb and brush her hair, adjust the straps on her filmy nightgown, rearrange things in her jewelry box, or just fiddle with her nails, employing every artifice she could think of to announce her availability. She knew she presented an alluring distraction, but Brock showed no glimmer of interest, chatting with her mundanely and walking about the bedroom seemingly indifferent to her beauty. Only when he stepped up behind her, leaned over, and gave her a polite good night kiss on the cheek—a ritual that he oddly had observed throughout the rift in their relationship—did he demonstrate any affection, but it carried no special feeling. It was never a precursor to lovemaking.

Or would he wait till they had turned out the lights, then without a word slide to her side of the bed? Every night she lay awake in the darkness listening. The slightest movement on Brock's side would send her heart pounding, her muscles twitching, while she held her breath, trying to decipher the movement and its meaning. Had he moved toward her? Or had he simply turned over? She listened intently, willing him to come to her. But to no avail. Soon she would detect the low regular rasp of his breathing and know that he was fast asleep, and she would succumb once again to depression, shed a tear or two, and fall asleep, resigned to try again the next night.

In time she realized that Brock would not respond to her seductive posturing at the dressing table. She had used that ruse before, only to slam his desire in his face by walking away from him. No, she could not expect him to interpret as serious overtures the same flirtations that had misled him before. It would take a more affirmative demonstration, and this she was resolved to do.

Two evenings later the two of them were again in the bedroom in their familiar routine. Eleanor, beautiful as ever, sat before her mirror filing her nails. Brock, fresh from a shower and a shave—it saved time in the morning, he said—stood beside her in his shower robe combing his hair.

"Did you notice the station wagon is dripping oil on the driveway again?" he asked, raising yet another banality that would serve to avoid the issue that hovered over them like a teetering giant.

"No, I didn't," she replied calmly. "Should I take it in tomorrow for a checkup? It's been back to the dealer two times already."

"I suppose you should. It must be a faulty seal."

"Well, they changed it once. Maybe it's something else."

"Whatever. We have to get it fixed."

"All right. I'll get to it in the morning."

"Good."

As he leaned over to give her the usual peck on the cheek, she turned her head and kissed him longingly on the lips. He started to draw away, but she placed her hand behind his head and pulled him to her. She felt his neck muscles tighten, and for a frightening second she thought he might disengage, but he didn't. He pressed his lips against hers. He answered! He answered!

The love she had stored up for two years poured through her lips, probing, reaching, flooding him with affection and yearning. She could hold back no longer. "Oh, Brock, I love you! I need you!"

He took her arms and, lifting her to her feet, embraced her, and they kissed for several minutes. He was back. He was hers. The waiting and loneliness were over....

Later, when Eleanor finally lay contented, drained of all desire, Brock looked down at her and smiled triumphantly.

The laurel wreath was his.

ELEVEN

During the next two months Eleanor experienced an inner contentment she had only dreamed about as a teenager fantasizing life with the perfect husband. If her relationship with Brock could be better, she didn't know how. Their marriage had come alive, both romantically and domestically, reaching new heights of sharing and loving.

Brock thrust aside the curtain of privacy that had cloaked his business activities from her and discussed them openly with her, listening for the first time to her ideas, for she was, as he was well aware, a highly intelligent person. He listened, and he confided in her his concerns and hopes for the firm. Never before in their six years together had he welcomed her into his world. The line had always been sharply drawn, and she had never ventured across, though D-M had been a deep fascination for her. Brock was amazed—and not a little intimidated—by her quick insights into the complexities of the firm's operations. It was not that he had underrated her mental capacity; that was one of the things he had always admired about her. It was the fact that, by discussing with her his business affairs, he acknowledged her competence and thus voluntarily forfeited the basis for his superiority in their relationship. He could not function without that feeling. To be her equal, to be anyone's equal, was an anathema to Brock. He had to be higher in rank and in control, and for that he had to believe he was better. Superior. He had to prove it constantly to himself and to others, and to Eleanor. So, for the time being, he would patronize her interest in D-M's affairs, though limiting her involvement to private discussions with him. No one else would know or need to know.

Meanwhile, their love life flourished. Eleanor became convinced

133

that, because she loved him and because she believed he truly loved her, he would no longer have an appetite for other women.

And so it went for two months…until Diego Martinez entered their relationship and changed it forever.

There was always an element of distrust and animosity between Brock and Diego. Not at first, of course. As so often happens, lasting enmity is born of quick friendship where two personalities thought to be compatible turn out to be diametrically opposed with no prospect of reconciliation.

The two men met in Santa Barbara through Kelly. Brock had gone there to oversee completion of a chemical firm's display in an industrial exposition. Kelly had landed the job but was obligated on another project and asked Brock to fill in, which he was happy to do because it gave him a chance to nose around in Kelly's backyard and check on his progress, or better, the lack of it.

Kelly had hired Diego, a thirty-year-old freelance specialist, to assemble the display, which featured a mechanical model of a new type of chemical processor developed by the client firm. He was working on the model when Brock arrived at the convention center.

"Martinez?" queried Brock, stopping a few feet from the display.

A tall wiry man stooping awkwardly over the complex array of clear plastic tubes, tumblers, and supporting gridwork turned his head in the direction of the voice. "That's me." His friendly dark-brown eyes measured Brock's face. "You must be Stowolski, Kelly's partner."

"Yep," replied Brock, concealing his ire at being lowered to Kelly's level. "I'm actually the senior partner. I founded the company. Kelly works for me."

"I'm sorry." A little perplexed at the stranger's response, Martinez stood up smiling and extended his hand. "Diego's the name. Pleased to meet you." They shook hands heartily, each feeling the other's strength. "I really mean that. You've established a fine reputation in the industry. I was tickled pink when Kelly asked me to help out."

"Why, thank you." The flattery soothed Brock's initial irritation. "Kelly is very choosy when it comes to subcontractors. If he picked you, you must be good."

Diego laughed, his genuineness and honesty making a positive impression on Brock. "But not good enough to make this contraption work!" He gestured dejectedly toward the model. "I'd like to blame it on the designer...which wasn't me...and which I hope wasn't you."

"You're safe. It wasn't me either."

Both men laughed.

"I'm glad of that," said Diego. "I followed the drawings exactly. But it keeps jamming, and I'm running out of time."

"You mean *we're* running out of time." Brock clapped him on the back chummily. "Let's take a look."

For the next several hours the two men labored to get the model machine running smoothly. Brock suggested several adjustments in the gear mechanism, and Diego made the changes, marveling at the result.

"Brock, you're a full-grown genius. It runs like a clock. Are you some kind of mechanical engineering wizard or something?" Diego's bony face opened into a wide grin that warmed his hard tanned features, weathered by years of working outdoors. "I can see why your company has been so successful."

"Nothin' to it, really. Do it all the time."

"I believe it."

They joined in laughter again; then Brock complimented Diego's work. "You've done an excellent job. You see, drawing a design on a piece of paper is one thing; building that design, making it come alive in three dimensions, that takes real skill. You're a fine craftsman, Diego. Kelly still has a good eye for talent."

"Don't applaud too loudly. I couldn't have put this thing together without your help. We did it together."

"I'll drink to that. Here's to teamwork."

They raised imaginary glasses and exchanged smiles. Brock began cleaning up the cubicle while Diego added the finishing touches to the exhibit.

"Listen, I've got to run," said Brock, putting on his jacket. "I have to catch a plane back to San Francisco. You've done a great job, and I'll tell

Kelly that. I'm sure we can use you again, if you're in the market."

Diego was flattered. "Anytime, Brock. Just call."

They shook hands, and Brock departed, feeling pleased with the project and with this fine craftsman Kelly had found.

But his euphoria lasted all of five days when an advertising agent with whom he regularly did business in Santa Barbara phoned to congratulate him on D-M's award for best display at the Santa Barbara exposition.

"What are you talking about?"

"Your exhibit. It won first place."

"When did that happen?"

"Three days ago. At the awards ceremony during the final banquet. Your guy accepted the plaque."

"Kelly?"

"No, I know Kelly. It was another guy."

"Tall, dark hair, thin face?"

"Yeah, that's him."

"What did he say?"

"Nothin'. He just thanked everybody and sat down. No big deal. Why? Didn't you know about it?"

Brock camouflaged his anger. It would not do to admit he was unaware of what his company was doing.

"Yes, of course. I remember now. Kelly told me about the award. I was thinking it was in Los Angeles. Sure, it was Diego Martinez. The chemical processor model. Beautiful set!" Brock lied convincingly.

They discussed other matters, and when their business was finished Brock hung up the phone and immediately buzzed Maggie on the intercom.

"Get me Kelly in L.A.," he snapped, tapping his fingers impatiently against their reflection in the dark polished surface of his desk. A minute later Maggie buzzed him back. He didn't bother acknowledging her but grabbed up the phone and barked, "What's your friend Diego up to?"

"Up to? Whataya talking about?" Kelly instantly recognized Brock's angry tone.

"The award."

"Oh, you mean the one from the exposition in Santa Barbara," said

Kelly innocently.

"Oh, the one from Santa Barbara," repeated Brock derisively.

"What about it?"

"Were you there?"

"No, I wasn't," Kelly said firmly. "You know that. That's why you went for me."

"Do you know what happened?"

"At the exposition?"

"No, at the banquet?"

"The banquet?" Kelly had no idea what Brock was angry about.

"Yes, the banquet. What—am I speaking Chinese?"

"Simmer down, Brock, and tell me what's bugging you."

"Do you know what happened at the banquet?"

"No! How could I? I wasn't at the stupid banquet! Why this interrogation? Are you off on one of your vendettas again?"

Brock would not countenance Kelly's impudence. One day Kelly would learn to keep his mouth shut and take orders like a junior partner should. "Did Diego tell you he'd won a trophy?"

"So that's what's eating you. Come on, Brock! What's another trophy? We've got shelves full of them."

"Did he tell you?"

"Yes, he did. He phoned me after the banquet. Big deal! You mad 'cause he didn't call you?"

"I'm mad because he took the credit for himself and not the firm."

"Maybe he did and maybe he didn't. I wasn't there, nor were you, but you obviously received a report. Are you upset because he didn't give *you* personal credit?"

Brock continued to ignore Kelly's attacks, which had become more open and aggressive since he moved to Los Angeles. Kelly was growing more independent, apparently under the delusion that as manager of that office, out of Brock's sight and hearing, he was not accountable to the main office. Brock would have to set him straight, but this was not the time. "Does he still have the trophy?"

"Yeah, it's a plaque. You want it?"

"You bet I do! I want it where it belongs, displayed with DESIGN METAPHORS' other awards."

"Then call him! He'll send it to you."

"No, *you* call him! He works for you, remember?"

Brock's anger ebbing, he began to get his temper under control, realizing how petty and fanatical he must appear. But he would not let Diego take credit for what he, Brock, had done. No one would do that. "Look, Kelly," he said, trying to sound reasonable. "It isn't the trophy. It's the principle. I'll not have a subcontractor taking credit for the inspired work of our staff and that includes you. It just isn't right."

"Okay, your point is well taken." Kelly could see the argument, though he was still suspicious of Brock's motives. "But I think you do Diego an injustice. I can't believe he knowingly took credit for something he didn't do. I've worked with him many times. He's as honest and straight a guy as I've ever met." *More honest and straight than you,* Kelly wanted to add.

"Perhaps, but I haven't time to debate his ethics. Just call him and tell him to send that trophy to me."

Later that day, Maggie hurried into Brock's office and handed him a letter. She had overheard his end of the angry conversation with Kelly and realized the moment she read the correspondence that Brock would want to see it.

"What's this?" he asked, scanning it.

"It's from Diego Martinez. By mistake it got put with the mail I'm holding for Los Angeles. It's my fault. I only found it now. It came in yesterday. He must have mailed it the night of the banquet." She withdrew as hastily as she had entered, not wishing to suffer Brock's reprimand for mislaying the letter.

Dear Brock,

This is to advise you, if you haven't heard by now, that your exhibit in Santa Barbara won first place. I'm writing instead of phoning because I'm embarrassed at how I mishandled it.

I had a great opportunity to do some free advertising for your company when they called me up to the podium to accept the plaque, but I'm terrified of public speaking and I froze. I couldn't think of a thing to say. I know it sounds dumb, but I've had this problem since I was a kid. My mind kind of went blank. All I did was thank them for the plaque and sit down.

I phoned Kelly tonight and told him about the award. I'll give it to him next time I see him. (It's not a very impressive plaque.)

Sincerely,

Diego Martinez

So that was it, thought Brock. The simple idiot got tongue-tied. He reread the last paragraph and wondered why Kelly had played dumb about the award. Was he trying to cover up for Diego? That was it! Kelly knew the whole story and was covering for Diego. Kelly probably wanted to keep the plaque down there for himself; hang it in his office.

Brock pressed the intercom. "Maggie, get me Kelly."

Maggie buzzed and Brock picked up the receiver. "Kelly?"

"Yeah, now what?"

"I just got a letter from Diego explaining the whole thing in Santa Barbara."

"What happened?"

"The poor guy's afraid to make speeches, but that's not important. He's a good worker and talented. I understand now what happened. Why don't you and he fly up here tomorrow and we'll celebrate? Have dinner. Mend some fences. Whataya think?"

"That's very generous of you, Brock." Kelly was surprised and, knowing Brock, on guard.

"It's been awhile since we got together. Why don't you bring Helena along? Ellie would love to see her and you, too, I'm sure. Is Diego married?"

"Yes. He has a lovely wife."

"Good. Invite her, too. I'd like to meet her. What's her name?"

"Raphaéla. You still want Diego to send you the plaque?"

"Naw, that's all right. He can bring it with him."

From the moment Diego's wife entered the dining room of the country club, Brock could not take his eyes off of her. She was tall, maybe five feet nine, wearing a tight, low-cut, brilliant red-sequined gown that accentuated her unusually large bust, narrow waist, and alluringly round hips. Thick jet-black hair, combed straight back, curled under at her bare shoulders, framing her gorgeous Hispanic face with its slim nose, square jaw, and high cheekbones. Her smooth, clear skin was dark, almost mulatto. Full moist red lips and black sultry eyes promised consuming pleasures of every sort. She was a ravishing beauty, surpassing even the sexiest models and filmdom starlets Brock had bedded. Lust, like a heavy boiling liquid, coursed through his body. He must have her, he thought. He must.

He went to her straightway, unleashing his maximum charm, focusing it on her like a powerful laser. She was dazzled.

"You're Raphaéla." He grasped her extended hand and, bowing slightly, pressed it gently to his lips, holding it there a moment while he took in her beauty close up. Diego, standing awkwardly at her side, reddened with embarrassment at Brock's unabashed leering. Eleanor, Kelly, and Helena were knotted together in raucous conversation on the other side of the room, oblivious to the adulterous interactions taking place behind them.

"And you must be Brock," purred Raphaéla, tilting her head saucily to one side as this handsome stranger's masculine magnetism reached inside her.

Diego recognized the childish fawning pose. It was, he had observed countless times before, the prelude to aggressive flirting. He cringed at the prospect of enduring her obnoxious spectacle throughout the evening. Kelly had intimated that Stowolski was a lecher, but Diego was shocked by such a blatant approach, which he was certain would enflame Raphaéla. He knew her well. Soon she would be unmanageable. He must speak with Mrs. Stowolski at once and somehow warn her of Raphaéla's untamed passions. He stole a glance at the attractive blond talking with Kelly and his wife. That had to be her. But first he had to disengage Raphaéla from Brock.

"It was good of you to invite us up here, Brock," he said.

"Thank you." Brock gave Diego an appreciative smile, then turned quickly back to Raphaéla. "Kelly told me Raphaéla was lovely, but I was totally unprepared for this."

140

"We would love to meet your wife," Diego suggested, wanting to derail Brock's flirting. "Kelly has spoken of her many times."

"Of course. Let me introduce you." He took Raphaéla's right hand and looped it under his arm. "Ellie!" he called. "Come and meet our guests."

Eleanor, roused finally from her lively repartee with Kelly and Helena, turned to discover the Martinezes had arrived. "How impolite of me!" she declared, reaching out to take their hands, only then noticing Raphaéla's wrapped tightly around Brock's arm. Rather than let go of him, Raphaéla offered her free hand, which Eleanor took hold of, and the four of them stood linked together in an indecorous chain while Kelly and Helena looked on uncomfortably. "I'm so pleased to meet you both."

"Thank you, Mrs. Stowolski," replied Diego, sensing her discomfort.

"Please call me Eleanor. We can't be good friends if we're so formal."

Raphaéla smiled but remained silent, staring at Brock with unconcealed fascination.

"I agree," added Brock. He turned to Raphaéla and, patting her hand on his sleeve, said, "Let me show you the 18th hole. It's a landscaper's dream." Pulling her away, he waved to Diego. "I'll have her back in five minutes!"

Eleanor was stung by Brock's flirtatious and insensitive behavior. Only moments before he had been the warm, solicitous husband. Then, suddenly, he walked off arm in arm with the beauteous wife of his guest, staring lasciviously at her cleavage. It was not so much the discourtesy of his manner that offended Eleanor as the glowing hunger in his eyes—the crass, undisguised look of lust devouring Mrs. Martinez. Eleanor had never before seen that look on his face. He had kept it hidden from her either out of kindness—or, more likely deceit. But it had surfaced without warning, forced into the open by his uncontrollable sex drive. How could he change so quickly and so completely? One moment the loving considerate husband, the next the unbridled womanizer. Unless these past months had all been a charade. But for what? A respectable family life? A wife's affection?

Then it came to her like a blast of cold air. Her sexual favors! They were the prize. The spoils. She saw it clearly now. It had been so obvious. She had been so gullible. Her father had lectured her as a child that "people don't change" and that "people are what they are." She had never accepted that fatalistic viewpoint till this moment. The stark truth of it pierced her heart. She gathered her composure and smiled through her chagrin.

Diego was saying something to her about the club's membership.

"Brock's a nut about the golf course," she replied, hoping her response made sense. Her heart was pounding so fiercely she thought she might faint. "He hardly ever plays, but he loves to show it off. You'd think he designed it."

"I'm sure he could have," said Diego politely. "He's very talented."

"In many ways," interjected Kelly. "Would anyone care for a drink?"

"Lead the way," said Diego, trying to be jolly and thankful for a break in the tension.

"I think we all need one," added Kelly.

"Be nice!" scolded Helena.

Diego came to his defense. "He is. We all need a drink!"

They ambled into the lounge at the rear, away from the noise of the crowd. A slim bleached blond in skimpy tights took their drink orders and disappeared among the milling patrons. It was Saturday night. A small rock ensemble began playing, and the dance floor soon teemed with gyrating couples old and young. The entertainment, although a bit expensive, had been one of Eleanor's brainstorms to liven up the club. It had paid off. The lounge had become a favorite nightspot for club members and guests and turned a generous profit.

"Do you smoke?" Eleanor asked Diego, grasping at something to dispel the conspicuous awkwardness.

"No."

"Good. Neither do we." So saying, she upended the circular blue glass ashtray on the small coffee table beside her and began running her fingers nervously around the lip of its base. "Your wife is very beautiful."

"Thank you."

"Have you been married long?"

"About two years."

"Any children?"

"None yet."

Diego was only half listening, entranced as he was by the aura of

Eleanor's own natural beauty. Glowing blue eyes and cool pink lips. He saw through the serene composure that hid her humiliation at Brock's lecherous display. He felt her pain and wondered how an intelligent man like Brock could forsake such a noble, attractive woman to chase after a trollop like Raphaéla. Diego knew that private relationships are rarely what they seem to outsiders and that a man can be driven to extreme acts by even the smallest strains, if they persist over time. He would have to learn more about Brock and Eleanor before he sat in judgment over either. *Who am I to judge others*, he thought. *Me of all people!*

"What is this?" Kelly laughed. "An interview?"

"Come on, Kel," said Diego, welcoming Kelly's attempt at humor. "Give her a break."

"I'll give her a kiss instead. You know, I love this girl. If I weren't married to this grouch here, I'd steal Eleanor away from her foolish husband."

Helena pouted. "Honey, don't let's talk about it. It only makes it worse."

Eleanor shook her head. "It's okay, Helena. It's just Brock's way of being friendly." It was a lie that none of the other three would embarrass her by challenging, knowing how deeply she was hurt. She spoke to Diego. "You must love her very much."

"Raphaéla?" He eyed Eleanor solemnly a long moment before replying. "She can be difficult at times."

Eleanor was trying to fathom the meaning of his reply when a strange sensation gripped her. A feeling she hadn't known in years. It was a compelling interest in Diego.

He was not a handsome man in a Hollywood sense, but he was immensely attractive. His features were jagged: his nose sharp and long, his chin jutting out below tight hard lips. His build was thin and bony, and he slouched a bit, probably a habit he acquired as a prematurely tall child not wanting to stand out among his shorter classmates. He appeared shy, though in a charming way, made more appealing by his quick broad smile and soft kindly brown eyes that watched her as she toyed with the ashtray. There was something about him that excited her, that made her avoid those eyes. His equanimity, modesty, the gentle but still masculine quality of his voice, and the calming way he looked at her. He was so different from Brock, so different from any man she had ever met. Perhaps that was the source of the attraction: he was different. Looking at him gave her a pleasurable feeling, but her conscience—alarmed by the adulterous images that blossomed in her mind—told her it was a feeling she must not encourage. She was a married woman and mother. She must purge such ideas from her head. Fearful that he and the others would detect her sudden captivation, she focused her attention on her fingers and fought down a blush she felt rising on her face.

Her self-reproach was interrupted by the return of Brock and his giggling, fawning companion, still clinging possessively to his arm. The sight of them angered Eleanor, who decided she had had enough. It was one thing to be embarrassed by one's husband and quite another to be insulted by a stranger in front of one's close friends.

She got up from her chair and met the pair as they arrived at the alcove. Forcing her mouth into a semblance of a smile, she reached out to Raphaéla's hand that clutched Brock's sleeve and, closing her fingers and thumb tightly around the wrist, pulled it loose. The two women's eyes flared at each other for a second, and Raphaéla's mouth opened to speak, then froze in a half smile. She recovered quickly, saying, "Your husband is a wonderful guide."

"Yes, I'm sure," replied Eleanor stiffly, still grasping Raphaéla's wrist. "I believe your place is here." She led her like an unruly child to the chair beside Diego's and stood by until Raphaéla had seated herself, while the others watched anxiously, expecting any moment the two women would be clawing each other's eyes. Thankfully Eleanor returned to her own chair and sat down, looking harshly at Brock and waiting for his reaction.

Brock was speechless at her boldly aggressive behavior. He had never seen her act this way before, and he was outraged. How dare she treat his guest in such a rude, highhanded way. It was a slap in the face to both him and Raphaéla. "You're in rare form tonight, Ellie," he snarled. "Something you drank, no doubt!" His voice chilled whatever warmth remained in the group. "Please forgive her, Raphaéla. She's losing her grip on her manners."

Raphaéla swallowed and looked wide-eyed at Brock, not knowing what to say.

Eleanor's fury reddened her cheeks as she riveted her eyes on the ashtray, holding it tightly to keep her hands from shaking. She had every right to be angry with this young woman for throwing herself so brazenly at Brock. Yet he had invited it with his flirting. Eleanor's thoughts were in turmoil. Their marriage had become so perfect, and now it was all askew. She wanted to run to him, embrace him, ask his forgiveness on this very special evening, but she was the wounded party. Doubly wounded. First by the realization that Brock had cunningly unscrupulously manipulated their marital relationship, pretending to be a faithful, solicitous, loving husband when his sole objective had been sex. And second by his insulting behavior with Raphaéla. It was he who should ask to be forgiven. It was he who should apologize. But she knew he never would.

Abruptly Brock turned, still standing, to address Diego in clipped blunt words. "So, Diego, I believe you brought something with you to give me."

"I sure did," he replied with equal harshness. "Just for you."

He bent down beside his chair and brought up a flat brown paper bag. No one but Brock had noticed him carrying it. Diego reached inside and withdrew a small wooden plaque bearing a brass plate inscribed with a curlicue logo and some unreadable words. He stood up and presented himself to the group. "On behalf of the American Chemical Industrial Association, for best display at the Santa Barbara exposition, I award this trophy to Brock Stowolski, founder and president of DESIGN METAPHORS." He handed the plaque to Brock as the others looked on nervously, not knowing what to expect, feeling they should applaud but not daring to. "It's all yours. Sorry you weren't at the banquet to accept it yourself. If I'd known it meant so much to you, I'd have seen to it you were there."

"All awards are important," said Brock.

"Not to me they aren't!"

They were face-to-face, eye-to-eye now, and Eleanor was frightened. She inferred from what Kelly had told her earlier that day about Diego that he was a physical man, a product of Los Angeles' tough inner-city streets. The small scars on his face and nose showed he was no stranger to violence. Uneducated but singularly ambitious, he had admirably raised himself out of that primitive, depressing environment by sheer hard work and determination and had set his life's course on a higher plane. She had a sudden frivolous notion that, if Diego struck Brock, it would be in her defense. *What nonsense*, she thought. The whole scene was ludicrous. Two grown, intelligent men facing off like two bulls. Then it occurred to her that their anger was too intense and personal to have been sparked simply by Brock's attentions to Raphaéla. She figured their hostility was rooted in something that had happened at the exposition; something Brock had not mentioned to her. She could not imagine that what she was witnessing was nothing more elementary than a barroom fight over a woman.

"That's why you'll always be a subcontractor," Brock jeered. "You don't appreciate awards. They are the standards by which excellence is measured."

"I know excellence when I see it. I don't need anyone to tell me."

"Plucky words from a guy who couldn't solve a simple mechanical design problem!" Brock grinned contemptuously, delighting in taking Diego down a peg in front of both Raphaéla and Eleanor.

"Touché." Diego nodded grimly, knowing that if he didn't quell his surging temper, he would lose control and deck the mighty Stowolski. If Brock needled him one more time, he would explode. He had to get out of there. There was no hope for the evening anyway. "Well, you have your trophy now. That's what I came for. So, if you'll excuse me, I have to be going."

"Going?" cried Raphaéla, her back stiffening.

"Now, now, Diego," Brock soothed. "Let's not be hasty." He decided to recoup the evening with a show of gallantry. It would make the evening tolerable and impress the luscious Raphaéla. It would also reinforce his feeling of superiority over this Chicano upstart. Brock smiled and offered his hand. "Maybe I spoke out of turn. Why don't we sit down and have a drink, like friends should?"

Diego pushed aside Brock's hand. "You're no friend of mine, mister, and you never will be! Are you coming?" His question was directed at his wife.

"No!" she snapped, making a show of her indignation. "How can you be so rude? We are guests of Mr. Stowolski."

"I'm no guest. I'm a delivery boy. Eh, Brock? Isn't that why I'm here? To bring you your precious trophy?"

"What's mine is mine, not yours."

Eleanor wondered if he was referring to her.

"Spoken like a true pragmatist," snarled Diego. "You coming, Raphaéla, or not?"

She pouted. "No, I'm not. You're acting like a spoiled child. If you leave, you leave without me. I'll spend the night with my sister Lucia in San Leandro."

"How will you get home?"

"She can ride to L.A. with me," offered Kelly, trying to avert another scene.

Diego shrugged. "As you wish." There was no point in pushing his defiance till everyone was hurt, especially Mrs. Stowolski. He definitely did not want to cause her any more pain. She had suffered enough this evening. He took a step toward her and, bowing slightly, said, "It was a real pleasure meeting you, Mrs. Stow...Eleanor. I'm sorry things didn't work out better."

"Won't you please stay?" she asked, a bit too earnestly for Brock's taste. He searched her face for some deeper feeling and thought he detected it. Something about her eyes and how they fixed on Diego's. Brock recalled now that when he and Raphaéla had entered the lounge, Diego was staring at Ellie in an admiring way. *Well, I'll be*, thought Brock. *He's coming on to Ellie, and she's falling for it.*

"No, ma'am," Diego was saying. "I think my welcome is worn out. I'll only spoil the evening for everyone." He waved dejectedly to Kelly and Helena. "See you in L.A." Then he spun around and disappeared into the noisy throng of revelers outside the alcove.

The dinner party limped on through the evening while Brock held forth on the bright future of the design industry, Raphaéla hanging enraptured on every word. The other three listened politely but made no effort to enliven the conversation. All three were repulsed by Brock's flagrant conduct toward Diego's wife. Kelly and Helena exchanged worried glances sharing their concern over how Eleanor was taking this indirect abuse. She sat woodenly erect, exhibiting no emotion but contempt as she sipped her wine and watched Brock's face and then the adoring Raphaéla's.

What was not revealed in Eleanor's impassive expression was the crumbling of her world within her. The warm affection and devotion Brock had lavished on her the past two months, she now fully realized, were but a cheap deception to seduce her. He had no more affection for her than he did for any of his inamoratas. He had used her like a toy for his pleasure and, having tired of the game, was shamelessly discarding her to pursue a fresh conquest. His behavior was insulting and despicable and beyond Eleanor's comprehension. Her mind was in such shock she could not reason clearly. Marriage for her was a precious, holy thing, yet what meaning did it have for him? Was it nothing more than a convenience? a pastime? a casual amenity to make him more acceptable to the upper social stratum and to prospective clients? What kind of a man was this she called husband?

From childhood on she had believed that one day a handsome suitor—her Lancelot—would meet her by chance, fall in love, and make her his wife, and they would live the rest of their lives together in blissful harmony. Although her body and mind matured and a hardheaded realism replaced her childhood fantasies about life and the world, she never quite rid herself of her cherished dream of matrimony, though she talked as if she had. She would caution her friends who were engaged that romance had little to do with a successful marriage and warned them not to be blinded by infatuation to the real personality hidden behind the sweet talk and romantic guise of their lovers. But talk was cheap. Each time she had made a new acquaintance with an eligible man, she could not help asking herself, *Is this my Lancelot? Will we fall in love? Will he carry me away to marital bliss?*

When she fell in love with Brock, she succumbed to the hypnosis of all new lovers. She lost all ability to assess him objectively. He was gallant, charming, devoted, protective, handsome, athletic, and sexy. He was everything she had dreamed of finding in a husband. Of course, he was not without faults. But in Eleanor's adoring eyes those faults had been mere eccentricities that showed he was human and made him more endearing.

Watching him now as he sat across the table boasting of his business successes, Eleanor saw him in a new light, as if for the first time. The events of the evening had unmasked the *real* Brock Stowolski. It was a heart-rending revelation. She had not wanted to see this person. For years

148

she had denied to herself his existence. Again and again she had denied it. During those many months when he had been unfaithful and had virtually abandoned her, she had become angry and wept and mourned her plight. Yet, when he returned to her, she had forgiven him, pretending that the person behind the mask did not exist. And when the closeness and vitality of their relationship as husband and wife were restored two months ago, she again erased the ugly memories and thought only of the good. Her repeated denials of the truth kept the mask firmly and safely in place. She had wanted to keep it there forever so the person behind it would never show himself. But the mask had now fallen away. She knew there was no hope or purpose in trying to retrieve it. Brock Stowolski had shed all pretense. His true personality was on display for all to see...and it horrified her. The man speaking was arrogant, obnoxiously egotistical, overbearing, and totally oblivious to the distasteful spectacle he was making of himself. How could she ever have fallen in love with such a self-centered, malevolent boor?

"So," Brock declared, finishing his brandy and addressing the group. "Why don't we all go over to Mineo's?"

"What's that?" asked Raphaéla enthusiastically.

"A small nightclub for the upper crust. The steep prices keep out the riffraff. It's a beautiful place. Mineo is a friend of mine. D-M designed the interior. Really nice job. The lighting effects are unusual."

Kelly patted Helena's hand beside his on the table. "No thanks, Brock. It's been a long day, and we're bushed." Helena nodded in agreement.

"Me, too," said Eleanor. "I've had enough for one evening."

"Aw, come on, you people!" Brock protested, ignoring her taunt. "You're all partypoopers."

"I'm not," chimed Raphaéla, her tone alive with eagerness.

"No," he replied. "We either go all together or we don't go at all."

Eleanor stared at him coldly. He didn't care about proprieties. He had something else planned.

"I'm sorry, Brock," said Kelly, "but the trip up here wore us out. Maybe next time. We're gonna call it a night."

"Okay. Next time. It was good of you to come. We should do this more often." He beckoned the waitress for the check, and they all rose to leave. "Say, Kelly, would you mind very much taking Ellie home? I've got a horde of contract papers at the office to review and sign before morning. I planned to swing by there on my way home, and Ellie would have to wait for me."

"Be glad to."

Eleanor instantly deduced Brock's sleazy little plan.

"And where did you say your sister lives?" he asked Raphaéla.

"In San Leandro."

"Oh, yes, that's east of Oakland. Actually I'll pass very close to there on my way to the office. Why don't I drop you off? Then Kelly won't have to make a long detour."

"That would be fine." She beamed her approval and gave Kelly directions to her sister's residence in San Leandro, so he could pick her up tomorrow and drive her back to L.A.

A pang of remorse shot through Eleanor's body. The last shred of hope for her marriage disintegrated. There would be no recovery from this shameful assignation. In full sight of their mutual friends he was trampling on her love for him, stomping it to death. It would not bloom a third time.

"Take me home, Kelly," she said. "Take me home now."

On the way home she wept uncontrollably. Helena sat with her in the rear seat trying to comfort her, but the tears flowed steadily.

"Eleanor, honey," said Kelly behind the steering wheel. "I love you like a daughter, and I wouldn't do or say anything to hurt you, but I've got to get this off my chest. I've known and worked with a lot of mean tough bastards in my life, and all I can say is that Brock is in a class by himself. I know you say you love him, and I don't doubt it. I don't understand it, but I believe you. Love is beyond explanation. It makes me mad, though...real mad...to see a crud like Brock mistreat a wonderful person like you."

"Please, Kelly." Eleanor raised her hand, while pressing the other over her eyes as if to hide her tears. "I know you mean well, but it doesn't help. It's something I have to work out by myself." Her voice trembled,

150

and another tear stole down her cheek.

"I thought you said your marriage was thriving, that you were happier together than ever."

"We are...we were."

"What happened? Did you have a fight?"

"Nothing happened! Nothing! He just used me. He pretended to love me. How could he do it? How could he be so callous and unfeeling? We were so close. Just last night we made love. I was going to make a grand announcement over dinner tonight. I wanted to tell Brock in front of everyone, so everyone could share in our joy." She broke down and threw herself across the seat into Helena's arms. "I'm pregnant again!"

TWELVE

The months of pregnancy passed in a blur. Eleanor kept herself occupied with club activities, caring for Paul, managing the household, and keeping to her tight regimen of prenatal exercises, dieting, and doctor's visits. As she teasingly told her obstetrician, she was too busy to have the baby. Keeping busy had quite another purpose, however. It kept back the tears. It kept her panic in check. It kept her so tired at night she fell instantly asleep with no chance of reliving the agony of Brock's cruel mistreatment of her. The awful memory of that night was so vivid that only by cramming her brain with the minutiae of everyday living could she blot out, if only temporarily, the image of Brock and Raphaéla making love. It was an image that reappeared again and again, reviving the pain and anger and humiliation Eleanor had suffered, and worst of all the despairing loneliness that followed, a loneliness that she expected would haunt her the rest of her life.

When she awakened the morning after that episode in the club and confirmed that Brock had not come home, she flew into a rage, angrily packed clothes for herself and Paul, gathered up a few of his favorite toys, tossed them into the back of the Mercedes, and sped off with no particular destination in mind, driving by instinct, unaware of where she was. Anger and vengeance displaced all other thoughts. Brock must be punished, be made to suffer, be taught a lesson. She was too loving and devoted and faithful a wife to be treated this way. Venomous unfamiliar words found their way to her lips. "Scoundrel," she muttered. "Pompous ass. Whoremonger."

Paul, seated behind her in his safety seat, turned his cherubic face toward her at the sound of her voice. "Mommy?"

His summons drew her out of the dark void into which her mind had sunk. She had forgotten he was there. "What is it, sweetheart?" She forced her mouth into a friendly smile.

He scrunched up his nose, as he did whenever he was nervous and uncertain. "Are you mad at me?"

"Oh, no, honey! No, sweetheart. Mommy's not angry at you."

"You sound angry," he protested.

"I was thinking of someone else, dear. Not you. Mommy loves you."

"Who are you thinking of?" He was quick-minded and observant for a three-year-old and read people's emotions intuitively.

"Oh, it's someone you don't know."

"I know Daddy."

His astute perception jolted her. She put on a sincere look. "Yes, you know Daddy." She laughed, forcing a lightheartedness that did not fool her son. "It's someone else. A man you don't know and wouldn't want to know."

"Will I ever meet him?"

"I hope not. The man Mommy's talking about is a bad, mean, nasty man."

"Are we going to see him?"

"No."

"Where are we going?"

"Just for a drive."

He swiveled around to look at the suitcase and toys in the rear. "Are we driving a long time?"

His innocence cut through her bitterness and defused it, bringing forth a genuine laugh from Eleanor. "I love you, Paul Stowolski. I love you because you make me see the truth. I'm such a foolish woman." She fell silent a moment. "Or is God speaking to me through you?" It was more of an afterthought to herself.

"God is inside me?" His sparkling dark eyes widened.

"In a way God is in all of us, and sometimes He talks to us through others if we listen." She knew that as keen as Paul's young mind was he could not comprehend such an abstract concept. "Let's stop here," she said, pointing to a fast-food restaurant. "We'll have a bite to eat and then go home. Okay?"

"Okay!" he yelled. His anxiety dispelled by the promise of returning to the security of his home, Paul began talking excitedly about what he would do when he got back to his room. Toys to play with, castles to build. "Can Tommy come over?"

"Of course he can."

Paul's enthusiasm resuscitated Eleanor's spirits and moved her mind to positive thoughts. It allowed her, for the first time, to begin thinking about dealing constructively with the crisis in her marriage.

She had been taught and she firmly believed that marriage was a sacred lifelong bond to be broken only at the peril of committing a grievous sin. It was a sin she could not and would not condone, no matter what sacrifices were demanded of her. The love that had spawned her marriage had been pure, uncontaminated by ulterior motives, or so she thought. At least from her side the love had been genuine, as were her wedding vows made before God at his holy altar. What God has joined let no man put asunder. She would not entertain notions of divorce no matter how flagrant Brock's adulteries. She was his wife, he her husband. That was an immutable legal fact that only death could alter. She would bear whatever burden was laid upon her. She would endure whatever privations, emotional or physical, that he inflicted on her. But she would never consent to a dissolution of their marriage. What troubled her more was that, as much as she was committed to remaining his wife, she no longer loved him enough ever to forgive or trust him again. He was a man without morals or conscience who could not comprehend the real meaning of love.

What lay before her now was the unhappy challenge of finding a way to live with Brock, some compatible midway between living separately and sharing a bed. She would set the terms, and he would have to accept them. She saw no room for compromise.

When she returned home from her impulsive ride and had parked the car in the garage, Paul gathered up his toys from the rear, jumped out, and ran gleefully inside and up to his room to begin his day's play, which their unexpected excursion had delayed several hours. He had much to do and left his mother alone.

Eleanor sat in the silence of the car for nearly an hour, analyzing her situation and the options it offered. There weren't many. First, she could leave Brock, get a divorce. Unacceptable. Second, live separately, she with

Paul, Brock with his playmates. Unfair to Paul. He needed a father and to be a member of a normal family. Normal? What would that be for a three-year-old? Concerned loving parents whose visible affection for him and for each other would give the security and confidence every child needs to face the hardships and uncertainties of life. Concerned and loving parents. Brock actually had shown real concern and love for Paul for the past eight weeks, or had that, too, been a deception? Brock was an excellent actor. Perhaps he would continue to play the loving father role. If he did, the only ingredient missing from Paul's perspective would be the visible signs of affection between his parents. That, she resolved sadly, he would have to do without, and she would try to make it up to him some other way.

So it came down to the third and only alternative: continue on as man and wife, mother and father, but with neither love nor lovemaking. She stared through the windshield into the dark shadows of the garage. Tears formed in both eyes and rolled down the sides of her nose, moistening her upper lip. She drew a hanky from her purse and dabbed at the wetness. She needed a loving husband. She needed normalcy. Why had he done this to her? What had she done to deserve this?

Bitterness consumed her, and she sagged, sobbing, against the steering wheel.

Oddly enough Brock gave no indication that he wanted to change the status of their relationship despite the hostile environment that greeted him upon his return home from his romp with Raphaéla. It was 7 AM when he entered through the front foyer wearing the same dark blue suit he had worn the night before. The pants had lost their crease, and one lapel on the coat was stained. His shirt was crumpled and unbuttoned at the collar. He could not remember what he had done with his tie, nor did he care. He needed a quick shave, shower, and a cup of strong coffee. Then he'd be off to renegotiate a contract with one of the firm's original clients.

Eleanor heard the front door open and came out of the kitchen to meet him. She had been baking Paul's favorite oatmeal cookies and wore a brightly flowered apron over a tight-fitting blue blouse and slacks. Her hair was pulled back by a yellow bandanna. But for her reddened eyes she looked radiantly domestic. "You'll find your things in the guest room," she said matter-of-factly, her face a mask of unconcern. "I'm sleeping in the master bedroom by myself from now on. Any problem with that?" She stared at him with ice cold eyes as she wiped butter from her fingers onto her apron.

Brock seem nonplused. "Anything you say," he said dully, shrugging and turning to go upstairs.

"Will you be home for dinner?"

He placed one foot on the first step and halted. "We'll be eating together?" he asked, not looking at her.

"We're still a family."

"I suppose." He frowned and resumed his ascent up the stairs.

"Suppose what?" she asked, her voice rising. "That we're still a family, or that you'll be home for dinner?"

"Both."

As he reached the top step, Eleanor watching from below announced, "Dinner's at seven."

He disappeared down the hallway, and she returned to the kitchen. They thus signaled more emphatically than they realized that from that moment on, they each would go their separate ways. Still married, still a family, but on parallel, not convergent, courses.

Weeks passed. She nurtured with secret delight the knowledge that Brock was still unaware of her condition. She got Kelly and Helena to promise they would tell no one. Brock was so wrapped up in his private world, so self-centered and uncaring, he never noticed the physical changes occurring in her figure. Even two months after she began wearing maternity clothes he still had not detected the transformation. His ignorance of the coming event amused and pleased her. She savored the prospect of telling him and watching his bewilderment, not that it would

156

have any recuperative effect on their relationship. She didn't want that, nor would she allow it to happen.

Her expectations were grandly rewarded. One Saturday morning, during her second trimester, Brock came into the kitchen for a cup of coffee and caught sight of Eleanor silhouetted against the glass door that led to the patio. His eyes fixed on her bulbous stomach, and his mouth fell open, perplexed. "Ellie! You're pregnant!"

"Not really," she replied, reciting carefully rehearsed lines. "I'm modeling some new maternity fashions for a friend."

"Bull," he said quickly. "I know a pregnant woman when I see one. You're pregnant!"

Eleanor felt her stomach with her hands. "Oh, you're right. I must have got it from wearing the clothes."

Brock laughed and walked over to her, taking her hands. "How long have you been pregnant? Why didn't you tell me?"

Her eyes flashed ominously at his. "I learned the afternoon we had dinner with the Barnabys and Diego and Raphaéla." She jerked her hands free and stepped away. "I was going to announce it that evening...but you were preoccupied."

"Look, Ellie. I'm sorry about that. It was—"

"No, you aren't, Brock. I know you now. I don't know why you do the things you do, but I know the kind of person you are. And the one thing you aren't is sorry. You aren't going to change. People don't change!"

"Oh?" His jaw tightened, his combativeness aroused and stirring. "And what kind of person am I?"

"It won't help our situation to start psychoanalyzing each other. There's an equilibrium in our marriage now that I can live with. It isn't what I expected or wanted when I accepted your marriage proposal, but it will have to do. I know it doesn't bother you because—"

"Because of the kind of person I am?" The bite in his words dared her to respond.

"I have come to accept the fact that we are different. I am reconciled to it. Let's leave it at that."

And so they did.

Brock's affair with Raphaéla had permanently changed the context of their marriage. There would be no rapprochement. No reconciliation. For reasons Eleanor could not fathom and Brock was willing to leave unexplored, he felt no impulse either to abandon their failed relationship or to heal it. He simply accepted the new status quo philosophically as one accepts a change in the weather, although in this case there was no indication the marriage would ever improve. No matter. He went about his life as though nothing had changed, and only close acquaintances were the wiser.

Eleanor, too, maintained an equanimity that concealed even from Kelly and Helena the emotional devastation within her. When mothering Paul and conversing with associates at the club, her cheerfulness and vivacity were captivating. She took on one project after another with a composure and vigor that gave an image of a happily married, well adjusted, contented, and secure woman.

It was a very different story at night. When she lay in bed, her abject loneliness stripped away pretenses and exposed her internal suffering. She longed to be held, to be comforted. She needed a man's affection. That was one of the many things that had attracted her to Brock: his sexuality and manliness, that aura under whose spell she had fallen as she traveled down the escalator that memorable day in the shopping mall, when she first glimpsed Brock working on his Santa Claus display.

Yet here she was, condemned to a celibate life by her moral commitment to her marriage vows and by circumstances over which she had no control. It was so unfair for her to be punished for Brock's misdeeds. So unfair and so irreconcilable. Night after night she sank into the same hopeless depression and wept, crushed by despair and by a wanton fear of the bleak, lonely years ahead. She moaned, bit her knuckles, and silently prayed to God for relief.

By and by, as the months passed, hardly noticing it, a change came over her, brought about by the new life growing in her womb. Its movements and kicks drove her thoughts away from loneliness and toward practical maternal concerns. They were not, however, the principal factor that revived her spirits.

Another event, totally unexpected and more compelling, revitalized her positive outlook on life. It was the visit to her home by Diego Martinez.

158

It was midmorning. Eleanor trotted heavily to the front door, supporting her potbelly with both hands. She had been sorting clothes in the laundry room and had not immediately heard the bell above the music of her stereo. She knew it was Alec, the deliveryman, bringing her groceries, and if no one answered he would not return with the bags till late afternoon. She flung open the door prepared to greet his usual intemperate scowl.

A tall lanky man dressed in a red plaid shirt and worn blue jeans stood in the doorway.

"Diego!"

"None other." His weathered smiling face met her wide-eyed expression.

"What are you doing here?" It sounded to her like a challenge, which she instantly regretted.

"I brought some things for the new baby." He pointed to a cardboard box at his feet. "Helena asked me to bring them by. They're little toys and stuff that she's had in her family for years. She thought you might like them. She didn't tell you I was coming?"

"No. No, she didn't. But how sweet of her...and you. It was very thoughtful. Come on in." She stepped back and let him carry in the box. "Over there by the closet is fine. Let's go into the kitchen. I'll make us some coffee if you like or would you prefer a cold beer?"

"Coffee's fine."

He seated himself on a stool, resting his elbows uneasily on the gorgeous green marble countertop as if it might break if he leaned too heavily. He felt out of place, an intruder. His last and only meeting with Eleanor had been unpleasant and traumatic for him and, he supposed, for her. He knew that seeing him again would revive those unpleasantries for her, and he wanted to put those behind them quickly.

"This is really a beautiful home."

"Thank you. We love it."

Diego supposed the "we" was a deft warning that, despite her differences with Brock, he was still her husband, and she was a married woman. But Diego didn't need the recollection. He was all too aware of her marital status. He watched admiringly as she loaded the coffeemaker with water and grounds. She was still as lovely as he remembered. He was about to remark how motherly she looked but thought better of it. He did not wish to remind her that the last time they met she wore an evening gown. Pregnant women were, he knew, sensitive about their figures and bulky maternity clothes. More than that, it would only bring back memories of that disagreeable evening and of Brock, whom Kelly had assured him was out of town, else Diego would not have come at all. It occurred to him that Eleanor would be thinking the same thing.

"How many months till the baby arrives?"

"Four weeks I'm told," she replied, casting him a warm smile. "The time has flown by so quickly. I've hardly noticed. It's been an easy pregnancy, more so than with Paul."

"Where will you go to have the baby? I mean, which hospital?"

"St. Vincent Paul General. It's only a few miles away and has a fine maternity staff. My doctor's a charter member. So how have you been these months? Getting lots of work? I've learned a lot about the business you're in. It's quite fascinating."

"Yes, you're right, fascinating and always different. No two days are the same."

Eleanor felt the question forming in her mind and could not fight down the compulsion to ask it. "How's Raphaéla?"

Instantly the calm air of informality between them tensed, and Diego's eyes fell to the counter, where he began polishing the surface absentmindedly with his sleeve. "I don't really know. We're divorced."

"Oh, Diego," said Eleanor with feeling. "I'm so sorry. She was..." Eleanor groped for the right words.

"A floozy," interjected Diego sourly. "So please don't feel sorry. I was a jerk for marrying her in the first place."

Eleanor flipped on the coffeemaker and sat down beside him. "We all make mistakes."

"Yes, I guess we do. As they say, her beauty blinded me. I thought I was a lot smarter than that, but obviously I'm not...or wasn't."

"How long were you married?"

"Two years. She was into partying and drugs and..." He paused and shook his head, uncertain how revealing he should be.

160

"Men," said Eleanor softly, finishing his sentence. "It's my turn to be frank."

"After...after what happened..." He looked to her for help, but her face remained expressionless. "She didn't come home for two weeks. When she did she was wild and mean. Tried to humiliate me with all sorts of tales about, you know, carousing. I just kept quiet and listened. The quieter I was the angrier she got. Finally she packed up her clothes and took off in her car. I didn't hear from her for a couple of weeks. Then one morning she calls and says she's suing for divorce. I laughed. 'On what grounds?' I asked. She babbled something about cruelty, and I told her to find another lawyer because it was me who was going to sue her. Well, two months later we settled without any big deal. She went her way. And me? I've just been happy to be rid of her."

Eleanor's sympathy reached out to him. She felt embarrassed by her strange attraction to this awkward, soft-spoken man with the jutting chin and crooked smile that charmed with its honesty and grit. But these feelings were easily explained. She was love-starved and lonely for male companionship. Her dealings with men—limited to her activities at the club—were by design highly structured and businesslike, bereft of any glimmer of romance. But here in the sanctuary of her home, away from the prying eyes of club members and neighbors, the temptation tantalized her, and she quickly thrust it away. She was no fool and would not be lured by what she knew were silly emotional reactions that could lead only to trouble.

She filled their cups, and they chatted awhile longer, both taking care to steer the conversation away from themselves. Then Diego rose, thanked her for the coffee, and wished her a healthy child. He walked out the front door without shaking her hand, merely waving good-bye, for he, too, sensed something drawing them together, and it made him uncomfortable. She was married with a family. He had no business being with her and was ashamed that he had allowed himself to be swayed by a whimsical desire to see her again. He had used poor judgment, but it wouldn't happen again. He would ensure that this was the last time he saw her.

When she closed the door and heard his car leave, she walked slowly back to the kitchen, her feelings charged with conflicting emotions. Relief and regret that Diego was out of the house and no longer an allurement. Shock and thrill that she could feel so drawn, even in pregnancy, to a man other than Brock. Pleased and abashed that even in her advanced deformed state of motherhood she could sense from Diego's looks that he found her attractive. For the first time since the Raphaéla episode Eleanor's heart held something more than the bitter dregs of a crushed and shattered romance. Diego's visit had planted there a tiny seed of affection, a dormant seed, but alive nevertheless. As she went back to her chores she smiled, knowing that something had happened. Something good.

Three weeks, four days, and six and one-half hours later, Eleanor went into labor. As she had expected he would be when the baby arrived, Brock was away on business closing a deal in Hawaii. She had summoned her regular babysitter, Edith, a strong-willed sixty-year-old grandmother who lived nearby. The woman treated Paul like a grandson and was delighted to take full charge of his care. She carried Eleanor's small suitcase to the car and settled her comfortably in the rear seat with Paul snuggled close beside her.

"Are you going to have your baby now?" he asked, a little unnerved at the idea of his mother's leaving.

"Yes, dear, very soon. Mommy's going to the hospital, and in a day or two you'll have a new brother or sister."

"Will your tummy be flat again?"

Eleanor chuckled and tousled his hair. "Flat as a pancake."

Edith got behind the wheel, started the engine, and gingerly moved the car forward.

"I won't break, Edith," joshed Eleanor. "Let's get moving. You don't want me to deliver here, do you?"

"Heaven's sake, Eleanor, be still. I'm not the surest driver in the world. We'll get there in plenty of time."

"Will Daddy be there?" asked Paul, scrunching his nose and eyeing his mother, anticipating her answer.

162

"No, sweetheart. Your father's in Hawaii. He doesn't even know I'm going to the hospital. Edith is going to call and tell him. He'll be along as soon as he can. She's going to phone Uncle Kelly and Aunt Helena, too."

"Didn't Daddy know you were going to the hospital?"

"No. How could he? Babies don't come like clockwork."

Paul frowned, while his keen three-year-old's mind worked on the facts given him. "But you knew. You packed the suitcase two days ago."

"Only as a precaution."

"Doesn't Daddy care whether you have the baby?"

Eleanor blanched at her son's probing insight. "Yes, of course, he cares, but he can't just stay at home every day waiting. He has a business to look after."

"But he has a—"

"That's enough now," said Eleanor, cutting him off. She didn't have the strength or patience at the moment to fend off his questions. It bothered her that the truth of Brock's indifference toward the baby was so obvious to Paul, but he was a very observant and intelligent boy. Why shouldn't he take notice?

Edith stole a glance at Eleanor's troubled face in the rearview mirror. "Paul, dear, your questions tire your mommy out. Best let her rest. She needs her strength. Why don't you tell her what we saw in the park today?"

Paul's eyes lit up, and he launched into an excited account of seeing a live cobra in a cage. Eleanor winked at Edith in the mirror and hugged her son closer to her.

An hour before midnight that same evening Eleanor delivered a beautiful baby girl.

"Mrs. Stowolski? Mrs. Stowolski?" A tall, attractive black nurse shook Eleanor's arm gently to awaken her. "Time for breakfast," she said cheerily.

Eleanor opened her eyes, trying to orient herself. "Breakfast?" She looked out the window; it was early morning.

"Yes, dear. Time for you and your baby to eat. The clipboard says you're breast-feeding. You want to eat or teat? It's your choice, honey. The baby's still asleep."

Eleanor rolled over, wincing. There was a lot of soreness in her abdomen. "Let me feed her first. I want to hold my baby. I can eat later. What time is it?"

"Six o'clock. Did you get to see her last night? I just came on shift."

"Yes, for a short time. I was pretty tired. She's so beautiful. Have you seen her?"

"I did indeed, and she's as pretty as you are. I'll go fetch her."

Eleanor found the push buttons that operated her bed and pressed the one to raise her upright. She adjusted the blankets and looked expectantly to the door. She had hoped there would be a note or telegram from Brock on the stand when she awoke, but there was none. It made his absence more telling and intensified her loneliness. She was not seeking a sign of his concern for herself. That didn't matter. It was for the baby. She was his daughter, his new child. He should be here to greet her, to show her he cared that she was born. But he didn't care and that was the cold hard truth. It saddened Eleanor.

You would think I'd be used to it by now, she thought. *He's never around. He pays no attention to Paul or me, so why should I expect him to act differently on this occasion.* But she wept anyway. Tears of frustration and anger and even self-pity. How alone she felt. Her closest relative was her brother in New York, a continent away. Her dearest friends were Kelly and Helena, but she had rejected their pleas to be with her when she gave birth. She had vowed the night of the Raphaéla affair that she would learn to bear her burdens alone, to stand on her own without depending on anyone else. Brock had taught her the necessity of self-reliance. What she had not known, but was learning at this moment, was that too much self-reliance brings isolation.

The door swung open and the nurse, beaming, entered carrying in her crooked arm the baby wrapped in a tiny blanket. "Hello, Mama! Have you ever seen such a beautiful baby?!" Easily, tenderly, with skilled and practiced movements, the nurse placed the youngling in her mother's cradling arms.

"Why are you crying? Happy tears? It does that to a lot of mothers."

164

Eleanor slowly shook her head, but the nurse misunderstood. "I agree," said the nurse. "She is a beauty. You go right ahead and feed her. I'll be back in a bit." Out of habit she felt Eleanor's forehead for fever and, finding none, left her alone with her newborn.

Eleanor opened her bed gown and nestled the baby's mouth against a nipple. Instinctively the mouth began making sucking movements, and soon mother and child were locked in the timeless embrace linking one generation to the next.

An hour later, the baby back in its crib in the nursery, Eleanor dozed fitfully, regaining her strength from a hearty breakfast but still troubled by Brock's insulting insensitive absence. Then something roused her. Something or someone in the room. A presence she knew. She fought off the web of sleep that cloaked her mind. She knew this person. They had been close. They had shared something. The face was dim and shapeless, but somehow familiar. Her vision gradually cleared, and she recognized it was the face of a man. He was sitting beside her watching her and smiling.

"Brock?" she whispered, blinking. "Is it you?"

"No, Eleanor." The voice was soft and soothing. "It's just plain ol' me. I was in town again when Kelly told me of the birth. He and Helena are driving up tonight. They insisted I visit you and bring you their affection and blessings for the baby. I brought a present for her."

Diego's sharp tanned features came into focus, and a broad smile of recognition broke across Eleanor's sleepy face. "It's you! Oh, I'm so glad to see you."

The unconditional affection in her voice brought a thrill to Diego's heart. Without a second thought she held out her hand to him. He hesitated a split second before taking hold of it. He was unsure of the rightness of his being alone with her once more in Brock's absence, and so soon after he had resolved not to see her again. But the warmth of her hand in his was tantalizing and irresistible.

Eleanor, now wide awake, sensed Diego's misgivings but refused to hide her happiness. Nor could she. If ever she needed a friend it was now. Someone with whom she could share her joy over her beautiful healthy baby girl. She squeezed his hand and asked, "Have you seen her yet? The baby?"

"Yes, on the way in. You were asleep, so I hung around the nursery until one of the attendants pointed her out. She's precious. She definitely has your looks. Have you chosen a name for her yet?"

Eleanor laughed, letting loose of his hand and pressing her fingers to her lips. "You know something? I forgot all about naming her. I wonder what—" She stopped. She was about to say "what Brock would recommend" but he wasn't there. By his willful absence he had forfeited his right to name the child. Eleanor would do the honors without him, and if he didn't like the name, too bad. "I wonder what would be most appropriate. What would you name her?"

Diego's brows knitted. "Name her? Well, let me think." His eyes brightened. "My mother, bless her, always favored the name Valerie, but she had no girls, just me."

"Valerie," she repeated, testing it like a new flavor.

"Do you like it?" he said.

"It sounds...feminine...and strong-willed."

"And artistic and kind."

"Honest and true."

"Loyal and obedient."

"Miss America."

"Miss Universe."

Their laughter carried down the hallway, causing curious heads to raise at the nurses' station.

"I like it," said Eleanor. "I really do. It's a fine name, and it fits. Valerie Stowolski."

"Stupendous," declared Diego, raising his arms above his head in a victory sign.

She grew serious, fixing her glowing blue eyes on his. "Your being here means a great deal to me. More than I really can explain."

Diego quickly directed his eyes away and shifted uneasily in the hardwood chair. The intimacy of her look alarmed him, warning of the risks that lay ahead on the course they were surely on. He should not have come. He felt a pulsing magnetism between them that would only grow stronger the longer they were together. He had no good reason to be here and certainly no right to be flirting with this beautiful but married woman whom he hardly knew. Stealing, he'd been taught, was a sin and that was what he was about. Anyone could see that Eleanor was an

166

abandoned lonely creature yearning for male companionship. Her husband obviously had forsaken her at the very moment a marriage is meant to exult, the moment the marital partnership brings a new life into the world. And where was the miscreant? Out playing with another Raphaéla? Diego had half a mind to search him out and beat him up. The law of the jungle, but fortunately not Diego's law.

"Eleanor." He hesitated, wanting to take her in his arms, yet mindful of the overwhelming wrong that would be. "I really shouldn't be here. You know that." His face grew solemn.

"We do what our hearts tell us is right," she said. "I know your intentions are noble and kind. You're an honest good person. One who—"

"C'mon, Eleanor, don't make me out to be a saint. Don't fantasize. I'm just as human as anyone. Human as Brock."

"You're different. You have a conscience."

"I have a mind and a heart, and they tell me I should go...now...before..."

"What harm is there?"

"I'm going." He stood up and stepped back to take one last look at her, to imprint her face in his memory. "I'm not coming back." He turned abruptly and left the room, the door easing silently back in place as Eleanor watched it.

She was grieved. She had failed to consider his feelings toward her, so immersed was she in her own troubles. *How selfish and careless,* she thought. *I should have been more sensitive to his predicament. Coming here alone. Seeing me vulnerable and in need of comfort. I was too receptive. If only he knew that I would never let our relationship go beyond a handshake.*

But her self-assurance wavered at the image of him embracing her, touching her, kissing her. Would she have stopped him? Would she have had the inner strength, the moral toughness? She didn't know. Perhaps Diego wisely sensed that she wouldn't. Perhaps it was best for everyone that he not return, that they renounce their relationship in its infancy before reckless emotions and chance allowed it to harm themselves, and Paul, and now Valerie.

Eleanor closed her eyes, reached deep inside her soul, and prayed that she would find the will to steel herself against her feelings toward

Diego. They would tempt her, she knew, to call him when she felt lonely, to reach out to him when she needed comforting. She had no other man to turn to. Kelly was a help but not a substitute. Every time she needed consoling she would think of Diego. Every time she needed to share a moment or feeling with someone she would think of him....

The elderly clerk at the counter searched the pigeonholes behind him for Brock's room number, found it, and spotted two envelopes. "Yes, sir," he said. "I believe there are messages." He reached up and withdrew them, handing them to the tanned good-looking gentleman standing on the other side of the counter. The clerk watched as the guest anxiously opened the envelopes and scanned the short typed phone messages.

"I'll be checking out at once. Please have my bill ready. I'll get my things and be right back. Can the concierge reserve me a flight to San Francisco?"

"Yes, sir, I'll see to it."

At the airport, awaiting the boarding of his plane, Brock phoned home, but there was no answer. Then he phoned the hospital only to learn that Ellie had checked out that morning, Thursday. Finally, he called the office, but Ellie had left no word. He hung up and reread the phone messages. The first was from Maggie, reporting Monday night that Ellie was in labor. The second, Tuesday morning, again from Maggie, announced the delivery of a gorgeous seven-pound baby girl.

Brock cursed himself for not calling the desk earlier for messages. People would talk about his absence, but it was of no serious concern to him. He would claim plausibly that the messages were not forwarded to him, which was true. He would say that the contract negotiations to design the interiors of a new community of luxury beach cabanas in Maui had been especially tough and that he had purposely isolated himself to concentrate on tactics and terms. No one would know that he had spent the past four days in a private beach residence ten miles from the hotel with two willing sisters, both in their twenties a year apart. He had befriended them in the hotel's disco Sunday evening after closing the

168

contract.

He wondered what there was about these random encounters with strangers that captured his fascination. It was not solely the pleasure. There was something more, something insensible which he could not put his finger on. Nor did it matter. He was powerless against his yearnings.

For the moment, however, there was a more pressing need—to see his newborn daughter. Having failed to locate Ellie, who he assumed was at the doctor's office or going to or from it and would be home soon, he decided to check with Kelly. Kelly, Brock knew, had become Ellie's confident and father figure. This didn't bother Brock as he felt it provided her an outlet for her misgivings about him and thus reduced the tensions in the family and made life at home more pleasant and tolerable. He dialed Kelly's office.

"Hello," said a familiar voice.

"Kelly?"

"Yes."

"Hey, it's me. Brock. I understand I'm a proud new father."

"Yes, you are," his partner replied coolly.

"I just got the message. How about that? Isn't it great?"

"It's marvelous."

"I phoned the hospital, but they said Ellie'd been discharged. Everything went okay then?"

"Perfect. No problems at all."

"That's a relief. I called home, but there's no one there."

"She had an early appointment with the obstetrician. I spoke with her an hour ago. She'll be home soon."

"Were you there when she gave birth?" Brock wanted to learn quickly the exact circumstances at the hospital in order to explain his absence in the most favorable light when he spoke to Ellie.

"No, we didn't go up. We stayed at home, much against our will. Eleanor stubbornly refused our offer to stand by."

"Who took care of Paul?"

"The babysitter, Edith. You know her. She lives a few houses from yours."

"Oh, yes, I know Edith. She's good. So you haven't seen the baby?"

"No, but Diego visited the hospital and called us afterwards. He said the baby's beautiful, just like her mommy." Kelly had purposely mentioned Diego, knowing it would enflame Brock. And it did.

"What was that creep doing around Ellie?" The words rang with rancor.

"Now don't get all steamed up. I asked him to go myself. He was in San Francisco, so I called him and said I'd appreciate his buying some gifts for the baby and dropping by the hospital to give them to Ellie."

"Maybe so."

"Whataya mean 'maybe'? I'm telling you he went on my and Helena's behalf."

"Well, I don't like that tamale messing around my wife. He may be a friend of yours, but he's a loser as far as I'm concerned. And I don't want him buying her gifts, even from you. If she needs gifts, I'll buy them myself."

"You're the faithful loving husband, eh?"

"Don't get wise, Kelly. It's none of your business."

"You're right it isn't. I've always kept out of it, and I intend to stay out."

"Good, then I'll say good-bye. I've got work to do." He hung up, resentful of Kelly's high-handed tone. Despite his animosity toward Kelly, Brock appreciated the man's frankness and honesty. He minded his own business, that was a fact. In the eleven years they had been associates Kelly had never interfered in Brock's personal affairs, which was consistent with Kelly's weak personality. He was so easily dominated. Brock's contempt for him was undiminished.

But Brock didn't want to think about Kelly. He wanted his mind cleared of all thoughts but one—his hatred of Diego. He was enraged that this Mexican had the audacity to visit Ellie in the hospital, to be alone with her when Brock was out of town. That was Brock's place! Who appointed Diego the surrogate father...or was it surrogate husband? It was humiliating and outrageous. Brock could live with the excuse that he was unavoidably out of reach on a vital business trip. The birth had come unexpectedly, a fact verified in Maggie's message to him. She didn't fault him for being absent, he was sure of that, nor did Ellie. Business was business. If he had known that the delivery was impending, he would have found some way to delay his trip. Ellie never mentioned it. How could he have known?

He phoned her again at home after rehearsing in his mind what he would say. She answered.

"Ellie? Brock. I've been trying to reach you. How's the baby?"

"Fine. Just fine. She's sleeping. I feed her every three hours like clockwork. She's simply perfect. Sleeps soundly, takes her milk easily, and she's so beautiful."

"I got Maggie's messages and one from Kelly when I got back from the meeting."

"Don't, Brock."

"Don't what?"

"Don't explain. Valerie is healthy and beautiful and that's all that matters."

That she had already named the baby jarred his train of thought, but he recovered at once. "Okay, but I want you to understand that..."

"I understand. I just don't want to discuss it."

Brock was just as happy to let the topic drop, and he moved on to the next. "When did you decide on a name? I thought we would talk about it like we did when Paul was born. If you remember, we liked the name Laura."

"That was then. Now is now, and I've named her Valerie. That's the name carried in the hospital records and that will be the name on the birth certificate."

"Okay, okay. It isn't important. I'm curious, though. Why Valerie?"

"Because I liked it."

"Diego didn't suggest it, did he?"

She marveled at Brock's intuition. How could he have known? "Why? Did he say he did?"

"No, I haven't talked to him."

"Then why would you think he proposed it?"

"Because he's pushy and arrogant."

"Oh, get off it, Brock! You're paranoid. I picked her name myself. Me. Her mother. When are you coming home?" She had to change the subject. Brock must never know that Valerie was Diego's suggestion.

"I fly out this afternoon. I should be home before midnight."

"I'll be asleep. Don't wake the baby. You'll get her off schedule. Have a nice trip." She hung up without saying good-bye. She knew for certain now that he had been shacked up with some babe. No one is that incommunicado, especially when their wife is on the verge of childbirth.

Brock slammed the phone down angrily. *She's out of control. Next thing I know she'll be telling me how to run D-M. I'm still the baby's father. I'll not be pushed aside and ignored. I'll make that perfectly clear when I get home. As for Diego, somehow I'm gonna fix him. Somehow. Someday.*

That day would be sooner than Brock expected.

THIRTEEN

T wo months later at a meeting in Brock's office Kelly, who had flown up from Los Angeles, was briefing him on a project that could net D-M enormous profits. It was the kind of high-stakes venture on which Brock thrived and which had become D-M's meat and potatoes.

"It's your type of operation," Kelly said. He was sitting on the arm of an easy chair opposite Brock, who was half prone on the couch with one leg hooked lazily over the other. Beyond the floor-to-ceiling windows San Francisco spread out below them in the bright afternoon sun, the Golden Gate Bridge standing regally in the background.

"Explain it again."

Brock's almost surly tone grated against Kelly, who felt Brock was baiting him. It had become a common occurrence in their dealings of late. Brock seemed compelled to make a show of his supreme authority, taking every opportunity to humble and humiliate Kelly even on matters of little consequence.

"Have I lost the power of speech?" said Kelly sharply. "I just explained all that."

"Then go through it again. I need to know the facts."

"Okay," grumbled Kelly, tight-lipped and glaring. "Once more from the top, slowly. Watch my lips. Universal Instruments Corporation is offering us 3.5 percent of all sales at this wholesalers' exhibit if we fund and stage it ourselves. They're marketing their newest line of communications and recording equipment, which uses top-of-the-line Teletron computer components. No one produces finer, more durable equipment, more reliable, sophisticated technology, or sleeker, more modern designs at fairer prices. Surveys show that Universal's wholesaler exhibits have always drawn well from the major retailers worldwide and have generated heavy sales."

"Why are they giving us a percentage of sales? Why not pay us to stage it and keep the profits for themselves?"

"As I said, Tom Tyson, their vice president for sales, told me it's a matter of incentives. He figures we'll do a better job and draw more buyers if we have a 'stake in the take.' That's a quote."

"And what do you figure it will cost us?"

"Two hundred thousand. One hundred for the exhibit structures, lights, flora, sound, and floor and security personnel. Fifty grand for advertising—trade magazines, worldwide mailing lists, the works. Fifty to pay our own staff and for miscellaneous. I don't have specific figures, but that's the ballpark. It's standard, routine, duck soup. We could produce the concept layouts in a week and have construction plans finished in two."

"What are the dates again?"

"Ten weeks from tomorrow," replied Kelly with mounting exasperation. "Three days running."

"You say Universal will give us 3.5 percent?"

"Yep."

"And they anticipate grossing ten million?"

"Last year as you'll remember we did the show, and they sold nine million dollars' worth. This year's line is better and higher priced. The market's alive. Tyson said sales might go as high as twelve million. Look, if they gross only six million, we'll break even."

Brock was torn. The offer had immense appeal because of the profit margin, but he could not bring himself to give Kelly the satisfaction of landing such a prize. It would undermine Brock's authority in their relationship and in the eyes of D-M employees. Junior partners didn't bag contracts of this size. That privilege belonged to the senior owners. Kelly was out of his class. Brock would have to invent some plausible reason for not accepting the offer.

He got up from the couch, paced to the window, and leaned against it with both hands, his back to Kelly. "No one gives money away. Not that kind of money. Something doesn't square. I'm uneasy about it."

"Look, Brock, if we don't take it, Universal will give it to Roger

Prentiss Associates or one of our other competitors."

"He specifically mentioned Prentiss?"

He hadn't, but Kelly hoped that mentioning Prentiss's name would goad Brock into action. "He implied it. He said he came to us first."

"But we take the risk. It isn't just a high risk; it's all the risk. Universal risks nothing. It's unnatural. It's queer." He turned, rising to his full height, and faced Kelly. "The answer is no. We'll pass."

Kelly jumped to his feet and confronted Brock, who stood inches taller. "Are you rejecting the offer because I was the intermediary? Because Tyson approached me and not you?"

Brock analyzed Kelly's tense face and erect posture. Signs of a showdown. Kelly would not back off on this one. "Nonsense. It's got nothing to do with you. A bad proposal is a bad proposal."

"Bull. You've been badgering me for weeks, Brock, and I'm fed up with it. Tyson is a smart honorable businessman. He's made us a legitimate lucrative offer. If you don't want it, I may accept it myself."

"On your own?" crowed Brock with a mocking air of incredulity. "Where will you get the funds? All your money's tied up in real estate."

"That would be my own business now, wouldn't it?"

"And who will help you? It's too big a job for one man."

"Oh, I know someone. He's very talented and has years of experience. I'm sure he'll be interested."

"I know him, too," said Brock, nodding. "Diego. You'll lose your shirt."

"But it's my shirt to lose."

"Indeed." Brock returned to his desk and sat down. The dispute was over. They were one giant step closer to severing their partnership. "No D-M funds are to be used. Is that understood?"

"Certainly." Kelly left the room and headed for the outer door.

"Not one dollar!" shouted Brock.

"Not a red cent!" came the distant response, and the outer door closed.

Brock monitored Kelly's progress through several well-placed and well-paid informants, one of whom was Kelly's own accountant. A number of Kelly's friends invested in the project, but their contributions amounted to only a fraction of the sum needed. It was Diego who turned the day. He liquidated his stocks and borrowed against most of his real estate holdings to raise the money. His enthusiasm for the venture and his willingness to risk virtually his entire financial estate were inspired, according to the accountant, by Diego's hatred of Brock. What better way to vent that hatred than to succeed where Brock had feared failure.

At first these reports consoled Brock, for they portrayed Diego as a headstrong, overconfident, high-stakes gambler whose good business sense had been co-opted by mindless vengeance. A sure recipe for disaster. But as the weeks passed, the reports by letter and phone grew more optimistic and complimentary—and from Brock's point of view unsettling. Diego and Kelly, it seemed, were well on their way to pulling it off, and brilliantly. A source at Universal Instruments told Brock that the Board of Directors was "jubilant" over the preparations and advertising and were "feverishly excited" about the prospects for huge sales.

Finally Kelly's secretary, whom Brock discreetly entertained whenever he visited Los Angeles, secretly made him a copy of the entire folder on the exhibit: correspondence, layouts, drawings, ads, contracts, and expense accountings. Alone one evening in his D-M office, he spread them out on his spacious crescent desk and studied them intently for two hours. When he had finished, he fell back in his chair and stared somberly at the ceiling. He was astonished at Diego's performance. Kelly was playing a valuable role as intermediary with Universal Instruments, but Diego was the prime mover. His command of the multitude of legal, technical, and financial details involved in staging an exhibition on this massive scale was truly impressive. Brock had greatly underestimated the man's talents. This was no half-baked amateurish affair. It was a full-scale, flashy, exquisitely designed, professional production. Every detail had been anticipated, studied, and addressed in the final plan. The central theme, highlighting Universal's new line of equipment, was woven into the plan in a dozen different ways, some subtle, some dramatic. The combination was scintillating. The exhibit would be a smash hit, and

Diego and Kelly would reap windfall profits as well as tremendous publicity in the design industry.

Brock was stricken with envy and self-condemnation. Had he been more astute and not let his hostility toward Kelly and Diego blind his business instincts, he could have owned the project himself and brought home the profits and the laurels. He had been stupid and would be made to look that way by the two of them. What cut deepest was that Diego had undertaken the project mainly to spite Brock. It was an act of retaliation, and to the degree that the exhibit succeeded—which looked to be large—Brock would be seen to have failed.

A strange feeling came over Brock. A feeling he had not known before. It was alien and foreboding. It gripped his muscles and organs, stifled his breathing, and produced beads of sweat on his brow and upper lip. Trembling, he wiped his face with his handkerchief and swallowed to quell a nausea rising in this throat. What he was experiencing for the first time in his life was fear. Fear for D-M. Fear that word of his reluctance to take on the exhibit would spread through the west coast industry and destroy his reputation. He had seen it happen before. A respected designer falters and at once the industry, which understandably respects only winners, turns its back on the now stigmatized unfortunate. It happens in the blink of an eye, like contracting a dread disease. One moment you're healthy, the next you're shunned like a leper. This was not simply a possibility to be considered; it was a near certainty. His chief competitors, most of all, Prentiss, would see to it. They would spread the word wherever they could that D-M had lacked the courage and talent to take on the exhibit; that D-M had been offered the contract but turned it down; that D-M was no longer a trend-setting leader but a frail and frightened follower.

How could I have let this happen? he thought.

All the years of work building D-M's outstanding reputation and its stable of solid wealthy clients could be swept away by the negative publicity and the whispers that would follow Diego's success. Of course, not all of Brock's clients would abandon him. Perhaps he was exaggerating the potential damage that the exhibit's success could cause him. It might be nothing more than a temporary loss of business while rumors badmouthing D-M's capabilities spent themselves. He would hang tough, wait out the period, and bounce back strong as ever. Then again, he thought, that's precisely what those now defunct or struggling firms, once leaders in the business, had told themselves as they fell from prominence under the weight of some monumental failure. They would be back, they said. They had done it once and they would do it again, but the again never came. They faded, shriveled, and died.

Whether D-M would be ruined as a consequence of the exhibit's success was uncertain. What was instantly clear to Brock, however, was that he could not take the chance when there was even the slightest possibility of a calamity befalling D-M. He must protect his company at all costs. But how? What could be done? What could he do?

It was too late to join forces with Kelly and Diego. They would never accept his partnership at this late stage no matter what he offered them in return. Brock doubted that, given their mutual hatred, Diego was approachable on any terms. Therefore the only practical alternative was to somehow cause the exhibit to fail. Failure. The idea had appeal. If he couldn't join them, then destroy them.

Quickly Brock's creative mind conjured up a host of scenarios ranging from an infestation of insects to burning the exhibit to the ground. None, of course, was feasible, much less legal. The act that would bring the exhibit to its knees had to be subtle, foolproof, and above all legal. Then a thought struck. Legal. A legal action. A legal technicality. Lawsuits painstakingly planned at prodigious expense by expert lawyers were frequently thrown out of court on the basis of minute procedural errors. Perhaps he could find such an error and throw out the exhibit.

Bolting upright in his chair, he clapped his hands together fiercely like a football player coming out of the huddle ready to execute a play. He gazed at the pile of documents on the desk before him, copies of the project files Kelly's secretary had clandestinely obtained for him. Somewhere in that pile, he told himself, might be the answer, the key. An error or loophole. Some detail overlooked. There had to be one. All he had to do was find it, that proverbial needle in a haystack.

He stood up and began organizing and arranging the papers in neat piles: drawings, layouts, photos of mockups, contracts, ad proofs, correspondence, and many more. Then he sat down again and set about reading and rereading each document, searching for some lever by which to topple Diego's exhibit. One by one he reviewed them as minutes and then hours passed. Still he read on, taking short breaks to relieve himself, fix a cup of coffee, stretch, then resume his search. At 2:30 AM, seven hours later, he finished empty-handed. He had found no cracks in the edifice. The exhibit's organizational and legal structure was impregnable. Yet his instincts, honed by his years in this highly competitive industry, encouraged him to believe there had to be a chink in the armor somewhere, some oversight that could be exploited. Brock had fed on such details over the years and had devoured many a competitor as a result.

Exhausted and discouraged, he sank back in his chair and studied the piles of documents. It had to be there. Somewhere. A point of vulnerability. He reconsidered the prime factors. Who wanted the show? Universal Instruments. Who controlled the products on display? The firms that manufactured them. Who...

Wait a minute!

He leaped to his feet, nearly falling off his chair, found the pile comprised of contracts and tossed it on the floor. He fell to his knees and rummaged through the documents with both hands looking for those that had technical amendments. He grabbed up half a dozen and threw himself onto the couch where he lay back and placed the contracts on the rug beside him. Something he had read in an amendment to one of them stuck in his mind. Something about "permission" and "re-use." His thinking was foggy from lack of sleep and confused by too many documents.

He picked up the first. It was a contract permitting use of the huge conference center at the Exeter Hotel for the exhibition. He scanned the legalese of its several pages but found nothing of significance.

The next document concerned use of the computer display equipment—the heart of the exhibit. He read quickly over the titles of the different paragraphs. Again nothing. He flipped the contract over, laid it facedown atop the first, and began perusing the next. As he did so, his eyes glanced back at the last page of the contract he had just laid on the floor. Its final paragraph related to maintenance and repair of the equipment.

"Aha!" he shouted, rolling off the couch onto the rug and seizing the document with both hands. On his knees he excitedly scanned the page for a sentence he only dimly recalled. And then he found it. His cunning and his intrepid faith in his own resourcefulness had triumphed again. There, in a small paragraph in the middle of the page, was a minor caveat that just possibly could spell defeat for the entire exhibition if Brock played it right. The sentence read: *To protect the manufacturer's guarantee of performance standards, this equipment shall not be used in any public exhibition without prior written consent of the aforesaid company.* Brock smiled. He would bet a million dollars that Diego, although a meticulous planner, had misread or possibly overlooked this tiny caveat just as Brock had originally, and Brock had even been looking for it.

The critical issue was "the aforesaid company." What was it? A casual reader would assume it referred to the manufacturer. He flipped back two pages searching for the first reference to "the company" and ran his finger down the page till it rested under the crucial text. It read: "the holding company."

"I've got you, Diego!" he shouted. "I've got you!"

Diego needed prior consent in writing not just from the manufacturer but from the holding company as well before he could use the Teletronix 460 computer display equipment in public. Without that equipment there could be no exhibit!

Brock lay back on the floor and rested the contract, clutched tightly in his fist, on his chest. The battle line was drawn but a long way from won. It was possible that Diego had after all acquired the holding company's permission. Brock would have to ascertain that information secretly without tipping his hand to Diego or to the holding company. He also needed to find some way, if permission had not been granted, to ensure that it wasn't.

He got up slowly from the rug and lowered himself wearily onto the couch. He needed sleep to clear his mind and regain his strength for the covert machinations ahead. He had been at this research marathon for ten hours straight and was physically and mentally exhausted. Knowing that he now probably had it within his power to block the exhibit, his self-confidence was returning, and the strange unnatural fear that had for a short while tormented him disappeared. As he closed his eyes his last thoughts before drifting off to sleep were of Diego—a sullen, dejected, defeated Diego. D-M would be saved, and Diego would pay the salvage fee. As Brock's fingers relaxed, the contract that now controlled Diego's fate fell to the floor.

The plan Brock conceived to sabotage the Universal exhibition was as daring as it was ingenious. He began implementing it at opening of business the next morning with a phone call to his longtime lawyer, Gordon Holly.

"Gordon. Brock."

"Yeah, Brock. What's up this morning? Are you still worried about the Hemperston suit?"

"No, I'm reconciled to it. I'll probably lose, but it won't cost me much if anything, right?"

"Correct."

"No, my purpose in calling you today is of a very different order. I need a surrogate to make a business deal for me. A confidential surrogate."

"To conceal your interest and involvement."

"You got it. I don't want my role visible to anyone, before or afterwards."

"No problem. What's the deal?"

"I want to organize an exhibit of a certain line of computer products—the Teletronix 460—manufactured by a company in Denver. The exhibit will be in Los Angeles in two weeks."

"That's cutting it close, isn't it?"

"All part of the game, Gordon. I play the cards I'm dealt."

"Fair enough."

Brock continued. "I need exclusive use of the Teletronix 460 line of products within a twenty-mile radius of the location of the exhibit. That's the key term. If I can't get that provision, there's no deal. But I don't want to make an issue of it in the opening stages of negotiations. It has to be low-key...handled with finesse and subtleness like a tight poker hand."

"We can handle it."

"I know you can. We've done similar things in the past. We need to take it one step at a time, nice'n'easy, so we don't spook the company that manufactures the Teletronix. If their suspicions are aroused, they'll pull out."

"Suspicion of what?"

"Another outfit, Universal Instruments, is planning to use that same computer line the same time I want to. But there's a strong possibility the holding company of the firm that makes this computer hasn't consented to Universal Instruments yet in writing like they're supposed to. If they haven't, and I can get sole rights, I can prevent Universal Instruments from using the computer."

"And then what happens?"

"It's curtains for Universal's exhibit. A TKO before round one. The exhibit is all about communications equipment, not computers. The computers are support stuff, like backdrops. It just happens that the communications gear Universal Instruments produces runs best only on Teletronix computers. It can run on other computers but not optimally, and it has to be optimal for the communications equipment to show off its main features. The buyers at the exhibit will be a very critical audience. Anything that detracts from the equipment's performance will hurt sales, in millions of dollars."

"I see," said the lawyer, impressed with the cunning of Brock's scheme. "Pretty nifty. What's the name of the holding company?"

"Circle Electron Incorporated in St. Louis. Chances are very good that Circle Electron knows nothing about Universal's exhibit. I'll have a messenger bring you the documentation."

"Let me repeat your instructions to be sure we're on the same page. You want the surrogate to inquire in a quiet businesslike way to Circle Electron about staging an exhibit in Los Angeles in two weeks, site to be determined. If they decline, we know the game is up. If they consent, we go the next step and ask for exclusive use. If they agree to that, we go the final step and request a twenty-mile radius. Is that it?"

"Exactly. And when Circle Electron grants the surrogate the rights to Teletronix, I'll give you detailed instructions to relay to him on making arrangements for our own exhibit. Now, none of this plan must leak out, especially my role in it. If it does, it could prove very embarrassing."

182

"Brock, I'm fully aware of the delicacy of this undertaking."

"I'm sorry, Gordon. Of course, you are. I just have a lot riding on the outcome."

"I'll get on it immediately. We should know something in a day or two. I'll call you the minute I have something."

"Use my private line or call me at home. I don't want Maggie or anyone else to know about this."

Two days passed without word from Holly, but Brock was unconcerned. Gordon, who had drafted the legal documents establishing D-M thirteen years earlier, was one of Brock's most reliable business associates. Throughout those years Brock had come to confide in Holly and to seek the lawyer's counsel on Brock's most private plans and activities. Never in all that time had Holly ever compromised the confidentiality of their relationship or failed to perform tasks which he had accepted. Some he declined on legal or personal grounds when what Brock had proposed skirted too close to breaking the law or violating a legal commitment Holly had made to another client. Holly regarded such commitments as sacred as he did the law. For that reason he served Brock well as a foil against which to test the legality, but not the ethics, of Brock's schemes. Holly considered acceptable any action that was legal. Whether it was unfair or unethical was irrelevant. For Holly the law spelled the rules of the game, which he conceded were inherently unfair, but he did not see it his duty to compensate losers. That was for liberals, social workers, and priests. Brock found solace in Holly's philosophy, for it legitimized and even encouraged Brock's ruthless business tactics.

Brock's private phone rang. It was 8 PM. He was in his apartment reviewing designs for the beach cabanas in Maui.

"Hello, Brock?" It was Gordon Holly.

"Yes, Gordon. Got some good news for me?"

"I do indeed."

"That's what I wanna hear!" He was thrilled.

"You must live right, Stowolski. Circle Electron took the bait, the line, and the rod. You got everything you wanted, and they never suspected a thing."

"Brock came to his feet and pumped his fist in the air. "How did you work it?"

"I engaged a client of mine, Clem Munson. He's a sharp, hard-driving businessman with loads of experience in computer sales and marketing from handheld calculators to million-dollar systems. He's made a fair-sized fortune in computer retailing. He agreed to be your surrogate, even without knowing who you are, because of the cleverness of the idea."

"You told him about it? About preempting the other exhibition?"

"I had to. It was a calculated risk. He insisted on knowing what the stakes were to be sure there wasn't a criminal conspiracy here and not just a skillful business ploy. So I told him."

"And he accepted it?"

"There's a bit of the killer instinct in him. I was fairly certain he would go for it. I've known him for years. He was like a kid with a new toy. I guess it was the challenge of it or the uniqueness. I don't know which."

"He didn't ask to know who I am?"

"Wasn't interested. Anyway, he agreed to do it and said you could pay him later what you think he's worth depending on the results. I told him you'd be generous if the plan succeeded."

"I'll be generous," said Brock. "You can count on that."

"I explained to him that he'd get further instructions from you directly through me as intermediary. I assume that's correct."

"You're right, and God bless you. I knew I could count on you. I think it's in the bag."

"I'm happy if you're satisfied. I hope you'll be as pleased when you see my bill."

They laughed, bid farewell, and Brock hung up. He was bursting with pride at his ingenuity. The operation was underway. He had proven once again that his intellect and will to succeed could overcome formidable obstacles.

The scheme unfolded much as Brock had envisioned. Munson rented an exhibit hall in a hotel ten miles from the site Diego had selected. Within one week, on Brock's detailed instructions relayed through Holly, the paraphernalia—the cheapest and quickest Brock could obtain on short notice—that would comprise the displays was constructed and erected and advertisements were placed in all of the Los Angeles newspapers. Then the day before Diego's exhibit was to open, Brock, again through Holly, triumphantly gave Munson the fateful order.

"Shut him down!"

Munson obediently faxed Circle Electron that he had just learned that a public exhibit to be held the next day within the agreed twenty-mile radius would use the Teletronix 460 computer in violation of his contract. He requested that Circle Electron contact the competing exhibitor at once and disallow him use of the 460.

In a late-night meeting Circle Electron's chief executive gathered his top advisers—as well as the forlorn officer who had approved Munson's contract—to examine the legality of Munson's demand and to explore the company's alternatives to shutting down Diego's exhibit. The company's legal counsel carefully reviewed the contract with Munson and adjudged its terms to be binding. The only alternative to denying Diego permission to use the Teletronix 460 was to negotiate a compromise with Munson. While the meeting recessed for an hour, the counsel reached Munson by phone at his home and offered a deal in which Munson would receive appropriate compensation for allowing Diego's exhibit to go forward. But Munson would not yield, insisting that the terms of his contract be observed to the letter. Circle Electron had no choice. The chief executive himself made the necessary phone call delivering the sad news, first to Universal Instruments, then to Diego.

As Brock had expected, the call to Universal's top management hit like a bomb, wreaking dismay, disbelief, anger, and vehement denunciations of Circle Electron. Following several hours of intense research by Universal's lawyers, they reluctantly admitted at 3 AM before the solemn scowling faces of its Board of Directors that Mr. Martinez had unfortunately failed through an oversight to secure proper authorization in advance to use the Teletronix computers as prescribed in the amendment to his contract, the very amendment Brock had discovered.

185

The lawyers deeply regretted this tragic setback for Universal, but there was nothing that could be done in view of Munson's intransigence. Universal, too, had appealed to him, making him an even more lucrative offer than Circle Electron's, but he flatly rejected any compromise. The intent, he explained, of his requesting exclusive use was to exercise exclusive use. If he had wanted a different arrangement he would have asked for it. As matters stood, a deal was a deal. Martinez would have to do without the 460 computers and, if that meant canceling or delaying his exhibit, so be it.

News of Diego's misfortune spread quickly and was carried in a brief item about Universal Instruments on the front page of the *Los Angeles Times* Business Section the next morning. There wasn't time to procure substitute computers, so Universal had canceled the exhibit and rescheduled it six months later under different management. Martinez and Barnaby were out. The Universal spokesman, seeking to mitigate the damage to the company's reputation, stated that Martinez's oversight had been an honest mistake and that no legal action against him was contemplated. Universal wished to put the debacle behind them as soon as possible.

Brock read the paper and telephoned Kelly at once. "That's a terrible thing," said Brock. "Terrible."

"Well," Kelly replied philosophically, "you predicted Diego would screw it up, and it seems you were right. Can't argue with that."

"Come on, Kelly, I thought he might have some problems, but I never expected nor would I ever wish such hard luck. I mean, from what the *Times* article said, the exhibit is a total bust."

Kelly knew Brock too well to be deceived by this show of sugary sympathy. He could tell Brock was delighted. "Let's face it," said Kelly. "It's a disaster. We've lost everything we invested. As you might guess, Universal's top brass are enraged. Their reputation is tarnished, and that translates into big losses in sales. The whole thing is a mess. I should have listened to you."

"Kelly," Brock said, oozing compassion, "I'm really sorry. Is there anything I can do?"

"I don't know what it would be. Diego and I are a sinking ship."

"Perhaps D-M's lawyers could appeal to the parties involved and work out some arrangement."

"Thanks, but that's already been tried. The guy running the other exhibit won't budge an inch. For some reason he wants our blood. A real tough cookie, and I can't blame him. We might do the same if we were in his shoes. You know...business is business."

"Did you lose much?"

"That's the saddest part. You remember when you said all my money was tied up in real estate? Well, you were right. I had very little liquid capital to invest, so Diego cashed in his resources and footed the lion's share of the cost. I'm sure he's ruined. I don't know if he has the resilience to bounce back from a defeat of this scale. He's taking it very hard."

"Too bad. A really tough break. My sympathy for him is tempered, as you know, by my dislike for the man. So I'm not going out of my way to help him. He got himself into this one, and he'll have to dig himself out."

The heartlessness of Brock's mentality was too much for Kelly to stomach on top of everything else. "You know what, Brock?" Kelly declared with uncharacteristic venom. "You're a lousy excuse for a human being!" He hung up without another word.

In the weeks that followed, Kelly sought to comfort Diego, to ease the pain of his friend's financial and professional setback, but Diego was inconsolable. He had gambled everything he owned on the project only to lose it all because of a stupid oversight of a contractual technicality.

"You'll come back," encouraged Kelly.

"It took me years to get this far, and it was a struggle every step of the way."

"So you've been through worse. You're a fighter. You know what it takes. You've got the skills and the experience. We all make mistakes, my friend, and we learn from them. Next time you'll pay more attention to the fine print."

"There won't be a next time. Who would hire me?"

"I would, you jerk! Like my father always said, don't worry about what might have been, worry about what will be!"

"You worry about it! I'm gonna get drunk!"

"Go ahead. Get it out of your system. And when you sober up, I'll be here waiting for you. When you're ready to go back to work call me. Okay?"

"We'll see." And so saying, Diego shuffled morosely out of Kelly's office and dropped out of sight for three months.

During that interval Kelly, nagged by the feeling that Brock was in some way involved in Diego's demise, made a few discreet inquiries to find out more about the competing exhibit and who sponsored it. Kelly had enumerable contacts in a range of business and professional fields, people who respected and trusted him. Over lunch, cocktails, and chance meetings, without making known his motives, he subtlety probed for knowledge of the Universal Instruments affair. As is customary in cases of dramatic failure or success, most everyone had an opinion to share about the lessons to be drawn from the fiasco. The incident was for weeks a hotly debated topic among persons directly engaged in the business of financing, staging, and managing exhibitions. They were the individuals Kelly targeted as most likely to have the information he wanted. And his effort did not go unrewarded.

A financial adviser in Kelly's bank confided that a high-ranking Universal officer told him, also in confidence, that the executives who decided to cancel Diego's operation believed the sole aim of the Munson exhibit was not to sell computers but to ruin Diego's show. They gave no credence to coincidence, not when sales worth tens of millions of dollars were at stake. Munson's intransigence in the face of Universal's handsome offer of a share of the profits from Diego's exhibit was suspicious, strongly suggesting that he was a stooge for one of Universal's chief competitors. Who the competitor was they didn't know, and there was nothing they could do about it any way. They would simply regroup, reschedule, and be a lot more careful in the future.

One Universal executive, a bit more grudging and vindictive than his colleagues, investigated Munson's business connections and obtained a list of names. They were unnoteworthy to him and nothing came of the investigation, which petered out.

Kelly, pretending to be only mildly curious, asked the financial adviser if he could get a copy of the list of Munson's connections. Two weeks later, when Kelly was visiting the bank on a wholly different matter, the adviser drew him aside and handed him an envelope.

"It's the list you asked for. A friend of a friend got it for me."

"Hey, thanks," said Kelly.

"No problem."

When Kelly was outside the bank he ripped open the envelope and hastily scanned the two-page typewritten list of Munson's close business associates. Midway down the second page under the title LEGAL was a name Kelly instantly recognized—Gordon Holly, Brock's lawyer. Kelly, not wasting a minute, went directly to a public phone and called Holly.

"Hey, Kelly, what can I do for you? My secretary said you have a matter of some urgency to discuss with me."

"Yes, I do. Is Clem Munson one of your clients?"

"Why, yes, he is. You realize I can't discuss my clients' affairs. That's all privileged."

"Was Brock behind Munson's exhibit?" Kelly hoped a frontal assault would catch Holly by surprise.

"Exhibit?" feigned Holly quickly.

"You know, his computer exhibit a few weeks ago."

"Oh, yes. And you want to know if Brock was involved."

"Yes."

"Well, you'll have to ask Brock." Holly was supremely calm.

"I think he was. I think it was a scheme from the get-go to ruin Diego Martinez. The Munson exhibit had nothing to do with business or money because Munson turned down a huge percentage of the profits from Diego's exhibit. No, it was all Brock's personal vendetta against Diego. And now Diego is financially ruined. It was a dirty, nasty thing, and I think you were involved, too. I always thought you were above that kind of thuggery. I'm ashamed for you, Gordon. Do you deny it?"

Holly, stunned by Kelly's revelations and his savage accusation, was silent for only a second as he formulated a reply.

Kelly didn't wait. "That's what I thought!" He slammed the phone down and dialed D-M.

"This is Kelly. Let me talk to Brock."

Maggie buzzed him.

"Yeah, Kelly, what's up?" said Brock guardedly, remembering Kelly's parting shot in their last conversation.

"I think it's time to dissolve our partnership."

Caught short, Brock's mind frantically analyzed the possible reasons for Kelly's demarche. It had to be the exhibit. Nothing else had happened since. But what about the exhibit? Did Kelly suspect Brock's complicity? Brock needed more information. "Why? What's happened?"

"You were behind Clem Munson. You put him up to it."

"Now wait a—"

"I can't prove it, so it makes no difference. That's not why I'm proposing we dissolve our partnership."

"Why then?"

"Because I don't like you. I don't like your philosophy or the way you treat people, especially Eleanor. I don't like working with you. I don't like my good name associated with yours." Kelly paused. "Need I go on?"

"Those are pretty strong words."

"From pretty strong feelings."

"How long have you felt this way?"

"It's been building over time."

"Months?"

Kelly was silent.

"Years?" asked Brock.

"Who knows."

They both fell awkwardly silent, neither knowing how to continue. Kelly, having expressed openly the animosity he had harbored for years toward Brock, was suddenly filled with a piercing sense of loss and regret. His early affection for Brock had been sincere and enduring. It was not something he could easily jettison, but in the past two years he had known this day was coming. Their partnership was fundamentally flawed by their diametrically opposed philosophies and temperaments. It could not survive under the punishment it was taking. It was time to part.

Brock had no particular feelings about it. Instead his mind was wrestling with the implications for D-M of Kelly's leaving. Who would run the Los Angeles office? Would Kelly request that Brock buy him out? How much was Kelly's share of the business worth in dollars?

Kelly spoke first. "Why don't you have the lawyers look into it and explain the options to us?"

190

"All right. I'll speak with Holly first chance I get. I'll have him prepare a brief and e-mail it to you by the weekend."

Their conversation lapsed again, then Kelly quietly remarked, almost to himself, "So that's it, I guess."

"Yes," replied Brock vacantly. "I guess it is."

They hung up, severing their connection. It was the last time they would ever speak to one another.

Only then did Brock feel a faint twinge of sentiment. It was merely a breath, a slight pang of regret, but it passed like a stranger, without recognition, and disappeared into the gray, faceless, self-centered world of Brock's ambition.

FOURTEEN

At twelve years of age Paul had grown into a sweet, loving child cherished by his mother and admired by his father, who saw traces of his own bloodline and character in the boy's looks and behavior. Handsome, boisterous, athletic, and single-minded, Paul seemed modeled in his father's image, a perception that troubled Eleanor. Their son was endowed with Brock's drive and set ambitious goals for himself that were usually beyond his youthful age. Even when a goal proved out of reach, he rarely admitted defeat, vowing with renewed determination that one day it would be accomplished. He was, like his father, a hostage to his dreams.

Almost in desperation Eleanor looked for attitudes in her son that were different from Brock's, and with great relief she found some. Tenderness, kindness, compassion, and a sensitivity to others' feelings. Granted, the boy's personality was still being forged with many years remaining till the mold hardened and his mentality and outlook as an adult were set, but the signs were promising and reassuring to her, and she meant to keep it that way by sheltering him as much as she could from Brock's misguided influence. When Brock was home—a rare occurrence, especially on weekends—she consciously planned activities that would keep Paul occupied, away from the house if possible. Brock did not seem aware of her subterfuge, as he was normally preoccupied with his own affairs, both business and recreational, including competitive ocean sailing which had become his obsession in the past several years. It offered him a brand-new arena in which to test his metal and prove his superiority and, naturally, his manhood. Yacht clubs attracted fun-loving, free-living people among whom he found a plentiful supply of willing, beautiful playmates, some married, some not.

Because sailing was normally an all-day activity, it was easy for Eleanor to forestall Paul's accompanying his father by simply scheduling the boy for some event or appointment, however brief, on that day. On occasions when Brock and Paul were together, Eleanor made sure she was close by to monitor and, if necessary, neutralize things that Brock would say or do that she considered potentially harmful to Paul's mind. She tried to be subtle, but at times she felt compelled to challenge Brock on the spot. Being intelligent and perceptive, Paul read his mother's purpose and learned to weigh for himself the right and wrong of his father's lifestyle. To his mother's delight, Paul soon began to question his father's statements and advice without any prompting from her.

"When you undertake a project," his father was explaining one morning over breakfast, "you can't let others get in your way. They have their own interests and agenda, which may not be the same as yours, and they'll want you to change your project to fit their needs."

"But what if their needs are more important than mine?" asked Paul with innocent sincerity.

"They can't be. Your needs should always come first."

"Even if that hurts someone else?"

"What?" asked Brock, unsettled by such mawkish thinking.

"If what you're doing hurts someone else," repeated Paul, "do you still go on doing it?"

Brock shook his head in wonderment. "Where do you get such ideas? Your mother?" He shot her an annoyed glance, but her face remained impassive.

"No," replied Paul guilelessly. "You said I should learn to think for myself. I am, and I think it isn't right to do things that hurt other people. What do you think?"

The child's bold, mature questioning put Brock on the defensive. He could not tolerate being interrogated by anyone, least of all his own child. Strangely, an image of Father Leonard at the seminary emerged in Brock's mind. "It isn't that simple, Paul. There are many other things to consider. Let's drop the subject. We can talk about it again when you're older and have more experience to draw on."

But they never did, and Brock quickly learned to parry Paul's questions or to avoid them altogether, because he had no answers to give that would satisfy his son. Brock would not justify his actions to a child. Life's rules were harsh and unforgiving. When Paul accepted that fact, he and his father could come to terms.

Meanwhile, to Eleanor's immense satisfaction, the relationship between father and son cooled, and the distance between them widened. Brock turned instead, partly as an act of reprisal, to doting on his daughter, Valerie, now nine years old, showily hugging and kissing her when he came home, bringing her small gifts and taking her with him whenever he could, even if it were only a trip to the drugstore.

Eleanor was not as watchful of the influence Brock was having on their daughter. There was a certain antipathy between Eleanor and Valerie that Eleanor could not define. Psychologists might assert that the two of them, being females, were competing for Brock's attention and affection. Where Paul was a striver, an athlete, and an achiever, Valerie was superficial, aimless, and self-indulgent. Her brash antics, impudent remarks, and generally unruly behavior—Brock called it "spirited"— irritated her mother, so that Eleanor actually looked forward to the child's outings with her father, because it relieved the tension she felt when Valerie was around.

And so it went for the next five years. Father and son somewhat estranged, mother and daughter in conflict, the two relationships developing on separate parallel courses. Although the dissonance between these pairings never reached levels that seriously threatened the family's cohesion, the attitudes they fostered became deeply ingrained and established patterns of behavior that no member of the family, even had they a mind to, could have changed. More significantly, as the differences between the pairs hardened, similarities in values and outlook within each pair grew. This was most profound in Valerie, who consciously modeled her behavior after her father's lifestyle. His worldly, sophisticated, hard-nosed view of the world appealed to her pubescent mind, which clamored to experience the thrills and pleasures she could see life offered. Being with him was always exciting and made her feel grown up.

"Paul!" she yelled, leaning out of the window of her father's white Mercedes convertible as he parked it at the rear of the house near the garage where her brother was shooting baskets. "Paul, you'll never guess who we met at the club." She threw open the door and ran to him. "Guess who it was."

Paul leaped high and looped the ball perfectly through the hoop with his right arm extended. "Whataya think of my sky hook?"

"Screw your sky hook. Guess who we met today."

"Valerie!" he scolded. "You'd better not let Mother hear you say *screw*. You know it upsets her."

"Braydon Beeler!" she screamed, ignoring his rebuke. "I thought I'd die. He was two feet away from me. I could have touched his gorgeous chest."

Paul retrieved the basketball and look at her amused. "Beeler the Peeler? The rock star?"

"In the flesh. I could have orged right there."

"Dad, can't you make her clean up her mouth? Girls shouldn't talk like that."

"Hey," said Brock, grinning approvingly at his daughter as he stepped out of the Mercedes. "We all express ourselves freely in this family. If you're offended, that's the price of free speech."

"Free speech is one thing. Foul language is another."

"Now, Paul," said his father. "She isn't that bad. It's only a phase. She's fourteen years old. It'll pass."

Valerie leaned against her brother. "You see, Paul dearest, I'm just in a stage, and if Beeler were any sexier, I'd die. You should have seen his bod."

Paul grimaced and playfully pushed her away. "You're oversexed, you know that?"

"Isn't it wonderful? Do you think he'd seduce me if I let him?"

"Dad!" wailed Paul.

Brock laughed. "C'mon you two. Time for dinner."

As the three of them went inside, Valerie walked backwards, her arms raised, pushing against Paul's chest. "Screw, screw, screw, screw," she taunted.

He grabbed her by the hair and clamped his hand over her mouth. She broke free and ran into the living room where her mother was watching the evening news on television.

"Mother," she gushed, "Daddy introduced me to Braydon Beeler this afternoon. Isn't that exciting?"

195

"Who's Breedon Baylor?" she replied dryly.

"No. Braydon Beeler. You don't know about him?"

"Should I?"

"He's only one of the top rock singers in the world! Fabulously rich and *so* good looking."

Paul sighed with relief that his sister had not used her more colorful vocabulary. "She expects a marriage proposal any minute," he said.

"I'd accept if he'd have me," she answered defiantly.

"Oh, Valerie," said Eleanor, "you talk such foolishness."

"It's a phase," said Brock, coming into the room. "Are we ready to eat?"

"Five minutes," replied Eleanor, getting up from her chair. "The potatoes aren't done yet."

"Hey, everyone," said Paul. "I'll bet you'll never guess where coach took the football team today."

"An X-rated movie?" cried Valerie gaily.

"No, dumbbell. Be serious."

"Medical checkups?" ventured Eleanor, standing in the kitchen doorway.

"Nope. Dad?"

"Let me think," said Brock. "Maybe...a swimming pool?"

"Nope. This'll kill you." He froze his expression, wanting to heighten the suspense.

"Well?" said Valerie impatiently. "Where?"

"A ballet school."

They all laughed.

"To watch or to dance?" Brock exclaimed.

"To dance."

More laughter.

"You know," said Brock more seriously, "I've read about that. Ballet training for football players and other athletes is supposed to improve balance and muscle coordination. I've always been skeptical, though. Does the coach really believe in that stuff?"

"I can't say. He seems to. The team's gonna take lessons once a week. The best part"—he winked at his sister—"is all the girls running around in tights."

196

"Go on, Paul," hooted Valerie. "You aren't interested in girls."

"No? They seem pretty interested in me."

The conversation continued in a lively fashion through dinner, after which Brock went to his study to review some financial papers. As he read down the columns of figures he thought about the football team's ballet lessons. Crazy idea. He didn't really like it. Ballet was for sissies and fairies. But he was comforted by Paul's normal masculine attraction to girls and the promise he showed as an athlete. His body was well developed for a seventeen-year-old. No wonder the girls were interested in him. They mature faster than boys, as Valerie had amply demonstrated that day by fawning over her rock idol.

Brock laid his papers down and gazed at Valerie's photograph framed on his desk beside Paul's. Ellie had disposed of her own photograph years ago. *How I love that girl,* Brock thought. *She's so like me. So full of life. Outspoken, brash, rebellious.* He smiled. *Her mother hasn't the first clue how to handle her. And that's good because you don't handle people like Valerie. You give them their head. Let them experience life's pleasures. Life is meant for adventure, not for conventional routine. Prudes like Ellie never understand that. Ellie and Valerie are from different planets. But that's all right. I understand Valerie, and that's all that matters.*

While Valerie's mental and physical maturation over the next year continued to please her doting father, his relationship with Paul had taken a turn for the better. Paul was a high school senior now and a member of the varsity football team, playing flanker. The season had just begun, and Paul, fast and agile with strong sure hands that rarely dropped a pass, was first string, an honor that instilled new pride in his father for his son's athletic prowess. Brock had even gone out of his way to attend one of Paul's games and admired his skills. Perhaps, thought Brock, the boy had promise after all. He wondered whether Paul was good enough to compete for a position on the football team at the University of Southern California. Its Office of Admissions had already accepted him for the coming fall under an advanced placement program.

Brock's newfound admiration for his son took an unexpected dive, however, one evening over dinner when Paul recounted the football team's latest visit to the ballet studio.

"You should've seen these guys. They were flying through the air like birds."

"With wings, no doubt," remarked Brock sarcastically.

"No, really Dad. It was amazing to see."

"Members of the football team?" cried Valerie with disbelief.

"No, the guys that take regular ballet lessons."

Brock put down his fork and looked directly at Paul. "You aren't getting serious about this ballet stuff, are you?" Everyone at the table sensed a toughening in Brock's voice. It was the familiar threatening tone that warned they were entering dangerous territory. "You'd look mighty weird in a tutu."

Valerie and Paul laughed, but not easily, while Eleanor listened and watched, concealing her reactions.

"C'mon, Dad. Guys don't wear tutus."

"I know. That's so you can tell the girls from the boys."

Valerie laughed.

"You think they're all fags?" asked Paul, not laughing anymore.

"Aren't they?"

"There are a lot of straight guys involved in it."

Valerie spoke up. "Very few, and you know it."

"You gonna gang up on me, too?"

"I'm not ganging up," she retorted, crossing her arms and straightening her shoulders. "It's a fact, that's all. Most male dancers are homosexuals. Why do you pretend they're not? Be honest about it."

Brock's eyes warmed as he watched his daughter take his side.

"I don't care," declared Paul. "Ballet is a tough, physically demanding sport that requires—"

"Sport!" cried his father. "Ballet a sport? You aren't serious."

"I am most sincerely serious."

"Ballet," said Brock, standing and shoving his chair back, "is an afternoon gig for prissy girls and queers, and no son of mine is going to humiliate us or himself by getting involved in it. You understand?"

Paul stared at his plate without answering.

198

"That's the end of it," continued Brock. "I won't hear another word about it. I'm going to call your coach and tell him what I think about his training program. Is he developing football players or fops?" He stalked out of the dining room and went to his study.

"I think Dad's right," said Valerie, breaking the lingering pall of silence. "You'd be a laughing stock at school if you did ballet."

"I never said I was going to do ballet," replied Paul defensively. "The only point I was making is that all the guys who do ballet aren't queers. That's all!"

"All right, now," said Eleanor. "That's enough. Valerie, will you get the dessert? It's on the counter next to the refrigerator."

They finished dinner without mentioning ballet again.

Later, as Eleanor cleaned up the kitchen, she felt elation over Paul's budding interest in ballet, which she had always loved for its surpassing grace, dignity, and refinement. She felt it was an activity that called forth the very best qualities in those who dedicated themselves to its fulfillment. Ballet, like other art forms, defied deception and cheating, laying bare for all the world to see those persons who pretended greatness and those who were truly gifted. It allowed no shortcuts to perfection but promised to devout practitioners the sheer unrivaled joy that comes with elegant and exacting performance. But more than that, Paul's captivation with ballet pleased her, because it signaled a further alienation between him and his father, and for that she was thankful.

She did not reveal her true feelings to anyone, maintaining an outward calm that would not make Brock suspect her. Instead she watched and bided her time. She recognized the unflinching look of resolve in Paul's intense dark eyes—so like his father's—and the way he cocked his jaw to one side when he had set his mind on something. He had done that since he was two years old. Now eighteen, he would, she was certain, do what he wished in spite of his father's opposition.

Brock knew he could not change Paul's mind directly, so he tried to use Eleanor as an intermediary since she was closer to Paul. "Do you want our son tiptoeing around in girls' slippers," he said to her later, "tripping the light fantastic like a fruit cake?"

"Now Brock," she soothed. "You've always said each person must learn from their mistakes, that we each pave our own road. Well, it's time

Paul made some mistakes. We can't shelter him forever."

Mollified by the logic of her statement and thankful she was not supporting Paul's interest in this fantasy, Brock backed off some. "Perhaps you're right. But I still don't like it."

"I'm sure it's a momentary thing," she added, feigning indifference. "I can't believe he's seriously interested in dancing. Somehow it doesn't fit with his other interests."

"Let's hope not."

When the football season ended in early November, Paul continued to drop by the ballet school occasionally on weekday afternoons and Saturday mornings just to watch. The director, Mr. Kúbokoff, recognized him as one of the football players and always waved to him and smiled a greeting. Since the young man had not paid for lessons, Kúbokoff did not invite him to join in the drills, but he did allow him to sit quietly and observe. *Who knows?* thought Kúbokoff. *The boy might find the courage, if that's what was holding him back, to enroll in a class.* It was a familiar scene: a boy captivated by the aura of dance but fearful of heckling from his friends if he donned tights and took the floor. *A pity,* thought Kúbokoff. *So many fine young athletes torn by the shallow prejudices of their national culture. Especially this lad.* When Kúbokoff was a youth in Russia, most boys vied with one another to be chosen for ballet class, which was a mark of distinction.

Kúbokoff remembered Paul well. Good posture. Excellent coordination. A certain aloofness and poise. A tall, lean, muscular body well proportioned for dance. Truly a pity. Like so many others the boy would visit the studio for a couple of weeks, then disappear, never to return, choosing some other avenue to athletic expression and self-fulfillment.

When the class was over, Kúbokoff went to the boy and said, "You enjoy vatching?"

"Yes. Yes, I do. It's very beautiful to watch."

"V'y don't you enroll?" He rolled his *R* with a heavy Russian accent.

"It vould be good for your body." Kúbokoff would not give him a sales pitch. One could not, he believed, persuade someone to enter ballet by reasoned argumentation. The motive had to be love of it, and it had to come from within.

"Well," said Paul, "I'm pretty busy."

"Vee start a new class in a veek. Give it some t'ought."

Kúbokoff departed. If it was to be, it would be.

Paul sat watching the class, mostly girls a bit younger than he, gather up their belongings and disperse. He tried to imagine what dancing, real dancing, would be like. The football players had merely learned and practiced a few basic movements to help their coordination. They never really danced. Paul wondered how it would feel, and then he realized why he was lingering, waiting for the class to leave.

The last girl ran from the room, pounding down the creaky wooden stairs, yelling after a friend. Her departure left the dance studio in eerie silence.

The late afternoon sun cast long shadows across the bare wooden floor, spotlighting the center like a stage. Paul studied the boards, mesmerized, watching invisible dancers whirl and twirl about the room. He saw himself among them, leaping, pirouetting, landing, thrusting his chest out, his arms spread wide, head held high, feet scissored apart.

He got to his feet, removed his jacket and shoes, and almost in a trance walked nimbly, self-consciously to the center of the floor into the circle of sunlight. As the recorded music to which the class had danced played in his mind, he began swaying in rhythm to its slow beat. He hummed the tune, and the sound energized his movements, which grew stronger and more expressive. His arms swung back and forth like two graceful palms in the wind, his fingers flicking in time with his singing. He began to move about the floor, twisting and turning, arms held out, leaning one way and then the other, deliberately at first, then faster and faster. He felt controlled by some inner force, obeying its commands, yielding to its passion. Then from within came the urge to leap. He felt unsure and slowed, then stopped and knelt in a coiled crouch, gathering his strength. And when the moment came the inner force unleashed his energy. He sprang up from the floor, took several short steps, and launched himself upward, holding his body in the dramatic position the dancers had used—arms wide, chest out, head up.

As if in slow motion he glided upwards higher and higher on a space-bound trajectory that he felt would have carried him crashing through the ceiling, had not the jealous fickle god of gravity regained mastery over him and pulled him back to earth. He landed softly, rolled on his back, and lay motionless, his eyes closed, his chest heaving from the exertion. Had he really flown through the air like a real dancer? Or had he only imagined it? It had been a fleeting dreamlike sensation, yet his hair had brushed the ceiling. He remembered that well. It had brushed the ceiling!

A smile formed on his lips as a profound happiness came over him. It was a feeling more intense and more satisfying than anything he had known. What could surpass it? He could not explain it nor did he understand it. But the implication was simple and unmistakable. From that moment on, ballet was his life. All of his life. The very essence of his life. He could not live without it.

He was born to dance.

In the shadows at the rear of the hall Alexéi Kúbokoff stood enthralled by what he had just witnessed. Tears streamed down his cheeks from the sheer joy of it. *Sláva bógu*, he thought. Praise God. Never in his fifty years in ballet—from his faltering steps as an eight-year-old in the Red Banner State School of Dance in Kiev, to his starring in the Kirov Ballet in Leningrad, to his much publicized defection in London, to his retirement here in San Francisco—had he seen such a marvelous display of raw natural talent. The boy had leaped so high his head nearly hit the ceiling. The positioning of his head, arms, legs, and body had been near perfect. And his "hang time," as the Americans called it, seemed like minutes, not half-seconds. Most dancers practiced years to attain such form. Surely he had training.

Kúbokoff suppressed an urge to run to the boy and embrace him. The boy would be embarrassed, for he obviously believed he was alone. No, the situation called for dignity and tact...and action.

Kúbokoff, wiping away the tears, coughed lightly to announce his presence. Startled and self-conscious, Paul spun around on the floor toward the sound, his mouth open as if to speak. The gray-haired teacher emerged from the shadows into the light and approached him. Their eyes met, and Paul at once relaxed, relieved that it was the dance master and not a stranger...or worse, a friend.

"I'm sorry...I'm..." Paul did not know what to say. "I hope...I mean..."

"How old are you?"

"Eighteen."

"How many years have you been studying ballet?" Kúbokoff spoke quietly in his throaty Russian accent, controlling his excitement.

"Two years with the football team."

"Yes," the master chuckled, "I remember you. But t'at vasn't study. T'at vas calest'enics. You obviously have had much serious training."

"You mean regular lessons?" Paul looked up at his questioner perplexed.

"Yes, of course. On t'e barre." He pointed toward the wooden railing on the mirrored wall behind them. "In pairs, routines, performances."

"Oh, no. Never," said Paul, shaking his head. "I don't know anything about that. Only what I saw the dancers do here in your class."

A tear formed in one of Kúbokoff's watery eyes as the enormity of what he had just seen hit him again. "T'en you have never been taught to fly t'rough t'e air as you just did?"

"No. I just made it up. It sort of seemed natural."

"T'en you have practiced leaping before?"

"Never. I'd be too..." He stopped.

"Embarrassed?" said Kúbokoff, smiling.

"Yeah. I guess I'm self-conscious. My family doesn't..." He raised and dropped his shoulders and fell silent. The dance master held out his hand.

"Velcome to ballet!"

Paul took his hand, and the man pulled him to his feet.

"Thank you," said Paul. He glanced about the studio. "I think I belong here, you know? I feel at home here."

Kúbokoff grinned. "I know. It is in your blood. A gift from God."

"Something's happened to me. I feel different."

"You vant to dance."

"Nothing else matters. I can't explain it. Everything else in my life suddenly has no importance. I knew it the moment I flew in the air."

"Ha, no!" roared Kúbokoff, throwing his arms wide. "You didn't fly. You soared! Like an eagle!" His joyous voice reverberated in the darkened hall as he strode about, gesturing theatrically with his heavy arms. "Like

Nureyev, Mukhammedov, Nagy, and Baryshnikov. You have t'e same talent. Now it is t'e talent of t'e vild beast. Explosive, passionate, and genuine. It must be tamed and cultured and refined. Discipline! Discipline! Discipline!" He clapped his hands on each word for emphasis.

Paul listened intently, moved by the man's ardor.

"T'e key qvestion," said Kúbokoff somberly, pointing a finger at Paul. "T'e key qvestion that must be answered is v'et'er you have t'e spirit and villpower to do it."

"I think I do."

"Tinking von't make it. You must be sure."

"I am. I want to dance...more than anything."

"And v'at vould you sacrifice?"

Paul fell silent, thinking, peering searchingly into the studio's dark corners as if the answer lay there. What would he give up to pursue ballet? Or turned around, what would he be unwilling to give up? He could think of nothing. All of his other interests, those things he did for school, for work, and for fun meant nothing. They now held no value whatever compared to ballet. He was meant to be a dancer. It was part of him, like being male and having dark eyes. It was something he couldn't change if he wanted to. He looked deeply into Kúbokoff's eyes and said, "I believe I would give my life itself to learn to dance."

"You vill pay a heavy price, you know. But t'e revards vill make up for it many times over, I promise. Do you know v'at it is to vork?"

"When it comes to that I take after my father. Work is his middle name."

"You started to say somet'ing earlier about your family. T'ey don't approve of ballet?"

"My father thinks all dancers are queers. He would kill me if he learned I was taking ballet lessons."

"And you vill still take lessons?"

"I said I'd sacrifice my life, didn't I?"

They laughed together.

"And v'at of your mot'er? She is also opposed?"

"I don't know. She and my father don't get on well, so she may support me. In fact, I'm sure she would."

"Anyvun else?"

"My sister, Valerie. I think she agrees with my father. My taking lessons would make her uncomfortable. She's very social and sensitive about what her friends think."

"So how shall we proceed? You vill take lessons?"

Paul made a fist and shook it. "Let's do it!"

"Vill your family know?"

"I'll have to tell my mother. She'll give me the money. I'll keep it a secret from everyone else."

"But not forever. Vun day it vill come out."

"When it does, I'll face it. Till then, I'll keep it private."

"You can afford private...secret...lessons? I'm expensive." Kúbokoff was skeptical for the first time.

"Don't worry. My family's loaded. I'll work it out."

"Good. So I am to be your teacher?" It was only proper for Kúbokoff to raise the question.

Paul looked around the room again. "I don't see anyone else."

"I like your sense of humor. You vill need it v'en t'e road narrows and t'e veight becomes heavy. Your name is...?"

"Paul. Paul Stowolski."

"Ah, Polish?"

"Fifty percent on my father's side."

"Your ancestors vere dancers?"

"Not that I know of."

"No matter. I am Alexéi Nikoláyevich Kúbokoff, dancer and Russian by birt'. Dancer first, Russian second. You may call me Mr. Kúbokoff. So v'en do vee start?"

"How about now?"

"It is late."

Paul's eyes pleaded. "Please?"

"Oh, vell. I suppose it von't hurt to teach you t'e first position."

"I think I already know it. You taught it to the football team."

"No, no. I taught you calest'enics. Now I teach you t'e first position. Here. Come to t'e barre, and I show you how to stand."

And so it began. The making of a would-be dancer. The making of a would-be star.

FIFTEEN

As Paul had expected, his mother was understanding and supportive and arranged secretly to pay for the lessons in cash, so neither his father nor Valerie would be the wiser. This makeshift conspiracy pleased Eleanor because it bound her and Paul more closely together in a way that excluded Brock, further diminishing his power to influence Paul's attitudes and lifestyle. There was enjoyment, too, for her in seeing Paul's excitement and dedication to this new venture. He lived and breathed ballet, talking of nothing else whenever they were alone. She bought him books on the history of ballet which they both read and discussed...and which he hid in his closet. He attended every performance of the San Francisco Ballet that he could work into his schedule. Sometimes she accompanied him and marveled at his total absorption. From the moment the curtain rose till it lowered he sat hunched forward in the box she had reserved for the season, his eyes never leaving the dancers, his hands and shoulders moving ever so slightly mirroring in miniature the movements of the figures on stage. On the way home he would relive the entire performance, animatedly critiquing the skills and artistry of each of the principal dancers.

Eleanor had not seen Paul dance. To keep his lessons secret he drove himself to the studio at night. She stayed away lest she be recognized and draw attention to him. Although she could watch him exercise daily in the "gym" in the basement of their home if she cared to, he never danced there. The room was a jungle of Nautilus equipment. One wall was mirrored, enabling him to monitor his stance and posture in each of the classical ballet positions.

Over the succeeding months Paul worked and practiced several evenings a week one-on-one with his sixty-year-old master, whose patience and physical endurance at the end of each long day in the studio were rejuvenated by his excitement when Paul entered. Kúbokoff would not reveal his continuing astonishment at his student's rare talent. Paul must, the Russian decided, remain humble to accept the discipline that was essential if he were to attain the stardom for which he seemed destined. Flattery and praise would only bloat his self-image and weaken his resolve. Kúbokoff agreed fundamentally with the famous choreographer, Paul Taylor, who said of coaching aspiring ballet dancers, "I think a little discouragement is the most I can do to help them." In fact Kúbokoff thought he might never tell Paul how he truly felt about his dancing, even if this young prodigy one day ascended to the very pinnacle of the ballet world. There must always be someone in authority to say, "No, not good enough. You can do better." Someone to drive the dancer not only to seek excellence but to surpass that level once it had been reached.

Paul's quickness as a student was an inspiration to his venerable teacher. Kúbokoff would hardly begin showing him a movement or technique when Paul would interrupt. "Yes, yes. I understand. Like this?" And he would demonstrate what his teacher had not finished explaining. It was, Kúbokoff observed to his wife, as if the boy were remembering something he had forgotten, not something he was learning for the first time.

Moreover, once "remembered," the lesson remained fixed in Paul's mind and in his dancing. He absorbed every detail of what Kúbokoff said and could repeat back the instructions word for word at any time. To his teacher's concealed amazement Paul mastered in a few months the basic skills that normal students required years to learn. Those skills quickly became second nature to Paul, who pestered Kúbokoff to teach him the more difficult moves—the cabriole, the ballotte, the gargouillade, the grand pas de basque. Though tempted to accede to Paul's craving to learn more and more so as to catch up with his peers to make up for the years of training he had missed, Kúbokoff held back. Ballet was a complex demanding art whose forms were mastered only through systematic monotonous repetition and gradual development month after month under the scrupulous correcting eye of the teacher. Trying to learn too much in too short a period without time to make second nature the smooth melding of one intricate maneuver into another could leave Paul with a dangerously superficial proficiency that could collapse when later put to the test of virtuosity.

The secrecy upon which Paul insisted frustrated Kúbokoff, who wanted his protégé to get exposure to an audience, for it was only in the fire of live performance that skills could be tested and tempered, and it was only in the presence of an audience that dance was transformed into art. Kúbokoff also fretted that the need for secrecy was preventing Paul from joining other students in a class in which he could learn, as he must, how to dance with a partner and how to interact artistically with a corps de ballet. The time had come to speak with Paul about it.

"You have done vell since vee began," said Kúbokoff, massaging a small knot in the gastrocnemius muscle in Paul's left leg which had cramped during his practice.

Paul, seated on a bench with his head and shoulders resting against a wall, feigned surprise. "A word of praise? I can't believe it! Five months we've been working together and never a compliment. The best I can hope for is an 'okay' now and then. What's the occasion? You want more money?"

"Money?" exclaimed Kúbokoff, disconcerted.

"Hey, I'm kidding."

"You kid too much. T'is is serious business."

"Okay, I'm serious...and I'm doink vell."

"Yes," replied Kúbokoff, ignoring Paul's playful mimicry. "You are doink vell, but not vell enough."

"So what do I have to do that I'm not doing now?"

"Join a class vit' ot'ers."

"Yes, I know. There are things I can learn only by dancing with others. Right?"

"You are alvays ahead of me." Kúbokoff shook his head. "Maybe you be teacher and I be student." The thought occurred to him that at the rate the boy was learning, before long the student might indeed know more than the teacher.

"So let's do it," said Paul. "When do we begin?"

"V'at about secrecy?" asked Kúbokoff. "T'e students vill talk about you. Vord vill spread."

"Then let it spread. Sooner or later my father's going to find out anyway. I can handle it."

I'm sure you can, thought Kúbokoff, but he did not say so. His admiration for this boy must not be evident.

"T'en four tomorrow afternoon. I have a class of fifteen advanced students. Tvelve girls and t'ree boys. T'ey may not know you. None, I believe, are from your school."

"That's good."

Kúbokoff slapped Paul's leg. "Stand up and valk around. Let's see if it's better."

Paul stood and gingerly tested his leg. He pursed his lips and paced slowly around Kúbokoff. "Okay so far. It feels good."

"Stretch before you dance! You're not stretching enough! Don't be impatient! I told you at t'e beginning and I repeat it. T'e limbering drills are as important in ballet as t'e movements and positions and technique."

Paul nodded. "I'll remember to be patient. Uh...there is something else."

"Yes?"

"Well, I just wondered...about the class...about the other students."

"V'at about t'em?"

"Well, am I really at their level yet?"

Bózhe moy, thought Kúbokoff. *If he only knew. He is a giant among dwarfs. He will intimidate them all. They will stand in awe of the power and majesty of his movements.* "Oh, I don't know," mumbled Kúbokoff, searching for the right words that would not inflate Paul's ego. "In some areas...you may even be...a little ahead."

"Really?" Paul was intrigued. Kúbokoff's habit of withholding praise had conditioned Paul to be more conscious of his faults and shortcomings than of his strengths. Paul truly had no way to gauge his progress because he had worked in isolation these past months. By practicing with others his age, by sort of coming out, he would see how he compared to his peers.

"It vould be perhaps vise if you...vell...observed a little...before you display...uh...before you take part."

"Observe?"

"Yes. T'e other dancers."

"So I can watch them?"

"Yes."

"I just observe and watch?"

"Yes. But no. To see first t'e level of skill demonstrated by t'e others so you can..." Kúbokoff groped.

"So I can learn from them?"

"No, not learn. So you can...match, yes, match t'eir level."

Paul instantly read Kúbokoff's implicit message. "I understand, Mr. Kúbokoff."

"Good. For example, v'en you do entrechats, do only quatre. T'at vill be enough for vork in class. V'en you are alone, you may do more."

"And my grandes pirouettes? How many revolutions?"

"No more t'an two. And v'en you jump, do not go so high."

"Only medium elevation."

"Yes." Kúbokoff nodded. "Medium."

"Anything else?"

"No, t'at vill do. You vill fit in nicely."

"I'm sure."

But he wasn't sure at all. Five months ago he had never even raised his arms in a graceful pose. To have done so in front of family, friends, or classmates would have subjected him to immediate ridicule. Tomorrow afternoon he would practice being graceful in front of fifteen of his peers. It was not, he knew, a performance before an audience, but it felt like it, and he could not shake his apprehension.

He fidgeted all day at school and could not keep his mind on his work. The last class seemed to go on forever till at last the hands on the clock reached three-thirty and the bell rang. He flew from his desk and raced out the door down the hall to his locker, and then to his car in the student lot.

"Hey, Paul!" yelled a friend. "We're going to Stu's for pizza. Wanna come along?"

"Can't! I've got a date." He slammed the door and started the engine.

"What's her name?" called the friend.

Paul gave an uncomprehending shrug of his shoulders and sped off toward the studio, arriving there twenty minutes later.

Many of the dance students—he saw only one boy—were already

there, warming up on the barre, stretching, donning their sweats, or tying on their ballet shoes. It was strange to see them all here in what had been his private practice hall. They seemed intruders. He'd been spoiled, he knew. Sharing Kúbokoff's attention with others would require an adjustment, but only a small one. Paul had come to learn, and learn he would.

He set down his athletic bag near the rear wall away from the nine or ten others, most of whom congregated near the windows on the other side. He pulled out his sweats and went into the boys' dressing room, more of a closet, to change his clothes. When he emerged, an attractive girl his own age was stretching on the floor outside the door. He nearly stumbled over her.

"Excuse me," he said, hopping over her back and putting his school clothes in his bag. It was obvious she had seen him go in and purposely placed herself in his way.

"You're new in class," she replied, touching her forehead to her outstretched knees.

"Yep. My first day." She was very good looking. Long blond hair coiled neatly behind her head. Pretty face. Green eyes. A gorgeously slim and curvaceous body. Wow!

"I'm Melissa Manford. What's your name?"

"Paul."

"Just Paul?"

"Just Paul."

She surveyed this handsome newcomer. He was sexy as all get-out, and every girl in the room was eyeing them enviously as they talked. Melissa wasn't a watcher. She went out and got what she wanted, and right now it was this new guy, Paul. "I haven't seen you before."

"Nope. Like I said, it's my first day."

"You been dancing long?"

"No, not long."

"Where do you go to school?"

"Other side of town."

What a perfect physique he had. Tall, muscular, well-proportioned, and tight. She wondered, as would all the girls, whether he was gay. He didn't act or talk like it, but she knew it was hard to tell sometimes. The girls more or less agreed that two of the other three boys in class were homos. The third was straight. Melissa was sure of that because she had seduced him a week ago in the backseat of his car. "Who did you study with?"

"Mr. Kúbokoff."

"When? I've never seen you. I've been taking from him for years."

"Well, I've had private lessons."

"Oh, ho! Big bucks. You must be rich."

"No, I just had a lot to learn in a short time. I only started five months ago."

"You wanna go out for a Coke after class?"

Paul's impulse was to accept, but he wanted to protect his identity, at least for awhile, and that would be difficult with someone as curious and aggressive as this Melissa.

"Thanks. I'd like to, but I really can't today. Maybe another time?"

"Like next time?"

"You are pushy, aren't you?"

"I just like to be friendly."

"Great. I can buy that. We'll be friends then."

Kúbokoff entered at that moment, followed close upon by the two other male students at whom he scowled for being tardy. He began shouting commands, lining up his charges and checking their shoe lacings. He carried a yard-long wooden stick with a rubber knob at each end which he used to point out his students' errors, tapping a shoe or touching an ankle or elbow as he moved among them.

Kúbokoff seemed to ignore Paul, who had expected his tutor to say something to him. But Paul was relieved that he hadn't. He didn't wish to call more attention to himself than he was already getting. As Paul later learned, Kúbokoff disdained greetings to his classes, feeling it eroded discipline. Every minute of class time was precious and not to be wasted. He rapped his stick on the floor and shouted. "Now t'en. Limbering drills. Take your positions. Qvickly now."

The master looked around the room and lost himself in thought for a moment. The dance studio. It was a magic cauldron in which natural talent was discovered, nurtured, and relentlessly painfully developed, session after session, repetition upon repetition, till the talent either broke

212

and folded or was transformed into true artistry. The outcome was never certain. For most of these aspirants it was bitter failure followed by a lifetime of regret for what might have been. For a few selected by fate, by God, or by whatever power they believed in, the fruit of their years of labor was fame and fulfillment as acclaimed professional dancers on the grand stages of the world. What would Paul's fate be? Failure or fame? Only God knew, for God was the only power Kúbokoff believed in.

As in Paul's private lessons, the class began with warm-up drills at the barre—plies, battements, ronds de jambe, developpes, and ports de bras—what Cyril Beaumont, the English ballet scholar, termed the "scales and arpeggios" of the ballet dancer. After a half hour of these preliminaries Kúbokoff called his students away from the barre for their "center practice" when they repeated many of the same exercises but without any means of support.

Because the dancers followed exactly the same routine that Paul had learned, he blended in immediately as just another member of the class, though many of the girls glanced in his direction out of the corners of their eyes to see how good a dancer he was. One could tell a lot by the way a person warmed up. Measuring one's own talent against others' was a given in ballet as in any athletic activity. Was the newcomer better than me? Where would he rank in the class? Ahead of Melissa? *I hope so,* thought one girl vindictively. Such were the rivalries in the class.

Paul found the barre routine and center practice exhilarating. He did the required movements easily and confidently. Those who could watch him admired his effortless control as he twisted his body and extended his sinewy limbs. One girl with long black hair tied in a single braid down her back lost her balance while staring at him and fell into the girl beside her, and they both tumbled to the floor to the laughter and hooting of their classmates.

"Irina!" yelled Kúbokoff, who had observed the reason for her fall. "Pay attention. Continue, one-two-t'ree-four. One-two..."

Her face reddened deeply as she regained her feet and took up the cadence.

Paul heard the commotion but had not seen what had caused it. He was glad for the diversion, conscious that everyone had been watching him.

Center practice was followed by the slow sustained adage movements, the pirouettes, and the fast allegro combinations of footwork and jumps. Then, while the girls practiced on full pointe, the boys worked on leaps, tours en l'air, and grands battements—the high kicks. But Paul, remembering Kúbokoff's admonition, kept his to "medium elevation."

As the drills became progressively more difficult, Paul began to discern the comparative skills of the members of the class. Most of the dancers were, to his surprise, a bit clumsy, though he would not have known that five months ago. Only two were advanced: one of the boys and Melissa. She showed great style and poise. However, he determined somewhat uneasily that none of them was at his level, and he silently thanked Kúbokoff for advising him to hold back.

A moment of tension arose for the whole class when it came time for partnering—the final exercise of the session. With only four boys in the group, eight of the girls would have to dance with each other. Four lucky ones would get male partners, and all eyes were on Paul. He felt like a piece of meat in a butcher shop. As if intentionally heightening the drama and suspense, Kúbokoff assigned partners to the other three boys first, leaving Paul last. Everyone held their breath, waiting for the final selection. Paul was delighted but not surprised when Kúbokoff chose his partner.

"Melissa," said the master, pointing his stick at her. "You vill dance vit' Paul."

A chorus of "aws" broke out among the remaining eight girls. Kúbokoff rapped his stick sharply. "Qvickly now. T'e rest of you choose your partners....Positions please...one-two-t'ree-four."

As the class commenced the exercise, Paul stood dumbly watching, not knowing what to do.

"Hold me, silly," said Melissa, taking his hands and placing them around her slim waist.

Paul saw what the other pairs were doing and copied them. Kúbokoff watched from the other side of the room and suppressed a smile at Paul's fumbling. *But not to worry,* thought Kúbokoff, *Melissa will teach him.*

Two afternoons each week Paul attended the group class. The other three days he practiced his positions at home after school and later had a private one-hour session with Kúbokoff at the studio. On Saturdays he worked with Melissa on a special routine they were preparing to perform in the show the class would put on at the end of summer. The routine was very demanding of both technical skills and artistry, and Kúbokoff coached them for about an hour each Saturday morning. The rest of the morning the two dancers were alone together in the studio. To Paul's annoyance Melissa was more interested in pursuing him than she was in perfecting their performance.

"Melissa," he snapped, "quit leaning on me. You're ruining the set."

"You don't like it when I rub against you?" she purred.

"I didn't say that. We have to practice and—"

"Then you do like it when I rub against you."

"Of course I like it. But we aren't—"

"Do you like it when I do this?" She ran her hand up the inside of his leg.

"Now stop that!" he scolded, grabbing her hand and backing away.

"Do you like it?" she teased, and in the same instant jerked her hand free and began to thrust it between his legs again.

Paul shoved her away violently with both hands, throwing her to the floor. "Not now, you jerk!"

Melissa lay on the floor dazed and shaken. "You didn't have to do that," she whimpered, rubbing an elbow with a pained expression.

"Yes, I did! I'm here to work on my dancing, not to fool around. Ballet is just a hobby with you. Something to kill time. For me it's my life!" He was shouting. "Do you understand that? My life!"

Paul gathered up his belongings and stalked toward the door. As he opened it, he stopped and looked back at Melissa, still sprawled on the floor. "If you want to change partners, I'll find someone else."

She lowered her head and pouted without replying.

"Well, do you or don't you?"

"I want to be your partner," she murmured.

"Then I'll see you here tomorrow morning at nine o'clock. We'll work till noon. And from now on keep your hot hands off me.

Understand?" He waited for a response.

She nodded dejectedly and watched him leave.

The next morning, and every time thereafter when they danced together, Melissa was all business, exhibiting the concentration and skills she had learned over years of ballet training. But her good behavior was motivated less by dedication to the art than fear of being publicly rejected by Paul, who was without question the premier dancer of the school and the idol of every girl there. For Melissa to be replaced as his partner was too humiliating a thought to even contemplate. There was, however, another motive. A motive she nourished with secret delight. For a brief moment on that Saturday morning he'd almost been hers. If she played along and waited for the right occasion, what might happen? In the meantime she would entice him subtlety, maintaining an outward composure that would make others believe that she and Paul were the closest of friends. No one must know of their tiff in the studio. And no one would.

Paul was unconcerned about Melissa's motives or the devious little games he knew she played. They were a nuisance, but as long as they didn't get in the way of his learning he would keep her as his partner. She was a fine dancer. His sole purpose in working with her was to learn the pas de deux and as many of its classical variations as he could. That was all that mattered.

His ballet training continued throughout the summer. Keeping it a secret from his father and sister was not difficult, because they were away from home most of the time. Valerie spent every day at the yacht club's swimming pool or sailing with her father when he was home from his business trips. Occasionally she accompanied him on these outings and returned with what Paul viewed as exaggerated tales of wanton life among the jet set. In any case his own life remained private, of no interest to either Valerie or his father, while his mastery of the art of ballet grew day by day, week by week, unaffected by events outside the ballet studio, the center and whole of his life.

He had become accustomed to the routine of his training and the

216

stability of the relationships he had with Kúbokoff and the dancers, particularly Melissa. He was therefore unprepared for what happened during the final rehearsal for the late summer show that Kúbokoff put on at a community theater to display his dancers' talents and encourage their parents to enroll them in the fall classes.

Paul and Melissa had finished their number and were standing together in the wings catching their breath while watching the next pair of dancers go on stage. They were pleased with their performance, he for the progress he'd made and she for her success in salvaging her relationship with him. He seemed to have put behind him the bad memory of that episode in the studio. He was kind to her, even protective, showing concern once when she twisted an ankle and again when she fell during a jump. It was only a matter of time, she was convinced, before she would win him over entirely. The cast party after the big show the next evening would be a perfect opportunity to make her move.

"I can't wait for tomorrow night," she told him.

"Me either. I'm really excited. It'll be my very first performance in front of an audience. My mother will be there, too. She's never seen me dance."

They continued to watch their classmates practice their routines.

"I think we make a nice pair, don't you?" she asked.

"I think so. Kúbokoff said our styles complement each other."

"Paul?" She rested her hand lightly on his arm. "I'll do my very best for you tomorrow night."

He turned, smiling, and absentmindedly patted her hand. "I will, too, Melissa. We'll blow 'em out of their seats."

"Thanks for being patient with me." She fluttered her eyelashes.

"Hey, no problem. You've been a trouper, and you taught me a lot."

Purposely turning her attention back to the stage, she casually linked her arm in his. "Aren't they doing well?" she said.

"They sure are."

Melissa silently gloried in her victory. She had played her cards perfectly. She and Paul were the star billing on the program, and now he was letting her get close to him by linking arms with her. She hoped others were watching. And tomorrow night she would be with him at the cast party. "Are you going to the party after the show tomorrow?" she asked, hiding her concern that he might not come.

"Of course. Wouldn't miss it. It's my debut, you know."

"We'll have so much fun."

Paul was about to agree when at that moment, for some reason he never comprehended, he swiveled his head far around to look behind Melissa at a line of dancers waiting to go on. At once his eyes fell upon the angelic face of a girl he'd seen countless times in class. She normally wore her long dark hair in a braid down her back, but tonight it was coiled neatly in a bun on the top of her head. Over the bun she wore a jeweled tiara that seemed to illuminate her large soft brown eyes—eyes that were looking straight into his. A sudden thrill shot through Paul's body as a sensation of discovery, recognition, and awakening passed between them, tingling his stomach. The girl instantly looked away, blushing. Paul was certain she had experienced the same feeling he had.

The pair dancing on stage finished, and the line of girls rustled past Paul in their white starched knee-length crinoline skirts and white stockings to take their places for the next number. He could not take his eyes off her. Her features were plain, yet she was the most beautiful girl he had ever seen. Why hadn't he noticed her beauty before?

He wanted her to look at him, but she kept her face averted, as if concentrating on the routine she was about to perform. *Look at me,* his mind commanded. *Look at me! You felt something as I did. I know it. I command you to look at me!*

To his shock and delight the girl tilted her head sideways and peeked at him shyly. He beamed a warm smile at her. Her head snapped down again, and her cheeks turned a brilliant red.

Paul laughed. "Who is that girl in the line with the red face?"

"Which one?" replied Melissa, looking.

"The...fifth from the left."

"Oh, that's Irina."

"Irina. Irina who?"

"I don't know her last name. She's very shy. I think she's Greek."

"You mean of Greek parents or herself from Greece?"

Melissa shrugged. "I really don't know. Does it matter?"

Paul looked at her strangely and was about to challenge her rudeness but decided to let it pass. No reason to spoil the evening. He was too thrilled about this Irina to care about Melissa.

Melissa bristled at Paul's sudden interest in this girl, but sensing his antagonism she quickly smiled to repair the damage. "Let's go see Kúbokoff and ask how we did," she said, tugging on his arm. He gave in, letting her lead him to the door to the seats out front where their teacher was directing the rehearsal. As Paul passed through the doorway he wheeled about and peered around the doorjamb. Irina had been watching him leave, and he caught her looking. He waved to her and smiled, and she again dropped her eyes, blushing, as Melissa pulled him away.

They seated themselves in the second row, behind Kúbokoff, and observed the girls' routine. As the stereo played a movement from Swan Lake, the dancers circled on their toes, swaying this way and that in ripple effect, forming chains and other familiar figures of a corps de ballet. Paul studied Irina closely and promptly concluded she was a mediocre dancer, a bit clumsy and stiff. He grinned at her awkwardness, which in his euphoric state only made her more attractive. She glowed with femininity, exuding a warmth and innocence that transfixed him. He was utterly, hopelessly, catastrophically in love.

When the routine was over, his impulse was to dash backstage and confront her, but he had to think of how Melissa would react. Her jealousy was already transparent. He had been aware all along that Melissa had designs on him and that she had been cunningly manipulating their relationship, or so she thought, to place him in a situation where she could seduce him. Clearly the cast party would be the opportune moment to hatch her little scheme.

But Paul had no desire to fulfill her aspirations. As he had made clear to her during the episode in the studio, ballet was his life and the sole reason for their being partners. And now that Irina had stolen his heart, pursuing intimacy with Melissa was the farthest thing from his thoughts.

He could not, however, pursue Irina and callously ignore Melissa's feelings. Melissa was his partner. "I'll do my very best for you," she had vowed. Now he must do the same for her. He owed it to her as much as to his development as a dancer. That must come first. Only when the next evening's performance was over would he be free to seek out Irina. In fact, prolonging his anticipation of that moment would make the encounter all the more satisfying. On the practical side, moreover, postponing their meeting was wise because Irina would preoccupy his thoughts, and he could ill afford to be distracted at this crucial time. He resolved therefore to put her out of his mind until after the show.

"Melissa?" he said, turning to her in the seat beside him.

She looked up at him adoringly. "Yes, Paul."

"Would you mind staying after rehearsal tonight to go through the routine a couple more times here on the stage? I want us to be perfect tomorrow."

"It's okay with me. Anything you say." She would walk on nails for him if he asked.

Her fawning behavior made him uneasy, but he purposely prolonged their conversation until he was sure that Irina had left the stage. He wanted Melissa to see that she held his undivided attention. Only the assurance that he would see Irina the next evening prevented his glancing at the stage for one more glimpse of her incredible beauty.

Melissa sat enraptured as Paul discussed their routine and reassured her how well it would go. He then took her hand and escorted her to the stage.

Kúbokoff saw them and called out, "Paul! Melissa! V'at are you doing?"

"We're going to practice the routine a little," Paul answered. "The opening's not quite right. It needs a little work."

"All right, and practice t'e first step. If you miss it...chort vozmi...t'e whole pas de deux is off, and you never catch up. But you practice only ten minutes. No more! Don't overdo it! Leave vell enough alone. And promise me no dancing tomorrow. Yes?"

"We promise," said Melissa.

"And something else. You don't see each o'ter tomorrow until t'e performance. Like bride and groom before t'e marriage. You relax. Vatch TV. Rest. No exercise. No see each other. T'en tomorrow night you vill be energized. At your peak. You vill see. Yes?"

"You got a deal," said Paul, nodding. "Right, Melissa?"

"Right," she said, thinking how apropos was Kúbokoff's analogy to a bride and groom. She would indeed make it a wedding night.

While Paul and Melissa practiced the opening of their routine, Kúbokoff, worn out by the day's exertions, trudged up the aisle and left

220

the empty auditorium—empty, that is, but for a lone figure wearing a tiara who stood behind a half-open door to the main foyer gazing dolefully at the splendidly synchronized pas de deux. Her heart grieved with envy for Melissa's talent as a dancer and for her role as Paul's partner. One could easily see the affection they held for each other in the intimacy of their interlocking movements. The way he held her. The way she looked at him. Irina could take no more. She closed the door and stood for several minutes staring forlornly at the aimless designs in the tile floor of the foyer, listening to the music from inside the auditorium. Then she shuffled to the main entrance and went outside, where her aunt was waiting in a car to drive her home.

The performance of Paul and Melissa was spellbinding and brought the audience to its feet with a roar, clamoring for an encore, which Kúbokoff strictly forbade as a matter of policy out of fairness to all the performers, as a footnote on the printed program indicated. The spectators, mostly parents and relatives, didn't care. They stomped, applauded, and shouted anyway, making the two dancers take two curtain calls. Some even threw flowers onto the stage.

Eleanor clapped her hands numb to the very last, weeping all the while. Not having seen Paul dance before, she was completely unprepared for his spectacular display of talent. She could not believe the transformation that had taken place in so short a time. With continued training how far might he go? The wonder of it was dizzying.

As soon as the final curtain closed, Eleanor went backstage and scrambled through the crowd to find Paul. Admiring parents and devotees of ballet thronged around him and his partner, clapping his back, shaking his hand, some just touching his arms reveling in the thrill of his presence. He spied his mother through the crowd and pushed his way to her, pulling Melissa behind him.

"Mother!" he called. "Did you like it? Was it okay?"

"Okay? Oh, Paul." She could find no words to express her feelings, so she flung her arms about him and wept again. Then, regaining her composure, she let loose of him and, wiping her eyes with a kerchief, turned to the girl. "This must be Melissa."

"Yes, ma'am," said Melissa formally, shaking hands and curtsying slightly as if in the presence of royalty. Eleanor's statuesque beauty had that effect on people.

"Forgive me, I'm such a cry baby. You've spent a great deal of time these past months with Paul. I see now why he's become so devoted to his training."

Paul squirmed inside at her suggestion, while Melissa blushed politely and leaned against him. To have her relationship with Paul acknowledged and even blessed by his mother was awesome.

"You're a very attractive girl," continued Eleanor to Paul's embarrassment, "and, I might add, a very excellent dancer."

"Not really, but thank you. Paul's the one with all the talent. He inspires all of us."

I'll bet he does, thought Eleanor, wondering if her son had succumbed to the sexuality of this shapely young woman.

"Are your parents here, Melissa? I'd like to meet them."

"No, they went to my little sister's piano recital tonight. They've seen me dance a hundred times. It's no big deal."

"I'm sorry I won't see them. Perhaps next time. Well, it was a wonderful program. Where's Mr. Kúbokoff? I want to meet him and tell him myself."

"Over there," replied Paul pointing. "By the lighting panel. Let me introduce you."

"No, sweetheart. That won't be necessary. You two go ahead and change for the cast party."

"You're coming, too, aren't you?" asked Paul with a frown. "All the parents are invited."

"Of course. I wouldn't miss it for the world. I'll drive myself. I want to commiserate with the other parents."

"Great!" Paul laughed. "And who do I commiserate with?"

"Oh, I think Melissa can handle that," his mother replied, winking.

Melissa gloried in the suggestive inference. Paul winced.

"How do I get to Mr. Kúbokoff's home?" asked Eleanor.

"His wife...the white-haired lady there standing next to him...she's

222

handing out maps."

"Good. I'll go meet her. I'll see you at the party."

"Okay," said Paul, kissing her cheek.

"And I loved your performance."

On their way to the dressing rooms Paul's eyes searched for Irina but did not spot her. He yearned to speak with her, if for no other reason than to hear her voice for the first time. Would it be weak and timorous? soft and feminine? shrill and grating? He grew anxious thinking about it, fearing that her personality would destroy the idealistic image her beauty had created in his mind.

"Are we driving together?"

"Huh?" grunted Paul. It was Melissa from the door to the girls' dressing room.

"Are you driving me to the party!"

"Uh...yeah...I suppose." He didn't know quite what to say. His mind was on Irina. "Sure. I guess so. I'll wait for you in the parking lot."

His lack of enthusiasm disquieted Melissa, but she brushed it aside and went in to shower, change, and prepare herself for her coming conquest. She would have him before the sun rose tomorrow. Envisioning Paul making love to her raised her adrenaline level to the point where her hands trembled so much she was unable to pencil her eyebrows without smearing the color. She sat back and closed her eyes, willing her body to relax. *Is this*, she thought, *how brides feel on their wedding night?*

She finally collected herself and finished primping. She had put on a provocatively low-cut, tight-fitting, black knee-length dress under which she wore no slip, only a lacy black bra and matching panties. Spraying on a touch of her favorite perfume and stepping into black high-heeled shoes, she hurried out to the parking lot. She knew Paul would be fretting over her tardiness, and she was right.

"What took you so long?" he said curtly from behind the wheel. But when she got into the car and sat down next to him, he saw how beautiful she looked and how alluring she smelled. "Hey! You look great!"

Melissa warmed to his reaction. "You look nice yourself."

He had put on a suit and tie in keeping with the customary formality of Kúbokoff's cast parties. They were special ceremonial occasions at which the master took great pleasure in honoring his students' accomplishments. It was a tradition he had learned in the former Soviet Union and that he perpetuated both to benefit his pupils and to preserve the fragile links to his cherished past.

"I'm sorry I kept you waiting," she said.

He started the engine, and the car pulled away.

"It's okay. Kúbokoff's is only ten minutes away. Anyway I was busy talking to a newswoman. She's a reporter or something from the *San Francisco Examiner.*"

"Is she writing an article about you?"

"No. Nothing like that. She comes to all of Kúbokoff's shows to spot new talent. Kind of like a scout for a professional football team."

"Who does she spot for?"

"The San Francisco Ballet Theatre."

"Wow!" Melissa shifted herself around to face him. "That's fantastic! Do you think you have a chance?"

"I dunno. You can't tell whether to believe these people or not. They probably say the same thing to every dancer. I know I'm good, but I'm not great, and you have to be super great to get into a top company like San Francisco."

"What did she say?"

"Oh, the usual stuff. You know. I have natural talent. With more training I could go far. Stuff like that."

"Did she say she'd recommend you to the Ballet?"

"Not in so many words."

"I bet she will. Really, Paul, you're a super dancer. You're way out of our league. The rest of us are amateurs. You're...you're phenomenal."

"Hey, let's not overdo it! You were great yourself tonight. You did everything perfectly."

"Thank you," she replied softly. "I did it for you."

The moment they entered Kúbokoff's house, crowded with performers and what seemed to be a large part of the audience, Paul broke away from Melissa on the excuse of finding them something to drink. Instead he went hunting for Irina. He plowed his way from room to room, upstairs and down, but she was nowhere to be found. Stopping a girl whom he had seen in the dance line with Irina, he asked if she knew whether Irina was coming to the party.

"No," she replied, shaking her head. "I don't think so."

Paul grappled with this bewildering and unwelcome information. Not here? Then he couldn't speak with her. He couldn't look at her beautiful face, look into her eyes, hold her hands or touch her, dance with her, and if the evening had gone as he fantasized it would, kiss her. He was shattered.

The girl to whom he was speaking noticed his troubled face. "Is there a problem?"

"Huh? Oh, no." He shrugged. "I just wanted to, uh...to talk with her." He fumbled to give a plausible explanation that would not reveal his true purpose. "Uh, I understand she's from Greece."

"Yes, she is."

"I...uh...wanted to talk with her about Greece. I've never been there. Was she born there?"

"Yes, she was. She's on a student visa."

Paul's interest in conversing with this girl quickly mushroomed. "Then you know her well?"

"Fairly well. We go to the same school."

"Great!" His enthusiasm overflowed.

"But I don't know anything about Greece," she said.

"Greece?"

"You said you wanted to talk to Irina about Greece."

"Yes, I did...and I do," he said, recovering. "It's a wonderful country. Does Irina talk about it much?"

"A little. She really wants to stay in this country. Her aunt, the woman she's living with, is working on it."

"Does her aunt live far from here?"

"I don't know where she lives."

"By the way, what's Irina's last name? I don't even know."

"Papagállou."

"Papagállou," he repeated. " Irina Papagállou. It sounds nice."

The girl laughed. "It sounds Greek to me."

"Yeah. Well, tell me more about her. Is she—"

"There you are!" cried a worried voice. "What happened to you? I've been looking everywhere." It was Melissa, a little wide-eyed and breathless. "You never came back. You were getting us something to drink."

"Sorry. I got sidetracked."

Melissa gave Irina's girlfriend a meaningless smile and grabbed hold of Paul's arm. "Come on. The food's in the dining room, and I'm famished, aren't you?"

"Yeah. See ya later," he said to the girl as he followed Melissa away. "Is my mother here yet? I haven't seen her."

"Yes. She just came in. I saw her in the living room talking to Kúbokoff."

They reached the buffet and began eating. Paul dug into the delicious food discovering he, too, was starved. Nevertheless, Irina's absence left him dispirited and robbed him of the enthusiasm he thought he would feel on this grand occasion. Melissa tried her best to liven him up, but as the evening wore on she became more and more disheartened and despaired of achieving her secret objective. She was angry at Paul's aloofness and the way he seemed to have withdrawn into himself. She finally gave up and flopped on a sofa in the living room where she pondered her next move. Paul meanwhile had found his mother and stayed close by her side both to introduce her to his ballet friends and to keep her company.

The party reached its climax when Kúbokoff summoned everyone to the large rec room in the basement where he would give out his awards—small trophies for the younger children and medals for the older—and make a speech.

When the last award from the card table before him had been presented and the applause subsided, the master went to a cabinet, withdrew a small flat box, and addressed his guests, his Russian accent somewhat thicker than usual from a combination of fatigue and a half dozen glasses of vodka.

"Everyvun of you dancers deserves praise for your hard vork t'is summer. I t'ank you all for t'at, and I hope all of you vill continue to study dance t'is fall and vinter...preferably vit me." He winked to a ripple of laughter. "But if not me, t'en someone inferior!" Now he led the laughter.

Then he turned serious. "T'ere is one among you, hovever, who vorked harder and longer t'an anyvun else. But he had reason to. He vas eighteen years old and had never had a ballet lesson in his life. V'at happened vas like a miracle. In nine months he learned v'at normally reqvires nine years. And tonight—" he recognized Paul with a motion of his outstretched hand—"you saw for yourselves how far he has advanced. V'at you saw, hovever, vas only a peek t'rough t'e vindow of his potential. He, of course, has much to learn and years of training ahead to learn it. Vet'er he vill do it, I cannot say. Only he and God know t'at. Maybe only God.

"So tonight t'e first chapter of his career comes to a sveet and triumphant end...just as it began. Eh, Paul? Vit' vun giant leap for mankind!" The eyes of the student and teacher connected briefly, sharing their private memory of Paul's first "leap through space" as Kúbokoff fondly called it. "I can say, as God is my vitness, t'at I have enjoyed every minute. If you, Paul, enjoyed every minute, t'en I didn't do my job."

The room reverberated with laughter and applause for both teacher and student.

"You did a *very good* job, Mr. Kúbokoff," said Paul, prompting more applause.

Kúbokoff opened the small box he was holding and withdrew a gold medal to the approving sighs of the onlookers. "Step over here, Paul."

Paul moved in front of the master.

"I vish to honor you tonight vit' t'is avard. On t'e front it has your name and t'e school and t'e date and all of t'at. Now let me read you t'e instruction...no, not instruction. V'at is it?"

"Inscription?" Paul suggested.

"T'at's it. Inscription on t'e back. It says 'T'is avard commemorates t'e end of t'e beginning. Good luck."

Applause rang out as Paul, embarrassed by this praise and attention, took the medal carefully from Kúbokoff and held it up for all to see. His discomfort was increased by his indifference to awards of this kind. To him they were meaningless. They were not the object or purpose of his dedication to ballet. Dancing itself was the reward, and attaining perfection in this most difficult and demanding of art forms.

As if reading his thoughts, Kúbokoff said, "I know you are not vorking so hard in ballet to receive medals. Dancing is in your blood and in your heart. Accept it t'en as a gift from your teacher and as a memoir of your time vit' me. I taught you as vell as I could. But I am old. You need

227

younger, stronger, tougher teachers t'an me to lead you up to t'e next..." He shook his head searching for the English word. "*Ploskogórye.*" He described two levels with his hands.

"Level? Plateau?" someone offered.

"Exactly. To t'e next plateau."

Paul frowned. "But I'm doing well enough with you." He wished he and Kúbokoff were alone. It was unfair of Kúbokoff to talk publicly of future plans, when they had not discussed them together in private.

"Ah, don't be upset, young man. I have a nice surprise for you. You have been accepted into t'e Montclair School of Ballet." The room echoed with sounds of approval. "For t'ose who don't know vat t'at is, let me explain. It is a special school here in San Francisco affil...affil...*chort vozmi...*"

"Affiliated," said Paul.

"Da, vit' t'e San Francisco Ballet T'eatre to develop t'e most promising dancers. It is, I believe, t'e finest school of its kind outside of Russia. Only my old school in St. Petersburg is better, eh?" He laughed. "But I vould never send you t'ere. They vould keep you for t'emselves."

Paul grinned as the packed room resounded again with laughter.

"Paul, I vill tell you all about t'e school later. It is a great honor for you and me, too, to have my student selected. I told t'em about you veeks ago, so t'ey sent t'ree delegates to observe you tonight. Von of t'em was t'e woman you spoke to. T'ere was no qvestion. T'ey saw you dance. T'at vas enough. T'ey told me aftervards t'ey can place you in t'eir September class."

"If you say so," Paul declared solemnly.

"I do. And I say somet'ing else. In Russia t'e student alvays addresses t'e teacher by last name: Gospodin Kúbokoff. Mister Kúbokoff. V'en student and teacher become good friends, teacher permits student to use first and second name. T'erefore, I vish to honor our friendship by permitting you to do t'e same. So, forever after, Paul, you may address me as Alexéi Nikoláyevich."

"Here, here," cried someone, and the crowd shouted its approval.

"So try it," urged Kúbokoff.

"Aléxi Nikoláyevich."

"No, no," the Russian groaned. "Alexéi Nikoláyevich. Alexéi

Nikoláyevich."

Paul tried again. "Alexéi Nikoláyevich."

"Forever after," uttered Kúbokoff emotionally and embraced his young protégé.

"Forever after," said Paul.

The next morning Paul awakened late, showered, gulped a quick donut with milk for breakfast, and raced to his car. His mind still churning with the excitement of the performance, his award, Alexéi Nikoláyevich's announcement of Paul's acceptance to the Montclair School, and, oh, yes, Melissa's outrage when at the end of the party she lured him to an upstairs bedroom and disrobed in a last desperate bid to seduce him. He called her pathetic and walked out, leaving her standing nude in the middle of the room, shouting obscenities and accusing him of being a fag. Case closed!

So much was happening so quickly, and on top of it all was his powerful yearning to meet Irina Papagállou. He said her name over and over, loving the sound and rhythm of it. He could not live another day without speaking to her, without hearing her voice or seeing her face. No one at the party knew her phone number or where she lived. She was a quiet, somewhat reclusive person, they said, staying pretty much to herself. But Alexéi Nikoláyevich saved the day. He said Paul could find Irina's number in the studio office. All of the students' names, phone numbers, and addresses were posted on a wall there. He told Paul the studio would be closed the next day, but that Paul could find the key in the mailbox as usual and to leave it there when he left.

Paul drove directly from his house to the studio, parked his car, vaulted up the few steps to the entrance, opened the mailbox, and found the key. He unlocked the door, threw it open, and bounded into Kúbokoff's— Alexéi Nikoláyevich's —office. The list was posted there as promised. Paul grabbed up a pencil and paper from the desk and hurriedly jotted down the vital information. He spun around to the desk and picked up the telephone, which he stupidly misdialed twice in his exuberance. He tried to calm down, but he was too worked up. With slow deliberate

229

motions he carefully redialed and waited...waited an eternity for the clicks and tones that would magically find Irina's home somewhere out there in San Francisco and form the electronic linkages to connect him with her voice.

A distant buzzing sounded in the receiver which, pressed hard against his ear, picked up the thumping of his pulse that beat out of time with the ringing of Irina's phone.

"Hello." It was an older woman's voice.

"Yes. Is Irina there?"

"No, she isn't. May I ask who is calling?"

Disappointment crushed his spirit. "This is Paul Stowolski. I'm in her ballet class. I...I wanted to speak with her if I could."

"Yes, I remember you. I was there last night when you danced. You were wonderful, truly wonderful."

"Thank you very much. Do you know when Irina will be back?"

"Oh, I don't know. Her aunt drove her to the dance studio to pick up her things."

"The studio?"

"Yes. Is there a problem?"

"Well, no," said Paul, both excited and troubled. "I'm at the studio, and she's not here. Did I miss her?"

"No, no. They left only a few minutes ago."

"Oh, I see." He slid down to the floor, his back against the side of the desk and, closing his eyes, heaved a great sigh of relief and exultation. At last! He would meet her, and they would talk, and..."

"Hello?" hailed the woman.

"Yes, ma'am. I'll wait for her here then."

"Very good, and good luck with your dancing. We very much enjoyed your performance."

"Thank you."

"Good-bye."

He paced about the studio nervously from wall to wall, watching through the windows for an approaching car. He had not thought to ask the woman how long it would take them to reach the studio or even if they were coming directly. Perhaps they would go somewhere else first. They might even...

230

He froze. A car had entered the parking lot. It carried two people—two women—and was heading for the entrance. He unconsciously stepped away from the window so as not to be seen. As the car drew nearer, he recognized Irina seated next to the driver, a woman in her forties.

The car stopped, motor idling, while Irina, beautiful as ever, got out and walked up the steps to the mailbox, her long braid of black hair flopping back and forth on her back. She looked fetching in her blue jeans, a pretty pink sweatshirt, white socks, and loafers. He presumed...he hoped...that her personality would be as unpretentious and unaffected as her attire. Certainly the black pigtail spoke for her consistency. He wondered, with a skip of his heartbeat, what she would look like if she unfurled her hair and let her shimmering tresses fall freely upon her shoulders.

She groped inside the mailbox, and her confused look showed she could not find the key. Turning back to the car, she made a quizzical gesture with her head and shoulders, then tried the studio door, which opened at the turn of the knob.

Paul swallowed in a sudden panic as to what he would say to her.

She put her head inside, squinting into the dark interior waiting for her eyes to adjust. "Is anyone here?" she called out with a slight Greek accent.

"Yes," croaked Paul. "I'm here."

"Who is it?" she asked apprehensively, not moving.

"It's me. Paul Stowolski."

"Oh!" A look of shock and embarrassment flashed across her radiant face, which she immediately averted, uncertain what to do.

"Come on in," said Paul hoarsely, trying to reassure her. "It's all right. I need to pick up a few things."

"Me too," she said barely above a whisper.

Paul thrilled at the delicate feminine texture of her voice.

In a quandary she waved uncertainly to her aunt, who returned the signal and drove off. "She has errands to run," Irina explained, still half in and half out the doorway.

"You can come in then." Paul smiled and began to feel more relaxed and in control. Her hesitation pleased and amused him. She was endearingly shy.

"I'll only be a minute," she said.

"Was that your aunt?"

"Yes." She was still rooted to the doorsill.

"Irina, for heaven's sake, come in! I won't bite. We've danced in the same class and in this same room for months!"

She hesitated, but the sensibility of his statement and the foolishness of her behavior resolved her ambivalence. She stepped inside and shut the door behind her, pressing her back against it.

"What are you afraid of?" he asked. "Me?"

"No," she replied, her eyes lowered avoiding his. "Not that. I...just feel funny."

"Can't you look at me?"

She blushed as she had on stage two nights before.

She's so adorable, thought Paul. "Please try," he said sincerely.

With great effort her eyes edged up ever so slowly until they met and held his.

Then time stopped.

Her beauty was more entrancing than Paul had remembered. Innocence and sweetness, purity and kindness, these were what he beheld. The long slender nose, full wide lips, dainty pointed chin, high cheeks, dark eyebrows, incredibly feathery eyelashes that veiled soft glowing brown eyes which in these timeless seconds stole whatever was left of his heart, leaving only a hollow aching shell.

Irina had studied Paul's face so many times from different angles during every class in the studio during the past months that she could envision his looks in her sleep. But she had never stood so close to him before and never had shared a moment like this with him...or anyone else. She was mesmerized. He was more strikingly handsome than she remembered, and his expression...he was looking at her with what...could it be adoration? Did she dare believe that what she saw in his piercing eyes was love? It could not be. She had seen that look or something like it when he danced with Melissa. Melissa was his constant companion and girlfriend.

Oh, God, Irina prayed, *tell me that look is for me! Make it true! Make it happen! I beg you.* She longed to be held in his arms, to feel their protective power around her, to feel his muscled body pressed warmly comfortably against hers.

Paul broke the spell, unable to withstand the tension of being so near her and not link his arms around her. "I missed you at the party."

"I didn't go," she said, swallowing and blinking, still unable to believe this was happening.

"I know. I looked for you everywhere. I went into every room to find you."

"Why?"

"To talk to you."

"About what?"

"About everything! About ballet and school and you...and me. Who we are and what we want to become."

"I'd like that." Her gentle voice masked the pleading in her heart.

"You would, really?"

The quickness and uncertainty of his question encouraged her.

"Yes. Unless...you're busy...with...other things."

Paul's unerring intuition told him at once she was referring to Melissa. "You mean my partner, Melissa."

"No, not her."

"Yes, her! I'm sure of it. You think Melissa and I are going steady and that...we're lovers. Let me clear that up. Kúbokoff had Melissa and me dance together because she was the best girl dancer in the class. No other reason. I don't even like her. She's a...well...I'd rather not say. I have no interest in her and never did. She isn't my type."

"I believe you," said Irina softly.

"We never dated. We have nothing in common. She's undisciplined and flaky. She has no ambition. Ballet for her is just a hobby." He was waving his hands to underscore his statements.

"I believe you." A bit louder.

"If our dancing together gave you the impression that..."

Paul stopped talking. Irina was grinning broadly at him.

"I think I get the picture," she said, feeling light-headed, knowing Paul was available and pursuing her. Her! Irina!

"What about you?" Paul challenged, recovering from his outburst. "You must be pretty busy yourself."

"Yes, I am," she said with exaggerated seriousness. "Out every night. Unending phone calls from admirers. Flowers and candy constantly. Never a moment to myself."

Being unfamiliar with her playful sense of humor, Paul gullibly swallowed every word and was dismayed. He should have known he was only one of dozens of guys swept away by her beauty. How could he have been so arrogant to believe she would not be involved with someone? Of course, she was. And yet...his intuition was sounding alarms...the way she had looked at him so shyly, blushing and avoiding his eyes. It didn't add up. Then it dawned.

"You're pulling my leg!"

She grinned and closed her eyes, bowing slightly to affirm his observation.

He shook a finger at her. "You know what happens to young ladies who tell fibs?"

She threw back her head and laughed merrily, releasing all of the pent-up tension and anxiety that had beset her for the past several weeks as her attraction to Paul had become mournful infatuation and now she was sure of it...love. He was easy to talk to. So open and sincere. So darling. *Thank You, God*, she thought, *for answering my prayer*. Her face came alive with merriment and coyness. "No. What happens to young girls who tell fibs?"

"I kill them with my bare hands!" He made a snarling face and curled his fingers menacingly.

"I thought you said I shouldn't be afraid of you."

He dropped the play-acting at once. "You shouldn't be. And you shouldn't play tricks on new friends."

"Why not?"

"It isn't fair."

"*Ola epitrepondai stin agapi kai ton polemo*," she said, enjoying his puzzled expression.

"Is that Greek?"

"Yes."

"What does it mean?"

"All's fair in love and war."

He feigned concern. "Are we at war?"

234

"Of course, not," she gaily replied, her graceful features aglow with happiness.

"Then what are we?"

The answer hit them both simultaneously. They were joyously in love.

SIXTEEN

Love takes root in different ways too numerous to count, and neither Paul nor Irina were of a mind to seek explanations. New love is its own reward and confirmation. It requires no rationale or justification, only recognition and nourishment as a seedling needs sun and rain and rich terrene in which to grow. They knew at once that their budding romance was a frail reed whose vitality could be crushed by carelessness or abuse or, worse, starved by indifference. They cherished it as a precious gift that answered the heartfelt prayers they each had made before this shining moment, expecting the worst while hoping for that miracle, that mysterious mutual attraction that eludes so many broken hearts and lonely souls.

And the miracle happened.

They felt wonderfully calmly secure in the durability of their new relationship. Again they did not need reasons. It was something they both felt without questioning the other, and it gave them time to patiently reinforce the thin but sturdy lines of attraction that had brought them together. No imperative moved them to rush hastily ahead, as so many lovers do, to savor the carnal pleasures of romance. They knew that those pleasures would be theirs in time as surely as the greening of spring follows the colorless desolation of winter. If their love was to last and flourish, it needed that rich loam of understanding and sharing in which to spread its delicate roots and build a rugged foundation that could withstand the winds and storms that life and human nature unleash against lovers.

For the remainder of that wondrous morning in Kúbokoff's studio where Paul had discovered months earlier his destiny as a dancer and now the girl he would love the rest of his life, they talked. Her aunt came and

236

left, assured that Paul would bring Irina home later. And they talked some more.

Paul recounted his family's history, his difficult relationship with his father, and how he had more or less stumbled into ballet, unaware until he made that first great leap in that very room that dancing would be his life.

Irina told him how her American-born mother had passed away when Irina was ten years old and how, when her father had died in Athens two years ago, she was alone. Although relatives in Greece generously offered to take care of her, her father's sister, a U.S. citizen living in San Francisco, invited her to come there on a student visa to complete her education. Irina jumped at the invitation because she spoke English fluently and wanted to see America. She also was fond of her aunt, who had visited Greece many times.

Irina explained that she led a quiet life centered around her academic studies and ballet. She rarely dated and, until Paul joined the class, she had no interest in boys or romance. But when Paul began attending ballet classes regularly, they became the focus of her life, where she could see him, watch him dance, and be near him—at least in the same room. She never approached him or had the nerve to speak to him. It mattered not that he was unaware of her infatuation, for she never dreamed that he would develop an interest in her. She was, she believed, quite plain and not a good dancer, which she presumed put her out of Paul's league. She could never compete with the likes of Melissa.

But that was yesterday.

She grinned sheepishly at him. "I used to watch every move you and Melissa made when you danced together. I knew every step of your routine. Oh, I envied her so, but I knew I wasn't good enough to be your partner. I'm still not, and I never will be, but it doesn't matter now."

"What are you talking about? We can dance together. Maybe not in performance, but I'd dance with you any time."

"Oh, come on, Paul. You're trying to be gallant. It's so like you."

"Look, I'm not trying to be anything but honest. You don't believe me?"

"I believe you're a gentleman."

"Then get your stuff on!" he said, getting up from the floor where they had been sitting for the past several hours.

"Now?"

"Why not?"

"But…"

"Let's go!"

He took her hand and pulled her to her feet, but he did not let go. It was the first time they had touched one another, and the contact of their flesh set off a wild interaction of electric emotions between them. They stood staring silently into each other's eyes for several long seconds before Paul pulled himself away.

"Do you know the pas de deux I danced with Melissa?"

"Of course."

"Good. We'll do it then. See you in two minutes." He dashed to the boys' dressing closet to change.

Minutes later, dressed in dancing togs, they stretched their limbs on the barre and shared amusing anecdotes about the different dancing styles of the members of the class, hiding from each other their mounting excitement as the moment neared when their bodies would touch. They drilled several minutes on plies, battements, and poses in arrondie and allongee. Finally, warmed and limber, they were ready to dance. Paul switched on the sound system, found the compact disk with the music for the routine he and Melissa had performed, and inserted it into the stereo.

Irina laughed heartily, shaking her head. "I can't do this!"

"If you don't," he warned with a heavy Russian accent, "I vill exile you to t'e coldest gulag in Siberia!"

He pressed the PLAY button and sprinted eagerly to the center of the floor to join Irina in the opening position. The music sounded and the five-minute pas de deux began.

They wheeled and stepped and turned around and around the floor, a yard apart at first, mirroring each other's movements, then drawing closer. He placed his hands about her waist and lifted her in a petit temps saute and twist which brought them close face-to-face for a split second. Steadied by his hands, she twirled on one toe and darted away. In and out of his arms she flew, tempting him, then fleeing.

She was, as they both understood, not a talented dancer. Her movements were stiff and choppy, and her positions lacked finesse and

238

precision, but neither of them cared. They were not performing. They were dancing, for the sheer pleasure of each other's company and, there was no denying it, for the physical intimacy of their bodily contact.

As the music crescendoed to a finale, she made a last pirouette and came to rest beside him, his arm about her waist, both of them in symmetrical fifth position en face toward an invisible audience. The music ended. They stood motionless and silent, side by side, breathing heavily, looking straight ahead.

Irina spoke first between breaths. "This is the happiest...I have ever been in my life."

"Me, too."

They still did not look at each other, neither wanting the magic of the moment to end. Paul was adrift on a cloud. He smelled the sweet perfume of her perspiration and felt the soft supple flesh of her waist beneath her blouse. "I have to tell you something," he said.

"Yes?" Her eyes shifted nervously.

"I'm madly in love with you. I know it's crazy. We don't know each other well enough for me to say that, but it's what I feel."

"I love you, too, Paul, with all my heart."

"How can we say this when we haven't even kissed yet?"

"Do you want to kiss me?" she asked demurely, her cheeks reddening.

"Of course, I do. Do you?"

"What if we do it wrong?" she replied in all seriousness.

Paul burst out laughing and turned her toward him with his arm so he could look into her eyes. "Then, Irina from Greece, we'll practice until we get it right."

She laughed at him. Then he took hold of her chin and guided her lips gently to his. They closed their eyes and kissed tenderly, without passion, for several seconds.

They parted slowly and Irina, trembling, quavered, "Was that good enough for lovers?"

"I think so. Have you ever been kissed before?"

"Once a couple of years ago. Like I said, I don't go out very much. Should we practice?"

Paul could feel the sexual tension building. But making love with

Irina now was unthinkable. It would ruin everything. It would cheapen their love and might even destroy it before it had a chance to mature. No, as much as he wanted to, he would not. Their relationship was worth far more.

"No, Irina. Let's not practice."

"Why not?"

"I love you too much. Things are moving way too fast. I don't think I can control myself."

"Oh." She half frowned. "You mean about sex."

"Yeah. My libido is off the scale."

"Mine, too."

"We better cool it before we do something we'll regret. How about a hamburger? Are you hungry?"

"I haven't eaten all day," she replied.

"Then let's go." He started to pull away.

"Wait!" She held on to his arms.

"What is it?"

"Just one more practice?"

Her beauty demolished his resistance. "I guess I can handle that."

They kissed again, as gently as before but longer.

"Now I know we gotta go!" he said. And they parted.

Their relationship evolved at a leisure but steady pace they both could control. The love they shared was so powerful that they feared, if it were not kept under tight rein, it would carry them away, upsetting their lives and handing their future over to the whims and wiles of chance. Love was never more favored by sensibility.

They were inseparable for the next several weeks before they entered college. She would attend the City College of San Francisco to seek a business degree, while Paul, with his mother's blessing, would major in dance at the California School of Fine Arts a few miles from the City College. His father, who was on an extended business trip to New York, would be furious when he returned and learned that Paul had withdrawn

240

his application from the University of Southern California, but it was Paul's education and Paul's decision. His father would just have to come to terms with it. It was that simple, at least in Paul's mind.

Paul was young and determined and had been taught by his mother to believe that true happiness and self-fulfillment can be found only by following one's heart. "It won't lie to you," she had told him when he was fifteen and struggling over a relationship with a friend at school who used drugs. "Your heart never lies if you listen to it carefully and honestly, for God is in your heart and He speaks to you through it."

"How will I know if it's God talking and not just me talking to myself?"

"All I can tell you," she said, "is that if you're honest with yourself, you'll know."

So Paul had listened to his heart and had decided to go against his father's wishes, giving up a career in the business world and rejecting his father's plan that he succeed him as head of DESIGN METAPHORS.

For now, however, the implications of his decision were far from his mind, which was preoccupied with his dear Irina. As the summer drew to a close, Paul picked her up at her home each morning and drove to a waffle house where they sat in their favorite booth and ate sinfully delicious blueberry pancakes for breakfast. And they talked. About Greece and America and ballet. About their future. About their love. After breakfast they walked hand in hand beside a creek, through a park, along the streets, and in the stores. The more they talked, the more congruence they discovered in their attitudes, living patterns, and life goals. And their love grew. They spent every waking hour of each day together, often doing nothing more than lying on the lawn of Paul's home watching the sky and the clouds and the birds. They talked of their class schedules in the coming year and planned when they would see one another each week. Because the Montclair School was affiliated with the San Francisco Ballet, the California School of Fine Arts would credit the Montclair classes toward his degree and exempt the dance classes he would otherwise have been required to take. It was a perfect arrangement but not unexpected, since everything in his life seemed to be falling into place. The future indeed could not have looked more promising.

Paul met Irina's aunt and her aunt's widowed mother-in-law, with whom he had spoken that first time when he phoned Irina. Paul introduced Irina to his mother, who was impressed and pleased with Paul's taste. Even though he professed to his mother that he would never love any other girl and would one day marry Irina, Eleanor remained reservedly skeptical. He was only eighteen and she was certain, notwithstanding his devout pledge, that with his good looks there would be dozens of other Irina's in his life and that one of them, to be sure, would become his wife.

Irina's introduction to Valerie in the Stowolskis' living room was more eventful, for it revealed to Valerie the secret of Paul's ballet training.

"You met each other in a ballet class?" Valerie exclaimed. "Ballet? Mother, do you know what he's talking about?"

Eleanor smiled reassuringly. "Of course I do. Paul's been studying ballet for the past ten months."

"Ballet?" Valerie made a gruesome face. "Ten months? I can't believe what I'm hearing. No offense, Irina, but I can't see my brother running around a stage in tights like a...well, you know."

"Valerie," said Eleanor patiently. "The issue is not whether homosexuals are dancers. That seems to be all that you and your father are concerned about. Yes, some dancers are gay. But there are homosexuals in every profession, even the most masculine of sports like professional football. What is important is Paul's doing in life what most satisfies him. God gave him enormous talent for dancing and that is what Paul is dedicating himself to doing. If you had seen him dance, you'd understand."

"You have?"

"Yes. A couple of weeks ago. He was absolutely magnificent."

"Then you approved of it from the beginning even though Daddy forbid it?"

"Certainly. With all my heart. I don't do everything your father tells me to. And you don't either."

Valerie shook her head in disbelief at her mother's blatant role in this conspiracy against her father. "Daddy will go bananas when he finds out. I hope I'm not around when he does."

"As I've said from the start," Paul retorted, "I'll face that when it happens. Are you going to tell him?"

242

"Not me, Paul! This is between you and him. I'm not involved, and I'm not getting involved. Personally, I think you're crazy." Then she smiled. "But I do like you, Irina, so I suppose ballet can't be all that bad."

When Eleanor left the room to check on the food cooking in the kitchen, Valerie whispered to Paul, "What does Mother say about it? Doesn't she know Daddy will go into a rage?"

"Yes, we've talked about it," he replied. "And she feels like I do. Dad's prejudice against ballet is as stupid and irrational as any other prejudice. I can't change what I am. I was born to dance. Mother understands that, and she's promised to back me up no matter what Dad thinks. What does she owe him anyway?"

Valerie was more acutely aware than Paul of their father's infidelities, having observed him firsthand at the club playing up to the ladies when he thought he was being discreet. Valerie missed very little and more than once detected the knowing intimate looks he exchanged with women. Although his behavior made her uncomfortable, she figured it was none of her business, just another aspect of the estrangement between her parents, which was something she had never understood.

"Some parents," she said, "just don't get along. I don't know why they stay married."

"For us, I presume," answered Paul.

"Yeah," Valerie replied, turning wistful. "I suppose."

The discussion of Paul's situation continued through dinner, in Irina's presence, and the conclusion was reached unanimously that the time had come to confront his father, however painful that would be for everyone. Despite her earlier remark about not wanting to be around when it happened, Valerie pluckily vowed to be present to lend support to Paul if he needed it. She loved him very much and would stand by him to defend his right to pursue his dream as she would want him to defend hers. It was a touching moment when the two embraced, bearing witness to the close bond they discovered existed between them despite the distance that had separated them through adolescence.

It was agreed then that, when their father returned in three days from his New York trip, they would sit down with him as a family and appeal for his understanding and support of Paul. That the secrecy of Paul's dancing would finally come to an end and with it the tensions of the past ten months was a great relief to both Eleanor and Paul. They had infused their discussion with an uplifting air of optimism. When the evening concluded, they all hugged one another, including Irina, and reassured themselves that everything would work out all right.

The next day Paul remained at home, as Irina was busy shopping with her aunt for new clothes for school and running errands, among which was a visit to the Immigration and Naturalization Service. When she returned home she would phone him to plan their evening. Meanwhile, he took advantage of the free time to practice ballet on the flat putting-green surface of the rear lawn to the music of a stereo CD player he brought outside. His mother, who never tired of watching him practice, looked out at him contentedly off and on from a window in the kitchen while she prepared the evening meal. Neither she nor Paul was worried that his father would walk in unexpectedly. He had phoned the night before from New York to say he would stop off in Chicago to attend an exhibitors' convention. They were unaware, however, that a blizzard had closed O'Hare field in Chicago, and that his father had flown directly to San Francisco. Eleanor, busy at her work, did not catch sight of Brock's car coming up the driveway until it reached the curve heading to the garage behind the house.

"Oh no! Please no!"

She dropped a cake pan on the floor with a clatter and rushed through the family room to the door that opened onto the patio above the yard where Paul was dancing. He would not hear the car's approach above the music blaring from the stereo. She dashed across the patio to the stone ledge to warn him. Too late!

The car was stopped in front of the open garage. Brock was behind the wheel, his head turned toward the lawn, his mouth agape, his face a portrait of bewilderment as his eyes followed Paul's smooth precise sweeping movements. Paul, lost in concentration on his technique, did not see him. Eleanor stood as a horrified spectator watching helplessly as the ominous scene unfolded below her.

244

Brock shut off the engine, got out of the car, and walked as if in a trance to the edge of the lawn where he stopped, feet apart, arms crossed, spellbound by the magnificence of Paul's leaps and turns. These were not the crude movements learned by football players at once-a-week frolics in a ballet school. Nor were they the childish play of an amateur. No, concluded Brock indignantly, these were the moves of a highly trained artist. Brock had a sense for artistry, whatever the art form, and a sharp discerning eye for talent. That eye instantly told him that Paul was not merely talented but gifted. Brilliantly gifted. Outrageously gifted! His son had defied him!

Brock felt a presence to his left and looked up. It was Eleanor, leaning over the patio ledge watching him. His eyes blazed with fury as he mouthed one word for her to read on his contorted lips. "You!"

"Please, Brock!" she cried, squeezing her fingers tightly into fists. "Try to understand!" But her voice could not penetrate the curtain of loud music.

"How could you!" he said to her. Then he screamed at Paul above the music. "Hey! Hey, you! Fag!"

The shouts broke through Paul's concentration, and he brought his movements to an abrupt controlled stop. He looked serenely at his father without speaking or making any sign of acknowledgment.

"What are you up to?" shouted Brock.

Paul, dressed in tight-fitting gray sweats, took several stiff-legged, even, heel-toe walk steps to the CD player and calmly shut off the music. "Excuse me?" he said innocently, rooting himself in the bras pas position, heels and knees together, toes spread wide apart, arms curved slightly at his sides, hands half-opened resting gently on his thighs. It was a daring premeditated pose of defiance.

Brock shook with rage, which was no more than Paul had expected when over the past months he imagined how this showdown would play out. "You've been taking lessons, haven't you?"

"Yes, I have. Every week for the past year."

"In spite of my orders!"

"Yes, sir. Most assuredly in spite of your orders."

"Why? What possessed you?"

"I love ballet. It's all I live for. I'm dedicating my life to it."

"Madness! Sheer mindless madness!" howled Brock. "No son of mine will ever, ever be a dandified ballet dancer! You understand that?"

"I was born to dance."

"You were born to be a man, to succeed me as head of D-M enterprises, to *be* someone!"

"I *will* be someone. I'll be one of the greatest dancers in the history of ballet."

"You're just a boy. You don't know what you're talking about."

"I'm training with the Montclair School of Ballet."

"Is that a news bulletin?"

"It's important."

"Funny, I didn't read about it on the front page."

"It's a great honor. Some of the finest dancers in the United States study there."

"And you're one of those finest, I suppose."

"They tell me I am."

Brock knew it was true from what he had just observed of his son's talent, but a career in ballet was unthinkable for Paul. There was so much more to life than prancing about a stage. Then a thought occurred. "Are you gay?"

Paul laughed. "That's really what's bugging you, isn't it, Dad? Afraid it will hurt your image with the ladies? Father of a fag?"

"Don't be insolent!"

"Well, you can relax. I'm not gay. I'm as sexually masculine as you are, which puts me in the top percentile, wouldn't you say?"

Brock disdained the slur. "Then all the more reason for me not to let you do something crazy that will hurt you in the long run. Who's been paying for all of this anyway? I assume it wasn't free."

"I have!" declared Eleanor from the patio above.

"That figures," said Brock scornfully. He looked up. "Trying to get even with me, Ellie? Is that what this is all about?"

"No, Brock, I'm not getting even with anybody. I'm doing what's best for Paul."

"No more you aren't! I control the money in this family and as of this moment not another cent goes for ballet lessons or anything connected with ballet." Then the larger meaning of Paul's declaration about ballet

246

being his life became clear. "You aren't going to USC to study business as we agreed, are you?"

"No, I'm not. I'm going to the California School of Fine Arts to major in dance."

"I'm not paying for that kind of education! If you want that, you can pay for it yourself. From now on, my accountant will approve and audit every expenditure you or your mother make with my money. But I won't stop there, buddy boy." He directed a finger at his son. "I'm going to fight you all the way on this. All the way! I'll use every ploy, every power, every weapon at my disposal to protect you from this...this disease! I'm going to stop you, Paul. Stop you cold! You'll learn soon enough you can't defy me."

"I *will* defy you!" Paul shouted.

"No, you won't," cut in Eleanor. "We will together!"

"Shut up, Ellie!"

"No, Dad! *You* shut up!" screamed Paul, and years of angry suppressed resentment spilled out. "You can take your loathsome whores and go straight to where people like you belong!"

"I see," said Brock, nodding as he looked back and forth between his wife and his son. "Where's Valerie?"

"At the club," replied Paul.

"Did she have any part in all of this?"

"No, she knew nothing. She learned about it only last night."

"I didn't think so."

Brock reexamined their faces. He saw hate and defiance there...and alliance. They were teamed against him. It was a murderous blow to his ego and pride. He had provided them a good life, all the necessities and then some. They wanted for nothing. And this was the thanks he got. Contempt and disobedience...and conspiracy. He might have expected it from Ellie, given their problems in the past, but it came hard from Paul, who was Brock's hope for the future of D-M. So, the boy would have to learn—Ellie relearn—that they could not trifle with him. "I see I'm not welcome here anymore," he said, more to himself than the others.

Eleanor's stomach knotted in apprehension that the turning point she had feared if Brock learned of Paul's ballet had come, and she quickly invoked a counterploy. "You have always been welcome," she pleaded, "and you always will be."

"Not on these terms...under these circumstances. You two violated the contract."

"What contract?" asked Paul.

"The unspoken unwritten contract in every family. The contract of mutual trust."

"You're joking!" scoffed Paul. "How can you speak of trust in front of Mother, whom you've cheated on for years?"

"Paul, please," implored Eleanor, afraid that her son's anger would worsen the predicament she saw threatening him. "The relationship between your father and me is of no concern here."

"It's of concern to me!" shouted Brock. "Or should I say it *was* of concern. This...this ballet thing changes everything. Changes them fundamentally." He dropped his head and shoulders as if surrendering to some difficult decision. "I'm leaving. But I'll tell you this, Paul." His eyes flared ominously. "Your ballet days are over!"

He returned to his car and drove away, while Paul and his mother watched in silence, numbed by the horrible finality of Brock's last words, which echoed in Paul's mind like a death knell.

"It's getting dark, Paul," said Eleanor sadly. "Come inside." She sighed. "We have much to talk about."

"What did he mean?" Paul asked minutes later as he set down the stereo on the kitchen floor. "He can't really stop me from dancing, can he?"

"Paul, sit down. Let's talk."

They took seats on opposite sides of the kitchen table. Paul leaned forward anxiously to receive his mother's encouragement and counsel. She was visibly shaken and needed consoling and support at this moment as much as he did.

"Things did not go as I hoped they would," she said. The corners of her mouth quivered, and Paul realized she was fighting back tears. It disturbed him and made the situation even more upsetting and uncertain. "I had always planned that, when the time was right, we would tell your father about your interest in ballet. Last night we agreed we would do it tactfully and calmly in a way that would allow him to understand your position before emotions interfered. Unfortunately that's not how it played out."

"I thought," said Paul, "that once he saw me dance, he'd understand. But he didn't. He's so unreasonable. Why does he hate me so much?"

"Oh, Paul, dearest, he doesn't hate you. I promise you that. Don't feel that way. Your father is a self-centered ambitious man. He's just transferred his ambition to you, that's all. He wants and expects you to share his dreams. Your passion for ballet is so alien to his thinking, and it clashes head-on with the plans he's made for you. Don't you see?"

"I suppose." Paul was not convinced. "So what happens now? I'm not going to stop dancing just because he doesn't like it. I couldn't."

"Of course not." But the distress in her eyes belied the comfort in her words.

"There's a problem though, isn't there? It's money."

Eleanor nodded.

"I won't be able to afford Montclair or the California School," he said.

"You'll be okay for the rest of this term. I paid in advance."

"And then what happens?"

"I don't know, son. Your father can be very determined. He'll nail down every dollar we have. He's extremely thorough, as you know, and he won't miss a trick. I have only a few thousand dollars of my own, but there are friends we can go to for help. Kelly and Helena will certainly lend us the money."

"No," said Paul emphatically. "I don't want them to know. I don't want anyone to know. This is a private family matter. Maybe after awhile Dad will change his mind."

"Don't expect that, Paul. I know your father too well. When he said he would fight you all the way on this thing, it means he won't rest until he wins...until you quit ballet. He'll never change his mind. Take my word for it. I've lived with him for nearly twenty years. I know."

"There's no way he can make me quit!"

"I pray to God you're right. And yet your father can be so...so fanatically ruthless and insensitive. I've never seen him so angry. Once he's set his mind on something, God Himself couldn't dissuade him."

"Look, Mother, I'm not giving up ballet no matter what he does. He can cut off the money if he wants to."

"He will. In fact, he's probably already used his cell phone to call his finance officer and give him instructions. By tomorrow morning we'll be on money rations."

"Not me. I'm gonna get a job so I can pay for my schooling myself."

"Paul, how can you do that? You don't have any free time as it is."

"I'll find a way. I have no choice. The combined tuition for Montclair and the Fine Arts School is nine thousand a semester. Eighteen thousand a year." He made some quick mental calculations, then continued. "That comes to three hundred fifty dollars a week. Where are we going to come by that kind of money if I don't work?"

"I can work."

"Never! I'd quit dancing before I'd let you do that."

"Why? Other mothers work to put their children through school. Why am I different?"

He looked at her with adoring eyes. "You'd do that for me?"

"I would do anything to make you happy."

"All right, but I'm still going to get a job!"

Brock never again lived under the same roof with Eleanor or Paul. Valerie spent weekends and holidays with her father when it was convenient to his schedule, but he effectively severed all contact with the other two. Valerie remained the link, however frail, that preserved their common identity as a family, offering only the slimmest hope to Eleanor of ultimate reunification. But it was not to be. From his narrow, inalterably biased perspective he was the injured party for whom restitution demanded that Paul and Ellie be taught a lesson.

His cutting off their funds was a meaningful gesture, but no more than a gesture, for he was sure—based on what he would have done in Ellie's shoes—that she had sufficient funds of her own stashed away in hidden accounts and stocks to finance Paul's college and continued ballet training indefinitely. But that wouldn't alter the situation. Brock was resolved to force Paul out of ballet...out for keeps. He therefore needed to attack the problem from another angle, where Paul's acceptability and standing among the aristocracy of ballet—the movers and shakers and

250

power moguls—were vulnerable. That would take some planning and perhaps a bit of luck, but Brock had always had plenty of that. Nor was he to be disappointed. His luck this time showed up in the person of Mrs. Catherine Dubeau.

He was unaware of the role she could play in his vendetta with Paul when they were first introduced at a cocktail party celebrating the opening of a new shopping mall in Monterey. It was a month after he moved out of the family house and took up residence downtown. She was a beautiful woman, tall, strikingly figured, with full dark shoulder-length hair. Her strapless gown accentuated the broadness of her shoulders and showed off her satiny unblemished skin.

She welcomed him to the affair explaining in an alluringly husky voice, whose elocution reflected a cultured upbringing, that her husband was one of several land developers who had financed the mall. She said she was active in California politics, and she tried to engage Brock in a discussion of candidates for the State Senate. He expressed his political views and then turned the conversation to the subject of interior design. They bantered a few minutes about the pros and cons of the mall's design, at which point she asked him if he were a patron of the arts.

"In your business," she said, "you must meet many artists."

"Oh, I do," he explained. "Mostly commercial artists looking for jobs and, of course, the artists I carry on my staff. Some of them paint and sculpt on the side." He chuckled. "From what I've seen of their work, they all need patrons. No one else would buy their stuff."

"My husband Reynolds and I are generous supporters of a number of projects, both amateur and professional. Repertory theater, exhibits by obscure but worthy artists, ballet, symphonies, recitals. We take the utmost pleasure in—"

"You say ballet?"

"Yes, are you a fan?"

"Can't say that I am."

"Well, each art form has its own devotees. Reynolds and I are rare eclectic birds. We enjoy all forms of artistic expression."

Brock's contempt for male dancers would, he thought, insult her, so he steered the conversation away from ballet. "I'd like to meet your husband."

"I'm sorry. He isn't here tonight. He could only come for the opening ceremony. Off to some business engagement. You know how developers are."

They were joined by two of her acquaintances, and Brock soon moved away, mingling with other guests. He was aroused by Dubeau's alluring beauty and wanted to talk with her some more, but he didn't see her again that evening.

Their paths crossed by chance late one afternoon two weeks later in the hallway outside a federal courtroom in San Francisco. Brock had been summoned as a material witness for the prosecution in a tax evasion case against Roger Prentiss, Brock's nemesis and the man who had insolently predicted that Brock would never make it in the design field. It was Mrs. Dubeau who saw Brock first.

"Mr. Stowolski!"

"Yes?" Brock turned and recognized her at once. "Ah, yes," he said, pretending to grope for her name. He did not want her to know what a memorable impression she had made on him, lest she think he was overeager. He liked to play hard to get. "I believe we met at the mall reception...uh...two weeks ago. Right?"

"Yes, and I'll buy you a drink if you can recall my name."

He smiled with great charm, savoring the husky seductiveness of her voice. "Pretty small wager. Would you care to make it dinner?"

"You're stalling," she said, smiling back, her cool blue eyes sparkling.

"Your name is..."

"Yes?"

Brock winked. "Catherine Dubeau, wife of land developer Reynolds Dubeau, political activist, patron of the arts...and I don't know much more."

"Bravo. I'm flattered you remembered me."

"Only a blind man would not remember you, Mrs. Dubeau."

"Thank you."

"Are you in the courthouse on business? Not on trial, I trust."

252

"Goodness no! Some innocent and unfortunately boring legal transactions, that's all. And you?"

Brock explained his summons.

"Well, aren't we the good citizen," she joshed.

"Yeah, good for me. I'm trying to run that sucker out of business. Could be worth a lot of money to me."

"Is that how you make your living?" She chuckled. "Running others out of business?"

"Of course, not. But I have good reason to dislike the man. It's something that happened long ago."

"I guess I should wish you luck then, and I also owe you a drink."

"Ah, but not today," he lamented. "I've got a full schedule until the wee hours. Maybe next time."

"Indeed. I'm sure we'll meet again."

There seemed to be a subtle invitation in her inflection, but Brock did not know her well enough to tell.

"I've gotta run," he said. "Court reconvenes in a couple of minutes. It's bad form to be late."

"Good-bye then," she said, shaking his hand, and walked down the hall.

He called after her. "I'll bet you a dinner you can't spell my last name!"

Without stopping or turning she replied in a loud clear voice, "S...T...O...W...O...L...S...K...I." She rounded a corner and disappeared.

Brock shook his head. *A slick gorgeous woman,* he thought. *Probably in her early forties. And if I know women,* he surmised, *she's on the make. Well, lady, I'm your man.*

Their next encounter was a month later and again unexpected. It occurred at a $100-a-plate fund-raiser for a congressman who was a fellow yachtsman and racing enthusiast at Brock's club. Brock loathed political gatherings but had condescended to attend as a personal favor to the candidate. Brock spied Mrs. Dubeau at a banquet table on the far side of the hall and kept his eyes on her throughout the dinner and speeches, halfheartedly keeping up his end of the conversation at his own table, while waiting for the right moment to approach her.

She seemed unaware of his presence, which made his reconnaissance all the more enjoyable, even salacious. There was a definite aura of style and high breeding about her that drew him to her. Her dazzling beauty, enhanced by her velvet rose gown and sparkling jewelry, attracted admiring looks from the men around the hall, and envy from the women. Brock also observed that she didn't just socialize with the others at her table; she held court, imposing herself and dominating the conversation. Brock wondered if she took a similarly aggressive posture when she made love. Something about her forwardness and that sly hungry Lauren Bacall look suggested she was approachable by the right person.

As the dinner drew to a close, he noticed something peculiar. There had been four women but only three men at her table all evening, which meant that one of the women was unaccompanied. Thinking about it, he further observed that the way the men and the three other women interacted suggested Mrs. Dubeau was the extra person and that her husband once again was away on business or otherwise detained. That she was alone and thus possibly available spurred Brock to action.

He was the first of the guests at his table to get up. He bid them good night and strode quickly across the hall to reach Mrs. Dubeau before she left. He made it to her table just before the departing crowd filled the aisles.

"Mrs. Dubeau," he said, announcing his presence as he stood behind her chair hidden from her view.

She turned in her seat, and her exquisite face lit up with genuine pleasure at seeing him again. "Why, Mr. Stowolski! How nice to see you." Then quickly before he could reply, she added, smiling, "If you've come to pay off your dinner wager, you're a bit late."

"So you remembered?"

"Of course," she said. "Have you been here all evening? I didn't see you."

"Yes, on the other side. Is your husband here?" *Why beat around the bush.*

"No. He despises these affairs. Claims politics is all nonsense. He's probably right."

"I wonder if you'd care to buy me that drink you owe me."

"That's right." She laughed lightly, all too aware of the effect her low-cut gown was having on Brock. "I'm still in arrears, aren't I. Well, I have a reputation for paying my debts. So why not? This seems as good a time as any."

Their affair blew white-hot for two weeks. From that first night they spent every evening in bed in his plush apartment. On this their fourteenth night he opened the refrigerator and withdrew a medium-size gold-capped bottle and two frosted thin-stemmed crystal glasses. Since their first night together it had become a ritual to sip champagne when their romp was over.

With an exaggerated flourish Brock uncorked the bottle, filled the glasses, and offered one to Catherine, saying, "*Joie de vivre*, mademoiselle."

She giggled and accepted the glass. "You know, you'd look good in tights. Ever think of joining my ballet company?"

"Can't dance." He sat down close beside her and drank thirstily from his glass.

"You wouldn't need to. That bulge in your tights would fill the concert hall with women. I know. For years I've watched women ogle the male dancers."

"You just watched?"

She smiled. "There's more to being a patron of the arts than patronage. Why do you think I contribute so much?"

"Does Reynolds know?"

"He doesn't care. We have, as they say, an understanding."

"How much do you contribute?"

"Nearly one tenth of the company's annual budget."

"That's a pretty big share. Have you always been a contributor?"

"No, not really. Ballet has been one of my passions since I was a child. It so happened that the year I married Reynolds the San Francisco

Ballet Theatre was in a financial crisis, on the brink of bankruptcy and closure. The dancers got citizens groups and businesses, TV and radio, movie stars, everyone to pitch in and save the company. Pretty soon I was deeply involved and committed. The company only barely survived the crisis. It still needed more funds. Private donations slumped because those were lean years economically. Fortunately Reynolds' income was unaffected; in fact he did very well, so I persuaded him to make a sizable contribution, which we've done every year since. As a result, I've gotten to know the dancers and the directors and the people behind the scenes. It was fun and still is. So you can see that very little happens in the San Francisco Ballet or the Montclair School that I don't know about or can't know if I choose."

A look of astonishment covered Brock's face as he choked on a swallow of champagne.

"What's the matter?" she asked.

"Montclair School?"

"Yes. What's wrong with that?"

He grinned joyfully. "Absolutely nothing! It's wonderful!"

"What am I missing here? You know something I don't?"

"A small thing you won't believe. The coincidence is incredible."

"What is it?"

"Are you ready for this? My son dances in your school."

"At Montclair!" Her mouth fell open.

"Yes, I think that's the name. In fact I'm sure of it."

"That's marvelous!"

"No, it isn't!" he snapped, rising from the bed. "It's insufferable!"

The depth of his feeling took Catherine by surprise. "You don't approve."

"No, I don't! Would you?" Then he laughed. "That was stupid. Of course you'd approve."

"Not necessarily. If I had a boy of my own I might feel the same."

"It's humiliating. I forbade him to dance, so he went behind my back and took lessons anyway with the connivance of his meddling mother."

"How old is he?"

"Seventeen. Or is it eighteen?"

"He must be good to have been accepted at Montclair."

256

"Unfortunately he is. I've seen him practicing. But I've cut off funds for it, though I'm sure his mother has enough money of her own to keep him going."

"Do you want him out?"

"Silly question. Of course I want him out of Montclair."

"That's not what I said. Do you want him out? Out of ballet."

The cold bluntness of her question caused Brock's eyes to narrow as he began to view this woman in a new light. He could see now that she was into power, which she acquired through the resourceful use of her husband's money, the force of her domineering personality, and probably her feminine favors...power she was unafraid to use when it served her purpose. She could be a dangerous adversary, he thought. A woman possibly without conscience.

"Yes, I do want him out, out of ballet altogether. Permanently. How do I go about it?"

"You don't," she replied. "I do. Leave it to me."

"I don't operate that way. I'll have to know more about your plan, how it will be carried out, and what the ramifications will be."

"You sound like a general planning a military campaign."

"Can you have him expelled outright?"

"Of course not! I can't just have someone expelled. There must be valid grounds. Open and shut. That's extremely hard to do."

"Then we'll invent some grounds."

"No. Too risky. Although I have considerable influence over decisions within the ballet company, I have to preserve my credibility and standing. My prestige and power would suffer if it were found that I manufactured a case against your son. No, this has to be done openly and with finesse, based on legitimate grounds."

"You sound like you'll enjoy it."

"I will. It's an intriguing challenge, but it won't be free. There will be a charge."

"Oh? The lady has a mercenary streak."

"Not money. Something else." She winked.

"From me?"

"You and you alone." She stuck out her tongue and wiggled it at him.

"If you put an end to my son's ballet career, I'm open to negotiation."

257

"Now it's my turn to say I don't operate that way. You start paying up front, then I'll deal with your son."

"Pay what? You said it wasn't money."

"That's right. You see..." She winked again coyly. "I have this insatiable fondness for a certain act that Reynolds refuses to perform for me."

Instantly Brock felt the power relationship between them shift. He was accustomed to wielding power over others. All at once the roles with Catherine were reversed. His immediate impulse was to throw her out of his apartment. No one would subjugate him. No one! But these were empty fruitless thoughts. Paul must be brought to heel, and the sooner the better. Catherine was the only person over whom Brock had any influence who was in a position to do it. Ironically, to get the job done, the controller would have to become the controllee, at least till Paul's involvement ballet had been permanently quashed.

Brock gave her a subdued look of resignation. "Okay. You got me. I want Paul out of ballet."

She sauntered toward the bathroom. "And just in case you're thinking of welshing on the deal, the moment I fix your son's wagon, keep in mind that I can open doors for him as well as close them."

SEVENTEEN

While Eleanor secured a low-paying position as a receptionist in a real estate firm, Paul, against his mother's wishes and with Irina's worried but loving support, took a job as a loader in a beer distributor's warehouse from 10 PM till 2 AM six nights a week. The work paid minimum wage—the most he could find for part-time employment—but left him so exhausted from loading trucks with hundreds of heavy kegs and cases of beer that he barely had the strength the next day to complete his morning calisthenics and perform well in his dance classes. More than degrading his physical stamina, the job netted him less than one hundred twenty dollars a week. This was nowhere near enough. He needed to earn three or four times that amount to finance his schooling. But he obstinately stuck with the job till he could find something better.

Paul's first weeks in college set him a lonely grueling pace. Lonely in that he missed the warmth and intimacy of Kúbokoff's private lessons. Grueling in that the Montclair School demanded as many hours of him as his academic work at the Fine Arts School, leaving little time to be with Irina, who lived at home as he did. Because they attended different colleges, they never saw each other during the day. In the evenings, if he drove at seventy miles an hour from Montclair, he reached her house in time to spend thirty precious minutes together before he raced home to eat dinner, do his homework, and get to the warehouse by ten o'clock. He went to bed at 3:00 AM, rose at seven, did his calisthenics and jogged, and began the whole cycle over again. It was a tight punishing schedule which he rather enjoyed, not masochistically for the self-torment it inflicted but for the lofty purpose it gave his life—to become a professional dancer and, of course, marry Irina and build a happy life together.

259

Seeing that his schedule was pressing him to the limit of his endurance, the staff at Montclair advised him to ease up and develop his skills and technique more slowly, assuring him that his chance to perform one day with the San Francisco Ballet or some other renowned company would come in time. He needed only to be patient.

But he was wary of such reassurances, because what he observed at Montclair told a different story with chilling clarity. Several male staff members were at least ten years older and more accomplished than he, yet they had never gained entry into the august ranks of any nationally recognized ballet troupe. Moreover, when they were his age they were, he presumed, far more advanced in their development. He logically concluded that he was years behind where he needed to be if he were to have any chance at all of reaching the top echelon of ballet dancers. There was no time to waste. He must make the most of every minute of every day, which included practicing on the sly in the warehouse during slack periods between the departure of one truck and the arrival of another. What inspired him to work even harder was his suspicion that the Montclair instructors as a group believed he was too old and were simply patronizing him out of admiration for his dedication and out of pity that he discovered his talent too late in life to take full advantage of it.

The cumulative erosion of his physical stamina finally took its toll. One morning four weeks after this enervating pace had begun, Paul slept through his alarm clock and did not awaken till midafternoon. He pulled himself out of his deep comalike rehabilitating sleep and sat up groggily on the side of his bed trying to clear his mind, which was dimly aware that his routine had gone awry. When he saw what time it was, he moaned and fell back on the bed.

I can't keep this up, he thought. *It's insane. I've to got to find an easier, better-paying job.*

He had already missed that day's Fine Arts classes, so he got up and dressed for his late afternoon dance session at Montclair. Perhaps one of the dance instructors there would know of a good-paying job that was not so physically demanding.

"Hey, Brad!" called out one of the instructors. "Paul here's lookin' for work. Ya' got any ideas?"

"Let me think," replied a heavy-set balding man who had devoted thirty years to a fruitless quest to be a ballet superstar. Though fame had eluded him, he stayed close to ballet in any capacity he could as a dying man clings to a life preserver. Like so many would-be's, he could never let go. "Good-looking well-built guys, especially dancers like you, Paul, are always in demand as male strippers. I'll bet there's a half dozen clubs in the Bay Area where you could find a job."

"Clubs?"

"Yeah, night clubs."

Paul winced. "What do they pay?"

"Depends on how good you are. Some guys have been known to pull in two hundred bills a night."

"Two hundred! For what?"

"For stripping, naturally. You know, like stripteasers. A piece at a time between gyrations set to music."

"Do they take everything off?"

"Not in the classy clubs. Avoid the sleazy joints. Especially the gay establishments. They're bad news. No, the place for a handsome stud like you is in one of the expensive high-class bars for women only. They cater to upper middle-class types who like watching half-naked weightlifters flex their organs."

"And they pay them that much?"

"Why not? The customers love it, and no one gets hurt. I mean it's not like the guys are gigolos, though some of that may go on. It's really just for fun. The women scream and laugh and carry on. I tell ya', it's a ball. Most of the strippers work on a low, fixed salary. The real money is in the tips the customers throw on the stage. Are you really interested?"

Paul swallowed hard, thinking. Night clubs had never been his scene. But could this be the answer—for now? Dancing had to be easier than what he was doing now. "Brad, I'm desperate. My night-shift job is killing me."

"Tell you what. I know a bartender at The Voyeur, one of the top women-only clubs. If you want an audition, I'm sure she can arrange it."

"Hey, that'd be great!"

"If I were ten years younger I'd be doin' it myself. I'll tell ya' this. It's a lot easier than making it as a ballet dancer. You should think about that."

There it was again, thought Paul resentfully. The insinuation that he was too old to succeed in a ballet career. Well, perhaps they were right, but he would have to find that out for himself.

Brad contacted his bartender friend that evening and then reached Paul at home during dinner to report that the audition was set for the next afternoon.

"Impossible!" exclaimed Paul. "I'm not ready. I don't know the first thing about it."

"Don't sweat it! Come by the theater around noon. I'll give you a demonstration. There's nothin' to it. You'll pick it up in five minutes. It's easy. I promise."

Right on the dot of twelve the next day Paul entered the empty darkened Montclair theater looking for Brad, whom he found dozing in the back row. He woke him, and they went up on stage and turned on some lights. Brad showed Paul the basic movements involved in a simple striptease, while Paul watched and mimicked each motion. As Brad had predicted, it took Paul only a few minutes to replicate the hip action and lewd posturing. Then the two dancers worked up a short routine which they choreographed to a rock CD Paul had brought with him. Within an hour he had mastered the routine and was ready. Brad gave him a few final pointers, reminded him to think of a sexy stage name—"Don't use your true name!"—and sent him on his way.

Two hours later Paul stood before the manager of The Voyeur, who was sitting on a stool at the bar. She was a thin, gaunt, white-haired, red-eyed woman named Kate, whose gravelly voice and constant coughing advertised better than any surgeon general's warning the hazards of smoking the lighted cigarette held between her yellowed fingers.

"Have you stripped before?" Her stale monotone had the emotion of an empty beer can.

Paul's impulse was to lie, but his intuition quickly warned him off that tack and onto a more promising course. "No, never. But I'm fresh and new. Young and sexy. I have that virgin look women love. I'm also a great dancer."

"So," she said dryly. She stared at his face coldly, as if identifying a cadaver in a morgue, then panned down his body. "Let's see whatcha got. You bring a CD or a tape?"

262

"CD." Paul held it out for her to see.

"Hey, Ernie! Com'ere. I got an audition for us."

A rotund black man waddled from behind a curtain at the rear of the semicircular platform on one side of the room and disinterestedly took the CD from Paul.

Paul removed all his clothes except for the white, silver-spangled, ankle-length tights he had worn in Kúbokoff's show. It was his sole costume. He vaulted barefoot onto the stage and assumed his starting position—standing, feet together, arms outstretched to his sides, hands clenched into fists, his face expressionless.

Bright stage lights came on only an instant before the music began, but Paul was ready, going into action without missing a beat, lurching from side to side in time with the fierce pounding rock rhythm. As the three-minute piece ended, he threw himself on the stage in a death pose, arms and legs spread wide.

The stage went dark again the moment the music stopped. Paul guessed that Ernie was not big on auditions, but then why should he be? There was probably a steady stream of guys auditioning for the high-paying jobs here. He hopped off the platform and began putting on his clothes while the manager, stoically watching him, sucked deeply on her cigarette and blew smoke upwards forming a ghostly cloud above her head.

"So," she said flatly.

Paul continued dressing, waiting for her pronouncement. There was none. Only silence. He glanced toward the bar to be sure she was still there. She was, staring straight at him, blowing smoke clouds. *She's weird*, he thought. He pulled on his shoes and walked over to her.

"Whataya think?" he asked. "Do I have a job?"

"If you can add a few minutes to your act."

"No problem there," said Paul, shaking his head.

"And you need a loose white silk shirt open to the waist."

"Okay." He nodded excitedly, sure that she was going to hire him.

"And a gold pendant on a thick gold chain around your neck."

"Okay." He nodded again.

"No other jewelry."

"No." He shook his head.

"And white pointed Italian shoes, but no socks."

"Shoes and no socks." He nodded again.

"And white gloves."

"Gloves."

"And a white scarf."

"Scarf."

"You start tomorrow night at nine o'clock. Be here at eight."

"Eight tomorrow."

"Twenty-five dollars a night plus tips. Two shows a night."

"Twenty-five and two shows."

"Three nights a week: Tuesday, Friday, and Saturday."

"Tuesday, Friday, and Saturday."

"You do well, I raise it to fifty."

"Fifty."

"Ernie will write you the contract."

"Ernie." He nodded.

"Don't be late."

"I would die first."

"That's not in the contract."

Paul peered skeptically at her stony haggard face, unwilling to believe she was kidding. Even when her mouth turned slowly up at the corners into an ingratiating smile, he reserved judgment.

"Can't an old lady make a joke?" she asked.

"Sure," he replied. "I just wasn't expecting it."

"What's your name?" A warmth suddenly infused her harsh voice, softening her face and her cold business mood.

"Paul...Stowolski."

"How old are you?"

"Eighteen."

"So. You're a nice boy, and I like you. You do what I tell you, and you'll make lots of money...and so will I."

"I...I don't wanna be known by my true name. I'm studying to be a professional ballet dancer, and it wouldn't look right. I mean, when I get good enough to audition with one of the big companies, they might hold it against me. You know, bad publicity."

"So what's new? Most of my dancers use funny names. You picked

264

one yet?"

"Yeah. Paul Car*nall,* as in carnal knowledge but with two ls and the accent on the second syllable."

"Did you think that one up yourself?"

"Yeah, why?"

"Nothin'. The ladies will go for it, and that's what counts. So. It's good luck, Paul Car*nall.* You're gonna do just fine."

Catherine, in a silk nightgown, lay curled on Brock's bed like a purring kitten after a full meal. They had just finished an hour of vigorous lovemaking, and she felt lusciously relaxed. Brock came out of the bathroom drying himself with a towel after showering.

"I have some news about Paul," she said, sipping her champagne.

"You don't say. Why didn't you tell me before?"

"I was saving it." She bit her index finger. "Sort of for dessert."

"So what's he up to? Are you any closer to dealing with him as we agreed?"

"A big step closer. I've learned that he's taken a job as a stripper in a nightclub."

"A stripper?" Brock winced. "Just as I suspected. He's a homosexual."

"No, you ninny. It's a nightclub for women and, I might add, one of the more fashionable. I've been there myself. Your son has class."

"Oho! I didn't know you went slumming in strip joints?"

"Hey, it's not what you think. It's for women to have a good laugh. But it may provide me the cause celebre I need to slander your son and get him expelled from Montclair. I mean, after all—" she winked—"we do have moral standards to uphold."

"You think his working there is sufficient grounds for dismissal? I'll bet he's not the first dancer from the school to find employment as a stripper."

"Oh, there have probably been others. There may be others now. What we'll need is a little incident to put Paul in the limelight so to speak."

"You've got a plan?"

"Not yet, but I'm thinking...."

Paul was an instant hit, and his popularity among the all-female customers grew rapidly. His artistry as a dancer and his physical attributes, magnified by his handsome face, combined as powerful attractions. Patrons knew which nights he performed, and within a month many came specifically to watch him. Kate, an astute manager, closely monitored audience reaction to each performer and, observing the stir Paul created, placed him later and later in the program to heighten the customers' anticipation and keep them in the club longer. Soon they developed a routine of chanting his name impatiently after each of the strippers before him had performed.

"Carnall...Carnall...Carnall," they cried.

As they chorused his name, the tension and excitement mounted until, when he finally appeared, near bedlam ensued. Cheers and screams and clapping filled the club. By the time he strode off the stage crumpled bills had been crammed into his jock by the "stocking stuffers," as the club staff called them. As Brad had predicted, they provided the bulk of his pay, which had risen to one hundred dollars a night...three hundred, sometimes four hundred a week.

He was on top of the world. In one year he would earn close to twenty thousand dollars—more than enough to finance his schooling. Now his mother didn't need to work, though he knew he would have difficulty persuading her to stop. He thought she actually enjoyed earning money after so many years as a member of the idle country club set. His work at The Voyeur not only freed him from the physically destructive routine he had been suffering with his other job, it also gave him time both to study for his courses and to be with Irina. For all these reasons, he endured the indignities of the strip club. There was, as he'd found out, no other way once his father had cut off his support.

One night after his act, Paul sat down on a chair at his dressing table and began pulling bills of various denominations from his jock strap, when a tall woman he didn't know entered the room. She wore an elegant white dress, and her long black hair hung loose about her shoulders.

"You can't come back here!" he warned.

She smiled unconcernedly. "Kate said it would be all right."

"It's not all right," he said, standing. "You have to leave!"

She visually inspected his exquisite physique. "I wanted to meet you. You're very good, you know. About the best I've ever seen."

A strip freak, he thought. "So you saw me. Now the show's over."

"I wanted a closer look."

Paul's anger was rising. For a second he thought he could rein it in while he found a way to get her to leave. But he was tired and her haughty self-indulgent manner burned him. "You want a closer look? Take it!" He ripped off his athletic supporter and stood spread-eagled before her.

"Well, well," she said, her eyebrows raised. "We certainly are endowed, aren't we?"

Her hand moved so quickly and unexpectedly that Paul had no time to think before her fingers closed firmly around his genitals. Nor could he control his instinctive defensive reaction. Terrified that she would crush his testicles, he slapped the side of her head with all his might. It was a powerful hammering blow that knocked her off her feet and onto the floor where she lay stock-still, a disheveled pile of white satin, black hair, arms, legs, stockings, and shoes.

Paul was too shocked by his reflex action and its result to move. Horrified at the sight of her crumpled body, he was certain he had killed her.

Then the pile moaned and moved and began to sort itself out. One arm reached out, grasping feebly at the air. The other found the head beneath the fold of the skirt and felt the deepening red welt on the cheek bone. The woman moaned again, lifted her head, and vomited onto the tile floor.

Paul threw on a bathrobe from the back of a chair and dashed out the door shouting for Kate. He found her in her office at the end of the hallway. "Kate! Quick! I hit a woman in my room. She's hurt."

Crushing her lighted cigarette in an ashtray, she leaped up from her desk and trotted down the hall behind Paul. When they entered his dressing room, they found the woman on her knees, crying softly, eyes closed, rocking back and forth, holding her head with one hand, covering her mouth with the other. Her white dress was splattered and stained with reddish vomit that filled the air with a sticky noxious odor.

"Close the door and get me a wet towel," ordered Kate, taking control of the situation. She knelt beside the woman and comforted her while Paul doused a towel with water in the sink. "You'll be all right," said Kate. "Let me see your face." Kate examined the nasty red area of swelling on her cheekbone. "That's going to turn black and blue, but a little makeup should cover it."

Paul handed Kate the towel and gawked at the woman he had brutalized. She was a mess.

"Now, honey," said Kate to the woman soothingly. "I think you should lie down. You'll feel better, and we can put some ice on that bruise."

"I'll get it," said Paul, darting out the door.

Kate helped the woman lie back on the floor and placed a rolled-up towel under her head. "We have to get you and your dress cleaned up."

Paul burst into the room carrying a plastic bowl filled with ice cubes from the bar. Kate quickly upended the bowl onto another towel which she folded into an ice pack and held against the suffering woman's head.

"Paul, go fetch Bertie from the kitchen. Then go to my office and stay there till I work things out here. Okay? Everything will be all right."

"Sure." He gathered up some clothes and did as she directed, though he was unconvinced that everything would be all right. The woman he had slapped appeared well-to-do. Her dress looked expensive, as did her jeweled necklace and earrings. She surely would sue him and the club for assault and battery, whatever that meant. He wasn't sure. But one couldn't go around bashing people and not get sued. A judge would probably award her a hundred thousand dollars in damages. Kate would fire him. He wouldn't find another job as well paying. It would be the end of his ballet career. The end of his future. Irina. Everything.

He sat dejectedly in Kate's office for nearly an hour and, as the minutes passed without her returning, his gloom deepened to despair. At last the door opened and Kate entered, weary but cheerful. Her sunny mood gave Paul immediate hope.

"What happened?" he asked.

"Nothin'. Ol' Kate knows how to handle these dames." She plunked herself down at her desk and reached for a cigarette. "Wanna drink?"

Paul shook his head. "Where is she?"

"Her girlfriends took her home." Kate read the unallayed apprehension on Paul's young face. "Hey, kid, cool it. I told you it would be all right. She won't make any trouble. She's a high-born lady. She can't make a stink without getting herself a lot of lurid publicity. The papers would have a field day linking her name to a common brawl in the dressing room of a male stripper in a place like this. I mean, I run a nice club, but you wouldn't hold Sunday school here."

"Is she married?"

"Yeah, I think so. She was wearing a wedding ring."

"What will she tell her husband?"

"Are you kidding? She'll tell him she walked into a door, fell out of a tree, anything, before she'll ever admit she was in a stripper's dressing room. Understand what I'm saying?"

Paul nodded as what she said made sense. "You're right. I'm being stupid. She can't do anything without exposing herself to scandal…."

"By the way, what did you hit her with, your fist?"

"No, my hand. I slapped her. Pretty hard, too."

"Hard? You're joking. You knocked her brains out. What did she do to make you hit her?"

"She grabbed my you-know-whats. I didn't think. I just smacked her. There wasn't time to do anything else."

"Then she got what she deserved. And you deserve a good night's sleep. So, go home and forget all about this. Just chalk it up to experience."

"All right. Just an occupational hazard, huh?"

"What happened to you?" Brock asked.

Catherine brushed past him at the door to his apartment and went into the bedroom. He followed her in and took hold of her shoulders, stopping her.

269

"Hold on." He turned her around and inspected the yellowish-green and black shiner that festooned her left cheekbone.

"A little accident," she said. "I don't wish to discuss it."

"Anyone I know?" He smiled, trying to brighten her mood.

"Let's not talk about it."

"Okay, but Reynolds isn't abusing you, is he?"

She laughed. "Oh, Brock."

"What's that mean? That he is?"

"Of course not."

"Someone else then? Do you need help?"

"No, I can handle it. In my own way...."

A week later a special Saturday feature appeared in the entertainment section of the *San Francisco Examiner*. Entitled "Baring Bods for Broads and Bucks: An Inside View of the Male Striptease Business," the article provided a sensationalized account of the Bay Area's booming business in male strip joints, from seedy, low-life bars to the ritzy, high-rent clubs like The Voyeur.

The author, Abigail Downing, took the readers on a far-ranging tour of the more popular establishments, highlighting the differences among them and their star performers, some of whom sat for personal interviews and photographs. The final stop on the tour was The Voyeur.

> "...the best in town with a showstopper who is fast becoming the biggest draw of all of San Francisco's strippers—Paul Carnall. This very sexy, pelvis-pumping stripteaser, whose bawdy and provocative act has made him a favorite of hundreds of sex-hungry housewives, is in fact Paul Stowolski, an eighteen-year-old college student from the California School of Fine Arts, where he is majoring in dance. He also attends the Montclair School of Ballet operated by the San Francisco Ballet Theatre.
>
> "Stowolski, who aspires to a professional career as a ballet dancer with the San Francisco troupe, was involved last week in a shocking

270

fracas in his private dressing room where he reportedly assaulted a female patron. The Voyeur's management would neither confirm nor deny the report, but several patrons—who understandably spoke on condition their identities not be revealed—disclosed that at the time of the incident Stowolski was naked and in the room alone with the victim.

"Stowolski would not grant an interview and was unavailable for comment."

Paul read the article in horrified silence after his mother had pointed it out to him over breakfast.

"Is that true?" she asked worriedly.

"Yes, as far as it goes."

"There's more?"

"This woman comes in my dressing room and grabs my—" He gestured toward his crotch. "I smacked her in self-defense. I didn't know what she'd do. I thought she was a wacko." Anxiously he read the article and then laid the paper on the table.

"Will it mean trouble for you?" she asked.

"I guess it depends on how you look at it."

"Did they ask you for an interview?"

"No, never. That's a big lie."

"Will the Montclair people be upset?"

"I don't know, but this is exactly what I didn't want. It's bad publicity for the school and the Ballet. How did the newspaper get all this information about me? Kate wouldn't have told them."

"Perhaps your father?"

"No, I don't think so. I asked Valerie only yesterday if he knew about The Voyeur. She was sure he'd have mentioned it to her if he knew."

"The instructors at Montclair know, don't they?"

"Yeah, that's true," he admitted. "One of them could have told the paper. But why?"

"You said many of the strippers in the clubs are dancers like you. If so, word gets around. It was bound to happen sooner or later."

"That sounds like I-told-you-so." Paul did not need a lecture from his mother at this point. He had known the risks when he took the job, but he needed the money. He had no other choice.

Eleanor recanted at once. "I didn't mean it that way. You did what you thought you had to."

"And you didn't agree with that?" Paul's tone sharpened.

"You know I support you in every way. I have from the very beginning...and I will in the future, whatever you do."

"I'm sorry, Mother. That was unfair of me."

She moved around the table and hugged him from behind, pressing her cheek against his. "I love you, Paul. I'm sure it will work out."

Eleanor was being only half truthful. She had been uneasy from the outset about Paul's working as a stripteaser. He was so young, and it was such a disreputable line of work that put him in the company of morally corrupting people. Where would it end? She had wondered but had kept her concerns to herself. She had supported Paul's taking the job because it was the only work he could find that allowed him to pay his own way through school and lead a more or less normal student life. "Perhaps," she continued, "the article won't have any impact at all except to increase your audiences, which I'm sure it will."

As if fate had been waiting for its cue, the phone rang. She let loose of Paul and picked off the receiver from the wall. "Hello?"

"Is Paul Stowolski there, please?"

"Yes, he is. May I ask who's calling?"

"Miss Billings at Montclair."

Eleanor, wide-eyed, held out the receiver to Paul. "Miss Billings from Montclair."

Taking the phone, Paul's expression instantly clouded as a premonition of disaster seized him. "Yes, this is Paul Stowolski."

"Mr. Conroy, the director, would like to see you in his office this morning, if that's convenient."

"Well, uh...yes...I guess so. What time?"

"Ten o'clock will be fine."

Paul's separation from Montclair was swift and surgically clean. At ten

272

o'clock he was a model student in good standing. At 10:05 he was neither. While dismissal had been only a remote theoretical risk when he accepted the job at The Voyeur, the reality was devastating. He had never fully measured the impact that dismissal would have on his life and his career ambitions. He should have.

Conroy informed him that the president of the San Francisco Ballet had phoned him at home that morning to express her outrage that the Ballet and its school had been publicly linked to an infamous striptease bar and, worse, to the nefarious incident in Paul's dressing room. Such despicable, shameful behavior was a disgrace to the Ballet, its sponsors, and to ballet enthusiasts and would not be tolerated. She demanded Paul's immediate expulsion from Montclair and directed Mr. Conroy to send letters at once to each major sponsor of the Ballet reporting the expulsion and reaffirming the school's high ethical and professional standards. Meanwhile, the *San Francisco Examiner* had already agreed to publish a letter to the editor from the Ballet disassociating itself from Stowolski and this deplorable episode and announcing his separation from Montclair.

"I believe," said Conroy solemnly, "that your little escapade as a strip-tease artist will cost you dearly. No self-respecting ballet school in the country will consider your application now. Perhaps after a few years they might, but by then you'll be years older and without qualified training. No, I would say your chances of a career in ballet have been effectively demolished. Foolishly, my boy. Foolishly." Conroy shook his head consolingly. "Whoever advised you to take that job did you no favor, no favor at all. I am truly very sorry."

Paul walked the streets of San Francisco for hours, striving to come to terms with this terrible turn of fate that he simply could not accept. Ballet was too much a part of his life to be suddenly wrenched from him. It was like tearing off an arm or a leg. It was just not possible. This couldn't be happening. There were other ballet schools, dozens, hundreds, maybe not as prestigious as Montclair but schools nonetheless. Surely one of them would accept him. He would apply to them all. Every one. In the whole country. He'd show Conroy. Paul Stowolski had talent. There had to be schools that rated talent over harmless bad publicity. He slumped dejectedly and continued walking aimlessly throughout the afternoon and early evening.

He eventually found himself in front of a noisy Gay Nineties bar. Laughter and music blared from the open entrance. He entered absentmindedly, drawn by the friendly atmosphere and wanting to lose himself in the happy Saturday-night crowd. An antique clock in the narrow vestibule showed 10:49. He stopped and stared at it, knowing that in about twenty minutes he would be expected to appear on stage at The Voyeur.

At first the other performers would notice he was late and pass the word to Kate. She would phone his home, and his mother would say she didn't know where he was. Then Kate would light a cigarette and the show would go on without him. Ballet would go on without him. Life would go on.

At that moment the hollow morbid thought of suicide introduced itself. It beckoned him, pushing aside all other thoughts, all other motives, all other needs, save one—to die, to draw down the curtain on this pitiful, painful drama. Then a burly beer drinker trying to enter the bar bumped into Paul. "Excuse me, fella. You're in the way." He went on in, leaving Paul standing in the vestibule looking after him.

"In the way?" said Paul. "In the way?" His face reddened with sudden anger. Customers at the bar inside turned toward him and pointed, laughing. "You wanna see a show? A real show?" he shouted. "Just watch me!"

He spun around and ran into the street, hailing down a cab, which drove him to The Voyeur. He raced into the lobby and through a side door to the dressing rooms.

Kate saw him sweep past her door. "You're late!"

He ignored her welcome and went directly to his room.

One of the other strippers who had just performed was there cooling off. "You're on in five minutes," he said. "Aren't you going to warm up?"

"Haven't time."

Paul pulled off his street clothes and put on his silver white-sequined jock strap, pants, and jacket. He slipped gold slave chains on both wrists and dropped a heavier version around his neck. Then he pushed his bare feet into a pair of shiny white leather loafers, wrapped a white silk scarf around his neck, and flew out the door. Kate had passed word to the emcee, a woman, that he was there and to be ready for him. No sooner

274

had Paul left his dressing room than he heard the tumultuous chant of his name.

"Carnall...Carnall."

The noise beat on his eardrums in shock waves. Alarmed, he stepped to the peephole in the backdrop and scanned the audience. Never had he seen such a crowd, all clapping in unison and shouting his name with a hunger and animal ferocity that were frightening. It was the newspaper article, of course, as his mother had predicted. They had read it and come to see "the very sexy, pelvis-pumping stripteaser" in the flesh.

Paul signaled the emcee by pushing a button on the wall.

"And now!" boomed the public address system. "Luscious ladies of The Voyeur!" A total silence fell over the crowd as every patron listened breathlessly for the magic name. "Our next performer...the epitome of male sex symbols...the Titan of teasers...San Francisco's own...the one and only...Paul Carnall!"

At the sound of his name, Paul vaulted through the curtain as his musical accompaniment blasted the audience through an array of speakers. The deafening shriek of two hundred hysterical women drowned out the music and was heard three blocks away. Had he not felt the beat of the music in the stage floor, he would have been lost. He pulled out all stops, spinning, lurching, leaping, savaging the audience with movements that were greeted with screams of approval. Playing to the audience's emotions, he smiled and winked each time his eyes connected with another pair in the crowd. Finally, as he entered the routine's climactic sequence, the crowd began cheering in time with each pulse.

"More!...More!...More!" they cried.

Paul was swept away in the fervor of his dancing and the music and the chanting. He kicked off his shoes and pulled down his slacks, revealing his sequined jock. As the music reached a new and dangerous level, Paul lost all touch with the music and with the gyrating mass of faces behind the glare of the spotlights. He saw only the dozen women leaning over the footlights, reaching for him as the woman had in his dressing room.

"You want me?" he screamed. "You want me?"

The last thing he remembered after that was the contorted face of a young woman screaming in pain as someone climbed on her back to mount the stage.

The jangle of the phone at 12:30 AM beside Eleanor's bed startled her, causing her to fumble the book in which was absorbed. It toppled to the floor as she scrambled for the receiver, praying it was Paul. He had not returned home or phoned all day since his appointment at Montclair. She had called Kate at The Voyeur around nine PM to speak with him, but Paul was not there yet. When Kate promised to have Paul phone home when he arrived, Eleanor demurred, feeling intrusive. Better to let her son work things out for himself. He knew she was there for him if he needed her. He would eventually call.

"Hello?" said Eleanor hesitantly. "Paul?"

"Mrs. Stovolski?"

"Yes," she replied, recognizing the caller at once. "Mr. Kúbokoff?"

"Yes. It is me," said the Russian expatriate in his ponderous rolling accent. "I am sorry to call you so late. It is very late and I..." He turned from the phone and addressed someone in the background. "*Izvinyayusya.*" He waited. "Yes, I apologize," he continued. "I apologize. I hope I did not vaken you."

"No, please. You didn't wake me. I was reading. What may I do for you?"

"Not for me, t'ank you, Mrs. Stovolski. It is Paul."

Her grip tightened on the receiver. "Is something wrong?"

"Yes. He vas injured in a...*narusheniye.*" Eleanor heard a woman's distant voice. "Yes," said Kúbokoff, "in a disturbance at t'e club v'ere he dances. T'ere vas pushing and shoving and many people on t'e stage. Paul vas in t'e middle of it all and vas knocked unconscious, but only for a moment. He got some bruises and vorst of all he ripped a muscle in his leg. I have told him many times to stretch and varm up before dancing. But, no! He's too hurry-hurry. And so he has hurt himself."

Too many questions crowded Eleanor's mind to ask all at once so she picked at random. "Does he have a concussion?"

276

"No, no. Do not vorry. A doctor came to t'e club and looked him over. It was a minor t'ing."

"Is the injury to his leg serious?"

"Not disabling. Oh, he vill be on crutches for a few weeks. T'en a cane. T'en slow exercises to rebuild t'e muscle. It vill be many veeks maybe mont's before he dances again. It vas a very stupid t'ing he do. I have scolded him."

Eleanor smiled at his quaintness. "Are you at the club? Is Paul there now?"

"No, no. His boss, she called me. T'ey vere going to take him to t'e hospital, but he knew v'at he had done and he vanted to come here."

"At your home?"

"Yes. T'ey brought him. He is here now."

"May I talk with him please?"

"Vell..."

There was a pause that drew a worried frown on Eleanor's face. "Something is wrong, isn't it?"

"Yes," Kúbokoff affirmed. "I vill try to explain v'at I know. Like I say, I vas not t'ere at t'e club, but he did somet'ing on v'ich he is greatly...*yemu stidno*...ashamed. V'en I suggest he call you, he screamed, 'No, no, never. I am too ashamed. I have disgraced my family and my mot'er.' T'en he cried and cried like a baby. He could not stop. I held him a long time like he vas my son. Finally he stopped and ve talked a little. I make him a deal. He can stay vit' me, and I vill doctor him and make him vell on one condition. T'at he lets you come and see him. At first he vould not agree, but I tell him how much you love him, so he gives in."

"So he wants to remain in your care until he recovers?"

"Yes. I vill fix him. I know t'is injury. It is common. Serious but common, and he vill recover under my...*nablyudeniye*...supervision."

"Do you know what he's ashamed of? Did he tell you?"

"Not exactly. He had a great setback today. Somet'ing about an article in t'e newspaper."

"He was expelled from Montclair!" It was both a question and an answer.

"Yes, t'at's right. He told you?"

"No, he never came home after his meeting with the director of the school. An article in this morning's paper about the nightclub identified him by name. I was afraid there would be repercussions."

"It is very tragic. Such a fine school. V'y vas he dancing naked in a nightclub? V'y such a place? You are rich people. He doesn't need t'e money."

Eleanor bit her lip. "Yes, he does. His father didn't want him to dance and cut off financial support. Working was the only way Paul could continue his ballet."

Kúbokoff restrained himself from condemning Paul's father. The Russian had witnessed much sadness in his life and much stupidity and had learned to accept injustice without complaint. "I see. Vell, ve all must follow our hearts. If Paul's fat'er does not see him as a dancer, t'en t'at is t'e vay it is. But t'at does not mean ve must remain...*slepiye*...blind to Paul's talent. I vill not be blind. Paul t'inks no ot'er ballet school vill have him now. I t'ink...I know...he is wrong. But if no one else will teach him, I vill do it myself."

"Mr. Kúbokoff, you're a wonderful person, and I want to thank you for all you've done. Paul is lucky to have such a friend and teacher as you."

"You vill come t'en tonight and see him? It vill mean a lot to him. He needs you."

"Of course. I'll bring some clean clothes and his schoolbooks. I'll be there in half an hour. Tell him I love him very much."

Paul's recovery was slow, retarded by the severe depression into which he sank as the enormity of his predicament and its inescapable consequences became clear. He had made himself a sideshow freak, debasing himself publicly...a lewd spectacle which all the papers had reported with clinical precision and exaggerated hype. If he had wanted to stigmatize himself and ruin any hope he might have had of achieving greatness someday on the stage, he could not have chosen a more effective way. He was a self-made pariah whom, he was sure, no reputable ballet school would grant an audition much less accept as a student. He had lost his pride and self-

278

respect and with them his desire to see Irina for, by disgracing himself, he had dishonored their love. His shame was so intense that he refused to see her or speak with her and, despite the pleadings of his mother and Kúbokoff, he would not return her calls. She visited Kúbokoff's home twice, but Paul locked himself in his room and would not come out till she left. Distraught by the mystery of his behavior, Irina sought solace from his mother, but there was nothing Eleanor could do for her except counsel patience.

At the same time across town in Brock's apartment Catherine was gloating over her triumph. "Are you a satisfied customer?" she asked Brock with a tinge of superiority.

"I certainly am. When you take on a job, lady, you deliver! I'm impressed."

"I did get results, didn't I."

"You know, Catherine, you're an intimidating lady."

"You mean ruthless, don't you?"

"Yeah, that fits, too, I suppose, as does the word *vengeful*."

She shot him a questioning look.

"I read about Paul's attack on you in the newspaper."

"Me?"

"Come on, stop pretending. You were the woman in his dressing room. That's where you got that shiner on your face."

She nodded. "Yeah, he punched me. It came out of nowhere. I've never been hit like that in my life. I thought I was going to die. It was awful."

"Why did he do it? What set him off? Something you said?"

"I grabbed his family jewels."

"You what!"

"I reached out and examined the goods. How was I to know he'd react violently?"

"Wonders never cease," said Brock with a shake of his head. "Is the show over, or are you making an encore? You sound like you're not finished with him."

"You can put money in the bank on that one."

"What do you have in mind?"

"I don't know, but I'll think of something...."

Catherine was determined to settle the score.

Catherine's wide circle of social and political acquaintances included an array of people in positions of diverse influence in both state and federal government of whom she could ask small favors without imposing on their friendship. She also enjoyed special relationships with a few very powerful figures, one of whom was the Honorable Walter B. Knox III, a California member of the United States House of Representatives. The request she made to him was sufficiently innocuous and compelling that he felt no compunction about acting on it.

Dear Walter,

My most reliable sources on the political scene in Washington tell me marvelous tales of your exploits on the Hill and of your growing reputation as an honest, fearless, and effective protagonist for California causes. My warmest congratulations. You have more than fulfilled the expectations of your constituents. You own, as always, our full support and can count me among your loyal contributors and campaigners next fall.

My purpose in writing is to bring to your attention a criminal act that, though a local matter and minor in comparison to the critical national problems that weigh upon your mind, is nevertheless a matter of concern to certain of your supporters. I refer to the blatant violation of alien status by one Irina Papagállou, a Greek citizen residing unlawfully in the United States. She entered the country on a student visa, but it expired a year ago. Moreover, despite not having been issued a work permit and in willful disregard of the prohibitions against her working, Miss Papagállou has been gainfully employed on a number of occasions since entering this country.

As you know, the movement in Los Angeles, San Francisco, San Diego, and other major California cities to grant illegal aliens asylum is gathering momentum again. You and your supporters have taken strong positions against asylum, chiefly because it will drain resources from welfare programs for legal immigrants and native-born Americans and, more important, deprive them of jobs to which they, not illegal aliens, are justly entitled.

Miss Papagállou's behavior, by contemptuously stealing employment from those who rightfully deserve it and by flaunting our immigration laws, places her beyond the law. If we are to stymie the asylum movement, we must make examples of all foreigners who abuse our laws and inflict hardships on our fellow Americans.

Anything you can do to punish Miss Papagállou for violating her visa status would be greatly appreciated. (I have enclosed a report that documents her illegal activities.) I personally believe that her swift deportation to Greece would best serve the interests of justice and the nation. I would be indebted as usual for whatever you could do to bring about that outcome.

Sorry I missed you at the fund-raiser in Pasadena. I was shanghaied by Senator Crestwall to entertain a group of Monterey investors. Next time you're in town you must allow us the privilege of hosting a dinner of your most ardent followers. Give our love to Betty and the children.

Sincerely yours,
Catherine Dubeau

The reference to missing him in Pasadena was an ad hoc deception meant to put any nosey secretaries or others who might read the letter off the scent of any scandal. In truth, Catherine had slept with the congressman the night of the fund-raiser, and the statement of being "indebted as usual" was a code word for favors rendered.

Catherine had been quite ingenious in discovering Irina's vulnerability. It had required persistence and imagination, but they paid off when Abigail Downing, the same feature writer who, at Catherine's confidential request, had written the article on male stripteasers, followed her advice and fished among Kúbokoff's ballet students for tidbits about

Paul's personal life. It was then that Downing, and in turn Catherine, learned of his Greek girlfriend and, under the guise of preparing an article on young ballet dancers, unearthed the story of her visa problems.

Fortune had smiled on Catherine's scheme when Downing encountered the cunning and vengeful Melissa Manford, Paul's unrequited dance partner. Melissa knew a great deal about Irina, which she recounted in delicious detail. She also served voluntarily as the reporter's clandestine agent in Irina's ballet class, quietly tracking down bits of confirmatory information and foraging for new leads. The result was the compilation of a fairly complete biographic report on Irina's life since coming to the United States, describing her family situation, her acquaintances, and her schooling. The report documented a number of occasions when Irina assisted her aunt's close friend, a hardware wholesaler, to inventory his warehouse. Although Irina viewed this work as a personal favor to him and to her aunt, he insisted each time that Irina accept compensation. "Call it a gift," he had said, each time pressing forty or fifty dollars into her hand.

Technically, she was in violation of her student status; in fact, the paltry sum she earned would not have interested the Immigration and Naturalization Service, had it not been for two factors. First, when her visa had expired a year earlier, her aunt enlisted a lawyer to appeal for an extension. The lawyer, the husband of a neighbor, took the matter more as a favor and, not planning to charge for the service, did not aggressively pursue the extension. As a result, the appeal languished in the INS bureaucracy for months. When Irina's aunt pressed the lawyer for action, he promised to pursue the matter but never got around to it. The second factor that energized the INS to act was, of course, the intervention of Congressman Knox.

A month after Catherine had written to Knox, a middle-aged man neatly dressed in a three-piece gray suit and matching tie rang the doorbell of Irina's home. Her aunt opened the door.

"Yes?" she said, thinking the caller was an encyclopedia salesman or a Jehovah's Witness missionary.

"Is this the residence of Irina Papagállou?"

"Why, yes, it is. And who are you, sir?"

He gave his name and said, "I'm a federal marshal." He pulled a flat black leather, wallet-size case from his coat pocket and opened it, displaying a bright gold badge and an official identification card. "Is Miss Papagállou in?"

"Yes, she is." The woman backed away, worried by the caller's official status, which could only mean trouble. Federal marshals don't make courtesy house calls. "Please come in."

"Thank you," he said, stepping into the living room.

"Take a seat. I'll go find her."

Irina entered the room shortly, deep concern written on her face. "I'm Irina."

He stood and shook her hand.

"Is there a problem?" she asked.

"Yes, ma'am, I'm afraid there is." He reached into the breast pocket of his coat and withdrew a small packet of folded legal documents which he extended to her. "It is my sworn duty to inform you, Irina Papagállou, that you are hereby notified to appear before the Federal District Court for a deportation hearing next Wednesday in room 926 of the Federal Office Building in San Francisco. Failure to appear will result in immediate issuance of a federal warrant for your arrest. You may be represented by legal counsel. The particulars of the case against you and the date, time, and place of the hearing are set forth in the documents I am delivering to you. Thank you and good day." The marshal bowed slightly to Irina and her aunt and without another word departed.

Irina remained standing in the center of the room with the document packet in her hand looking in disbelief at her aunt. "What is it?" gasped Irina. "What have I done?"

Her aunt gave her a quick comforting hug but had already guessed what the documents would say. "Let's see the papers."

For the next half hour they huddled together on a couch anxiously reading and rereading the papers. Despite their confusing format and complex legal terminology, the documents presented a clear straightforward case against Irina. She had broken the law by remaining in the United States after her visa expired, and she had been gainfully employed when she was prohibited from being employed.

"We need a good lawyer," her aunt declared. "I'll phone Paul's mother. She'll know what to do."

"I'm not going to contest the charges," said Irina flatly without emotion.

"What?" Her aunt did not understand. "That means deportation? Is that what you want?"

"I have no desire to remain in the United States."

Paul's rejection of her had wounded her irreparably. She had not spoken with him in six weeks...since the night before the article exposing him as a stripper appeared in the newspaper. He had severed all communication with her. All she wanted now was to get away from him and ballet and everything that reminded her of him...to flee from her pain and sorrow. She had no reason to stay. It would be better for everyone if she left.

The hearing was conducted in a formal but nonchalant manner in a small wood-paneled courtroom in the Federal Office Building downtown. It lasted no more than five minutes. The presiding judge read the indictment and calmly ruled against her. "Do you wish to appeal this verdict?"

"No, sir, I do not."

"So be it. It is the order of this court that you be deported by federal marshals to Athens, Greece on Monday of next week. Until that time you will, on the recommendation of the Justice Department, remain on your own recognizance. You will present yourself to the marshals at your home as directed by them. Do you understand this order and agree to fulfill its terms?"

"I do, Your Honor."

"Case closed." He turned to a woman seated at a desk nearby and said, "Next case, please."

At Irina's insistence Paul had not been informed of the hearing, but Eleanor attended and tried to console Irina and her aunt in the corridor

284

outside the courtroom following the judge's decision. But Irina firmly rejected Eleanor's sympathy.

"For reasons Paul alone understands," Irina told his mother, "he has chosen not to see me or call me. That is not an act of love. The only reason he would see me now is out of pity, and I don't want or need his pity."

"But Irina," pleaded Eleanor, "I'm sure he loves you. He loves you very much. He's depressed by his dismissal from the school and ashamed of what he did at that club, but it's only a temporary thing. He'll come out of it, I know, stronger and more confident of himself and more in love with you."

"You don't understand. If he withdraws from me every time he faces a crisis, then what kind of a relationship can we have?" Irina's bitterness and hurt shown in her eyes. "When two people are truly in love, they look to each other for strength to meet life's challenges. They draw closer together; they don't turn away from each other."

Such sage words from one so young impressed Eleanor but left her without a response. She and Brock had done the very opposite, never gaining strength from each other, always turning away from one another. What could she say?

"It's just as well I return to Greece. Living here..." She was about to say "close to him" but even that hurt too much. "Living here would be difficult. I am Greek. My place is in Greece, not America."

But when Eleanor returned home from the hearing, she disobeyed Irina's wish and phoned Paul to tell him of the tragic turn of events. Witnessing Irina's suffering convinced Eleanor the two young people were after all in love and that Paul should know of the deportation order. He would never forgive his mother if Irina were deported and he were not told of it in advance.

"I don't believe it!" he cried. "They can't do that! You don't just exile someone because their appeal for a new visa gets lost in red tape or because they accept a few bucks as a favor to someone else. That's crazy!"

"Paul, dearest," his mother said. "It's all over and done with. Ranting about it won't change anything. She made foolish mistakes at an unfortunate time when illegal aliens are a hot issue. Irina is being made an example for others. Anyway, she refused her right to appeal the judgment. I spoke to a lawyer about it, and he said he was sure he could overturn the decision, but she refused."

Paul cocked his jaw as he reached a decision. "I have to see her. Will you drive me?"

An hour later Paul stood propped on his crutches in front of Irina's door anxiously waiting for her lovely face to appear. He rang the bell a second time as his mother watched from her car in the street. Footsteps sounded, and the door opened.

When Irina saw it was Paul, her impulse was to throw her arms about him and cry out her love, but the pitying look on his face instantly angered her. "If you're here to express condolences, you came to the wrong address."

"Irina, please, listen to me! I'm sorry I shut you out. It was dumb and foolish of me. I was terribly upset, but I love you. I truly love you. You're the only thing that matters to me."

"More than ballet?"

"That isn't fair! Ballet is a profession. You're my life. These aren't things one chooses between. They go together."

Irina understood perfectly what he meant, but it had no relevance to her situation. "Maybe so, but it's too late. Your country is deporting me next week. I violated your laws. I'm a criminal."

"You make it sound like I'm the one deporting you."

"What's the difference?"

"The difference is I love you. Won't you appeal the verdict? You can win, you know. What you're charged with is trivial."

"No. I want to leave the United States. I'm unhappy here."

"You can't leave! I need you! I want you to marry me!"

Marriage? She looked at Paul afresh, standing before her on his crutches, muscular and tall, dark flashing eyes, endearingly handsome. How she loved him. In all of their many conversations they had envisioned a happy future together, loving each other, raising a family. Yet they had avoided the specific topic of marriage. They both felt they were too young and inexperienced for it. Too vulnerable. Too lacking in confidence that their love could triumph over life's adversities. Paul had been scarred badly by the breakdown in his parents' relationship. They, too, had been in love once, yet their marriage had crumbled under the weight of their problems. Irina herself had been abandoned through the

286

untimely death first of her mother and later her father, underscoring the fragility of life and its partnerships. She carried with her the ever-present fear of again being abandoned, and it had undermined her faith in the durability of marriage. Paul's refusal in the past several weeks to see her merely reinforced and legitimized this fear, which under the present circumstance was a lethal blow to Paul's sudden proposal.

Irina's eyes brimmed with tears. "Would you close me out of your life every time you suffered a setback or faced a serious problem? Would you set our love aside like...like an old pair of shoes that you'd outgrown? Would you abandon me?"

"Of course, not. I love you."

"Did you love me last week and the week before?"

"Yes. Oh, yes. I swear I did, but I was..." He stopped in midsentence, seeing where her reasoning was taking him.

"You see, Paul?" Tears streamed down her face. "You're not ready for marriage."

"I love you. That's—"

"Would you have asked me to marry you if I weren't being deported?"

Paul hesitated. "But that's different. Irina! Why can't you see I love you?" He reached for her but she pulled away.

"No. Don't touch me. That will only make it harder."

"After all we've been to each other, all we've talked about, all our plans, you can't let this happen."

"*You* let it happen! *You* did! If we were as close as you say we are, you would have come to me. We would have worked it out together. But you didn't."

"I will next time. I promise. Irina, please, I love you. I want you to be my wife. I want..."

"Go away, Paul." She began to cry. "You don't know what love is...and you certainly don't know anything about marriage." She looked at him wistfully a long moment. "Go away and leave me alone." With that she bowed her head and shut and locked the door.

Paul teetered on his crutches staring at the closed door before him. Then his face contorted, and he wept. Softly, uncontrollably. His shoulders shook, and he staggered. By his own foolishness he had lost the one person he held most precious in all the world. He started to reel drunkenly, when two hands took him by an arm.

"It's all right, Paul," said his mother gently. "Come back to the car. I'll drive you to Mr. Kúbokoff's."

"No," he muttered defiantly, shaking his head. "Not Kúbokoff's. Take me home. I'm not going back to Kúbokoff's. I'm not going back. I'm through with that. I'm through with ballet, and I'm through with school."

"Paul, this isn't the time to make decisions. You're upset. You're—"

"Mother!" He took her by the shoulder and aligned his eyes with hers. "Look in my eyes."

Her face paled at the fierce bitterness she saw there. They were Brock's eyes, and they shown with his single-minded determination.

"Mother, it's over! Strike three!" His voice turned suddenly soft while his reddened eyes still held hers. "I'm out...it's over."

Her lips trembled as her heart-breaking anguish reached out to him but could not penetrate the grim remorse that blanketed his mind. He looked away to the maples and oaks swaying in the late afternoon breeze across the lawn as an empty desolation came over him.

Aside from Catherine the only person in the world pleased with the outcome of the tragic chain of events that had wreaked havoc on the lives of Paul and Irina was Paul's father. Catherine had pulled the right strings, and Brock had gotten his way again. They had celebrated this denouement with champagne, but the crowning glory was the sight of his son standing before him at his D-M office one month after Irina's deportation.

Paul had come in unannounced. He just waltzed in—still limping slightly—like a curious passerby, only he wasn't curious. Solemn and withdrawn would better describe him. He was there out of the blue to pay homage to his father's superior wisdom, to beg his pardon for having disobeyed his wish that Paul not pursue a career in ballet, and to find out if the offer of a job were still open.

"Of course it is!" said Brock jubilantly, almost yelling in his elation as

288

he rose from his chair to walk around the desk. "It's always been open." Brock was ecstatic at the prodigal's return. "Paul...son." Brock put his arm around Paul's shoulders and walked him to the glass wall with the panoramic view of the bay. "I know you've had some pretty tough times lately. It was in the newspapers...about your...dancing job. Were the stories anywhere near close to what actually happened?"

"Pretty close," Paul replied in a subdued voice.

"I'm sure it was painful. Your coming here took a lot of guts. I admire you for that, I truly do. You've shown great character."

"I'm really sorry about everything."

"Let's make a deal," his father exhorted. "Let's set aside the past...all of it...and start fresh. Father and son...on a new course into the future...friends and partners. Whataya say?"

Paul cocked his jaw and looked up at his father, who was three inches taller. "I guess it's worth a try."

"Let's shake on it. Our first business deal."

They shook hands and embraced, awkwardly at first, but then more vigorously as the barriers erected between them by years of estrangement began to fall away.

"Come with me," said Brock happily. "I'll introduce you around."

He led Paul from room to room, making introductions, beaming with fatherly pride, basking in the warm feelings that Paul's handsome presence at his side generated among the staff. When the tour was finished, Maggie brought them coffee, and they settled down on the sofa to talk about Paul's future.

First, he would continue at the California College of Fine Arts. It was a respected institution with a reputable design department that would furnish him a solid grounding in the fundamentals. Meanwhile, he would work part-time at D-M learning the ropes. He would have a desk in Brock's spacious office where he could observe, listen, and take notes as his father went about managing the firm's diverse projects and interests.

Although he made a valiant effort to share his father's excitement, Paul's apprehensions showed through. Brock read his son's thoughts. "Hey, I know this is all strange and foreign to you. A whole different world of bids and contracts and deadlines and trial designs. It's complex, but I promise you it's exciting. It will give you more challenges and more feelings of accomplishment than you've ever had."

Seeing his son's fatigue, he shifted gears. "Look, let's call it a day. Why don't you have dinner with me tonight? You can visit my new apartment. I moved six months ago. We can talk some more, and I'll fill you in on the firm's financial picture."

"I really can't. Mother's expecting me for dinner. How about tomorrow night?"

Paul's response gladdened Brock's heart. "Splendid. Tomorrow it is. Get a parking permit and mag-card from Maggie so you can use the garage and elevator. It's more convenient than looking for a space on the street. She'll give you directions. How about seven o'clock?"

"I'll be there," said Paul with strained enthusiasm.

They shook hands again, embraced warmly, and Paul departed, leaving Brock smiling.

Brock sat down in his chair and lay back to savor his long-delayed triumph. Why is it, he wondered, that some people like himself were perpetual winners and others unavoidable losers? Many of the losers worked as diligently as the winners and made the necessary sacrifices. Many were as smart. What then made the difference? Luck?

Naw, he dismissed that idea. Luck was blind. If you place your faith in luck, you're no more in charge of your fate than a cork bobbing in the ocean. He decided the difference between winning and losing lay in ruthlessness or, in the rousing words of his high school football coach, "taking no prisoners." To be unafraid to hurt people's feelings, unafraid to make enemies, to cause others to fail, to profit from their setbacks and downfalls—that was ruthlessness. Lack of compassion. Lack of sentimentality. Lack of concern for others. Lack...he felt uneasy thinking it...lack of love. These were the qualities that most often separated the victorious from the defeated.

This train of thought disturbed him for some reason, so he got up to leave. It was near quitting time, and the office staff was shutting down operations for the day.

"I didn't make life's rules," he said aloud belligerently to no one. "I just play by them...and I play to win."

As he reached for his coat in the closet, a pain that had been nagging his groin off and on for the past two weeks flared sharply, doubling him over, bringing him to his knees. He exhaled convulsively and groaned. He had passed off the discomfort as a muscle pull, probably from tennis or working on his yacht, but this time it would not yield to rationalization. It was intense and real, burning in his belly like a tiny blowtorch consuming his flesh. Seconds passed but, unlike before, the pain did not subside. It persisted, contemptuous of his stubborn effort to quell the burning by sheer willpower.

When the searing pain continued, Brock, hidden by a waist-high planter, crawled into his private bathroom, kicked the door shut, and sagged onto the tile floor in a fetal position, eyes tightly closed, waiting for the agony to pass. It came in waves, ebbing and flowing, relenting with a promise of relief, only to return with merciless intensity, racking his groin till he whimpered like a child.

While Brock suffered in the privacy of his bathroom, D-M's employees were leaving, turning out lights, wholly unaware of his plight. Maggie had donned her coat and was approaching the exit when Valerie entered with a bright face and saucy grin.

"Hi, Mag! Is Daddy still here?"

"Hello, Valerie. Yes, I believe he is. Go on in."

"Thanks."

The lithe and beautiful sixteen-year-old, whose graceful looks and figure were beginning to emulate her mother's, sauntered into her father's empty office, then ran back to the foyer. "Maggie? He isn't there."

The ever-composed matron was unconcerned. "Maybe he left already."

"His car's still down in the garage. I saw it."

"Then try the bathroom."

Valerie jogged to the bathroom door and knocked. There was no answer. "Daddy, are you in there?"

Brock heard her summons, but a paroxysm of pain paralyzed his lungs, blocking his speech.

"Daddy?" She rapped lightly again, about to try the knob.

The pain suddenly mercifully subsided, and he gasped for air to fill his lungs enough to reply in a weak tremulous voice. "Yes, I'll be out in a minute."

Valerie scowled. "Are you all right? You sound funny."

His ordeal had left him drained of energy and with soreness throughout his abdomen. He got shakily to his knees, resting his elbows on the closed toilet seat where they remained for several moments. "I'm okay. Give me time to clean up. It's...been a rough day." He was dizzy and nauseated and concerned that he would faint. When in a few minutes the feeling passed, he struggled to his feet and rinsed his face with cold water from the tap. The shock of its coldness pumped adrenaline into his veins, restoring some of his vitality. He looked at himself in the mirror and groaned, not from pain but dismay. His bloodshot eyes stood out starkly against the sickly yellowish pallor of his cheeks and the bluish tint of his lips. He was a hideous sight.

He sat down heavily on the toilet seat and, closing his eyes, slumped back against the water tank. He hadn't felt this sick since he drank three bottles of cheap red wine with a woman friend in an Oakland motel two years before. He had since sworn off red wine of all kinds as a preventive, not a penance.

With five minutes' rest and only a lingering twinge of pain deep within his groin he rose unsteadily to his feet, a little wobbly but under control. He doused more cold water on his face, combed his hair, and made himself moderately presentable. The mirror showed he had regained a little color, so he took a deep breath and opened the door, prepared to meet his daughter's close inspection.

"You look awful!" she said with her usual bluntness. She never minced words. Doing so was commonplace and unexciting, and she enjoyed shocking people.

"I'm okay. Some bad food, I guess." He prayed the pain would not return and embarrass him in front of her. He had worked hard to portray himself invincible to her and others. Groveling on the floor like a sick worm was repulsive and degrading.

"Vince is downstairs. I want you to meet him."

"Who's Vince?" he asked with disdain.

"Vince D'Ambrosio. I told you about him. We've been dating several weeks. You said I should bring him by so you could have a look at him to see if he was—" she put on a playfully haughty air—"worthy!"

"Oh, yes, I remember." Brock was not in a playful mood. "Tell you what. Why don't you two drive me to my place. I'm not up to driving myself. My stomach's a little queasy. Do you mind?"

"Of course not. I'm sure Vince won't mind. I was hoping we could have a drink at your apartment and talk, so you could get to know him. He's really a neat guy."

"Oh, not tonight, kitten. That's real sweet of you, but I'm just not up to it. Maybe another night."

"Sure, Daddy, I understand. Let's go down. We're parked in front."

"I've got fantastic news to tell you," he said. As they rode the elevator, Brock related Paul's surprise visit to the office that day.

"Are you kidding me?" she howled.

"Of course not. Your brother and I sealed the deal. He's going to work for D-M part-time and occupy a desk alongside mine. It's the answer to my prayers."

"He up and quit ballet? Just..." She snapped her fingers. "...like that?"

"Apparently." Brock savored his secret knowledge of the entire affair.

They reached the lobby and exited the elevator.

"Was it because of that incident at his club and being kicked out of dance school?"

"I'm sure they were part of it, but I didn't press him for an explanation. I don't need one. He's going to join the firm. That's all that matters."

"I can't believe it."

"He seemed a little despondent. How has he been acting at home?"

"Well," replied Valerie, avoiding her father's eyes, "I haven't seen that much of him."

"Oh?" Too much time with Vince, he suspected. "What does your mother say?" Brock thought this was an excellent opportunity to find out how much, if anything, Paul and Eleanor knew about Catherine's role...and Brock's...in forcing Paul out of ballet.

"Uh..." Valerie shifted her eyes away again. "She didn't say anything."

Her evasiveness alerted Brock. "Young lady, when's the last time you spoke with her?"

"Day before yesterday," she replied and then continued, anticipating his next question. "I spent two days with a girlfriend up near Lake Tahoe."

She was not a convincing liar, and Brock immediately surmised she had been with Vince, not with a girlfriend.

They reached the main entrance and stepped out onto the sidewalk. The flashy ornamented all-red, fully restored 1985 Cadillac Eldorado Biarritz convertible parked outside was a natural extension of the flamboyant personality and wanton lifestyle of the young man leaning against it. Vincent D'Ambrosio, of medium height with curly black hair, tanned brown skin, heavy dark eyebrows, razor sharp nose, and an ivory smile. The spoiled only son of a successful and widely known San Francisco restaurateur, he was as close to the archetype playboy as one could find outside the advertisements in *Gentleman's Quarterly*. His pseudo-employment as his father's "director of promotional activities" enabled him to frequent yacht and athletic clubs on the thin pretext of developing business contacts, though the connections he sought were all personal and all female. He displayed his virile masculinity shamelessly by means of tight pants, gold chains about his neck and wrists, open-collared shirts that exposed his tanned hairy chest, and an audacious, almost insolent aggressiveness toward attractive women of all ages. His appetite and prowess as a lover were legendary among the clucking wishful gossips in the clubs who made much of the fact that he didn't restrict his affairs of the chamber to women his age but pursued young virgins and older women with equal zest. It was more his indiscriminate taste than his profligate lifestyle that offended them. The irony was not lost on Vincent, who reveled in their indignation, flaunting himself before them, going as far at times as to flirt with the more austere and aloof among them, some of whom later vindicated his contempt of their moral snobbery by propositioning him by phone.

Brock typecast him on sight as a restless, unprincipled womanizer. Such men plied the playgrounds of the rich and famous like hungry stalking lions prowling the fringe of the herd until they spotted a tempting quarry, then drove in boldly to purse and devour. In Brock's experience these sexual predators were endemic to any locale habituated by beautiful women. The reason he could so quickly and confidently identify Vincent as this type of person and know instinctively what was going on in Vincent's mind was that Brock was a member of the same species.

"Daddy, this is Vince," said Valerie.

The two predators shook hands firmly, Brock returning with bland indifference the other's broad toothy smile.

"It's a pleasure to meet you, sir," gushed the young man with unctuous sincerity.

"I'm sure," Brock replied coldly. "Let's get going. I need to get to bed."

Valerie signaled Vince with her eyes. "Daddy's not feeling well."

"I see. Mr. Stowolski, why don't you sit in back where you'll have more room?"

"Fine."

Vince opened the rear door and Brock gingerly climbed in, concerned that any robust movement would trigger another attack of whatever it was that had afflicted him.

As he sank back into the cushioned seat, he watched Valerie get into the front and was struck by her appearance. In his pain-ridden state he hadn't taken a good look at her. The person he saw was no longer the little girl he had played with on his yacht and who had accompanied him like a cuddlesome puppy on business trips to Hawaii and San Diego. This was a blossoming woman. How old was she? Fifteen? Sixteen? So young, yet her breasts and hips were already well developed, and her slender legs had filled out and were more shapely than he remembered. She was gorgeous and provocative like her mother—an obvious target for lusting lions like the black-maned wop behind the wheel.

"How old are you, Vince?" he asked, more as a challenge than a query.

"Twenty-one," replied the driver quickly, sensing Brock's purpose. He was actually twenty-four.

"Aren't you a little old to be chasing after girls Valerie's age?"

"Oh, Val and me are just good friends. She's a lot of fun. We aren't serious or anything. She plays a mean game of tennis, though."

His lame attempt to divert Brock's line of questioning was wasted.

"Is tennis the only game you play with her?"

Valerie twisted around to glare at her father. "Daddy, that's awful! Vince and I are just friends like he says."

"Yeah, I know all about friends. You make sure your lover boy keeps his in his pants."

"That's crude!" rejoined Valerie, turning abruptly to the front.

"So is getting pregnant. Make sure you don't."

The atmosphere in the car remained tense and silent the rest of the way to Brock's apartment building. Valerie was too humiliated to speak, Vince too intimidated, and Brock too sick. He wanted only to get to bed. They let him off at the entrance to his building and, after a perfunctory exchange of meaningless good-byes, they drove away.

As soon as the car was out of sight of the building, Valerie scooted across the seat and nuzzled against Vince. He smiled at her and sent her a kiss.

"Let's go to your place," she whispered, "and play those games my father said we shouldn't."

As soon as they entered Vince's condominium Valerie ran to the phone and dialed home. Her mother answered and barraged her with probing questions.

"Where are you calling from?"

"A restaurant downtown."

"Who's with you?"

"Vince. We'll have dinner, and then he'll drive me home."

"I thought your friend Jessica was bringing you home."

"She was, but she got asked out by someone, so I phoned Vince and he came and got me." It was a lie, but her mother wouldn't believe anything she said anyway, so what did it matter?

"I don't believe you," said Eleanor offhandedly. "When will you be home?"

"Oh, I don't know. Around midnight."

Eleanor preferred that she be home earlier, but she had no control over Valerie. Her father had seen to that years before. "All right, but don't be too late. Please?"

"Hey, what's this I hear about Paul quitting ballet and working with Daddy? Is it true?"

"I'm afraid so. Who told you?"

"Daddy did. I took Vince by his office this afternoon to meet him. I

296

still can't believe it. Paul was so dedicated to ballet. What happened? Why did he give it up?"

"It's a long sad tale. I'll tell you about it when you come home tonight. Maybe then you won't stay out so late. What did your father think of Vince?"

"Not much, I guess. I was hoping they'd get on better."

"What did he say?"

"He told me not to get pregnant."

"Brock, for heaven's sake! Haven't you got any better advice for your daughter than 'don't get pregnant'? She's just a child." Eleanor was furious at Brock's laissez-faire detachment from Valerie's life. "Don't you care about her?"

"Yes, I care." He shifted the phone to his other hand. "It may have slipped your mind, Ellie, but I've spent more time with Valerie the past ten years than you have, and I'm a lot closer to her."

"All the more reason for you to exercise more control and discipline in her life. God knows I've tried, but she won't listen to me."

"Ellie! Don't you ever let up? Must you control everything in her life? Is that why you phoned me? She's not like you, you know. And she doesn't run like a clock on a set schedule like Paul. She's a free spirit like me, living life as it should be lived with an open mind and, if I may say so, an open heart."

"Empty words, Brock. Empty words. The same words you've spoken to me a hundred times. They didn't help our marriage, and they won't help Valerie. It's because of her uninhibited lifestyle patterned after yours that she's headed for trouble. It's a pity you can't see that."

Eleanor, losing patience, hung up.

Paul had been restless after dining with his mother and went for a long drive making the grand tour of the bay: west across the Oakland Bay Bridge, past the Presidio, south along the Bayside Freeway, then east across the bay over the San Mateo Bridge, and back to Oakland on the Nimitz Freeway. As he drove, he examined his new situation over and over again, seeking a final reconciliation with his former but still lingering ambition...a final compromise that would appease his heartbreaking disappointment.

Giving up ballet and losing Irina were the most traumatic things he had ever experienced...maybe ever would experience. It required total reprogramming of his entire rationale for living. Not easily done. Before his life went awry he had laid out a careful tightly scheduled plan for his future that accounted in a logical and loving fashion for Irina, the family they would raise, and his progression through the ranks of dancers to the highest rung of his profession. That plan had been utterly obliterated, torn apart by the series of calamitous unrelated events which one after another had struck him like bolts of lightning, shattering his dreams and reshaping his life. He desperately needed a new foundation on which to rebuild his future, whatever it was to be. He could not coast aimlessly through life. He was the type of person who lived by a master plan and for a purpose. Without purpose or plan he could not function rationally. There had to be an objective in his life, an important goal toward which he strove and from which he drew inspiration and strength.

It was therefore predictable that he would latch on to the first promising opportunity that availed itself. It was also predictable to his mother, who understood his situation and motivations, that he would immediately fall back on his father's longstanding job offer. It was at hand, in easy reach, full of opportunity for growth and riches and even power if he liked. She saw it coming the moment he declared his intention to give up ballet. She saw it coming and she hated it for what it would do to her devoted and impressionable son...for all the reasons she despised Brock. And there wasn't a thing she could think of to prevent its happening.

When Paul passed the sign denoting the Oakland city limits, he thought of his father's invitation to dinner that evening and wondered what they would have talked about. Future projects? D-M's finances. Paul's professional development? It was important for Paul to begin

298

shaping a new strategic plan for his life. He must put aside his former ambitions and the memories they evoked and fix in their place a whole set of new prescripts to guide and govern his actions. He wished now that he had accepted his father's invitation. He wondered whether it was not too late to call on his father, who was probably still awake. It was only 10:30.

Paul made a sweeping U-turn and doubled back to the exit that would bring him to his father's apartment building. He pulled into the garage entrance, identified himself to the uniformed security officer behind the glass window, and asked if his father's car was still in the garage. When the guard confirmed it was, Paul thanked him and slipped the magnetic card Maggie had given him into the gate control box. The black-and-white wooden arm saluted. He drove through a narrow tunnel and down a steep ramp to the underground parking area where several visitor spaces were vacant. He parked in one, got out of his car, and walked to the elevator. Again, as Maggie had instructed, he inserted the mag-card into a slot in the elevator control panel. A whirring sound came from the door, then a thump, and the door slid open. He entered the wood-paneled compartment and pressed the button for the tenth floor. When the door closed, the elevator rose swiftly and quietly, slowing, then halting gently, the number 10 illuminated on the side panel. The door glided open, and Paul stepped out, looking to the right, where Maggie had said he would find his father's apartment toward the end of the corridor.

He took two steps on the spongy carpeting and stopped. There was only one door in that direction, and a woman with her back to Paul was standing in it talking with someone...almost certainly his father. Paul made a move to proceed when he stopped again. There was something familiar and arresting about the woman. Then the shock of recognition propelled him backwards into the elevator and out of sight. He flattened himself against the paneling and slammed his fist against the button marked G for garage. The door closed, and the elevator began its descent.

The long black hair. The nose and chin. The figure. There was no question about it. She was the woman he had slapped in his dressing room at The Voyeur. Thank God she hadn't seen him. But why was she there? Had she decided to sue him? Kate was wrong. The woman would make trouble after all. He had to talk to Kate at once. But first he must verify his identification.

He returned to his car and hunched down in the rear seat where he could watch the elevator door without being seen. He assumed—he hoped—that she had been leaving the apartment, not arriving. When she came out, he would get a front view of her face. That would clinch it.

A hundred rampant thoughts besieged his worried mind as he waited, pondering the possible ramifications of her contacting his father. Was she seeking an out-of-court settlement? Would a lawsuit affect Paul's improving relationship with his father? Would his father cancel their deal?

The elevator was moving. The lighted floor numbers above the elevator door showed it was rising. He stared hypnotically as the light behind the numbers inched to the right, finally stopping at the tenth floor. The number held unchanged for a few seconds, then began moving to the left. She was coming down. His mouth went dry, and he slunk down farther in the seat. She mustn't see him.

The elevator reached the garage and opened. When the woman emerged, he stole a quick look, then dropped down again. His mind recorded the image of her face, then retrieved from memory the face of the woman at The Voyeur and compared them. They were the same. She was the dingbat he had slugged in his dressing room.

He pushed himself to the floor and listened for her footsteps. The clicking of her heels on the concrete echoed through the garage as she crossed the floor drawing nearer to Paul's car. The clicking stopped, and a car door opened, then shut. An engine revved, dropped into gear, and moved away, its noise diminishing rapidly as the car ascended the ramp and passed through the tunnel. She was gone.

Paul opened the rear door and got out, looking around to confirm that no one had seen him. He felt a bit paranoid, as if spying on the woman had been illegal. He shrugged off the feeling and got behind the wheel. A minute later he stopped the car in front of the guard's window.

"Hi there," he said.

"Yeah, what can I do for ya'?" replied the guard.

"I, uh, wonder if you could give me some information."

"Depends."

"Well, I went up to see my dad, and the woman who just left was with him, so I came back down. I didn't wanna barge in, you know."

"Yeah, I watched you on the monitors." He pointed to a row of TV screens mounted on one wall of his cubicle.

Paul's mouth fell open when he saw them and realized his every movement and reaction in the elevator, hallway, and garage had been on display. He felt foolish and embarrassed.

The guard spotted Paul's chagrin. "Hey, man, don't worry none about it. I'd do the same thing I catch my old man messin' 'round some chick. I mean, it's private, you know?"

Relieved, Paul half-smiled. "Yeah, it's embarrassing. At first I didn't know what to do."

"You did right, man. You was cool."

"Do you know who that woman is?"

"No. Mr. Stowolski brought her in one night and told me she could come and go whenever she liked."

Paul was confused. "Whenever she liked?"

"Yeah. You know, man. You know how it is."

"When was that?"

"When he brought her here the first time?"

"The first time?" Paul didn't understand.

"Oh...I gotta think...maybe six or seven months ago."

"Months?" exclaimed Paul. "Six or seven months?"

His mind floundered in this new and perplexing information. She and his father were old friends! Lovers! She wasn't here to press her case against Paul. Paul had nothing to do with their relationship. And yet...

"At least four," said the guard. "She's been comin' in here two or three nights a week regular. She never says nothin'. Just drives through. Hardly pays me no mind."

"And you have no idea who she is?"

"Zero, man. She's Madame X, the mystery woman."

Paul thanked him and drove away, pondering the meaning of this discovery. Was it sheer coincidence that a woman having an affair with his father came backstage at The Voyeur? Maybe...maybe not. Did the woman know at the time that he was her lover's son? His identity had not yet been revealed in the newspapers. Again maybe not, but only maybe. The woman's connection to his father was suspicious and unsettling, since his father had vowed to run him out of ballet.

Paul had to learn who she was. He stopped at a phone booth and called The Voyeur. Kate was there as always and took the call the instant she was told it was Paul.

"So," said her raspy voice. "What are you up to? Wanna job?"

"No thanks, Kate. I've hung up my jock for good."

"You're one of the greatest, you know that."

"Thanks, but I need some information."

"Sure thing."

"What's the name of the lady I slugged in my dressing room? Do you remember?"

"Of course I remember, but I'm not telling you. I can't reveal the names of my customers. That's like...privileged information. If word got around I was giving out names, I'd be out of business overnight."

"Kate, I have to know. It's urgent."

"What's so urgent?"

"That woman's having an affair with my father."

"So, women have affairs. That's not urgent."

"You don't understand. My father may have put her up to going to my dressing room to create some kind of an incident."

"Why would he do that?"

"To create an incident for the newspapers."

"So? It was reported in the papers and that night the place was jammed. Biggest crowd I've ever had."

"That's not the point. Mainly because of that incident I was kicked out of the Montclair School of Ballet and my future as a dancer is down the toilet. I think my father caused all of this to happen, and that woman was a key player."

"Why would he do that?"

"Because he promised to run me out of ballet, to end my career."

"He's that mean and devious?"

"Mean and unscrupulous!"

Kate fell silent. Paul knew the phone connection was still open because he could hear music playing in the background. He waited for her answer.

"Her name is Mrs. Catherine Dubeau." She spelled it for him. "That's all I'll tell you."

302

"That's enough. Kate, I owe you for this. I won't tell anyone where I got her name."

"You better not. So, you owe me, huh?"

"Yep."

"Then come back and dance for me."

"I don't owe you that much!"

"You're right, Paul," she said gently. "You don't. So...you take care of yourself." She hung up without another word.

Paul dropped another quarter into the phone and dialed Kúbokoff's home. The phone rang half a dozen times before a groggy Russian voice growled, "Who's calling so late?"

"Alexéi Nikoláyevich. It's me. Paul."

"*Dorogoy. Byedny.* How are you?"

"Fine. Fine."

"V'y you call me so late? I am sleeping already."

"I'm sorry. I know it's late. I need some information. It's very important."

"Important. Okay. You ask. If I know, I tell you."

"Do you know a Mrs. Catherine Dubeau?"

"Katerina Dubeau." He spoke in Russian to someone, his wife Paul guessed, and repeated the name. "Ah, yes, I remember. T'is woman is very rich. She helps...*dobivayet dyengi*...yes, she helps raise money for t'e San Francisco Ballet. She is very...*vliyatel'naya*...influential."

There it was, thought Paul. Another connection. "You don't know her yourself?"

"Maybe I have met her. I don't remember, but I know t'e name and t'e face. I have seen her at many ballet functions."

"One more question. Do you know an Abigail Downing?" She had written the exposé in the *Examiner.*

"Abigail Downing? Of course, and so do you."

"Me? I don't know her."

"But you do! You talked vit' her after t'e show at my school. She vas vun of t'e people from Montclair t'at came to vatch you dance."

"That was Abigail Downing?"

"Of course. You don't remember?"

"I don't think she ever told me her name, and if she did I forgot it."

"V'at is t'is all about, Paul?"

"I'm not sure. It has something to do with my father. I'll tell you when I figure it out. I'm sorry I bothered you."

"It's okay. I go to bed now. You come and see me, yes? And maybe ve talk?" He still held out hope that Paul would reconsider his decision to quit ballet.

"One of these days we'll talk, I promise. Good night."

The next morning after his history class Paul phoned the *San Francisco Examiner* and asked to speak with Abigail Downing. The operator thanked him and rang the woman's number.

"Downing," snapped a harried female voice.

"Ms. Downing?" Paul swallowed nervously. "This is Peter Hall. I'm a friend of Catherine Dubeau. She asked me to do a special favor for her, and to do it I need a copy of the article you wrote for her. I tried the library, but that section of the paper is missing. She said you would have a copy. Could you fax it to me?"

"You mean the one on the stri—" She cut herself off. She was rushing to meet a deadline on an article, and her mind was distracted. Catherine's role in the strip-joint feature was confidential. Catherine would never have revealed that to anyone. "I don't recall doing any article for Mrs. Dubeau. I'm very busy."

The line clicked dead, but Paul had what he wanted. Good ol' Abigail had given it away. She had started to say "stripper" or "striptease" or "strip joint" but caught herself. And she admitted she knew Dubeau, although she probably would have known her anyway as a fund-raiser for the ballet.

He was pleased with his cleverness. He had established undeniable linkages between Downing, Dubeau, and his father. That could mean only one thing. His dismissal from Montclair had been a conspiracy masterminded by his father. Paul could never prove it, but he knew it all the same, and that's what mattered. And what was more, his father knew it and had lied to him at his office that very day.

Paul had read about sinister people who did not live by the same code of ethics the rest of society did. They shrewdly portrayed their misdeeds as acts of courage, of artistic self-expression, even of love...but they never admitted to themselves and certainly never to others that these were acts of pure selfishness. They crushed a rival in the name of free-market competition. They betrayed and were cruel to their friends and deliberately, recklessly violated their trust either due to circumstances "beyond their control" or as retribution for alleged wrongs. The sinister people were psychologically flawed creatures—destructive and dangerous to their fellow humans whom they willfully, even politely injured without remorse. Life for the sinister was a succession of rationalizations and self-delusions, of half-truths and lies, of cruel vengeful deeds.

From all that Paul knew from his childhood and from the recent tragic events in his life he concluded with both sadness and regret that his father was one of the sinister people. Deceit and guile were the trademarks of his father's success and of his lifestyle. Callous and merciless, he blinded himself to the pain and suffering he caused others just as he feigned ignorance of the circumstances that had crippled Paul's dreams of ballet stardom. Only a man obsessed with self-gratification could remain so insensitive and oblivious to the needs of others, especially his family. Only a father devoid of love could behave so cruelly toward a son. Brock Stowolski was indeed a sinister person with sinister motives.

Paul swore never again to set eyes on his father or to communicate with him in any form. Appealing to his father's humanity and decency was doomed to fail because Brock Stowolski possessed neither. He was a classic case of someone who could not distinguish right from wrong in a moral sense. Being morally blind and motivated only by his own self-interest, he lacked a conscience and thus was forever beyond the reach of human persuasion.

Paul had but one alternative: disown and disavow his father. Not out of vengeance—his feelings had carried him beyond that angry emotional state—but for Paul's own survival. He could never coexist with his father. Coexistence would mean living on his father's selfish terms, which was servitude, and that Paul could not accept, nor would his father ever tolerate anything less. It was time for Paul to leave home, to break away, to find peace in obscurity far from his father's clamoring influence and his mother's aching heart.

He drove home and packed a suitcase with jeans, sweatshirts, underwear, socks, casual and work shoes, and toilet articles. Nothing fancy, nothing formal, and nothing to do with ballet. He then sat down with his mother and calmly lovingly explained to her what he was doing and why. He would head for Oregon, he told her, where he could drop out of sight in the anonymity of odd jobs and strangers and cheap hotels. She tearfully pleaded with him to change his mind, but when she saw his iron resolve...his cocked jaw...she lapsed into a dazed quiet and said no more. He tried to prolong their conversation, but she shook her head and would not raise her eyes to his.

It pained him to see her in such distress. Not once in his memory had he ever intentionally hurt his mother. Having witnessed the loneliness and suffering his father had inflicted on her over the years, Paul had always gone out of his way to be kind, loving, and solicitous to her. This time, however, the circumstances as he viewed them offered no other option. He could not remain in San Francisco. He needed time and distance and solitude to sort out his feelings and reconstruct his future.

He pressed his cheek tightly against hers for a long moment and kissed her hair. Then he tore himself away and left her slumped in an easy chair in the darkened living room, alone and heartbroken.

EIGHTEEN

Eleanor remained seated, grieving over Paul's departure as one mourns the death of a loved one. His future and his happiness were the bulwarks of her life, the only things that gave it purpose and value, that made each day worthwhile and filled with promise and love. Now, on this darkest of all days, all that remained was her heartrending pain for her son. Everything else had been swept away by Brock's cruel hand like a fearsome tornado in the night. How she hated Brock. Were he with her now in this room and had she a weapon, she would kill him, God forgive her. If she were armed with nothing more than a stick, she would beat him with it till he was dead, till the evil in his heart could cause no more suffering to anyone.

She suddenly made an animal-like sound and, losing all control, threw herself from her chair onto the rug, beating her fists on the floor and sobbing to vent her unbearable frustration. She carried on insanely for nearly a minute until the surge of wild rage passed, taking with it her strength. Her body finally went slack, and she rested her head on her arm and closed her eyes as tears continued to trickle across her lips onto the rug.

She felt desolate and helpless. Each time before when Brock had wounded her she had stiffened her resolve and toughed it out, digging deep within her for the inner strength and will to face the new adversity and overcome it. She had rebounded again and again over the years on the simple conviction that things could be worse and would get better. She never lost hope nor stopped praying that she could change Brock, never surrendered her conviction that she could find happiness by living her life according to the Christian tenets on which she had been reared. And she had been reasonably successful...till now.

This time the blow was too severe, the damage too deep and disabling. This time she would not recover. Her resilience was exhausted, her reservoir of faith in a better tomorrow depleted. She was hopeless and helpless, feeling like a child again, wanting someone to tell her it would be okay, to soothe her, to fix it, to make it right again.

She rolled onto her back and opened her red swollen eyes to stare at the empty shadowed ceiling. *Like a child*, she thought. *Like a child.* And when things went wrong when she was a child, what had she done?

She filed through her memories of a golden childhood in a small town in New Hampshire. Of family picnics in summer and sledding in winter on the hill behind the old barn. Walks after school with girlfriends in spring to pick wildflowers for their dinner tables. Raking autumn leaves into piles for jumping contests in which the dogs noisily joined, yapping and licking dirty laughing faces. Roasting marshmallows in the kitchen fireplace while singing the favorite old rounds. Listening to the mournful wail of the north wind on bitterly cold January nights when the moon turned the snow-covered hills into sparkling fairy kingdoms where eight-year-old Eleanor imagined bearded elves danced and caroused among the towering pines, leaving their tiny footprints in the snow. Each morning Eleanor found the footsteps and followed them around and through the trees. Her playmates scoffed at her belief in elves, telling her the footprints were those of small animals, but she knew better. Even so, they ridiculed her and made her cry.

And what did she do when things like that went wrong? To what did she resort? To whom?

The cloudy images of those early years sharpened, and she began to remember...how she stayed in her room alone, angry and morose, waiting for someone. Someone to come home. Yes, that was it. Waiting for her brother Charles to come home from high school. He was nine years her senior, kind, generous, and serious-minded. He loved her and patronized her affection. She would run to his arms and sit in his lap, recounting to him in minute though exaggerated detail all the events of the day, both happy and sad. He had limitless patience and never seemed too busy to share her joys or to console her when things went wrong. How many times had he kissed her tiny tears? Too many to remember, for romantic sensitive little girls like Eleanor cried a lot and took everything very seriously. Yet her brother was always there to soothe her and set things right.

How long had it been since she had spoken to him? Four months since Christmas Eve when she last called him.

Wiping her face with her hands, she got to her feet unsteadily and went to the kitchen where she kept her Rolodex. She found his number, picked up her cell phone, and with trembling fingers punched the numbered buttons.

"St. Ignatius. Father Morrison speaking. How may I help you?"

She asked for Father Charles, and after some calling and footsteps he was on the line. "Charles! It's Eleanor." She struggled to sound natural, even flattening her hair with her hand as if he could see her disheveled appearance.

"Eleanor! It's great to hear your voice. How's everything?"

"Well..." She need not lie. Charles could always sense when she was not telling the truth. "Not good, which is why..." Her voice quavered, and tears reappeared as she choked back a sob. She fought to keep control.

"It's all right, honey," said her brother. "It's all right. I'm here to listen and help. Just take your time."

"Like we...used to...when I was...little?" Her words came halting through her sobs.

"You remember that, do you?" He chuckled, trying to soothe her.

"Of course. That's why I called." She wiped the tears from her cheeks with her free hand, already feeling calmer. "I was remembering how you would listen to my woes. Somehow they never seemed as dire after we talked."

"That's because they weren't dire to begin with."

"This time they are. Oh, Charles, I really need you." The tears flowed again.

"Talk to me, honey." His heart went out to her. "What's on your mind?"

For the next ten minutes, amid tears and sobs and moments of inhibited silence, she related the history of Paul's contrived discharge from the Montclair School and his expulsion from the ranks of ballet hopefuls. Charles listened, patiently as always.

"Brock is Catholic, isn't he?"

"Yes," she replied, "but in name only. I don't think he's been to Mass since our wedding more than twenty years ago."

"Have you talked to a priest about this?"

"That's what I'm doing now, silly." She laughed, straining to be lighthearted.

"You know what I mean. Your parish priest."

"No. What good would it do? Brock is beyond the influence of the Church."

"Dear Eleanor," said Charles, trying not to admonish. "No one is beyond prayer. Let's be constructive."

"I'm sorry. You're right. Say, I just remembered there was a priest that Brock told me about years ago. He was Brock's mentor at St. Charles College?"

"St. Charles?"

"Yes, where he studied for the priesthood."

"Priesthood?" exclaimed Charles. "You never told me he was a seminarian."

"It was never important, and Brock never liked to talk about it."

"Well, it may be important now. Who is this priest?"

Eleanor dug deep in her memory. It was so long ago and so many memories past. She was good at names, however.

The letter *L* came to mind. Louis. Leo. Leonard. "Father Leonard. That was it. I remember. My first beau in high school was named Leonard."

"Do you know where this priest is now?"

"I have no idea."

"Well, let me check. I'll contact St. Charles. If they don't know, I have access to several fairly reliable databases for locating priests. One of them is sure to work. I'll find him, explain the situation, and have him call you. Okay?"

Eleanor thanked him and wept some more while she answered his further questions about her life and how she was bearing up.

He reviewed his plan to contact Father Leonard, then said good-bye, promising to pray for her and her family...including Brock.

310

The next day Charles phoned her shortly after breakfast to report his quick success in tracking down Brock's seminarian mentor through St. Charles College, with which Father Leonard had maintained close ties over the years. The administration office furnished Charles with his address and phone number. Charles contacted him at once, talked about Eleanor's problem, whether Father Leonard could recommend a suitable course of action, and whether he would be willing to speak with her.

"Not only is he willing," reported Charles, "he's flying out to see you! He's on the faculty at Notre Dame University and said he's earned a little time off. He seemed concerned. I judge from the way he spoke of Brock that they were once very close. That could help."

"I hope so," she said. "Brock never talked about him after that one time. When did Father Leonard say he'd be coming out here?"

"Today. This morning. He said he had a number of old friends he'd wanted to visit in California for years but had never gotten around to it, and this was a good excuse, before they all died. I asked him jokingly if any of them were Protestants and whether he's worried he might not see them later in heaven. He said it wasn't the Protestants he was worried about."

They ended their conversation laughing.

At four o'clock that afternoon Father Leonard phoned Eleanor from the rectory of St. Dominic's Church in San Francisco where he was staying as a guest of the parish priest, an old school chum. Father Leonard introduced himself and invited her to dine with him that evening. She offered to pick him up at the rectory, but he said it was too out of the way and that he preferred to meet her downtown. She named a landmark hotel, and they agreed to meet in the lobby at seven o'clock.

She spotted his black clerical suit and white collar the moment she passed through the revolving door of the lobby. Her smile caught his eye, and he rose from his chair to greet her. He was in his late fifties, maybe older, taller than she had expected, well over six feet, with thick graying hair but a bright intelligent face that radiated vitality and kindness. She liked him immediately.

"Eleanor."

"Yes, and you are Father Leonard."

They shook hands as the priest said, "I am most sorry that we should get acquainted under such trying circumstances. Your husband was...is still a special person to me. I had always anticipated meeting his wife and children...well, in sort of a family reunion, even though we would not have met before."

"He spoke well of you, Father."

"I'm happy then. You must tell me what he said. I have a lot of catching up to do, but I mustn't keep you standing here. Shall we go into the restaurant?"

She nodded.

During dinner she did most of the talking as she recounted at Father Leonard's request the history of her relationship with Brock. Halting now and then to blot a tear with her napkin, she described their chance encounter in the shopping mall, their romance and marriage soon after, and then Brock's episodic infidelities and cruelty.

Cruelty. That word had become so hackneyed from overuse in media coverage of celebrated divorce cases that Eleanor, before her marriage, had been skeptical of women who claimed such abuse as grounds for legal action. After twenty years with Brock, however, she was no longer a skeptic.

"And you're certain," questioned Father Leonard, "that Brock engineered Paul's dismissal from the school?"

"There's no question about it. I also suspect he had a hand in Irina's deportation, though I can't prove it. It's the kind of thing he has a special talent for. He's at his best when it comes to bringing others down, whether it's a business competitor or a member of his family."

The priest's eyes saddened at her description of his erstwhile protégé. He shook his head slowly in disbelief.

Eleanor continued. "He can't stand to be outdone or second-best or to be defied when he has given an order or made a decision. It's more than

312

an ego thing. He feels personally threatened, and then he strikes back without mercy or regret. I sincerely believe, Father, that Brock has no conscience and that..." She wept unashamedly as her eyes searched the priest's face for understanding and hope. "...and that he is beyond the healing power of the Church."

"No one, Eleanor, is beyond Christ's healing."

She bowed her head. "My brother, Charles, reminded me of that, too, but neither you nor he have lived with Brock Stowolski."

"You must surely believe in Christ's healing power. Or perhaps..." He hesitated to follow his line of reasoning.

"Perhaps what?"

"Well, it's possible, even likely, that your enmity toward Brock has narrowed your perspective. It's only natural that you feel he should be punished for the pain and suffering he has caused."

Eleanor considered her feeling. "I admit that I may lack objectivity, but..."

"I won't ask you to change your feelings. After what you've been through, no one could expect you to feel differently. I am truly amazed that you've stuck by him all these years."

"I have strong moral convictions."

"So I see, and God bless you for them. But you're thinking you need more than blessings."

"I don't know what I need. Not for me personally. For Paul. My situation was hopeless long ago. Paul's is not. He has the talent to become a great dancer, if only he would realize it. He's still young with all kinds of opportunities ahead of him."

"Perhaps I could talk with him."

"If only you could. I don't know where he is. He went off to Oregon and left no address."

"Then we'll just have to find him."

"How?"

"Oh, I've had some experience with runaways."

"He isn't a runaway, Father. I mean, not like teenagers who flee home."

"I spent several years in Baltimore's inner city working with disadvantaged children. I realize Paul is not your typical runaway. Yet, like all of them, he's escaping from an oppressive situation. Adults can be runaways, too. Time and distance have an uncanny way of buffering the pain we humans suffer. But when the pain subsides, loneliness sets in. I think that will happen with Paul, and in no time you'll be getting a phone call just so he can talk with you and be reassured you still love him and for you to know he loves you. How strong a will would you say he has compared to your own?"

Eleanor lifted her shoulders. "I would guess he's as determined as I am about things."

"When did he leave? Yesterday?"

"No, the day before."

"Then I wager he'll call before the week is out, maybe sooner. When he does, you tell him an old priest, a friend of his father, wishes to meet him. No obligations. No recriminations. Just talk."

"All right."

"Good," said the priest cheerily. "Now, how about an extravagant dessert?"

Father Leonard was a blessed elixir, instilling in Eleanor a renewed faith not only in Paul's future but her own. He saw her life objectively, unfettered by the emotions and bitter lingering memories that blurred her own outlook. He held nothing back, speaking his mind honestly, openly, and confidently. Every time she was with him, at least once a day for the next week, she felt spiritually renewed, and her hatred of Brock diminished...but only marginally. She tried, as the priest urged, to nourish an attitude of forgiveness for Brock's misdeeds, but it was of little use. The wounds of her marriage still festered and tormented her. She needed some sign, however small, of Brock's remorse, some sign of regret, before she could bring herself to forgive his countless transgressions against her.

The more Father Leonard talked about Brock and their close relationship at the seminary, the more convinced Eleanor became that over the years the priest had carried an unshakable regret, perhaps a guilt, for having allowed the seminarian whom he described as clearly destined

314

for greatness in the Catholic Church to fall by the wayside by default...Father Leonard's default. Was this journey to California the priest's atonement for having failed the Church by not detecting the obvious warning signs of Brock's spiraling disenchantment with a vocation in the clergy? she wondered. Was the priest's self-condemnation now more severe because he was learning of the evil to which his former student had succumbed, to which Brock had become vulnerable without the protection of the faith he left behind at St. Charles?

Had Father Leonard confided in Eleanor his true purpose, her suspicions would have been validated, for it was his intention—the real object of his trip west—to hear Brock's confession, to cleanse his old friend's soul of its accumulated sins, and thereby expiate the priest's own feeling of complicity in them. The issue, Father Leonard told Eleanor, was not whether he would meet with Brock, but how and when. The encounter must not happen accidentally nor, the priest cautioned, should Brock know of his presence in San Francisco. Surprise was vital if the priest were to have any chance of penetrating Brock's mental bulwarks and influencing his thinking. Nevertheless, the obstacles appeared daunting.

Father Leonard's lengthy conversations with Eleanor throughout the week at St. Dominic's rectory armed him with much of the information he needed concerning Brock's life over the past thirty years. But he felt he needed more, from the perspective of Brock's children, and asked Eleanor if he could speak with Valerie. Eleanor was opposed to the idea. She persuaded the priest that the girl could not be trusted and would almost certainly alert Brock to Father Leonard's presence. A conversation with Valerie's brother, however, was a sensible necessary step to better understand all that had happened and why. It would also be therapeutic for Paul, letting him vent his anger and depression, drawing from his mind the poisonous resentments which his misfortunes had sown there. The face-off with Brock therefore would be delayed until Paul's whereabouts could be determined.

That step was accomplished sooner than either Father Leonard or Eleanor expected but exactly as the priest had predicted, by a phone call to her from Paul. It came coincidentally while Father Leonard was with her in her kitchen preparing a light lunch. Valerie was in school.

The conversation was brief and emotional, mother and son tearfully reaffirming their love and concern for one another. Father Leonard was touched by the strength of the affection he witnessed, a memorable demonstration, he thought, of the power that human love can wield in people's tangled lives and how love, a steadfast beacon showing the way out of troubled darkness, rises above life's turmoil to link people's hearts together.

As their conversation neared an end and Paul promised to keep in touch by letter and phone, Eleanor told him of Father Leonard's visit and his desire to meet Paul to learn more about his father. At first Paul resisted, rejecting anything associated with his father. But when his mother explained Father Leonard's purpose, Paul relented and agreed to meet the priest the next day in Portland at the apartment where Paul was staying with a former high school football teammate. Eleanor took down the address and phone number, then looked to Father Leonard for a sign that he wished to speak with Paul on the phone. He read her intent and shook his head, so she bid her son good-bye and exacted his promise to keep in touch with her.

The relief she felt at knowing where Paul was and that Father Leonard would be speaking with him on the morrow was abruptly shattered by another phone call an hour later as she and the priest were lunching.

"Yes," she said to the caller. "This is Mrs. Stowolski." She listened intently as Father Leonard looked on, her face showing the range of emotions the caller's message induced—curiosity, then surprise, then shock and concern.

"Which hospital?" she asked, her expression still troubled but under control. She waited for a reply. "Yes. All right. I'll be there as soon as I can, and I'll have a priest with me. A Father Leonard. Yes. Thank you." She hung up and gave the priest a somber pathetic look. "It's Brock. He's very ill."

Father Leonard rose from the table and went to her. "What's the trouble?"

"They aren't sure. That was Tom Shepley, our doctor. He said Brock has been suffering extreme abdominal pains with some rectal bleeding for several weeks. Brock thought it was gas and hemorrhoids or something

316

equally harmless, but late this afternoon the pain was so bad he called the doctor to his apartment. After only a brief examination the doctor had him taken by ambulance to the emergency room for tests and X-rays."

Her eyes watered and she turned away. "The doctor said it could be very serious...possibly cancer. I feel confused...and guilty. I've hated Brock so these past few years. At times I could have killed him."

"Eleanor, please. Don't talk nonsense."

Her eyes flared as she spun around. "It isn't nonsense!" she screamed, tears gushing. "You have no idea of my hatred for him. He's an evil person! Hateful and evil! I've wished him dead over and over. Even now!"

The priest went to her and grasped her hands in his. "I understand. I really do, but why are you crying if you despise him?"

"I...I don't know. I think..." She paused, trying to make sense of her confused and conflicting emotions.

"What?"

"I think I'm afraid...afraid he'll die...before he changes back to the man I fell in love with. I've always prayed he would change."

"We must go to him then," said Father Leonard, almost in a whisper, taking hold of her arm. "I know you love him despite his abuse of that love, and now he needs you, maybe really for the first time in your marriage. We can phone Paul and Valerie from the hospital."

By the time they reached the emergency room forty minutes later Brock had already been moved to a private room. Eleanor had prepared herself during the drive to the hospital for the emotional shock of seeing Brock in the Emergency Room. When the receptionist informed them his room was in the Intensive Care Unit, Eleanor clasped her hands to her breast and moaned, "He's going to die."

"That isn't certain at all," comforted the priest. "They're simply treating him, evaluating his condition, taking the normal precautions. It may not be as serious as you think. Let's go find the doctor."

They walked briskly down the hallway to a bank of elevators and took one to the second floor of the hospital tower that was the centerpiece of the sprawling medical complex. When the door opened, they expected to be greeted by an air of excitement and orderly commotion with nurses rushing from room to room carrying medicine and equipment, tending to patients, obeying doctors' hurried clipped commands studded with medical jargon unintelligible to the layman. What they found was a hushed, tranquil, seemingly leisure environment. Two white-uniformed nurses conversed inaudibly at the nurses' station at one end of the shiny waxed hallway, their white caps bobbing up and down as they talked. The doors to all of the rooms were closed, and the only noticeable sound was the low whirring of the refrigeration unit on a drinking fountain.

They hurried to the nurses' station, and Father Leonard inquired of Dr. Shepley and Brock.

"Yes," replied one of the nurses. "Dr. Shepley said to call him when you arrived. If you'll have a seat over there in the lounge, we'll notify him you're here."

"Are public phones there?" asked Father Leonard.

"Yes, Father. On the wall to the rear."

"May we see my husband?" asked Eleanor, impatient to learn of his condition.

"I think Dr. Shepley wants to speak with you first. His office is nearby. He'll be here shortly."

Father Leonard politely intervened. "Let's wait, Eleanor. The doctor will have information for us."

"I suppose so." Seeing the phone on the wall she said, "I'm going to call Paul and Valerie to tell them. They'll both want to come."

Eleanor reached her son immediately and gave him the news. He was bowled over. His father had never been sick before except for hangovers. Paul said he would fly to San Francisco on the first flight he could get and then take a taxi to the hospital. He was glad Father Leonard was there with her.

Valerie could not be located. To Eleanor's surprise and irritation, she was not at school. She had called in sick. So Eleanor tried the country club, but there was no trace of her. She assumed Valerie was off somewhere with that sleazy D'Ambrosio character. She left messages at the club, the high school, and on their home answering machine for Valerie to call the hospital. Meanwhile, she and Father Leonard sat stiffly on a sofa in the small richly appointed waiting area opposite the nurses' station. Minutes later, as Eleanor was rising to make another phone call, Dr. Shepley came round the corner in his white starched linen coat, a silver stethoscope yoked around his neck.

"Hello, Eleanor," he said, smiling. He was in his forties with a large forehead whose baldness was made more prominent by a shaggy red beard that wagged as he spoke. He shook her hand and introduced himself to Father Leonard. "I know you're both very worried, and there is reason to be, but we don't yet know the nature or severity of Brock's illness."

"Is it cancer?" Eleanor challenged, driving to the heart of the issue.

"Perhaps. He shows many of the signs. Swelling in certain areas of the body, bleeding, severe pain, nausea. We'll know more in an hour or so when the initial test results are in. We've run a blood test, chest X-ray, and an MRI. Depending on what they show, we may order up a longer series of exploratory tests...barium, more X-rays, a CEA, urinalysis, biopsies."

"Can we see him?"

"Of course. However, he's sedated and only semiconscious, so he probably won't know you're here. You can stay with him as long as you wish. Just keep out of the way of the nurses. They're a very efficient but dogmatic crew, and they take umbrage at anyone who gets in their way." He grinned. "Including doctors. I'll bring the test results to you as soon as they're in."

"How long will that be?" asked Eleanor.

"Perhaps an hour. Maybe longer."

The doctor escorted them to Brock's room, then departed to look after other patients. Eleanor went to the bedside while the priest stood near the door where he could watch without interfering in this intimate moment between husband and wife.

Brock lay faceup in the bed, intravenous tubes connecting his wrists to two plastic bottles dangling from a chromium pole. His face seemed to have aged ten years since Eleanor last saw him only weeks before. He was fifty years old, but the hollowness of his cheeks and the pallor that showed through the tan of his face made him look much older. There was gray among the dark curls of his hair, and his jaw was slack, depriving him of his usually noble profile.

Eleanor stepped to the side of the bed and laid her hand lightly on his hair, stroking it gently as she studied his face, trying to remember when she had last touched him. Months? Years? What did it matter? He lay there decrepit and vulnerable...and at rest. All the vile passions and obsessions that had ruled his mind and his life were now stilled by the illness in his body, that so-called temple of the soul.

You can cheat people, Brock, she thought, *but you can't cheat Nature.* She felt a certain vindication in seeing him physically immobilized. He was a man who gloried in his manliness and physical attributes, flaunting them before anyone whose attention he could attract. His compulsion to parade himself had long ago become for Eleanor not merely obnoxious but tiresome. She had thought he, too, might one day weary of such childish displays, but they were a habit too deeply ingrained to be shed easily.

She shook her head. Poor Brock. She wondered if he had ever known true happiness. His lifestyle had been guided by flimsy, self-centered, hedonistic principles that gave no lasting spiritual nourishment, only temporal pleasures. In point of fact, Brock's life was devoid of any spiritual component she knew of. When you came right down to it, she thought, he's a pretty pathetic creature, and she wondered again why he never realized it. Why he could not see himself as God surely did. Then Eleanor rebuked herself for presuming to know what God thought. Only God could fathom Brock's spiritual character.

"Who knows?" she said aloud. "Maybe in His eyes you're a saint."

"Who's a saint?" asked Father Leonard. He confessed inwardly to a wry fascination in analyzing the changes time had wrought in his old friend's features. Time had not been kind.

"I was merely speculating, Father. Do come over and see him. Stand here with me."

The priest approached the bed and stood beside her.

"Would you say a prayer for him?" she asked.

"I would be honored."

He knelt down and Eleanor followed, resting her head on the mattress, while her fingers remained touching Brock's hair.

"Oh, fair Jesus, our Lord and Savior, You who healed the sick and raised the dead to manifest Your divinity as God's only Son, we pray You

320

will endow this afflicted man, whom we both dearly love, with the power and grace to see anew the miracle and sacredness of life and to accept Your heavenly Father's precious gift of love to be shared among all people. Grant to our beloved husband and friend a new lease on life. Cleanse him of his disease. Spare his life. We pray in Your Holy name. Amen."

They got to their feet, and Father Leonard viewed Brock's face up close for the first time in thirty years. Time and travail had indeed left their marks. Gone were the innocence and purity that had shown so brightly at St. Charles. Gone were the youthful pride and nobility, the promise and commitment. The sleeping face—a tired, traveled face—was that of a stranger. Brock's profligate ways had taken their toll. Eleanor had grown accustomed to the incremental changes in Brock's appearance, but their cumulative effects over three decades jarred the priest, whose own face had changed very little outside of a few wrinkles.

"We have much to talk about, my friend," he said solemnly to the unconscious figure in the bed. "Much to talk about indeed."

They stayed with Brock for an hour or so, watching him, chatting amiably with each other to ease their concern, waiting for Dr. Shepley's return with the test results and the dreaded prognosis. The afternoon dragged on as the clock edged toward 5 PM. Eleanor had just come back from the ladies' room when Shepley returned.

He wasted no time on preliminaries that might prepare Eleanor and the priest for bad news. It wasn't his style. He figured people wanted to hear the verdict straight out without a lot of beating around the bush.

"Well, it isn't good," he stated flatly, seating himself in a chair opposite them with the bed behind him. "There is foreign matter in the blood, bleeding in the intestines and the bladder, lymph nodes swollen and inflamed and, worst of all, malignant tissue everywhere. Biopsies confirm a contagion of cancer throughout the body. It's cancer in a fairly advanced stage. We will, of course, run further tests to validate these initial indications and pinpoint precisely the state and prognosis of the disease. But there's no question about the cancer."

He paused, waiting for their reaction.

Eleanor's mind was blank. She was unable to speak.

"What are his prospects?" Father Leonard asked.

"You mean how long will he live?"

The priest nodded.

"Only additional tests can tell us reliably. If I were to guess, based on my knowledge of such cases, I'd say weeks not months. At worst, days."

Eleanor was stunned. "Will it be painful?" she asked, wiping her eyes with a hanky.

"We will do everything possible to alleviate his pain. There will, however, be discomfort. It's unavoidable."

A comely overweight nurse came through the door and began preparing Brock to be moved to the X-ray room. While she checked his pulse and blood pressure, Dr. Shepley rose and beckoned Eleanor and Father Leonard, leading them out into the hallway.

"The tests will take an hour or so. You can wait in the lounge or, if you'll accept the advice of a friend, you'll go home and get some rest. His condition won't change overnight, and you both can use the break. The strain on you is showing."

"You're right," Eleanor agreed. "You will call us if there's any change?"

"Certainly, but I don't expect any. We'll know the full dimensions of his situation tomorrow morning for certain. We will have stabilized his condition by then, so he'll be conscious and lucid, and you can talk to him. Why don't you return here around nine in the morning?"

Eleanor phoned Father Leonard at 8 PM to say she would be late in the morning and for him to meet with Shepley alone. Valerie had not come home that night. Eleanor spent hours calling her daughter's friends and checking with the police. There was no word of her whereabouts and no report of an accident, nor did any hospitals list her among their emergencies. Eleanor rang Vince's apartment a number of times, but no one answered, so she surmised Valerie and her man friend were shacked up somewhere else. Paul had phoned from the Portland airport around ten. All flights to San Francisco were booked solid, so he'd catch the first one out in the morning.

Eleanor was severely depressed and after only a few hours' sleep was

322

in no shape to face the harrowing news she was certain awaited them at the hospital. She decided to rest in bed till noon. A few more hours' sleep would not change the doctor's assessment. Paul was going directly from the airport to the hospital. She would meet him there.

Dr. Shepley greeted Father Leonard in the hospital's main waiting room where dozens of people were quietly gathered for the opening of general visiting hours.

"Good morning, Father. Let's go find some privacy." The doctor led the way to one of the consultation offices and found an empty desk where he seated himself, while Father Leonard pulled up a chair. "The tests confirm the worst. Cancer is widespread throughout his midsection. Numerous vital organs appear to be involved. The diseased area is so extensive and in such an advanced stage that arrestive treatment is not signified."

"He is dying then," said the priest solemnly.

"I give him a week, and that's generous."

"Does he know?"

"I told him an hour ago."

I'm sure you did, thought the priest. "And about me? Does he know I'm here?"

"I said nothing about your presence or the absence of his children. Have you located them yet?"

"Valerie didn't come home last night. Eleanor tried to find her but was unsuccessful. She'll keep trying. Paul's flying in this morning."

"Good. There isn't much time. If Brock's condition continues to deteriorate, as it rapidly will, we'll be forced to administer painkillers that will virtually anesthetize him, making it impossible for you and the others to communicate with him effectively. I pray Valerie will be found in time."

"Thank you. May I see him now? Eleanor said it would be all right. She'll be along later. She had a tiring night."

"Certainly. By the way, Father, we moved him to the Terminal

Ward." He said Terminal Ward as he might have said cafeteria or library. "Room 222. It's better equipped to handle his type of illness. He's awake. I'll check on him later in the morning. We've got him on a mild sedative through an IV, but he's alert and conversant. Does he know you, Father?"

Father Leonard's eyes seem to glaze over for a moment. "Yes...from many years ago."

The priest walked to the second floor and opened the door to Brock's room without knocking. He stopped in the doorway, waiting to be recognized and invited in. He would not force himself on Brock and was fully prepared to leave, if that were his former friend's wish. He sensed for no good reason other than his memory of their last conversation thirty years ago—which he could recite verbatim—that his unannounced arrival would be greeted with hostility and suspicion. For that, too, he was prepared.

Brock lay on his back, his eyes closed. Dr. Shepley had said he was awake, so the priest decided to announce his presence.

"May an old friend enter?"

Brock opened his eyes and squinted at the door. The voice was familiar, but he could not make out the face. "Who is it?" he asked weakly.

"Father Leonard. The old wiseacre who called you friend and colleague when you had thoughts of becoming a priest."

Brock's face gave no sign of welcome, freezing instead into an implacable unreadable mask. "So. You've come to condemn and bury the sinning seminarian. I should have known Ellie wouldn't miss this one last chance to nail a few more spiteful spikes in my coffin."

"May I come in?" the priest repeated, not responding to Brock's challenge. He would not enter unless invited.

"By all means. Join the fun."

Father Leonard stepped into the room and closed the door, while Brock continued speaking. "You believe no doubt that I have lived a life of self-enrichment, debauchery, and wantonness and that Mother Nature is justly putting an end to it."

The priest moved a chair to the bedside and sat down, setting a briefcase on the floor beside him.

"Know any good exorcist jokes, Father? I know a limerick about one.

There once was a man with a demon, who promised to make him a he-man...."

Father Leonard interrupted in a soft, even, firm voice. "I came, Brock, to hear your confession, to anoint your flesh, and to pray for your salvation."

"Bull!" Brock's mouth sneered. "You came to gloat. The sinner is getting what he rightfully deserves. Isn't that what you think? Punishment for quitting the seminary? Isn't that why you came, you self-righteous hypocrite!" Brock winced from the pain his outburst caused him internally.

The priest, showing no emotion, continued to speak softly and compassionately. "I came to visit an old friend in Christ, to reaffirm that friendship and, if he wishes, to grant him absolution."

"Absolution for what?"

"For our sins. For what we have done and for what we have failed to do."

"So it's *we* all of a sudden. How noble...and sanctimonious!"

"I haven't come to censure you, Brock. I'm here out of love and compassion."

"Compassion for a sinner? Not likely. I can read it all over your face. Sweet vindication is what you're here for. Well, you know what you can do with that...."

"I understand your anger..."

"No, you don't. You only understand the world through the rose-colored windows of an idyllic philosophy that has lost its relevance. It may still play well among the pygmies but in downtown Frisco it's passé. I play the game of life by the rules of life, not by some wishful pie-in-the-sky dogma of goodwill. Life is competitive. Survival of the fittest. To the victor belong the spoils. It's the way of the jungle, the way of the world. God's world! The world He created! Psalm 119 says it very well: 'Happy are they who follow the law of the Lord!' Am I to ask His forgiveness for playing by His rules? I lived my life according to my convictions based on those rules. What one does out of moral conviction cannot, by definition, be immoral."

The words tumbled out as if bottled up under pressure. They were the rationale for Brock's lifestyle, the rationale he coveted and had invoked again and again over the years to justify his actions.

Father Leonard replied, biting each word. "You would define your own morality?" A testiness crept into the priest's voice as his stern self-control began to weaken under the fusillade of Brock's insolent assertions. "How convenient. Now you will doubtless define your own life eternal and take up residence there upon your death, which is in the offing."

"Why not?"

"Why?" The priest laughed derisively. "Because God Almighty alone defines morality. Not you! He and He alone judges...and He alone condemns. You've made up your own rules, haven't you?" His voice was rising. "When you left the seminary, you found life's rules not quite to your liking, so you bent and reshaped them a bit, made up new ones, more accommodating, more suitable to your aims. Then you pretended they were justified. And now—" he was yelling—"you have the audacity to ascribe them to God?"

Brock rose on one arm and angrily shouted back. "Who are you to tell me what the rules are? Who gave you that right?"

Father Leonard stood up, rising to his full height as he had in Brock's room years ago. "I am a priest! An ordained priest! With the holy power invested in me by Jesus Christ, our Lord and Savior, to forgive sins...or *not* to forgive sins!"

Brock's face blanched, either from fury or chagrin, the priest couldn't tell which.

"I tell you, Brock Stowolski, that your rules are as corrupt as your life has been. You have done great harm—unconscionable harm—to others...your family...in your merciless quest for power and pleasure."

Brock fought back. "I worked hard. I earned every penny of everything I ever got. With the sweat of my own hands I built a multi-million dollar company from scratch. I achieved things!"

"At what price?" scoffed the priest, who began pacing about the room as he used to at St. Charles. "The price of Eleanor's happiness? The price of your son's fulfillment in ballet? Is there no limit to what you would force others to sacrifice for your 'achievements'?"

"You're distorting the facts."

"I think not. I think you're a sinner, Brock. Pure and simple. Your philosophy blasphemes all the principles Christians hold dear and holy.

Your deeds mock real love and justice. You masquerade as an achiever when in fact you're a spoiler, an exploiter, a pillager of others' lives. Don't you realize what you've done...what you've become?" The priest paused, thinking, measuring his words. "I will anoint your body when you have passed on, but I will see to it that your sins are not absolved unless you confess them to me or another priest."

Brock's stony visage gave no inkling of his thoughts as he stared hostilely into Father Leonard's unwavering, resolute eyes. "I have nothing to confess to you or anyone else."

The priest nodded gravely. "As you wish. Then you will die with your sins darkening your soul. You will go to heaven's gate, your shoulders bowed under their weight, to pass before God's judgment. Were I in your shoes, I would fear God's justice and retribution, and I would pray for His mercy." He leaned down, opened his briefcase, and withdrew from it a light-blue Bible, which he set on the nightstand beside Brock's bed. It was the very same Bible Brock had left behind in his room at St. Charles. "Perhaps this will help you find the right path."

"I won't be needing that!" Brock snarled, irate that his former mentor had saved the Bible.

"Maybe not, but I leave it with you all the same."

The priest closed the briefcase and turned as if to go, then stopped. With a weary look that made no effort to conceal the mournful sadness in his heart, he glanced back at this pitifully stubborn, dying man. "I really hoped we might spend time together reliving some old but good memories...and perhaps clarifying what happened in your life...and why. But I see there's no point in it." He would give it one last try. "You're sure you won't make confession?"

Brock, his face turned toward the wall to avoid the priest's eyes, shook his head once very slowly.

"I'm sorry," muttered the priest. Then barely above a whisper, to himself. "Sorry for both of us."

When the priest had gone, Brock summoned a nurse by pressing the button on a cord slung over the headboard. She promptly appeared in the doorway.

"I don't wish to see anyone but my doctor and my daughter, Valerie. Is that understood?"

327

"Yes, sir."

"No visitors except those two. Not my wife, not my son, and not that obnoxious priest who just left. See to it!"

Cowed by his ferocity, she scurried off to inform her supervisor.

Good riddance, thought Brock. *Vicious miserable people. Come to persecute me, knowing I can't fight back. Scheming against me. Waiting for me to die. Father Leonard's unctuous superiority and sanctimonious demagoguery. Hypocrite. And then there's Ellie, the conniver, parading around as the grieving wife, waiting for me to die while she secretly counts the treasure she'll inherit. Oho, is she in for a surprise. I've fixed her wagon. I'll have the better of her. I always do...in everything...even my death.*

In fact, despite his present pain and the near prospect of death, he was pretty well satisfied with his life. He had accomplished everything he had set out thirty years ago to do. He had created DESIGN METAPHORS from nothing, building and expanding until D-M dominated the industry, providing him fame and fortune throughout his mature years. In the long run, of course, D-M will have flourished like Camelot for only *one brief shining moment.* It would, with his death, fall into decline and perish. No matter. He had despised the thought of obscurity during his lifetime. He had always yearned to be seen, to be visible and noticed, admired and envied. To be bigger than life. He had wanted heads to turn when he passed...and they did. Now that he was nearing the end, he supposed he really didn't mind if D-M withered and died with him. He had achieved his goal—he was a millionaire who quaffed expensive wines, dined in the finest restaurants, drove exquisite cars, lived in sumptuous surroundings, socialized in the most exclusive clubs, and slept with the most beautiful women. What more could he have wanted? His standard of living had long since risen past the level of highborn luxury.

But, yes, as he came to think about it, there was one thing, one objective unattained, the one whose accomplishment he had vowed the day he first rented D-M's suite in the Calvert Plaza—the ruination of one Roger Prentiss, the arrogant old man who had said Brock would never make it in the design business. Since that confrontation twenty-five years ago in Prentiss's office not a day had passed that Brock had not been ready to seize any opportunity to ridicule Prentiss's work, undercut his fees, steal his clients, and cripple his business...ultimately to destroy Prentiss Associates. Over the years Brock had clashed with him repeatedly, bidding on contracts, recruiting talented designers, renting prime floor space at exhibits. The two companies had vied for awards and especially the Institute of Interior Design's Best-of-the-Year Trophy, which each had won several times. In spite of Brock's campaign, Prentiss Associates had thrived, surviving every assault. Once, two years ago, Prentiss seemed in real jeopardy when he was indicted by a federal court for tax evasion. Brock had not been instrumental in exposing him but did testify for the prosecution—the day Brock met Catherine Dubeau outside the courtroom. Brock had been convinced that his die-hard adversary was guilty and that the court would find him so, levying enormous fines plus interest and maybe even sentencing him to prison. Brock had reveled in his adversary's predicament. But Prentiss was a shrewd tactician and in the end wriggled free of the charges on legal technicalities.

So where did the rivalry stand? wondered Brock, lying in his hospital deathbed. Where was that old reprobate Prentiss? The last Brock had heard, Prentiss, now 73 and suffering from Alzheimer's disease, had retired to his residence in San Diego where he lay in bed helplessly succumbing to the steady deterioration of his brain. Were the two of them similar in other ways? Perhaps, thought Brock, but he wished he had just one more chance to crush Prentiss Associates. Just one more chance. If only...

He closed his eyes and under the influence of his medication fell asleep.

Eleanor was in her bedroom putting on makeup when Dr. Shepley phoned to inform her that she, Paul, and Father Leonard were *personae non grata* in Brock's hospital room. She was dejected by the news but not surprised.

"Now you see what I've been putting up with these many years," she said, when the priest arrived for lunch at her home an hour later. She had reached him in the waiting room and invited him over.

"Yes, I do see. He *is* obstinate and vindictive, isn't he? It seems we two outcasts will be deprived of the pleasure of his company...and sadly he of ours. You do know he needs us desperately, you especially, but his iron pride and prickly ego won't allow him to admit it. How lonely he must feel with death stalking him and no one there to comfort him, to assuage his fears."

"Father, is there nothing we can do? Can the hospital really prevent us from seeing a dying member of our own family?"

"Oh, I suppose if we forced the issue legally they might relent, work out a compromise, but Brock would only make a big scene and embarrass everyone. Anyway, it would serve no purpose and would probably make matters worse for him emotionally. I'm concerned as much about his mental state as his physical. No, the invitation must come from him. By the way, I didn't see Paul at the hospital. I thought he was flying in this morning. He *is* coming, isn't he?"

"Yes, of course. I'm sorry I forgot to tell you. He phoned from the airport after I spoke with you. I explained the circumstances...the prognosis." Her mind drifted off as she thought of Brock's dying without ever speaking to her or Paul again. It was unthinkable that anyone would be that heartless. But not Brock.

Father Leonard waited politely for her to continue. When she didn't, he prompted her. "So Paul is coming here?"

She broke out of her trance. "Yes. I'm sorry. He should be here soon. Then you two can finally have your tête-à-tête." She started for the kitchen. "I better get lunch going. Come and keep me company."

"Any news of Valerie?" he said, trailing behind her.

"Not a thing. I left messages everywhere for her to contact the hospital. I've stopped worrying about her. She'll eventually turn up. There's no controlling her. She's so like her father. She adores him, you know." Eleanor gazed into a plate she was about to set on the counter. "She'll be devastated when she learns about his condition. They're very close."

They heard the front door open and a voice call out. "Anybody home?" It was Paul.

Eleanor burst into tears and ran to him.

"Excuse me. I'm Valerie Stowolski. I was told my father is a patient here. I'd like to see him."

The receptionist showed her a thin superficial smile. "Well, I'm not sure. We've been given strict orders about who can visit him. I'll have to check with my supervisor."

She put a phone to her ear as Valerie asked, "Is he in quarantine?"

The receptionist waved the question away and punched a button on the small switchboard before her. "Mrs. Dunbar, please. This is Sarah in Main Reception...Well, could you get her please? It's about Mr. Stowolski in 222. He has a visitor....Yes, I know....Okay, I'll wait."

Valerie leaned over the desk. "What's wrong with my father?"

"I really can't say. You'll have to speak to his doctor. Let's see here." She pulled the patient's file up on her computer screen. "Dr. Shepley. I can ring him for you if you like."

Just then a voice spoke in the earpiece and the receptionist replied. "His daughter, Valerie...yes, I'll send her up." She replaced the phone on its carriage and addressed the worried young woman hovering over the desk. "You can see him in room 222. Second floor. The stairs are over there."

Valerie thanked her and proceeded to the stairway. Moments later she found the room and entered after knocking lightly. The sight of her dynamic vigorous father lying flat on his back connected to two intravenous tubes was shocking. He was alone and appeared to be asleep. She was taken aback by the paleness of his skin and his haggard expression. He seemed much older.

"Daddy?" she whispered. "Are you asleep?"

"Valerie?" His eyes opened and searched the room for her.

"I'm right here," she answered as she approached the bedside, unaware that she was in the Terminal Ward. "What's wrong? Are you ill?"

"Nothing I can't handle." He grimaced in defiance of the dull unrelenting pain that knotted his stomach despite the powerful painkiller dripping into his artery through one of the IV hookups. "A bad case of ulcers, that's all. It was nice of you to come by."

"Mother's been trying to reach me. I came as soon as I got her message." She patted his hand and surveyed the room. "Are your ulcers serious?"

"Just a precaution. Nothing to worry about. So where have you been? Out with that creep Vince?"

"Yes, but we've split up. You and Mom were right. He turned out to be a lousy crumb."

"Why do you say that? Did he mistreat you?"

His daughter looked away anxiously. "Sort of."

"I'll kill him if he hurt you."

"He didn't hurt me like that. It's something else."

Her delicate features tightened in a peculiar apprehensive way unfamiliar to Brock. It was more the concerned look of a woman than of the child he still considered her to be. For a fleeting moment he forgot his own misery and felt something inside him reach out to her.

"What is it? Did he jilt you for someone else?"

"No, not that. It's kind of something I did to myself. I mean Vince was part of it. He got me the stuff. I don't blame him. It was my choice."

Stuff? The answer burst in Brock's mind, sending a shock wave of adrenaline into his system. Simultaneously, a sharp pain bit deeply into his groin. He stifled a groan and pursed his lips tightly. "Are...are you on drugs?" he grunted. "Is that it?"

Valerie's lips trembled. "Yes, and I'm scared." Starting to cry, she reached for his hand but he withdrew it and slapped hers away.

"You stupid idiot! Why did you do a dumb thing like that? Haven't you any sense?"

Taken aback at his angry reaction, she leaned lightly against the bed. "It was just a game. For fun. I didn't know it would turn out like this."

"How bad is it? Are you hooked?"

Valerie broke down completely and, sobbing into her hands, sat down on the edge of the bed. "I can't stop. I can't. And the lines cost too much. I don't have the money, and Vince won't pay for it anymore."

"Lines? You mean cocaine?"

"Yes. He says I have to deal for it myself now, but I don't know how...and I'm scared."

332

"Are you addicted?"

"I can't stop!" she cried, flinging her head back and forth wildly. "I can't! I need money!"

"No money! I won't give you money for drugs. You just have to stop."

"Don't you understand? I can't!" she screamed. "I need it too bad! I'm hitting ten lines a day. It's...it's fifty dollars a line."

"You're a junkie!"

"I'm your daughter, and I need your help."

"A kick in the ass is what you need!"

"I was only doing what you told me to."

"I never told you to take drugs! Never!"

Tears flooded her cheeks, though she made no attempt to wipe them away. "You talked all the time about living life the way it was meant to be lived. 'Full throttle,' you'd say. Remember our talks on the yacht? You said 'experience and savor...experience and savor.'"

"I never said drugs."

"You never said I shouldn't!"

"Did you ever see me do drugs?"

She shook her head.

"Don't try to blame me for your own failings. We all have to accept responsibility for our actions, and there are rules we have to follow."

She glared at him. "When have you ever followed the rules?"

Because in all the years they had been together she had never challenged her father, her accusation caught Brock unprepared and stung hard. He had, he knew, been more permissive with Valerie than her mother approved of, but he accepted no one's criticism, least of all from a member of his own family.

"You watch your mouth, young lady," he warned. "I'm your father. You don't talk to me that way."

Valerie drew herself away from him and stumbled backwards to the foot of the bed. "You have no right to talk of rules," she retorted, her courage and anger mounting. "You've always done whatever you pleased."

"Don't preach to me! What I do is none of your business."

"You've always said 'do as I do.' 'Model your life after mine.' 'I'm a success; be like me.' So now you can't all of a sudden change everything because you might dirty your hands in your daughter's mess."

"You've no right to say that," he declared, rising on one elbow and pointing an accusing finger. "I've been a good father to you. I've given you everything. I've tried to be an example to you."

"Oh, you were, Daddy," she mocked, "but not the example you think. Remember all those women you brought on the boat and in the hotels where we stayed on your 'business' trips? You pretended they were 'business associates.' You think I didn't know what you were doing with them and cheating on Mother? I told myself it was okay, because I loved you and I wanted to be like you, to be part of your world, not part of Mother's."

Brock looked at her in amazement, afraid to comprehend the judgment implicit in her words. It had never occurred to him that the little girl who tagged along on his recreational trips had seen through his deception.

"Where do you think I learned about sex?" she continued. "From you! I snuck into your closet one night in Honolulu when you were out, and later, when you came back with two women, I watched everything."

Brock was speechless, appalled that his daughter had witnessed his depravity, that she had known of it all these years, that she had seen the side of him that he thought was hidden from everyone except, of course, his willing partners. He was horrified that Valerie had secretly penetrated the privacy of his bedroom. She had seen him naked, stripped not only of his clothes but of his decency. She had seen her father, the dignified, self-respecting role model in her young life, unmasked as nothing more than a common whoremonger and debauchee. More humiliating still was that she had kept silent and thus become a party to his deceit.

His imperious, wounded pride instantly counterattacked, driven automatically by the same instincts for power and survival that had ruled his behavior since he quit St. Charles. And as was his habit, the counterattack was vicious and unyielding. "You spied on me like a conniving thief behind my back. What were you going to do, blackmail me?"

"Of course not," she replied, shocked and uncomprehending.

"Did you take photographs?"

"What are you saying?"

334

"I'm telling you to get out of here!"

"But I need your help!"

"I said I won't give you money."

"It isn't only money."

"Then that's your tough luck, because I can't help you any other way. Wanna know why?"

"Yes!" she cried out defiantly.

"I'm gonna die! I lied about the ulcers. It isn't ulcers. This is the Terminal Ward. I have cancer. All over my body. I'm a dead man, Valerie. I'll be in my coffin within a week, so you'll have to look elsewhere for someone to bail you out of your stinking mess. Try Vince. Try Mother. Try anyone," he shouted, "but leave me alone!" He winced from a wave of pain in his groin and chest and looked away from her.

Valerie grabbed hold of the metal railing of the bedstead to keep her balance as her mind reeled from the shock of her father's outburst. The one person in the world she thought she could count on refused to help her and was dying before her very eyes. She couldn't face the thought of her father dying, and she couldn't face her predicament. To whom could she turn? Who was left? Or did it really matter?

She turned away from the bed in a daze and ran out of the room.

It was 12:30 the next afternoon when the phone next to Brock's bed buzzed crankily, its ring mechanically muted per hospital regulations against loud noises in the Terminal Ward. He was half asleep, a gift of the nurse's administration of drugs two hours before. The buzzing stopped, then resumed...on...off...on...off. He could not escape its persistence. Slowly he opened his eyes and, recognizing the source of his annoyance, reached painfully to the phone and picked off the receiver.

"Wha' is it?" he mumbled in a hoarse whisper.

"Brock, this is Leonard. Don't hang up. I have news for you. Are you still there?"

"I dun wan' talk t'you," said Brock thickly, his speech slurred by the painkillers and sleep.

"I had to call. Something terrible has happened."

As Leonard paused, searching for the right words, Brock answered more alertly and caustically. "Worse than dying of cancer, you dumb priest?"

"It's about Valerie." Leonard paused again.

Irritated, Brock snapped, "So tell me, all right?"

"I'm sorry, Brock, to be the one to tell you. She's...dead."

Brock's already dull expression was suddenly erased of any emotion, as if he had lost all sensory perception. He heard the word *dead* echo in his head like a far-off church bell ringing mournfully in the night. Pushing through a mass of confused and agonizing thoughts, he managed to utter one word. "How?"

"She drowned...yesterday afternoon they think."

Brock lay inert, traumatized by this horrifying news and by the realization that his brutal rejection of his daughter's plea for help possibly—no, almost certainly—sent her to her death. The terrible question had to be voiced.

"Suicide?" he asked, his eyes pinched closed, afraid to hear the answer.

"It appears so. Her car was abandoned on the beach."

Brock replaced the receiver cutting off the connection. He had no more to say to Father Leonard and absolutely no more to hear. There was nothing more he needed to know. He had murdered his daughter!

He lost all track of time. When a nurse came in at 2 PM to check his condition he realized Father Leonard had not called back. While she took his blood pressure and temperature, he was conscious again of his surroundings and his constant pain. When the nurse left after injecting a strong painkiller into an IV tube, he withdrew once more into his thoughts, leaving his body behind as if it belonged to someone else. He wanted to rid himself of it, to distance himself from the memories inherent in his body, for he now confronted the cold hard fact that he had evaded and denied repeatedly over the past twenty years. Brock Stowolski was an evil person.

Valerie's suicidal death had broken through his defenses, his rationalizations, his excuses, and his specious self-serving philosophy that endlessly justified wrongful and malicious acts. Her death showed them for what they truly were: lies. All lies. All self-deceptions.

And then something Catherine Dubeau had said to him once during the first weeks of their affair surfaced in his mind. "I think you're the devil in disguise." He recalled at the time being irritated by her remark, then quickly sloughing it off as he always did to disparaging statements about his motives and ethics.

Now more than ever before, Brock wanted desperately to escape from the truth, to escape from this diseased and tormented body and more particularly from the person that resided in that body, that had committed these evil acts, these sins. With the help of his narcotic medication he thought he could retreat safely to the inner recesses of his mind, but the dark ugly guilt for his sins followed, attached solidly to his soul like a bloodsucking parasite whose powerful grip only God alone could loose by an act of mercy.

A question blared in his mind as if trumpeted by a thousand bugles: Was he worthy of God's mercy? He had killed his daughter in a single, blind, selfish act so commonplace and natural to him that he never weighed or even considered weighing its evil versus its good. Such comparisons were alien to his thinking. He had come by some process he did not understand to make decisions in his life based on the merits of power and pleasure, money and sex, riches and happiness. Inherent goodness and inherent evil were never factors to be weighed in his decision making.

Why did he only now perceive his rejection of Valerie's call for help as outrageously cruel and evil? he wondered. Was it because he was terminally ill and the prospect of imminent death raised the specter of his day of judgment? Would he have been conscious of the enormity of his sins were he healthy? He thought not. Death's imminence has a pernicious way of cutting through false rationales that serve only the living. *If I were not dying*, he thought, *I would probably not feel the guilt, though it would exist nevertheless, bound to my soul as tightly as bark to a tree. I am therefore doubly guilty. Guilty for all the evil I have committed and guilty for the evil I would have committed if I weren't dying.* What was it Father Leonard had shouted at him? The words had penetrated to his very soul. *"Don't you realize what you've done...what you've become?"*

Oh, yes, Brock realized it all right. He had simply refused to acknowledge it. It had become his lifelong pattern after St. Charles to deny and reject, deny and reject, because it was inconvenient to admit and accept the unpleasant truth, the soul-damning truth, that truth Father Leonard had spoken when he condemned Brock as an exploiter and pillager of others' lives. It was the truth Father Leonard had spoken when he accused Brock of having done great harm, unconscionable harm. Yet Brock had automatically rejected the condemnation and denied the accusations. And when his old mentor had offered to hear his confession and forgive his sins, Brock again denied he had sinned and rejected the offer of confession just as he later rejected his daughter's desperate appeal.

Would God grant mercy to such a sinner? Should He grant mercy?

Brock saw and heard and felt the inescapable answer. There could be only one. His crimes against his fellow man, against his friends, against his wife, against his son...against his beloved daughter...were crimes against God because they were crimes against love. He knew better. He had always known better. His greatest crime was in choosing not to know, symbolized by his leaving his Bible—the word and testament of God—behind when he walked out of the seminary. For such crimes he was undeniably unworthy of God's mercy. Unworthy.

Unworthy.

Unworthy.

Unworthy.

It was 8 PM. Eleanor slipped quietly into Brock's dimly lit room, fearing that her presence against his wishes would provoke a belligerent tantrum. She had come in spite of her fears, unable to stay away. All day she had been at home mourning Valerie's death. Father Leonard and Paul were a comfort, but she was drawn by a compulsion to be near Brock, Valerie's father, Valerie's flesh and blood. Eleanor knew Brock was heartbroken and in need of someone with whom to share his grief. He was alone at the hospital...secluded...self-exiled. Her compassion for him, a person in physical and mental anguish, overrode her enmity. Whatever she thought of him, whatever his harsh feelings toward her, he was a father whose daughter had tragically taken her own life.

Eleanor tiptoed to his bedside and stood watching him. He was asleep. Strangely, almost disappointingly, she felt no love for this man, only compassion for him as a fellow human. He was in extreme suffering, his body grossly disfigured already by the spread of the cancer's swellings, his life at death's threshold, ebbing away cell by cell, organ by vital organ.

Sensing her presence, his eyes slid open, working to identify her. As they came into focus, she tensed, anticipating a hostile reaction, but none came. "It's me, Brock...Eleanor...I came to be with you. I know you don't want to see me...but our daughter is dead....Father Leonard called you....I wanted to come to be with you for awhile...please don't be angry."

Without any sign of emotion he shifted his eyes away from Eleanor to a landscape painting on the wall beyond the foot of the bed. He knew every inch of that painting.

Eleanor continued softly. "We both know we lost the love in our marriage years ago. I don't know where it went, but we've lost our daughter, too, and more. I need to be here with you. Do you mind? May I stay?"

"Why not," he replied indifferently in barely a whisper. "Don't expect conversation. I'm not in the mood."

"That's all right," she said, relieved.

"While you're here," he said, "would you witness a contract addendum for me? I need to wrap things up before I die. It's in the envelope there on the table."

Reaching for the envelope, she continued to unburden herself to him about Valerie. "I'm tormented by the thought she might be...this sounds silly, I know, but...she might be alone, isolated, in limbo, maybe purgatory, for her sinful way of life. Worse, she killed herself, which as you know is in the eyes of the Church a mortal sin. I know you don't believe in such things, but I do, and I fear for her. I've been on my knees praying almost every minute since we were notified. Paul has been with me the whole time. Paul had to go to the morgue to identify the body and all. I suppose Father Leonard gave you the details. I can't speak of them. They're too painful."

A nurse opened the door and looked in. "Time for your bath and medication, sir."

"Oh, I see," said Eleanor. "I think I'm in the way." She stood and faced Brock as the nurse entered and began wrapping the inflatable bag of a blood pressure meter around his arm. "Well, I'll see you later."

When Brock neither looked at her nor answered, sadness enveloped her face. She left the room downcast and uncomforted, wondering why she had come. He didn't want her sympathy or consoling. He was too preoccupied with his imminent death.

She found the stairs and descended to the main reception area. Seeing the receptionist reminded Eleanor that she had meant to ask Brock if he had spoken with Valerie. Valerie never came home or called. Perhaps she had received one of the messages Eleanor and Paul had left with her friends to call the hospital. Perhaps she had spoken with Brock by phone before her death. If not, it would only deepen the tragedy.

Eleanor stopped at the receptionist. "Excuse me. I'm Mrs. Stowolski. My husband is in the Terminal Ward."

"Yes, ma'am?"

"If someone telephoned a patient in the Terminal Ward, would that call go through your switchboard here?"

"Yes. All calls to patients are routed here. The receptionist then connects the caller to the right room."

"Would you happen to know if my daughter, Valerie, telephoned my husband in the past two days?"

"I'm sorry. I work evenings, and I don't remember any calls to Mr. Stowolski from a daughter. You see, we don't keep records of callers, only visitors."

"It's important that I find out. Who was on duty here during the day?"

"Sarah. She's still here. I saw her having dinner in the cafeteria. Hold on."

The receptionist pressed a switch on the panel before her and dialed. "Hi, this is Margie. Say...yeah, I could hear it down here. We need to complain to housekeeping. Sure...sure. Say, is Sarah still down there? Good, call her over to the phone. I need to talk to her."

Margie smiled at Eleanor. "They're getting her."

"Yeah, Sarah. Margie. There's a woman here wants to know if her daughter telephoned Mr. Stowolski in Terminal during the past two days." She held her hand over the mouthpiece and looked up at Eleanor. "What's her name again?"

Eleanor told her.

"Valerie Stowolski...Yeah, he's the one...his wife. She did? In the afternoon....Okay, I gotta run. Talk to you later. Bubbye." She hung up. "She says your daughter didn't phone; she visited. She was here yesterday afternoon."

"She's certain about that?"

"She talked to her. She asked to see him, and Sarah gave her directions to his room."

"Thank you."

Eleanor walked out the exit and down the marble steps of the hospital to the sidewalk below, turning over in her mind the information the receptionist had given her. Valerie had visited Brock in mid-afternoon. That was about the time, according to the police, that Valerie arrived at the beach. That meant Brock was very likely one of the last people to talk to her before—Eleanor halted. An alarming suspicion was forming in her mind. Clenching her fists, she turned back toward the hospital.

Some thirty hours after Valerie had raced down these tiered marble steps, her mother grimly ascended them, her face etched with bitter resolve. She strode through the entrance, past the gabbling receptionist, and climbed the same stairs her daughter had used the day before. Proceeding directly to 222, Eleanor shoved the door open violently with two stiff arms and literally blew into the room.

Brock was alone, dozing. The nurse was gone. Eleanor's stormy entrance jolted him awake.

"Wake up, Brock!" she commanded, assuming a defiant position with hands on hips at the foot of the bed in the same spot where, unbeknownst to her, Valerie had stood. "I wanna talk to you!"

There was menace in her voice, the growl of a wounded lioness.

Brock recoiled. "I told them to keep you out of here," he said unsteadily, more out of self-defense than of pique.

"It doesn't matter what you want," she snapped. Her eyes blazed with hatred. "There's something I need to know, and you're going to tell me, and I don't care how sick you are or that you're gonna die. I need some answers!"

Her verbal barrage swept away the cobwebs and brought him fully awake.

"Valerie was here yesterday afternoon. What did you tell her?"

"None o' your business."

"She came to you for help, didn't she?"

"Is that what she told you?" He watched her for clues.

"No, I figured it out myself. What did you tell her? She was desperate, wasn't she?"

"If you know so much, you tell me."

"I know the answer. I just need to hear it from your venomous lips."

"Is that so? All right then. She got herself in trouble and was looking for easy outs."

"And, of course, you told her to fix things herself and not to bother you, that it was her own fault, not yours."

"She talked to you then?"

"No, she didn't, you stupid selfish miscreant!" Eleanor's lips were curled so tightly with rage she could barely speak.

"When she left the hospital she drove her car to Pompino Beach, walked down to the water, took off her shoes, and went straight in fully clothed. She swam out into the ocean farther and farther till her strength gave out. Then she drowned. The shore patrol discovered her car later. They found her shoes in the sand and began an air search. A couple of hours later they found her body floating a mile offshore." Eleanor recited the chronology in a sad tearful monotone.

"They recovered the body and confirmed at the morgue last night that the cause of death was drowning. But they confirmed two other things you probably already know. She was a heavy user of cocaine and other drugs, probably an addict, and she was three months pregnant with our grandchild, who is also dead."

An invisible hand as cold as ice seized Brock's heart and squeezed it.

"The coroner asked if I wished him to perform an amniocentesis to find out the sex of the child. I said no, that it didn't matter. What good would it do? Valerie already had gone through enough. She'll be buried carrying the child, and her tombstone will read simply 'Valerie Ann Stowolski and Child.'"

Eleanor wiped her eyes and fixed them coldly again on Brock's stupefied face. "I married you out of love, which you destroyed just as you destroyed our marriage. But I stayed with you because I believed marital vows were sacred and because I hoped and prayed that one day, God willing, your soul would wake up and you would change. God did not choose to answer my prayers. So now I have a new prayer, a new hope, which is that your death will be slow and painful, unbearably painful, and that after you die, you'll rot in hell for all eternity! Rot in hell! God damn you. God damn you forever!"

Brock heard her fearsome imprecation but did not know when she departed. The shock of her words left him catatonic. His sins were even more heinous and deadly than he had thought. He was a double murderer. He had killed two people, his beloved daughter and her unborn infant, his grandchild. He *should* indeed rot in hell as Eleanor hoped. There must be a special place there for monsters like him, he thought. How could he reject a plea from Valerie for help, from Valerie whom he loved? What kind of madness made him do such a thing? Egotism? Pride? Fear of guilt? Fear of complicity and responsibility? He was unworthy of God's mercy.

For another hour Brock gazed at the ceiling, reliving his life, recounting his sins, weighing their severity, and condemning himself over and over according to his conscience, which burned in his heart like a white-hot torch.

His dinner, untouched on the tray beside him, was retrieved by a glowering gray lady who mildly chastised him for not tending to his nutrition. She hastily withdrew when he turned on her menacingly and snarled, "Get out of here!"

The idea that had been forming slowly in his mind congealed. It was logical, fitting, and just. He would not die quietly in the serene sanctity of a sterile hospital bed, pampered till the last minute by a hovering cast of overattentive nurses and doctors. He was undeserving of that consideration. Valerie had not been so blessed. No one had eased her death. Brock deserved only God's anger and punishment, and the plan he had devised would justly render that punishment...in the dark cold pitiless waters of the ocean, where he had sent Valerie and her unborn to die.

Padding down the darkened corridor in her dingy white, rubber-soled nurse's shoes, Judy Harrison studied the patient list on her clipboard and noted the time on her wristwatch. It was fifteen past midnight and except for the rhythmical thumping of the respirator in room 220 behind her and the steady drumming of rain on the windows, the ward was quiet. This was unusual for terminal patients, some of whom seemed always to be coughing or thrashing about cantankerously to ease their discomfort. But only fifteen of the twenty-five beds were occupied, and many of the patients were heavily sedated, released if only for a few aimless hours from the torment of their bodies' inexorable decay.

She stopped before 222 and pressed her shoulder gently against the solid wood door. Mr. Stowolski, next on her list, should be sleeping soundly. The door silently gave way, and she leaned into the shadowed room to check on the motionless figure in the solitary bed, barely visible in the ghostly glimmer from a small floor lamp in one corner. She wrinkled her nose and thought sardonically, *You old fart!* Stowolski was one of the "losers," a title the nurses in the ward maliciously bestowed on the few patients who approached their rendezvous with death with savage bitterness. Angry, sullen, irascible, they begrudged their mortal fate. Disqualified and condemned, they had lost the contest, the race was over. Life with all its joys, thrills, and sensations would go on without them. They bore only malice for those who would survive them, including the nurses.

Caring for the terminally ill tried the patience of even the kindest members of the hospital staff, and Judy was not among the kindest. She normally worked in Intensive Care where her expert skills and knowledge were daily put to the test, a challenge that gave purpose to her life and, she felt, reconfirmed her worth as a human. She had volunteered to help out in the Terminal Ward for a few days when sickness and maternity leave created a shortage of nurses there. Still, she despised caring for dying patients, those the Terminal Ward nurses cynically referred to as "circling the drain." It was only dedication to her profession and compassion for her colleagues that had compelled her to volunteer.

Staring fixedly at the blanket covering Stowolski's chest, she looked for the gentle rise and fall that would confirm respiration. He was turned on his side away from her, making it difficult to detect the telltale movement. She squinted, impatient to complete her rounds and return to a romance novel awaiting her at her station. She would have to make sure he was sleeping...for the hospital's records. She moved silently into the room, leaned over his head without touching the bed, and listened for breathing. She jerked upright.

"What the—!" she said aloud, touching his "head." It was a T-shirt stuffed with a towel. She threw back the blanket. Pillows for a body. He was gone.

With a quickness made instinct by years of practice, she flicked a light switch above the bed with one hand and with the other grabbed the bedside phone and punched in Security.

"Charlie?"

"Yeah, what's up?"

"Judy in Terminal. I've got a missing patient in 22." Her eyes flitted up and down her clipboard. "Brock Stowolski. Fifty-two years old. Terminal cancer. He was last checked at eleven o'clock for his sleeping dosage."

"Think he's still in the hospital?"

"Not a chance. He put pillows under his blanket to conceal his getaway. He's gone. Maybe caught a cab in the rain. He only has one or two weeks, maybe days. Probably went home to die like many of them want to. Wouldn't be the first. I'll look around anyway."

"Good. I'll inform the superintendent. He should be the one to phone the guy's family. He'll also want to call the lawyers to make sure we're covered. They'll probably be in touch with you to get particulars. Okay?"

"I'll be here. You gonna have the guards search the hospital, just in case I'm wrong?"

"Sure thing."

NINETEEN

Brock's sudden unexplained disappearance from his hospital room dealt another emotional blow to Eleanor and Paul, already shattered by the death of Valerie and her child. Beside herself with grief that her relationship with Valerie had been so adversarial that the girl had chosen suicide rather than confide her problems to her mother, Eleanor was ridden by guilt that she had failed her daughter. She had, out of anger and frustration, deliberately abrogated her parental duties. Countless times over the years Eleanor had rejected Valerie's appeals.

"Ask your Father!"

"I don't care!"

"Do whatever he says!"

Almost from the moment Valerie was born, Eleanor's attention had been so riveted on Paul, protecting him from his father's evil influence, that she had spared little time to tend to her daughter's needs. So the child had looked to her father for guidance and love and a role model...and it had cost her life. It was ironic, thought Eleanor, reproaching herself, that Brock's sinister influence, which she had feared would harm Paul, had through her very own action concentrated its evil effect on Valerie with tragic results. Had Eleanor been a better mother, would Valerie be alive now? Or would Paul then have fallen under his father's spell? There was no way of knowing nor any purpose served in anguishing over what was passed. It was over and done. Eleanor sank into a well of despondency.

Father Leonard and Paul comforted her, soothing her grief and bewilderment and helping her through the onerous task of selecting a casket for Valerie and arranging for her funeral and interment. Death had been so far from Brock's and Eleanor's concerns that neither of them had

346

ever given thought to a burial ground for the family, so picking a grave site was another burdensome chore.

The funeral Mass two days later was, at Eleanor's request, restricted to family and close friends. Father Leonard was the celebrant and delivered a short prayerful homily that mentioned neither the cause of Valerie's death nor her father. When the service was over and the small group rose to make their way to the cemetery, Eleanor discovered that Diego Martinez was sitting alone in a back pew. As she passed him, their eyes connected for a second. She smiled and instantly felt a disturbing but comforting warmth in her breast. They had not seen or spoken to one another since the day Valerie was born years ago and he chose her name. They had shared a special moment that day in her hospital room, a memory that had resurfaced in her mind whenever she heard his name or saw a picture of a maternity ward. Something electric and uncontrollable had lain beneath the politeness that had passed for their feelings. But he had left, severing all contact with her.

In the years that followed she learned indirectly from Kelly of Diego's activities, but she made no effort to contact him, nor he her. The truth was, she confessed to herself as she got into the limousine for the ride to the cemetery, that Diego's only real connection with her was his naming Valerie. Then it dawned on Eleanor that it was not she but Valerie who had brought Diego to the funeral, and she sank back in her seat in the limousine reproaching herself for her foolish thoughts.

Eleanor bore up well under the stress of Valerie's tragedy. Years of marriage to Brock had conditioned her to such trials. His slipping away in the night from the hospital was the final indignation, but predictable if she had thought about it beforehand. It was simply his refusal to accept responsibility for Valerie's suicide. Brock would deny his culpability to his death, which the doctor told her could come at any time. God only knew where Brock was now.

The hospital had phoned her at home minutes after his absence was discovered. The police were called in and looked for him in all of the most likely places—his office, his apartment, the country club. With discretion, using information provided by Maggie, they visited the apartments of several of his regular female acquaintances without telling Eleanor. He was nowhere to be found. It was only then that Eleanor remembered the

Gigolo, Brock's racing yacht.

At her suggestion a police officer phoned the security guard in the harbor attendant's office and confirmed what she already had guessed. Mr. Stowolski had passed through the gate on foot around midnight and boarded his sloop. The guard had wished him a good evening but received no reply. Mr. Stowolski had said not a word and looked real bad. The guard never expected him to take the boat out in such terrible weather, but it wasn't his business to tell boat owners what to do. He was there to protect the boats from thieves and vandals. If they wanted to sail to China in a typhoon that was their business. He was a simple watchman and knew squat about sailing anyway, never set foot in anything larger than a rowboat.

As Brock had anticipated, the Coast Guard broadcast emergency alerts to all ships within a hundred miles of San Francisco to report any sighting of the *Gigolo*, but there was none. After a week the alert was canceled. Some Coast Guard and police officials believed Brock had not ventured out into the ocean at all but had used that impression as a ruse. Instead, they theorized, he had hugged the coast and hidden the boat in one of a hundred inlets where sailboats numbering altogether in the thousands were moored. From there he could have taken a taxi or hitchhiked to some hideaway on land. They advised Eleanor that they would begin checking with taxi companies and each and every harbor, inlet, and sheltered water on the coastline fifty miles north and south of San Francisco. It would take days, probably weeks. Boatyards were also notified to report the presence of the *Gigolo*, but if experience were any guide, many of them would ignore the notice. There were just too many reports of stolen and missing boats for yard masters to pay attention to a wacko dying of cancer.

Eleanor listened politely to the sincere and ostensibly knowledgeable explanations by the police and Coast Guard, but she paid them no heed. She knew Brock was far away by now somewhere in the Pacific Ocean, probably dead. He was too proud and vain to die like a rotting piece of contaminated meat in a hospital bed. It was beneath his dignity. The high-powered wheeler-dealer, the master manipulator, the mighty cocksman die like a mere mortal? Like a common man? Never! Brock would cheat Death's plan as he had cheated everything else during his life. It would be

Brock's way or no way. She listened and nodded patronizingly to the officers, but she knew they were wrong. Brock was at sea, and whether he was alive or dead was of no concern to her any longer. Or so she thought until she met with Brock's attorney, Gordon Holly.

A thundering ice-cold wave crashed upon the beach and washed over Brock Stowolski's raglike body, stunning his comatose mind into semi-consciousness. Choking, he flailed about on hands and knees in the churning eddy, struggling to keep his head above water. As the wave receded amid the steady roar of the storm, he coughed, sending a searing stab of pain through his cancer-ridden loins and chest. Moaning and clutching his stomach, he fell forward, rolling in agony on the sand. Another powerful wave steamrolled up behind him, smashing his body down, tumbling him up the sand a dozen yards before he could right himself. His mind bolted awake from the shock.

He looked about at the dark heaving water and the sand and sky that merged seamlessly in a gray-black continuum. Another spasm of pain paralyzed him, stealing his breath and slamming his eyes shut. Hearing and feeling another wave approach, he rolled over on his hands and knees, shuddering helplessly from the cold, and braced himself in the sand against the hammering that at once engulfed him, then as quickly fell away. Gagging on the salt water, he coughed, gasped in pain, then retched. Warm, sticky, dark reddish fluid he knew was blood splattered onto the wet sand and trickled down his chin.

Where could he be? He vaguely remembered his secret departure from the hospital. Forgoing a taxi, whose movement could be traced, he had made his way uncertainly and painfully on foot the six blocks to the marina where his thirty-foot Bermudian sloop was moored. He had resolved not to die in the hospital. Instead, he would steal away in his boat at night, ditch it far out in the ocean, and drown without a trace...drown like Valerie.

But where was he now? Somewhere on the California coast, he was certain. He looked at his wristwatch and, noting the date, was alarmed. If his watch was correct, he had been without food, water, or medication for ten days. He commanded his mind to remember what had happened, but his thoughts were too foggy and chaotic. The last thing he could recall clearly was setting a course due west. He must have blacked out at that point.

But why hadn't he died? The doctors had given him only a few days, a week at most. By all rights he should be dead.

He *would* die! Now!

Summoning what little of his strength remained, he feebly got to his feet, staggering to keep his balance. "I wanna die!" he screamed, turning his contorted face into the wind and spray. Fluid oozing from his anus restained the rear of his soggy white pants a dark widening red and ran down one leg over his bare foot and into the sand. Rivulets of blood trickling from his nostrils and one ear met at his chin and disappeared in the sodden stubble of his unshaven whiskers. Lurching toward the water, he plunged headfirst into a towering wave, but its force hurled him back. Writhing in pain, he wrestled himself to a stand, spit out red water from his mouth, and toppled back toward the waves. A giant wall of water and foam like the mouth of a mammoth sea creature curled above him as its undercurrent tugged at his legs. Feeling its power seize him, he thankfully surrendered to it.

"Now, now!" he shouted. "Let it be done! Take me!"

The whirling, suffocating water wrenched and pummeled his shriveled, wasted body, cartwheeling it along the sandy bottom like a burly clump of seaweed. He could neither breathe, nor see, nor feel. Darkness...death's darkness...invaded his mind. He embraced it, cherished it, and finally succumbed to it.

But Death's door remained sealed. Brock did not die. The black rampaging waves, in defiance of his wish, cast his crumpled corpselike body high onto the beach, then gradually subsided as if to rest, their task complete. The raging wind that had battered him with stinging pellets of ice-cold rain throttled down to a gusty breeze, and the black clouded sky brightened to a dull gray.

He lay facedown, his limbs and head twisted unnaturally. His bluish, paper-like skin had the look of death about it, but he was ruefully alive if only by the weak arrhythmic pulse of a weary heart whose faint beat he would command to stop if he could.

Brock had wanted a violent, lonely death at sea as just punishment for the contemptible wrongs he had committed. He had no defense for his sins, and he offered no excuse. There was none. He wanted only to die in the empty reaches of the vast ocean away from doctors and nurses and their unwanted sympathy and care, away from Eleanor and Paul and their painful memories and accusing hate, away from Father Leonard and the Church's unrequested forgiveness, away even from God and His undeserved mercy.

Brock writhed from the withering pain inside him. Was this then how he would die? Like a beached whale, his life ebbing away slowly, agonizingly, hour by hour, minute by minute, till life had diminished to a single futile heartbeat, and then the final release—Death's cold embrace. His body would decompose in the sand, and the rising and falling tides would leach it, perhaps carrying it out into the ocean for scavenging schools of anonymous fish to strip to the bone. This was not how he had envisioned his execution.

He had motored smartly out of the small harbor in San Francisco in the driving rain, heading westward against five- to six-foot waves. He had guided the helm by the luminous dial of the domed compass mounted in front of the wheel, pointing the bowsprit into pitch darkness as black as his boat, for he had purposely switched off his running lights. He did not wish to be found. There were no other craft or ships in the area. Only a man as desperate as he would be foolish enough to venture to sea in such a storm.

In the next hour he would pass across the transcoastal commercial shipping lanes where he would watch for freighters and the like. Only if he spotted one close by and felt certain his yacht could be seen would he turn on the running lights to avoid a collision. As soon as the people ashore discovered he had taken the *Gigolo*, they would alert all vessels in the surrounding waters to be on the lookout. If he could get across the shipping lanes undetected he would be home free, at least until daylight when search-and-rescue aircraft would surely be looking for him if the storm passed. By then, however, he wouldn't care, for there would be nothing for them to find. He and the boat would be gone, swallowed up by the ocean.

From time to time he looked shoreward, watching the lights of the coastal cities grow smaller and smaller till they merged into a thin wispy ribbon marking the horizon. His plan was to pull the plug on the *Gigolo* as soon as the lights ashore disappeared.

The harsh rain beat incessantly on his face. He lowered his head to shield his eyes so he could view the compass and keep the boat on a westward heading as the *Gigolo's* sleek racing hull, driven by its throbbing engine, cut cleanly through the heaving waters. Brock, a proud and skilled sailor who shunned resorting to engine power even in stormy weather, would have preferred to be under sail, but he lacked the physical strength to raise canvas.

Peering astern now and then to check on the coastal lights, he blinked stinging spray out of his eyes and checked the compass heading again. Still due west. He glanced behind to check on the ribbon of shore lights. They had vanished. Except for the bluish-green glimmer of the compass, he was now shrouded in a world of total darkness where ocean and sky were one, where he was the sole human in a water expanse of perhaps one hundred square miles and probably more. It was time, he told himself with grim finality, to join that dark world, to become part of its sightless, shapeless, soulless gloom. It was time to die, to put an end to his mental and physical torment. To pay the price for his sins.

The sea cocks he would open to let in the water were located in the hull forward of the keel. They were intended for draining the bilges in dry dock but, if opened at sea, would let in enough water in five minutes to scuttle the boat.

Without another thought, navigation ceasing to have any importance, Brock let loose of the wheel and crawled unsteadily on the heaving slippery deck toward the cabin hatch, feeling his way with outstretched hands in the darkness. He reached the hatch, stood up, grasped the handle, and was about to pull it open when a huge wave, which he could not see coming in the blackness, hit the boat abeam. The deck lurched crazily, knocking Brock off his feet and slamming his head against the brass coaming around the hatch. His left temple took the full brunt of the impact, which knocked him out, dropping him into the well of the cockpit...unconscious...but still alive.

How long had he lain there? Ten days according to his wristwatch.

352

And how many miles had he traveled? Tens? Hundreds? There was no way of telling. He knew only that when he regained consciousness he was out of the boat and on a beach in a fierce storm and in unbearable pain. All of the tranquilizing effects of the drugs he had been taking in the hospital had worn off, leaving him unprotected against the merciless pain of the cancer's savage attack spreading contagion through his vital organs. Sharp, burning, throbbing, lingering pain pierced him in a thousand places deep inside his swollen torso and limbs. He could not bear it. Death was his only deliverance. Immediate death.

He scrambled to a wobbly hands-and-knees position and surveyed the beach in the near darkness. He saw no lights or buildings or structures of any kind. Only sand and palm trees. He looked seaward, but didn't see the *Gigolo*. Most likely the storm had carried the boat down the California coast, and the boat had foundered on some shoals, throwing him overboard. Perhaps it had sunk.

A blinding, mind-shattering pain thrust deep into his abdomen like a red-hot sword. He screamed and fell forward, vomiting blood onto the wet sand.

"I wanna die!" he moaned, hugging his stomach and rolling on his back. As the wave of pain subsided, he lurched to his knees and visually searched the beach inland but saw only a ridge of sand, windblown palm trees, and gray sky. Then about fifty yards down the beach he noticed a small clifflike promontory that jutted some twenty feet above the water. At its base the waves crashed and churned against a solid wall of rock lacking a beach. Surely he could die there!

Clutching his stomach, Brock struggled to his feet and staggered head-down toward the edge of the cliff determined to put himself to death. "I am unworthy," he muttered almost in a chant. "I am unworthy." He repeated the phrase again and again as he neared the edge.

Kelly and Helena had flown up from Los Angeles the minute Eleanor informed them of Valerie's death and in the same phone conversation Brock's disappearance. She insisted over their mild objections that they stay in one of the guest rooms in her home. To her they were part of the family whose sympathetic support she sorely needed. Kelly, moreover, would be indispensable in keeping DESIGN METAPHORS on an even keel. He knew the inner workings and personnel and would understand its business operations, which had to continue if D-M were to meet its payroll and other financial and contractual obligations, which were vast and varied. Brock's appetite for large-scale high-risk business ventures had grown in the past several years in direct proportion to his ever-expanding ambitions.

With Eleanor's approval by phone to Maggie, Kelly spent three days at D-M going over Brock's private investments and the firm's projects including both those on-going as well as the dozen or so which had not been started but to which Brock had committed the firm over the coming months. Digesting the details and financial implications of these myriad activities was a challenge, but Kelly had thirty years' experience in the interior and industrial design fields, was intimately familiar with Brock's modus operandi and, most important of all, was a far better businessman than either Brock or even he himself believed. Kelly interviewed each member of D-M's staff to verify which projects they were working on, when they would be finished, and what the projects entailed. Finally, he obtained from D-M's accountant a full financial statement on the firm's monetary position.

On the fourth day, armed with this information, Kelly accompanied Eleanor to Gordon Holly's office for a determination of the legal ramifications for D-M and for Eleanor of the situation created by his absence.

"I'm afraid," said Holly to Eleanor, "that Brock's action has created very unfortunate circumstances for you and the firm."

Eleanor was troubled. "What do you mean? Is D-M failing? Is it bankrupt?"

"No, certainly not. At this time, at least, the firm is in excellent shape both in liquid and capital assets and in contractual business."

Kelly nodded vigorously in agreement. "Of course it is. D-M is as sound financially as its reputation, which is unsurpassed on the West Coast. I can vouch for that. The net assets amount to close to twenty-five million dollars, not counting real estate held in the company's name with a current market value of four and a half million. Brock was a shrewd venture capitalist and land buyer. According to the figures I got from the accounting firm, some of these properties will double and even triple in value over the next several years."

"No question about that, Kelly," affirmed Holly. "Brock built a commercial and real estate enterprise of considerable size and renown. But you will also agree that D-M has a hefty debt burden. While the number of its creditors is small, the amounts owed are not."

"True," replied Kelly, "but D-M's assets and earning power are more than enough to cover any debts. D-M is one of the most profitable companies of its kind in America."

"Certainly. D-M ranks among the top design firms. Brock labored thirty years to achieve that enviable status...and that's the problem. D-M's reputation rests on Brock. He and D-M are one and the same in the eyes of his many prosperous clients. But without him, without his masterminding the firm's production, D-M is just another design outfit. A good outfit, mind you, but back down among the crowd, not standing high above it. Brock was the source of D-M's sparkle, its aura, its genius. Without him the firm loses its singularity and attraction. Without him it will suffer. D-M's competitors will swarm like locusts to cut into D-M's share of the market. What do you think, Kelly? Am I right? You've seen this before, I'm sure."

For Eleanor's sake the burly, dapple-haired, sixty-four-year-old artisan resisted agreeing with the savvy lawyer. More trouble she didn't need, but he couldn't lie to her. There was too much at stake. "Unfortunately I have. And it obviously could happen to D-M. But I've seen plenty of companies survive the loss of their founder. It happens all the time! New leadership, new ideas, a new look, and you're back in the game."

Holly made a wry face. "I wouldn't say 'plenty.' A few would be more accurate. But to make up for such a loss of creative energy and charisma you need a quick, smooth transition to new leadership...and that's the second problem."

"Why?" asked Kelly, still feeling a strong need to protect Eleanor. "I know several guys who could do it. Guys who know design and who have a good head for business."

Eleanor was sure that one of them was Diego.

"I'm certain you do, Kelly, but that's not the problem. The difficulty is that Brock is the sole owner of D-M. There is no board of directors, no vice president, no partner. You were the sole partner for a number of years, but Brock severed your association with the firm and had me draw up a special property agreement between him and Eleanor, which both of them signed. You may recall it, Eleanor. Here it is." He handed her a multi-page document.

"No, I don't. What is it?"

"It's an agreement between the two of you in which you disavow all interest in DESIGN METAPHORS and grant Brock sole ownership of the firm."

"No, I don't recall signing such an agreement. I'd remember something that important."

"Are you sure about that?" said Holly, unsettled by her quick denial. "He never discussed with you a property agreement?"

"Absolutely not. I'd remember. I assure you I never knowingly signed a property agreement!" She returned the document to Holly.

"Could he have tricked you into signing it?" asked Kelly. "He's not above something that scurrilous, as we all know."

"I don't know. It's possible. I've witnessed Brock's signature on his business documents for years. It was routine, especially while he was living at home, that is, before our separation. He normally worked late in his study, and before going to bed he'd bring me documents to witness, sometimes half a dozen or more at a time. He could have slipped in this property agreement. I would have signed it without knowing its importance."

"In this case," said Holly, picking up his theme, "you weren't a witness to a signature. You were the signatory."

"No, never."

Kelly patted her hand. "I think Brock pulled one on you. So what's new?"

"What does it mean?" she asked Holly.

"In a word, trouble. Maybe big trouble. Here's how it comes down. The document before me which you signed stipulates among other things that no one other than Brock has authority to make decisions regarding

356

D-M's business operations, and that means every aspect from buying a new pencil sharpener or hiring and firing employees to signing new contracts with clients. He went so far as to specify here that even in his absence that authority remains his exclusively and is not to be usurped by anyone. That means D-M can't replace him or delegate his authority."

Disbelief and concern seized Kelly's face. "That's utter nonsense! You mean there's no one in command of D-M as long as Brock's absent?"

Holly nodded. "In a nutshell."

"Can we accept new contracts?"

"From existing clients, probably yes. From new clients, no. I'm afraid not. Brock retains sole authority for committing D-M's resources. As I said, Brock is the company. The company is Brock. They are one and the same."

"Then what can D-M do?" declared Kelly. "There's a staff of thirty people to pay and support. We can't just ignore that fact."

"Our options are very limited, which was exactly Brock's intent."

Kelly vented his frustration at the lawyer. "How could you let him do something so dangerous and irresponsible?"

"Kelly, may I remind you that it is not my place to question the motives or intentions of my clients. I defined the limits of my responsibility to Brock carefully and explicitly at the outset of our relationship thirty years ago. My duty was nothing more than to ensure that the transactions he wished to undertake were legal. He did not seek, nor did I feel it my place to offer, my personal advice on the wisdom or ethics of those transactions."

Having been Brock's partner, Kelly needed no brief on the strong-headed single-mindedness of D-M's chief executive. Brock had always been a one-man show who resented advice from others, especially unsolicited advice. "I'm sorry," said Kelly. "I had no business getting on your case. I know better than to blame you."

"No problem." He frowned and directed a soulful aspect at Eleanor. "This is a very unfortunate situation."

"You can say that again," said Kelly. "So what you're telling us is that D-M can't accept any contracts from new clients."

"That's about it."

"But," said Eleanor, confused and alarmed, "D-M can still undertake new projects from clients already under contract, can't it?"

"As long as the contract provides for it. You see, Eleanor, some of D-M's contracts contain open-ended provisions for follow-on projects, so if the customer remains satisfied, D-M can continue to undertake new projects indefinitely for that client, Brock already having in effect approved future projects. But that scenario applies to only a handful of clients and is, as I say, dependent on their continuing faith in D-M. What is more, all of those contracts have escape clauses and could very well be terminated by the clients, if they believe D-M can't do the job anymore."

Kelly insisted on being positive...his standard outlook on life. "Then we'll just have to prove to them we can do the job."

Holly shook his head. "I want to shield Eleanor from the pain of this situation as much as you do, Kelly, but we've got to be coldly objective about this. The loss of Brock will be devastating to D-M. As I said, for most of the clients Brock *is* D-M."

"Then the firm is hamstrung, isn't it?" said Eleanor.

The lawyer shrugged and cast a hapless look at the two of them. "Well, it doesn't look good."

Eleanor was beginning to appreciate the magnitude of the crisis looming before them. "You know the business," she said to Kelly. "How long can D-M stay afloat?"

His answer was matter-of-fact. "Until current contracts are completed. Of course, the payments on them will keep rolling in for awhile, but eventually..."

Eleanor was impatient. "So how long?"

"What do you think, Holly?" ventured Kelly. "A year? Two years at most?"

"Yes, I'd go along with that. Keep in mind that each of these particular contracts contains an escape clause. The minute those customers lose confidence in D-M, you can kiss them good-bye."

"Then D-M really is doomed," said Eleanor.

"Not necessarily," replied Holly. "It depends on several things. First of all how fast D-M loses clients. Some may stick with her, at least for awhile. Secondly, how soon Brock's fate is revealed and confirmed and, thirdly, what latitude the court-appointed trustee of Brock's estate will have in overseeing the business in his absence."

"What trustee?" asked Kelly uncertainly.

"In cases like this where a person is missing, the law protects that person's interests in his property by having the court appoint a temporary administrator until the person is found. The statutes provide that Eleanor can petition the Superior Court to appoint a trustee after Brock's been missing ninety days. Under the unique circumstances of his terminal illness, I think we can move the court to waive that waiting period and to appoint someone immediately."

"Who would it be?" asked Eleanor.

"It's really your choice. The court must prefer the wife's nominee."

"Could I nominate Kelly? He's an obvious choice."

Holly pouted as he mulled over the idea. "You could, but I seriously doubt the court would approve him. The court's responsibility is to care for the estate as the missing person would. Given the well-known animosity between Brock and Kelly, Brock surely would not want Kelly to be trustee, nor would the court acting as Brock's surrogate. The court normally operates on the assumption that the missing person will show up any moment to resume full control of their estate. Therefore the court won't sanction any action it believes the missing person would disapprove of. No, I think Kelly would never sell as trustee."

"What about Diego Martinez?" asked Kelly, knowing that Eleanor would be shy about suggesting his name.

"That's hard to say. I suppose it would depend on how widely known was Brock's dislike of the man. I know for a fact Brock despised him. But there is nothing on record that I know of that could be construed as Brock's making a case against Diego's involvement in the firm. If Eleanor, the wife, strongly endorses Diego's nomination, the court might go along. It's worth a try."

"What if Brock—" Kelly broke off his sentence looking worriedly at Eleanor.

"What if he dies," said Eleanor without emotion, finishing his thought, "and his body is never found? Is that what you're saying, Kelly? Because that's exactly what will happen, you know." Her voice suddenly became angry. "He's sailed off to God knows where to die by himself. He doesn't care about us or D-M or what will happen to it all when he's gone. How will we ever prove he's dead?"

"The law provides for that, too, in its way," explained Holly. "Unfortunately the statute says that, if death is suspected but there is no proof, no redisposition of the deceased's estate can occur for five years, at which time death is presumed and probate commences."

"Five years!" exclaimed Eleanor.

"Five years?" repeated Kelly dismally. "D-M could be long buried by then."

"Maybe," said Holly. "But you said yourself that with new leadership and a new look D-M could be, I think you said, back in the game. Do you think this fellow Martinez can really work that kind of magic?"

"If he can't, no one can!" affirmed Kelly.

"I pray you're right. It won't be easy for him as trustee."

"Why not? He's an excellent manager with a keen business sense and with years of experience."

"Yes, Kelly, I know that. He's eminently qualified. That's not the issue. The problem is that Diego won't have carte blanche to do whatever he thinks is necessary. As I said, the trustee's power is strictly defined and limited by the court. In light of Brock's adamant insistence on being the sole person to make decisions for D-M, the court is unlikely to grant expansive powers to Diego or any other person serving as trustee of Brock's estate. Moreover, the power the court does grant will be closely monitored, and Diego will be required to account periodically to the court for his actions. For many of these actions he will need prior approval. And if the court were to become displeased with his performance, they could unilaterally replace him. They have that kind of arbitrary power. The court is within its right to remove a trustee any time it believes he is failing to uphold the missing person's interests."

"I see your point," said Kelly. "Diego may not have the flexibility of action he'll need to pull it off."

"It's worse. D-M's creditors will be watching, too. The more they are owed, the more jumpy they'll be. At the first sign of a risky move by Diego, they'll petition the court to remove him. It happens all the time. They'll hound him like a pack of yelping dogs gnawing on his shoes, constantly reminding him of his precarious position. You see, the trustee is personally...I mean all by himself...legally responsible for any breach of duty that causes a loss to the estate. That's why trustees tend to be a very

360

cautious and conservative lot, very risk-averse. Yet taking risks is probably what Diego will have to do to prevent D-M's collapse."

Kelly shrugged. "Despite all those limitations he's still the best man for the job."

"I hope the court agrees. But are you sure he'll take the job, given the legal liabilities it involves?"

"I know he will," replied Kelly. "I've already talked to him about it."

"There is another matter, however, I want to discuss." Holly paused, gathering his thoughts. "Eleanor, do you have any private funds, properties, or sources of income separate from Brock's? Assets of which you are the sole owner?"

She thought for a moment. "Not really. I have a checking account and credit cards. That's all I've ever needed. Brock's accountant makes monthly deposits in my account and pays all my bills. I never really want for money. I'm not a spendthrift, so it's never been an issue between me and Brock. When I've had to make more expensive purchases like a car or jewelry, I've simply informed the accountant. We are comfortably wealthy. Money was only a problem for me when Brock refused to finance Paul's ballet training, but we found ways to get around his objections, at least for a time." A hollow bitterness leached through her words.

"Then you have no resources of your own?" Holly seemed alarmed.

"No, none. Why?"

He frowned and shook his head. He appreciated in full for the first time Eleanor's financial dependence on D-M and the crisis it foretold. "I thought you had other resources. I thought..." He was incredulous that an intelligent, educated person like Eleanor Stowolski had failed to protect her own financial security. She evidently had deferred entirely to Brock's judgment, trusting his largess implicitly, despite her firsthand knowledge of his selfish and deceitful ways. As a lawyer and legal tactician, Holly made a practice of exhaustively analyzing every facet of his clients' financial affairs to uncover vulnerabilities and to prescribe protective measures, a service he had provided Brock. Eleanor's carelessness was thus all the more appalling to him. All of this could have been avoided by a few simple precautions. He wanted to scold her, but there was no point in it. The time for that had long passed.

"Well," he continued, "we've got a serious problem here. These financial records show that everything you have—your home, your car, your clothes, your jewelry—was bought and paid for by D-M, not as gifts but as company property."

"Company property!" Kelly was astounded. "You mean they're not hers?"

"They are listed as company-owned tangible assets. Your house, the car, the whole shooting match are as much a part of D-M as the copying machine next to Maggie's desk. D-M owns everything you have. Brock was obsessive in his drive to build up the company's assets in whatever way he could. I advised him time and again of the danger of this policy, which placed at risk to creditors the entire estate of his heirs, but he refused to heed my warnings. Like I said, my job is to do what the client wishes, having explained to him the full legal ramifications."

"D-M will continue to support me, won't it?" asked Eleanor uneasily.

"It's a little complicated. The law ensures that dependents of missing persons are supported during the period of absence. That's one of the trustee's sworn duties."

Kelly was relieved. "Then Eleanor will be cared for."

"Yes...and no. In point of fact it's the discretion of the court, not the trustee, to determine the amount of financial support rendered to the missing person's spouse and dependents, in keeping, as the code says, with their station in life. You need have no concern there. Your standard of living will be unaffected...that is unless D-M falters."

"Falters?" she repeated.

"Well." He sighed, not savoring his role as bearer of continuing bad news. "You see, when the firm loses business—and it surely will as word of Brock's disappearance spreads—revenues and profits will drop, maybe sharply. At some point the trustee, with the court's permission, will be forced to sell assets to pay off taxes and debts and to fund the payroll. The sale of D-M's assets will become public knowledge. Bad news like that travels at the speed of light in investment and banking circles and will further undermine confidence among clients. Their loss of confidence will result in further loss of business. The loss of business will force further liquidation of assets, and the cycle will spiral downward. At some point creditors will petition the court for a Chapter Seven bankruptcy, declaring

D-M insolvent, freezing all its assets for ninety days, and voiding any sell-off while bankruptcy proceedings are prepared."

"That sounds awful," said Kelly, wincing.

"That, of course, is the worst-case scenario. We hope it never reaches that stage. Long before D-M reaches bankruptcy we would sell the company, or at least try to, to preserve as much as we could of its value. So you see, the very real danger is that, if D-M goes bankrupt, you and Paul will stand to lose everything but maybe your clothes."

"You're kidding!" cried Kelly.

"Not in the least! Jewelry, furniture, art objects all would go."

"The cars, too?" said Eleanor. "Even the house?"

"Easily the cars. As for the house, the homestead is generally not subject to a forced sell in bankruptcy cases, but the property agreement Eleanor signed, albeit unwittingly, defeats the law's normal protection. There's no question about it. The creditors would take the house."

"But if Eleanor was hoodwinked into signing the property agreement," said Kelly, "couldn't we contest it in court?"

"Sure, but it would be costly, and proving she was hoodwinked would be extremely difficult. Not impossible, but difficult."

"What can we do?" she pleaded.

"Pray that Diego can turn back the storm," replied Holly.

Kelly still looked for an alternative. "What about his will? He must have left her something. Doesn't that enter into this somewhere?"

"I can't comment because the contents of the will are privileged information until the will is enacted, and that won't happen until there's proof of death or the statutory five-year waiting period expires."

Kelly tried another tack. "Didn't Brock carry life insurance making Eleanor the beneficiary? Perhaps there's something we can make out of that policy."

"As a matter of fact he didn't carry any life insurance."

"You aren't serious! A man of his prudence?"

"He didn't believe in life insurance, especially on his own life. He told me once when I raised the matter with him in much the same tone as yours that he had better ways to spend his money and that, when he died, D-M would be his legacy and his heirs' inheritance, not some annuity benefits from life insurance."

"He's already dead!" said Eleanor, more as an announcement than an opinion.

"Now, Eleanor," said Kelly in a soothing voice, "we don't know that."

"I feel it." Her crystal eyes stared icily ahead. "It's his final insult." She dropped her eyes. "God forgive me, but I hate him so."

Kelly and the lawyer exchanged sympathetic looks that betrayed their mutual feeling of helplessness.

"I can't help but pray," she said, recalling the last words she had spoken to Brock in the hospital, "that his death was prolonged and painful. Very prolonged and very painful."

TWENTY

Stumbling over the edge of the promontory, Brock's deadweight body plummeted headfirst into the swirling black cauldron of bone-crushing waves that crashed explosively against the jagged rocks at the base of the twenty-foot-high cliff. His fall carried him deep into the powerful undercurrent streaming laterally like a freight train across the face of the cliff toward the beach from which he had just dragged himself. The cannonball current propelled his limp form along the bottom, hammering him against the sand again and again, narrowly missing deadly outcroppings of razor-sharp rock. Then the black roiling water coiled around him and, with a roar, hurled him upward out of the waves and, like a stomach regurgitating indigestible food, disgorged him on the beach, where he lay exhausted in the sand, his arms and legs all askew.

For ten minutes he lay unconscious in the grip of a terrifying nightmare of his slowly sinking and drowning in the foul-smelling bilge of hell. He flailed against the downward pull of slimy entrails that wrapped around his arms and legs. Bound and helpless, unable to resist, he tried to scream, but no noise came from his wide-open, twisted mouth.

A wave of ice-cold water broke over his body and shocked him back to consciousness. As his senses returned, the horrific pain from the cancered erosion of his internal organs doubled him over, and again he vomited blood that gurgled through his animal-like cries of anguish.

When the throbs of pain lessened, he regained his bearings and remembered the promontory and his plunge to what he had hoped would be certain death. Yet, once again, he was still alive, his death wish rejected by the ocean as if it had a will and purpose of its own. Every time he had tried to kill himself, the ocean had denied him.

The pain of his suffering from the rampant corrosion inside him reached new heights. He could literally feel the cancer eating away his organs as one watches a time-delay movie of vermin devouring the insides of a dead animal, except Brock wasn't dead. The pain of one organ's decay vied with that of other organs, until the unbearable became tolerable only because it could not get worse.

What little mental faculty he retained he concentrated on one single objective: suicide. He decided the only way to ensure his drowning was to weigh himself down with rocks tied like an anchor to his legs. He struggled to his feet again, dribbling blood in the process, and scanned in both directions along the beach for rocks and something to tie them with. The sun unseen had nearly set behind the blanket of clouds, which had turned ever darker, making even more wretched the pelting rain and cold, steady wind.

He staggered drunkenly along the beach toward the promontory, the crashing waves spilling over the sand and grappling his legs. Then, in the dim light, he made out the fuzzy shape of a tall beam...a mast...to a sailing craft. He couldn't tell at first for sure in the murkiness if it was the *Gigolo*. Then he recognized the familiar telltales on the stays—red and white streamers salvaged from a filmy nightgown left on the *Gigolo* by a lady friend. He hobbled up the beach and spied the boat lying on its side twenty yards off shore in a small inlet of relatively calm waters protected by the promontory. It was the *Gigolo* all right. Her port beam was stove in as if by a huge hammer. She would never sail again. Her mainsail, still secured to its boom, had been torn loose from the mast and was floating on the water. More important to Brock, her rigging was still intact and would be perfect for binding some heavy object to his feet.

Bent over in pain, he staggered through the shallow, foam-covered water. Maneuvering around the sail, he ducked under the bowsprit and, like a sick jellyfish, slithered over the gunwale onto the forward deck, noting as he did so that his wristwatch was gone. Leaving a trail of bloody ooze behind him, he crawled snail-like along the steeply angled deck to the wheel aft, where he found the small emergency axe mounted in metal clamps on the bulkhead facing the wheel. He pulled the razor-sharp axe out of its holder and clumsily hacked several lines that were tied to the mast and that hung down into the water. They came free and, as they began to sink out of sight, he grabbed them and began reeling them in.

When he looked to pull them through their pulleys at the top of the mast, he saw that the spar spreading the shrouds apart at right angles to the mast formed a cross.

Suddenly an idea flashed. A cross...a crucifixion cross. As Christ had died on a cross for mankind's sins, so should Brock die for his. It was a shrewd and sensible idea. So fitting and deserved. Justice would be paid its due after all, and there would be no waves to cast him back from Death's door. His spirits lifted at the prospect of self-execution. Death on the cross! Yes!

Weak and suffering, he blotted out all distractions and directed his inventive designer's mind to the single problem of building and erecting a cross and raising himself on it. The obvious solution for the cross was the *Gigolo*'s forty-foot oak mast. Specially constructed by a Swedish family-owned boat-building company in Los Angeles, the mast was sturdy, tall enough for the purpose, and already fitted with the necessary crosspiece near its top.

It took him half an hour but, wielding the axe, he eventually managed to sever the mast from the *Gigolo* and floated the beam to shore. From there, using rapidly diminishing strength, stumbling, falling, and finally crawling on hands and knees, he dragged the timber up a sandy slope to a flat open area among some tall palm trees. The exertion left him totally exhausted. He lay still for fifteen minutes scraping together what little energy he had left and working out in his pain-ridden mind how he would engineer his crucifixion. Having finalized a plan, he tottered to his feet and stumbled back down the slope, falling and rolling onto the beach. He flopped into the water and paddled back to the *Gigolo*, leaving a sludge of blood and other bodily effluents floating like oil on the surface in his wake.

He gathered up a half dozen ropes, some cord, a small shovel, two heavy-duty pulleys, two empty sail bags from the sail locker, and a sharp paring knife from the galley. Fumbling and lashing these items to several life jackets, he slowly towed them to the beach and then on hands and knees, halting every ten seconds from fatigue, dragged them to the clearing among the trees. There, in a stupor induced by exhaustion and pain, lying on his stomach, he laboriously dug a deep hole in the sand and positioned the foot of the mast beside it. He filled the two sail bags with sand and tied a length of rope to each, vomiting thick red sticky liquid onto everything he touched. He bound the pulleys to either end of the crosstree near the top of the mast, threaded the ropes from the bags through them, and fastened several guy lines midway on the mast, stopping now and then to catch his breath and restore his depleted energy.

Gathering himself, he heaved the mast up, letting the base drop into the hole, then staked down the guys to secure it upright. Lying on his back and using his feet for shovels, he gradually filled in the hole around the base, then collapsed flat on his back onto the sand for ten minutes. He wound one of the two pulley ropes around his waist and, leaning forward to put the full weight of his frail body behind it, slowly, step by step, hoisted one of the two sand-filled bags to one tip of the crosstree, making the haul line fast to the base. After resting for another ten minutes, he repeated the grueling process with the other bag. Now fully spent, he lay on the sand almost comatose for half an hour trying to summon the strength for one final exertion. Flat on his back and wriggling like a dying insect, he stripped off his shirt and pants, leaving on only his sodden undershorts matted with feces, urine, blood, and other bodily fluids seeping from his orifices. He was now ready for the final challenge of raising himself spread-eagled to the top.

Gasping for breath and doubled over with agony, he took two short lengths of rope and tied one end of each into a loop barely big enough to fit over his hand. The other ends he lashed with slip knots to the haul lines. Turning his back to the mast, he tied his ankles together with cord and slipped his hands into the two loops. Then, after a momentary pause, he used the paring knife to simultaneously cut both haul lines below the loops.

The two sail bags instantly dropped, jerking Brock's arms above his head. Instinctively he flexed his biceps, bending his arms as if doing a chin-up. At once his body levitated, pulled slowly upward by the combined weight of the bags, which descended toward the sand. Up and up his limp sacklike body rose, his back rubbing against the mast, until the knots on the loops around his wrists jammed the pulleys at the crosstree, whose separation by five feet spread his arms apart in the classic pose of Christ's crucifixion.

Brock had succeeded. The "unworthy" was crucified and would die at last.

Strangely the words of St. Luke came to his mind. He began to repeat them like a chant. "For everyone who exalts himself shall be humbled.... For everyone who exalts himself shall be humbled....I am unworthy...I am unworthy...For everyone who exalts himself shall be humbled."

As he chanted, his natural impulse was to resist the traction of the sandbags, which he did for several minutes by contracting the muscles of his upper body. However, they were already spent from his exertions and, having no reserve, they quickly gave out, at which point he relaxed and let the skeletal structure of his arms and shoulders, not the muscles, bear the weight of his body. But the pull of the ropes on his arms constricted his lungs, making every gasp of air a struggle, and a losing one.

For an instant, but no more than that, he felt a queer elation, as if now he would experience some relief from the physical pummeling his body and organs had been suffering. So steady had been the grinding pain that he had become almost insensate to the white-hot coals burning his insides away. Yet within minutes a new aching began, first in his compressed lungs, then at his wrists where the rope loops bit deeply into his skin and tendons, and then at his shoulders where the weight of his body gripped the joints and pulled on the balls and sockets, twisting them unnaturally. The throbbing of his upper body set off stabbing muscle spasms in his diaphragm and legs as the gore from his internal bleeding and the fluids oozing from his decomposing organs accumulated in his distended abdomen and seeped out his anus, trickling down his legs and puddling the sand thirty-feet below at the base of the mast. Every part of his organism was in violent torment, every breath a torture, every movement an agony. Brock lost himself in a world of incredible pain.

By this time darkness had enveloped the island. He was unconscious of the roar of the ocean, the whirring of the wind through the trees, and the creaking of the guy ropes as the mast shifted back and forth, pulled by the pendulum motion of the sail bags swinging freely in the wind. So complete was the blackness that he was in effect sightless. Nevertheless he continued to stare dully ahead, as if expecting to see something, a light, a movement, but there was only blackness, and incredible pain reaching higher thresholds than he ever imagined possible. He prayed to pass out, but it was not to be. He remained conscious, looking blindly into the darkness.

All at once the wind died. It simply gave out, as if someone had closed a window or turned off a fan. At the same instant the waves abated and the ocean becalmed. Even with his suffering Brock was suddenly aware of the eerie silence. He thought for a moment he had died, that he had started his journey through the empty blackness of space to his rendezvous in hell. He imagined from the fiery pain of the ropes cutting into his arms that he was in the grip of two giant red-eyed mastiffs, each holding one of his wrists clamped in iron-vise jaws. Delirious and comatose, he was unaware of time as the night passed.

The sun rose in a cloudless sky heating the sand as well as his swollen inert body, which dangled uselessly from the crosstree, a sorry, dried-up, wasted sack of skin and bones. Not a breath of wind or a ripple on the water appeared all day...for twelve tortuous incredible hours. As his skin temperature rose, his body looked for water in muscle and skin tissue but found little, it having been depleted by loss of fluids through seepage and hemorrhaging. He breathed in short painful gasps, barely enough to sustain his life. His pores had ceased perspiring hours earlier. His entire body was dehydrated. His skin took on a yellowish deathlike pallor, his lips turned blue, swelled, cracked, and bled, and his glazed eyes sank in their sockets. By dusk his breathing and pulse were so shallow, they would not have been detectable by casual inspection. Brock thus teetered on the border between life and death...but he did not die.

He could not see it, but had he remained conscious he would have witnessed a magnificent sunset lasting a full hour with spectacular bursts of color of every hue fanning across the sky like giant curtains of fine silk, waning, pulsating, glowing, merging. Ancient prophets would have interpreted such a display in the heavens as a harbinger of some marvelous event. And so it was, but far beyond anything Brock could have imagined.

As the chromatic extravaganza faded into night, a cool breeze came up, ruffling the placid water. Clouds blew in from the east blanking out the stars, and waves rippled on the beach. The temperature dropped, and the westward wind grew brisk, then strong and steady, bending the palm trees and testing the mast's creaking guy ropes. The waves increased in size and power, the noise of their crashing on the beach rising to a roaring cannonade. Rain began falling, lightly at first, then harder and harder till it came in torrents driven by a howling wind that had now reached gale force.

The shock of icy wind and water on Brock's withered body broke into his fevered mind and brought him into a dreamlike consciousness in which he was dimly aware of the night and the storm and of his condition on death's door. Distant lightning illuminated the heaving ocean and set off delayed rolls of thunder that even in Brock's hazy awareness seemed to presage some major happening. He then knew that he was about to die and, expending the last miniscule reservoir of strength, he repeated in a weak and quavering whisper his self-condemning affirmation. "I am...unworthy...Everyone...who...exalts...himself...shall...be...humbled."

In Brock's delirium he had not quoted the passage from Luke in full. Had he been able to, he might have sensed what was to happen, for the rest of the passage reads, "...and he who humbles himself shall be exalted."

At that second a colossal lightning bolt struck the tip of the mast, suffusing Brock and the entire structure in a blinding ectoplasm of blue-green light, splitting and burning the mast and vaporizing the ropes. Brock, cut loose from his bindings and knocked unconscious, plummeted down, thudding onto the sand. The entire mast was enveloped in flames that hissed a staccato snare-drum beat in the driving rain that soon extinguished the fire, blanketing the area again in total darkness.

In minutes the sea calmed, the wind fell off to a wafting breeze, the rain clouds dissipated, and stars twinkled brightly against the blue-black sky. The air turned from cold and dank to mild and dry. The sour, dead-fish smell of the storm was replaced by the flowery fragrance of blossoms. All the while Brock's body lay inert at the base of the mast.

Gradually, a bluish translucence formed on the horizon due east of the island. The light expanded and brightened, sending rays of color across the smooth mirror-like surface of the water. Finally the orange ball of the sun broached the far horizon, and a beam of dazzling sunlight shot across the ocean illuminating the crosstree of the mast and the tops of the palm trees. As the orange globe rose, the shafts of light spread out, coloring the mast, trees, bushes, rocks, and beach a lustrous life-nourishing gold.

Brock lay facedown, one arm under his forehead. The sunlight seemed to activate his consciousness, and he began to stir. He opened his eyes and, not moving, focused on the sand two inches from his face.

Something had happened, he knew. He couldn't remember what. Pain and darkness had engulfed him. He barely remembered the storm and wind. It was like a dream, vague and formless but very real.

Then it all came back. The mast. His ascent up the mast to the crosstree. His self-crucifixion. The burning sun, then wind and rain beating against his body. The excruciating pain. His struggle and finally surrender to death. Then...his memory lapsed. A blank spot. Something had happened.

Suddenly he realized there was something different about him. He didn't know what, but there was a difference. Not something wrong exactly, just different. Then it hit him. No pain! His pain was gone. No, it was more than gone. He felt good. He felt...relaxed...content...no, there was more. He felt...healthy!

He rolled on his back and began to examine himself. The lumps on his arms and face and chest and abdomen and thighs and ankles were gone. Not only had they vanished, but there was no soreness, not even tenderness. Hesitantly he breathed in and out, expecting the torturing pain that had been his constant companion on the cross. His lungs were clear. The thrill of this discovery was held in check by a disbelief, an expectation that any movement of his body would trigger the usual chain of nerve-stabbing blows to his joints and diaphragm. He brought his knees slowly up to his chest...no pain. The muscles functioned smoothly...even strongly. He stretched his legs out...no pain. Raising his knees to his chest again, he could feel the strength of the muscles, and a smile broke across his face. He sat up and rolled forward crouching on the balls of his feet. No pain. Moreover, there was a certain youthful spring in his legs that surprised and delighted him. Giggling, he carefully stood up, waiting for his accustomed wooziness, but his head remained clear, and his sense of balance was sharp. He raised up on his toes and felt the sinews in his thighs and lower legs pull tightly and evenly. Relaxing his muscles, his heels sank an inch or so into the sand. Flexing his soles, he rose up on his toes and down again, up and down. Then he began to jump, playfully at first, then more vigorously, leaping and throwing his arms above his head. Yelling and laughing, he broke into a run down the beach, splashing into the water, careening in and out, feeling like a twenty-year-old filled with power and stamina.

His route had taken him to the promontory to the very edge from which he had tried to kill himself the day before. He looked over the precipice into the quiescent blue-green water that what seemed like only minutes before had been a cauldron of death. It was now a placid pool, the water so clear that even from this height he could see small colorful rocks on the bottom.

Sometimes one becomes uncannily aware of another's unseen presence. No one quite knows how, though some claim its an inherent psychic ability, but Brock suddenly became so aware. His eyes moved slowly from the rocks below, to the water farther out, to the glistening light rays dancing on the surface, and finally to the horizon which lit up his face with a display of colors and patterns and hues of wondrous beauty. It was the Fourth of July, the Northern Lights, and the Dawn of Mankind. The cascading colors transfixed his mind, reached into his being, took hold of his soul, and caressed it...and he wept...for from without and from within at the same instant came the awesome realization that he was cured. His cancer was gone. His entire body had been rejuvenated. Even his undershorts were dazzling white again.

He fell to his knees and sobbed, covering his face with his hands and shaking his head as he struggled to comprehend this miracle. It defied reason and rational explanation. To what did he owe his incredible transformation from a dying decomposing slug to a robust healthy man? He looked skyward and, clasping his hands together prayerfully, intoned, "My heavenly Father, why me? Why have You bestowed on me, a worthless, hopeless sinner, this miracle of miracles? I have done nothing to merit it. I treat my wife, son, and daughter cruelly, thoughtlessly, selfishly, even hatefully. I use every means at my disposal, immoral or unethical, to beat down my competition. I coldly turn away good souls like Father Leonard, Kelly, and Diego who showed me only friendship and kindness. I am in every way, as Catherine said, the devil in disguise. I am unquestionably, inarguably, indisputably, undeniably unworthy of Your mercy. Unworthy!" he shouted. "Unworthy! I am the prototype sinner who knows right from wrong and good from evil, yet defiles everything he touches. My life mocked everything good and holy. My despicable life deserves only condemnation and retribution, not...not..." He broke down sobbing, shaking his head, flailing his arms helplessly. "Not mercy," he whispered. "Please not mercy. I don't deserve it."

Suddenly a memory came into his mind. It was a phrase from the Bible. *For everyone...* It faded, only to return more clearly. *For everyone who exalts himself shall be humbled.* But there was more. He prodded his mind to see what it was. Then it came to him fully. *For everyone who exalts himself shall be humbled, and he who humbles himself shall be exalted.*

He fell forward on the sand, his head resting on his hands. A loving warmth surrounded him like a cloak. It was the most exhilarating feeling he had ever experienced. He luxuriated in its comfort, knowing in his heart that it was either God's love or the Holy Spirit. He remained motionless praying for a half hour.

Gradually he recovered from his reverie and became cognizant once more of his surroundings. He got up and walked resolutely down from the promontory and up the ridge to the mast to examine it and analyze how he had been cured. The two large bags of sand lay where they had fallen, while the ropeless pulleys were still secured to the spars. It was obvious. He had been struck by lightning. The beam was split its entire length right into the ground but somehow remained standing. The surfaces of both halves were charred, and the pungent escharotic odor of wet cinders hung in an invisible cloud around the site. He could only wonder at the nature and power of this phenomenal occurrence.

Beginning to take an interest in his location, he turned from the mast to look inland to see if he could determine where he had landed on the California coast. He guessed the storm had carried him south, probably north of Los Angeles. He was stunned by the sight before him. He spun around, peering in every direction. Water...endless water. He was on a small island with no land in sight. Lacking a sextant with which to fix his position, he could only wonder where the island was located and how near the mainland. Where was he?

He pondered this question as he looked about. His new home was a gorgeous paradise featuring a number of tall palm trees and an assortment of flowered plants—orchid, hibiscus, bougainvillea, and the strongly perfumed gardenia-like pandanus. The ground rose at the middle of the island to maybe thirty feet above sea level.

He surveyed his new domain. The island was tiny, less than half a mile long, and narrow, no more than a hundred yards at its greatest width about midway. It seemed to be more or less boat-shaped, its two convex sides meeting at sharp ends pointing north and south. There was less sand on the western shore than the eastern where Brock had landed and where the *Gigolo* was beached. On the western side was a small lagoon of coral and volcanic rock, substances uncommon to the California coast, suggesting the island was at a much greater distance in the Pacific than he had supposed.

A flock of twenty or thirty seagulls perched lazily on one of the two fingers of rock that formed the lagoon. As if to demonstrate for him their independence, the largest bird in the flock—the kingpin, he presumed—took off from the lagoon and circled the island. The others followed, swooping across it, putting on a show for the visitor seemingly to lay claim to the airspace in case Brock had any notion of seeking dominion there, too.

"You may have the air!" he called to them. "And the fish the sea. But I lay claim to this island in the name of..." It was the usual thing in history for explorers to claim newly discovered territories, but in whose name should he claim this tiny isle? Certainly not his own. Then thinking of his miraculous cure, he knew. "I lay claim to this island in the name of miracles. Miracle Island!"

He was feeling youthful and vigorous. Perhaps, he thought, this is the magic place that Ponce de Leon, the Spanish explorer, had sought, where resided the fabled Fountain of Youth, except here it was mystical lightning, not Circean water, that did the trick.

Thinking of fountains, it occurred to Brock that he had not seen a source of fresh water. He spun around, scanning the island again, all of which was visible from the hillock. There was no pool or basin in which rainwater could collect. There were, however, palm trees and the flowering flora, but he had read somewhere that certain species of plants, whose roots stored water, could survive on very little moisture. There probably was just enough rainfall here to replenish the roots but not enough for lush greenery. The runoff from any rain would soak quickly through the sand and volcanic soil. The coral and volcanic rock underpinning below probably created small pools of water that only deep roots could reach.

So what was he to do for water? He had no idea how often it rained here, wherever he was. The rain might be seasonal with droughts as long as four or five months. Fish looked to be the only source of food he had seen on the island aside from the birds and a few coconuts, but the latter wouldn't last long. Perhaps if he ate enough fish, they would furnish him with the water his body needed, but he didn't know how much that was, and he doubted it would be enough. Then he remembered there was a water tank aboard the *Gigolo* and decided to check on it at once.

Running vigorously down to the beach, he waded through the three-foot depth of cool, clear, azure water and lifted himself effortlessly over the gunwale and into the cockpit, his muscles flexing powerfully and painlessly. The hatch was open. He hopped down the steps into the rancid, fishy smelling cabin below, taking a quick inventory of equipment and fixtures as he went. Everything was helter-skelter. Cabinets open. Dishes, pans, utensils, and paper cups on the deck. Some of the cups were floating in seawater pooled in one corner. Even though the deck was canted at forty-five degrees, he effortlessly with his newfound strength crossed the sodden carpeted floor to the forward compartment, where the water storage tank was housed. It had a capacity of five gallons. He had not filled it before leaving the marina in San Francisco and had not drunk from it during his ordeal at sea. Fresh water had been the last thing on his death-obsessed mind. Now it was uppermost, the difference between survival and extinction. Had God miraculously cured his cancer only to let him die of thirst? Certainly not!

Out of habit Brock flipped on the light switch but, of course, the compartment, which had no portal, remained dark. He found a flashlight hanging in its accustomed place on the bulkhead beside the doorway and directed its beam at the tank. A glass tube on the outside of the container indicated its water level. It read a fraction more than one gallon. One gallon! Actually less because the tank, like the boat, was listing. Brock was dismayed. How long could he survive on less than one gallon? If he rationed his consumption to even a cup a day, he was doomed to run out in a week or so.

And what about food?

He opened the food locker. He had not sailed the *Gigolo* in two months nor restocked its provisions. There was a can of tomato soup, an opened half-filled bag of soggy potato chips, a sodden package of Morton's salt, a bottle of Tabasco sauce, a small box of cocktail toothpicks, and a crumpled carton of paper napkins. Nothing of sustenance on which to survive except the soup.

He chuckled. "Survive? For how long? Till I'm rescued? No one knows I'm here, wherever that is, and from the looks of this island no one ever comes here." So, a can of soup and one gallon of water. Not enough. He needed to develop a plan for survival.

He turned first to devising a way of collecting rainwater. He rigged a sail to serve as a catch basin among the palm trees on the ridge and put a bucket at the lowest edge to catch the runoff, should it rain. Then he searched the shores of the island for fish but saw none. He pulled up some underwater greenery growing near the rocks on the lagoon and laid it out on the sand to dry. He'd try eating it later. He picked different leaves and roots and blossoms and touched them to his lower lip. He remembered an article he had read about hiking in wilderness that advised the neophyte to put a bit of any unknown leaf, berry, root, or herb on the lower lip. "If it stings or is rancid, don't eat it! And don't eat what birds eat. They have a bird's digestive system. You don't!" He lip-tested every type of vegetation he could find on the island and determined, his lip nearly numb from the acidic substances on the leaves, that none was fit for consumption.

So he turned his attention to the seagulls. Twenty-two in all. They wouldn't last long as a food source. Still, there must be fish around, because isn't that what seagulls feed on? It was apparently not the nesting season because he saw no eggs. Prospects for food were grim...and so was the outlook for his survival.

With his new health and vitality came an immense appetite and likewise an immense hunger. So he decided to have a feast. What was the point in stretching out what little food he had? He might as well use it up and starve, if he were going to starve anyway. Meanwhile he would try to catch some fish.

He extricated the gas stove from the galley and set it up on the beach alongside a deck chair and a TV tray for a table. He found a lone half-filled bottle of red wine in the liquor cabinet. He and his yachting friends had finished off all of the other bottles in a night-long bash to celebrate their victory in the club's final race of the season two months ago. He got a coconut, put the soup on the stove, tore open the bag of potato chips, and served himself a glass of wine. While the soup was heating up, he set out three fishing rods with spinners and later, as he ate and watched the rods, he thought more about his cure.

New doubts about its being a miracle began to creep in as they always do about supernatural events. What would skeptics think? That the lightning bolt was an act of Nature, not of God. An enormous charge of electrical energy had apparently passed through him, encasing his body in a powerful highly charged field of electrical flux with all kinds of interactions with the cells in his body. Could not that exposure have killed off the cancer cells and revitalized his muscles and energy? Could anyone prove otherwise? It was a plausible explanation. After all, use of electrolysis to revitalize skin and muscles was widespread among athletes as well as the aging and aged. Microwaves were proven to cure all sorts of ailments. In a hundred years, medical experts might be using lightning-type charges to cure millions of people of everything from lumbago to hay fever. Who knows?

He hastily devoured the soup, chips, and coconut meat, then spent the rest of the day fishing...without success. As the sun set in the west within a dazzling panorama of color that spanned the horizon, Brock settled into his deck chair on the beach and, for the first time since his cure, thought of Eleanor and Paul and the situation he had left behind in California. The memories were vivid and emotionally wrenching. Despondent, he cast his eyes around the starlit heavens. He said aloud to himself, "Perhaps I've died, and this is heaven. But if so, heaven has the

378

same star system as earth." No, he thought. He was still alive and somewhere in the Pacific. He fell asleep in the chair wondering where he was.

The next morning he checked his fish lines, but they were empty. No bites. He tried again, walking the beaches and casting with one of the rods. He varied the bait—roots, spinners, leftover potato chips, some soaked in Tabasco sauce, even some colorful flower petals. Nothing worked. He would like to have experimented with insects as bait, but he could find none.

Although survival was now uppermost in his thoughts, he still groped for an explanation for his cure. If it had been a real miracle, he—like doubting Saint Thomas—would need to see some concrete proof, an unmistakable sign.

He fished all day without success and without food, but he did drink two cups of water from the *Gigolo*'s tank. At dusk, seeing no alternative, he cracked open another coconut with the axe, wolfed down the meat, and went to sleep on the sand.

The next day he followed the same routine, fishing at different sites along the island's shore while looking ever more hungrily at the seagulls, figuring how he could snare one for a meal. He ate two coconuts and drank two cups of water.

By the third day he was getting desperate. He was going to die of starvation, of that he was sure. He hunted for more coconuts, but there were only three left in the trees. He knocked them down and ate all three, but they were green and tasteless, and he doubted they had the nutrients he needed for survival. Their bitterness made him thirsty, so he drank four cups of water.

When he awoke the next morning and realized his supply of coconuts was exhausted, he put aside his fear of eating poisonous plants and started to gingerly experiment with the flora. Attractive and seemingly edible roots and leaves were sour beyond his tolerance and gave him stomach cramps. So he quit eating them and went instead on a seagull hunt, trying various traps and snares to catch one of the birds. He even played dead on the water, floating faceup along the rocks where the gulls roosted, but they were not fooled and skittered away whenever he approached.

Day after day passed. Still no food. On the fourteenth day he awakened with severe stomach pains. He got to his feet, wobbling a bit from malnutrition, and dizzily made his way across the island to the lagoon. The seagulls, instinctively alert to his hunger and wary of his intentions, took to the air at his approach and soared safely in the sky above the island, coming to rest at the far tip. Confused and depressed, he walked dejectedly back across the ridge, past the mast, and down to the eastern beach, where he plopped down on his rump in the sand, slumping forward, his arms on his knees, his head hanging down in resignation. He reflected on the unlikely chain of events that had brought him here, from San Francisco to this very moment.

The storm at sea knocks him out, preventing him from scuttling the *Gigolo* and drowning. Beating all odds the boat runs aground on this lonely island, a microdot in thousands of square miles of empty ocean. But the boat doesn't sink nor does he drown. Somehow he falls overboard and is washed ashore. Again an unlikely scenario. He tries to kill himself—by walking into the waves and by throwing himself off the promontory— and each time the ocean pitches him up onto the sand unharmed. An even unlikelier scenario. Lastly he crucifies himself and instead of dying, which his terminal physical condition warranted, he is struck by lightning and is somehow cleansed of his cancer. An atheist would contend that none of these events was unnatural, that all were quite normal and unremarkable. No laws of physics or natural science were abridged or violated.

Brock knelt again and prayed aloud for God to send him a sign. "I am hopelessly like Thomas, Lord. I have lost my faith over the years that I ignored You. I need just this one favor. Please, God, grant me this one wish, that I may understand whether my cure and all these bizarre events are Your work or simply an extraordinary sequence of natural happenings which have no spiritual meaning. Grant me a sign of Your understanding. Grant me a sign. Please."

He remained praying for twenty or thirty minutes. He wasn't sure how long. He had no reckoning of time, when distantly he heard a strange flapping noise. At first he thought it was the wings of the seagulls, but there was splashing as well.

He got to his feet and ran up the rise, tripping and falling in his haste,

380

then racing on hands and knees to the top of the ridge. Down below the lagoon was teeming with fish, so many they churned the water's surface.

Brock jumped to his feet, electrified, and ran down to the lagoon whooping and hollering. He dove headfirst into the seething water and grabbed one of the small silvery fish in his two hands and threw it onto the beach. Then another, and another, and another. Ten, fifteen, twenty. Shouting and laughing, he forgot his prayer. He forgot his wish for a sign. All he could think about was food. Now he would eat...he would survive.

Suddenly he froze, his chest heaving, brine running into his eyes and down his face and dripping from his three-week growth of beard. He looked at the beach. Piled there was a glistening, flapping heap of shiny silver fish with white bellies. The enormity of what had happened dawned on him. His mouth fell open and his eyes widened. He raised his arms and walked slowly out of the water, oblivious to the thrashing water around him. Falling to his knees on the beach, he grasped a fish in each hand and clasped them to his chest. Then he looked heavenward and, with tears coursing down his cheeks, fell forward weeping. It was the sign! Not merely that God was behind all of these events, but that Brock was forgiven...forgiven his sins. God's love abounded for all of His children, even the least of them. Strangely the words of the prophet Isaiah rang out in Brock's mind as clearly as if a voice were reading from Scripture. "Can a mother forget her infant? Even should she forget, I your God will never forget you!"

Brock wept, out of thanksgiving for his salvation, out of remorse for his sins, out of love for the many people he had harmed and wronged. He wept most of all out of humility and wonder that, despite all the heartless things he had done, God, his heavenly Father, still cherished him as one of His own.

It was difficult for Brock to reconcile this proof of God's abiding love with Brock's feeling of abject unworthiness. Could God love someone who was so clearly unworthy of love? Then all at once the truth showed itself. "Of course," he said aloud. "Why couldn't I see it?" Father Leonard had lectured on it once in class. "It is God's love that makes us worthy!" Redeemed and renewed, Brock got to his feet amid the pile of fish around him. "Thank You, O, most merciful and benevolent Father."

Seeing that there were thirty or forty fish flapping around on the sand about him, he laughed. "Sorry, God. I don't mean to squander Your gift." He threw back all but four and sauntered joyously back to the other side of the island to clean, cook, and eat them. As he reached the ridge, the fish in the lagoon went out of sight as quickly as they had appeared. The silence halted Brock, and he turned to stare at the calm quiet water in the lagoon. Another miracle!

As he was cleaning the fish, he wished he had a bucket of fresh water to wash them in, and then he had a sudden revelation. The one gallon! How could he drink water for two weeks and the tank not run dry?

He dropped the fish and dashed wildly through the shallows to the *Gigolo*, vaulted over the side, and clambered below to the water tank. The indicator still read one gallon. He hesitated a moment, then with the daring self-confidence that comes with true faith, he threw open the valve and let the water pour freely onto the deck in a steady stream. He watched the indicator breathlessly, thrilled at his own recklessness. The level stayed at one.

He knelt and placed his palms in the thin ribbon of water, letting it wash over and through his outstretched fingers. The indicator held at one.

Tears again streamed from his eyes as he felt the touch of water...holy water...a third miracle...run across his skin. He ducked his head under the water and crossed himself. Then, laughing delightedly, he gathered every container and receptacle he could find and began filling them and taking them up on deck. Two buckets, dishes, glasses, pots, pans, plastic food containers, even a rain hat. On and on. When he finally shut off the spigot he had collected maybe ten gallons of water...and the indicator on the tank still read one gallon.

He leaned back against the railing and looked at the hodgepodge of containers crowding every space on deck, some balanced precariously over the gunwales, some stacked and teetering atop others. His faith in God, now turned to warm unconstrained affection, glowed at the sight— the living proof—of not merely God's unimaginable power but of His very existence.

On a sudden impulse Brock grabbed one of the brimful buckets and upended it over his head, drenching his body with holy water. "I love You, Lord!" he shouted exuberantly. "I love You with all my heart...and all my soul!" He laughed merrily and spontaneously as he took up another bucket and doused himself with it. He couldn't help it. The purist joy filled his senses. The God of the Universe had reached out to him, had spoken to him, and shown him love.

Brock sank down in the well of the cockpit and eased into a more contemplative mood, reflecting on the wonder of what had happened. It was beyond his understanding—the why of it. God had acted for His own reasons. It was not for Brock to know or question. That God loved him was enough. Nay, it was everything. The greatest gift of all. Pity the poor souls who die without knowing God's boundless love for each of them. *Peace be on me*, he thought. *I am like Thomas, who cast aside his doubts when he saw the proof of Jesus' resurrection. As St. John wrote, "Blest are they who have not seen and have believed."*

Brock felt the urge to read the Bible, to refresh his memory of the Scriptures and to find new meaning in them from his experience here. Only then did he remember taking his blue Bible with him from the hospital. Strange, he thought, that while his feverish mind had been bent on suicide he should have bothered to bring along his Bible. Why would he have done that? Unless God's hand had been at work again. But, of course, it had been. And where was the Bible now? Brock had stowed it in the clothes locker.

He heaved himself up out of the cockpit and threaded his way through the maze of containers to the cabin. There he found the Bible, safe and dry. Holding it high above his head, he waded ashore and laid it down beside the fish. He then returned to the boat and detached the water tank from the bulkhead and took it ashore, setting it down alongside the Bible. Humming and whistling, he proceeded to clean and cook on the gas stove. He ate the fish and drank and bathed in the water from the tank. Then he seized the Bible and walked up the ridge and seated himself before the mast-cross, where he prayed and read from St. John for an hour or so.

When he finished, out of profound gratitude and wonder for what had happened, he went to work constructing an altar. After all, didn't Abraham build an altar in thanksgiving for God's gift of the Promised Land? If it was good enough for Abraham, surely it was good enough for Brock. It was a simple structure fashioned of flat volcanic rocks that he lugged up from the beach to the promontory. Atop the rocks he erected a

383

cross fashioned out of wood splinters from the *Gigolo*'s gashed hull. He knelt and prayed and, taking a glass of water from the *Gigolo*'s tank, sprinkled it over the cross and altar. Then he prayed again silently.

As he formed words of thanksgiving in his mind, the sky darkened and clouds appeared. In minutes the wind picked up and the ocean became choppy, whitecaps rising. The weather quickly worsened and before Brock could grasp what was happening, lightning struck the water a hundred yards offshore followed by thunder and heavy windblown rain that pelted his body, forcing him to abandon the promontory and seek shelter among the trees on the ridge. He grabbed the water tank and the Bible and dashed up the slope. He was halfway up when a full-fledged storm broke, and a hurricane-force wind out of nowhere blasted across the island, knocking him to the sand, bending the trees, toppling the altar, scattering the stones and crucifix like playing cards.

Terrified, Brock crouched behind one of the larger palm trees. This was a different sign, no question about it. The sign of an angry God displeased by something Brock had done...or not done.

"What have I done?" he shouted. "How have I displeased You?"

The howling wind lashed the beach, tearing down the sail Brock had rigged to catch water and throwing up sand that stung his face and arms. Covering the Bible with his body, he flattened himself on the ground quavering in fear that he would be struck again by lightning as he had been on the cross. Would God revoke the miracle? Would He kill him after all?

The storm raged for twenty minutes, battering the island, while Brock huddled on the ground behind the trees fearing the worst. Then as quickly as the storm had come, it left. The wind fell, the rain stopped, the ocean calmed, and the sun reappeared.

Brock lay motionless for several minutes, wondering if it were truly over, then he cautiously raised himself on his arms and peered through the grass to the promontory. The altar had been demolished. He hung his head and sighed in relief that he was still alive, wondering aloud if violent storms regularly lashed this island. Regaining his composure, he chuckled and got to his feet. He had never been a comic, a raconteur, someone who cracked jokes or made entertaining wisecracks. No one would ever have described him as humorous, yet all at once he felt impish and jocular.

Looking upward and addressing himself to God, he said, "So, You didn't like the altar. Hey, I never said it was my best work. I didn't know You were such an art critic, but I'm easy to work with. Just tell me. I don't need to be run over by a freight train...or a typhoon. But look, an artist deserves some latitude."

A gust of wind tousled his hair.

"All right, all right! Just kidding. No latitude."

He began walking along the beach, a grin on his face, his heart light as a feather. "I'll make You another altar. You'll like it. I promise. Something special. More intrinsically worthy. More appealing to the eye. And look, if You don't like what I build, how about a small roll of thunder? I'll get the message. But please, no more storms."

Brock looked down at himself. He was covered with wet sand from head to foot. "Now look what You've done. I'm a mess. What will people think?" He frowned playfully, enjoying this repartee with his Creator. He raced down to the water and dove in, washing the sand from his body. When he emerged from the water, he spied a gigantic three-masted schooner resting at an angle on its bottom about thirty yards from shore on the opposite side of the promontory from the *Gigolo*. "Where did that come from?"

He ran down the beach toward the schooner shouting. "Ahoy! Is anyone aboard? Hello! Hello!" The name on the schooner's prow was *Bali*, suggesting she was from Indonesia. He jumped into the water and swam toward the vessel. Reaching her, he pulled himself over the gunwale, which was half under water. Clambering around the deck, he quickly determined no one was on board.

He spent the next hour examining her. Clearly she was crewless and unseaworthy. Her ragged wind-torn sails and rigging hung down in great folds and shreds. Diving underwater with a snorkeling mask from the *Gigolo*, he checked her hull, which seemed undamaged as far as he could tell. Her crew obviously had abandoned her in the storm. He surmised that she was an old vessel—maybe fifty years or more—and the wrenching of her hull by the storm's pounding waves must have opened her seams, letting in more water than the crew could pump out. When she started to sink, they would have piled into lifeboats and left her for dead. The davits were empty, the lifeboats gone. But the schooner hadn't gone down. Her hull had filled with water, but there apparently were enough air pockets in her compartments to maintain buoyancy. The storm's waves did the rest, carrying her right up to the beach where she lodged sideways and healed over. Or so he surmised.

His investigation completed, he waded ashore and sat down on the beach to think about the ship. "I ask You for a sign, and You give it to me double-barreled—first the fish, then the water. When I try to express my gratitude, You blow a storm up on the island, scatter Your altar all around, and dump a derelict schooner on the beach. So now I'm deserted with not just one but two useless ships. I think You're telling me something, but I don't know what it is. What is the message? Or is this island gonna be a maritime junkyard. Is that what You have in mind for me? To be custodian of derelict ships?"

He stared sullenly at the schooner, pondering its significance, when he spotted a bit of white fluff on one of its yardarms. It was a bird, but not a seagull. He had looked at enough seagulls the past several weeks to recognize one. No, this was another species. He stepped to the water's edge for a better look, but the sun was setting and the light dimming. If he had to guess, he'd say it was a pigeon. "Well, there's no point in bothering about it today. I've got all the time in the world. We'll see about it in the morning. The bird will probably be gone by then anyway."

He went up among the trees and lay down on the sand near the mast, the site of his miracle. Just being close to it was comforting. Oddly enough he didn't feel lonely. How could he be lonely when God was here with him? He was neither hungry nor thirsty, but he did feel worn out.

Before he closed his eyes he prayed, wondering whether there would be another storm during the night and whether he would be warm enough. Then it occurred to him that, with the exception of the brief storm today, the weather had been absolutely perfect day and night, neither too warm nor too cold. He said to himself, "Faith, Brock. Have faith. God knows what He's doing. If He thought you needed a blanket He'd have provided one." With that comforting thought he closed his eyes and fell soundly asleep.

The next morning he rose fully rested and ravenously hungry. His first thought was that the miraculous appearance of fish in the lagoon had been a coincidence. A natural event that could be plausibly explained by...

386

"It was God's doing," he said aloud. "There's no point in looking for other explanations. The God of the Universe is at work here through me and perhaps for me. I don't know why, but there it is!" His faith restored, he headed directly for the lagoon to procure his breakfast. And his faith was rewarded. The second his toes touched the water its smooth surface erupted in a massive school of flapping, swarming fish. Gleefully he snared four and carried them back to the other side of the island, stopping on his way to witness again the school's magical disappearance. "So much for doubting Thomases," he said, crossing himself. "Thank You, God, for this food." He cleaned the fish with water from the inexhaustible tank, cooked them, prayed, and ate.

Only then did he remember the white bird in the tattered rigging of the schooner. He looked over at the foundered vessel and sure enough the white pigeon was still perched by itself on a yardarm...a lonesome blossom on a leafless limb. Brock picked off a piece of fish from his plate and, walking to the beach opposite the schooner, tossed the food on the sand. "Hey! Bird! Welcome to Miracle Island! Come down and have a bite. Introduce yourself, and we'll get acquainted."

To Brock's astonishment and delight the bird sprang from the spar and glided effortlessly across the water with wings outstretched, landing gracefully twenty feet away.

"If you're that friendly, then I guess God must have brought you here, too."

As if disinterested in Brock's presence and unafraid, the bird waddled directly to the fish and began pecking and tearing it apart, swallowing small bits.

"You're welcome...I guess. And you're obviously hungry. Bet you haven't eaten in days." Brock squinted, looking more closely. "What kind of pigeon are you? A homing pigeon? You're a long way from home, wherever that is. I'll bet you're a castaway like me. I'd say that storm blew you off course. Where were you headed? Hawaii? California? It's a wonder you survived that wind and rain. Of course, if God was your Protector, you weren't in any danger. Right?"

The snow-white bird continued its feasting, paying no attention to Brock's idle conversation.

"You came to the right place to survive. Say, pardon me for asking but, if you're planning on staying awhile, you'll need a moniker. I can't address you as 'bird.' Let's see. What would be appropriate? Saved from death by the grace of God Himself. How about Jonah?" Brock frowned. "Naw. No good. Jonah was inside a whale, which is no place for a bird. Then there's...Lazarus. Christ brought him back from the dead. Yeah, I like that. Lazarus. It kind of fits."

Brock walked back to his breakfast.

"So, Lazarus. If you choose to stick around, I promise you a steady diet of Holy Mackerel!" He stopped and laughed, then looked skyward with a playful scowl. "Only kidding, God. Only kidding." Brock turned back to the pigeon. "You see, Laz, baby, God furnishes the meals here. I mean it's like a drive-in. You step in the water and, whammo, fish everywhere. You'll love it. It's a fish-eating bird's paradise." Brock saw that the pigeon was unconcernedly laboring over his piece of fish. "I don't think you heard a word I said."

In the days that followed, Brock became accustomed to the sight of the snowy bird and noticed that it didn't mingle with the seagulls but stayed apart. A lost and lonely sheep, thought Brock. The gulls showed neither fear of nor interest in the newcomer. They were monumentally indifferent. The pigeon had given them no cause to feel threatened, because Brock fed it every time he ate a meal, so it was not in competition for the gulls' food supply. As a result they coexisted nicely.

For Brock, Lazarus was a welcome companion with whom to share his meals and his observations about their new life on this tiny dot of land surrounded by the endless expanse of the Pacific Ocean. As the weeks passed, he kidded the bird a lot because it would not approach him, remaining always at a respectful distance. "You think I bite or something? Well, you're right. I mean, day after day I've eaten nothing but fish. I would really savor a juicy roast pigeon! Hmm-hmm!" He rubbed his stomach and licked his lips. "But I shouldn't threaten you, should I? It isn't hospitable of me as your host. After all, we're going to be good buddies, you and I."

Brock gave a slight look of surprise and grinned. "What if you aren't a buddy but a buddess? How can I tell if your name should be Lazarita instead of Lazarus?" He studied the bird's physique for some clue to its gender. "All birds look alike. Look, Laz, old girl, or whatever. I'm gonna gamble that you're a stud who got lost on his way to a romp with the boys. Any problem with that?"

The bird stopped bobbing up and down over the fish it was chipping away at and cocked its head, seeming to look directly at Brock. Then it resumed its feeding. Brock guffawed at the bird's antics, pleased that his new companion was tickling his humor. "I take it then you have no objection to being addressed as Lazarus."

Brock had never felt so full of amusement or so primed to laugh at the predicaments that faced him. He could not account for this unfamiliar humor. Perhaps it sprang from the new joy he discovered in being alive and healthy.

"Be that as it may, my friend, our task today is to fathom why God sent us this ship. Are we to build from it a raft or some type of boat in which to sail back to civilization? Am I to parade myself around the world as a living testament to God's power of salvation? On the face of it I'd say that would be a little tacky, wouldn't you? I mean, who would believe me in the first place? And secondly I'd come across to most of the world as a freak, a weirdo. No, I don't think that's what God wants me to do."

Brock ambled along the beach musing on the meaning of the schooner. It had been delivered to the island by the hand of God. But for what purpose? The storm that brought it also destroyed the altar. Is there a connection? Brock had to admit that the altar had been a pretty shabby gift. Was God therefore mandating the erection of another altar, larger and more ornate? Of course, that was it! He stopped walking, excitement lighting up his face. The significance of the schooner was obvious. As the schooner was larger and more pretentious than the *Gigolo*, so would be the altar compared to the first. Brock's eyes gleamed with pleasure at deciphering God's message.

"I hear You, Lord, loud and clear! If it's an altar You want, then it's an altar You'll get! I'll make it special...a prize-winner....You'll love it."

Brock's inventive mind instantly envisioned a variety of possible designs and, while he compared them one to another, he stumped the island looking for the ideal location. His artistic instincts led him to the highest point—the clearing among the trees where the mast-cross stood. Lazarus followed along, alighting atop one of the taller trees.

"Here's the spot! No other would do the altar justice. A beautiful altar."

The palm trees towering above him rustled in a sudden gust of wind. Brock's head snapped upward at the sound, and he warily eyed the fluttering palm leaves, reading in their movement another message.

"Hmm. So You don't like that idea. The location's okay, so it must be the altar idea. Yeah. Something better than an altar."

He paced around the mast-cross thinking.

"Something better...no, bigger."

He continued pacing.

"Something bigger...a shrine...a small temple...maybe a chapel." He stopped and gazed up the length of the tall mast-cross. "That's it! A chapel! Right here...around the mast on which Your lightning cured me." His mind opened to a new vision of a wonderful chapel with stained-glass windows, a carved stone altar, the mast-cross standing majestically behind it.

He looked toward the schooner resting peacefully offshore and laughed, falling to his knees. He opened his arms wide and raised his eyes. "You've sent me this wreckage to use as building material for a chapel. That's what You want me to build...a gorgeous chapel to celebrate the miracles You've performed here and to express my gratitude. A chapel! Oh, You will be pleased, Lord. Very pleased, I promise!" He threw a worried look up the trees to their palms. They were motionless. He checked the water surrounding the island. It was still. He grinned and laughed. "Okay, then. You're pleased."

It was midmorning with many hours of daylight left. He would begin at once. He first considered using the palm trees on the island for wood. He walked among them comparing their different sizes and potential. But he was disinclined to use it because he knew from experience that palm wood is tough barklike material difficult to tool.

He discovered, however, that there were twelve palm trees on the island. Five were in a scraggly line at the southern end, six larger and more stately trees were grouped Stonehenge-like around the mast-cross at the top of the hillock, and near the northern tip of the islet stood the twelfth, a frail scrawny tree that seemed to cling rather than be rooted to the ground. Its palms were weathered and brown, probably from lack of fresh water, its roots being so near the salt water.

390

Twelve? Pondering the unlikely coincidence of finding twelve trees on a holy island, he pursed his lips and sighed. "Nothing on this weird island is coincidental." He stood in the clearing around the mast-cross and gazed up at the tall trees above him. "Twelve, huh? You must represent the Twelve Apostles. I mean, why not? It fits. Don't you agree, Lazarus?"

The bird clung stoically to its roost atop the closest tree.

Brock smiled at his winged companion. "The lightning, the fish, the water, the whole thing. It all has a certain biblical flavor, don't you think, Lazarus? So why not twelve living monuments to the Apostles?" He looked out over the ocean. "Okay, God, I won't chop them down. I guess if You'd wanted me to use them in the chapel, You wouldn't have sent me the schooner with its tall masts."

Brock wagged his head in wonderment at everything that had happened. "What next? The Second Coming? Now that would be a spectacle! But like everything else here, who would believe it? I'd be the sole witness, and if I told people what's been going on here, they'd certify me a lunatic. Oh, if only you Apostles could talk."

Thinking about that, he surveyed them again and wondered who was who. "Which of you is Simon Peter, the Rock? Ah, that would be you there, the tallest." He stepped forward and laid his hands on the rough saw-toothed bark of the giant tree. "Peter! Ah, yes, I'd recognize you anywhere. Robust and assertive. Let's see, who else?"

Like all well-versed teenage catechists, he had memorized the names of the Apostles, but again like most catechists he could recall their names only by reciting the entire list, which he did aloud. "Peter, Andrew, James, John, Philip, Bartholomew, Matthew, Thomas, James, Jude, Simon, and Judas. As you obviously don't know, Lazarus, being as you are an uneducated illiterate wandering pagan fowl, these were Christ's chosen Apostles. And the twelfth was that ignominious traitor, Judas Iscariot."

"Aha!" cried Brock, energized by the fun of his game. He pointed an accusing finger at arm's length toward the small sickly tree at the northern tip. "There you are, you mongrel! Pity your soul! All alone. Frail and wasted. It is you, Judas! A contemptible outcast, your thin spidery roots clinging to the coral like a woeful creature on the verge of extinction. Yes, Lazarus, we will shun Judas as the other trees have, so don't go sitting on his palms. And mind you! No pooping on him. He's suffered enough."

Brock laughed and mischievously scanned the other trees. "Which of you then is Andrew, Peter's brother? They were Christ's first disciples, Lazarus. They would be standing side by side, I suppose. That would make—" he eyed the tree nearest Peter—"you there. You must be Andrew."

He continued his game, assigning each tree an Apostle's name. Thereafter he conversed with them as he went about his daily routine, addressing each by name and thus enlarging the "family" of his island companions. It was fun and fed his newfound appetite for humor.

"So, Laz, it looks like all the wood for the chapel will have to come from the two boats. No problem, eh?"

The first priority was finding construction equipment and materials. Ropes and pulleys abounded on the schooner with a few more on the *Gigolo*. Together with the masts and spars they would provide levering devices, lifts, and a derrick...machines Brock would need to erect the chapel.

He boarded the schooner and tugged at a heavy wooden hatch cover six feet on a side that he presumed led to the cargo hold. He removed the cover and found that he was right, but the cargo, consisting of dry goods, radios, TVs, and stereo equipment, had been ruined by the seawater. Little was salvageable. He converted the hatch cover into a makeshift raft fitted with outriggers to which for added buoyancy he strapped six empty five-gallon drums he found in the hold. He tied the raft alongside and loaded it with ruined goods. Then he loosed the raft from the schooner and paddled two hundred yards from the island and dumped the goods overboard into the ocean. It took several days repeating this maneuver over and over to dispose of the unwanted cargo. The ocean was a perfect disposal machine consuming every load without a trace. It was a marvelous convenience that kept the island clean. There would be no room on the island for junk, once he began constructing the chapel. More than that, he felt a moral obligation to preserve the island's original unblemished state. He would not defile its sacredness and beauty by littering it with trash.

Among the schooner's cargo he discovered several bolts of heavy cloth, all but one of which were hopelessly ruined. The bolt untouched on the top of the pile was of a heavy brown, double-mesh, wool-like material. He washed and rinsed it thoroughly with water from the tank, then hung it on a rope strung between Simon and Thaddeus, the two southernmost trees, to dry in the sun. He thought he could make some type of robe out of the cloth.

As he was unloading the hold, he found a cache of tools of all kinds—hammers, saws, planes, files, calipers, mallets, chisels, honing stones, augers and bits, and an assortment of knives. These items tokened not only the presence of a skilled shipwright among the schooner's crew but the likelihood that Brock would find construction materials and hardware aboard as well. He donned the snorkeling mask and explored the water-filled compartments, finding sure enough a large storage cabinet filled with boxes and cans of assorted nails, screws, and other hardware. Behind the cabinet was a long narrow storeroom in which bundles of lumber of various sizes and types were stacked. God had indeed provided well for the chapel.

Brock removed all of the tools and carried them ashore where he methodically cleaned, dried, and oiled each one. Then he extricated the building materials and laid them out on the sand to dry, binding them tightly together to prevent warping and arranging them in neat logically organized piles for cleaning and more importantly inventorying, for the kinds and quantity of material available would determine the design of the chapel he could build.

It did not take long for Brock to conclude that the stock of lumber aboard the schooner was inadequate for any sizable structure. For a reasonably sized chapel he would need large timbers for supports and braces, and the only such timbers available were in the hulls of the schooner and *Gigolo*. He had no alternative. He would have to completely disassemble the two vessels, and he lost no time getting started.

Each day he followed the same routine with no concern for calendar dates. The passage of time had lost its meaning. There was no clock here to press his schedule, no calendar to keep, no deadlines to meet. He didn't know the date or even which day of the week it was. It mattered not. Spared from death, his new life was cut off from the grinding toils elsewhere on the globe. His world had shrunk to this islet on which he was dedicated to a single purpose: the building of a chapel as beautiful as he could make it in the sight of God, Who furnished him water to drink and fish to eat, and all-encompassing love, which brought him inexpressible peace and contentment. Brock had no other human needs.

Although he was the happiest and most contented he had ever been, the sins of his past shadowed his every movement and thought. Three times each day he prayed—at daybreak, midday, and before sleep at night—devoutly petitioning God to right the terrible wrongs he had committed against his family and friends. He never mentioned their names aloud to himself, to Lazarus, or the Apostles. They were no longer part of his family, and they had no role here. They were of a different lifetime, a different life.

Brock had no way of knowing how they were faring, though he feared the worst. He pleaded with God to show them the same mercy He had shown Brock, but Brock knew that God's purpose was unfathomable and that the evil Brock had sown could well endure forever, rolling on endlessly like a giant wave in the ocean, destroying lives and breaking hearts.

The more he thought about it the surer he was that the misery he had inflicted on others would endure. Were he somehow to return to them now after all he had been through, he would doubtless make amends and redeem himself in their eyes. But that was not to be. That silent voice within his mind which is called Understanding had made known to him that the miracles which had taken place on this small bit of land were endemic and personal. He had not been healed, he believed, so that through him God could help others. The miracles had been for him alone. It was his egregious sins, not those of others, that God had forgiven. For that reason the memory of the miseries Brock had caused his family lay heavily upon his heart and drove him each day in his prayers and in his work to give God reason to grant mercy and relief to the afflicted ones. He prayed each night until he wept, beseeching God to intercede in the lives of Eleanor and Paul and the others as a final act of forgiveness.

When Brock's thoughts gave way to despondency, he reminded himself of the water and the fish and the power of faith to which they gave testimony each day, and his spirits revived...and his work on the chapel proceeded.

394

TWENTY-ONE

In the gloomy aftermath of his father's disappearance Paul sank into isolation and depression, reeling from the corrosive rapid-fire blows of his scandalous performance at The Voyeur, his expulsion from Montclair, the inexplicable deportation of his beloved Irina and, most devastating of all, the death of his sister, Valerie, and her unborn child. He remained at home close to his mother, supporting and consoling her. She was emotionally drained by Valerie's death and now D-M's problems, all brought on by his father.

Paul felt no loss, nor did his mother, from his father's disappearance...only hatred and a needling hunger for revenge. His mother forced him to talk with her about his feelings and loss, and she told him of hers, knowing that doing so was good therapy for them both. Their mutual hatred of Brock seemed to intensify by exposing it to each other. They cursed him and reveled in exchanging stories about his outrageous lifestyle. It was good for them, releasing their pent-up venom, purifying their emotions, and allowing them both to redirect their minds and energies to the problems of living and planning for the future as they must.

To help rid themselves of Brock's memory they methodically purged the house of anything that reminded them of him—his favorite chair, his desk, photos, books, clothes, golf clubs—every vestige of the man was removed. Brock became nothing more than a bad dream, a nightmare, whose memory faded a little more each day. He was not easily forgotten, however. Brock's deeds lived on, complicating and tormenting their lives and sustaining their hatred of him.

But two events occurred two months after he disappeared that took their minds off Brock and gave them sorely needed happiness and hope.

It was after 9 PM when Kúbokoff heard the front doorbell and got up from his rolltop desk where he was balancing his monthly accounts. He despised bookkeeping and welcomed the interruption. The mother of a student had said she would come by late to discuss her daughter's future as a dancer. Kúbokoff mentally rehearsed the lecture he would give her, about talent being as elusive to predict as tornadoes, that a child might be clumsy one year and blossom overnight into a gifted star—or maybe never blossom—and that only through hard work and persistence could it happen at all, but there were no guarantees. It was the same lecture he had delivered a hundred times before, but he never tired of it. For him it was a labor of love, a paean to the exalted art of ballet. He opened the door prepared to greet the mother, his mouth beginning to form the first syllable of her name. Instead his jaw dropped.

"Paul!" he exclaimed. "I feel so good to see you. Come in, come in." The aging ballet master had forgotten his conversation that day with his protégé.

The once aspiring dancer gave a halfhearted smile and stepped into the small poorly lit foyer. His face had the forlorn nostalgic look of a traveler returning after many years to a place of cherished but painful memories.

"I'm glad you came," said Kúbokoff. "Come into t'e parlor and sit. Ve vill talk."

"If it's about dancing," said Paul combatively, "I told you on the phone I'm through with that. It's over."

"Yes, yes. Sit down. Here. Good."

Paul seated himself on a heavily upholstered sofa as his former teacher drew up a wooden three-legged stool in front of him and enveloped it with his ample posterior.

"Anyway, my leg hasn't healed yet, so I couldn't dance if I wanted to."

"Yes, yes. I know all of t'at. You told me."

"So? You asked me to come, and I'm here."

Kúbokoff studied the young face before him and saw in the dark

396

passionate eyes the residue of pain and sorrow left by the recent tragedies in Paul's life. "I vanted to look in your eyes and see for myself."

"See what?"

"T'e trut'. To see if your eyes say v'at your mout' says. Eyes are t'e window to t'e soul, you know."

"And what do my eyes tell you?"

Kúbokoff smiled and his eyes misted. "T'at you are dancer...deep in your heart...and t'at no ot'er life vill satisfy you."

Paul turned anxiously away and shook his head. "Not true."

"Yes true! I can see it. You vere born a dancer. You love ballet. You can deny it all you vant, but t'ere it is."

"I'm too old and too much has happened. I keep telling you, I'm through with ballet."

"T'en v'y are you here? V'y did you come?"

"Because..." Paul's thoughts collided with his words. Why had he complied so willingly with Kúbokoff's invitation to talk when the subject was predictable: Paul's returning to ballet. Was there any point in discussing it? Was there any hope?

"What chance is there of my ever succeeding?"

"No chance at all if you don't try, but t'ere is alvays t'e chance if you dedicate yourself and vork." Kúbokoff's standard lecture began, though his sincerity was never greater. "Life never promises us anyt'ing. Ve vork and get v'at life gives us. Life. She is...*neohotnaya.*" He swiveled on the stool and shouted to his wife in the kitchen. "*Shto znachet neohotnee po angleeskee?*"

"Grudging," came the reply.

"*Da, zhizn...*life is grudging and...how you say...ah yes, stingy. You slave for years in hope of greatness and maybe you get only crumbs from t'e czar's table, and maybe you get jeweled crown. But if you don't try, you get nothing but emptiness. Is t'at not true?"

Paul's eyes found Kúbokoff's. "All right, Alexéi Nikoláyevich. Okay. It's true. I'm here because...because I'm a dancer. That's what I am. I am also out of money, out of school, and I have a game leg that isn't healing. So what can I do?"

"For one, you can stop feeling sorry for yourself."

"That's not easy." Paul thought of his favorite metaphor: *I've got a dozen strikes against me. It only takes three to put you out.*

"Maybe I've got somet'ing t'at vill change your mind," said Kúbokoff with a smirk, his eyes twinkling.

"What are you talking about?"

Kúbokoff's face beamed. "I have news! Vonderful news!"

"What kind of news?"

"Money news. A patron of t'e arts, a donator, saw you dance at our show last fall and heard of your difficulties. She called me and asked about you. She said she vas going to arrange a grant in aid for you t'rough me. A lump sum."

"Who is she?"

"Her name is Louise. To be exact, Eloisa Mikhaylova Vigroff."

"She's Russian?"

"By family name only. She speaks no Russian unfortunately. I tried, but she knows nothing. She said all four of her grandparents were Russian, but her own parents never spoke t'e language enough for her to learn. Actually, her name should be Vigrova. In Russia it would be."

"Have you met her?"

"No. She is handling t'e whole t'ing t'rough her bank. She vants to remain in t'e background."

"It's incredible."

"Not in t'is business. Happens all t'e time. Rich people see a talented young performer and t'ey vant to help, but anomon...amon. You know, without being known."

"How does the grant work?" Paul's enthusiasm was mounting.

"It is simple. I sign agreement to use money for only your ballet training, and she me sends check." His English was deteriorating in his excitement.

"When does it happen?"

"It already did. I got agreement in mail two veeks ago, signed and sent it back. And today I got check in mail."

"How much is it?"

"Fifty t'ousand dollars."

Paul shot to his feet, his mouth agape, his face aghast. "Fifty thousand!" he shouted.

"It means you can vork full-time on your dancing. Full-time, Paul.

Right avay. Tomorrow."

Paul paced around the cramped room limping noticeably. "Tomorrow? I don't know if I'm ready."

"I know. You are ready. I teach you. Ve vill vork toget'er. No more Montclair. I teach you myself, and I bring in best coaches. I charge you regular fee, yes, for private lessons. I know good muscle t'erapist who vill treat your leg. You vork as you did two summers ago. Vit' devotion and concentration. Strict regimen. Food, sleep, exercise, drills, practice. I make schedule and you follow. Okay?"

Kúbokoff rose and held out his arms. Paul hung back, still reserving judgment, unconsciously reluctant to let go of his self-pity and resignation but thrilled at the thought of returning to ballet. Kúbokoff gestured again, smiling, entreating Paul to come to him. "Ve can do it, you and I."

Paul's resistance collapsed. "Okay, Alexéi Nikoláyevich." And he fell into Kúbokoff's bear hug.

Paul resumed his ballet training with maniacal dedication, working first with the therapist to heal his leg and then with Kúbokoff and other seasoned coaches to regain the dancing skills and form which had begun to atrophy. It was not too late, though Kúbokoff had privately feared it might have been. Paul was young and resilient, and his natural talent was so immense that, as before, it was more a process of rediscovery than of learning. Watching him dance, working him hour after hour, witnessing the blossoming of an artist who could well become one of the great dancers in America was an experience few people ever have an opportunity to enjoy. Knowing this made the enjoyment all the more pleasurable for the former Russian star.

In six months Paul reached a new significantly more advanced stage in his development, and Kúbokoff decided to showcase Paul's "return to ballet" in the Christmas exhibition that Kúbokoff's school presented each year. As usual, ballet critics and representatives from some of the top ballet companies in the country, drawn by Kúbokoff's renown as a teacher and by his personal invitation, would be there to look for new talent. His letting the word out that Paul would make a "comeback" appearance did not hurt ticket sales.

As Kúbokoff expected, news of Paul's debut reached the press, and items reporting the event appeared in all of the San Francisco newspapers with lurid recountings of the riot at The Voyeur eleven months earlier and Paul's subsequent dismissal from Montclair. Both teacher and student had expected the notoriety and were prepared to endure it. It was a necessary rite of passage to Paul's acceptance in the world of ballet. If the talent were there, however, the critics and patrons of the arts would forgive almost anything, even stripteasing. And in Paul's case his talent radiated like the sun.

Because Kúbokoff wanted to let the audience's anticipation build, Paul's solo was placed before the grand finale in the third act. It was good showbiz. The show fortunately was going well, and the audience was in a happy forgiving mood. Paul sensed this as he warmed up in the wings, and the tension he had felt all day gave way to elation. Adding to his excitement was the presence in the audience of his mother, Kelly, and Helena, but especially his mother. Without her unflagging support and encouragement from the very beginning, when he first became interested in ballet, he would not be on this stage. He owed her everything, and dancing for her, displaying the talent which her faith had liberated, would be sheer joy. But he also would not be performing were it not for his anonymous benefactress, and he hoped that she, too, was in the audience.

As he took up his position at center stage and the houselights dimmed, his thoughts resounded with Kúbokoff's final instruction. "Don't t'ink so much. Be yourself. Trust your feelings. Listen to your body. It knows what to do. Let it. Let it dance."

The introductory music began and the curtain opened, quieting the audience that buzzed at the sight of him and then became silent, watching for the first movement of his sinewy body.

He raised his arms and one leg and powered into a temps leve. His routine, specially choreographed by Kúbokoff to show off the broad range and artistry of Paul's remarkable skills, was underway. His pirouettes and leaps brought forth wild cheers and almost continuous applause, ratifying Kúbokoff's conviction that the young man displaying phenomenal talent on the stage was a star in the making. And then a strange thing happened.

As Paul entered the final series of movements in his performance, spinning round and round, focusing in each revolution on a single spot in the audience, he saw Irina's face. It caught his attention but did not surprise him because, since she had returned to Greece, he had seen her face in crowds everywhere. In theaters, stores, restaurants, on the street, even in his dreams. But it was always an illusion. It never was his beloved Irina, just look-alikes. How could it be otherwise? She was thousands of miles away in Greece. So he knew the face was not Irina's, and he kept on dancing.

But it was Irina!

His concentration mentally derailed, he stopped abruptly and froze in 5th position as the taped music continued on without him, through the climax, and ended. Utter silence filled the auditorium as Paul stepped cautiously to the footlights and peered out into the darkness toward the face. The perplexed audience, in muffled turmoil, began to murmur and strain their necks and point in the direction of his line of sight. Some patrons stood to get a better view. Kúbokoff walked anxiously onto the stage from behind a curtain in the wings to see what had caused Paul to cut short his performance.

Irina, alarmed that Paul had discovered her, sank down in her seat, but then he saw her clearly and cried out.

"Irina! It's you!"

Eleanor gaped uncertainly at her son, wondering why he was calling Irina's name. Kelly and Helena looked at each other in confusion.

Irina, frightened and embarrassed, rose to her feet and began pushing her way toward the center aisle through the people seated in her row. Some stood clumsily to let her by, but they only blocked her escape.

All eyes were now on the two of them, first Irina then Paul who, abandoning the stage, had leaped gracefully into the center aisle and was racing toward her. When she reached the aisle, she saw him coming and, realizing she could not escape, gave up and turned to face him. He stopped ten feet away.

Oblivious to the presence of the spellbound audience watching the unfolding drama, Paul spoke to her in a soft plaintive voice heard distinctly throughout the theater. "I've missed you."

Confused and discomposed, Irina looked at him with anguish, then glanced furtively at the beaming faces around her. "Paul..." She shook her head as if doing so would prevent his speaking.

"Why didn't you call me?" he asked.

"I didn't think you..." She looked anxiously at the audience again.

"Cared? Irina, I love you. I want you to marry me. I always have."

"I can't talk here," she whispered. "Not here!" Her hands gestured in frustration at the enthralled audience.

"I don't care who hears me," he said, gleefully raising his voice. "I'll shout it from the highest mountain. I love you!"

Scattered applause and yelps from younger members of the audience emboldened him. "Yes," he cried, pointing a finger at her. "And you wouldn't be here tonight if you didn't love me, too."

"But..." Unable to speak, she began to weep.

"You do love me. I know it."

"Oh, Paul!"

Even as she continued to shake her head in denial, she took a small step toward him, her heart propelling while her mind resisted.

"We belong together," he said, moving toward her and holding out his arms.

Her shoulders sagged in resignation, and she threw herself into his embrace. The enraptured audience rose as one and exploded into cheers and applause. Then Paul pushed Irina gently away and, holding her shoulders at arm's length, shouted excitedly above the din. "Do you still dance?"

"Every day," she replied, her tearful face aglow.

Paul turned to the stage to find Kúbokoff, who was standing at the footlights applauding with the others. "May we?" he called, wiggling the first two fingers of each hand to depict two dancers.

Kúbokoff nodded affectionately. He, too, was swept away by the heart-moving display of the two young people's love. Anyway, it would be good theater, which appealed to his showman's mind.

Paul took Irina's hand and amid continued clapping and whistling led her down the aisle and onto the stage.

"Paul, I can't dance now. I'm not dressed, and we haven't practiced."

He looked at her loose white blouse and stockings and flowing pleated Blackwatch skirt. "That'll do. Kick off your shoes. This isn't

Carnegie Hall. It's Kúbokoff's show! That's a friendly audience out there."
He held up. "You do remember our pas de deux in the studio, don't you?"

"I've danced it every day since we parted!"

"Then come on!" He looked to Kúbokoff. "Alexéi Nikoláyevich, can we find shoes for her?"

A teenage girl called out, "She can use mine."

As Eleanor, Helena, and Kelly and the rest of the audience applauded excitedly, the girl quickly untied her shoes and handed them to Paul, who had run up the aisle to her.

Shrugging in disbelief at what she was about to do, Irina hastily donned the ballet shoes and began stretching her legs and torso, while the audience babbled loudly in anticipation.

Offstage, Paul rummaged through his carry-all for the CD for the pas de deux he had danced with Melissa Manford. He had saved it, carrying it with him as a remembrance of Irina. He found it and ran across the stage to a smattering of encouraging calls from the audience. "Put this on," he told the wide-eyed woman in charge of the music.

Walking confidently to the center of the stage, Paul held out his hands inviting Irina to join him. She got up from the floor and went to him, as a hush blanketed the jabbering patrons, every eye fixed on the pair. The music operator waited till the dancers were set, Paul holding Irina in 5th position on pointe ready to perform the opening fouette rond de jambe en tournant. Then the music began.

Just as they had danced that day in Kúbokoff's studio, the two lovers wheeled and circled the stage, matched figures mirroring each other's movements. Paul lifted his beloved in short jumps which, though inartistic and unathletic, pleased the audience no less for the sheer romance of it. Again she flew in and out of his arms, tempting and taunting him with her love. Then the five-minute routine crescendoed to a finale, and the two came to rest side by side breathing heavily, again in 5th position, his arm about her waist, facing the audience, which rose, shouting and clapping. Eleanor, standing with the rest, wept for joy to see the two young people together again at last. The ovations continued as the pair stepped to the footlights and made a decorous bow, while Kúbokoff himself applauded enthusiastically from the wings.

Looking down at Irina beside him, Paul spoke loudly to make himself heard above the applause. "Don't ever leave me again!"

She smiled. "I promise." She stretched up and kissed his lips, and the crowd roared its approval. Paul waved to them and strode happily offstage, pulling Irina with him. They ran to his dressing room and fell into each other's arms, not unclinching till minutes later when Eleanor, Kelly, and Helena joined them.

Later that evening in the living room of the Stowolskis' stately home, Irina related the strange story of her return to the United States some six months earlier. She had given up all hope of ever seeing Paul again, convinced by the ill-fated events that led to her deportation that he did not truly love her and that she was destined to live out her life in Greece without seeing or hearing from him again.

She had moved in with a cousin in Athens and taken a job in a dress shop where her meager salary barely sustained her. Inconsolably depressed, having surrendered herself to her desolate fate, she was taken aback one day by a phone call from a Greek lawyer whom she did not know who asked her to come to his office to discuss her situation. She was alarmed at first, thinking that by her deportation she had somehow violated Greek laws. Only when the lawyer insisted that she was in no danger, indeed quite the contrary, did she finally consent to meet him.

He was very cordial and businesslike. After seating her on the balcony of his fashionable office with a splendid view of the Acropolis and bringing her a glass of lemonade and a dish of cookies, he sat down in a chair beside her and explained the purpose of his call.

"I have very good news for you," he said. "The U.S. Embassy has informed me that your deportation case has been readjudicated." He withdrew a document from an envelope, flourished it in the air, then held it before him and read from it. "It is the decision of the Review Board that the original judgment revoking your visa was unduly harsh and that you be granted a new visa with a conditional work permit, the conditions being that you secure sponsorship by a U.S. citizen in good standing and that you acquire self-sustaining employment. Both the sponsorship and the employment must be confirmed and notarized in writing to the U.S. Embassy before the visa and work permit will be issued."

A multitude of questions erupted in Irina's mind amid this flood of new and exciting information. "What made them review my case?"

"I don't really know, but I would guess that someone of influence caused the case to be reopened."

"Who could that be? I don't know anyone of influence."

The lawyer stood and stepped to the railing of the balcony to admire the view. "It may have been the U.S. ambassador here in Athens."

"I don't know him, and I'm certain he doesn't know me."

"Not personally perhaps," he said, turning her way. "But he definitely knows of your case."

"How do you know that?"

"He told me himself."

"The ambassador? About me? But I'm nobody!"

He smiled knowingly. "Not to your benefactor. He's the one who advised the ambassador about your circumstances."

Irina's quizzical expression relayed her confusion. "I don't understand. What benefactor? I don't have one."

"Benefactors don't always announce themselves, my dear." He sat down again as if his closeness to her would help convince her.

She grew suspicious. "Is this person expecting some act of gratitude from me in return? Some favor?" Her eyebrows lifted.

The lawyer made a smacking sound with his tongue and tipped his head back, the Greek way of saying no. "No favors at all. It's all quite proper and aboveboard."

"Who is he? Have I met him?"

"Possibly. He claims to know a great deal about you. His name is Seigolo Paeresnis, a wealthy and obviously influential man."

"What interest could he possibly have in me?" Irina's discomfort increased. How did this man know such much about her. Had he been probing into her private life?

"He didn't tell me, and it would have been impolite of me to ask."

"What's he like?"

"I can't say. I've never met him."

"Never in person?" She was now deeply concerned and a little afraid.

Sensing her anxiety, the lawyer reached out and laid his hand gently on hers. "No. He transacted all of his business concerning you by telephone."

"What sort of business?" she said, drawing her hand away and sitting back in her chair.

"Please, Irina, there is nothing to fear. I promise you all is well. Indeed I haven't gotten to the best part yet, have I?"

"What is it?" asked Irina.

"An outright gift of five thousand dollars to finance your trip back to the United States and to help you get settled there. I have a check for you right here."

"I can't accept that!" Her suspicions aroused, she pushed her chair back, got up, and pressed her back against the railing from where she stared at the lawyer.

"Why not? He expects nothing from you in return. But there's more. He also arranged for your employment as a clerk in an export-import company in San Francisco owned by a longtime friend of the ambassador. I have here a letter of introduction for you and a letter of agreement from the company. It's all set. The job doesn't pay much to begin with, but there are opportunities for advancement. Anyway, it's a start until you can find something better. Are you planning to become an American citizen?"

Her fear turned into hope. "I had no plans at all before you told me all of this. It's overwhelming."

She slowly returned to her seat, her mind in a whirl. Her first thought was of Paul. The bitter disappointment she had felt at his failure to confide in her and share with her his setbacks had gradually faded, crowded out by her abounding love for him. Because of her own stubbornness and childish pique she had foolishly rejected his overtures. Was it too late now to resurrect their relationship? Of course it was. Paul might sulk a bit and lose his way for a time, but he was iron-willed and self-disciplined and would by now have come to terms with their breakup. Perhaps he had found someone else. The thought made her despondent. He would write off Irina and the past, like bad investments, accept his losses, and look confidently to the future of which she would not be a part. She must learn to live with the fact that Paul had by now erased her from his life, and she should get about planning her own.

"Yes, sir," she said with a sudden new confidence. "I do intend to become an American citizen. And I don't care who this benefactor is. I'm going to take his money and go back to the United States."

"I think that's a splendid decision," he said.

Irina and the lawyer worked out the details, and three weeks later she resumed her life in San Francisco, staying again with her aunt, who became her sponsor. She worked at her clerk's job by day and attended ballet classes—not with Kúbokoff—three nights a week both for the physical exercise and for love of the art. She held no illusions about her talent; she would always be an amateur. But most of all the classes kept alive her dearest memories of her wonderful summer with Paul. Memories were all that remained. That and the sadness at what never would be.

Irina could not bring herself to believe there was any chance Paul might still love her. Why should he after her cold rejection of his appeal to her on her doorstep nine months ago? Nevertheless, her heart yearned for him, so when she saw the flyer on the bulletin board in her dance class advertising Kúbokoff's show, the chance to see Paul, to see if he had changed, was irresistible. She slipped into the auditorium as unobtrusively as she could. Having no intention of confronting Paul or even making her presence known, she was completely unprepared for what happened.

Paul sat cozily beside her on the couch as she related her story, and when she finished he took her hand and gently kissed it.

"It's like a fairy tale," he said. "I thought I'd lost you forever. Then suddenly you appear out of nowhere. How I ever spotted you in that dark theater I'll never know."

"I guess it was meant to be," she said demurely. "But I wouldn't have been there if it hadn't been for Mr. Paeresnis. It's strange. I owe him everything, but he's remained anonymous. The lawyer told me that wealthy patrons like Paeresnis prefer to remain in the background because they're not doing it to gain publicity for themselves."

"I know. My sponsor's the same way."

"Your sponsor?" she said, shaking her head in confusion.

Paul explained the grant from the Russian woman who had contacted Kúbokoff.

Irina hugged him and cried, "Oh, Paul, I'm so happy for you. It's like a dream come true being here with you and your family." Irina could tell by the uneasy looks exchanged among Paul and the others that something was wrong. She blushed and frowned. "Did I say something I shouldn't have?"

Eleanor allayed her fears, relating the tragic events which had upset their lives—Valerie's death and Brock's disappearance.

"Oh, I'm so sorry. I didn't know."

"It's all right," said Eleanor kindly. "We've adjusted. We're still a family of which you are now a member, and we're pleased that you are."

"Thank you, Mrs. Stowolski. I don't know what to say. Such a terrible thing. Have you heard anything of Mr. Stowolski?"

"Not a word," replied Eleanor. "He isn't the most popular person around here. He left us high and dry."

Eleanor sent Paul a commiserating look as she addressed Irina. "Some things Paul's father did and failed to do have made it very difficult for us. We're all very bitter over it. You see, until we can establish—get legal proof—that my husband is dead, all of his estate remains in a kind of legal limbo. Meanwhile, his company is losing business and having to sell its assets to meet the payroll and pay off creditors. He won't be presumed dead for five more years. By then we'll almost surely be bankrupt, so you see it isn't a pretty situation."

Irina was glum. "I wish I could help. Maybe my benefactor could do something. He's very rich."

"That's kind of you to think so," said Eleanor. "I wish he could, but it's beyond that now. We've considered every alternative. The fact is we're stymied by the laws."

"Our predicament is filled with ironies," said Paul. "Dad did everything he could to prevent me from pursuing a career in ballet, and he probably had a hand in your deportation. And look what's happened. Two people, my Russian lady and your wealthy Greek, two people worlds apart, appear like angels of mercy and overturn everything my father tried to do. If he hadn't sailed off into the ocean, if he were here now, he'd have gone on fighting us, I know it. He'd have used every trick he could think of to prevent me from resuming my ballet studies and to block the State Department from allowing you to reenter the country."

"How could anyone be so mean?" Irina asked.

"Evil men like him have a gift for using their money and influence to spoil others' lives. In the end they always seem to get their way."

Irina smiled. "Not this time!"

TWENTY-TWO

A profound calm took charge of Brock's emotions and drive. He had no urge whatever to leave the island so at peace was he with himself and with his loving God. He had been given a second life, a life he would devote to a merciful Creator who had spared him a cruel death.

The days and weeks passed for Brock in blissful labor from sunrise to sunset according to a set routine. He slept in a bunk salvaged from the *Gigolo* and placed between Peter and John on the ridge outside the perimeter of the chapel site. He awakened with the first rays of sunlight—it never rained—and knelt beside his bed to pray thankfully for the miracle of another day beginning. He then walked down to the eastern beach amid rows of neatly aligned piles of planks and beams and various structural members—all that remained of the two vessels now fully disassembled—and went out on a flimsily constructed fifty-foot pier he had thrown together out of scrap lumber. At its end was a bench in which he had installed an open toilet seat over the water. He relieved himself and trod back across the island to the lagoon, where an enormous school of fish, on cue, leaped about on the surface as his feet touched the water. He waded in, nonchalantly grabbed two in each hand, and made the sign of the cross. "Thank You, Lord," he said, bowing slightly toward the future site of the chapel on the ridge.

He took the fish to a coral ledge on the rim of the lagoon where he had chiseled out a small pit for a fire. The ledge served as his kitchen and dining area. The few culinary utensils he needed were kept there on a table taken from the schooner. He gutted, cleaned, and deboned the fish, sliced them lengthwise into filets, and laid them in a frying pan. Because the gas stove had run out of fuel, he used a small magnifying glass—

previously used for reading maps on the *Gigolo*—to concentrate the sun's rays on a clump of dry seaweed, setting it afire in the pit. Then he placed the pan on a metal grill over the flames. He had found a single book of matches on the *Gigolo*, but he was holding them in reserve, should he need to start a fire at night or on a cloudy day, though he was beginning to believe that the sky over Miracle Island was never cloudy.

While the fish cooked, he filled a glass with water from a plastic bottle that he replenished every few days from the *Gigolo*'s water tank, which he had installed atop two timbers fastened seven feet above ground between Matthew and James-son-of-John on the edge of the chapel site. In its new location the tank served both as a source of drinking water and a shower for bathing.

After eating his fish and feeding Lazarus, he cleaned his utensils in the ocean brine, rinsed them under the water tank, and placed them on the table to dry in the warm sunlight. He then mounted the ridge and, doffing the brown robe he had fashioned from the bolt of cloth salvaged from the schooner, hung it above his bed on a peg inserted in John for that purpose, and resumed work on the chapel.

He labored all day, stopping only once at midday for half an hour to rest and to pray for Eleanor and Paul, that his cruel treatment had not ruined their lives. He ate nothing and drank water sparingly depending on how much he sweat. Off and on during the long workday he held one-sided witty conversations with Lazarus or broke into song with a melodious baritone voice singing Gregorian chants he had learned at St. Charles and whose Latin lyrics, by the grace of God, he unerringly recalled word for word.

At dusk he bathed in the ocean, showered beneath the water tank to wash off the salt, donned the brown robe, and prepared and ate his supper, which like breakfast consisted of fried fish, which he unfailingly shared with Lazarus. After supper he watched the ever-beautiful ever-changing sunset and went to bed. Each night before he lay down on his bunk, he knelt and prayed. "Heavenly Father, I am most thankful for this day which has passed in which I dedicated myself to Your chapel, my gift to You for Your mercy. I shall now retire to my bed and, as I have since You delivered me to this holy ground, place myself in Your loving hands. And if it be Your wish that tomorrow I shall awaken to continue my

411

work, I will do so with a joyous heart. But, if You should summon my soul during the night, that, too, will bring me joy. I seek only to do Your will. Amen."

One morning as he prepared to eat his breakfast he noticed Lazarus was not joining him. He called to him.

"Hey, Laz! Wake up you lout! Time for breakfast!"

He took a few bites of fish and, chewing the delicious delicate food, cast his eyes up and down the beach looking for his pigeon companion. He was nowhere to be seen. When Brock finished eating and had cleaned his cookware, he searched the island for the bird, scanning the tops of the trees, particularly Matthew, the pigeon's favorite roost. He was nowhere in sight. Perhaps he had taken ill and was nestled among the palms asleep...or worse.

Brock stood at the base of Matthew's tall curved trunk and yelled, "Lazarus! Come forth!"

His spontaneous mimicry of Jesus' summons to the real Lazarus to emerge from his tomb struck Brock as hilarious, and he exploded with laughter, falling backward onto the sand roaring in delight. Recovering somewhat, he wiped his eyes and said, "Forgive me, Lord. I wasn't making fun of Your Son's miracle, but You must admit it was funny. I'm sure You enjoy a good laugh. After all, You invented it."

He stood up and brushed the sand from his robe. So where was that indolent fowl? Where had he gone? Flown away to wherever he was headed before the storm diverted him to this island? Brock hoped not. He had grown very attached to the little fellow.

He made another round of the island searching under bushes and among the flowering plants. Then, looking to the beach on the southeastern side, he spied something white on the beach. His heart gave a twinge. Let it not be a dead pigeon floating on the surface, he prayed. He ran to the spot and found to his relief that the white object was not Lazarus at all but an oddly shaped bluish-white stone, about a foot long and three or four inches wide. Its smooth irregular surface had been burnished to a high sheen by the constant grinding of sand and water.

There was something familiar in its contours, something he had seen before. He turned the stone over in his hands and inspected it from different angles. All at once recognition dawned. The serene downcast

412

face, the head cloth draped over the shoulders. It was a natural impressionist sculpture of the Blessed Virgin, or so it appeared to Brock. He vowed to find a special place for it on the island. And so he did, on the northern tip of the lagoon where he discovered a small niche in the coral. He enlarged and shaped the niche into an attractive alcove in which he set the stone upright. He sprinkled it with holy water from the *Gigolo's* tank and thereafter treated it as a shrine to Mary, the Mother of Jesus.

No sooner had he finished reciting a series of Hail Mary's on his knees before the shrine than Lazarus reappeared, landing beside the shrine and waddling back and forth to signal his readiness for breakfast. "So, there you are! And where have you been, may I ask? While you were out skylarking, I've been dogging the whole island looking for you. I thought you'd flown the coop...or maybe died. I even summoned you back from the grave, you twit. Lazarus, come forth!" He roared again with laughter, to which the pigeon, as Brock expected, gave no response as it continued its waddling cadence. "And I suppose now you want something to eat, despite the fact the kitchen is closed till dinnertime?" Brock chortled and threw up his hands. "Ah, it's a bird's life! Okay, Laz old boy, stay put while I fish something out of the pantry. By the way, do you see what I found here? A nature-made sculpture of the Blessed Mother."

Lazarus stopped and seemed to look at the shrine...or at Brock. Brock couldn't tell which.

"Well, at least she got your attention. Oh, Laz," he said laughing, "you kill me! I'm so glad you didn't leave me. I'd have been lonely without you."

Brock stepped into the lagoon and snatched up a fish, which he cut into small morsels and left for Lazarus to eat raw while he went to work on the chapel. A short while later the pigeon wheeled overhead and resumed his accustomed place atop Matthew, watching Brock labor below.

Subsequently, each evening before retiring, Brock knelt before the shrine and prayed a Hail Mary. Then as a final orison he sang a Gregorian chant. His rich baritone enveloped the island like a father's gentle caress, lulling the seagulls and Lazarus and conceivably even the trees and flowers to sleep as in a Grimm's fairy tale.

Six days a week he faithfully followed this routine without any variation, finding both inner strength and peace of mind in the unvarying repetition day after day. The regimentation freed his mind, unleashing for six days the full power of his creativity and skills. The seventh day he arbitrarily identified as Sunday, though he had lost track of actual calendar dates. On Sundays he rested, prayed, ambled about the island, chanted Gregorian, and read his blue Bible aloud to Lazarus, engaging in mock conversations both with the pigeon and with the towering Apostles as a way of analyzing the Holy Scriptures and also entertaining himself. His favorite reading was Psalm 23 because of its parallels with his life and experiences on the island.

> The Lord is my shepherd. I shall not want. In verdant pastures He gives me repose. Beside restful waters He leads me. He refreshes my soul. He guides me in right paths for His name's sake. Even though I walk in the dark valley I fear no evil, for You are at my side with Your rod and Your staff that give me courage. You spread the table before me in the sight of my foes. You anoint my head with oil. My cup overflows. Only goodness and kindness follow me all the days of my life, and I shall dwell in the house of the Lord for years to come.

For years to come, thought Brock. To dwell here on this island in the chapel he was building. The idea enthralled him. For years to come. With God as his protector and provider.

His miraculous cure had not transformed Brock physically. He was still fifty-one years old with a fifty-one-year-old body, though a strong, healthy one. His muscles still tired and grew sore from too much heavy labor as would anyone else his age. He bruised from bumps and falls and bled from cuts and splinters. His hands blistered from the ropes and developed calluses from continuous handling of tools and rough wood. Although his stamina probably exceeded that of men in his peer group, he needed every minute of the nine hours he slept each night to restore his reservoirs of energy. But they were peaceful hours of sleep undisturbed by dreams or worries.

414

Brock methodically inventoried the motley assortment of lumber recovered from the disassembled *Gigolo* and schooner. He measured each piece, meticulously detailing every shape and dimension in a loose-leaf notebook he had kept in the *Gigolo* for navigational log-keeping during races. When the inventory was completed, he analyzed what kind of chapel design was possible with the available materials. Plumbing his creativity for ideas, a fount of architectural images swam before his mind's eye. Round structures, hexagons, rectangles, domes, pyramids, steeples, naves, aisles, and altars paraded before him, weaving one through another in endless variation, while his artistry critically appraised each combination looking for the right one, the best one, the one that would be worthy of memorializing his gratitude for God's miracle. And then it happened. The image in his mind sharpened, the shapes and pieces suddenly fit together, and his intuition cried out, *That's it! That's the design! That's the chapel!*

Once he had a fixed conception of what the chapel would look like, bringing it to three-dimensional life was a straightforward undertaking, for Brock knew well how to build things. He was not only a trained designer of thirty years' experience but a creative artisan whose innate talent would now be put to its most difficult but rewarding test. "Which I devoutly and happily accept, Lord," he said to the unblemished blue sky. "I'll build you the most beautiful sanctuary on this globe. And I don't need any blueprints or sketches. I've got it all up here in my head." Brock strode through the sand toward the ridge. "And I'm going to put it there, among Your Son's Apostles, on the very spot Your lightning bolt cured me. You know?" He stopped and laughed. "Dr. Frankenstein would have been impressed with that display of Yours." He resumed his trek up to the ridge. "I mean...*bang, zap, boom*...it really must have been something to see. I can imagine Boris Karloff erecting masts all over the island and dangling his Leggo bodies from them, trying to score a live one with one of Your bolts. Pretty funny, eh?"

Brock's rollicking laughter disturbed the gulls, whose lively wailing turned Lazarus's head. He was perched on one of the spreaders atop the mast-cross.

Brock reached the ridge and walked to the split mast in the center of the group of Apostolic trees. Lazarus dove from the mast and wheeled overhead. Brock saw the bird and called out to him.

"Hey, Laz, come down here! I'm gonna start work on the chapel today."

As if understanding Brock's invitation, the bird landed near Matthew and strutted about, stopping now and then to preen himself.

"I suppose you have better things to do than help me, huh?"

The pigeon ignored the jibe.

"If you pay attention, you might pick up some pointers on building yourself a nest. No self-respecting member of the Aves Family would remain homeless. You are self-respecting, aren't you?"

The bird cocked its head disdainfully and turned about, lifting its tail feathers toward Brock, who burst out laughing. Unmoved and unworried, Lazarus toddled away to the beach apparently to hunt for sea life in the sand.

TWENTY-THREE

Kelly and Eleanor rode the elevator up to the D-M suite in the Calvert Plaza.

"Why are you being so mysterious?" she asked smiling.

"I'm not being mysterious. It's my natural state in the presence of a beautiful woman." He winked at her.

"Then why won't you tell me why I'm here?"

"Just for fun, I guess. I figure you could use some merriment. You've had very little to smile about, so today I've got something I think will make you happy."

The elevator stopped at the 18th floor and opened opposite D-M's pretentious entrance. Kelly took Eleanor's arm in his and walked her across the hallway and into the reception room. Maggie, seated at her desk, spotted their approach and went to the door to greet these two people for whom she held great respect and affection.

"Here she is!" bellowed Kelly to Maggie.

Eleanor kissed Maggie's cheek and laughed. "You know I'm too old for this."

"Bother!" said Maggie. "You go right in. We have a surprise for you."

Kelly took her hand and led her down the short corridor to Brock's corner office with its panoramic view of San Francisco Bay and the Golden Gate Bridge in the distance. Just before they turned the corner into the office Kelly stopped and said, "Eleanor, it is my esteemed pleasure to introduce you to D-M's newly appointed trustee." He bowed and beckoned her to proceed.

For a split second she hesitated, having suspected that her meeting the long-awaited trustee was the object of Kelly's little game and also having prayed it would be Diego, whose candidacy Kelly had been championing so aggressively. She held her breath and walked into the office, remembering vividly her first visit to Brock's sanctuary—he sitting benignly behind his desk smiling at her, enjoying her surprise that the "common workman" she had spent time in the mall coffee shop talking about O'Henry was in fact the proud owner of DESIGN METAPHORS. But no longer. That owner was long gone, dead she hoped, suffering in hell she hoped.

Diego was sitting in an easy chair by the window reading some documents in his lap. He grinned broadly and stood up when he saw her. "Eleanor! How wonderful to see you."

She was thrilled. He still had that enchanting crooked grin that she had remembered ten thousand times. It dimpled his cheeks and wrinkled the skin at the corners of his piercing brown eyes. His tanned face had aged very little. He was forty-seven, two years older than she. His hair was as thick and black and curly as it had been in the maternity ward sixteen years before.

He tossed the documents onto the chair and strode to meet her in the middle of the room. They stopped a few feet apart and shook hands.

Eleanor's calm smiling face concealed the excitement churning inside her. "And you." She feared the quaver in her voice was noticeable. "How have you been?"

"Very well, thank you."

"Congratulations on your appointment as trustee. D-M is fortunate to have someone with your experience. Kelly told me he was lobbying for you."

"Too much perhaps." Diego aimed a finger at his promoter standing in the doorway.

Eleanor motioned with her head toward Kelly. "He told me he'd seek an audience with the Pope, if it would help make you trustee."

Kelly cheerily chimed in. "I was ready to, but Diego's reputation needed no pumping up. He was the front-runner the minute Holly put his name in the ring. Hey, why don't you two sit down and catch up on old times, while I check the mail. Maybe someone's paid their bill." He turned and went back to the reception room, wanting these two people to be alone for awhile. He felt they needed each other, and it was time they found that out for themselves.

418

Eleanor and Diego stood stiffly looking at one another like two teenagers on their first date. There were so many things she wanted to tell him, things sealed up within her heart, but she felt naive and foolish. What if he didn't share her longings? After all, it had been sixteen years! Too many to hope that the attraction which had drawn them together so long ago had survived. She knew from her regular elicitations of Kelly and Helena that Diego had not remarried. But neither had the Barnabys ever suggested he carried a torch for her, though it was not his nature to be self-revealing. Now here he stood, a few feet away, and she honestly did not know what to say. Her lips started moving anyway and she spoke.

"The last I heard a year ago you had not remarried." What a fool thing to say, but she couldn't help herself.

"Yes, that's still true. I had no desire to after my sad experience with Raphaéla."

"Too bad. Life can be lonely by oneself." Then she wished she hadn't said that either. It was judgmental and prying.

"Some things a man can live without. Maybe when the right woman comes along I'll reconsider."

She avoided his eyes, afraid she would see indifference there, a hint that she was not that woman.

"I'm sorry, Eleanor, about all this trouble. I know it's been hard on you."

"Thank you for coming to Valerie's funeral. That was very kind. I never had a chance to thank you."

Diego blushed at the memory of his having stolen away without paying Eleanor the courtesy of acknowledging his presence. But his embarrassment warmed her and reminded her both of his sensitivity and of how cold and distant Brock had been.

"I'm sorry," Diego said. "I truly am. It was impolite of me."

"Oh, no, please."

"I thought it wasn't the right time to..." He didn't know how to say it. "I mean...it wasn't the best time to talk with you...in your moment of grief."

"Yes, I understand. Anyway I appreciated your coming. Valerie never knew how special she was to you." She wanted to say "and how special you are to me."

She smiled. "You gave her her name. No one knows that, of course, but you and I. I've never forgotten that day in the hospital when I needed someone to be there with me and you appeared. I've never forgotten."

Diego looked down at his shoes in a boyish manner. "I haven't either."

There was a long awkward pause while they separately relived that perilous moment in her hospital room so long ago, when they were two heartbeats away from doing and saying things that would have changed the course of both their lives. Diego had wisely backed off, departing her room before his feelings for her overrode his common sense. But the memory of that close encounter had remained vivid for both of them as had their latent mutual attraction, which now burned intensely, given new life by the circumstance of Brock's absence and presumed death.

Then Eleanor recalled another old memory...an unhappy one...Diego's terrible financial loss shortly after Valerie was born. "That was a difficult period for you, too," she said. "As I recall you were wiped out by the failure of that exhibit in Los Angeles. Kelly told me about it."

Diego made a wry face. "Every penny I owned. I shot the works on what I thought was a sure thing. I suppose you know that Brock was the mastermind behind the exhibit's downfall?"

"Yes," she replied blankly. There was nothing more she could say.

"It taught me a bitter lesson: there are no sure winners. Life is a gamble. I learned to value each day for its own sake and to give of myself the same way."

"You dropped out of sight for quite awhile."

"Yeah, I bottomed out, bummed around, drank a lot. It took me a good three years to get myself together. Then I came back to L.A."

"You got a job as a carpenter in Paramount Studios, didn't you?"

Diego's brows lifted. "How did you know that?" He smiled. "You been keeping tabs on me?"

Eleanor's face reddened. "Oh...no, Kelly always talked about you and what you were doing." She needed to change the subject. "The years have been kind to you, Diego. You look wonderful."

"You too...but more than wonderful." He held back his next thought, then changed his mind. "You look even more beautiful now than you did then, if that's possible."

420

Their eyes met, and a craving to be held tightly in his arms seized Eleanor. Her hands began to tremble. This would not do. She moved away toward Brock's crescent marble desk to escape the tension. "So much has happened," she said, afraid to respond to his compliment. "I think maybe I'm a different person than I was then."

"I think not. I know it's bold of me to say this but…I'd know if there were a difference. There isn't. You haven't changed, nor have I. We're just a bit older and maybe a lot wiser."

Sensing her uneasiness, Diego shifted gears. "Eleanor, I'm honored to be trustee and to manage DESIGN METAPHORS until this thing with Brock can be resolved. I promise I'll do my very best."

"I know you will. I can't think of anyone I'd rather have running things. Have you had a chance to study the company's situation?" It was a relief to talk business.

"Yes." Diego went behind the desk, opened a side drawer, and pulled out a blue folder. "Kelly filled me in pretty well before he proposed my name. Wanted me to know what I was getting into before I consented."

"What do you think? Do we have any chance at all of saving D-M?"

He leafed through the papers in the folder and withdrew a several-page report. "These are the bottom-line figures that Kelly worked up." He gave out a half-laugh of resignation and handed the report to Eleanor. "It's grim. You can see for yourself. The fall-off rate of clients is sharper than Kelly's worst projection, and that complicates everything."

"I'm sorry, but these figures don't mean anything to me."

"The short of it is that D-M's days are numbered. You see, we need time to rebuild client confidence, but the sharp drop in revenues puts us deeper in the red every day. If only the court had appointed me trustee when Brock skipped out."

"You think it would have made a difference?"

"Perhaps, but it's irrelevant now. Water under the bridge."

As Holly had foreseen, D-M's major clients quickly lost confidence in the firm's reliability following news reports of Brock's disappearance. Holly had petitioned the Superior Court to appoint a trustee, arguing forcefully with a stack of financial records as exhibits that the absence of the company's sole decision maker left D-M in perilous straits. He urged the judge to waive the statutory waiting period of ninety days, citing the

421

inevitable loss of clients and the crucial need for strong leadership to preserve the company's financial position, which would be seriously weakened. But the judge wasn't moved, being unpersuaded that Brock was dead and being unwilling without supreme cause to take hasty action on the estate of a man who placed so high a premium on controlling it himself. "We'll keep an eye on the situation," declared the judge. "Meanwhile, the court must deny the petition."

And so D-M had carried on, making do without the firm guiding hand of its flamboyant founder. Kelly quietly held things together, staying unobtrusively in the background, directing the day-to-day operations of the company's thirty employees within the narrow limits permitted by Holly's stringent instructions. Although the court, keeping a benign watch over D-M, might learn of Kelly's role, Holly was confident they would not intervene as long as D-M continued to function reasonably well and Kelly remained invisible. Nor were creditors concerned as long as D-M made payments on its debts. Under these unwieldy constraints, and fearing for its future, D-M struggled through the ninety days while its situation, as predicted, steadily worsened. Finally, on the hundredth day after Brock's flight from the hospital, the Superior Court heard Holly's petition to have a trustee appointed. The judge reviewed the evidence of D-M's financial decline and decreed that a trustee be designated and empowered as soon as possible.

"Section 263 of the probate code," the judge proclaimed, "provides that in appointing a trustee the court must prefer the spouse or the spouse's nominee. Given that Mrs. Stowolski cannot legitimately assume the position of trustee herself, because she forswore any interest in the missing person's estate in a property agreement, the court sees fit to invite her nomination of a trustee."

Holly on her behalf nominated Diego, and though it took the court nearly two weeks to issue its decision, it finally came, and now D-M was officially and legally under Diego's direct control.

Eleanor, concerned over Diego's pessimistic forecast, sought more information on alternatives, knowing that he almost certainly had explored every option. "Can't we borrow money somewhere to tide us over till we can recover our clients?"

"Unfortunately the court has me on a very short leash. They fully understand our situation and gave me explicit directives in writing for the court's record telling me what I can and cannot do. One of the things I can't do is borrow funds from any source to sustain D-M's operations."

"Then what are we to do?"

Diego shrugged and gazed at her glumly. "Give up."

"Declare bankruptcy?"

"Heavens no! D-M isn't bankrupt, but if we keep operating in the red we eventually will be."

"How soon will that be?"

"It depends on a range of things, all variables. In any case I think our best...no, our only option is to sell the firm."

"Will the court go along with that?"

"Not only along. They'll probably recommend it. Their job is to preserve as much of Brock's estate as possible to satisfy creditors, and selling D-M is the only way to do that at this juncture."

Eleanor was disheartened. "Does Kelly agree?"

"More or less. He agrees that at some point, if we can't turn the corner on our downward slide, we have to call it quits. He wants to give it one more go, pitch each client, appeal for time."

Eleanor understood. "When will you have to make your decision?"

"It won't be my decision. It will be yours. The company is rightfully yours, even though the court doesn't recognize your ownership, and I have no intention of infringing on your rights."

"All right, then, when do I have to make that decision? How many months?"

"Kelly and I agree that, if we don't see positive signs in twelve months, you should pull the plug."

"Twelve months," she repeated, not relishing the dismal prospect of watching D-M sink slowly month by month to its demise.

"Meanwhile, we're going to give her everything we've got. Design is our business. We're experts with proven abilities and solid track records. We're not licked yet."

The courage and conviction in his words gave Eleanor new hope, and his honesty and compassion were refreshing. So unlike Brock. She smiled, thinking how enraged Brock would be if he knew that Diego was now at D-M's helm.

"Eleanor?"

"Yes." His mood seemed to be different, as if he had made some decision.

He swallowed and licked his lips. "I've kept my distance from you for sixteen years out of respect for your marriage vows and your decency. It hasn't been easy. Kelly and Helena kept me posted on events in your life, your sufferings. Many times I've wanted to pick up the phone and console you, to lighten your burden. Perhaps I should have. I don't know. When Brock left your home to live by himself, it took heroic self-restraint for me not to call you, knowing you were alone and perhaps needing someone. But you were still a married woman. It wouldn't have been right."

Eleanor listened wide-eyed and enthralled at Diego's impromptu confession...what she had secretly longed to hear over the years.

"Although the courts won't certify for another four years that Brock is deceased, all of us—you, me, Kelly, Helena, Gordon—we all know he's dead. So I no longer consider you a married woman. Therefore..." Diego began nervously rubbing his hands together as he gathered the courage to ask her the question he had been waiting these many years to pose, but whose answer he was suddenly afraid to hear. "Would you be interested...that is, would you like...could we perhaps..."

"Yes!" said Eleanor.

Diego smiled. "Let me finish. Could we pick up where we left things in that maternity ward?"

Eleanor started to reply but her excitement stalled her.

"Oh, I understand," said Diego quickly, sensing rejection. "If you feel this wouldn't be the right time. I mean with all that has happened, I'd understand."

Eleanor regained control of herself and replied calmly, "Diego, I would like very much to pick up where we left things."

He did not answer at once. Instead he reached out and took her hands and looked into her eyes for several seconds, seeing what he had known these many years was a shared affection. "I've been waiting sixteen years to hear you say that."

"So many years," she said sadly, knowing he felt the same loss she did. Years they could have spent together. Years never to be retrieved.

"Let's not lose any more."

424

"No more."

"Would you dine with me tonight?" he asked, squeezing her hands.

"Tonight and every night."

He let go of her hands as he heard Kelly approaching.

"You two getting reacquainted?" asked Kelly, rounding the corner with an armload of mail.

The spell broken, Eleanor breathed deeply and, looking endearingly at Diego, said, "Yes, we were recollecting old times and thinking about the future."

"Good. And did he brief you on the situation here?"

Diego replied. "I think we're all in agreement that, if things haven't turned around in twelve months, we throw in the towel."

Eleanor gave the two men a doleful look. Kelly laid the mail on the desk and put his arms around her, hugging her gently. He kissed her cheek and stepped back. "I'm really sorry that it's come to this. We'll try to save as much as we can. But, as you well know, you may come out of this mess with nothing more than the clothes on your back. That's the worst case, of course. If Diego here is true to his reputation, we can do much better than that. It's a long shot, but once in awhile a long shot comes in. What makes the odds so poor is that the whole industry knows about Brock's escapade. His cancer. His running off in his boat. His leaving D-M moribund. If he had gracefully retired, formally passing the reins of the company to a successor, D-M's future would have been promising. But his acting like a lunatic leaving behind the mess he did has tarnished the company's image. And it's been further warped by the garbage the newspapers have been dredging up about him. One story referred to the whole rigmarole as D-Mentia."

Kelly picked up Brock's silver nameplate and studied it for a second. "Some legacy you left! You miserable..." He wrapped the fingers of both hands around it and squeezed till his knuckles turned white. The metal plate snapped in half.

TWENTY-FOUR

ay by day, timber by timber, the skeleton of the chapel took shape. Brock had been cast upon the island in April, and by the end of May the dismemberment of the *Gigolo* and the schooner and the sorting and stacking of the building materials were completed. In June, he surveyed the construction site in the clearing where the scarred mast-cross remained in its original position. The chapel's shape was to be hexagonal. Using the three masts and ropes from the schooner, he devised a simple but workable lifting apparatus, which he could manipulate with lines run through pulleys attached to the tops of Peter, John, Matthew, and Philip, the tallest trees around the site. With this ingenious derrick in place, he raised the hexagonal chapel's six main pillars and seated them firmly in the ground atop large flat rocks placed at the bottom of each hole to ensure that the base of every pillar was at precisely the same elevation and as flat and stable as his surpassing carpentry skills could make it. He adjusted its pillar's verticality using plumb lines until all six were perfectly perpendicular. Then he filled in the holes around their base with rocks and sand, packing the composite down with a heavy timber to seal the feet of the pillars tightly in place. Then he cut, planed, and chiseled six crossbeams, lifted them deftly into their positions atop the pillars, and secured them with stout hardwood pegs. The sturdy framework of the chapel was in place around the lightning-charred mast-cross, the site of his miraculous cure.

By the time he began work on the dome it was July and the summer sun had tanned his legs, arms, and upper body a golden bronze and bleached his dark hair and beard a pale blond. Before the month was over, the dome was finished, and by the end of October, he had built an apse behind the mast-cross on the eastern side, constructed a doorless entrance on the western side with a mahogany marquee supported by two fluted stanchions, and enclosed the remaining four sides with decorative wooden walls, each of which like the apse contained a round hole ten feet across. A smaller hole was in the short wall above the entrance.

Into each of these six openings he emplaced a circular wooden frame that would later contain stained-glass windows which, owing to the formal symmetrical geometry of the building, would be its dominant features. However, fabricating the glass and the lead webbing to hold them and designing and assembling the windows would be the most difficult and chancy part of the entire project. Their artful execution was crucial to the fulfillment of Brock's design.

Brock had never made glass from scratch. He had learned the basic process from the elderly French priest at St. Charles who had taught him ancient techniques for repairing the stained-glass windows in the seminary chapel. Later, out of curiosity as part of his self-education in the art of interior design, Brock had read numerous books on stained-glass windows, books that covered the history of glassmaking and the evolution of the process. His knowledge of glassmaking was therefore fairly extensive but unpracticed, for knowledge and skill are two very different things. Moreover, whether he could find on this tiny isle the necessary materials for glassmaking was highly questionable. Even more dubitable was whether he could build a furnace that could achieve and sustain the extremely high temperatures needed to convert a batch of silicon sand and other ingredients into molten glass. Finally, even if he could surmount these enormous difficulties and succeed in manufacturing glass, there was no certainty he could produce glass of different colors and of radiant quality. The odds of his succeeding were therefore overwhelmingly against him. Nevertheless, his faith in his vision of the completed chapel persuaded him to proceed blindly ahead. God, he was confident, would lead the way.

On the morning after he finished the last window frame he knelt before the mast-cross and prayed for God's guidance and inspiration in how to go about producing the glass. His meditation done, he rose and strolled around the interior of the chapel pondering the task ahead. The early morning sun sent a blazing shaft of light through the large empty window frame in the apse, casting the shadow of the mast-cross on the uneven sand floor dimpled from wall to wall by the imprints of his footsteps and the traces of construction work.

"You see, Lord, I know how to make glass. That isn't the problem. It's the materials I lack. For example, a glass founding furnace is built of fire bricks, but there aren't any here." He stopped in the entrance, leaned his shoulder against the buttress, and gazed thoughtfully upon the shimmering blue-green ocean whose surface sparkled with the sun's dazzling reflections. "Where should I begin, Lord? Where do I look? What do I do? I know You will show the way as You have so far. All I need do is wait."

Lazarus, seeing Brock appear in the doorway, left his customary perch atop Matthew and glided down to the marquee over the entrance.

"So, Laz, my friend, have you come to console me?" Brock stepped out of the chapel and looked back to the roof where the bird was contentedly preening its tail feathers. "Small chance of that, eh? I think the only thing that moves you is hunger. I never saw a bird so small, who does so little, eat so much." He grinned and waved. "All right. Come along, you feckless fowl. I'll get you your breakfast. As our Lord said, 'whatsoever you do to the least of mine you do to me.'" He chuckled. "I would say you qualify among the least of His." Then quickly, "No insult intended, of course, my dear friend."

Brock ambled down the now well-worn path to the lagoon and strode directly into the water, whereupon fish appeared all around him leaping and splashing. The daily repetition of this remarkable phenomenon had dulled Brock's wonderment at the miracle of it, and he casually grasped four fish and waded out of the water, which instantly quieted. He bowed, crossed himself, and said, "Thank You, Lord." Then looking to the trees for Lazarus, he shouted, "Come and get it!"

Sure enough the bird shot out from the drooping palms and wheeled above Brock for several minutes, finally alighting on a spur of coral ten feet from the small fire pit where Brock routinely cooked their unvarying diet.

As Brock watched the filets sizzle in the frying pan, his focus came to rest on the soot-blackened bottom and sides of the pit. He had been burning dried seaweed in it now for months, yet there was no erosion or decomposition of the coral rock. Nor should there necessarily be erosion,

428

since most of the heat of the burning seaweed was released into the atmosphere, not concentrated in the rock. The question was whether the coral could withstand really high temperatures. He wondered. And could the seaweed burn hot enough to serve as fuel for a founder?

Then he remembered reading how eighteenth-century glassmakers in Normandy had used kelp, a type of coarse brown seaweed that grew abundantly along the French coast, as both an intensely hot-burning fuel for their furnaces and, in its ash form, as a flux which, when mixed with the other powdered ingredients, lowered the temperature at which silicon fused into molten glass.

"Do you think it'll work?" he said to the bird, which was waddling impatiently back and forth waiting for its breakfast. "We haven't missed yet." He dropped his voice to a whisper. "Of course, we've had a little help from you-know-who." Grinning, he pointed heavenward.

After breakfast he gathered an assortment of heavy tools, the principal being a sledgehammer, and set to work breaking up a massive chunk of fifty-thousand-year-old coral in the lagoon. He hammered the rock into roughly shaped one-foot bricks and assembled them into a small test furnace, using a mallet and a heavy blunt chisel to make the edges of the blocks fit tightly together. He crammed this makeshift oven with bundles of dry brittle seaweed and set them afire with the magnifying glass, restoking the fuel as it was consumed. The extreme intensity of the heat impressed him as did the durability of the coral.

"I think we're on to something here, Laz, old boy!"

Before the flames in the furnace had burned out, Brock was already at work on a full-scale version designed as best he could remember along the lines of those used by Norman glassmakers.

It took four weeks—into late January—and over one hundred seventy blocks to complete the six-foot-high structure with a vaulted ceiling and apertures in the top and sides for feeding fuel to the fire, venting the smoke, and inserting sand that he hoped would melt into glass. Gathering and drying ten huge stacks of seaweed took another two weeks, followed by yet another to collect and sift sand and store it in sail-cloth bags.

When he examined the sand on the island, he discovered there were four distinctly different kinds in four separate locations. The lagoon sand was white and of fine grain. That on the beach at the northern tip of the island next to Iscariot was brownish and gritty. The sand around the bluff was gray and granular, while that at the southern tip was as fine as the lagoon variety but of a reddish hue. He collected twenty large bags of sand, five of each type—having no idea whether these sands could be turned into glass—and in mid-February began the tiresome and tricky process.

While Lazarus looked on at a safe distance atop Matthew, Brock stoked and fired the furnace till the heat radiating from its mouth forced him to don a hooded poncho-like garment he sewed together out of canvas to protect his skin from burns. Wearing canvas mittens, he opened a wrought-iron door, taken from a stove on the schooner, on one end of the roaring furnace and using iron tongs inserted a heavy earthenware pot containing a one-inch-deep batch of sand and ash in a ten-to-one ratio. The pot was one of a dozen he had found in the schooner's galley. He clanged the door shut, waited for half an hour, then reopened it and withdrew the pot, setting it on the ground to study its contents. The condition of the sand-ash composite was unchanged. He touched a slender shoot from a bush to the batch to test its temperature, lacking any kind of thermometer. The shoot instantly burst into flame.

"You're hot, all right," he said, making a disappointed face. "But you aren't hot enough...or I don't have the right mixture of sand and seaweed ash."

Assuming it needed longer heating, he scratched the letter *A* on the side of the pot and replaced it in the furnace. Then he picked up another pot, marked it *B*, poured into it the same size batch but in a smaller ratio of sand to ash, and placed it in the furnace alongside the first pot. An hour later he retrieved both pots. No change. And so it went by trial and error, pot after pot, different sand, different amounts, different ratios, longer durations of heating...week after week...without success.

It was midday the third week of March. Brock sat dejectedly on a bench he had built ten yards from the furnace outside the blister range of its radiation. He had just removed a set of six pots after cooking them for four straight hours and consuming two full stacks of seaweed. He was physically exhausted and dispirited.

"Look, God, I'm doing this for You, but I'm not getting anywhere. I don't even know if I'm close. What if I'm not on the right track? Maybe this sand won't fuse. Maybe the chemical composition of the seaweed isn't right for a flux. I feel like a witless alchemist trying to make gold out of sand. I've tried everything I can think of. I've altered the time in the oven, the ratio of sand to ash, the total size of the batch, and the different sands. None of the four brands fuses."

He jerked upright. "Wait a minute! I haven't mixed the sands. I've been working with each brand separately." He looked skyward. "Stick with me, Lord! We ain't licked yet!"

He emptied the six pots and poured into them measured amounts of different combinations of the four brands of sand, adding an equal measure of ash to each. He then fired up the furnace to its maximum heat and inserted the pots, leaving them there for about two hours, which he computed roughly with a crude sundial he had built nearby for that purpose. It was nearly sundown when he removed them and eagerly examined their contents. Nothing! The sand and ash in each one remained sand and ash. No chemical change had occurred.

He threw his mittens down angrily and kicked the sand. "I'm getting nowhere! I've been at this for almost seven weeks!" *Maybe it's time*, he thought, *to forget stained glass and design something else for the windows in the chapel walls.*

He shuffled dejectedly up the path to the ridge, weary of failing and demoralized by the growing suspicion—edging toward certainty—that what he was trying to do was chemically impossible. As he passed the chapel, intending to proceed to his offshore privy on the other side of the island to continue his usual nighttime routine, he stopped and stared through the open circle of the wall before him. He had planned to fill that and the other openings with beautiful stained glass. That was a pipe dream. He had overreached his capabilities. He was plum out of miracles. His faith in God's miraculous powers had gone beyond reason.

Then he laughed. "Hey, Lazarus! Where are you? Wanna hear something funny? I just told myself that my faith in miracles was beyond reason. Isn't that one for the books!"

The bird was nowhere in sight.

"Well, I don't blame you for ostracizing me. Any guy who believes that miracles are reasonable is off his rocker any way. Miracles, as you probably don't know, are inherently unreasonable. That's why they're called miracles. I know that! I know that!"

He looked about for Lazarus among the deepening shadows of twilight.

"After all that's happened to me on this incredible island, you'd think my faith would be stronger. Eh, Laz? Isn't that right? Of course, some people would also say that a guy who talks to birds is off his rocker. But God understands. He knows. He knows."

Brock left the path and entered the darkening chapel. Night was descending rapidly, and he could barely make out the outline of the mast-cross. He walked across the nave and knelt before the symbol of his cure.

"Dear Lord, forgive my lassitude and my flimsy faith in the power of Your mercy and love. Where Your will deems it, all things are possible. In that fact I do believe, as events on this island bear witness. I promise to be patient and to persevere. Tomorrow I shall begin again with renewed resolve. In Your Son's holy name. Amen."

Weighed down by fatigue, Brock decided to abandon his nightly regimen. Instead he lay down at the foot of the mast-cross and fell deeply asleep with total peace of mind, content with his apology and ready to resume his glassmaking experiments on the morrow.

Around four in the morning he was awakened by a fluttering winglike sound and opened his eyes. At first the dark interior of the chapel ceiling looked strange and confused him, accustomed as he was to sleeping outside beneath the canopy of stars. As he came out of his slumber he remembered where he was, though he wasn't sure what had bestirred him. He listened now, wide awake, for some express sound. There was only the whisper of the night breeze through the trees and the distant muffled lapping of the ocean on the rim of the island.

Brock got to his feet. Alert and needing to relieve himself, having earlier missed his nightly visit to the privy, he made his way down to the eastern beach and the pier. He saw to his bodily needs, then reclimbed the ridge intending to go to his bed. Before doing so he surveyed the lagoon on the western side, taking in his feckless glass-making furnace where tomorrow he would resume his experiments. His eyes were drawn immediately to a spot of light on the roof of the furnace.

Curious, he thought. It must be a glow of red-hot coral inside reflecting through the chimney opening. He never realized how long the interior of the furnace remained at such a high temperature. But that shouldn't be. The fuel would have been consumed and the fire extinguished. Unless, of course, something in the furnace had absorbed the heat, keeping the internal temperature high.

He jogged down the path to the lagoon to investigate, seeing his way easily with the light from the stars. As he approached the furnace, he saw dimly the five pots he had removed before sulking off in a despondent funk.

"Five?" he said aloud. He recounted them. There were only five. He peered sharply about in the half light for the sixth pot. Nowhere to be seen. Then it must still be in the kiln.

He put on the canvas poncho and mittens and threw open the iron door, lighting the area in front with the reddish glow of the interior. A blast of heat pressed against him as he reached inside the furnace with the tongs and withdrew the sixth pot from the rear. As it cleared the door and emerged into the darkness, amazement and triumph came over Brock's hooded face. He stared unbelieving at the glowing contents of the pot, whose incandescence bathed his face an eerie yellowish red.

"Now I know how Madame Curie felt when she discovered radium."

Smiling, he closed his eyes and let the lacy fingers of heat radiating from the molten mass brush lightly against his forehead and cheeks.

"I did it!" he cried. "I did it! I baked me some glass!" Quickly realizing the relic of his lifelong egotism in his statement, he bowed his head. "Okay, *we* did it, God. But You couldn't have done it without me."

Finally, the truth prevailed and in a wave of emotion he sank to his knees laying the searing pot on the sand. "And I," he whispered, "could not have done it without You." He wept, moved yet again by the inescapable feeling of God's presence and love. "It was Your Son who said, 'For man it is impossible but not for God. With God all things are possible.' Forgive my arrogance, Lord. It is a lifetime habit hard to break."

Brock collected himself and scrutinized more closely the red-glowing molten material in the pot. He was certain it was glass. But what to do now? Would he forget in his excitement the exact composition of the batch in the sixth pot?

He rolled back on his haunches and contemplated his next move, mentally walking through each of the steps in glassmaking. He remembered that molten glass would crystallize, becoming useless, if it cooled too quickly. It had to be cooled slowly—annealed—in a furnace called a lehr, in which the temperature is reduced gradually. The idea of hammering another hundred blocks out of coral for a third furnace was depressing. Perhaps, he thought, he could build an extension onto the side of the existing furnace and devise some way to regulate its heat, which would come from the single fire.

But, he recalled, the glass must first be shaped into its final form, in this case flat sheets which he would later cut into pieces of exact shapes and sizes to make up the designs depicted in the stained-glass windows. The finished glass would then be stored in boxes by color, ready for final trimming and insertion into the windows.

Relieved at this marvelous breakthrough, he walked up the path to his bed. By God's grace Brock would, after all, complete the chapel his imagination had conceived.

He lay down in his bunk and relaxed his tired aching muscles. For seven weeks he had driven himself relentlessly and blindly in search of the magic formula...and God had answered his prayers. Certain that he now could produce the glass he needed, he closed his eyes, happily envisioning the windows he would construct and what each would portray. As Brock drifted off to sleep, Lazarus circled the trees and took up his roost for the night atop Matthew.

During the next ten weeks Brock added an annealing oven to one side of the furnace and through another lengthy tedious series of firings found he was able, by selectively combining the four types of sand on the island, to create every color of the rainbow. He was not surprised at the astonishing quality of the glass or the brilliance of the colors.

"I should have expected it," he told Lazarus. "I mean, when God's own hand is mixing the batch, you don't figure you'll get a lousy product." He chuckled, then grew reflective as he wondered what he might have accomplished during his life had he let God "mix the batch."

Completion of the chapel took six months devoted mainly to the six stained-glass windows. Using exact measurements, Brock outlined in charcoal on six large sections of sailcloth what each window would portray. Atop the sail cloth he constructed the lattice-like lead framing that would hold the hundreds of pieces of glass to create the images he had drawn. The lead was formed by melting heavy lead ingots that had been used as ballast in the schooner's bilge and pouring the molten lead into long thin wooden molds. When all of the framing was done, he set about the painstaking process of selecting the precise color glass needed for each aperture, however tiny, then trimming and filing each piece to fit perfectly. His artistry flourished. He lost himself totally for hours at a time in this absorbing and exquisitely satisfying labor as bit by bit each window came to life. When he was finished, he dragged the windows, each weighing several hundred pounds, by sled to their assigned walls and raised them into position with the derrick.

The penultimate step in completing the chapel was laying the floor, which entailed crushing hundreds of pounds of coral into small bits and pounding them flat inside the chapel perimeter to form a solid durable foundation. On this subflooring, using as glue a sticky substance he squeezed out of fresh seaweed, he laid a mosaic of tiny, tightly packed, glossy sea shells of different colors and shades to form sweeping varied patterns: spirals, filigree, interweaving vines, and fanciful flowers. The result was a glistening marble-like surface of immeasurable beauty that would have done homage to the finest mosaic artists in the world.

The final step of construction was tidying up the surrounding landscape to make the chapel's setting as clean and picturesque as the geography of the island would permit. He spent two weeks towing tools and unused materials out on the raft, dumping them a good distance from the island. He dismantled the derrick, the glass oven, likewise disposed of them in the ocean. Little by little he returned the island to its original state as he had found it.

The restoration completed, he made a final inspection of the island, assuring himself that all was in order, and then saw to cleaning himself up. He bathed in the ocean, rinsed off under the water from the tank, and dried off seated naked on the rim of the lagoon in the late afternoon sun. Refreshed and content, he put on his brown robe and entered the chapel.

As the sun set, Brock sat facing the entrance, his back against the altar, and luxuriated in the gleaming beauty of the stained-glass windows. Their bright colors, which tinted his fingers different hues as he playfully wiggled them in front of his face, bathed the chapel in a mystical light, as he had conceived it would. Nothing he had ever done in his life came close to giving him the satisfaction he was now experiencing. He took pleasure in knowing he had merely been the implementer, the tool in God's hand. God was the real architect and builder, and for this Brock was supremely satisfied, for he was sure that God was pleased. No hurricane, no wind or wave would God unleash to tear down this holly sanctuary erected over the site of His miraculous intercession.

A profound peace of mind and inner contentment settled upon Brock, instilling in him a wondrous sense of well-being, a feeling of unparalleled goodness and total fulfillment. He thought this must be how Christ felt after His resurrection. He recalled Jesus' last words on the cross before giving up His spirit: "It is accomplished." *Indeed,* Brock thought, *God's purpose here has truly been accomplished.*

The dimming light in the chapel told of dusk's approach. Brock got up, bowed to the mast-cross, crossed himself, and ambled out the entrance. He strolled down the path to the lagoon and, kneeling before his shrine to the Holy Virgin, recited the Beatitudes, while a glorious sunset muraled the western sky. When he finished, he walked back up the ridge amid the darkening shadows of night and lay down on his bed. He would skip dinner. He had no appetite at all and hoped Lazarus would forgive him this one time for not providing his evening meal. He had not seen the bird all day and presumed he was reposing in his retreat atop Matthew. Within minutes Brock was asleep.

He slept deeply without stirring and awakened late the next morning to bright sunlight, a cloudless blue sky, and a strange silence. Neither gulls, nor waves, nor wind made a sound. Brock rose from his bed and scanned the horizon. The ocean was totally becalmed. No swell or eddy marred the water's mirror-like surface. The entire environment was in a peaceful almost mystical hiatus. It intrigued him, because every happening on the island had some special significance hidden at first from his understanding but ultimately revealed. The eerie silence, he was sure, tokened some major forthcoming event. But he was unconcerned. He was in God's hands, and whatever would happen was God's will.

Still lacking an appetite, he passed up breakfast and set about the day's special ceremonies which he had been contemplating for some months as work on the chapel neared completion. He would perform two final acts—consecration of the chapel and the entire island with holy water from the *Gigolo*'s tank, and celebration of an inaugural Mass at the altar.

He removed the tank from its perch between Matthew and James-son-of-John, hoisted it onto his left shoulder, and entered the chapel. Operating the spigot with his left hand, he caught water in his right and cast it about as he walked to the mast-cross, to the altar, around the nave, and to each window. He went outside and around the building, sprinkling the holy water, through the six Apostolic palm trees near the chapel, down the path to the shallows where the schooner had lain, to the promontory, to the beach where the *Gigolo* had run aground, to the northern tip where Judas remained a forlorn outcast, back along the ridge to the southern tip and the other five Apostles, and then along the western shore to the lagoon and the shrine to the Holy Mother. He knelt before the natural sculpture in its nook and recited the Hail Mary three times, each time sprinkling holy water on the rocks and the niche.

As he rose to purify the shrine once more, a startling thing happened. No water came from the spigot. He shook the tank and worked the handle vigorously with his left hand, but not a drop came out. He set the tank down, opened the top, and peered inside. It was bone dry. He plunked himself down in the sand with the tank between his knees and rested his hands and chin on it, pondering the meaning of this development. For twenty-one months the tank had faithfully supplied water. Now it had suddenly and inexplicably run dry, emptying itself. What did that signify? The answer, painfully unwelcome but logically expected, was obvious. As the work on the chapel was finished, so was Brock's mission here.

To test his hypothesis, he walked to the lagoon where twice daily for nearly two years his entry into the water had triggered that magical eruption of his private churning school of fish. He extend his foot and lowered it into the quiet cool green water. The surface remained tranquil and undisturbed. He dipped his hands in and swished them about to summon the fish. There was no response. The fish did not appear.

He made his way dolorously to the beach and stood pensively over the water tank. The miracles were finished. The water and fish which had sustained his life had vanished to return no more, signaling an end to his adventures on the island.

He unscrewed the spigot and dropped it inside the open tank. Withdrawing a jackknife from a pocket of his robe, he poked a hole in the bottom of the tank, walked to the water's edge, and heaved the tank as far out as he could. It floated on the surface for a few seconds, drifting away from the island with the current, then filled with water and sank out of sight.

Brock's heart was heavy. He had supposed he would live on the island for years, praying in the chapel, robed in God's grace, eating of the fish and drinking of the water, in perfect harmony with his Creator. "And I shall dwell in the house of the Lord for years to come."

He had grown to love this place. Its clear green water, the golden sunrises and dazzling sunsets, the Twelve Apostles, the seagulls, his bathing in the *Gigolo's* water, his fun-filled conversations with Lonesome Lazarus, his Gregorian chants, his prayers at Mary's shrine, and most of all the chapel. His beautiful sacred chapel, the crowning achievement of his life. That more than anything would be difficult to part with.

Thinking of Lazarus, Brock wondered where the bird was. He hadn't seen the little rascal in the past two days. Had the pigeon's instincts sensed what was happening? Had it already flown away, resuming finally the journey which the storm had interrupted? Brock was saddened to think that his inscrutable companion had departed without letting Brock bid him a friendly final farewell.

Brock spent the next several hours dismantling and removing from the island by the raft the appurtenances of his daily life—his bed, the offshore privy and pier, his cooking utensils, even his jackknife—everything he had used for life support and hygiene. His final act of cleansing was to disassemble the raft and shove its components out into the currents, which carried them away out of sight. Then, making a last circumference of the island on foot to ensure it was as he had found it when he was cast upon its shore, he trudged slowly up the path to the chapel and stood barefoot at the entrance with only the few things he had saved: his blue Bible, the hooded brown habit he was wearing, two candles, the book of matches he had kept for emergencies, a wafer of coconut meat, and a tin cup containing the last few swallows of wine from the bottle he had found on the *Gigolo*. He crossed himself and stepped inside. He went to the altar, where he deposited the Bible, mounted the candles on either side, and lit them.

It was only fitting that he should be the first person to say Mass in this holy sanctuary. He was sure that someday someone would discover his masterwork, and then priests would come and conduct Masses here. But he wanted to be the first. It would not, of course, be a real Mass because he was not an ordained priest, and that bothered him. He would go through the motions, but without the sacred power conferred from one priest to the next by the laying on of hands, there would be no transubstantiation, the changing of the bread (in this case the coconut wafer) and wine into Christ's actual body and blood. It would be merely a symbolic simulation.

Brock wished God could lay hands upon him, to ordain him a priest before he died. But no, he thought, God already had given him more...much more...than he ever deserved. The tank's running out of water and the disappearance of the fish had signaled an end to miracles here. There would be no more.

At that instant Lazarus flew in through the chapel door and landed on the altar, inches away, facing Brock. It was the closest the bird had ever come to him. Brock stared at the bird, astounded, as a great door to understanding opened in his mind. "You!" he gasped. Lazarus was not a pigeon. He was a dove. The Paraclete. The embodiment of the Holy Spirit. Brock was as sure of it as he was of God's hand in all the amazing events on the island. It was Lazarus who had watched over Brock and comforted him. It was Lazarus who had brought God's miraculous power to the island. Brock recalled the words of St. Matthew's Gospel describing Jesus' baptism and how afterwards Jesus saw the Spirit of God descending as a dove and coming upon him. "It *is* you!" whispered Brock.

He fell to his knees and bowed, touching his forehead to the mosaic tile floor as the pure white dove spread its wings flat upon the altar and

439

lowered its head. The bird then lifted itself and launched into flight, circling the interior of the chapel three times, coming to rest on Brock's right shoulder. The dove's light weight pressed on him like a finger, its touch radiating a strange sensation through Brock's body. It was, he knew, the laying on of God's hand. Brock was now a priest.

Tearfully he got to his feet with the dove perched on his shoulder and walked around the altar, facing it with his back to the mast-cross. The Latin words of the Mass, which he had not heard or spoken in over three decades, came instantly to his lips.

"*In nominee Patris et filii et Spiritus Sancti.*"

Brock felt exalted, raised to the highest estate of human and moral consciousness. God had ordained what Brock had entered the seminary to become—like Melchisedek who blessed Abram—a priest of the Most High God. Reverently, confidently, Brock celebrated Mass. It was the solemn confirmation of God's covenant with Brock, the final reconciliation in which Brock's gratitude became divine gratefulness and through which he was spiritually reunited with God through Christ.

As Brock concluded the Mass, he remained kneeling at the altar for several minutes basking in the light of God's love and the warmth of Christ's presence. He rose, kissed the altar and, crossing himself, intoned the final blessing. *"Per ipsum, et cum ipso, est tibi Deo Patri omnipotenti, in unitate Spiritus Sancti, omnis honor et gloria per omnia seacula saeculorum. Amen."* He kissed the altar again, walked around to its front and, facing it, looked up at the imposing, coal-black mast-cross.

"Almighty God, my heavenly Father, please accept this chapel, inspired by Your divine intercession, as a testament of my gratitude for Your love. May this chapel be acceptable in Your sight, and may it inspire others to believe as I do in Your mercy, compassion, and generosity. And through it may others come to experience Your healing power and blessed forgiveness. My soul magnifies You, my spirit rejoices in You. With acute sadness at leaving my beloved hallowed isle, where I have been at utmost peace with the world, with myself, and with You, but with a contented trusting heart, I surrender myself to Your loving care."

Brock's eyes clung a moment longer to the majestic cross. Then, with a consoling smile on his lips, peace on his face, and God's sweet dove still perched on his shoulder, he prostrated himself facedown on the mosaic floor, his arms outstretched to either side, his head toward the altar.

Then he closed his eyes.

The candles flickered for a moment, then simultaneously went out, white smoke from their wicks curling to the vaulted ceiling. Seconds later the wicks stopped smoldering, at which instant the dove flapped its wings softly and lifted off Brock's lifeless shoulder. Swooping out the doorway into the brilliant sunlight, it circled around the chapel and came to rest atop the gleaming silver cross at the peak of the dome. The dove remained motionless for a time, as if watching and listening, the only sound the renewed rippling of the ocean on the beaches.

Then a foreign noise invaded the peacefulness...the low rumbling of a motor launch approaching from a small freighter anchored a half mile offshore.

The bird dived from the cross at the sound of the boat, wheeled about the island three times, then ascended high in the sky and flew away.

TWENTY-FIVE

One week earlier Gordon Holly swept past Maggie's desk without his usual friendly hello and strode purposefully into Diego's corner office. Holly had come directly from the Superior Court. Kelly looked up from his work at a desk near Diego's and greeted the lawyer with a question. "What's the verdict?"

Holly stood ramrod in the center of the room holding his briefcase. "We lost it! We go to hearing in seven days."

"Oh, no!" exclaimed Diego, throwing his pencil across the room, cracking it off the panoramic glass wall.

Kelly's shoulders buckled as he slouched against the back of his chair, his eyes staring blankly ahead.

"Why now?" declared Diego. "We've got a lock on the contracts! We can do it! We're there! We all thought D-M would be on the ropes six months ago, and here it is December and we're still alive. We've battled back. Don't they understand that? Don't they see it? Are they blind?"

Kelly waved his palms limply at Diego. "Whoa. Take it easy. They know all that. Holly presented our case."

"I know, I know," said Diego, exasperated and scowling, tormented by the injustice and illogic of it. "You did your best, Gordon. No, you *are* the best. If you couldn't pound some sense into their dense heads, no one could."

Holly laid his briefcase on the rug and sat his heavy frame down on the sofa, tilting his head back against the cushions. The strain of the hearing had sapped his energy. He was getting too old for tense courtroom battles. He closed his eyes to relax, but his mind was still running at high speed. "You have to appreciate, my friends, that the law is very restrictive on the court's prerogatives. Just as the court keeps you tightly reined, so the statutes bind the court's hands."

Holly leaned forward, resting his hands on his knees and turning toward the two men. "You negotiated the contract with Marlow Builders for the Heathrow Project."

Diego nodded. "And Marlow agreed and signed the affidavit you furnished the court confirming the agreement. D-M holds off the creditors for three months, at which time Marlow hands us the two-million-dollar contract, and D-M is out of the woods."

"Yes," said Holly, "that all sounds terrific from D-M's point of view. But not that of the creditors. On the one hand, it's a boon to them because part of that two million belongs to them. But what if the Heathrow thing runs into code violations or a strike or some unforeseen litigation?"

Diego started to object.

Holly interrupted. "It can happen! You know it can! If it does, will the contract stand? Will Marlow default? Will D-M get its money? The creditors are fearful. They want their money now. It's all right for D-M to gamble on its future, but the creditors will have none of it. The court must respect and give precedence to the claims of the creditors. The court can't gamble with the assets of the estate."

"What are they asking for?" said Diego sarcastically. "Accelerated payments on our debts? They wanna bleed us dry and then throw what's left to the sharks out there in the bay?"

"Worse," replied Holly coldly, his eyes closed. "They've petitioned for a Chapter Seven. As you know, if the court grants the petition, it means D-M will be declared insolvent, all its assets will be frozen for ninety days, and any sell-off of its assets in progress will be voided."

Diego and Kelly looked at each other mournfully.

"The coup de gras," moaned Diego.

Holly opened his eyes. "They're also asking for your removal as trustee, turning the firm over to the court's direct control during the ninety-day freeze or till a successor is appointed."

"Can't we stall them?" said Kelly. "Delay the hearing on their petition?"

"We've stalled as much as the court's patience will allow. I'm afraid we've reached the end of the road."

Diego turned toward the window. "We should have sold the firm six months ago when we had originally planned to."

"That's spilt milk," said Holly. "Hindsight won't change the situation. Let's work with the conditions we're facing now. We do have one viable alternative."

His two friends perked up, ready to cling to any straw, however frail, that held out hope for the firm's survival.

"We can counterattack by petitioning for a Chapter Eleven bankruptcy. Let me explain." Holly got up and took a seat near Diego's desk. "Under Chapter Eleven we would submit a plan to revitalize D-M and repay the creditors."

Kelly was confused. "Won't the creditors object?

"Absolutely, but we could embellish the plan, make it innovative and impressive, add new dimensions to it. New directions. New concepts. I admit that, even with such a plan, it will still be an uphill fight to ward off a Chapter Seven."

"What are our chances?" asked Diego.

"Slim, but I see no other choice. It's that or Chapter Seven."

"When is the hearing?"

"A week from today."

Diego grit his teeth and dug down for the strength and resolve to mount yet another battle for D-M. "Holly, buddy, take off your coat and pull up a chair. We've got one more lap to go. Maybe our last."

The houselights in the magnificent baroque theater dimmed, alerting the formally attired patrons who thronged the aisles that the overture was about to begin. The noisy babbling crowd seemed at first to ignore the signal, but gradually the chattering diminished though not to silence. A low buzzing continued—a symptom of the audience's unconstrained excitement at the next and final number on the evening's program. It was the moment for which the San Francisco Ballet community and well-informed ballet aficionados around the country and from abroad had waited for several weeks. The debut of a new dancer making his first solo appearance.

Not since 1974, when Mikhail Baryshnikov appeared in the American Ballet Theatre's production of *Giselle*—his first performance in the United States following his defection from the Soviet Union—had the ballet world made such a fuss over a single dancer. Reporters and dance critics from around the globe were in the audience to witness and record this historic event which ballet notables in a rare instance of accord had unabashedly proclaimed the advent of an uncontested star of Olympian stature. The press and ballet journals had greeted his inaugural performance with the kind of jubilant fanfare normally reserved for the art's aristocracy. They had chorused his talents which, though late in developing for reasons politely unspoken, had thankfully matured and would now favor the world with a level of artistry that, according to the column published that very day by San Francisco's leading ballet critic, "promised to surpass that of the luminary dancers of our time." The international ballet community was poised to welcome into its hallowed fold this shining new star who stood behind the curtain alone in the center of the darkened stage, rigid but supple, his mind in full control of every muscle and movement of his beautifully proportioned, finely sculptured body. Months of rigorous training and endless grueling rehearsals had brought him to this glorious threshold to his life's goal.

But not as he had expected. He had always assumed he would begin as a secondary member of a company and perhaps, if he were lucky, the partner to some promising ballerina. But his dreams never conceived of the incredible strides he would make in the past year and a half when, through the generosity and kindness of a patron of the arts, he had been allowed to dedicate himself full-time to his development as a dancer. It was the merging of two parallel channels in his life: his marriage to Irina and the joy and contentment they shared, and his relationship with Kúbokoff, now as much father as teacher, instilling in his eager protégé the knowledge and insights acquired in a lifetime of performing and teaching.

Paul had digested every morsel of Kúbokoff's instruction, taking ownership of it, and with it the heir's responsibility to use this new treasure to reach new heights, both figuratively and literally, for Paul's physical maturity had invested him with the astonishing ability to leap higher and remain in the air longer than any other dancer on record.

445

When he leaped, he soared, boasted Kúbokoff to reporters, recounting Paul's first attempt in Kúbokoff's studio.

As the curtains opened to the final strains of the overture, and the dim claylike faces of the spellbound audience came into view, Paul remembered the unexplainable urge he had felt that afternoon three years earlier in the studio, the urge to dance, to express through the movement and posturing of his body the feelings deep within him that he could express in no other way. From that primitive yearning he had labored and suffered to reach this moment, to reach this stage. If this was his destiny, he would not forsake it. He was ready.

The overture ended. The conductor paused, arms up, baton frozen in midair, the object of each musician's attention. The baton twitched, the arm fell, and the opening chord thundered into the spacious hall.

Paul whirled and posed, performing a smooth harmonious enchainment of classical steps vividly expressed and faultlessly executed with vigorous pas de ciseaux mixed with light gliding pas de bourree and gargouillades...all of it controlled, exact, continuous, interconnected, flowing from step to step with flamboyant style and striking aplomb. He circled the stage with a series of flashing sissonnes tombee, building artistic and physical momentum for the leap which was a famous part of this classic piece...to many the ultimate test of a male dancer's prowess. The music rolled on, building, rising, escalating to a throbbing crescendo. He took four short lead-off steps and launched himself with all his might toward the heavens in perfect form...head up, chest out, arms spread, fingers gracefully curled, legs widely split leading with the right. He was airborne two full seconds, covering more than twenty feet, and his head reached eleven feet above the floor. The audience gasped and, letting loose a roar, rose en masse to its feet.

The shock wave of their ovation nearly broke Paul's concentration, reminding him for a split second of the riotous crowd at The Voyeur. But that was a bygone memory. He had risen above and beyond that episode. Here on this stage was where he belonged, fulfilling his destiny before an adoring crowd. The shock passed, burying the memory, as Paul attacked the remainder of his routine with the power and daring of a Dandelion warrior. Awestruck, the audience remained on its feet till the end, when Paul stepped proudly to the footlights to receive a tumultuous ovation, his

446

face aglow with the joy of one who has found his place in this world. The crowd stood for five minutes of continuous applause, demanding Paul take a dozen curtain calls.

When he made his final bow and retreated behind the curtain, he was gleefully mobbed by the people whom he now considered his family: Irina and her aunt, his mother, Kúbokoff and his wife, Kelly and Helena, and Diego, whose involvement in the family's activities had made his mother happier and more content than Paul had ever seen her. Amid hugs, kisses, and handshakes the group pushed through the crowd of well-wishers and found sanctuary in his dressing room.

When the door closed, Paul shouted, "Listen everyone! I have something to say."

They quieted, gathering around him with unspoken admiration for the wonder of his talent.

"I would not be in this room tonight, if it hadn't been for the love and support of everyone here." He looked into each person's eyes. "God gives talent to lots of people. In most cases it's wasted and for all kinds of reasons, most of which aren't anyone's fault. It just doesn't pan out. My case was different. I was lucky. First, I had a fantastic mother who cared. From the very beginning she encouraged my interest in dance. She lied for me, deceived my father for me, got money for my lessons, shielded me from his dirty scheming, propped me up when I needed it most, and..." Tears showed in his eyes. "...and loved me when I needed a parent's love."

"And you, Irina!" he continued, pushing aside his emotion. "You gave me the inspiration, the will to sacrifice my body. And oh..." He moaned playfully as the others laughed. "...how I sacrificed! Those sore muscles you massaged back to health, on their behalf I thank you."

"And thanks to the Barnabys. Helena. Kelly. You stood like Gibraltar behind my mother through all her troubles. Without your support she would have crumbled, like the song says, and I'd have gone with her, and this day would never have come."

"And I owe a special thanks to you, Diego, for the moral support you've given her." Eleanor blushed slightly and eyed the floor, embarrassed that her closeness to Diego and by implication their private intimacy had been so apparent. "Also for the strength and leadership you've provided to all of us, as we struggled through the mess my father left. We're all very glad you're here."

"Thank you, Paul," said Diego. He was standing beside Eleanor and took hold of her hand. "Those are warm and most welcome words."

"And most of all, thanks to you, Alexéi Nikoláyevich. Where would I be without you? My dearest friend. My teacher. My master."

"*Dorogoy!*" cried Kúbokoff. He stepped forward and hugged his student manfully. "You are one in million. But it is I who t'anks you. I put my visdom in your brain. Now I live again in you. V'en you dance, I dance. God never gave anyone such a gift as you have given me. Bless you."

"There is," said Paul, "another person to thank who is not here. Madame Vigroff, without whose financial support I would never have had the chance to train and develop. Ballet as you all know requires total dedication. Without her grant of money we wouldn't be here. I'm sorry to say, I've never met her. She prefers to keep her distance. She may have been, probably was, in the audience tonight. I hope so. And at our dinner to celebrate this marvelous occasion, we will toast her health...and, of course, her wealth!"

While they all laughed and Paul excused himself to shower and dress for the evening's celebration, there was a knock on the door. Eleanor was nearest and opened it. A young man handed her an oblong box.

"They arrived during the show," he said.

Eleanor thanked him, closed the door, and opened the box, which contained a dozen gorgeous red roses and a card, which she picked out and read.

Paul,

So what's a hunk like you doing in a ballet? The tips are lousy and the dames can only dream what you look like in a jock. If they don't give you ten curtains, they don't deserve you. Just remember, you've always got a dressing room at The Voyeur with a star and your name on it!

Break a leg!
Love,
Kate

448

Eleanor grinned. "Look, Diego. It's from Kate, the manager of The Voyeur, that nightspot where Paul...uh...danced. He speaks fondly of her. She comes across as a tough old bird, but she's kind and warmhearted underneath. He'll be so pleased to know she remembered him."

"That's great," replied Diego. "And so are you."

Their eyes locked together, and they shared a silent moment while the others in the room chattered away loudly in the background.

"I have such mixed feelings tonight," she confided. "I'm overjoyed at Paul's triumph. He's a sensation and so deserving of it after the sacrifices he's had to make. I won't worry about him anymore. He's on his way now, and a whole career lies ahead of him. A new life filled with excitement and promise and fulfillment. But for me...tomorrow." Her voiced trailed off. "I have this awful foreboding about the hearing. Diego, isn't there something we can do? Some legal technicality we can use."

"Eleanor, please don't look for miracles. We've been over this many times. We've done everything that is doable. Everything! It's now in the hands of the lawyers and the court. Without your control over D-M we can't make the kinds of financial deals that could save the company. If we controlled D-M's assets—if they were free of judicial oversight—we'd have no trouble getting a loan to carry us over till the Heathrow contract is sealed. We've come back a long way. We've stemmed the exodus of clients, and we're on the verge of recovery. We're that close!" He held up his hand describing the distance between his thumb and forefinger. "Holly did everything he could to convince the judge to deny the Chapter Seven motion, but the court was unimpressed. The judge said our business is too changeable, too unpredictable. He was totally intransigent."

"Then it's over," she said with a desolate tone of defeat.

"Not till we see what happens at the hearing. Holly will appeal for a Chapter Eleven. I've explained all that to you."

"Yes, and you said the outlook is grim."

"I was only being truthful. No sense kidding ourselves. Look, Eleanor, we gave it one heck of a shot. It's just that Brock stacked the cards too high against us. But after all, it isn't the end of the world."

"It's the end of mine! Tomorrow the judge will declare D-M financially unsound and remand D-M to the Bankruptcy Court. Isn't that what you said would happen?"

"Probably." Then sadly, hanging his head to avoid her eyes, "Yes."

"Everything I have—my home, my car, my jewelry, my furniture, my paintings—will be auctioned off. Brock saw to that. I think he knew this would happen. It was all part of his crazy scheme. If only I had divorced him years ago, I could have won a fair settlement. But I was too sanctimonious, too faithful to vows that meant nothing to him. And look what I'll get for it. The home I've lived in for…" Her bitterness gave way to self-pity, and she turned away to hide her face. "I know I sound selfish, when so much more is at stake…D-M, the employees, all that."

Diego took her by the shoulders and turned her around, hugging her to him. "I know what you're feeling," he said, pressing his cheek against hers.

"It's just that I'll be dispossessed of everything I used to think was mine when, in fact, I never really owned it. I've never owned any of it. It was all an illusion, a deception by Brock. He knew all along exactly what he was doing."

"You're not alone, Eleanor," he said quietly. "You have friends."

"To pity me? Give me charity? You know I can't tolerate that. I'm too proud. I have to learn to fend for myself."

Her comment evoked the same thought for both of them. Since they had acknowledged their mutual feelings, they had discussed many times the subject of marriage. Both saw the dangers of moving too swiftly to formalize their relationship. They really didn't know each other well. Their initial contact sixteen years ago had been brief and superficial, and much had happened to each of them in the intervening period. They had to be sure their feelings for each other were genuine and not simply a revival, a reliving of an infatuation they shared in the distant past. Because both had experienced the pain of an unhappy marriage and of years of loneliness, they could unconsciously be using each other now as a kind of life preserver, a convenient cure-all. In short, they both mistrusted their feelings, not quite able to accept the fact that they were truly deeply in love. They needed time and frequent close association to assure each other that their love was real and that their relationship would endure. If they eventually married, so be it. But they were in no rush to matrimony.

"Maybe I'll start my own business," said Eleanor, still in Diego's embrace.

Kelly joined them. "That's my girl!" he said jovially. "Come out fighting!" He had watched her from across the room and recognized her depression. "No matter what the court decides tomorrow, you'll come through this thing okay. You'll survive. Look what you've been through up to now. You'll make it because we'll all be behind you every step of the way."

Helena appeared, taking Eleanor's hand. "You bet we will," she declared. "All of us love you, and that's what counts in the end."

Paul came out of his dressing room in suit and tie ready for the dinner party. He spied the downcast look on his mother's face and guessed its reason. He addressed her cheerfully. "This is no time for a sourpuss! Brighten up, woman! Rejoice! Your only son has this night conquered the kingdom of ballet, which he lays at your feet." He knelt on one knee and grandly kissed her hand with a graceful flourish only a ballet star could give such a simple act. "Fair lady! Wilst thou accompany me to yon dining hall, where 'tis reported gay festivities await thee?"

Eleanor forced a smile and looked down at her son through loving tears. "I love you, Paul."

He got up and hugged her tightly. "I love you, too, Mother. Let's go celebrate, and no more of this gloom stuff about tomorrow."

"Ooráh!" shouted Kúbokoff. "And I vill toast you a hundred toasts till all but one of us is...ne *soznayushchee.*"

"What's he saying?" asked Diego.

"Unconscious," said Mrs. Kúbokoff, grimacing, as the group followed Paul out the door laughing and talking. But each of them was privately worried about the next day's hearing, a dread that stayed with them through the evening like an unwanted guest hovering nearby in the shadow cast upon their merrymaking by the hateful memory of Brock...the architect of Eleanor's and D-M's financial ruin.

The formal oak-paneled hearing room had a funereal atmosphere about it. Dreary brown floor-to-ceiling drapes over large windows shut out most of the light from outside, where the drizzly gray weather had collaborated to set a depressing atmosphere in which the black-robed justice, seated behind a raised platform, would proclaim the demise of DESIGN METAPHORS. His gray hair and wizened countenance suggested he had presided over many such hearings, but they gave no hint of his fairness or grasp of the tangled legal issues in question whose interpretation would decide D-M's fate, and Eleanor's with it.

His riffling of the legal documents he was reading was the only distinct noise in the otherwise silent room. Eleanor, ever the picture of class and dignity in her brown suit and suede pumps, sat sullenly at a long wide highly polished oak table in front of the judge's dais. She was mentally removed from the proceedings and resigned to the fateful denouement over which no one she could call friend had any influence. The bitterness and self-pity she had felt so intensely the evening before had worn off overnight, leaving only a flat indistinct tension. She was blank. Numb. Psychiatrists would describe her condition as withdrawn, mentally coiled in a self-protective fetal position shielded by a benign aloofness.

Gordon Holly, seated beside her, was not fooled. His familiarity with her personality and behavior penetrated her blank facade with X-ray precision and sensed her fearful desolation. What his intellect perceived was a proud, beautiful, middle-aged woman abandoned by her husband and condemned by him during the past twenty-one months to watch helplessly while the forces he had set in motion gradually decomposed her estate and her way of life. Holly placed his hand over hers and squeezed ever so gently. *Dear woman,* he thought, *what did you ever do to merit so unworthy a fate?* Her empty eyes remained fixed on some distant invisible object or thought. He could almost feel her withdrawing further into herself.

"Eleanor!" he said softly but sharply. "Snap out of it! I won't have you escape from reality this way. It isn't like you, nor is it fair to you or your friends and family. But more important is that, if you give into despondency and melancholy, you concede victory to the cretin who did this to you. Do you concede him the winner? Do you? Is that what this is about? He trashes your marriage and the vows that made it sacred. He steals your equity in his fortune, which he amassed while you stood loyally by, caring for his children and preserving his public image as a respectable provider and family man. He may have won the battle financially, that's true. We ran out of time and options. But he doesn't have to win the moral victory as well. Morality is on your side, if you seize it, and you do that by spitting in his eye, by proclaiming that he may have stolen your tangible assets but never your spirit, never your self-respect. As long as you live, you must never concede him those intangibles. They are priceless...worth a million times more than the material assets he's deprived you of. You can lose those intangibles only if you give them away. Is that what you're doing? Just giving them away? Just handing them over without a fight or a struggle?"

Eleanor placed her other hand on top of Holly's and turned to face him with clear comprehending eyes. The suddenness of her recomposure startled him.

"You're right," she said, smiling. "I'll never surrender those precious intangibles. They're my most sacred possessions. Thank you for reminding me. They are what's kept me going all these years. I can't abandon them now, can I? I'll never give them up!"

Holly felt like grinning, pleased to see that familiar fire in her eyes, but it was not his style to show emotion in court. Instead he nodded soberly. "That's more like it."

The judge cleared his throat, at which signal the small group of spectators—Paul, Irina, Diego, Kelly, Helena, and Holly's wife—on benches at the rear of the room alertly straightened up and cut off their muted conversations. "The court has reviewed the depositions, declarations, and affidavits and is prepared to hear the plaintiffs' arguments for liquidation of DESIGN METAPHORS. You may proceed."

One of the three attorneys seated at the other end of the table from Holly and Eleanor rose and addressed the judge in a slow ponderous voice. "Your Honor, the plaintiffs contend that the business enterprise known as DESIGN METAPHORS..."

Holly listened as the lawyer entered into a lengthy circuitous discourse on D-M's faltering fortunes. Holly leaned over and whispered in Eleanor's ear. "Get comfortable. This is going to take awhile."

She was about to reply when a motion behind her caught her attention. It was Maggie, harried and breathless, peering around the half-opened door to the hallway looking for Eleanor. As their eyes met,

Maggie frantically beckoned Eleanor to come outside. The thin, white-haired, sixty-year-old secretary—D-M's oldest and most loyal employee—had gained a little weight since she was hired by Brock thirty years ago but had not lost the spunky grit and indomitable stamina that made her the revered grande dame of the firm. She had retained that special look of elegance that had captured Brock's fancy the day she interviewed for the job, the look that had personified the high style and prestige of the company he sought to build.

"Excuse me, Gordon," Eleanor whispered. "Maggie's here and wants to see me. The way my luck's been running, my house has probably burned down."

Holly grinned at her humor but maintained his formal demeanor. "Go see what she wants. I'll hold down the fort."

While the other attorney droned on, Eleanor left her chair, slipped behind Holly's and tiptoed down the marble aisle to the door, where she was met by Diego who held it open for her. He had seen Maggie signaling her. Outside in the hallway they found Maggie waving a paper note.

"What is it?" asked Eleanor.

"I'm sorry to barge in, but a priest phoned the office and said it was absolutely urgent that he speak with you right away. I told him you were in court, but he said I was to find you immediately and have you phone him."

"Did he say what it's about?" asked Diego.

"No. I asked him, but he wouldn't say."

Maggie handed Eleanor the note, which she read aloud while Diego looked over her shoulder. "Father Deaver, Bishop Merrindon's residence." A phone number was written at the bottom. She looked up at Maggie. "Who's Father Deaver?"

"I don't know."

Diego spoke. "Merrindon is the Catholic bishop of the San Francisco Diocese."

"Yes," said Eleanor. "I've seen him on TV a couple of times. Well, I guess I better call."

She retrieved a cell phone from her purse. "What could be so urgent? Maybe the bishop heard about the hearing and decided to excommunicate me for marrying such a heathen." The number was ringing. "Or maybe he's excommunicating Brock!"

Her two companions smiled but stayed close by, sensing in the priest's summons a real emergency.

"Bishop Merrindon's residence," said a young man's voice. "Deacon Hewitt speaking. How may I help you?"

Eleanor introduced herself and explained the purpose of her call.

"Yes, I know, Mrs. Stowolski. Father Deaver is expecting your call. Please hold."

There was silence on the other end and then the heavy rumbling voice of a much older man. "Mrs. Stowolski?"

"Yes. Are you Father Deaver?"

"I am, and thank you for returning my call. I realize this is a bit unusual, reaching you in court this way. I hope I didn't upset the proceedings."

"That's quite all right, Father," impatient with his small talk. "What is it you wanted?"

"Well, that's pretty unusual, too. Are you in good health, Mrs. Stowolski?"

"Yes, very. Why?" She was puzzled.

"Is someone with you there?"

"Yes. Two close friends standing right next to me."

"Good. Because the news I have for you is quite shocking. It concerns your husband."

"Brock?"

Maggie and Diego, intrigued, drew close to her at the mention of that infamous name, and Eleanor, alarmed, unconsciously seized Diego's hand and held it tightly.

"He's been found," said the priest.

"Alive?"

The voice hesitated and replied, "No, ma'am. I'm very sorry. Your husband is deceased."

"Thank God! You have proof of that?"

Baffled by her insensitivity, he stated boldly, "Incontrovertible."

"Oh, my God!" she cried. "Thank God! Thank God!"

The priest was dumbfounded by her reaction. "Are you all right, Mrs. Stowolski?"

"It's a gift from heaven, Father. The answer to my prayers."

Overwhelmed, she lowered the phone and began to cry, blindly clutching Maggie and Diego to her breast. While Diego grabbed for the phone with a free hand, Eleanor sobbed and shook, overcome by relief and joy and an odd mixture of remorse and guilt. A hundred thousand times she had wished Brock dead these many months, but now the realization of that prayer brought ironic twisted satisfaction.

"Hello?" said Diego into the phone. "Father Deaver?"

"Yes, what's happening? Who is this?"

"I'm a close friend of Mrs. Stowolski. She's been under a terrible strain. She can't talk right now. I take it that her husband has been found."

"That is correct, but he is not alive."

"Oh, I see." Stunned, Diego paused to collect his thoughts. "Could you give me some details? Better yet, let me get her lawyer. He should hear this directly. It bears mightily on the legal proceedings going on this very moment."

While Maggie walked Eleanor to a wooden bench nearby and sat down with her, Diego ran into the hearing room and summoned Holly, who hurried to the phone after gaining a brief intermission from the judge. Holly listened intently to the priest's report, asking questions now and then to clarify points of information. Finally, after arranging to meet at the bishop's residence that evening when more information would be available, he hung up and ushered Eleanor, who had by then recovered from her shock, back into the hearing to the curious anxious looks of her family.

Holly stood before the judge. "Your Honor, we have just received an important message from Bishop Merrindon of the Catholic Diocese of San Francisco that bears mightily on this proceeding. An official representative of the Hawaiian Islands has advised the bishop that a dead body confirmed to be that of Brock Stowolski, husband of my client, was found five days ago on a small island in the Pacific."

A muted outcry burst from the covey of spectators, to which Eleanor turned about and directed a contented, not quite victorious look at her friends, whose expressions showed a mixture of surprise, joy, and uncertainty as to what import this shocking news would have.

456

Holly continued. "Although the circumstances and the cause of his death are still being investigated, there is no question, Your Honor, that my client's husband is deceased. We therefore submit that the basis for this hearing is no longer valid and that dissolution is in order."

Holly sat down and awaited the judge's ruling.

The judge reflected silently for a few seconds on what Holly had said, then spoke. "Given this information, the court will seek to verify the death of Brock Stowolski. This hearing is therefore adjourned until such verification has been established." He banged his gavel on the table and got up and left the courtroom. The plaintiff's attorneys eyed each other, shrugged, and left the courtroom, looking back resentfully at the celebration of the defendants.

Eleanor no sooner rose from her chair than she was engulfed in the joyous embrace of Paul and Helena. The others circled the couple in uncontained jubilation. The monster was dead. The source and mastermind of the family's prolonged suffering had at long last been summoned by his maker to face final judgment.

Kelly spoke for all of them. "May he burn in hell for all eternity or at least until he's paid his debt."

"If there's any justice in heaven," swore Diego.

Paul kissed his mother's cheek and turned excitedly to Holly. "It's over then, isn't it? Isn't that what this means?"

The lawyer's sturdy aristocratic face remained as solemn and implacable as when he had addressed the judge. "I'm afraid nothing is as simple or as good as it first sounds in this business."

Paul's expression darkened. "You mean this is a setback? That somehow my father's death complicates matters?"

"It could, but let's save that interpretation for later. Listen, everyone! I've scheduled a meeting this evening at eight o'clock at Bishop Merrindon's residence to learn more about Brock's death and to read his will. I think the reading will answer many of your questions about where this takes us. I have some things to do in the meantime, so I'll meet all of you at the bishop's at eight."

He gave them the directions Father Deaver had given him, and they left, bewildered by the long-awaited news of Brock's demise and the new uncertainties it apparently raised. Everyone had questions, beginning with

Brock's connection with the bishop, and looked to the meeting at the latter's residence as a time for resolving mysteries and hopefully healing wounds. But Holly's parting words had not been encouraging.

Gordon Holly sat uncomfortably in the chair next to Father Deaver's in a good-sized sitting room in the bishop's residence, a three-story yellow stucco building with red terra-cotta roof tiles.

"First," said the somewhat overweight priest in a soothing basso profundo, "I would like to thank Mr. Holly for arranging this meeting on such short notice." His visitors studied the priest, whom they variously judged by his thinning black hair and lined face to be between forty and fifty years old. He wore a tight-fitting black blazer and black vest with a white collar. "I know the report of Mr. Stowolski's death has left you all in a quandary. I think I can shed some light on the circumstances of his death but...I must confess..." He shook his head despairingly. "Some things about it will probably never be understood. Even now Vatican representatives are rushing to the island to join the investigation already underway."

"What island?" asked Paul, perplexed like the others by the mounting mystery. "And what does his death have to do with the Vatican?"

Holly intervened. "Why don't we hold all our questions till Father Deaver has told us what he can?"

"Yes," agreed the priest. "It's quite a story, and I have some remarkable slides to show you." He pointed to a projector behind him; then he sat back heavily, inhaling deeply as if storing up air for a long delivery. "Let me preface my remarks by stating on behalf of the bishop, who incidentally is flying to Hawaii this very moment to meet with civil authorities and church members there, that we have at this point no official explanation for the events that occurred on the island. None whatsoever."

Father Deaver took a small red notebook from his coat, which strained against the movements of his portly figure. He perused the pages of the notebook through his bifocals to refresh his memory. "On April

458

14th of last year Brock Stowolski, as all of you know, slipped away unnoticed from his hospital room in the dark of night, walked or taxied to the marina a short distance away where he kept his boat, and sailed out into the Pacific in a heavy storm. Where he was headed, we don't know. We do know where he ended up. A tiny uninhabited island five hundred miles south of Hawaii and three thousand miles from the California coast."

The group, hanging on every word, gasped.

"Let me run down what else is known and unknown. We can then speculate on explanations. We know to begin with that Brock was terminally ill with cancer, which had infiltrated his entire body, and that he was not expected to live more than a week, possibly less. We know that he died on the island five days ago...December 13th...twenty months later!...and that his body—"

The group came alive with questions.

"Please, please, everyone!" cried Holly, waving his hands up and down. "Let Father Deaver finish. Then we can ask questions."

"Thank you, Gordon," said the priest. "As I was saying, we know he died five days ago, which is twenty months after he left the hospital, and that he showed none—I repeat, none—of the visible signs of the disease that, according to doctors at the hospital, had ravaged and swollen parts of his body. We know that he built a magnificent chapel on the island during those months."

The group, enthralled by his monologue, held absolutely still, barely breathing.

"We know that he used the mast from his boat as the cross above the altar in the chapel and that the mast was split from top to bottom and charred, as if struck by lightning. He secured a pulley to each end of the crosspiece at the top of the mast and ran ropes through them tied to two large bags filled with sand. One can only speculate—and I will directly—on the purpose of this contrivance. We know he manufactured beautiful stained-glass windows for the chapel. How he did this, like everything about the island, remains a mystery so far. Finally, we know he died only minutes before his body was discovered. We do not know the cause of death. At the moment he gave up his spirit, he was in the chapel, wearing a monk's hooded habit. We don't know where he got it. He was lying prone with his feet together, arms spread-eagled, head toward the altar—the traditional position of supplicants during the sacrament of ordination to the priesthood. The fact that he was once a seminarian enhances the intriguing implications that can be drawn from the dramatic and peculiar setting of his death. It goes without saying that a full-scale investigation by the Vatican is underway to obtain facts that will unravel the mysteries surrounding these unusual events. As far as we know, he left no written record that would explain these bizarre circumstances.

"These revelations began when a small Japanese merchant ship en route to Hawaii from Tokyo navigated a southern course to avoid a severe storm and passed a few miles north of the island. A seaman, casually viewing the island through binoculars, made out the unexpected presence of the chapel. The ship's captain altered course, anchored nearby, and sent three crewmen ashore, one with a camera, to investigate. The slides I will now show you are copies of those taken by a crewman. They were flown here this morning. Why don't you turn your chairs around to face the screen."

The group did as he asked, then waited in rapt silence while he got up from his chair, turned off all but one of several table lamps, and switched on the projector, which illuminated a screen on the opposite wall. It showed a brightly colored photograph of the island taken from the merchant ship's launch as it approached the promontory. Eleanor, Paul, and the others were entranced by the beautiful sight of the chapel on a hill at the center of the island.

"You mean my father's been on that island all this time?" said Paul, his disbelief tinged with anger. "While Mother's been suffering through the hell he left her in, he's been taking life easy in the South Pacific?"

Father Deaver's deep voice answered calmly and deliberately. "I don't believe I made clear to you the full nature of what has occurred on that island or perhaps earlier on your father's journey to it. You see, it seems that he was cured of his cancer."

"Cured?" repeated Eleanor. "How?"

"We don't know yet. We may never know. His body is being held in a freezing compartment aboard a U.S. Navy ship pending your authorization to perform an autopsy to determine the cause of death. The ship's doctor reported that a preliminary examination revealed no sign of

460

disease whatever. Certainly no external evidence of cancer. The doctor describes the deceased as appearing in the bloom of health."

"What's the Navy doing there?" asked Kelly.

"I'll explain momentarily. Let me show you what the Japanese ship's landing party found."

The priest ran through the slides. A shot of the chapel from the beach. A closer rather artistic view of the chapel through the palm trees showing the entrance and the presence of stained-glass windows on the two walls visible. A shot of the interior of the nave showed the altar with the lower half of the split mast-cross in the background. A close-up side view of the mast-cross showed the ropes dangling from the two pulleys on the spreaders. Another photo showed the two sail bags full of sand at the base of the mast. And then, to the breathless silence of the onlookers, the next slide showed Brock pronated before the altar, his forehead pressed against the mosaic floor, his face barely recognizable behind the twenty-month growth of beard.

Eleanor gasped. "I don't understand. What's going on?" She began to weep, but no one moved to comfort her, so captivated were they by this eerie photograph of Brock's dead body.

"Is that Mr. B?" asked Maggie. "It doesn't look like him."

Eleanor confirmed the identity. "Yes, Maggie, it's him. It's Brock."

"He looks so healthy and alive," said Helena.

"He died only minutes before this picture was taken," Father Deaver explained. "The body was still warm. The crewmen, apparently frightened by the sight of Brock's body, sped back to their ship to report their amazing discovery. Thankfully they were so awed...and deeply superstitious, I might add...that they disturbed nothing except the sand they walked on. The ship's captain was fortunately an intelligent man and guessed at once the possible importance of their find. He radioed Hawaii and passed a message to the U.S. Coast Guard, which alerted the Navy. Several U.S. Navy ships maneuvering in the vicinity were diverted to guard the island against looting. Within hours they had more or less cordoned off the area, while word of the discovery made its way up through the chain of command. A tight lid has been placed on the story, because the Navy fears, if word gets out, an armada of sightseers and reporters and religious people will descend on the island. The ships there lack the means to control such an onslaught, although additional military forces are being deployed to assist."

"Was it then that the Church was brought in?" asked Holly.

"Yes. In fact, it was Brock's clothing and Catholic Bible that triggered the decision by Hawaiian authorities to contact the Church."

"His Bible?" said Paul.

"Oh, yes, I forgot. The landing party did take back one thing with them to the ship. His Bible. You can see it in the shot of the altar." The priest reversed the sequence of slides and displayed the altar. Brock's light-blue Bible could be plainly seen resting between the two flameless candles. "There's an inscription inside the cover to Brock Stowolski from Father Leonard daVinci of St. Charles Seminary. Under the circumstances and given the evidence at hand, the Coast Guard logically concluded that Brock was a Catholic priest. They conferred with Hawaiian authorities, who informed Church officials in Honolulu, who immediately made inquiries and determined that Brock was not a priest, but that Father Leonard was...that is, he *is* a priest. He was contacted this morning at his residence at Notre Dame University and is departing for Honolulu on the first available flight."

Eleanor spoke up. "We know Father Leonard. He was a friend of Brock's at the seminary. He came to see me a few days before Brock fell ill."

The priest nodded. "Meanwhile, a fast oceangoing Coast Guard cruiser set out for the island carrying several technical specialists from the University of Hawaii including a marine biologist, a medical scientist, and a Catholic priest on sabbatical. They reached the island last night and have since telephoned us several reports which are the basis for most of what I'm telling you."

"How did you get the slides so quickly?" asked Holly.

"The same Coast Guard cutter out of Hawaii raced to the island shortly after the captain of the Japanese ship radioed his discovery. The crew surveyed the island, interviewed the ship's captain and his crew, and returned to Honolulu with the undeveloped film. The film was developed and copies were flown to San Francisco. We got the slides shortly before I spoke with you this afternoon."

Holly stroked his chin. "Show us the outside of the chapel again, if you please."

"Certainly." Father Deaver clicked back through the slides till the photo of the chapel was on the screen.

"Could he really have built a structure that size and complex all by himself?" asked Holly skeptically. "He must have had help. That would explain the absence of tools and other things, would it not?"

"Perhaps," replied the priest reservedly. "That would be a logical explanation...until one poses the consequent questions. I've been giving the matter a good deal of thought. For example, it is extremely unlikely that the deceased planned in advance to rendezvous on the island with someone. He was dying and knew it. He almost certainly believed that death was imminent when he slipped away from the hospital, his ostensible purpose being to die at sea rather than in a hospital bed."

Holly interrupted. "That's a presumption, of course."

"True enough. We really don't know. And I hasten to add that these are my own personal views and not those of the Church. The Church will withhold all official comment until the full report of the investigating team has been thoroughly studied by experts in Rome. But back to what I think. I believe one can rule out the notion that Brock ever intended to go to that island, if he even knew it existed. You may recall there was a severe storm in the middle Pacific at that time lasting more than a week. In all likelihood the storm, not Brock's hand on the tiller, deposited him and his boat on the island."

Holly nodded. "A fair and logical conclusion, but then there could have been others on the island when he arrived, or they could have come later. Strangers there by coincidence and happenstance. He was there for twenty months."

"Exactly," said Father Deaver. "Then the questions are who were they and why have they not come forward to proclaim their achievement and Brock's cure?Here it is difficult to assign motives for keeping silent. But not just silent...secretive. Like master burglars, they left no evidence, no trace. Only footprints in the sand.

"Then we return to the question of motive for keeping the chapel secret. Why not tell the world? What they allegedly did was not illegal or immoral. They were not trespassing. Of course, they could have been fugitives from the law, but now we're stretching plausibility."

"How big is the chapel?" asked Kelly.

"Forty feet high at its center and about eighty feet in diameter. It's in the shape of a hexagon."

"That's a large building!" observed Diego. "Is it possible Brock erected it by himself?"

"Why not?" said Kelly. "He's done the improbable all his life."

"Indeed," said the priest, continuing. "It's a magnificent structure, a work of art, an achievement worth telling the world about. One explanation is that Brock asked his helpers not to tell anyone. In that case he wished his presence on the island and his miraculous cure to remain a secret, at least until someone stumbled onto it, as the Japanese merchantman did. But here again the thread of logic unravels. If he knew, as he must have, that eventually the chapel and his presence there would become known, why keep it a secret? If he truly wished to hide his identity, why leave his Bible with his name in it where it would surely be found? Oh, the questions go on and on without end and without satisfactory answers. Who were these alleged helpers? Sailors? Vacationers? Fishermen? Natives from some Polynesian island? Even if they agreed not to speak of their experience, how long would they remain silent? A secret that momentous tears at the human conscience to be set free."

"Pardon me, Father," interjected Kelly. "You said 'miraculous cure' a moment ago. Was that just a figure of speech or are you saying that Brock was cured by divine intervention? an actual miracle?"

"My personal belief? Again I'm not speaking for the Catholic Church. Yes, a bona fide miracle. A real live one like in the Bible." The priest picked up a black-bound Bible from the table beside him, opened it at a red ribbon to Matthew, and read aloud. "'And behold, a leper came up and worshipped Him, saying, Lord, if Thou wilt, Thou canst make me clean. And stretching forth His hand, Jesus touched him, saying, I will. Be thou clean. And immediately his leprosy was cleansed. And Jesus said to him, see thou tell no one, but go show thyself to the priest and offer the gift that Moses commanded for a witness to them.'"

"If that is what happened," offered Holly, "if he was cured miraculously, then it's possible, if he took that biblical passage as a guide, that he did indeed wish to keep it secret. 'Tell no one,' said Jesus. Brock

464

may have sworn the alleged helpers to silence about the miracle."

"Very good," said the priest, nodding. "I can accept that, but that is not my own interpretation. I believe Brock was cured through God's intercession and that the operative phrase which applies from the testament I just read you is 'offer the gift...as a witness.' In other words Brock single-handedly built the chapel as a venerable gift to God, an act of contrition, an offer of thanks and more importantly a witness, a testament, a proof, a monument to his cure."

"What evidence is there to support your interpretation?" asked Holly. "I grant you it's logical, even compelling under the circumstances, but is there more?"

"You're perceptive or intuitive, Gordon. Yes, you're right. I do have more, and I didn't mean to purposely hide it from you. I was coming to it, but your questions simply got ahead of my recitation. The evidence is found, I believe, in the stained-glass window over the altar."

As he clicked rapidly through the slides the group had already seen, he said, "The Japanese crewmen photographed only one of the windows, apparently frightened and wanting to return as fast as possible to their ship. Here is the window above the altar." The resplendent beauty of the window evoked an immediate *oooh* from the group. It depicted the mast being rent by a blazing bolt of lightning against a dark rich blue background whose deep color intensified the light-greenish glow that encased the mast. Around the curved bottom edge of the window were inscribed two biblical phrases: "BE MADE CLEAN" and "THY SINS ARE FORGIVEN."

"The quotations," said the priest, "are from Mark. You see, the erection of the chapel shows that Brock experienced a deeply religious event. The biblical quotations confirm it, and the window recounts it pictorially."

"So," questioned Paul, "the lightning struck the mast and that cured Dad's cancer?"

"Not exactly," replied the priest. "I believe the lightning struck your father."

"What? But how? I don't get it."

"Your father was at the top of the mast. You see, he tried to crucify himself."

"He did what?" exclaimed Eleanor in disbelief. "What are you saying? Put himself to death on the mast...on a cross...like Christ?" The idea of Brock conceiving of such an extremely religious self-sacrificing act of contrition was preposterous. "Brock?" She shook her head fiercely. "Never! You're saying that faced with his sentence of death by cancer, he hopped in his boat and sailed to this island to crucify himself? Father, please! You don't know Brock Stowolski!"

Undeterred the priest replied, "You are right, Eleanor. I did not know your husband. I gather from all I've been told that he was a selfish, cruel man. But I ask you with deep humility and respect if you know the man who labored twenty months to build that chapel? Do you know the man that made that window with its biblical inscriptions? Do you know the man who prostrated himself before God's altar and gave up his spirit so calmly and trustingly? Do you know him, Eleanor? I am glad, Eleanor, that I never met your Brock Stowolski." His eyes filled with tears and his lips quavered. "But I wish to God I had known the man who raised himself upon a cross on that island and was saved by our heavenly Father. I wish I had known him." He halted, unable for the moment to continue. The priest's outburst put Eleanor in a quandary. How was it possible that the man she and her loved ones had come to hate was revered by the priest. She was stunned into stony silence.

Father Deaver wiped his eyes and continued. "We cannot fathom the depth of God's mercy or the capacity of the human soul to redeem itself. Nor can we underestimate God's power. Man seeks redemption...and punishment as well...for his sins. God forgives sins and does so mercifully and in His own way."

Eleanor bowed her head and wept, as did every person in the room, which held a reverent soul-searching prayerful silence for several minutes.

Then Father Deaver resumed in a clear and steady voice. "There are two other things about the island that reinforce my conviction that a miracle occurred there. I'm sure believers and nonbelievers will be arguing over them for years to come, but not I. They are too surprising, compelling, and unexplainable to brush aside as pure accident. The first is the shape of the island. The Navy took aerial photographs of the island soon after the initial report of the chapel's presence there reached Pacific

466

Fleet headquarters in Hawaii. Those pictures were then compared with aerial shots taken a number of years ago as part of an oceanographic study. The new photos showed that seaweed around the island had grown into the sharp, unmistakable shape of a fish. Skeptical marine scientists in Hawaii have passed it off as a meaningless one-in-a-million natural phenomenon. But to believers like me it is the unmistakable sign of Jesus' presence."

Eleanor nodded. "You're referring to the sign of the fish that early Christians used to signify their religion and faith in Jesus."

"Exactly. The letters of the ancient Greek word for fish...IChThYS...formed the acronym for 'Jesus Christ, God, the Only One, Deliverer.'"

Paul was intrigued. "And the seaweed actually forms this fish shape?"

"Indeed it does."

"What was the other thing?" Paul asked.

"Fish bones." The priest, enjoying himself, smiled at the perplexed looks on the faces of his guests. "The floor of the lagoon at one end of the island is littered with fish bones. Ichthyologists at the University of Hawaii have determined they are all from the same species. They apparently were what kept Brock alive those many months."

"I don't understand," said Holly. "Fish are fish. What's so miraculous about it?"

"Well, Gordon, these aren't just any fish. They have been indisputably identified." The priest referred to his notebook. "They come from the wide-mouthed six-inch-long silvery fish called *mousht*, a species of freshwater carp (members of the Cyprinidae family) indigenous to Israel's Lake Tiberias, which in biblical times was known as the Sea of Galilee. The mousht by local Mideastern tradition is called 'St. Peter's Fish.'"

Holly's mouth fell open. "What do the ichthyologists make of that? Have they any explanation?"

"None at all. They're at a total loss to explain it. They have no idea how these freshwater fish came to be so far from their habitat, how they managed to survive in seawater, and why not a single fish of that species has ever been seen in the Pacific Ocean. I, of course, have an answer for them. Plain and simple. The fish were brought there by God to feed

Brock."

"And that," said Eleanor, "is why you are so convinced that a miracle occurred on the island...a crucifixion...a miraculous cure."

"That and all the other evidence. But I do not believe, Eleanor, that your husband left the hospital to crucify himself. No, I...I think he wanted to drown himself, perhaps as your daughter Valerie drowned, but for some reason...we will never know why...he failed or changed his mind, and the storm or God's guiding hand deposited him on that island. God is omniscient and omnipresent. He is with us in this room now as He was with Brock in the hospital where he lay near death. He was with him in the boat as he sailed out to sea in the storm. God was with him every moment, and if God's plan was to cure your husband, then one can posit that all the events that occurred were of God's doing.

"I can envision Brock finding himself on the island alive and in pain, both from his ailments and his sins. I don't find it difficult to believe that he survived the storm with the idea of suicide still on his mind and that he followed through on that idea by using pulleys and ropes and sand bags to lift himself to the top of the mast, there to die as a fitting punishment for his sins. And then it happened! God's lightning struck, Brock was cured and spiritually resurrected. He built the chapel in a spirit of thanksgiving. You're the experts, Kelly and Diego. Tell us. Could he single-handedly have built that chapel in twenty months?"

The two designers exchanged looks.

"He was a master craftsman," said Kelly.

"Inventive, artistic," added Diego. "But where did he get the building materials? And the tools?"

"I don't know," answered the priest. "We may never know. But I have no doubt that an autopsy will find no cause of death. Mark my words. The medical experts will conclude that to all appearances his heart simply stopped beating."

"Oh, Father Deaver," sobbed Eleanor as she wiped her eyes, "I hope your explanation is true, that Brock did in the end find himself and God. I prayed for years that he would."

"I do too, Eleanor."

Sensing that the priest's description of the island had come to an end, Holly said, "If that's all you wanted to tell us about the island, Father, I

468

think it's time to read Brock's will." He reached for his briefcase beside him and removed a large blue envelope.

"Yes," said the priest. "I've no more information to share with you. I'll shut off the projector."

While the priest busied himself with the projector, Holly switched on the table lamp next to him and unfolded the Last Will and Testament of Brock Stowolski. The others, still confounded by the photos of the chapel and what the priest had told them, watched his every move intently. He read aloud a lengthy preamble—"enjoying good health and being of sound and disposing mind"—and a detailed description of the testator's complete estate. The language was saturated with the arcane legal terminology which by custom makes such documents unintelligible to laymen. Finally Holly reached the paragraphs dealing with the bequeathal, and the listeners became keenly attentive.

"Paragraph 15. I hereby do give and bequeath to my beloved daughter, Valerie Stowolski, and to no others, my entire estate, all of its assets and properties, with all household furniture and other personal property used in connection therewith and situated thereon at my death."

"Paragraph 16. I make no provision in this will and testament for my wife, Eleanor Stowolski, she having waived her rights to and interest in any part of my estate by written instrument."

Holly raised his head from the document and said as an aside to Eleanor, "That was the property agreement you unwittingly signed."

"Paragraph 17. Nor do I make provision for my son, Paul Stowolski. My discrimination against my son, Paul, has been made with careful consideration of the welfare of all persons involved and concerned."

When Holly had finished he looked for reactions in the faces around him.

Eleanor was troubled. "Then he left everything to Valerie?"

"Yes," replied Holly. "I'm afraid so. Everything. And that's part of the problem. Valerie is dead, so you both have a viable claim to the estate. No judge or jury would deny you what is rightfully yours as Brock's faithful wife of twenty-four years. He can't just give your entitlement away to suit his whimsy. The trouble is that by the time we contest the will and it clears probate—a process that could very well take a couple of years, maybe longer—DESIGN METAPHORS will be in receivership."

"Why didn't you tell me about the will last year?" asked Eleanor, alarmed and confused.

"Because by law I couldn't reveal the contents of the will. Besides, it wouldn't have made any difference. The only way we could have avoided all this was for Brock to have made you a co-owner of D-M. Then upon his death D-M would have been yours alone and exempt from probate."

"So what we do now?" she asked.

"The only thing we *can* do: appeal to the judge to grant you ownership of the estate. Like I said, Brock's estate is rightfully yours. At least that will be the basis of our claim."

The door opened, and the deacon who had greeted them upon their arrival reappeared. "Excuse me. We have just received a message from a Father Leonard." The group riveted their attention on him, eager for news about the island. Reading from the notes he made, the deacon said, "He wants the entire Stowolski family and close friends to come to the island as soon as possible. He has arranged through the Navy to fly you to Hawaii, where you will be transported to the island on a Coast Guard ship."

"I stand corrected," said Holly, smiling. "Appealing to the judge is not the only thing we can do. We can see for ourselves what Brock has erected on that island."

470

TWENTY-SIX

Captain Beaufort "Buck" Eakins, the forty-nine-year-old commander of the U.S. Coast Guard cutter *Inverness*, gripped the shiny brass railing of the starboard bridge and scanned the southern horizon dead ahead. They had been underway at a steady twenty-five knots since leaving Honolulu the day before. The weather and sea had been perfect, making the journey a pleasant one for his crew and their nine passengers.

He had been on more special missions in his twenty-three years in the Coast Guard than he could remember, but this was the kind of assignment whose memory would stick with him the rest of his life, one he would recount to his grandchildren when they were old enough to understand. For among the Kowalski party of nine lounging comfortably in the bright sunlight below him on the foredeck were two people whose names were the talk of households around the world: Eleanor, because she was the wife of Brock Stowolski, and Paul, because he was not only Brock's son but was emerging as one of the leading ballet stars in the world.

Word of the island, its chapel, and the alleged miracle had leaked out only minutes after the initial report reached Hawaii four weeks earlier. Major newspapers and popular magazines, television programs, and radio talk shows in nearly every country on the globe were covering the story from every conceivable angle, telling and retelling the strange heart-warming story of Brock's reconciliation in death with his family and his God. Hollywood could not have created more self-generating conditions for celebrity. Everywhere it was the main topic of conversation and endless speculation.

The departure of the Stowolski family for Honolulu by air from San

Francisco had been a quintessential media event broadcast by satellite to TV stations in every part of the globe with live interviews with each member of the party: Eleanor, Diego, Paul, Irina, Kelly, Helena, Maggie, and Gordon Holly and his wife. The crush of photographers, screaming reporters, and ogling bystanders at the airport brought home the raw reality of their newborn notoriety. Want it or not, for better or worse, they had become integral parts of the exalted tale—already legend—of Brock's miraculous cure on the mast-cross and his heroic inspired construction of The Chapel, replicas of which were already being planned in several countries as objects of veneration.

The Stowolski family was relieved to be sequestered on the *Inverness*, away from the crowds, to begin to adjust to being famous and to have time to think through the tumult about what it all meant, to them, to Brock, and to humankind. Even so, a small flotilla of motor cruisers, many carrying reporters and photographers, accompanied the Coast Guard cutter. Their presence was a constant reminder of the price that fame exacts.

Captain Eakins slid nimbly down the ladder from the bridge to the foredeck and joined the family. They were conversing amiably, their voices raised to be heard above the wind and the steady rumble of the cutter's powerful diesel engines.

Eleanor smiled to him. "Welcome, Captain. We were sharing our expectations about what we'll find on the island and how it will affect us. We're all very anxious, as you can imagine. It's so hard to deal with. We feel uprooted by forces we have no control over. It's frightening, and at the same time exciting. It's hard to put into words."

The smartly uniformed officer took a seat in a cushioned deck chair beside hers. Not the usual furnishings on a Coast Guard vessel, the chairs were requisitioned especially for the passengers and pointed up for the crew the uniqueness of this mission. "I can imagine, ma'am, how disconcerting all of this must be for all of you." He gestured toward the other eight who were standing close by, monitoring their conversation. "I hope the crew has made you comfortable."

All nine passengers nodded their satisfaction.

"Well, I'm glad," he replied with a robust smile that enriched his square, tanned, clean-shaven face. "We are proud to have you aboard."

472

"Captain," said Gordon Holly, "can you tell us what the current situation is on the island? What we're likely to find?"

"Frankly I've never seen anything like it. I've been there almost from the first day. Because of her speed the *Inverness* was dispatched within hours after word of the discovery reached our headquarters in Honolulu. We arrived at the island at about the same time as the first three Navy ships. We rendezvoused with the Japanese merchantman whose crewmen investigated the island. They gave us the film they shot, and we raced back to Honolulu with the film and the Bible. We no sooner reached Honolulu than we were ordered back to bolster security. The top brass feared an onslaught of sightseers and souvenir hunters once word got out, as it was bound to. We were under strict orders to keep the lid on the story, but you know how long that lasted. A sensation like that? No way it would remain a secret."

"How many official ships are there now?" asked Kelly.

"Naval and Coast Guard?"

"Yes."

"The Fleet Summary I read this morning listed twenty including, I might add, the *Reagan*...the nuclear-powered aircraft carrier. She's gargantuan. Towers over the other ships and the little island like King Kong, which has had the desired restraining effect on the civilian boats and ships that have gone there."

"Are there many?" asked Paul.

The captain chuckled. "Would you believe two hundred and counting!"

The party of nine was astonished.

"Where do they come from?" exclaimed Maggie.

"Who knows? All over. Pleasure yachts from Hawaii. Fishing boats from the Marshalls, the Marquesas, the Phoenix. Merchantmen out of Singapore, Japan, Ecuador, Mexico. A German oceanographic ship. The Pacific Ocean is dotted with ships and boats of every description, and all of them have radios." He shrugged. "It's simple. They hear the news, and they come. Worst of all we have no way to stop them or to know how many are coming. We've broadcast messages warning ships to stay away, that there isn't enough anchorage. It's a tiny island, and the floor around it drops off steeply after a mile. But the warnings are having no appreciable effect. More vessels are arriving every hour."

"How are you protecting the island then?" asked Holly. "Are people from the boats roaming the place freely?"

"No, absolutely not. That was anticipated. The first Navy ship to arrive sent a small security force ashore with the team of examiners."

"I believe," said Eleanor, "that's the team Father Leonard is in."

"Yes, I recall that name," replied the captain. "Then three days later a detachment of Marine infantry was rushed in and took full charge of the island. I mean really took charge...with guard dogs and loaded weapons and orders to use them if necessary."

Eleanor was shocked at the incongruity of armed Marines guarding the holy chapel. "How awful!"

Paul was curious. "Have they used them?"

"The weapons?" said the captain. "Once. The second night they were there four young guys from an American yacht swam ashore on a lark to take a look around. A beach sentry saw them in the moonlight and fired three rounds in the air, per his orders, and pinned them down. Another sentry fired a red signal flare and within seconds searchlights, Marines, guard dogs, rubber motor rafts, the whole shootin' match descended on the poor guys and apprehended them. They were later released and returned to their yacht, but the incident, which was witnessed by people on boats anchored nearest the island, gave a vivid demonstration of the Marines' power and sent a clear message to every onlooker not to venture ashore."

"Has it worked?" asked Paul.

"So far. I've seen no reports of further incidents."

Irina motioned for the captain's attention. "Do they just stay offshore watching the island day after day?"

"Yep. They gawk and train binoculars at each other and at the comings and goings of the official traffic in and out, which hasn't been much until the past week. We set up a cordon of Navy and Coast Guard ships around the island interspersed with buoys and rafts. No one is permitted inside the cordoned area without permission of the admiral aboard the carrier. I tell you, I don't know which is more intimidating, the Marines on the island or that steel mountain of a carrier. Add to that the launching and landing of jet aircraft and helicopters on the carrier, and you begin to appreciate that we have the island and the growing population of visitors under tight control. No worry there."

Holly was thinking ahead to what would happen once visitors were allowed ashore. "How will you handle sightseers when the island is eventually opened to the public? I presume it will be. Won't there be immense problems of crowd control?"

"That's what they've been working on in Honolulu. A task force has been looking at the problem. It was established by the special commission set up by the President about three days after the discovery. The United States claims the island as a possession...part of the Hawaiian Island chain...and no country has chosen to dispute it. The Secretary of the Interior chairs the commission. He appointed the Governor of Hawaii to head the task force, which includes representatives from a whole range of organizations and authorities with interests and equities in the island."

"Like who?"

"Oh, the Catholic Church, of course. The State of Hawaii. The National Science Foundation. The U.S. Congress. The Pentagon. The University of Hawaii. The diversity of the membership is amazing, but from what I've read in the papers and in the official Coast Guard traffic, they seem to be working well together."

"Yes," agreed Holly. "I read about it. As with anything else there's been controversy about the membership. Congress yesterday passed emergency legislation to make the island and the water surrounding it for twelve miles an historical site to be managed by the Department of the Interior."

"And a wise move, if you ask me," said the captain. "The legislation prohibits the erection of any structure on the island except hidden lighting for night illumination and security and a small unobtrusive communications booth linked by radio and cable to the command ship offshore. The aim is to preserve the island exactly as it was found."

Holly was unconvinced. "How will they preserve it with tourists traipsing all over the place? The environment must be extremely fragile. If the tourists aren't controlled, they'll take bits of rock and handfuls of sand as souvenirs, and in no time at all the island will be denuded. God only knows what relic hunters will do to the chapel."

"Like I said the task force is working the problem. I read their preliminary recommendations last night. I have a copy in my cabin you can borrow, if you like."

"Yes," said Holly, "I would. Thank you."

"They plan to erect a decorative barrier a quarter mile offshore fencing in the entire perimeter. It will be impenetrable below and above the waterline and be equipped with electronic sensors to detect underwater swimmers and anyone trying to scale the fence. A network of detectors will be planted on the bottom inside the perimeter to alert the security force to anything in the water larger than a minnow."

"How will visitors be handled?"

"Well, they're thinking of two types of short tours. One is a boat ride that would circle the island close ashore for photo taking. The other would be a guided tour on the island itself. They'd run like every fifteen or twenty minutes around the clock, twenty-four hours a day."

Paul was incredulous. "Around the clock? Every day?"

"Yes, sir. Seven days a week, every week of the year. It's the only way to handle the numbers of visitors they expect...more than two million a year."

"Two million!" chorused Eleanor and the others.

"Are you serious?" asked Diego.

The captain laughed. "Folks, you have no idea. No one did until air patrols from the *Enterprise* began reporting ship sightings. Reconnaissance of the ocean within a radius of one thousand miles shows over seven hundred vessels approaching."

"Holy moly!" exclaimed Kelly.

"Amen to that, sir. And then there's the cruise lines. They've been literally swamped with bookings for cruises to the island. Christian churches, both Catholic and Protestant, have booked entire ships. The world public's fascination with the island is epidemic. It's romance and religion both rolled into one. I read in yesterday's paper that five movie producers—two Americans, a Japanese, one Brit, and an Italian—are planning separate films, three for TV, about all of you, the island, and Mr. Stowolski's adventure."

"But won't this fascination eventually wear off?" asked Eleanor. "It's the rage now, but it's a long way to travel to see a little island and a chapel in the middle of nowhere."

476

"Ah, Mrs. Stowolski," the captain said, shaking his head. "You haven't been there yet. I think you'll have a different opinion when you've experienced it. When you've felt it."

"Felt what?" asked Helena.

"It's inexplicable. Mystical. Even the toughest Marines sense it and talk about it. You see..." He hesitated, unsure how to explain it. "Chapel Island is truly a holy place. You can almost touch it, the atmosphere. It makes everyone speak in undertones. All those boats and hundreds, thousands, of people, and there's hardly a sound. No honking. No yelling. No racing of engines. No wild parties. It's a totally hushed self-constrained reverential environment like you find in church. The reason, of course, is the chapel. It radiates a kind of, I don't know, mystical aura? If anything, world interest in the island will only grow."

Eleanor was staggered by the scale of operations foreseen by the task force. "It all sounds too fantastic. Millions of people? Barriers? Crowd control? Cruise ships? I don't think I like it. Is that what Brock would want? Would he be pleased knowing his passionate work of art, his tribute to our Lord, has become nothing more than a tourist attraction?"

"On the contrary, ma'am," the captain protested politely. "Like I said, this is no common tourist site. Don't you understand? A miracle took place there. A real miracle in modern times. Not something that happened a hundred, five hundred, or two thousand years ago where the few recorded facts have been distorted and embellished beyond recognition and belief. Chapel Island is a modern-day Lourdes. The Lourdes of the Pacific. Already there have been three claims of miraculous cures of people on boats at the island who drank the ocean water. God knows if the cures are real. The point is that word of the cures will spread, and millions of the faithful and sick will hear of it and come to pray for healings, or maybe just for forgiveness of sins. Mr. Stowolski, your husband, with the Lord's help, has made the island with its chapel the holiest site in the entire Pacific Ocean. Wait till you experience it. Then you'll know what I'm talking about."

"Island in sight, sir, dead ahead!" called out an officer above.

The captain and his passengers rose together. While he excused himself and ascended to the bridge, they rushed to the railing on the prow where, shoulder to shoulder, they strained to catch a glimpse of the island

and Brock's holy structure.

"Do you see anything?" someone asked.

"There's something dark and low...straight ahead. See it?"

"No."

"I think I do."

"It must be the carrier."

"I see a jet."

"Where?"

"Over there to the right and low."

Suddenly a Navy fighter loomed into view and roared overhead, its deafening sound crashing over the cutter. The aircraft banked and disappeared in the sky. The group followed its trail for a few seconds, then turned their attention back to the island.

"I see it now," cried Paul, one of the three in the party with binoculars. "The carrier. It's giant."

"I see it, too," said Diego. "Here, Eleanor, look through the glasses."

Chattering excitedly, the group passed binoculars back and forth giving everyone a magnified view. Soon binoculars were not needed, as the carrier and the larger ships could be seen clearly with the naked eye. At that point the group fell silent, as they prepared themselves emotionally for the sighting of the chapel, their minds drawn to the holy place where God had touched one of their own. Unconsciously, one by one, they joined hands and pressed close together, sharing the thrill and joy of entering this sacred domain. Then like each one of the millions who would follow in their path, they felt an indefinable spiritual aura.

"I can feel it, can you?" called Eleanor to Diego beside her. "Or is it my imagination?"

"No," he agreed. "You're not imagining it. There's a certain indefinable presence."

"I sense it, too," said Maggie, clasping Eleanor's hand tightly. Her action pulsed through the group, as all hands gripped one another more strongly.

Like an apparition, the chapel came into view, indistinct at first, then in sharper focus. Finally in full panoramic view its astonishing beauty engulfed them. They all wept openly, saying nothing, drinking in the glory of Brock's exquisite handiwork. The photographs they had seen could not do justice to the chapel's utter magnificence.

They remained nine lifelike statues frozen to the railing as the ship churned through the dark green brine toward the islet, where the giant hulk of the carrier was anchored amid a veritable armada of smaller ships, boats, and yachts of every description, packed tightly together by the Navy into pie-slice groups separated by waterways that converged on the island. A few giant merchant ships, unanchored because of the depth of the water, lay farther out, maintaining their stations with their engines.

Hour after hour boats and ships carrying the curious and the faithful were arriving seemingly from every quarter of the compass, swelling the armada and further complicating the Navy's problems. The commander-in-chief of the Pacific Fleet had dispatched a dozen fast patrol boats to police the waters and maintain order in the teeming anchorage. The arrival of this flotilla was expected in the hour.

Because word that the Stowolski family was aboard the cutter had reached the anchorage hours earlier, the arrival of the *Inverness* sparked a spontaneous celebration. As the cutter drove slowly up one of the waterways, the entire anchorage, belying Captain Eakins's statement about the serene atmosphere, exploded into honking and sirens as people crowded onto the decks on either side waving, whistling, and yelling jubilantly as if they and the passengers on the *Inverness* had just won some great victory. Eleanor and the others waved back.

The tumultuous welcome continued unabated while the cutter's engine throttled down, the ship slowed, the anchor plummeted into the water, and bells rang below deck. As the noise of the celebrating diminished and finally subsided, a team of crewmen ran to the fantail and lowered a launch into the water. One of the seamen leaped into its cockpit and, starting up its engine, steered the launch alongside the cutter. The D-M party lined up at the gangway and were helped into the launch, bidding farewell to Captain Eakins as they left. He affirmed that their luggage would be transferred to the carrier where they would be billeted, and he promised to deliver a copy of the task force report to Holly.

Safely aboard, they took their cushioned seats along the gunwales, and the launch sped off toward a portable pier that naval engineers had placed on the eastern shore of the island beside the promontory. It was a short run, and before long they were jumping onto the pier and walking unsteadily, after twenty-three hours at sea, down a ramp onto the beach.

Breathless, dazed, and slightly dizzy, the feel of the sand strange beneath their feet, they peered up at the ridge and at the chapel rising above it, its pinnacle silver cross gleaming over the six adjacent palm trees. The group mutely took in the sight, when a familiar figure appeared on the ridge waving and smiling. It was Father Leonard in black suit and white collar. They returned his greeting, and Eleanor and Paul ran up the path as he loped down. They met, nearly colliding, and embraced.

"Dear Eleanor! Paul! How wonderful to see you!"

"We're thrilled to be here," said Eleanor. "At last. Come down and meet everyone."

She took the priest's hand and led him to the others waiting on the beach, where she made the introductions, leaving Diego for last. "And this handsome man is Diego Martinez, my fiancée."

"Diego." The two men shook hands. "I am happy you came and that you are to wed this wonderful woman."

"Thank you, Father."

The priest was flushed with excitement. "Come, come, come. There's so much to tell you and show you. I feel like a young kid with a huge secret he can't wait to reveal."

"Have you seen Brock's body yet?" asked Eleanor, leaping to the thought that had preoccupied her and the others as the cutter approached the island.

"Yes, dear. I've visited the ship several times. I'll take you out later, if you wish."

"Which ship is it?"

"The *Faraday*...there...pendant number 723. His body is in a freezer locker."

"Did they perform the autopsy there?" asked Diego.

"Yes. The ship, as you know, has a well-equipped operating room. A team of doctors, mostly medical examiners, shipped in last week and did it. Their findings were out yesterday and are exactly what we predicted. Brock died a perfectly healthy specimen in every way. Not a single cancer cell could be found, nor any sign of illness."

"What was the cause of death?"

"Unknown officially. Unofficially? We all know. Brock simply lay

480

down and gave up his spirit lovingly to the merciful God who cured him. I tell you, folks, I've never been so happy in my life. Brock was redeemed. His soul was saved. I feel redeemed myself." His eyes watered, but he was unashamed.

Eleanor hugged him. "Father, before we go to the chapel, I have something to ask you."

"Yes?"

"Is the chapel a real church yet? I mean, Diego and I would like to be married in the chapel, by you. We know Brock would be pleased if you would."

Father Leonard beamed. "Nothing would make me happier. If I could experience greater joy than this, I'd surely be in heaven."

"You mean it would be all right before the Papal consecration?"

"I'm certain that in God's eyes the chapel is a most sacred site. When would you like to do it?"

"Not today, but sometime this week before the Pope arrives. We brought all the paperwork with us."

Diego placed his arm around her shoulders and drew her close. "How about tomorrow night by candlelight?"

Eleanor gave Diego an approving smile. "Yes. Tomorrow."

"That will be perfect," the priest replied. "So, everyone!" He looked to the others in the group. "I believe you're ready to visit Brock's masterpiece." He straightened as if proud of his role as guide. "Please follow me."

As the others stepped forward, Eleanor, instantly somber and tearful, remained rooted in place, blocking everyone's way.

"It's all right, Eleanor," the priest said, understanding her hesitancy and extending his hand to her. "The chapel is filled with an all-embracing love, in every nail, for you, for me, for Diego, for everyone...for God and Jesus. I could spend every moment there. I've had to tear myself away from it to perform my duties that brought me here. So, come. Take my hand."

Eleanor relented, and with the priest in the lead the group of nine trailed up the ridge to the chapel past several armed Marines. They assembled in a circle around him at the entrance, stealing side glances into its multicolored interior.

481

"Let us pray," he said. Holding hands, they bowed their heads. "Our Father in heaven. We have come to visit the shrine erected by Brock Stowolski in testament to Your mercy. Purify our hearts and minds so that as we enter this sacred house, we may be worthy to behold the magnificence which Your love for Your children has borne. In Jesus' name we pray. Amen."

With that the group filed through the entrance, knelt, crossed themselves...and entered another world.

The nave was awash in colliding colors radiating magically from the translucent stained-glass windows on every side. Overcome with emotion, no one said a word as tears flowed from every eye. The group broke up, wandering individually from window to window. After a few minutes, Father Leonard called them together in the center of the chapel. "Let us focus on each of the windows one at a time, beginning with the small rosette above the entrance. Unlike the others, it has no inscription, but it's absolutely gorgeous, isn't it?" He waited a few seconds as the beauty of the window dazzled the group's admiring eyes.

"The window to the left of the entrance is dedicated to Valerie about whose death Brock learned the very day he decamped from the hospital." The window was light green and bore Valerie's name at the top in white letters above two bright red hearts, one within the other, from which issued a glistening blue teardrop. The inscription in vivid pink letters said in Latin: IN MEMORIAM CUM AMORE.

"He loved her very much," said Eleanor quietly, almost to herself. "One heart is for her, the other for the child she carried."

The priest continued. "The next window is dedicated to Irina." It was a lush canary yellow, displayed her name at the top in green letters, and featured a radiant red rose in full bloom with stem and leaves above the inscription: SINSERE APOLOGIES.

"Oh, dear," muttered Maggie. "He's a better speller than that."

Kelly came to his defense. "Maybe he didn't realize the error until the window was too far along to correct. That happens, you know. An easy mistake to make."

"God will forgive him," Father Leonard threw in, smiling.

Everyone chuckled.

"What was he apologizing for?" asked Irina.

482

"Probably your deportation," answered Paul. "You know we always suspected he somehow had a hand in it. It was never clear who was behind it."

"I think you're right, Paul," chimed Eleanor. "It was so like Brock to punish his enemies indirectly through others. By victimizing Irina, he probably felt he was punishing you."

"The next carries Paul's name," said the priest. A wonderful bluish purple, it showed a male ballet dancer leaping across the face of a white moon beneath which was the inscription: FFORGIV ME.

"Oh, not again!" wailed Maggie. "His spelling is atrocious, and so unlike him. Maybe the cure affected his mind."

"Wait a minute!" said Holly. "Maybe those aren't errors. Those misspellings could be intentional."

"What do you mean intentional?" asked Paul. "Why would he misspell them?"

"I don't know, but look again at the words as if they were a puzzle, like the letters on personalized license plates. FFORGIV...two *F*s and no *E*. Forgive me twice?"

Suddenly Paul leaped to his feet and screamed. "Of course! I've got it! Don't you see it? Read it backwards. FFORGIV ME is E. M. VIGROFF, my benefactor. My patron. The woman who..." Paul crumpled to his knees on the floor and covered his face with his arms. He sobbed, unable to speak, as Irina went to him.

"She is the one," said Eleanor, excitedly picking up where Paul had stopped, "who financed Paul's lessons after Brock disappeared. She made it possible for Paul to resume his training. Without her help he never would have achieved..." She too succumbed in tears as the startling revelation seized her that the father and husband they had reviled all these months had sought anonymously to redeem himself. "He did it..." She choked back her tears, struggling to share her incredible insight. "He did it anonymously because he felt unworthy of our forgiveness."

She knelt beside Paul and Irina and crossed herself. "I forgive you, Brock. I forgive you for everything."

Father Deaver said, "Then let us go back to Irina's window. Can any of you decipher a meaning from that misspelling?"

Irina cried out. "I see it! It's backwards again. The name of my sponsor. SINSERE APOLOGIES is Seigolo Paeresnis. Paul, it was your father! Your father brought me back to America!"

Paul smiled through his weeping. "It's all too wonderful to believe...that he would do these things."

"But how did he do it?" asked Kelly. "Did he contact you, Gordon?"

"No. He said nothing to me. In fact I never saw him in the hospital. I was busy at the time on a pressing matter with another client. I had planned to visit Brock the day after he disappeared. I never dreamed he would take off like that. It took us all by surprise."

"I know how he did it!" Paul declared with finality. Everyone in the room looked at him with surprise. "His woman friend. The one who..." Paul had never told anyone, even Irina, about the incident in his dressing room or mentioned Catherine Dubeau by name. "Anyway, a woman friend. She'll have the answers, I'm sure. I need to call her. Father, is there some way I can contact her?"

"Yes, I'm sure the Navy can make the necessary connections. I'll see to it as soon as we arrive on the carrier."

For the next few minutes in a lively high-spirited session the group discussed Brock's uncharacteristic acts of altruism and their significance. Finally, Father Leonard felt it appropriate to move on. "There is one more window. It's Eleanor's."

The group studied its stained-glass artwork, consisting of the logo of DESIGN METAPHORS, a multicolored plumed bird of paradise under the arch of a rainbow resting on a bank of white clouds against a light blue sky. Beneath it were the words: PRESERVE D-M WITH MY LOVE.

"Well," observed Kelly, "there's no misspelling there, but what does it mean?"

Holly offered an opinion. "That Eleanor is to keep D-M in business, keep it prosperous."

Kelly unconsciously raised a hand as if he needed permission to speak. "How can she preserve D-M, if she isn't a co-owner of the company? Brock intentionally arranged it so she would have no ties with the company, no influence over its affairs."

"He must have had a change of heart," said Paul, "as he did with Irina and me."

"That's very likely," said Holly. "Perhaps he wrote an amendment to

484

his will." He looked to Father Leonard. "You said no documents have been found on the island, isn't that true?"

"Yes. We specifically inquired about that, and the team was thoroughly briefed to look for documents of any kind. None has been found. It's possible they're buried somewhere on the island, but that seems a real long shot. Moreover, if Brock wanted Eleanor to know that he made her a co-owner of D-M, why would he bury it, hide it out of sight?"

"I agree." Holly stroked his chin. "Nevertheless, when he created that window, he clearly believed that Eleanor was in control of D-M. So he must have executed a new property agreement or at least he thought he had." Holly's head snapped upright. "Wait a minute! Eleanor, did you witness any documents for Brock in the hospital?"

She thought back to that tempestuous period. "As a matter of fact I did. It was the night he disappeared. I remember now. He asked me to witness a handwritten document. I didn't read it."

"And did you sign it?"

"Yes."

"What did he do with it?"

"I don't know. I left, and then I learned Valerie had been there the day before, and I went back to his room and confronted him. I was nearly hysterical. I never asked him about the document. I don't know what happened to it."

Holly became excited. "Then I absolutely and without any reservation believe that, just as Brock concealed his role in helping Irina and Paul, he concealed from you his amending your earlier property agreement."

"Run that by me again," said Paul.

"I think your father tricked your mother into signing a new property agreement that made her co-owner of D-M. In other words, there is a document somewhere that says she is now, this very moment, owner of D-M."

"That fits with the window," said Kelly. "Only if she's a co-owner can she preserve the company. But why wouldn't he tell her about it there in the hospital room? Why keep it a secret?"

Father Leonard cleared his throat. "I believe I can answer that." They

485

all turned to him. "He was ashamed. He had persecuted Eleanor over and over in different ways throughout their marriage. Because of his granite-like pride, he simply couldn't bring himself to acknowledge it, and making her co-owner of DESIGN METAPHORS was an unmistakable, self-damning admission of his horrendous guilt.

"If she were co-owner," Diego cried, "it would solve everything! But where's this document? Where could it be if not here on the island?"

"Finding that document isn't the issue," said Holly gruffly. "Finding it in time to save D-M is the problem. Even if the estate enters probate, we can institute stalling tactics to prolong the proceedings until we can locate the document. But D-M needs a loan now, immediately. Marlow's deadline is only ten days away. Without the loan the firm goes under, probate or no probate. It's imperative we find that document."

"Where do we start looking?" asked Eleanor.

"In San Francisco!" declared Holly. "We can take the *Inverness*, the Coast Guard cutter that brought us here. Captain Eakins told me he's returning to Hawaii tomorrow morning."

"I'll speak to him about it," said Father Leonard, "when he transports us to the *Faraday*, where Brock's body is being kept."

Eleanor caught Diego's attention and frowned. "Father?" The priest came to her. She took Diego's hand and drew him to her side. "If we're leaving tomorrow morning, would it be possible for you to marry us tonight. I don't want to wait."

Diego kissed her cheek. "Nor do I."

The priest smiled broadly. "My dear ones, I will be only too happy to bind you together in holy matrimony. We'll do it right here, this evening."

Eleanor's eyes gleamed. "Thank you, Father. But let's limit attendance to the family. No outsiders. The ceremony will be all the more special that way."

"I agree," said Diego.

"As you say. In the meantime, let's enjoy the chapel. I can't get enough of it."

The members of the group meandered from window to window. Eleanor knelt in consuming prayer before her window—the D-M bird of paradise wreathed in a rainbow. Irina knelt before hers of the weeping

486

heart. Paul at first stood before his ballet dancer, his eyes closed, his head pressed against the base of the window frame, then he, too, knelt and prayed.

While Father Leonard remained inconspicuous by the entrance, the others—Diego, Maggie, Helena, Kelly, Gordon and his wife—instinctively congregated before the altar, gazing in wonderment at the ethereal sight of the three kneeling figures praying before their windows. Eleanor, Paul, and Irina were each bonded to the chapel unlike any other persons on earth ever would be. Their names would remain emblazoned in the windows for centuries to come, to be witnessed, honored, and revered by hundreds of millions of people in future generations.

After a time the three rejoined their friends and, as if by prearrangement, they moved to the mast-cross where they were joined by Father Leonard.

"Imagine," he said softly. "God's holy finger touched this mast and cured Brock."

Eleanor slowly carefully, stretched out her right hand and, trembling, laid it gently upon the rough charred wood. She felt as if she were touching the imprint of God's hand. One by one the others joined her until all ten stood together, their arms outstretched, an ensemble of souls in touch with their Creator through the blackened antenna of the riven cross. It was Brock's final and most perfect gift, an offering not of atonement but of love in its purest form.

The group toured the island, visiting the promontory on which it was conjectured Brock watched the sun rise each morning, the beaches on which he strolled, the lagoon from which he viewed the sunsets in the west, and the niche in the coral where they figured he prayed each night before the impressionist nature-made statue that was unmistakably an image of the Blessed Virgin.

Father Leonard described to the best of the investigative team's knowledge how Brock had managed to construct the chapel. Although much of the team's interpretation was sheer guesswork at this stage, to be confirmed later, physical evidence discovered by the Navy on the sea floor around the island provided solid corroboration for some conclusions. The Navy, using sophisticated bottom-scanning sonar, had located in the surrounding waters a large amount of debris believed to be construction equipment and materials. Secretly, so as not to precipitate a frenzied clawing mob of divers from the civilian boats and ships ransacking the bottom for souvenirs, Navy divers working at night had begun retrieving items. They were being scientifically examined aboard the *Faraday*.

"In time," explained Father Leonard, "if we're lucky, investigators may be able to piece together what actually happened here. One thing we won't need to know, however, is why it happened. We know that. But it has been authoritatively established that Brock obtained the materials for the chapel from two sailing vessels, his own yacht and a Indonesian schooner, which the Indonesian government reports foundered at sea during a storm and was abandoned by its crew. The schooner must have washed ashore here. To lift and maneuver the pillars and buttresses and other components of the chapel, Brock engineered some type of derrick using the schooner's masts and pulleys. These and other items have been recovered, cleaned, and preserved in the *Faraday*'s hold. I'll take you to see them later.

"The Navy has taken hundreds of underwater photos of all kinds of other debris, including elements of a huge oven constructed of coral bricks that Brock must have used to produce the stained glass for the windows. I'm confident, as is the team, that in time the world will have a clear and complete picture of how Brock constructed this magnificent monument."

The D-M party attended Mass aboard the carrier later in the afternoon celebrated by the ship's Catholic chaplain, then visited their quarters to unpack and shower. Paul took the opportunity to contact Catherine Dubeau. The ship's communication division connected him with San Francisco information, which provided Dubeau's home number. He dialed it and asked the woman who answered, presumably a maid, if he could speak with Mrs. Dubeau.

"I'm sorry. She is taking no calls at the moment. May I take a message?"

"No, I have to speak with her this very minute. It's an emergency.

488

Tell her it's Paul Stowolski who wants to talk to her about Madame Vigroff. She'll understand."

"Paul Stowolski? About who?"

"About Madame Vigroff." He spelled it for her.

"Vigroff," she repeated.

"Yes."

"All right. One moment, please."

Less than a minute later Catherine Dubeau was on the line. "Yes, Mr. Stowolski. What may I do for you?" Her voice sounded tense and wary.

"Mrs. Dubeau, I know now that my father was the true sponsor of Madame Vigroff's donations to my ballet training, and I believe you are Madame Vigroff. Are you?"

Fifteen minutes later Paul returned to his family waiting for him in a library and recounted what she had told him.

"It seems Dad phoned this woman the afternoon after Valerie died. Father Leonard had phoned his hospital room and told him of my sister's death. Dad was overcome with remorse and wanted to make amends but, like Holly said, he felt ashamed and preferred to work anonymously through this woman, to have her be the instrument of his atonement as he described it to her."

"Who is she?" asked Helena.

"I'm sorry, Helena, but she asked that she not be identified. The past has passed. Let's let it rest. The point is the woman helped both me and Irina. For that we owe her anonymity. Dad gave her precise instructions over the phone, and she carried them out to the letter. He supplied her with the combination to the wall safe in the bedroom of his apartment, to which she had a key, and told her to take from it a packet of money—sixty thousand dollars in cash. She said it was his rainy-day reserve. He laid out how she was to use the money and dictated the exact spelling of the names of the two fictitious patrons—E. M. Vigroff and Seigolo Paeresnis. He never told her the secret of their reverse spellings, and she never guessed. She just did what he asked. She played Madame Vigroff herself, contacting Mr. Kúbokoff by phone directly. She also arranged the reinstatement of Irina's visa through people she knew in Washington and a wealthy Greek business friend in Greece. He handled matters at that end without revealing his identity. It really wasn't very complicated, just secret."

Eleanor was overcome with wonder. "Brock went to these extreme lengths because he was deeply ashamed of what he had done to us. So ashamed and guilt-ridden that he couldn't face his family to apologize and ask our forgiveness, which we would readily have given. His shame was so great he couldn't bear to even display the words in the stain-glass windows, instead hiding their meaning in anagrams."

A ship's officer entered the library and announced that a launch had come alongside to take the family to the *Faraday* to view Brock's body.

It was a wrenching solemn occasion. Wearing heavy down jackets loaned by the crew, the D-M visitors filed into the *Faraday*'s freezing compartment, Eleanor first, then Paul, Irina, and the others. As they approached the long cream-colored plastic container in which the body was kept, they stopped, allowing Eleanor to proceed alone. As a courtesy to the visitors, the lid of the container had been removed and placed against a nearby bulkhead.

Father Leonard took Eleanor's hand and brought her to the container's side. She rested her hands on the ice-cold rim and looked down at the body. A foil-like cloth was pulled up to the shoulders to conceal the ugly surgical incisions made during the autopsy. The head, untouched, was exposed.

She gazed soulfully at her husband's face with its thick bleached-brown beard which she remembered from the photo of him lying on the mosaic floor before the altar. The beard gave him a holy priestly look. Were it not for the deathly pallor of his deeply tanned skin, she would have thought he was sleeping and that a slight nudge to his shoulder would awaken him. Instead she touched his cold, dry cheek tenderly with her fingers and said softly, "Sleep with God."

Several hours later Eleanor and Diego snuggled cozily against a railing on the carrier watching as the fiery orange-and-blue sunset behind the island silhouetted the chapel and trees. Neither of them had spoken for ten minutes, each mesmerized by the beauty and majesty of it all.

490

"When I look at the island," said Eleanor, breaking their silence, "I imagine him working on the chapel. Cutting and sanding, hammering, fitting the pieces lovingly together. He must have been very happy here. Happier and more at peace than he had ever been, probably for the first time in his life. I still love him, you know."

"I understand," said Diego. "He was two people really. The one you fell in love with and the one you lived with. This one—" he nodded in the direction of the chapel—"is the one you loved."

"But I love him now in a different way. Not as my husband but as a special human being, for what he's done here and the gestures of kindness and love he extended to Paul and Irina. I just feel so good when I think about him. It's very strange, after all the evil things he did to me and others. I sense Brock's presence here so strongly and his love, for both of us."

"He's all around us," said Diego. "It's as if he were standing here beside us, embracing us, blessing us."

She took Diego's hand and kissed it. "Do you think he knew we'd be married in his chapel? Or is that just a silly notion of a bride-to-be?"

"Maybe not married here, but he probably expected we'd find each other one day. That was in the cards from the moment we first met. There's no question in my mind that the Brock of this island blesses our marriage. Our love is true and heaven-sent." He kissed her gently on the lips. "And by having the wedding ceremony in his chapel he becomes a part of it...part of us...with us always."

Eleanor set her eyes on the chapel and studied its symmetrical outline against the fading light, a silhouette now world-famous and instantly recognized by people everywhere. "I feel drawn to the chapel. It beckons me. Do you feel it?"

"Yes, like a magnet."

In a private candlelit ceremony performed by Father Leonard and attended only by the other seven members of the group, Eleanor and Diego were married, kneeling before the splendorously sculptured altar

Brock had hewn from the bedrock of the island. In the ghostly flickering light of two dozen candles placed at either end of the altar and those carried by each of the others present, Father Leonard, dressed in crisp white vestments, conducted the Nuptial Mass and joined the two lovers in the bonds of lifelong matrimony.

TWENTY-SEVEN

Upon passing through the security exit at the San Francisco International Airport, the family, to their astonishment and fright, was confronted by a howling milling throng of reporters with microphones, tape recorders, and TV floodlights and cameras. They had gotten word of the family's return. Journalists vied with one another in shouting questions to members of the beleaguered family.

"Follow me!" shouted Diego, who launched himself into the crowd, pushing and shoving to make way for the others behind him. It took them five minutes, jostled and pummeled, to pass through the mob and pile quickly into two limousines to take them away to D-M.

On their way Holly called Maggie on his cell phone and told her of their escape from the news media.

"I've got news for you, Mr. Holly. They're here, too. A bunch of them are outside. I kicked out the first of them to arrive and locked the door. It's a mob scene. When I told them the family wasn't here yet and that the firm's attorney was on his way, they calmed down, though their numbers have continued to grow by the minute, filling the entire hallway. I imagine they're downstairs in the main lobby, too, waiting for you."

"Okay, Maggie," he said. "Thanks for the warning."

"How soon will you arrive?"

"Give us thirty minutes. And tell you what. We'll have the limos drop us off in the underground garage. We'll take the elevator to the 17th floor, walk up one flight, and enter D-M on the other side of the building. Can you hold them off till we arrive and I can talk to them?"

"No problem."

Bypassing the media, Eleanor, Paul, and the rest of the family took refuge in Diego's office, where Maggie served them coffee and pastries. Shortly they were joined by the entire D-M staff, followed by Gordon Holly.

"I'm going to put together a brief news release for the media. I'll assemble them in the conference room, handout the brief, and answer their questions," he said. "I spoke with Father Deaver on our way here. He said the news people have been everywhere scavenging for anything remotely connected with Brock and the island—Navy and Coast Guard bases in Hawaii, the Catholic Church's offices here in San Francisco and in Honolulu, the Navy Department in Washington. Some guy even telephoned St. Charles Seminary in Maryland. If any of you are approached by journalists, the best reply to any question is 'I have no comment' and refer them to me. Does everyone understand?" He saw nods all around. "All right, then. You can get back to your work." Then to Maggie. "Come with me and we'll get started on that news release."

As Holly dictated, Maggie typed a one-paragraph statement, made fifty copies, and opened the conference room to the waiting horde. Jamming into every available space, they set up their recording equipment and lights.

Holly entered from the inner office, identified himself, and asked if everyone had a copy of the handout. One newswoman did not, so Maggie passed one to her. Then Holly began.

"Because you already know the background to Brock Stowolski's death on Chapel Island, the brief statement I have provided you skips over all of that and brings you up to date, as best I know, on what is new from Chapel Island. Nevertheless, let me review the scenario, as we know it.

"Brock Stowolski was terminally ill with cancer twenty-one months ago when he left his hospital room and sailed through a terrific storm, or was carried by it, to a small uninhabited island some five hundred miles south of Hawaii. There he erected a cross constructed from his boat's mast and attempted to crucify himself. Lightning apparently struck the mast, splitting it and miraculously curing his cancer. In thankfulness for this

494

miracle he constructed the chapel, using wood from his own boat and that of an unmanned, abandoned Indonesian schooner that washed ashore. Some time later, we're not sure when, he cleaned the island of everything to return it to the condition in which he found it. Then ten days ago he lay down in front of the altar and died.

"Shortly thereafter, perhaps minutes, a Japanese merchant ship, diverted by a storm out of the normal shipping lanes, came upon the island and discovered the chapel. Intrigued, a party of crewmen went ashore to photograph the building and found Brock's still warm but dead body lying prone in front of the altar. Frightened, the crewmen fled back to their ship, whose captain radioed their discovery to the U.S. Coast Guard in Honolulu.

"An official investigation by Hawaiian authorities and the Catholic Church is underway. To avoid wild speculation on the circumstances surrounding Mr. Stowolski's death, the investigators will reveal none of their findings until the final report of the investigation has been completed, printed, and released to the public, which may take months.

"Meanwhile, an ever-growing armada of sightseers has descended on the tiny islet. A squadron of U.S. naval ships has set up a cordon around the island to prevent its being vandalized and to support the investigation. That is my statement. Now I'll try to answer your questions."

Twenty reporters spoke at once with hands and recorders raised. Their questions ranged from basic fact-finding to the ridiculous and macabre. Holly declined to comment on nearly every one, but he did expand factually where he could to clarify points in the handout. In closing, he announced to their eager satisfaction, their pencils poised, that there was one development related to Brock's death that he wished to speak about that the handout did not mention. It was about the missing document. He explained its importance and appealed to anyone having knowledge of its whereabouts to contact D-M. He gave the reporters a phone number to call, but their interest rapidly faded when they saw no connection with the island or with the circumstances of Brock's death. Holly urged them to mention the document in their write-ups, then thanked them for coming and exited through the door to Brock's office.

The mob of newspeople quickly departed, scrambling to board the elevators to return to their press rooms. A few lingered in the reception room vainly plying Maggie with more questions, but she refused comment, and within minutes they, too, were gone.

Holly invited the family into the vacated conference room. When everyone was settled, he said, "In order to find the missing document we need to get organized. May I serve as commander of this operation, Eleanor? One person has to be in charge if we're to use our time and resources to their maximum efficiency. I'm not seeking control for its own sake. I just happen to have some experience in locating missing documents."

Eleanor reached out and touched Holly's arm. "I think I can speak for everyone. We will be happy to follow your lead. What would you have us do?"

"Let me work up a plan of action. We've all been through the emotional wringer and need a good night's rest before we begin the search for the document. Let's meet here in this room at eight o'clock sharp tomorrow morning. We'll use D-M as our command post. Maggie will serve as coordinator. There will be lots of phone calls to make and people to visit, so...that's about it. Oh, there is one other thing. Say nothing to anyone about the island, Eleanor's and Diego's wedding, our viewing Brock's body, our almost supernatural experience as we together touched the mast-cross, and so on. That includes relatives, close friends, and especially D-M's staff. I want their minds fully focused on the search for the document. We can tell them everything once the document is found. In the meantime plead ignorance." He grew quickly solemn. "My friends. I have never been a religious person, but tonight I'm going to kneel down at my bedside and pray for Brock's soul and to ask God's help in finding that document."

The plan Holly devised to search for the putative document covered every possibility he could think of. The obvious first target was any visitor to Brock's room who was not an employee of the hospital. The next target was the staff of doctors and nurses in the Terminal Ward who treated Brock and were in regular contact with him. The third was the hospital's general staff on duty at any time during the three days Brock was there. This amounted to several hundred people—doctors, nurses, administrators, cooks, cleaning crews, even other patients—anyone to whom he might have given the document. The prospect of identifying, contacting, and interviewing each of these persons was mind-boggling.

"We have to marshal every D-M employee," Holly explained to the family group gathered in the conference room the next morning. "Nothing else D-M is doing has a higher priority. I've prepared a detailed list of tasks and assigned them to individuals. Maggie is in charge of all phone calling, assigning jobs to the staff, and keeping track of who is called, when and where appointments are scheduled, who does the interviewing, and what the results are. I leave all that to you, Maggie. I'm meeting with the hospital's chief administrator in an hour to seek her cooperation in giving us access to time and attendance records while Brock was in residence. There are protections under the Privacy Act that will limit our access, especially to former patients, but I believe suitable procedures can be worked out to accommodate our needs without violating any laws.

"Kelly, I'm giving you the job of combing through D-M files on the chance that Brock mailed the document to his office from the hospital. It would be ironic if the document we're looking for were right here under our noses. Maggie will assign staff members to help you.

"And you, Diego, I want you to check with the post office's dead letter section. If Brock mailed the document to someone—one of us, a friend, an acquaintance—he might have misaddressed the envelope or forgotten to put a stamp on it. We don't know his mental state at the time, but he was on painkillers and could have been dazed and incoherent. Also, inquire if there is any way to determine if he sent any registered letters. I doubt they keep records by name, but it's worth checking. I'm sure you can handle that by yourself, but if you want help, ask Maggie.

"Eleanor and Paul, your job is to check with Brock's friends and business associates to learn if they received any letter from him for safekeeping. We know he didn't leave the hospital during banking hours, so we can rule out the possibility that he placed the document in a safe-deposit box himself, though he might have enlisted someone to do it for him. Why he would place it in a safety-deposit box is beyond me, but we can't exclude the possibility. He could have asked someone to put the letter in a safe place until a specific date, at which time the letter would be unsealed or mailed. Knowing Brock's love of theatrics, it's conceivable he planned something like that. Again, Maggie will assign people to help you. And one more thing. Speak with the hospital's phone operators and the phone company itself and see if they can identify any calls he made from his room and to whom.

"Can anyone think of anything else we should investigate?" Holly waited while the group pondered his query.

Kelly raised his hand. "I think you've pretty well covered it. Why don't we go with what you've planned, and if we don't find the document, we'll just have to think of something else."

"Good enough," said Holly. "Then let's get going. And remember to keep Maggie informed. This office will be our base of operations. Unless you hear differently, we'll meet here again at eight o'clock tomorrow morning to evaluate our progress and make whatever changes are recommended. Good luck." He held up a finger to indicate he had more to say. "And may God bless our search and help us to find what we're looking for." Everyone in the group nodded.

Over the next hour Maggie called D-M's thirty employees together in the conference room and briefed them in general terms on Holly's plan of action. By now all of them were aware of Brock's death on Chapel Island in the Pacific from the news media coverage. A few of them had worked closely with Brock for nearly twenty years, during which time they had come to respect him for his professional talents. Although his after-hours liaisons had generated a steady flow of juicy gossip that circulated among the staff, it had no real impact on D-M's business affairs.

Holly entered the room and gave them a pep talk on how vital their participation in the search for the document was to D-M's future and indeed their own. It was simple. If D-M went bust, they'd all lose their jobs. He instructed them to continue to play dumb to reporters and to refer all press inquiries to him. He asked the staff if they had any questions, but there was none. Then he left to meet with the director of the hospital.

Maggie immediately took control, barking out commands and instructions like a crusty drill sergeant and forming squads of telephone callers, interviewers, records searchers, and general gophers. Within an hour she converted D-M's sedate suite into a bustling clamorous command center with herself in charge.

Responding to Holly's appeal to the media to report D-M's search for the missing document, all newspapers and TV news ran stories about it. They were newsworthy and of human interest. As a result, the phones in D-M began ringing with inquiries of all kinds from kooks as well as citizens trying to be helpful, though none was. Maggie wanted to stop answering incoming calls to the suite, but Holly feared someone with useful information about the document might phone in, so she put two staffers to work answering phones and taking messages, which Holly would screen and give instructions on whether and how to reply.

Eleanor and Paul sat down with Irina and Helena to go over a number of lists Eleanor had brought from home containing names, addresses, and phone numbers of family friends and business acquaintances with whom she and Brock, before their separation, had exchanged Christmas cards. The four of them copied the information for each individual onto three-by-five cards which they gave to Maggie, who then assigned them to the telephone callers. Irina and Helena volunteered to be in charge of refreshments and set about planning for lunch, which they would set up as a buffet in the reception room. Meanwhile Diego rushed off to tackle the post office, while Holly went to negotiate with the hospital for access to their records.

The hospital's management, as Holly anticipated, opposed granting him access to employee time sheets, doctors' visits, and patient listings. Instead the administrator proposed that a bulletin be distributed to all employees explaining Holly's purpose and inviting anyone with information to contact him voluntarily. Holly favored this approach, but he pressed the administrator for a more direct immediate method of surveying doctors and particularly the nurses who had attended Brock. Holly thought the latter were the most likely to have been given the document.

He also wanted the names and addresses of the patients who were in the Terminal Ward while Brock was there. Although none of them was still alive, they could have received the document and passed it to others or in some way put it in safekeeping. The administrator resisted, citing the Privacy Act, but Holly made an impassioned appeal in his finest courtroom style, explaining the unique circumstances of Brock's disappearance and painting a harrowing picture of the consequences that would befall D-M and Brock's family if the document were not found quickly. A compromise was finally negotiated whereby an official of the hospital would contact each of these individuals first and advise them of their right to answer or not answer Holly's questions. As soon as Holly and the administrator shook hands on the agreement, Holly went to work with the hospital's personnel office to begin the process, exhorting them to move with all speed.

At eight o'clock the next morning Holly met with the entire staff in the conference room to hear status reports and reassess their strategy. Kelly had found nothing of relevance in the D-M files. Diego had struck out at the post office and had joined Eleanor back at D-M in identifying Brock's associates. Diego had gotten keys from Maggie to the two apartments Brock kept—one in downtown Oakland where he lived week nights, the other on the shore near Salinas for weekends. Diego spent the afternoon scouring the apartments for the document or for clues to where Brock might have sent it. The results were negative.

Holly had amassed a daunting list of two hundred employees of the hospital who had volunteered to be interviewed about the missing documents. A good many said they volunteered after watching TV news stories about Stowolski's death. Telephone teams then worked until eleven that night contacting the volunteers, explaining the situation, asking if they had any knowledge of Eleanor signing a document for

Brock. Many of those contacted were no longer employees; some now lived in other states. One former nurse had moved with her husband to Germany. These responses, too, proved negative.

"We must keep trying!" Holly implored. "Someone out there knows of the document. We've got to find that person. And one other thing. Newspeople have been besieging Maggie with questions and requests for interviews. She is rejecting all such requests as all of you should as well. Let me repeat yesterday's directive. Please do not speak with reporters or anyone outside our staff about Brock or anything to do with the firm. Whatever you say will inevitably be distorted and sensationalized. If pressed, as I said yesterday, simply disavow any knowledge and refer the questioner to me. In deference to Mrs. Stowolski, if for no other reason, we must not fuel rumors and wild stories. Is there any question about that?" The room was silent. "Good."

Maggie stood and clapped hands. "Okay, teams, let's hit those phones!"

The D-M crowd broke up and went busily about their assignments. Holly pulled Maggie aside and praised her performance, then departed for the hospital to oversee the continuing screening of employees, doctors, and patients.

By the morning of the fourth day, two days before Christmas, gloom had descended over the D-M staff as it assembled in the conference room for the morning meeting. Not a single contact or lead had panned out. No one had seen Eleanor sign any document, and no one had been given a document or letter to mail or place in safekeeping. Everyone who had volunteered to speak with the D-M staff had been interviewed.

After each team had reported its negative findings, Holly gloomily summarized the pessimistic outlook. "It's pretty clear from these reports that we are very nearly at the end of the line. I believe there are only five individuals, all on the hospital staff at the time Brock was there, whom we have so far failed to contact." He consulted the summary list he had prepared at home late the night before. "One was out of town. A message was left on her answering machine, but she hasn't phoned in yet. In three cases roommates or family members answered our call and promised to pass on the message, but again no response has yet been received. The other one has no answering machine and could not be reached."

He slowly set the list down on the conference table with a finality that seemed to signal an end to the search. "Actually, there's only one person among the five employees who in my estimation is likely to have knowledge of the document. That's Judy Harrison, the nurse that discovered Brock was missing. She was on duty alone in the Terminal Ward for several hours before he slipped away. The personnel office told me she's returning home this morning from a vacation for the noonday shift. Let's pray we hear from her when she listens to our message on her machine. Although the other four were working in the general area of Brock's room, there's no reason to believe they had any contact with him. One is a building maintenance worker, another an electrician, the two others are members of the cleaning force but not in the Terminal Ward."

Maggie had been checking her own ledgers while Holly was talking. "Hold on a minute! What was the nurse's name again?"

"Judy Harrison."

"She called!"

"When?"

"Half an hour ago. Just before our meeting. She's supposed to call us back in an hour."

"That's good," said Holly with restrained enthusiasm. There had been too many blind alleys. "Let me talk to her when she calls. She's our last hope. Who spoke to her?"

"I did," said one of D-M's graphic artists seated at the table.

"What did she say exactly?"

"Here it is," the artist replied, checking her abbreviated notes in a three-ringed binder in her lap. "I gave her the standard spiel. She didn't remember any document or anything like that. She was in a big hurry to get to work early. Said she had some things to do before her shift and that she was going for a shower. Said she'd think about it and call us back at nine."

Holly heaved a sigh of resignation and shook his head. "Thank you. That may be the ball game." He sat glumly in silence.

The assembled throng followed his lead, lapsing into deep gloom.

After a few moments he looked around the room. "I think it's time for desperate measures. Anyone got any ideas? I'm plum out."

"We could go on TV with a public appeal," said someone.

"We could offer a reward for information on the witness," said another.

"Maybe we've already talked to the witness, and he or she is holding out on us."

"Maybe give 'em lie detector tests."

"Maybe there's no document."

That offhand remark stunned the group into silence again. It was the thought that had been on everyone's mind as the search turned up empty. It was a case of Ockum's Razor—the theory that the simplest explanation is the correct one—meaning *there was no document!* The whole operation was a wild-goose chase. D-M was doomed.

Eleanor, seated beside Holly at the conference table, was disconsolate. "Oh, Gordon, what's the use? Maybe we've been chasing pipe dreams. Maybe I didn't sign a document. Maybe I just dreamed it. On the other hand, couldn't the words in the stained-glass window have a totally innocuous meaning? Maybe *preserve* simply refers to the memory of D-M and not the reality."

"Look," he said gravely to the assembled, "I've tried to remain optimistic throughout this thing, but it's time, as Eleanor suggests, to face reality. I think we've reached the end of the line. There are other avenues we could explore to locate the document, but the chances of success are less than remote. In fact, they aren't worth the candle." He stood up at the head of the table. "I wish to thank all of you, each and every one. We had to give it a try, and you've all worked so hard. It was Eleanor's and D-M's only hope. Tomorrow the deadline for securing the loan expires, and I'm afraid the outcome is foregone."

He looked wearily at the sullen faces around him, many of which were downcast, avoiding his eyes and his unwelcome message. "This isn't a good Christmas present, but Merry Christmas anyway to each of you. Diego, do you wish to say anything?"

Diego went to the head of the table as Holly took a seat. "My dear friends, the end, as Gordon said, is near for DESIGN METAPHORS. We've exhausted every recuperative measure we could think of and then some. What makes the demise so tragic is that we are two or three months away from winning a contract that would save the firm. But our creditors are afraid the contract could fall through, so they've persuaded the court to close us down. As Vince Lombardi, the famous coach of the Green Bay Packers once said after a painful loss, 'We didn't lose. We just ran out of time.' So here we are on the verge of defeat. Only a miracle can save us." He smiled and glanced at Eleanor. "But I've become a believer in miracles, so don't count us out just yet." He paused and grew serious again. "We will continue operations for two weeks at which time, barring some change, I will release all of you. Everyone will receive one month's salary. As Gordon said, that isn't a welcome Christmas present. I don't know if you want to hold our annual Christmas party tomorrow or not. It will be more of a wake than a party, but I'll let you all decide."

"We'll have the party!" cried Maggie loudly and defiantly. "If it's gonna be a wake, it should be a happy one. I'm Irish, you know!"

"She's right," added Kelly. "We'll give the company the send-off it and her fine staff deserve."

"So be it," said Diego. "In the meantime you all would best be looking for new jobs." He wanted to say more but could think of nothing appropriate. "Thank you again." He bowed to Eleanor. "Sorry, Eleanor. We truly did the best we could, but it just wasn't enough."

"I know you did, and so does Brock and everyone here."

The meeting dissolved gradually. A few people hurriedly left, unable to bear the sorrow. Some, not knowing what else to do, walked lethargically back to their desks to resume work on the last of D-M's projects. Others remained seated, staring numbly at the table, unwilling to accept D-M's death sentence but helpless to do anything about it. Within ten minutes they, too, withdrew, and the conference room was empty, as empty as the all-out no-holds-barred effort to find the elusive alleged document that would have saved the company.

Holly ruefully shook hands with Eleanor and Paul and the others in the reception room and departed, his shoulders bowed under the unaccustomed weight of failure. His friends watched him through the glass wall while he waited for the elevator. No one spoke. The elevator arrived, its doors opened, and Holly stepped in and turned, paying them a final farewell with a forlorn wave of his hand and a halfhearted smile. Then the door's shut, bringing to a close his valiant but fruitless effort to rescue D-M.

"I think I'll head home," said Eleanor, moving to get her purse. "I have stacks of ironing waiting for me. It will give me time to think, so Diego and I can make plans."

"I have some Christmas shopping to do," said Helena. "Wanna join me, Eleanor?"

"Not really, but thanks. I'm just not in the mood, and we're going to have to stretch our pennies from now on."

"Oh, Eleanor," cried Helena. "I'm sure..."

"Please don't say it. Please. Diego and I have to work this out for ourselves."

"All right, if you say so. Are you staying, Kelly?"

"Yes, Diego and I have things to wrap up."

The friends parted, going their separate ways, concealing from each other their common foreboding of the collapse of D-M. The weeks ahead would be no more than a deathwatch over the company which, like a sick loved one, ill beyond hope, would slowly slip away.

Left alone, Diego and Kelly walked into the corner office to begin preparations for tomorrow's probate. The intercom buzzed and Diego answered. "Yeah, Maggie."

"That nurse is on the line. Judy Harrison."

Kelly motioned to Diego. "Let me talk to her." He yelled to Maggie, "I'll take it." He pushed the lighted button on his desk's phone box. "Hello, Miss Harrison?"

"Yes, who's this?"

"Kelly Barnaby. I'm working with DESIGN METAPHORS to find a missing document."

"Like I told the woman this morning, I don't know anything about a document. I'm very sorry. I wish I could help you."

"Maybe we could get together today and chat a bit. You might remember something that would be important to us. How about lunch?"

"Well, I can't leave the hospital."

"That's okay. I'll meet you in the cafeteria."

She was skeptical and had better things to do with her lunch hour. "Well, I guess so. No harm in talking."

"Good. Will you be wearing your name tag?"

"Always."

"I'll find you. What time?"

"Twelve fifteen."

"I'll be there."

Kelly sat across from Judy Harrison while she munched on a large salad. She was an attractive fortyish single woman. She explained she had just returned from a two-week Caribbean cruise and was having difficulty adjusting to her first day back at work. Tanned but tired, she was impatient with Kelly's questions.

"Please think back. Do you recall seeing any member of the staff or a visitor sign a document in Stowolski's room?"

"No, I don't!" she retorted emphatically. "I already told that person on the phone I didn't."

"I realize that, Miss Harrison," said Kelly in a courteous and friendly voice. "I'm just trying to be certain. We're at our wit's end on this thing."

"Have you talked with the others on duty then?"

"Most of them." Kelly brought out a list from his briefcase and placed it on the table before her. "You're one of the last five we hadn't reached."

She picked up the list and perused the names.

"You know all those people?" asked Kelly.

"Sure, but I don't remember if they worked during my shift that night. It's a wonder how anyone can keep straight who's on what shift. There are so many changes, and it was well over a year ago. It's a real pain."

"Why so many changes?"

"Oh, people take leave. They get sick. They take off on special occasions. You know, the regular stuff. The schedules are made up weeks in advance, so each person is responsible for finding their own replacement if they have to take time off like the woman I replaced. It puts the burden on the nurse, not on the administrative staff. It's only right, and no one objects to that system."

"You replaced someone?"

"Yeah. She became ill early in her shift and called me to ask if I'd stand in for her."

506

"Who is she?"

"I don't remember. It's been over a year!"

"Is she on that list?"

"Lemme see here." She read down the list of five names, noting her own.

"No, it wasn't any of these. I'd remember. Her name isn't there."

"That means we've already spoken to her and she had nothing to say. Those on the list, as I said, are the five we haven't talked to, except now you. But you don't recall her name."

"No. Maybe I'd remember it if you had the names of everyone on the duty roster for that day. Do you have that?"

Kelly rummaged in his briefcase, found the computer listing, and set it before her. "That's everyone that worked in the Terminal Ward the three days Stowolski was there. Like I said, we've spoken with all but five—four that is, now that we've talked with you."

"There's a lot of names. I never realized how many people work here."

Kelly waited while the nurse scanned the names.

"No. I don't recognize any of them."

"But that's a comprehensive list of every hospital employee in the ward those three days. We got it from the personnel office. Why isn't her name there?"

"I dunno. I guess the hospital deleted her name and put mine in instead. Here's mine right here." She pointed to her name. "Maybe 'cause she didn't work a full shift. I don't know. Ask them."

"But wouldn't we already have talked to her? I mean she was on the staff serving that ward, wasn't she?"

"Let's see...I don't think so. No, I remember now. It was her first duty up there. She was from ER. Yeah, that's it. It's coming back to me now. I remember, because I don't like working in Terminal. She asked me to do it for her as a favor, which I did. Fact is, I haven't worked Terminal since then."

"You mean she was working in the Terminal Ward that day, and there's no record of it here?"

"Man, we're only human. Whataya want?"

"Is she still on the staff?" Kelly would not relent.

Harrison thought for a moment. "No, I don't think so. I haven't seen her around since then. I didn't know her well, and she left that night before I got to the ward."

"But you don't recall her name."

"Let me think. Oh, it's been too long. Let's see...she worked in ER...with Phyllis and Arlene. I think her name began with a *D*. Doreen? Dorothy? Doris? No, it was Dorothy. That's it. Dorothy. Dorothy Hines. That's it."

Kelly got Dorothy Hines's address and phone number from the personnel office. Having taken another nursing job a year ago, she was no longer employed by the hospital. He telephoned her at once when he returned to D-M. Beating all odds, which he knew were dead set against him, she answered.

Restraining his excitement, he introduced himself and explained the purpose of his call.

"I'm sorry, Mr. Barnaby. That was a long time ago, and I was sick that night. I remember being feverish and nauseous and calling Judy. She was real sweet and agreed to take my shift. Before she could get there I fainted. When I came to, they had moved me to the nurses' lounge. They figured I had the flu, so they sent me home."

"Do you remember being given a document by one of the patients? Please try. It's very important."

Kelly waited, tense and hopeful, while she tried to revive her fuzzy memories of that night.

"I don't know. I don't think so."

"Did a patient give you anything to mail or give to someone else?"

"Like what?"

"Oh, like an envelope maybe."

"An envelope? Wait. There was an envelope."

Kelly's heart leaped. He had so convinced himself she would not be helpful that he was incredulous. "You remember an envelope?"

Diego, working at his desk, jumped to his feet at Kelly's mention of an envelope.

"Yes," she said. "I remember now taking something from someone, a patient, I think. Yeah, it was an older guy. He had cancer. Some woman was there with him. I don't remember who she was, maybe his wife. I don't know. It was after she left. I remember because she was so beautiful. Like a queen or some kind of royalty. A really nice refined person. She was signing something for him. And when I returned after she left...yes...he put it in an envelope, a white envelope, and gave it to me. That's funny. I never remembered that till now."

Kelly was nearly exploding with excitement. He made a victorious fist and waved it above his head to signal Diego. Diego ran out to find Maggie and tell her the news.

"Anything unusual about the envelope? What size was it? Was it addressed?"

"It's been so long, Mr. Barnaby. I don't remember. My memory is pretty hazy."

"Hey, you're doing great, Mrs. Hines. So what did you do with the envelope? Did you mail it?"

"I don't remember. I really don't."

"I tell you what. Let's walk through what you did that night. Maybe it will come to you."

"Is all of this really that important?"

"A fine company and the future of that royal lady you saw in the hospital room depend on it. Okay?"

"All right."

Over the phone Kelly led her step by step through a verbal re-enactment of the events of the fateful night. It was her first tour in the Terminal Ward. She reported to the nurses' station and signed in around 8 PM. She felt dizzy and upset. She went to the bathroom and threw up and felt better. She thought it was food poisoning. She proceeded with her rounds. She checked on Stowolski. The woman was there at his bedside signing a document of some kind. When she came back to check on him later, he put the document in a white envelope and gave it to me.

"But why did he give it to you? To mail? To deliver somewhere?"

"I'm sorry, sir. I honestly don't remember. I remember now putting the envelope in the pocket of my sweater, which I had put on because I was chilled. And I remember taking his temperature and blood pressure and going back to my station. That's when I began to feel real sick. And that's when I phoned Judy and asked her to complete the rest of my shift. She said she would, but before she could get there, I passed out and was taken to the nurses' lounge. The doctor checked me over and decided I had the flu. They phoned my son to come and drive me home."

She fell silent a moment.

"Let's see. Oh, yes. He met me at the front entrance. I was terribly ill—fever, nausea, aches and pains. A bad case of the flu. And when I got home, I went to bed."

"You didn't stop to mail the envelope?"

"I don't know. I slept the whole time. Maybe my son, Jim, would remember."

She turned from the phone and yelled to her son. A conversation ensued of which Kelly caught only bits and pieces.

"Here he comes. I'll put him on."

Kelly explained to him what he wanted to know.

"I dunno, mister. I remember Mom was sick and I went and got her. Let me think. A mailbox? I have no idea. Maybe we did. Mom was awful sick. They told me to put her to bed right away. I don't think I'd've stopped to mail a stupid letter. No way!"

"Jim, maybe she gave you the letter the next day?"

"It's possible, but I can't remember. Shoot, that was over a year ago."

Kelly thanked the young man, then requestioned his mother, but she had nothing more to add. Kelly hung up depressed and dismayed. The ups and downs of the past few days had worn him to a frazzle. Sullenly he recounted to Diego and Maggie what Dorothy Hines and her son had revealed. There had indeed been a document, that much was now confirmed. Holly had been right all along. But they were no better off than before. The document was still missing.

"Maybe it fell out of her sweater pocket when she fainted in the hospital," suggested Maggie. "God only knows where it is now. It was probably thrown in the trash. Long gone!"

"Maybe," said Diego, "it fell out in the car."

"In the car?" Kelly's face brightened. "Why didn't I think of that?"

He was on the phone in an instant.

510

"Mrs. Hines? Kelly Barnaby here. Could I speak with your son again?"

"Sure thing. I'll get him."

"Thank you." Kelly waited.

"Yes, sir."

"Jim," he said, speaking very deliberately to ensure his question was clearly understood. "Do you still drive the car you drove your mother home in from the hospital that night?"

"You mean do I still own it?"

The young man's response sent a throb of despair through Kelly's chest. He had sold the car. "Yes. Do you still own it?"

"Of course, it's a valuable car, but I'm sure your envelope isn't in it. I clean it real good once a month, under the seats, too. It's kind of an antique. And I've never found an envelope."

Kelly tasted bitter defeat again. Another up, another down. "Look, Jim, do me a big favor. Take another look. This is really important to a great many very fine people."

"Okay, but don't hold your breath. I know it's not there. You wanna wait while I check or should I call you back later?"

"No, I'll hang on. If it's bad news, I want to hear it right away."

"Sure thing."

The phone went silent while Jim Hines left to search his car for the envelope. Hours seemed to pass while Kelly, Maggie, and Diego each in their own way prayed that God would grant them another miracle. Kelly tapped his thumb nervously on the green marble desktop. Maggie huddled on the couch, feet together, head down, hands in her lap, her bony fingers tightly intertwined like a ball of yarn. Diego paced like a caged feline before the panoramic windows.

"So it all comes down to a young kid and his car," Kelly cynically observed. "It seems incredible. How did this happen? The fate of a thriving successful thirty-year-old company hinges on how well this kid cleans his car each month. Did he find the envelope eighteen months ago and pitch it? Or did it lodge under the seat and remain hidden all these months? Or was it ever there? Maybe it fell out in the hospital and got thrown away."

Jim Hines, having completed his search, closed the car door and walked back from the garage to the kitchen, where the phone lay patiently on the countertop waiting for his portentous report. As he lifted the receiver to his mouth with one hand, his other presented to his eyes a sealed and stamped, crumpled, grease-stained envelope addressed to a Gordon Holly.

"Mister?" said Jim. "You're never gonna believe this!"

TWENTY-EIGHT

G lorious sunlight greeted the approach of the launch carrying the Pope of the Holy Roman Catholic Church and his entourage. As the boat neared the pier, a boys' choir in the chapel began a dulcet Gregorian chant heralding his arrival. The graceful sonorous harmonies like high-pitched bells pierced the tranquil silence across the still blue-green water to the attentive ears of the many thousands of onlookers aboard the flotilla of ships and boats whose numbers had swelled to over three thousand. The white-robed Pontiff led his small cortege of red-frocked cardinals and bishops down the gangway onto the pier and directly up the ridge in a colorful formal procession televised worldwide.

Awaiting the procession was a symphony orchestra comprised of eminent Catholic musicians from around the globe seated on a platform erected outside the chapel facing the entrance. On bleachers behind the orchestra was a chorus of men and women from Catholic cathedrals in Latin America. Inside the nave seated stiffly in folding chairs on either side of a wide center aisle were over a hundred foreign and U.S. dignitaries including the President and First Lady of the United States in the front row on the left. On the right was the Stowolski family. Standing along the walls behind the congregation was the boys choir, whose members came from East European nations.

The somber guests had been waiting half an hour, shifting their attention between the stained-glass windows and Brock's shimmering sealed mahogany casket in front of the altar. But it was the split cross in the apse that most captivated the congregation. Its wonder, mystery, and invisible power evoked images in every mind of how the man lying in the casket before them must have looked suspended on the cross like the crucified Christ and how the lightning bolt depicted in the window in the apse had struck him. To be only feet away from the remains of this holy man in front of the very cross on which it all had happened and inside the sanctuary he single-handedly built was an experience that would leave a lasting imprint on the lives of every person present.

When the procession reached the entrance, the orchestra and chorus struck up the final movement of Beethoven's choral symphony, and the dignitaries rose to their feet. While the music resounded about them, the Pope walked around the outside of the chapel sprinkling holy water from a gold aspergillum borne by an attendant priest. Halting several times to pray and to read from a missal held before him by an aide, the Holy Father completed his circuit and solemnly invoked the blessing of the chapel in the name of the Holy Trinity.

The consecration completed, the Pope exchanged his white outer vestment for a deep violet chasuble festooned with heavy gold brocade. The cortege then processed up the aisle of the chapel and divided at the casket, passing on either side to the rear of the altar where the Pontiff and his entourage turned and faced the congregation. The music ended, and the Pope stepped to the altar and began the funeral service.

"Our instinct of self-preservation makes us shrink from death, but our faith sees beyond the grave. Death is holy, a part of the gift of life. It is God's way of gathering His family to Himself. Precious in the eyes of the Lord is every living soul. Death is not the end of life; it is the end of the beginning. Life is not ended by death, merely changed. Thus death is the end of preparation and the beginning of life's fulfillment. It is the end of danger, of all wavering between God and His creatures, of all warring between spirit and flesh. It is the prelude to eternal joy with God."

With that invocation the mass proceeded, culminating an hour later in the formal sealing of the casket which was then lowered into the grave dug beneath it on the very spot where Brock had died six weeks before. The Holy Father stepped around the altar and stood over the grave. Looking to heaven he delivered a prayer.

"Almighty Father, we lay to rest here on this small isle, remote from civilization but not from Your divine mercy, the remains of Brock Stowolski, one of Your faithful, who in spiritual desolation hung himself from this cross and was healed of mortal illness by Your blessed hand. To

You he paid homage for his cure by building this wonderful chapel. We pray that You will grant him eternal life. Amen."

The Pontiff cast his sparkling eyes over the congregation and said, "This man was not a saint. He was raised a Catholic, entered the seminary before he was twenty, then left two years later to pursue a profligate, self-indulgent life. Whether God interceded in Brock's life to bring him to this denouement is immaterial. It was Brock who changed, not God. Brock showed that sin can be conquered if we love God enough. Indeed, through God anything is possible. Clearly this man felt and believed in God's love. We see its affirmation in the window behind the cross. 'Glory to God in the highest...who takes away the sins of the world'...the God who took away Brock's sins. Without question Brock erected this chapel, this holy place, as a monument to bear witness to his thanksgiving and love for the Father Almighty. And we have today consecrated this chapel with the same thanksgiving and love.

"We can only wonder what marvelous events took place here and what communications passed between Brock and God. There is no record. No one will ever know. All that is here, all that remains, is the chapel and the surpassing beauty of its workmanship. After his cure Brock could have used the same skills and tools and materials to repair his boat and return to civilization, but he did not. He chose to remain here, to die here, in God's favor, leaving the island as clean and pure as he had found it, as he himself was made clean and pure. May the love that inspired him to build this chapel live on to inspire all those who see and visit it to likewise love their God in all things, always. By his actions this man exalted himself in God's eyes. And in exalting himself he exalted all humankind."

Bowing, the Holy Father returned to his chair behind the altar and seated himself to hear the orchestra and choir perform the "Hallelujah Chorus" from Handel's *Messiah*.

Paul, seated in the front row next to his mother, was deeply moved by the Pope's words. As the music swelled and filled the chapel, a compulsion to dance welled up within him. Dancing was his instinctive outlet for his feelings, which now pulsed with adoration for his father, reverence for the Pope, and faith in God. At that moment, with the grave open and the Holy Father looking on, Paul desperately needed to release his emotions. He could not keep them inside. His heart was bursting. He clenched his fists fighting the compulsion, but the music called. He could resist the summons no longer.

He suddenly stood up and removed his coat and tie, startling his mother, who instantly understood and began to weep. All eyes in the chapel were riveted on him as he kicked off his shoes and strode resolutely, arms at his side, head held high, to the railing around the grave. He bowed low to the Pope, holding this position several seconds in proud reverence. Then he spun about and quickly joined his sweeping movements to the rhythm and grandeur of the music. The choreography of his dancing, though extemporaneous, was flowing and masterful. He flew up and down the aisle and around the altar, pirouetting, bending, expressing through the grace and beauty of his powerful movements the love he felt for his father. His spontaneous performance spellbound the priests, the congregation, and the millions watching on television.

As the chorus sang the final "hallelujah," holding the chord to the very last beat, Paul raced down the aisle from the entrance and leaped...up...up...soaring...soaring...high toward the vaulted ceiling of the chapel, landing prostrate before his father's grave as the music ended.

EPILOGUE

Chapel Island became a world-renowned religious site attracting over three million visitors a year. To manage such numbers an elaborate administrative organization was created employing hundreds of people—technicians, accountants, boat handlers, multilingual guides, security officers, communicators, managers, food service people, medical staff, and a contingent of Catholic priests, deacons, and nuns to minister to the faithful. A small cruise ship anchored offshore served as a residence for the entire support corps and contained fully equipped medical facilities and offices for confessions and consultations with the faithful.

A research unit was formed to study artifacts from the island and the surrounding waters to shed light on the methods and materials Brock Stowolski used to build his chapel. Found strewn on the bottom half a mile around the island were the tools, ropes, pulleys, and miscellaneous gear he had used. To prevent souvenir hunters from stealing the artifacts, teams of scuba divers from all over the world, mostly volunteers who gave freely of their special talents without pay to aid in the research unit's work, plied the ocean bottom around the island, mapping, photographing, tabulating, and retrieving all of the debris scattered there by Brock Stowolski. After being photographed and thoroughly examined, the items recovered were taken for storage and display to a brand-new museum established by the Catholic Church in Hawaii dedicated to the chapel and its builder.

Construction engineers called in to examine the materials established what they believed was an accurate understanding of the process by which the chapel's components were formed and assembled. The engineers described the process in a best-selling book with artists' depictions of the various stages of construction. Proceeds from the book's sale went to fund the administration of the island and the research unit's operations. As the unit's functions evolved, it was also called upon to investigate visitors' claims of miraculous cures. The staff thus became experts on the question of miracles at the site, and its offices became the official repository of the evidence collected on each case.

As at Lourdes, the issue of miracles was unresolved. The Vatican's investigators never gathered sufficient hard evidence to warrant an official affirmation by the Catholic Church that Stowolski's cure was the result of divine intervention. Respected scientists offered alternative explanations. Nor were any of the hundreds of alleged cures at the island in subsequent years validated as miracles. In the end the question remained, as it always had in the past, a matter of individual religious conviction.

For years scientists expert in preservation of wood were regularly consulted on how to prevent wearing and corrosion of the chapel's timbers and the mast-cross from constant exposure to damp sea air. Consideration was given to encasing the entire structure in a protective dome and applying chemical preservatives to the wood annually, but neither the chapel nor the mast-cross ever showed any, even microscopic, deterioration. The island's administrator eventually ceased worrying about it.

The region around the island was unaccountably free of storms. Rains occasionally fell, cleansing surfaces and replenishing the scant underground water supply needed to sustain the palm trees and other flora, but storms never came closer than the horizon. Nonbelievers pointed out that it never rained in the desert either and that the Law of Probability would eventually dictate that a storm pass over the island. None ever did.

DESIGN METAPHORS prospered under the direction of Diego Martinez. The firm's notoriety resulting from media coverage of events on Chapel Island brought D-M instant fame, and clients by the hundreds from all over the world sought the firm's services. Twenty years later Eleanor and Diego sold the company to an enterprising group of young innovative designers and retired to their home in Hawaii.

Paul became one of the world's foremost ballet dancers, raised with Irina a wholesome and happy family of three boys and two girls, then

518

retired from the stage to become director of the San Francisco Ballet Theatre.

Until their passing fifty years later, Eleanor and Diego attended the memorial service celebrated annually in the chapel by a Vatican emissary on the anniversary of Brock's death. At the end of each of these Masses the celebrant said a special prayer of thanksgiving and remembrance over the small unpretentious headstone that to this day marks the grave in the chapel floor in front of the altar. The stone bears the following terse inscription:

This Holy Chapel
Is Dedicated to the Memory of
BROCK STOWOLSKI
Its Builder—Whom God Favored

About the Author

MORGAN D. JONES was born in Evanston, Illinois, in 1932. During the Korean War he enlisted in the U.S. Army where he learned Russian and was stationed in Vienna, Austria. Upon separation he attended the University of Illinois, obtaining a bachelor degree in economics.

Immediately after graduation he joined the Central Intelligence Agency where he served for 36 years, mostly as an intelligence analyst of Soviet military affairs. During that time he learned Greek. With other analysts he wrote intelligence reports for the President, Cabinet members, and top policy makers. For several years late in his career he was chief of the Agency's Analytic Training Branch. As an offshoot, with a fellow CIA officer, he taught a course on analytic methods for four semesters in Georgetown University's Master of Science Foreign Service graduate program. Upon his retirement in 1993 he wrote *The Thinker's Toolkit: 14 Powerful Techniques for Problem Solving* and founded with another CIA officer a Virginia company, Analytic Prowess (www.analyticprowess.com), which conducts workshops for federal agencies and private companies on the book's techniques.

He now resides in Florida with his wife of 47 years. He has two children: Stephanie Duran, a real estate agent in Santa Fe, NM, with a husband and two small children; and Christopher Jones, cofounder of Mediaworks LLC, in Brambleton, VA, with a wife and two small children. Jones' favorite pastimes are writing novels, building wood models of old cannon-toting square-rigged ships, and singing in choral groups.

For more information on Morgan, go to **www.capstonefiction.com**. You can also contact him by email at **www.culpa@atlantic.net**.

Printed in the United States
87516LV00003B/55-147/A

9 781602 900554